Petrichor (n.) the smell of earth after rain.

[and]

Pluviophile (n.) a lover of rain; someone who finds joy and peace during rainy days.

Colson Herzog

For those who suffer from **anxiety**.
For those who **love** too much.
For those who can´t **let go**.

[and]
To all introverted and creative dreamers. **Wake up.**

CONTENTS OF

[Petrichor and Pluviophile]

BRFORE, YOU READ

This story isn´t resembling a healthy or normal relationship. It is a work of fiction and not a role model for love. You should learn from and reflect on it but not replicate, romanticize, or internalize it.

[…]

TRIGGER WARNINGS

This book contains heavy Triggers.
The following contain huge **spoilers** of the story so be aware.

Social anxiety, anxiety, blood, car accident, cheating, abuse, depression, sexual molestation, borderline, emotional abuse, pregnancy, choaking, death, grieve, suicide, suicide ideation, cutting, self-injurious behavior, mention of eating disorders, scars, knife play, dealing with loss, drug abuse, sexually explicit scenes, miscarriage, adoption, stalking, bullying, derealization, nightmares, sleep disorders, attempted suicide, and vomit.

[If I missed anything feel free to contact me]

~~Pain~~ Rain

An old legend says that there is a place where it rains only. Where everything is peaceful. And where the rain is so loud that the pain inside falls silent.
It is being said that there lives a creature that carries so much pain, which can only be relieved by the rain. That is why the creature has never known any other place. It was too hurtful to move away from the familiar safe space. Some say it is a lost soul, others say it is a fallen angel. And some even say it is a demon or the devil itself.
But the pain was only in his head. He was so afraid of daring to do something, that he did nothing. He chose to be in pain because he thought it defined him. He chose to suffer instead of healing.
Every time the rain washed away the pain, he created new pain. It was like a drug. He even hurt himself to ease the pain.
Some say he could only survive because of the rain.
For him, it was the pain that kept him alive.

- unknown soul -

SPOTIFY PLAYLIST

[Petrichor and Pluviophile]

YouTube main songs

When the party´s over - slowed humming part by Billie Eilish

Berlin by RY X – humming part

PART ONE

[Petrichor]

Prologue

Would you change anything if you knew how your life would turn out? Or knew which people you lose, regret or love? Or would you still want the same ending?

For me, I know I´ll do the same. Because not meeting him would have been worse. The only thing I would do different is how I lived those moments. I would live them and would be nowhere as in the now.

H*ow easy do you find love? And how easily you lose it? What says that about you?*

I´m an addict of love. I craved the love I never got in return. I used to give myself up for love and lost myself for love. And got broken. *Shattered.*

But now I´m an addict of isolation. I shut down and rather stay alone than letting someone in. I had chosen myself. At least I thought I did.

And with that I lost the chance of love. *I lost him.*

I got from one extreme to the other. And ended up with nothing.

Ended up with losing him.

And there is that thing that happens to me. That people stay longer in my mind than my life. I was afraid it might happen with him too. And maybe that was my mistake. Cause in the end that happened. *I lost him.*

But I still remember the darkness I saw in his eyes. Remember the saltiness of his kisses, filled with hot tears. Feel the rain on my skin like his hands on me. See him every time I close my eyes and feel him in the rain, as if he´s crying on me. Feel the pain when he kissed me. I still feel him everywhere. I remember everything like it happened yesterday. And he happened to me like it was yesterday. Love happened. But something so lethal can still be your cure. But in the end, it´s your downfall.

The darkness in his eyes were my abyss. The abyss I fell into and got lost in. The abyss, I grieved ever since and never let go of. The abyss I lost. *Him.*

And to deal I kept daydreaming and got lost in thoughts. In lyrics. In books. In the stars. Lost in him. As an introvert, that´s what you do. *Creating. Escape.*

I dreamed to run from reality. And at some point, the imagination got better than the real world. Boundaries were blurring and I lost the touch to real life. But I got in touch with him.

Nothing is impossible. But the worst thing about dreaming is you never know you do until you wake up. But eventually you do. *Wake up.*

And you´re left with the aching pain of the loss. *The loss of him.*

I dreamed and never came back since. Since I lost him. *Yesterday.*

1

"Welcome.
Come and find yourself,
run down the rabbit hole with us,
straight on 'till morning."

August 2020

As I rub my fingers over the Polaroid, I remember the things Nina told me when she invited me to that party.

...

"You know, we party a bit different." She said, and I looked at her questioning, because what should *different* mean?

"It´s more of a mindset we all share." She told me like she just shared some secret. "But I think you'll fit in." She considered searching my face. "But once you joined us, you can´t turn back to the way you´ve been before." She warned me but it sounded more like she meant it in a good way. That sounded drastic, but I´ve been desperate for a change. Now that I start to study in three months. And the summer isn´t over yet. It didn´t really began for me. But every summer has a story, and that party or mindset seemed like a start. So, I smiled at her and agreed to come.

- 27 -

I was never good at keeping friends. I also wasn´t good at keeping the boys I love. I always lost them in ways and never got over them. *Not fully.*

But this time it had to be different. At least, I hoped it would.

How easy you make friends? How easy you lose them?

What says that about you?

As a person who always had few to no friends at all, finding friends is dangerous. Because they can leave you. It is out of your hand. They can abandon you. And you can distance yourself. They can hurt you. And you hurt them.

But this time it would be different. At least, I hoped it would.

It can be the time of your life and you´re happy. But when you part, you´re back to the loneliness you´re used to. And I know you´re never *really* alone. You just feel like it. And I felt a lot like it.

But again, I thought this time it would be different. At least, I hoped it would.

I had more conversations in my head than with actual people. I´m *that* lonely.

Even if I had friends, deep down I was lonely. It was always there.

I just covered it. *And still I hoped.*

But what she didn´t know back then is that how you think the world is, always turns out to be the way it is for you. But you always can change the way the world seems. You just must look at it differently. *And think differently.*

But I already agreed to come and opened the door for new friends to come. So, I had no other choice than to let myself be vulnerable. *And let people in.*

2

I probably won´t know anyone except Nina and her boyfriend Leon. I met her at a club. She was crying because of him.

I saved her from a perv. Then I listened to her. And after that I held her hair while she vomited.

Afterwards, I gave her a pep talk, and I helped her find her boyfriend.

The next weekend I was at the same club. I´m not really into clubbing, but maybe it was fate I went a second time. And Nina recognized me. I was surprised she remembered me; cause she was pretty wasted. And she´s insanely beautiful aka she´s popular. Not that I´m ugly. *Cause I´m not.*

But she´s the kind of pretty you know that she´s the center of a party. Guys hit on her constantly. Girls try to be just like her. And on top she´s intelligent and charming. Roundabout, someone who easily makes friends. *And not at all like me.*

I´m not one of those people, who easily talk to strangers. Nina was one of those you just want to be friends with. And she wanted to be friends with me.

That day she gave me the invitation. And after that she kind of adopted me. She´s that extroverted friend an introvert needs to be the best version of themselves. Or at least the confident and outgoing one. She´s like alcohol to my system. She gives me the push I need to act like I normally would around friends.

People I trust. *Like myself.*

- 27 -

I had never been to that part of my village before. It´s a beautiful area. Rich to be exact. I did hear about the parties, though. There were rumors. *There were a lot.*

Those parties are different from others. They say they give you the *project X* vibe. The *euphoria* feeling. At least that´s what I heard.

Because everyone wants to be invited. But hardly anyone is. They´re playing games you played as a child with your neighbors until dawn. But they do it with drugs. At least that´s what I´ve seen on social media. There are just glimpses of what happens. But what you´ve seen makes you want to go to one of those parties.

But since I´ve never been popular, and I don´t really have friends, I wouldn´t know. Luckily, I met Nina, who insisted that I´ll come partying with them.

I text Leon, hoping I don´t have to go in alone.

For a while, I stare at the chat. *No answer.*

Five minutes pass. *Still, no answer.*

I send Nina a message but also *nothing*.

So, I decide to just go in.

I can do this. I can walk in there by myself. No big deal. It´s just a party. No reason to freak out. Actually, it´s a good thing. Now I can decide if I´ll be the silent one. As I´m always anywhere I´m new. Or I´ll be myself without checking the people first. Without knowing if they won´t judge me. Or like me. As me.

Just do it.

I clasp the photo in my hand. When I open the gate, I see *how* huge the property is. A large garden and at the center of the lawn a recessed pool, which definitively confirms my assumption of being rich.

On the covered terrace is a sofa area with a shisha on the table. A group is playing beer pong. Others stand on the terrace talking, drinking, smoking, or dancing.

I was so focused on the surroundings; I didn´t realize I was already in the middle of the party. To my relief, hardly anyone stares at me. They´re all busy minding their own business. Otherwise, I *always* feel all eyes on me, and not in a positive way. Social Anxiety ways. My little demon on the shoulder. But now it´s pleasingly quiet instead of whispering to me, so I take the place in.

All wear glow sticks. There are girls skinny-dipping on the shoulders of guys playing wrestling. And, as if the facade were not impressive enough, I discover on the terrace a whirlpool with a couple. Taking a closer look, I realize they´re not cuddling. They *fuck* in front of *everyone*. Taking the risk of getting filmed. But no one seems to care except for the guy next to them watching closely.

This party is clearly different.

There are even people reading on a blanket. And there´s that couple humping each other in the pool. Some sit on the ground or lie in the grass. Others play volleyball in the backyard. And some guy to my left, basketball. It´s like all random stuff you´d do on a daily pared with music, drugs, and sex. There are people who laugh and have the time of their life´s and some are throwing fists. Like all emotions collected at one place. Like everyone is living their own definition of a party. It doesn´t feel like the other parties I´ve been to. *Which aren´t many.*

This is different.

Lost in my thoughts, I didn´t realize Leon was coming towards me, until he blocks my gaze. "Hey Lia." He says. "Hi." I answer. He points to the other half of the semi-detached house. A gateway joins the two gardens. "That´s where I live. And this house belongs to my friend Kai. It´s where the parties at." He tells me smug. "Must be nice to live next to your mate" I suggest. "It is." He says nodding. "Most of the time." He adds. I give him a smile.

"Let me introduce you to my little brother." He heads for the couch. I follow him. The music is changing. The best songs are the ones you know you like from the first few seconds. That´s how it was with this one. Looking back, I´ve never forget those lines along with the blackish eyes I saw.

Juliette – Slush Puppy

Because at the same moment, I catch the gaze of a guy sitting in the corner of the sofa. He holds a joint *(Pot, I guess)* and wears a black t-shirt. His hair is dark brown and messy. The typical, I woke up and went through look. Still, they look done.

Simply fine.

His face is distinctive. He´s got a look that I can´t read. His dark eyes pierce me. Red shot to be exact. He´s high. *Definitely pod.*

He frowns at me. I can´t really keep eye contact for long. *Shy and all.*

Especially not with guys I think are hot, but I can´t get away from his look. He´s fucking beautiful and looks like the personification of darkness.

He takes a train and doesn´t keep his eyes off me. But he seems to be not at all amused. *Pissed even I´d say.*

Like he hates me already.

But before I can think about it, someone gets in my sight.

3

Next to him a guy stands up who also has brown hair but fluffier and lighter. He holds his hand out to me. "Aidan. You must be, Lia." I look at his hand in front of me.

He wants to shake hands? I´ve always wondered why people do this.

But he grins and seems happy to meet me, so I take his.

"Yes. Heard a lot about you," I say, grinning. *Little brother* isn´t the right description.

Rather hot brother.

"I only hope for good" he responds but looks at his older brother. "Sure," says Leon with a broad grin.

The two are talking now. So, there´s another eye meeting between the guy and me. He looks sexy and arrogant. And he looks at me like he knows *exactly* I don´t belong here. It´s hatred and disgusted. But also, indifference and coldness. He looks at me directly but doesn´t say a thing so, I sit down. Leon and his brother talk about something I can´t catch up with, so I´m silent for a while.

I start to feel uncomfortable. It comes creeping in. And it feels like I´m the only person who doesn´t talk to anyone. *Which is the hard truth.*

I feel misplaced, but I can´t follow-up in their conversation, so I´m a bit lost. I´m extremely aware of myself. Like I see myself from the outside. *Disconnected.*

I fiddle with my arm wrist and my rings. And then the urge to play alibi on my phone comes over me. But I don´t because I´m too self-conscious about that too. *Duh.*

So instead, I keep spinning my ring.

That was *exactly* what I was afraid of. That I´d be awkward cause I can´t talk to strangers. I mean, I can, but I don´t. *What should I even say? I´m such a weirdo. I can´t even think of some small talk nor who I could talk to.*

My face heats awfully and I´m afraid I might turn red. I take a breath and look around.

You don´t have to get on your phone. You don´t have to do things with your hands all the time. You can just do nothing. You don´t have to seem busy or not like a loner. No one pays attention to you. Don´t make everything about you.

I can´t spot Nina anywhere, either.

I check my phone. No messages. *Like always. That´s nothing new.*

I´d like to crawl back into my bed. But I´m too self-aware to walk past all of them. I consider going to the toilet, but I don´t know where it is and maybe inside are more people.

My face tingles. *God, I hate this feeling.*

I don´t recognize *anyone* at this party. *My ears grow hot.*

After a while I take my phone and do unnecessary stuff. It feels like *hours* until Aidan addresses me, but it´s probably just been minutes.

"If you want to grab a drink, go inside, you can have whatever you want." He assures me. "Yeah, thanks." I say and get up, although I don´t drink alcohol anymore, but I take every chance to recharge my social battery now already.

The fact that he had to tell me. *Of course, I could get some drinks.*

Didn´t I plan on being someone else? Not the shy creep I´m currently am.

But, as always, I fail. *Cause anxiety is greater.*

So, I run and hide. *Avoid.*

4

Once inside, I´m relieved cause I see no one. I close my eyes and take deep breaths.

This house is a dream. And this party too, but I can´t find my place in it.

When I open them, I see puppies lying on the sofa. Two Yorkshire Terriers. I can´t help but sit with them. They´re too cute. And they won´t care if I´ll talk or not. Or I´m weird and a social phobic.

One is firm asleep. The other welcomes me and starts to play with my hand. *Pups make everything okay. They love you no matter what. They don´t talk and sense how you feel. And you can communicate without needing to. Just how I like it.*

For a party you need an invitation to, no one seemed to care if I have a right to be here or not. I hope Nina gets her ass here soon or I´ll die on socially awkwardness. *Can you die out of embarrassment, like in the sims? I hope not. That would be my end,* I laugh to myself.

"Spirit" I hear someone behind me say. I flinch and turn around to see who the rough voice belongs to. The guy from the sofa is leaning against the door frame. He´s really tall now that he stands.

"What.." I stammer, caught off guard. "That´s her name." He nods his chin towards the puppy. "The dog you´re petting." He states and as I say nothing he goes on. "I´ve always hated people who just pet other people´s dogs." He scoffs. "You don´t want strange guys touching *you* either just, because they think you´re pretty, right?" He asks. My hand stops. *What the fuck?*

I mean, he has a point. *But still. And did he just call me pretty?*

"It´s a puppy." I retort. He shrugs. We stare at each other.

"Lia, right?" He asks, squinting his eyes at me with a frown.

How casual he stands there. Even that looks hot.

I´m already annoyed by him. Something we have in common.

I wonder how long he´s been watching me talking to the dog like a baby.

"Eh, yes," I say. He lifts his chin slightly. "I´m Kai, Leon, and Aidan´s friend." He says and another deep line forms on his forehead.

"So, you´re the host?" He nods, folding his arms. I can´t help but sample his tight upper arms.

"You got invited?" He asks, with his frown deepening. I´m tempted to point out to stop, otherwise he will get wrinkles. *But I keep my mouth shut.*

I nod and show him the Polaroid. *He eyes it.*

"Who gave you this?" He asks his voice filled with anger. "Nina." I respond, and he closes his eyes, inhaling. He´s annoyed. He doesn´t even hide that fact.

"Thought so." He says. I just look at him, not sure what to say.

"Didn´t you want to grab a drink or something?" He asks. I look at him unsure what to do cause he´s pissed for no fucking reason besides having a heart for pets. "So, you want a drink or are you going to keep *harassing* my dogs?" He asks with a raised brow, challenging me. "*Hassle*? Seriously?" I laugh and get up. He´s twisting his eyes.

"Then a..?" He´s waiting for my answer. *Oh, now he wants to make me a drink? What´s the matter with him? Is he being sarcastic?* I don´t think so.

I walk up to him but keep my distance.

"Mojito." I say choosing something that must be prepared. "Good choice." He hisses and straightens up. He towers over me. *Now he´s even taller.* My throat tightens. His gaze feels intimidating. I have to look up. He stares down at me for a sec before he heads towards the island.

"Without alcohol," I add. "You don´t drink?" He asks over his shoulder. I shake my head, feeling dumb because he can´t see. So, I say "No" and follow him into the kitchen.

There is a quote on his hoodie.

"Nobody cares about your fake life on social media."

I like that statement.

His back muscles play while he walks. *Stop staring at him.*

"You know you´re at a party, right?" He asks, looking at me. I shrug. "Don´t drink that often." I say. "Why?" He asks the question they all do cause *how can you not drink*? *Maybe because it´s a drug and unhealthy*?

"Don´t really see a point in it." I say *(despite it gives me confidence, but I must learn to be myself without any drug, so no alc for me today).*

He nods once. Maybe, I should have, cause if he´ll keeps making remarks I´ll need some.

He starts by washing limes and mint. Undecided what to do, I sit down on one of the bar stools across him cause I´m not allowed to ~~play with~~ no *harass* the dogs.

I roll my eyes. *He´s a jerk.*

With a serious look, he seems to be immersed in preparation.

So, I get a chance to take him in. My eyes wander to his forearm where´s black ink. A fine line Scorpio. I have to grin but press my lips together. *Is that his zodiac?*

Yet, I don´t know a guy with mine. *That makes me curious.*

Maybe, it was just a design he liked. But I certainly won´t ask. Especially since most people think astrology is stupid. Which is, but just the ones in newspapers or weird websites. But on the deeper level, it makes sense. *Like, why else has the moon effects on the tides? We´re basically made of water. Why shouldn´t the stars have an influence on us too, then?*

Maybe I can find out his birthdate. I think of my list I made ages ago, where I wrote down the compatibility with every zodiac sign. Scorpio and Scorpio.

Dark abysses or total fusion I think was the bottom line. *Sounds fun.*

Honestly, his tattoo has similarities to mine. Which is also a Scorpio. I wonder if he has any other tattoos. Leon has lots, on his covered arms, throat, neck, and chest.

If Aidan has any?

He doesn´t seem like the type to have some. Nina´s got a few for sure. She probably has one above her ass which reads *love me* or *divine.*

I blink to regain focus. He doesn´t notice my analyzing looks. *Anyway, I hope so.*

Either he´s so focused because he likes to mix *or* because he doesn´t want to talk to me. *Probably the latter. But he offered, so his bad.*

He puts the drink in front of me and starts mixing another cocktail. "Thanks." I let out. This time he looks up. Again, wrinkles form on his forehead. He should really stop. I know what I´m talking about. Because in ten years from now when I´m almost thirty, I´ll have deep lines between my eyebrows. The great thing with light eyes and sun.

Exhausting.

"Where are you from?" He asks and I wonder if Leon hasn´t already told him about me. "I live here. But at the other end of the village," I reply. He looks at me for a moment. "Never seen you before." He says and pulls his eyebrows together. *Neither did I.* It´s funny how small the world is sometimes. *Even in a suburb.*

"Ditto." I reply. Our village is not small, but neither huge. But apparently big enough not to run into each other for nineteen years, at least not that I know of. *How old is he?* Guess not much older than Leon, who´s twenty-two. Nina is my age nineteen.

"What´s your last name?" He asks, ripping me out of my thoughts. He squeezes a lime between. His arm tightens and veins emerge. I try not to stare. *Really, I do.*

"Sky" I say. "Lia Sky" he repeats. "Never heard of it." He shrugs. "Yours?" I ask. "Kai Dark" he says, and I shake my head. In any case, his name matches his appearance and personality. *Lia Dark Sky*. That would be too iconic, I laugh into myself. *Oh my god.* I didn´t just do that. I haven´t even known this guy in ten minutes, and I´m already checking to see if our names match. And he´s clearly a dick.

There´s definitely something wrong with me.

"You have storm?" I ask to get away from the thought. He seems even more unfriendly than before. "Businesses." He answers. "Plural?" I ask what I regret in the same moment.

It just slipped.

He holds his breath. "Are seldom at home." I guess I hit a sore spot. I don´t rake further and he would probably not answer. I can´t blame him because we don´t know each other.

"Look.." He says. "I´m not into small talk or some shit so.." He snaps. "Yeah *clearly*." I respond and leave him on that.

I´m generally good at reading people. I´m sensing vibes, but I can´t read him. *Not at all.* All I get are mixed signals. And one that screams *leave me the fuck alone*.

So, I grab my drink and thank him again, but he doesn´t respond neither looks at me, so I go outside. *Can´t believe they´re friends.*

5

I don´t have to look long for Nina since she sits on Leons lap. She gets up as she sees me and hugs me. "Hey sorry.." She begins, but someone speaks up behind me. "She just wanted to leave." He says. She breaks the hug. It´s Kai who followed me. *What?*

"You did it again." He says fiercely. She glares at him. "She doesn´t fit. You shouldn´t have invited her." He goes on talking about me as if I´m not even here. And maybe I´m not because I´m rooted like cement. Just watching because I don´t know *what the fuck* just happened.

"You can´t just keep doing this." He tells her. "Don´t be a dick." Nina hisses.

I face him. "Did we get off on the wrong foot or something?" I ask. He stiffs a laugh. "Yeah.. sure." He mocks. I frown at him. "She told me you have sort of a mindset. She told me I *would* fit in." I try to defend myself, even if I´m not sure for what.

My existence?

"Well, she´s wrong. You don´t. Nina´s naïve." He spits madly.

What is wrong with him?

"Come on cut it." Nina glares at him. "There are *rules*. You´re not just *simply* invited." He tells me but looks at her. "It´s no mindset. It´s no house party. It´s a *way* of living. It´s a promise. *Fearless.* Something you *clearly* aren´t. And you can´t just become a part of it." He keeps going.

"Then I´ll better go." I say feeling my skin heat and fingers tingle. "I think so." He says. "She just came." Nina presses. "Don´t do *this* shit." He snaps, stepping closer. "I invited her." She insists. "I *am* allowed." She says in a low voice. "But *I* decide *who* stays and she´s *not*. And I don´t *want* her here. So, she´s leaving. *Now*." He growls. I walk past them totally disgraced as Nina continues to argue with Kai, but I don´t care cause I´m humiliated. I´ve always felt uneasy on parties and had the feeling people don´t like me. But he actually doesn´t like me, and he *fucking* told me.

But someone blocks my way. Leon now stands in front of me. And next to him his brother. "Come on Dark, let her stay. She´s been here for half an hour or so." He says. "Don´t be a dick." He adds. "You *serious*?" Kai rages. "Just *one* Party." Aidan joins in. Kai gapes at him. "Give her a chance." He adds. *I think, I don´t want that chance.*

"She´s my friend." Nina pleads him. "Yeah, like *every* chick." He scoffs. I try to walk past Leon, but he gets in my way again. "She *stays*." He demands. Kai and Leon glare at each other for a moment. He looks at Aidan and shakes his head. He faces Nina again, pointing at her. "You haven´t even familiarized her with our rules." Kai snaps. "I forgot." She hisses, but he already walks past us.

"*Rules*?" I ask confused. "Yeah, we have *some* rules." She says smiling apologetic. "*Why* didn´t you tell me?" I ask upset. "Cause every time I try to bring my friends, he throws them out." My eyes widen. *Every time? Wow. She knew that would happen?*

Great.

"I´ve prepared them and told them the rules and all, but he always played big dick. Now I thought.." She continues, but I cut her off. "You thought you just leave me in the dark and throw me in?" I yell, even if I´m not a yeller. "Where I *obviously* am unwanted let alone fit." I add furious. "*Thanks*." I tell her. She looks at me, feeling sorry. "It´s his party, his house, and he doesn´t want me here." I list. "It´s not *his* party." She says but the way she said it tells me in ways *it is*.

"Doesn´t matter. I´ll go." I say attempting to walk away just to be blocked by Leon and Aidan again. I exhale annoyed. "Stay please." She begs. "He´s a dick, but he´ll leave you alone." She assures me, but I don´t believe her.

I turn to her, lowering my voice. "This.." I begin gesturing with my hands. "Makes me feel uncomfortable and anxious. I´m embarrassed Nina. And I just want to go home. I *don´t* want to stay." I say. "I know and I´m sorry I won´t let you down. Please just stay, okay? Our parties are really fun." She tells me. "*Fun*." I laugh. "Just *one* party." She insists. I inhale annoyed and give in because I know she won´t let me off so easily.

But I know already I won´t dare to come a second time here.

6

She smiles and draws me to the couch. We sit down and the boys too.

I take a look at Kai, who stands next to some guy who looks a lot like him. Same dark hair and dark eyes. *Same face.* Just a bit older and taller. *Brothers?*

But unlike Kai, he´s dressed up. He wears a white suit shirt with black trousers and black lacquer shoes. As if he just came out of a meeting. He doesn´t seem *that* unfriendly to me.

The only thing they have style wise in common is a wristwatch. An expensive one. *Rolex*. Matches the house and the cars. *And the shit personality.*

The other thing they have in common is the frown on their faces. *They argue.* I didn´t want to get *any* attention. Now I offended the host. *Great.*

Party life officially cancelled. Not that I had one.

"I´ll send you the rules." Nina chirps, regaining my attention.

I take out my phone. She texted me *the rules*. Their house parties have *rules*.

Twenty-six to be exact.

Dark rules

1. Know your limits + Don´t drink and drive
2. Music = dance
3. Play the games or go home
4. No smoking inside (except for weed)
5. Everyone is free to expose anatomy (skinny-dipping, free the nipples etc.)
6. Use a condom + Don´t leave used condoms + Screw at the guest room
7. Go big or go home
8. Don´t be a cock block
9. What happens at the Darks, stays there
10. No posts on social media
11. No police
12. Bring drugs, food, games, or anything new
13. Don´t bring random people
14. Don´t break shit + Don´t steal shit + Don´t snoop around
15. No one goes upstairs unasked
16. Treat your "insert pronoun" with respect
17. Leave the dogs alone
18. Don´t shit in the pool/hot tub
19. The house rules on any of the games should never be questioned
20. Sleep at home
21. If Nina cries, go find the tattooed guy who´s called Leon
22. Don´t burn the house down
23. "No" is a complete sentence
24. No phones (seriously)

25. Be in the now
26. Disrespect the rules and you´re banned

…

Glow stick colors:
Red = single
Blue = complicated
White = taken
Black = don´t talk to me
Lilac = I don´t know
Pink = flirt mood

That explains the glow sticks. Leon wears a white one and Nina a blue one. Seems like they´re having an agreement there. Aidan wears a pink one. Kai obviously a black one. And the guy next to him, none. I take a lilac one from the table.

"Those are.. a lot of rules." I state. "There are more." She waves me off. "But those are the main ones." She says. "*More*." I repeat. She nods.

"Don´t tell me someone.." I begin and she finishes. "Shit in the pool? Yeah." She answers. "We keep adding stuff." She says with a grin. I snort.

"What games?" I ask. "You´ll see." She brushes me off.

"No phones?" I ask. "Yeah, just for a quick text, pics, or videos. And, of course, for the games." She explains. I nod.

Now I know why I was the only one on the phone. *I already broke rules.* I touched the dogs. I´ve been on my phone, and didn´t bring anything. And I´m *random people*.

Great.

I glance at Kai, who stares at me, anger in his features.

Nina and I talk, but I don´t know about what. All I can sense is him. The death stare I get. And his eyes on me feel like *all* of them. On top of that he´s shamelessly beautiful, which is *not* helping.

We play a drinking game. Some rounds and shots pass. Leon must chuck two beers; Nina jumps into the pool in her underwear and Aidan shares his body count. Quite a lot. *A classic fuckboy?* He doesn´t look bad; he *knows* that, and the girls obviously too.

But when it´s my turn, my social phobia kicks in. *Like, what did you expected?* Of course, you´ll have to make a turn.

"Kiss Aidan" reads Nina with a broad grin. "Tongue and at least 60 seconds", she adds by herself, I can tell smile. For a moment, I´m annoyed that Kai didn´t play. At the same time, I wonder where *that* thought came from.

Hot to kiss, not hot enough to miss, I guess.

I must smile and so does Aidan, but then his mouth becomes a flat line. His jaw flexes. *Why didn´t I drink?* But my stomach flutters anyway. I feel lightheaded.

He looks at me hungry. My heart beats faster, and insects are going sane in my stomach. I lean over, take his jaw, and kiss him. Because after I got yelled at and yelled back, I´m *not* shy anymore. *Not tonight.* For one night.

His lips are soft. He tastes of Shisha flavor and cherry liquor.

Fortunately, not after beer.

When he takes my face in his hand, I drop mine on his leg. Our lips part further. The kiss is better than I´d admit. Hard and lustful. He shoves his tongue into my mouth. Others cheer on us. I´m sure we´ve been kissing for more than just a minute.

When we finally let go, we grin.

I see Kai and the guy watching the show. Especially Kai seems to watch *closely.* I look away. I think I´ve pissed him off more with *that one*, but I don´t care at all. Nina filmed us.

More rounds pass. But not once Kai´s eyes leave me like he waits for me to run, and on the inside, I´d liked to. *But I don´t.* Because I know it´s just one night. I´ll never see them again. *So, I tune him out.* But I still feel like I don´t belong, despite he´s the only that makes me feel that way. And with that, it feels as bad as if the whole party wants me to leave. He´s *that* intense. But I try to ignore him as good as I can.

The others are fun, and Aidan and I vibe and have the same sense of humor. And contrary to what I thought at first, I´m not alone tonight. Or awkward cause no one judges me *accept of him.*

She didn´t know yet, but this party would change her for good. And indeed, there was no turning back after.

7

Next evening

Nina invited me over to Leon´s. And despite I said I won´t come back I had a great time. Besides the almost getting kicked out part. But we´re not at Kai´s so.. *whatever.*

I´m glad they were okay with my best friend coming. We´ve known each other since kindergarten. We had lost sight, as with so many friendships. Somehow, I lose them all over time. Even though I know I was partly to blame because I have periods in which I isolate. From everyone. *Everything.*

But for two years we have been in contact again we´re as close as never before. Luca understands me and is also the quieter person. We don´t find it weird not to talk all the time. Or don´t get mad if we´re on radio silence for a while. We just know that we´re there when we need each other.

I wanted her to come yesterday too because I hate being new somewhere. And although she won´t admit, but she forced me to go alone, so I could step out of my comfort zone. We both knew she didn´t have anything else to do. At least not other than reading and binge-watching. But I love her for that. And in the end, it really wasn´t *that* bad. I was even one of the last to leave.

- 27 -

Arrived in his garden, the fireplace already burns. The sun is about to set. We sit on the tree trunks. Leon next to us.

Nina wraps bread on a stick. And I put a marshmallow on the skewer and hold it over the flames.

Summer nights like this are the best. The crackling envelops me, and the smell of coal fills my lungs.

The garden door opens, and I hear guys talking. Bottles clink and I can hear at least three different voices. I shift, uncomfortable and pull strands out of my bun. *I thought there were only the four of us. I hate plan changes. Not knowing everything. Controlling the outcome. Managing my anxiety. Or people. New people. Or myself.*

I swallow, trying to stomach my anxiety. They sit across from us. I´ll count five. Aidan grins at us. *He grins a lot.*

Aidan greets us. But then Kai sits next to him, followed by the tall well-dressed guy who was hanging out with him. *Shit.* My face heats. *Why´s he here?*

The guy also says hello, and it turns out his name is Finn. Kai remains silent.

Of course. What else?

He´s giving me a hard look. Like *I* insulted him twenty-four hours ago and not the other way around.

Two other guys sit between Finn and Nina. "Hi, I´m glad Ryan." He introduces himself with his guitar in his one hand. But I forgot the other guy´s name the second he said it. *Oops*. He seems to get along with Finn though. He´s also dressed chic with dark jeans and a white suit shirt.

Kai sits in my eyesight. He´s wearing black hoodie and training shorts. If I´d known the boys were coming, I would´ve at least gotten *a little* ready. And not yesterday´s bun and one of my fathers´ gray shirts. But that´s where I feel most comfortable. I don´t sweat because they´re oversized, and I don´t have to fiddle around wondering if everything sits right. But at least I´ve got my nicest jeans on, and my eyelashes curled. No mascara though. I shouldn´t care what I look like. But with those guys around, I cannot wonder.

Excited heartbeat spreads. Unlike at the party, where my concern all eyes might be on me, was unjustified. Is it not so easy here in the group of eight other people. Especially with Kai across from me.

I´m talking to Luca to calm my anxiety. And slowly I feel the shame slipping and relax a bit. Ryan tunes his guitar, and Nina talks to him a bit flirty. Unknown guy sticks between the roasted marshmallow chocolate and biscuits. Leon´s gone inside to get something. And Aidan talks to Finn. Kai keeps silent, just pokes around in the fire with the metal rod. He´s bent forward and now has the hood of his sweater on. I must pull myself together not to stare at him constantly.

Leon sits next to me with an electric guitar, distracting me. “Any requests?” Asks Ryan. “What about the new ones?” Dimples play around nameless boy´s mouth as he looks more at Luca than me. She thinks and names one.

They both sing. And I´m getting goose bumps.

I see in the corner of my eye how Kai smokes weed. *Is he a stoner?*

I glimpse his way and see his Adam´s apple wandering while swallowing beer. This is so hot, I don´t know why. *I turn away.* Looks aren´t everything.

8

The sun has gone down a while ago, and the flames make everyone look orange. They play *Creep by Radiohead* and Leon´s electric guitar solos are paying off.

The text hits me like a slap in the face. I usually feel like *the creep* somewhere. But *this* is different. The only one who makes me feel that way is *still* Kai.

I feel a hot burn on my face, but it´s not the fire, but Kai´s gaze. Who´s staring right at me. As if he *knew* I was just thinking of him. His features are a mixture of indifference and anger. *Why is he so pissed at me?* It´s not his gathering.

I painfully press my tongue against my teeth, and he flexes his jaw so his muscles play.

What´s his problem?

I decide to ignore it and wrap some dough around the stick and keep it on fire. I don´t have much to talk about anyway, because Leon sings, Nina is on her phone, and Luca is talking to Aidan. Somehow, I´m even grateful because I just want to enjoy. I don´t have to talk just to talk. Sometimes talking is even weirder than silence could ever be.

\- 27 -

The next hour they play more songs and for some we all sing along, because the alcohol starts to kick in slowly. Eventually, only Ryan plays, humming. And I´m getting the chills.

Why didn´t I bring a jacket?

Nina puts her legs over Leon´s while kissing. That´s all they ever do.

Besides fighting.

Ryan stops playing, moves to the other lock and talks to nameless guy.

My eyes are locked on the fire. The others have become a little quieter. And as I look up, I meet Kai´s eyes. They seem almost black in this lighting. His expression is just cold now. For a moment, we stare at each other. But then he stands up and pulls his sweater over his head. His white shirt slips upwards exposing his muscles. His boxer hangs over the waistband. And before I can picture the memory, the fabric slips down. Without taking his eyes off me, he hands it to me. He doesn´t say anything, and I swallow hard. My heart beats in my throat as his charcoal eyes swallow mine. I take it. "Thank you" I say hardly audibly, and I consider repeating myself.

Why do I always have to speak so quietly?

I don´t want to be rude. Well, he´s the rude one here. *Or he was?*

He turns around, and I look at his muscular back. His gaze searches mine as he sits down, and I quickly put on the sweater to escape. But a new cocktail of emotions runs through me as my nostrils fill with his scent. A combo of him and something I can´t place. *But fuck, I like it.* I´d like to keep my head inside and never come out, but *obviously* I can´t.

I bury my hands in the sleeves and try to avoid his stare. But he´s burning holes in me.

I eat my bread and zone out on the flames.

Kai´s phone has rung. He gets up and puts it to his ear. Then he walks over to his and slams the door. On the one hand, I´m relieved he´s gone, but on the other.. *Whatever.*

\- 27 -

The air smells like a rain shower. Swallows fly low, I feel a drop on my cheek, and I close my eyes, smiling. *I´ve always been a rain lover.*

As it starts to drizzle, the others get up to go inside. "I´ll follow," I say, and stay seated. When they´re gone, I close my eyes, shutting everything out. Even if I have a hood now, I don´t wear it. Especially since my hair isn´t done anyway.

It feels like I can breathe again. I focus on the crackling of wood and the rain pattering against the roof. My senses are intoxicated.

I´m torn out of my meditative state by a rough voice. "It´s raining." I open my eyes to see Kai, who sits now again across me. He looks at me with a frown. "You´ll get wet." He says as if I didn´t understand what he was implying. "That´s the point" I say a little annoyed and wait for a reaction. *In vain.*

He´s just staring at me. *How long has he been there? And how long have I been?*

He still wears just his t-shirt. He must have been one of the students who wear no jacket but shorts during winter. The desire to give it back creeps up on me, but I resist. Especially since he would refuse it.

So, we just look at each other.

The dripping has turned into spray rain. The air is steamy. The campfire has halved and will go out soon. But we´re still just sitting. *No talking.*

I´m trying to focus on the drizzle instead of the guy in front of me.

Why doesn´t he just go?

"You´re getting wet." I say challengingly. I think I can see a grin through the rain, but I´m not sure. "That´s the point, right?" He returns. I suppress a smile.

He won´t get the satisfaction.

It´s only now that I recognize his T-shirt is soaked. My chest heaves and I´m thankful to be covered with his sweater, so he won´t see. *I hope so, at least.*

As I lift my gaze, he saw me checking him out. *Shit.*

"Aren´t you cold?" I try to justify my gaff. "You?" He throws back with a knowing grin. *Can he answer questions? And did he just smile?* I´m not sure because it disappeared so fast like the memory of a dream in the morning.

"Lia?" Luca calls out and I jerk my head in her direction. *Longed-for salvation.*

I get up and walk towards the terrace. "What are you doing?" She asks, grinning with big eyes. *What am I doing?*

"I´m going home. I´m soaking." I say as I look down on myself. "I can see *that*." She´s laughing. "Are you coming?" I ask. "No, I´ll stay a little longer." She says. "Okay, text me later and say goodbye to the others." I save her a hug.

When I turn to the fireplace. I find it empty. *He´s gone.* Like he´s never been here.

I ride my bike home. In his sweater. *In the rain.* Feeling alone. *Again.*

I chose to be alone. But he sat with me. *Until he didn´t.*

I thought there was a moment of bonding, but I was wrong.

When Nina texted, Kai is taking me to the party, I immediately wanted to cancel. It was a mix of excitement and annoyance. *And a bit of fear.*

I´m not that sure if he despises me. But he can´t hate me *that much* if he agreed to pick me up. *Right?*

The others have been there for a while, and Kai had some work to do, which is why he´s taking me. At least, that´s what Nina told me. I´m sure she forced him to. That´s why I´m already adjusting to an even worse mood than before. Even though I don´t know if I can stand a moodier version. But it´s Friday and I have nothing else to do. Since I don´t have the number of friends who would want me to join a lot of parties, so *I am* going. I just have no idea *what* awaits me.

He didn´t say goodbye as he left Sunday. But I still have his sweater. With which I did not at all slept the past five nights. *This did not happen.* I also didn´t wash it afterward because I feared it would smell like me. *No that did also not happen. Not at all.*

I´m waiting at the fence because, I hate punctuality, and I don´t want to give him any more reasons to be unkind. I´m sure the gesture with the sweater was an exception. It was handsome, but maybe that´s just a thing to do as a guy. Offer your clothes to girls who are freezing.

The matte black BMW turns in. I feel awkward as I stand here like a weirdo waiting on him. *Why didn´t I wait around the corner?* I wouldn´t have to stand around until his car pulled up. It´s even more uncomfortable since he seems to drive on purpose slowly. It´s as bad as walking towards each other from a long distance. *Just unpleasant.*

He doesn´t look at me when he stops by the gate. I´m rooted for a moment and feel my heart beating way too fast for just a drive. *We´ll be alone.* That´s what I´m realizing.

This is a bad idea. What if he just drops me somewhere to piss me off?

He lets down his window. "Won´t open that door for you." He snaps. *Nice. This will be great.* He won´t even look at me. *Asshole.*

I don´t want to have a ride with him either. And I didn´t expect him to open my door either. Besides he´s not the type to open doors. *But the type to offer his hoodie?* I´m not even sure *what* kind of guy he is. *Because I don´t know him.*

Before he addresses me again, I get in. "I´ve got your sweater. I washed it." I tell him and lay it in the foot well. *Silence.* All right, no talking then.

He´s moving fast but controlled. Add to the note, *he´s the guy who´s good at driving*, but that´s what I expected. He has nice taste in cars *and* style.

The whole drive, he ignored me, or we both did. Although I wanted to ask him tons of questions. *I didn´t.* I decided it would be the best to just keep my mouth shut. But there wasn´t even a chance to talk since the car vibrated with the bass.

We park next to a football field. Kai gets out and heads towards the building. His car locks up while I watch him leave. He doesn´t bother to look for me.

Thanks for that, sucker.

On the back of his black T-shirt is a quote.

"Psycho by birth. Bastard by choice."

I almost burst in laughter. *How fitting.*

We´re on someone´s birthday that´s what I know. I don´t know who´s birthday. There are too many people in the clubhouse to make out the special guest. I have no present, but this seems like a huge party anyway. Like every person invited people. There are a lot of guys. *The soccer team?*

I don´t know anyone here besides Nina, Leon, and Aidan. Well and Kai, but I won´t count on that.

- 27 -

Aidan tried to teach me waltzes, and the boys were playing beer pong. Most of the night I was with Aidan and Nina. Kai drove me home. Along with some guys I´ve never seen. But before we got in, he walked a few steps next to me. "You sit front." He said so only I could hear him. Then he rushed ahead and got in.

I sat in the front. Even though I would have loved to piss him off. But something told me I should do as he said. *So, I did.*

I don´t know why. He didn´t want me to sit between them. He´s not bad as he seems.

At least not in every way.

He tuned the volume as loud as he could. Just as before but even a bit louder. But I was glad. It saved me small talk and having to talk to stoned or drunk guys.

10

Next evening

We´re watching a basketball game. *At Kai´s.* And he´s been shooting at me all night and letting me feel that he doesn´t want me here. I´m out of place because of him. *Again.*

Nina said, she would be there too but she wasn´t. *Damn her.*

So, I´m in fact a bit misplaced without her. At least, that´s what *he* makes me feel since I´ve gotten here. I don´t know much about the game but I like the company of the boys, so I decide to stay. Even if he doesn´t want me to. I just hope Nina will be here soon.

When Kai gets up to get some more beer, I take the opportunity to confront him. I follow him into the kitchen.

The quote on his back makes me laugh.

"I was atheist until I realized I´m God."

No, you´re not, fucker. God needs some grounding. He should come back to earth realizing he´s not at all special.

"You don´t know me." I say. He turns to face me. "Right." He replies as he opens the beers with his fist slamming on the edge of the counter. He´s relaxed watching me as if he´s enjoying my upset. Like he´s watching a show or a toddler having an outburst. But I ignore that and keep going.

"Then why are you acting like an *asshole* all the time? I didn´t do you *anything*." I say and his mouth twitches. *Fuck him.*

"Believe me, *yet* I´m nice." He looks at me, making my knees buckle. "*Nice*." I repeat, laughing. "Yes." He says with his eyebrows raised. "Nina invited me over." I state. "Well, *I* didn´t." He replies, sipping on his beer. "And she´s not here, so why don´t you just *leave*?" He asks. To be honest I don´t know. *Why am I not leaving? Do I like being insulted? Is this some sick kink or something?*

As he watches me pondering, he lights himself a joint.

Does he have to smoke pod now?

"You smoke a lot, don´t you?" I ask. "None of your business." He snaps and blows smoke in my direction. "Crack head." I mutter coughing. "Insecure bitch." He laughs, showing his teeth. *What the fuck? Did he just?*

"You´re so pathetic." He scoffs before I can process what he just said. "Get over yourself." I shout, still shocked. "I bet you´re so scared of what other people might think of you. You want to be liked by everyone, which is *why* you care about what *I* think of you." He says and steps closer. "But I have to disappoint you, cause not *everyone* you meet has to like you." He gets in my face. I shake my head in disbelief. *Well, that´s what he thinks of me.* And the worst part is that he´s right.

"I don´t give a *shit* about what *you* think." I defend myself, but my lie is obvious. "Sure." He says knowing he´s right. "Let me give you a piece of advice." He says between a puff. "*If you make decisions based upon people´s reactions or opinions, then you make really bad choices.* Heath ledger, a smart man." He quotes leaning against the counter. I don´t know what to say, so I just blink at him as he smokes his blunt with satisfaction.

"You know you have *your* opinion about me, and I have mine about *you*. The only difference is that *I´m* right. You´re not." He continues.

“Guys come on.” Aidan intervenes. *Finally, one of them speaks up.* The whole evening, they just let him stomp me down. They even laughed like it´s his way of communication or some shit.

“Avery, stay out of this.” Kai´s glaring at him until Aidan raises his hands and turns his attention back to the game. *Great.* So, I´m by myself. *As if it were anytime different. Why did I think they would help me in this?* I´m not one of their friends, just cause I´ve partied with them twice. They stood up for me last week because Nina *wanted* them to. *I feel so stupid.* Of course, they´d be on his side when she´s not there. I mean he wasn´t calling me names but he wasn´t friendly either.

Not at all. He´s just rude for no reason.

Anger boils inside of me, which out drains the anxiety I should feel right now.

I don´t know what gets into me as I speak. “You are a rich *bastard.*” I howl. “Fuck off.” He laughs like I´m a joke. *And somehow, I feel like that.*

But I keep going. “Looks like you´ve got it all shoved up your ass, the best proof is in front of your garage or on your wrist.” I gesture to his Rolex, and he just shakes his head mockingly. That´s when I realize. *He´s right, I am pathetic.*

“You have *no* idea.” He laughs, taking another drag. *He´s not taking me seriously.*

I wouldn´t either.

“Yeah, *I* know. So do you. So shut up about things you simply have no idea about.” I say heated. He chuckles. *Seriously?* He´s way too confident and arrogant.

“It´s obvious that I have, or you wouldn´t be freaking out like that. Just because I called you out on your insecurities.” He says amused. “Confident people are the most insecure people.” I say in return and I´m proud of that one. But this blows as he nods like I´m a child. *God, I hate this guy.* He´s beautiful on the outside, but his personality is *ugly.*

“I can´t stand this.” I say. “I get it, you *clearly* don´t want me here.” I add. “That´s right.” He answers, straightening up. “Okay.” I nod, swallowing the lump in my throat. *Fuck, I can´t cry now. I can´t give him that.*

My face heats painfully. “Then I´ll go.” I say and rush outside, ignoring the looks of the others. *I am embarrassed.* I can´t wrap my head around what just happened. *But he´s right. Fuck, he read me like a book. Why can he read me, and I can´t read him?*

I accused him with nothing but sad attempts. I squeeze my eyes shut. *I feel stupid.* I made a fool of myself.

The door opens. For some reason, I know it´s him. *He´s got to be kidding me.*

"Wait." He demands. I stop and turn around. "What?" I ask furiously. "Come back in." He says as if none of it happened. Like it was indeed *just a game*. A sick way of making fun of me. *Feeding his ego or some shit.*

I shake my head in confusion. "What? Why? No!" I shout. "Just come back in." He says again. I look at him in amazement. *He does not apologize. I know he won´t. Well, I won´t either. But I don´t have to. He on the other hand..*

"I´m not gonna beg, so do what you want." He shrugs and walks back in.

The guy clearly has mood swings.

I shouldn´t care that he doesn´t like me. *But I do.* And he´s the leader. He´s their friend.

So, I have to deal with him.

After a few minutes of processing and considering what to do, I go back inside, but Kai´s already gone. *Better so.*

11

Aidan apologized for his behavior. Leon said *he´s the way he is*. I made a sarcastic remark on that, and they laughed. In ways, I´m proud I stuck up to him even if I failed in the end.

But I got back in. Although he wasn´t there anymore. I don´t know where he went but I didn´t ask.

As the next ad starts, I get up and go to the bathroom. I dial Nina´s number and wait for her to answer.

She didn´t pick up but called me back after two minutes. "Hi sorry Lia, I couldn´t make it." She wines. She got my angry texts, cursing her for letting me down today.

"It´s okay. But you should have told them." I say upset. "I did. I told Leon." She points out. "Well, he didn´t tell the others." I say annoyed, and with others I meant him. "Kai was rude to you." She guesses. "*Rude*?" I yell. "He kicked me out after he gave me death stares and assaulting remarks all night long." I say irritated.

"Lia I´m sorry." She apologizes again. "He hates me." I say. "He doesn´t hate you." She says. I laugh. *I bet she doesn´t even believe that.*

"Of course, he does." I scoff. "He just.. He hates *new* people." She tells me. "*New*?" I ask. "I got the impression he hates *all* people." I say. She laughs. I do to. "He doesn´t hate his friends." She states. "Don´t see us there." I try to joke, but I know it´s true. *We´ll never be friends.* Even if I wanted to. Cause he *clearly* wouldn´t. But even despite his rudeness he´s someone I´d liked to get to know. Which is *exactly* the proof why I´m *indeed* pathetic.

"Well, he´s a bit narrow-minded." She agrees. I laugh. "Did not pass me." I say. "Look.." She begins. "I´ve told you about the rules, right?" I frown. "Yeah." I say unsure where she´s going. "There are *simple* rules. Don´t talk to him for example." She tells me and I stiff a laugh. "How should I not talk to him when he´s around all the time? And when we´re hanging at his?" I ask. "I´m just saying Kai´s someone you shouldn´t fuck with. He´s used to *his* people." She adds but causes just more questions.

"Couldn´t you have warned me before I´ve upset him?" I ask fed up. "Well, I think either way, you would have. He hates all my new friends. He hates me bringing them, to be exact." She mutters. I let out an annoyed and upset sound.

"But don´t worry about him. Either you ignore him, or you stand up to him. Either way, he´ll be the way he is." She says, and I shake my head cause Leon said the same thing. "Asshole? Arrogant? Offending?" I list. She laughs.

"How can you be friends with him anyway?" I ask confused. "He doesn´t like most people." She says. "That´s nothing new." I interrupt her. "He likes us cause we´ve grown up together. Or rather, *they* did. It took a time for him to tolerate *me*. Mostly for Leons´s sake. And cause, he realized I won´t go no matter how many times we broke up." She tells me.

"And now he has to get used to you too, because I won´t get rid of you." She assures me. I smile weakly. "He´ll make hell out of it." She warns me. *I bet he´ll do.*

"See it as a challenge." She chirps, on which I stiff a laugh. "He´s not *that* bad." She says in a way she means it; I can tell. "I doubt it." I mutter and she laughs.

"He´s really fun. Besides Aidan, the funniest guy I know." She says. "I don´t know who you´re talking about." I retort. "You´ll see. Get to know him." She says. "If he lets you." She adds with a laugh, and I sigh.

"He´s sarcastic. But his rudeness is just a façade. You´ll see if you´ll get along." She says. *If we´ll get along.*

12

We played a game called Paranoia. Which was one of *the* games they play. From what I´ve heard they usually play worse games, but I´m glad we start with something light. We sat in a circle. One person starts and flips a shoe. If it lands face down; the person won´t say the question out loud but whispers to the player. If it lands face up; the question is asked out loud. In both cases, the player must answer loudly and truthfully.

I didn´t really get what the point was since I didn´t know all the players, but because of the rules I kept my mouth shut and played. First round I got lucky and could answer without them knowing what I got asked. *Who´s most likely to have a beautiful voice?* I said Kai. He looked at me. I was glad he didn´t know. But the way he stared holes at me, he wanted to know. *His bad.*

Who´s the dirtiest in the group? A girl got asked. Kai, she said. They all agreed.

I got whispered; W*ho is capable of robbing a bank?* I said, "Leon, for sure." He frowned at me.

Some asked; *who´s most likely to become a phone sex operator?* Nina was the answer. She threw her cup at that guy. Then she had to answer *who´s more likely to have a body buried in their backyard?* She said Kai. They laughed. "He would." Aidan agreed. And to the question *who´s more likely to sniff at their partner´s undies,* Kai said Leon. They smirked. Nina just shook her head.

That game was fun, but every time someone said my name and I didn´t know why, I freaked out on the inside. Especially when Aidan and Kai said it.

Somehow, the shoe often landed face up. Vans land almost every time the right way. At least, that´s what I´ve come to conclusion.

And with the time, they asked questions without the whispering thingy, so you had to answer *plus* everyone knew. It became more of a group play. Cause everyone who wanted could guess. We just asked random questions.

Who´s most likely to say I´m born in the wrong generation? Kai, they said at the same time. *I would do that too.* But I didn´t say my name. *Who´s the smartest?* I got asked. I caught his eyes before I said it. "Kai." I don´t even know why I said it, but it just came out. "Doubt it." Leon mocked him. They grinned at each other. His eyes fell on me after that for a second.

I got asked; *who´s more likely to eat their birthday cake alone?* I said "Me." *If I only got one.* But I didn´t say that one. There was an awkward silence. "I would do that too." Some girl joined in, trying to make it less weird for me.

What stung with me was the question; *who´s most likely to break hearts?* Kai, a guy said. Everyone agreed. And what felt like an assault was the answer to the question *who´s likely to fall in love without hesitation?* Kai stiffed a laugh and said blonde girl, as if it´s been an insult. And it´s ash blond I wanted to tell him. *But I didn´t.* But it was the truth, but it did fucking hurt. It hurt even more because he doesn´t know shit about me but guessed right. Or judged right.

He also said my name when he got asked *who´s the most sensitive and insecure? And I called that prick intelligent.* It occurred to me that he used that game to pick on me. So, I decided to hit back.

The girl next to me asked *who I think would die first at the hunger games*? I said Kai. The boys laughed. "I would win." He said. *I know he would.* "Nah." Leon said. "You heard her you would lose." He grinned. Kai shot me a look.

The funniest in the group? Aidan. Nina would create a fake profile on social media. *Who would host the best party?* Kai.

Lie about their age? Nina. *Most sexual partners?* Aidan. *Foot fetish?* Leon. *Perfect kisser?* Kai. *Partners name tattooed?* Leon showed Nina´s name under his chest. My eyes widened. *That´s serious.* She cried last month because they broke up. Now they´re back together. It´s a back and forth. One that´s been *inked.*

To have a side chick? Aidan. *Biggest pervert?* Leon. He smacked Kai´s chest. *Be a nymphomaniac?* Aidan and Nina. *Be a screamer?* Nina. *Who´s going to hell?* Kai. *Who had the worst childhood?* Aidan. *Needs to see a therapist?* Kai. He flicked Leon his finger. *Meanest person in the circle?* Kai. *The most spiritual?* Kai. That stung with me too, but his dog is named Spirit, so maybe it´s true.

Become a millionaire? Kai. *Who will die first?* Nina because she´s clumsy or Kai who´s careless. *The worst superhero?* Kai. *Fart and blame the dog?* Leon. *Socks that never match?* Leon. *Who looks the youngest for their age?* Lia. *Tell their teacher their dog devoured the homework?* Aidan. *Creative one?* Kai, they said. "Lia." Nina said. He looked at me.

The worst driver? Kai said Nina and I thought he would say my name even if he wouldn´t know. But he would say *anything* at this point.

Get kicked out of a museum for touching the Art? Kai. *To think a plane is a shooting star?* Nina. *Walk around their house naked?* Aidan. *Freakiest in the circle?* Kai. *Have the most kinks?* Kai. *To have a threesome?* Aidan. *Owns the most sex toys?* Nina. *Watches the most porn?* Leon. *Laugh during sex?* Nina. *Cry during sex?* Also, Nina. *Daddy issues?* Nina.

Prude of the group? "Lia." Kai called. "Not at all." Nina said, knowing me. I just grinned. Kai looked at me for a beat.

Sex Playlist? Nina. *Mirror on their ceiling?* Leon. He has one.

Horniest in the group? Aidan. "Lia" Nina said loudly. "Shut up." I yelled. Again, Kai looked at me. But they all did.

Sex in public? Aidan. *Sleep with their boss?* Aidan and Nina. *Sex tape?* Leon.

13

Next evening, Golden Brown – The Stranglers

"We call em the lost boys." The girl says. "Like in the movie?" I ask. "Yeah." She grins. "And all this." She lets her gaze wander between the people. "This is Neverland." She says as if it was real. "They created it." She adds. *They?*

"Okay?" I ask not sure how to respond to that. Nina disappeared with Leon and left me with that girl. Who wanted to tell me more about the parties.

"Our parties are different." The girls says. "Yeah, I´ve heard that." I retort. "But what does that mean?" I ask. "There are the lost boys and the pirates." She explains leaning forward. "They crash each other´s parties. Call the cops. Mess with each other." She tells me. "One night they came with water bombs. The other, they hit back with nerve guns. They did paintball. They do car races. Have fights. Do bets. All kinds of stuff." She says with a shrug, and I try to process.

"Then who´s Peter?" I ask laughing. "The lost boy itself." She nods towards Kai who´s smoking across from the terrace. I knew she meant him.

"Who´s Wendy?" I grin. "There´s not *one* Wendy." She says. "We all are." She shrugs.

What does that mean?

I thought Wendy left Neverland eventually. The only one who stayed was his fairy. "Who´s Tinker?" I wonder. "Lost boy has none." She says as if he´s sad for that.

And maybe he is.

"And who´s Hook?" I ask. "*That* you must ask the flying devil itself." She says as if we were in some play. "Aka the lost boy known as Peter Pan?" I assume. "You got it." She smiles. I shake my head. *She´s weird.*

I narrow my eyes. "You´re high on something?" I ask. "And don´t say pixie dust." I warn. "No." She laughs. "Just some weeed." She grins. And I believe that right now she´s running from Captain Hook, with her head in the stars, flying through Neverland.

She´s definitely on another planet right now.

I get up and let her be in dreamland. This party gets weirder and weirder. *The lost boys.* I shake my smile off as I walk to the boy of the moon. *The boy who wouldn´t grow up.*

I sit down. "So." I begin watching Kai inhaling his blunt. He frowns at me, followed by a slight chin tilt. He blows smoke in the air. *No insult as a greeting.* I guess that´s some progress. *Or just the weed.*

“Who´s Hook?” I ask right from the back. His frown deepens for a moment before it disappears and his mouth twitches. So, he *knows* what I´m talking about.

Means Neverland is a thing?

“Whoever you need him to be.” He says, gesturing with his Jibbit. I roll my eyes. All those people have an inner philosopher. *Can they just answer questions? Or is that part of the games? Keeping the newcomers in the dark to play with?* Maybe I´m part of the game. Part of *his* game.

“He´s your greatest fear.” He clarifies. Now I´m the one frowning. “For Peter, it´s growing up.” He tells me. “And death for Hook. That´s why you hear the ticking clock whenever death is near Hook, who hunts Pan to ban him from Neverland.” He explains. “I don´t understand.” I say. “You didn´t watch the movie as a kid?” He asks offended. “I did.” I say.

He takes a drag and speaks with a deeper voice due to the smoke in his lungs. “What´s your biggest fear?” I inhale pondering. “L..Losing control, I guess.” I say. He nods with a grin. “So that´s Hook for you.” He tells me. I search his face. *Who´s this guy? Didn´t he hate me?*

“What´s yours?” I ask. He hesitates for a moment. His jaw hardens. And he looks past me. Looking at *someone*, but just as I want to turn, he speaks. “Time.” *So, death.*

I look at his Rolex. *He notices.*

He shows me his arm. I look at the watch. “It stopped.” He says.

Indeed, it stopped at four in the morning.

“I never look at the time.” He adds. “Cause something as time doesn´t exist?” I guess. He smiles, narrowing his eyes. As if he didn´t expect me to get that. *Dick.*

“Exactly.” He says nodding. “Time is a prison I don´t want to live in.” He adds. I smile. *“Time is an illusion.”* I quote *Albert Einstein*. His mouth twitches. “*In Medias Res*. Life is *always* in medias res.” He nods.

We look at each other for a moment.

“Come with me where dreams are born, and time is never planned.” He quotes the movie, I assume. “And *this* is Neverland? Your parties?” I ask. He tilts his head wanting to nod but also shake his head. “No. Not the parties. The people. The time you spend with them. That´s why we don´t allow phones. In Neverland, there´s no time. No growing up. Just dreaming. Fun and friends.” He responds. *He´s so talkative right now.*

It´s unusual but refreshing.

“So, like mindfulness.” I consider. “Yeah, kinda like that.” He agrees. “Be in the now.” I repeat one of the rules. He nods like I got it. “Cause *once you´re grown up, you can´t come back.*” He quotes again now I know for sure it´s what Peter Pan said. “Is *that* why you keep playing those games?" I ask. "Cause at Neverland you'll do those things?" I ask. "We do what we want to." He shrugs. "If we want to play hopscotch we do. If we want to do a race, we do. If we want to rub a Bank, we do. If we want to jump in the pool from the roof.." He lists, but I cut in. "Okay, I get it." I say. "So *actually*, Neverland is an escape." I say. "Nah." He dismisses. *But I'm sure it is.*

"It's a way of living. A mindset. A religion or a belief system." He says. "But when Hook is your greatest fear, and you run from it while doing what you want in Neverland.." I begin. "You *are* running from your problems instead of dealing with them." I point out. "Yeah, like all people do." He shrugs. *So, they do run.*

"No one wants to deal with their shit. But we do it with fun." He smirks. "And we know *exactly* what we're running from." He adds. "If it's work. Our relationships. Parents. Ourselves. We know. We're aware. Which most of the people aren't. That's why they never reach Neverland." He speaks as if he tells me the meaning of life. *And in a way he does.*

I'm always down for spirituality or an open mindset. So, I listen.

"Cause, they don't acknowledge their fears. They run from the unknown. They don't deal. *We do.* We get that we can't outrun those. They're with us all the time even in Neverland they follow. But we won't let them overpower us. We live with them. Like dancing with death. You can't run if you walk along with it." He explains, and I memorize all the letters. He keeps talking with such an excitement I want him to never stop.

"The ticking never stops. But you can decide to not listen." He says, tapping on his watch. "To make it stop. To draw your attention to the now, the people, and the things you want." It gushes out of him, and there is a way of how he's talking that I want to know every opinion he has.

He stubs out his Joint because it burned down while he held his monologue. He leans back, crossing his arms behind his head watching me taking in. And he does it with curiosity. Like he enjoys enlightening people.

A smile fights to surface. *But he beats it.*

"Welcome to Neverland." He says, with the head in the clouds. *He's extremely high.* Maybe that's why he keeps talking with me.

"Aren't there no rules in Neverland?" I ask. "From what I've seen, you've got a long list." I joke. "Rules can be bent." He says smug.

"And there *are* rules to Neverland. The lost boys follow Pan. Which is the main rule." He says with a grin. That's why he's the one who decides who stays ~~in Neverland,~~ I mean the parties. *Maybe, he's the one who invites people too?*

"So, what do you wanna do *now* that you´ve reached Neverland?" He asks. *He´s way too friendly now. When does he kick me out or offend me again?*

"I don´t.. know." I say. Just as he opens his mouth to respond, Aidan sits down next to him. *He shuts his mouth.*

"Sup?" Aidan asks. I look at Kai. He looks from me to his friend. "Someone´s new to dreamland." He says. Aidan smiles, lifting his eyebrows understanding. "Dream big." He nods. "Huh?" I ask. "I haven´t gotten to that part yet." Kai intervenes and Aidan nods.

What part?

"So, the next big thing we do is up to you." He says. I look at them questioning. "Like a game, an activity, a trip, a place, or something like that." Aidan explains. "But chose wisely. We all must do it with you." He tells me. "Like the *whole* party?" I ask. He nods. My eyes widen. *All of them. No pressure at all.*

"Your first wish is valid for all of us. After that you can choose the people, you want in with you." He states. "Cause not everyone has the same dreams." He points out. "*If* you´re staying." He adds. But I think *allowed* is the better term.

"What were your wishes?" I ask them. They grin. "That´s a story for another day." Aidan brushes me off. "But most of the things we do are our ideas. And we do a lot of stupid things." He grins. They exchange looks, having a conversation without words or something. And it´s now that I realize they´re best friends. They keep talking and goof around. And it´s the first time I see a different side of Kai. *A side I really like.*

"I´ll think of something." I say. But they´re not paying attention anymore. So, I smile watching them crack up.

This party is something I never would have expected. *But maybe all I need.*

Hopefully, I can come up with something for them to want me to stay.

She wasn´t aware, but Neverland was a dark place. Pan trapped her. And she would never leave him. *Nor Neverland.*

14

"You´re friends with Nina, right?" A girl speaks up next to me. "Yeah." I say. She nods to herself. There is an awkward moment. I don´t get often addressed neither from guys nor girls, so I just look at her.

"You´re the new one. I´ve seen you around." She says. "Yeah." I say. "Most of the newies don´t make a night here." She points out. *So, it´s really a thing that he scares people.*

My eyes wander to him for a sec, but she caught me. "He´s hot right?" She gushes and nods towards Kai. He sits across us talking to some guys. "He is." I say intently. "But.. a dick." I add. She laughs. "Words." She laughs. "But demons must be beautiful to make sins." She agrees. We smile at each other.

"I know you´re new and since you made it so far, I´ll tell you this to spare you some shit." She offers. I look at her thankfully. *Finally*, someone who wants to help me instead of that cryptic stuff they feed me. *At least, I hope she will.*

"If I were you, I would stay away from him." She says. *That´s not what I´ve expected.* But Nina told me the same. And he did that in ways, too.

I watch him for a moment, the way he laughs with his friends. *Why can´t he laugh with me?* I mean he did the other day, but that was because he was high. Now he´s back to whatever he´s doing. *Hating me.*

"He´s trouble." She says. I look at her. Her friend speaks up behind her. "Better listen." She laughs as if she knows what she´s speaking of. I frown at them. "He´s a psycho but a gorgeous one. That´s why you fall for him." She says. *Fall for him?*

"Who would fall for that guy?" I laugh. *You. Idiot.*

"Believe me, we´ve fallen for him too. It always ends bad with these lost boys." She says with a smile. *We? Lost boys?*

"So, this is a thing here, huh?" I ask and she nods.

"You know they say it´s a fairy tale. But it´s darker." She says. "The darlings aren´t for playing. They are for fucking. For sharing and possessing. To mess with." She tells me. "They play with them, yes, but not in the way you´d think." She says and I blink.

"They get them to break them." She tells me. "The guys here have all kinds of kinks." She looks around. "But they´re the worst." She says. "Who?" I try to make him out, but she faces me. "Hook and Pan." She says. *Kai.*

"He likes hurting. He breaks hearts. He´s cold. He´s rude." She lists. "Arrogant and selfish. And he rejected every girl." She continues and her friend finishes. "And those who get the chance to date him or at least what comes close to dating end up with high hopes and hurt." She reveals. "He did some fucked up shit." She says as she eyes him. "He kicked a girl he had something with, out of his car and dumped her that day. Her knees and hands were bleeding. She wasn´t invited after that day anymore." She tells me. "What?" I ask looking at him and our eyes meet. I rip my gaze off him.

"Yeah." Her friend joins in. "He has beaten some guy just because he looked at him. He went to the hospital. He fights. Thy play games with the girls here. Mess with their feelings. With their minds." She says. "That´s why here are more guys than girls.

Eventually they must replace them. If they aren´t claimed or leaving by themselves." She goes on, and I try to process what she´s saying.

"He even tried to commit suicide on one of the parties. In front of everyone." The other girl adds. *He what? Why are they telling me all this?*

I catch his gaze a second time but regain my focus as they keep talking. "Most girls still try. Cause he´s fucking beautiful, funny, smart and a born bad boy. Tempting to lose your heart to. But they end up like the other girl, bleeding and broken. With nothing." She shrugs.

"So, save yourself that." The other one warns me. "He won´t treat you good." She says. "He used to fuck a lot. But then he stopped. Hasn´t fucked for a year or so. Seems like he doesn´t care anymore." She says with a smile. "I think it stopped after he fucked someone´s girlfriend." The other one shrugs. I gape at her. "A rumor." She grins. "But that doesn´t mean he won´t fuck you otherwise." She says.

"But one thing that´s good about him, he´s honest. *Brutally.* He doesn´t want a girl, and he makes that *very* clear. But they stick to him like trapped in honey. Hoping, they´re the exception. But he´s heartless. No one to fall in love with. He just sucks the honey and drops you." She tells me.

"Unspoken rule of the girls here." She smiles. "T*ry not to fall in love with that guy. And not his bed.*" She says with a laugh. "But some girls can´t resist." The other says. "Yeah, because he *fucks* so good. He´s kinky." She hums. "But the hurt isn´t worth it." She says shaking her head. "He might be lost boy. But there´s a dark side to the fairy tale." She says. "Remember that. And here are other lost boys to choose from." She smiles. *Lost boy.* So, it´s true then. It´s no joke. The people here *know* about this. It´s not just games, it´s *more.* It´s dark and twisted. And hurtful. *And he´s the worst.*

They go on and on. Gossiping and telling me all the horrible things he has done. Why should I stay away. But all I can do is stare at him, wondering. He catches me and holds eye contact for way too long to be comfortable with. *Dead eyes.* Eyes of a lost boy. There´s no happy lost boy. I should have kept that in mind. *Because even Pan has reasons why he is the way he is. There might be a dark side, but how dark can it be? Where fairies are real, and you believe in them?*

He looks at the girls next to me, still chattering. And back to me. He straightens up. Still holding my gaze. The girls have noticed and walk off, giving me a small smile. I return it, looking after them. *Weird.* They didn´t even tell me their names.

As I turn, Kai´s eyes are on me as he strides towards me.

Seems like Pan made out his victim.

"Made friends?" He asks. "Don´t think so." I say. "They just.." I shake my head. "Whatever." I say. "You know those girls?" I ask instead. His eyes narrow. "I know *all* the people here." He says. "It´s my party, my house, my drugs, my people." He says intently. "You like them?" I ask. As if he likes *anyone* but himself.

He stiffs a laugh, shaking his head. "No, I don´t like them *much*." He says, fighting a smile like he knows I´m beating around the bush. "But that´s not what you want to know, right?" He looks at me, waiting. *Did he hear what we talked about?* Cause he acts like he knows *exactly*. But he couldn´t due to the music and the distance. He just *saw* us talking.

Or he has his own fairy watching the island.

"No." I admit. "What is it?" he asks towering over me. "People talk." I begin. "They do." He nods. "They.. talk about *you*." I clarify. He nods again. "And.. *you* believe them." He assumes, but it´s more of a statement. "I *don´t* believe them." I say, but he cuts me off. "You believe them enough to ask me if it´s true." He spits. *So, he knows?*

He leans against the post, crossing his arms. My eyes wander to his biceps for a sec. But he speaks up. "What do they say about me?" He asks, as if he knows. "They say.. you tried to.." I stammer. "Commit suicide?" He finishes, raising his eyebrows. "Yeah." I lower my eyes. *Why did I ask him that?*

"Why?" He asks, lifting his chin. "Why what?" I wanna know. "Why do they spread those rumors?" He clarifies. "I don´t know." I say. "Think about it." He tells me straightening up. But he doesn´t wait for me to think. "They talk *shit* about me, cause they know *nothing* about me." He tells me. "I´m a *mystery* to them." He does those air quotes. "I´m a closed book to them, so they start smearing the cover. That´s what people do when they know shit. *Quack*. Desperate to know something. Desperate for attention. But they get *shit*." He spits. "I did hit that guy, cause he harassed Nina. They think I´ve tried to kill myself because I sat on the roof. I just chilled and smoked pod. I didn´t drink, and I didn´t attempt to jump. I didn´t try to off myself. That´s what *they* made out of it. I sit up there all the time. Which they would know if they were friends with me." He explains.

"And.. that girl you dated and threw out of your car?" I stammer, already feeling like an idiot. He exhales annoyed. "I kicked her out because she grabbed my *dick* without permission. Not every guy wants any girl to suck their dick." He says irritated. "And *fuck* no, I didn´t date her. I just gave her a ride, cause she was plastered and wanted to drive. She knew the rules. And I didn´t *throw* her out. I asked her to get out. I told her to fuck off and I left. But I didn´t kick her. She felt embarrassed cause I rejected her. But she made all that up. The bleeding and all." He says spitefully. "Why didn´t you clarify then?" I ask. "Why should I?" He asks fed up. "I don´t *fucking* care about those who believe assumptions. I care about my friends, nothing more." He spits. *That´s what I thought.*

"I asked you about that one because it was the one I cared about. The one I was afraid of being.. true." I admit, feeling ashamed. "What if it were?" He shrugs and looks down on me. "What if I wanted to? But not on the roof but in my bathroom. Or the pool or on the highway?" He asks, glaring. I look at him, unable to answer. *He tried to..? I´m such an ass.*

"Nothing. Cause I´m still here, so doesn´t matter." He mutters. "It´s disrespectful. And none of their *fucking* business." He says hateful. "And *you* listen to their bullshit. They´re just jealous cause you´re friends with Nina. They fear you. Cause you´re close to the inner circle. They just want to mess with you." He says. *Fear me? Close to the..*

"I´m sorry." I say, but he shakes his head. "Don´t be." He shrugs. "Own it." He demands. "It´s easier to think what others think." He says, nodding, and it feels like a punch in the gut. More in the throat, because I feel sick and guilty. *Deserved.*

His chin shots back as if I offended him, which I probably did. "For some reason, I thought better of you." He scoffs and walks past me. I squeeze my eyes shut.

He did think better of me? I´m confused.

So, was Nina right and *his rudeness is just some sort of defense mechanism?*

Either way, I fucked up. And pissed him off. *Again.*

[NOTEBOOK ENTRIES]

We all have that mindset of not giving a damn. Of living in the moment and knowing death is around the corner waiting. It´s a way of surviving in a world where polar bears die. It´s a way out of life, an escape, and a hideout. It´s a bond we can´t escape. A pact we made. A place we´re home, hide and stay. There are the lost boys. Aidan and Leon, Ryan and Andi, Finn and me and Nina since she´s with one of us. She´s not one of the Wendy´s. She counts as a lost girl. But we´re the center. The others are just players. And there are the pirates. The enemies. Who we fight. We made those games up. We found people who would follow, play, and do risky shit. Who liked it fast and aware. But no one enters our group. At least not the closest. And they know. But we have some rule breakers under us. One especially. She likes to invite people trying to widen our circle. Play wingman. But they are just people to play with. No bond. No exception. And she knows it, but she keeps messing with me. And I keep messing with her friends, as she calls them. I get it she´s lonely with all the lost boys around her. There are few girls at our gatherings. She wants a friend. Someone who stays. But she has us. There's no need for another lost girl. . A lost girl isn't anyone either. We're the founders. And she can invite as many as she wants. They don't stay. Because Neverland isn't for everyone. It's for those who have no family but their friends. And in the beginning, it was fun fucking with the newie's. But now it's just annoying. The fun stopped since Hook tried to kill Pan. But she can't decide who's in. I decide. Because I am Neverland. This is me. I'm the lost boy. Peter Pan.

There was that girl Leon warned me about that Nina would bring. I know how to deal with them. As soon as they get I'm not into their stuff they fuck off. Sometimes they need a little help. But they don't stay and we don't play anymore. But Leon said she's okay. Which made me mad. None of her friends has ever been okay. Does that mean she's inner circle, okay? I hope not. I can argue with Nina but if the boys agree too I'm not sure. And I hate when the guys try to set me up with someone. Never gonna happen.

That girl showed up. She looked good. Ash blonde hair with blue puppy eyes. Nice ass little tits. All fine. Fine to fuck and to play with. But not enough to be part. And I knew Nina would try to implant her but I'm sick of her trying to find someone who would fit. They never do. One worse than the other. And that girl got on my nerves. The way she looked at me like she already wanted me to fuck her. She's been insecure. But what dived me mad was the way they stood up for her. They don't even know her. Leon just wanted to please Nina, but they were against me. And they never do. I hated her the moment they turned their backs on me. I let her stay though. She will run anyway because most people don't agree with our way of living or partying. They are boring and she seemed exactly like that. She made out with Aidan. He did it to piss me off and partly cause he found her hot. But the worst was they seem to get along. We were already enough people. We didn't needed more rule breakers. Or someone who would quack about the things we did. The illegal stuff, the car races or the break-ins and other stuff I won't write about. Those things happened before. With all the people Nina invited. Those were people who don't get what we do. We break rules, do drugs, are selfish and broken. Pain is our fuel. We see the world through eyes of a child. Still colorful and as an adventure. We love the thrill and do the stupid and dangerous stuff no one would dare. We are in the now. And nowhere else, and I don't want her in. So let's hope she won't stay long. Or I'll have to make her go. And there's the simple and the hard way. It's up to her. But some say lost boy loves a great game, blood and pain so let's see how it ends.

Nina is convinced she's her next bestie. But it's been always that way. She thinks they fit. Surprise they never do. And in addition, blond girl brought a friend of hers. It couldn't get any better. Since we don't play with the girls as we used to, I'll have to scare them off differently. It won't take long. Although, she didn't stare at me like the others did. But I knew I got under her skin. The pain will be greater then. Wendy's get attached so easily. Tinkers and lost girls are the smart ones. But the latter are rare and the former a myth. I gave her my hoodie because she wasn't smart enough to bring one herself. And despite my indifference towards her, I'm not an asshole. But just as I thought the night couldn't piss me off more, father called. Business wise. That I even thought otherwise. When isn't it about that? I must admit she surprised me. She sat in the rain. While the others were inside partying, she sat there and looked peaceful. I sat with her until I realized what the hell I was doing, so I left and got back to hating her because it was always just the six of us. Then came Nina and with her the problems. Not only for Leon, cause they fought a lot but for us too. She invited people who would call the police, post on social media or mess with our dynamic. But what was worse was when they fell for us. We played games with them. It was fun, but some of us got hurt in ways we could never take back. I kept playing with Andi. We always hated each other, what kept the games exciting. He's part of us because he's my brother's best friend. And even though Leon and Nina are always on-off, she's part too. And that was an exception. And that girl won't be another. Even if she sat in the rain and didn't care. Even if she looked beautiful with the rain on her skin. Even if I liked her in my hoodie. Even if I got curious. She's no exception.

Nina tries to do it differently. But that doesn't mean she's different too. She's as boring as all the other Wendy's. Wendy's who want to grow up. All the things I don't want. I had to take her home, but I went with some pirates. Weed wise and other stuff. Places she shouldn't go. So, I told her to sit next to me. Because I know the guys. Especially one of them. She listened. Lucky for her. I wouldn't have hesitated to force her. Putting her next to Wren or the other two idiots would have been corrupt. But he must know she's special, even if she isn't. For her being in my car, she was kind of. No one drives in my car without me wanting them. So, he knew. But he kept shut. They all did. They would have made her join us. But that was the last thing I wanted, so I put the volume up. I had no choice but to keep her from them. Besides she's mine to fuck with. They didn't question her. But silence in Wren's case is never good. Silence in his case means war.

I was looking forward to a non-girl's night. But blond girl was there, and she annoyed the shit out of me. The others had no problem with her being here, but mostly because they knew it pissed me off. I was wondering when she would fight back. Cause most Wendy's dare not. And I needed fun. Although her punches were weak, at least she tried. She's full of shit. The fact that she used the pod and money to shoot at me was almost funny. She didn't even defend herself. But Aidan took her side. Again. Some fuse blew, and I made her go. It made me rage, cause I know he likes her. Even Leon. Why do they like her? But I felt weird afterward. I never felt that way. The boys told me to get her back. They took her side over mine. A-fucking-gain. If they want her in. I'm out. Aidan told me I should give her a go. That she's different. But how would he know? He doesn't know her. And I don't want to know her. She isn't different. She's worse.

We argue mostly over dumb shit. But it's fun. The way she gets angry or annoyed with me. I like toying with the mouse before I eat it. It's more fun when the prey fights back. She tries to offend me, but I find it amusing. It's sweet really. It's too easy for me to make her mad. She's shy and fights like a pup. Like a little fairy she tries to stick up. Pathetic.

The other girls tried to make me fall for them or to please me. Bash their eyelids. Cry even. But she didn't. Despite her shyness, she stuck up to me. At least tried to. With me, she wasn't so shy. Kinda liked that. The way she looked at me like she wants to kill me. Exactly what keeps my dick going. A pain in the arse that ash girl. She's the most exciting I played with. I think it's not hard to crack her, but to break her will be. Because I have a feeling, she can bear great pain. But I found the right buttons to push. She knew points in me too. I must give her that. Which was refreshing. I know there's more in her. I just need to keep stabbing for her to stab back. And then, I'm closer to get what I want. Pain, scars, and blood. Because that's what makes Pan fly without a fairy. I never had one. I learned other ways to keep me going. Who needs Tinker when I can kill Wendy's?

They say Wendy's can become lost girls. But for me, they never did.

Her friends before were boring but that girl wasn't. So, I found my pastime. My next prey. My next game. My next blood to make me fly.

15

Since yesterday, we've been arguing constantly. He insults me and I try to fire back. He makes it obvious to everyone he doesn't like me, and I despise him either. We make fun of each other, but in a *funny* teasing way, sarcastic and mean.

It's fun sometimes and sometimes not, cause his strikes hit deep.

When he'll make it a hard time for me, I'll do the same in return.

"With your damn blue eyes." He scoffs. "I have green eyes." I say cause that´s not the first-time people assume that which is incorrect. And I´m stubborn as hell even over minor things as eye colors. *But that´s a personal one.*

"Nah. They´re blue." He says stubbornly. "My eyes are green." I say stolid. He shakes his head. "They are." I get into his face, so he can look. He steps closer. Squinting his eyes. "They are." He says. "See." I say with proud. He notices the proximity as he still stares into my not at all blue eyes.

"They are gray too." His voice deeper than before. *My smile falls.*

He clears his throat, backing away. "Stick that *shit* grin up your ass." He shots. Whereas I grin. *As I said, it´s funny sometimes.*

\- 27 -

The music roars through my ears. I´m standing in the kitchen looking out. It´s getting dark. It has started to rain. I rest my palms on the edge of the sink. And suddenly, my social battery is dead. Like someone flipped a switch. I´d like to go home, read or just sleep. But before Nina wants to have another shot, I better sneak out.

I push past the people and head towards the front door. It doesn´t rain much, but for some it would be too much to be outside. Rain is cleansing for me. It is soothing.

I sit on the step breathing. I look up and realize the garden gate is open.

Some idiot must have left it open.

I´d better close it. The Dark´s house is secure. Cameras and security codes everywhere. Only the Yorkshire puppies doesn´t fit. But the small ones have the biggest mouth. I must smile when I think of my dog.

But as I try to close the gate, I see someone sitting on the sidewalk. *It´s Kai.*

In his right hand, he holds a joint. And he said he´s no crack head but every time I see him, he´s smoking.

His hair is damp, and his clothes seem darker. *He´s been sitting here for a while.*

The white letters on bis black hoodie read.

"Nothing is ever Lost."

And just as I try to think about that, he turns his head to the side. Maybe he noticed or just sensed that he´s not alone. "I thought someone left it open." I explain. "I did." He states.

Obviously.

He takes the blunt to his mouth and blows smoke into the rain. His legs are bent, and his forearms on his knees. He´s still looking at me. Then he nods to the ground next to him. For a second, I wonder if I was wrong, and he just moved his head or something.

Do I even want to sit next to him after the past weeks?

But before he changes his mind, I sit down.

He looks ahead as I do so. Water collects in the grooves.

"What are you doing out there?" He asks between a puff. That´s what I´m wondering too. *What am I doing out there? Escape from social contact? Enjoy the rain? Go home without saying goodbye?*

"You?" I ask instead of answering like he often does.

"Being alone." He says after a moment. "Same." I give back.

Even if I have a thousand questions, I´ll keep quiet, and so will he. It´s pleasant. We´re just the two of us. *In the rain.*

We even sit beyond the shower. Occasionally, we look at each other. *But still no talking.*

And I think it´s a good sign. No talking is better than fighting.

They liked their silence. Sometimes they needed it more than their words. The bonds they made through their silence.

16

Two weeks later

"I´ll drive you." Kai says, from behind. "No need, I can walk." I say shaking him off. "I´ll drive." He offers again. "I´m fine I´ll walk." I insist. He steps in front of me. "Sorry if I´m mansplaining but the way you´re dressed you´re not going *fucking* anywhere alone." He says. "Well, but you *are*." I say. "And I am going to walk." I add and move around him. I wear a black dress, white sneakers, and a leather jacket. *The way you´re dressed.*

He unlocks his car, and I hear his trunk open and closing. His car locks again.

I hear his footsteps on the gravel. I roll my eyes.

As I turn around, he throws his jacket over. I grab it to save it from falling and snuck in. His scent drowns me. *Missed that.* Even if I smelled it only once. Well, five days in a row since I slept with his sweater like a stuffed animal.

He puts his hands in his front pockets. "I´ll walk you." He says.

He´s just in a T-shirt. *It´s chilly.*

"But your car.." I begin. He shrugs. "I´ll get it tomorrow or later." He replies. "You can´t walk *twice* its three kilometers." I say. He just shrugs. *He does that a lot.*

The party guests are gone, so we are the only ones walking home. So, he doesn´t *have to* walk me. *But I guess he wants to?*

He´s not that of an asshole. *Maybe. Sometimes.*

Now I feel bad refusing. But I don´t want to give in. *So, we walk.*

In silence. No bad silence, though.

His gaze is lowered. And I look anywhere but at him. He kicks a stone along. He even does some tricks with it. Not once putting his hands out of his jeans.

Normally I walk fast. For me, there is no such thing as strolling. But right now, I catch myself walking *extra* slow. *That´s stupid. I´m stupid.*

H carried the stone until we reached my street, then he picked it up and flipped it in his hands. I thank him, and he shrugs it off. "Sleep well." I say. He nods once. "Never do." He mutters and waits until I´m inside.

When I switch the lights on I glance out the window and see him walking down the street, kicking the stone. *He waited for me to enter my room.*

For a guy I´ve heard the worst about, he´s kinda okay. Even more than that.

She didn´t realize yet, but she was falling for him. Despite his rudeness. Because what she also didn´t realize was that he stopped being rude to her.

17

We´re at Kai´s again. It is becoming a habit. Every weekend we´re here. It feels like a frat house but a rich one.

And as soon as I enter the house, my eyes search for him. Automatically. No matter how hard I try to fight it, I catch myself looking for his gaze. *I wonder if that´s how he feels too.* But you *know* when someone´s into you. And Kai is obviously not into me.

Right? I would know. Because I can´t tell.

Sometimes he´s rude and in the next does something not so rude at all. I´m confused.

He was that boy in school who yanks your ponytail because he´s into you.

I sit with my back to him forcing me to look away. I try to follow the conversations, but all I hear is Kai talking to his buddies. I hear him laugh and wish he would never stop. His laughter is deep and honest. Not like Aidan´s, where you just must laugh. I can´t name it. It gives me goose bumps. He´s also the type who hides his smile or laughter. Like he´s embarrassed of it. But it´s the most beautiful thing. The way he covers it with his hand, fist, arm or how he turns away makes it just admirable. *This guy.*

Now he´s at the other end of the room, staring at me. I let my eyes wander around to avoid his. *In vain.*

I hate that feeling. I hate the way he takes over my thoughts. I hate losing control. I don´t want to like him or find him attractive. The problem is, I behave differently towards people I like. Usually I´m sarcastic, humorous, teasing and sometimes insulting. That´s how I show my affection. But somehow, I can´t be myself if I like someone. And I want to be myself when I´m with him. I want him to see me.

So, I decide not to like him more than a friend. Well, *if* we could become friends. I don´t even know if I want to be or he wants to.

I don´t want you to like me. You don´t have to like me. I try to tell him telepathically.

I don´t care what you think of me. I tell myself.

- 27 -

We haven´t talked once, but our eyes crossed a thousand times. I watched him talk to a girl. His gaze was no less hard than for me. For whatever reason I liked that fact. Maybe because he´s just as unfriendly to everyone else. Except Aidan and the others. Or maybe it would have sucked to see *him* smile at the girl.

That´s when I realized I want to make him smile.

18

We´re playing a drinking game. And it´s Kai´s turn. He reads out loud, "Text the person you last stalked on social media." Aidan groans. "Easy." Kai takes out his cell and leans forward with his forearms on his thighs. *He´s typing.*

"What´s your favorite position?" That´s Aidan´s question.

Kai´s gaze meets mine; he leans back and puts it in his front pocket. Something else is in his expression. But I can´t put my finger on it. He holds my gaze.

My phone vibrates, but I ignore it.

"Doggy and probably rider or 69." Explains Aidan and hands the phone to a guy I don´t know. It´s been weeks and I still don´t know *any* of the people. There are just too many and a crowd of guys I´ve never seen. *Maybe those are the pirates.*

That guy chucks three shots and the girl next to him takes off her bra.

I check the time and my heart sinks. I have a message. *From Kai.*

I can tell by his profile picture, cause I´ve looked at it many times before. Since I´m in that group chat for the parties.

"Psst."

That´s all.

I look up. He´s already looking at me. He smiles a little. Barely noticeable. But it´s there. *A smirk.* I think so, at least. Because as soon as the smile wants to fight it´s way to the surface, the corners of his mouth move back down to a line. And the cold face is back. As if he noticed, he smiled at me.

I put it back and get up to avoid both, one my task and two Kai. *I can't figure him out.*

He's not quiet, but I wouldn't call him extroverted either. He's not a clown like Aidan, but he's indeed funny for what I can tell. I wish he'd be that easy on me, too, and not that asshole he's been showing so far. Or that ambivalent version of himself. *And now he was looking for me on social media?*

Just as I want to go back outside with my drink, Kai's suddenly in front of me. He's got his hands in his pockets, blocking me with his body. He doesn't say anything but has that intense look I've seen on him.

I try to move around, but he dodges me. He towers over me. I swallow the feeling he's causing. I look away. "Do I make you nervous?" He asks. I can tell he's pleased by it. I say nothing and look up at him. He smirks. *This time really.* It is barely visible. *But I see it.*

He has a look on his face. Like he wants to *fuck* me. But that look disappears, as if he noticed. But his heaving chest exposes him. My face burns.

Our eyes won't let go of each other. "No." I answer, but my voice sounds weird. He nods. "Okay." He grins like he knows I talk shit.

Is he linked to my brain, or why can he call bullshit that easy?

I wonder what he thinks right now. I take the initiative before our conversation ends. Because I know for sure he'll end it just to be rude.

"So, you're stalking me, huh?" I raise my chin. "I wouldn't call it *that.*" He says. "Why didn't you send me a request?" I ask him. "Why should I?" He asks in return, as if it were the last thing he would do. *And I believe that.*

He's raising a brow. Either he won't admit it, or he's is just an asshole.

"Don't imagine it." He adds, stepping closer. *Clearly the second.*

"I don't." I lie stiffing a laugh. "Good." He says bluntly. "Good," I repeat and move around him. He doesn't bulge, so I brush past him. *He lets me.*

Outside, I face Aidan, who talks with someone, but engages me in the conversation. Aidan and I are fooling around. When I talk to him, I'm always happy. We laugh a lot. When the song changes, he takes my hand and pulls me to his chest. "Dance with me," he says and grins. I put my arms around his neck, and we dance. His grin widens and brings out his dimples. *His smile is gorgeous.*

Some songs we dance. Sometimes slower, sometimes more exuberant and to my surprise he can dance well. And with his lead, I forget that I can't dance.

When Aidan goes to the bathroom, I catch Kai staring at me from the couch.

Has he been doing that all the time?

I sit next to him, waiting for Aidan.

And as others sit on the sofa, I slide up to make room. *Our knees touch.* Our eyes meet, but none of us makes any attempts to move. He leans back and spreads his legs further, so our thighs touch. *That* was on purpose. *Right?*

I can´t deny how electrifying that little touch feels. I try to focus on other people´s conversations but all I notice is us touching. I can feel his gaze on me but avoid looking at him.

When Aidan comes back, I get up, and we continue to dance. And this time Kai isn´t looking, or he didn´t in the first place.

19

Next evening

On the way out, a drunk guy pours his beer over my top. Anger rises. "Sorry. Sry." He slurs and wants to touch my arm. I back away. The guy tries to touch me again, but before I can fight back, Kai stands behind him and grabs his shoulder. He turns, and now the two are talking. I hardly understand anything since I stand next to the speaker and try to get a handkerchief out of my bag. I´m relieved, that I don´t have to deal with that guy. They´re arguing. He tries to provoke by pushing Kai. *Unsuccessfully.* Because he´s a wall.

Kai grabs him by the shirt, whereupon Leon steps between them and drags the guy to the gate. Better so he has been looking for stress.

"You all right?" Asks Kai with a frown. "Yes. Only everything reeks of beer." I moan but must laugh. "I *hate* beer." I wine. "Come with me," he says amused. I follow him. He´s going upstairs. *No one goes upstairs unasked.* I guess rules can indeed be bent.

I smile as I read the quote on his shirt. *He always has one.*

And it´s a different way to get to know him.

"Are you alive or just existing?"

That´s so him, I guess.

"Back to the left is the bathroom." He points at the door. We´re in front of each other. He´s looking at me with that look again. "Here." He reaches behind and pulls his shirt over his head. I can´t look away. Even if I wanted to. He´s got an eight pack. *Why does it look hot when guys take off their shirts like that? And why am I staring?*

He catches me doing it but doesn´t make a remark. He hands it to me. "Thank you" I answer. When he disappeared, I lock the door. I think about what just happened. First, he scared off that guy. I didn´t even know he was near. And then he offered me his shirt. He did before, but he stripped for me now.

I inhale his scent getting goose bumps. I take off my top, soap it in and wash it out. Then I put it on the heater and throw on his T-shirt. After a last look in the mirror, I take another deep smell on his shirt before I open the door.

Like the smell isn´t in my nose for the rest of the night anyway.

The door to the room he went is ajar. I slip through and see him hitting a black punching bag. *Still shirtless.* Seeing his muscles in action is so hot.

When he senses me, he looks at me. And I think to see a smile on his face, which disappears, as so often. *It is like he doesn´t want to grin because of me.* Like he tries to remind himself he despises me.

"Suits you better than me." He says and keeps boxing. *Sarcastic?*

His room is big. He has a box spring bed covered with white bedding. On the right side are three black bookshelves. *He reads?*

"Neat collection. What are you reading?" I ask. He speaks squeezed between the blows. "Thrillers and Psychology. Classics, Buddhism, finance, and stuff like that." That´s somehow impressive and not at all what I expected. I suppose he can see my astonishment. "That´s not what you´d think of me, is it?" *Yes.*

"No. I think it´s nice. I also read a lot." I say. "What are *you* reading?" He asks and I´m surprised by his sudden interest. "Mostly novels, spiritual stuff, poetry, and psychology." I say and as he does not answer I continue. "I hated reading until two years ago. But I just didn´t know what I was interested in."

He turns to me. *Why did I tell him that?* He doesn´t want to know such stuff about me.

"It´s the same with me. My parents wanted to force me to read, so I hated it even more. Or rather pretended." He smirks. *His parents.* Last time we talked about his family, he was cold. So, I ignore my curiosity and look at the punching bag. "I´ve always wanted to do kickboxing. But I never went through with it." He must laugh, but he tries to suppress it. I look at him pissed. "What´s so funny? You think I can´t do that?" He snorts. "No. I think it´s *nice* honest. I just didn´t expect *that* from you." He mirrors my words. He looks at me with pierced eyes, as if he were thinking about me.

"Apparently we have some wrong prejudices about each other.," I say. "*It´s easier to split an atom than a prejudice.*" He quotes *Albert Einstein*. And again, he impresses me.

Who´s this guy?

He turns to his closet and takes out a T-shirt. *That´s too bad.* But at least no more distractions. Next to a black wardrobe, he has a flat screen. Besides the window a desk with a gaming setup and lots of notebooks. The walls are painted white. He´s got a lot of pictures too. Photographs. Cars, buildings, roads, nature, animals, and his friends. I also discover cameras on a shelf. It´s almost creepy because we have much more interests in common than I thought. *More wrong prejudices.*

Even though his furniture is mostly black, I feel comfortable in his room. It´s got something. Apparently not only his style is based on black, white, and gray.

"Do you photograph?" I ask. "As a hobby." He shrugs. "And what are you gambling?" I want to know. "Do you *always* ask so many questions?" He asks. "I´m just showing interest, asshole." I roll my eyes. "Called me worse." He shrugs, and without waiting for me, he walks out. I preferred the protective shirt gifting Kai. Nevertheless, I follow him without a word.

And that quote on his new gray shirt fits even more.

"Do I look like a fucking people´s person?"

No, you don´t.

- 27 -

The rest of the evening, we play more drinking games, and I must force myself to not keep looking at him all the time. *But our eyes meet often.*

On the way home, I realize I forgot my top. However, I do not turn around.

Once I´m home, I remove my makeup, shower, and get in bed, dressed in one of Kai´s cloths. *Again. This must stop.*

That night. He texted her. "*You´ve left your top.*"

"*You´ve gave me your shirt.*" She responded. "*Hah.*" He texted.

And they kept texting. *The whole night.*

And they haven´t stopped since.

20

Two weeks later

We don´t talk much, but after the parties when I walk home, when I lay in bed, we text. A lot and about everything. Not the kind of *what are you doing* or *how are you* shit. Rather, *do you think plants can feel* or *are they conscious* type of texts.

When we party, we share brief looks. He stares at me from across the room. Frowns at me. Still insults me. And I flick the finger. Or try to ignore him. Try not to stare at him too. As if we never text. As if we don´t share sleepless nights. As if we´re not philosophizing about the meaning of life. *We´re strangers.*

And I don´t know why we do it and why it´s a secret. And why we´re barely talking to each other when we *clearly* have a lot to talk about. But it seems like our thing. The thing no one knows. They think we don´t like each other. And in ways we don´t, but in ways we do. *I think at least.*

The time smartphones were *the* new thing. It was addictive. I texted a lot. I had a lot of people to text to. And after I had none, I just had my ex. But after our breakup, my phone got empty. *Silent. Mute.*

After I lost the friends I´ve gained, it got dead. I even got scared that it would ring. That´s *how* lonely I was. I even kept it at silent 24/7. *I don´t know why.*

To pretend there could be messages and I just didn´t hear them. Or to silence everything. Silence the world when all I do is scream.

What I wanted to say is I lost the excitement I felt back then. I got tired of texting, responding, and connecting. *I stopped waiting, hoping, caring. Stopped texting.*

Until this rude guy texted me. And we haven´t stopped.

My phone is still mute. Cause just as in real life we shut up, I shut up the texts too. Like they´re not real. Not happening. *But they are.*

And I wait for them. Hope for them. Care for them. And pray that one day they go over into real life. *Come true.*

I feel that excitement I felt back in 2013. Cause he texted. *We texted.* Not just meaningless phrases or shallow affirmations. We texted *whole* paragraphs. Most guys don´t do that, or just to get into your pants.

He did text them. But not at all to get into my pants. *But to get into my mind.*

He never uses emojis. I stopped since I noticed he doesn´t. He uses his words. He expresses himself well, pays attention to grammar and punctuation.

It felt surreal. It was a parallel universe. *Ours.*

Were we didn´t despite each other. Were, we did talk. Were it felt nice to talk to someone when the world slept. *When the thoughts cut deep.*

- 27 -

The last few times our conversations consisted of teasing, making sarcastic remarks, and making fun of each other. But still arguing. He´s still rude. But somehow, it´s fun. It´s cause I´ve seen another side of him. The side who´s been texting me every night. Or I´m just stupid and I imagined the texts. Or he just plays games. *But would he be that into it then?*

It has become more a game now. I think, slowly he loosens up.

"Are you insecure about your height?" I ask with a grin. "What?" He snaps. "I´m like ten heads taller than you." He laughs, raising his eyebrows. "Nah, you´re not *that* big." I shake my head in amusement. His hand grabs my jaw stepping closer, making my heart shiver. "Kai" I warn and roll my eyes at him. His expression changes and he let´s go of me. And that´s when I realize. This is the first time I addressed him by his name. For a second, I see *something* different in his gaze. *His eyes soften a bit.*

But then his expression hardens, and his black eyes fix me. There´s the wall again. Before I can do something, he grabs and pushes me full force into the pool, giving me tinnitus.

When I surface, he´s gone. *Asshole.*

I stomp through the house. I don´t care that I leave a trail behind me. I must smile at the idea of annoying him. I want to mess with him.

I push open his bedroom door and head for the closet. *Fuck the rules. Fuck him.*

I take out a pair of shorts, boxers, socks, and search for a hoodie. I take a black one and read the back.

"Pretty girls like trap music."

This should make it.

I go to the bathroom, take a quick shower, and wash my hair with a five in one. *Shower gel, shampoo, conditioner and what else?* Honestly, it is still missing that you can rinse your mouth with those.

After the shower I change, wring out my clothes over the bathtub and throw them in the basket. I´m dressed all black except for the white tennis socks. I comb through my damp hair with my fingers and open the window. *I smell like him.* On my body, hair, face, and clothes.

As I leave the bathroom, I feel bad about the hardwood floor. But not *too* much. But still *enough*, so I get a sweater from his closet to wipe the floor. I stand on it to dry the track. In front of the patio, I pick up the dripping sweater and step outside.

Kai´s gaze shoots in my direction after looking twice. I walk towards him. He scrutinizes me in his clothes. I slap it against his chest. "Wiped," I grin. He grabs it. Without waiting for an answer, I settle down on the couch. *I caught him off guard.*

I smile to myself as he just stares at me for a moment. A few seconds later, Kai sits down next to me, throwing the hoodie on the floor. He interlocks his hands and props them behind his head. He turns his head to me and grins slightly. This time it doesn´t disappear. His eyes wander over my face. I can´t interpret him. He seems amused. *Which makes me angry.*

"What?" I ask him as he pokes holes in me. He just shakes his head and presses his lips together. "I feel like driving. You wanna come?" He gives me a look and stands up. He adjusts his hood and at that moment I realize we´re in matching outfits. Black is my fav color. *Even if it´s not actually one.*

He nods to the garage and puts his hand in his training shorts. His key jingles. "Come on," he urges, and I stand up before he changes his mind.

As we pull onto the highway, the sun begins to set. *Freakin´ Out on the Interstate by Briston Maroney* blares through the car. Kai accelerates as we have a clear path. I love our country for that. No speed limit. Even if it can be dangerous. But right now, I feel anything but in danger. *Free. Happy.*

In the corner of my eye, I watch him enjoy it. It´s the first time we´re driving alone. At least *wanting* it this time. Because he offered. I think he does like me. But he also doesn´t like me. *For whatever reason.*

I was nervous about the fact that we would be alone. I had worries we wouldn´t talk despite our nightly texts. But he took that fear since he put the volume on max so even if we wanted to, we couldn´t. *Which I´m fine with.*

We pull into the drive in. He orders us some fries and vegan nuggets.

We eat in the car.

He looks at me. "What?" I ask. He squints his eyes. "You showered. Did you?" He asks. I nod. "Obviously Sherlock my hair is wet." I say. He leans into me, smelling me.

My heart flutters.

"Yeah." He begins. "You smell like me." He says leaning back as if he wasn´t just *that* close to me. "Finally, you don´t stink." He says. I flick him off. "Fuck you." I scoff. He chuckles. On which sound I must grin.

Now we are quite easy. I enjoy fooling around with him. I like the real life with him. Maybe after all dreams do come true. *Maybe.*

21

We sit in the back of the car. Kai in the middle between Aidan and me. His knee touches mine because he´s sitting with his legs wide. His hand on his thigh. The sight of his arm covered with veins makes me dizzy. And even when I force myself to look out the window, his body radiates a heat I can´t ignore. And somehow, I have the feeling that he´s sitting more wide-legged than he must. As if he *wants* our legs to touch. *Again.*

But I must admit that I sit more towards him than I need to.

Our arms touch. Even through the clothes, my skin tingles.

- 27 -

Kai pushes a blue cup into my hand. “Just accept these from me.” He demands. “I can take care of my own drinks.” I return, rolling my eyes and pressing it against his chest. He breathes in through his nose. “I don´t want *anyone* putting anything in your drink.” He presses. And before I could even think he´s worried about me, he adds “I´m certainly not going to *babysit.* I know the people here. If you´re lying unconscious in the corner later..” He stops himself mid-sentence. “Wasn´t planning on it” I snap. “Just watch out or Nina will kill me.” He justifies and gulps the cup. Then he disappears between the crowd.

The quote on his shirt catches my eyes.

“Allergic to people.”

I have to grin. *Yeah, me too.* Me too Kai.

After a few shots I dance with Nina, Luca, and some other girls. I always need a bit alcohol to be able to dance. *And for once my anxiety´s gone.*

As I look around, I spot Kai´s figure. He´s standing across the room, leaning against a black piano. I don´t dare to look again.

Nina asks if I need to go to the bathroom. I shake my head. But Luca joins her. A girl named Elena takes my hand, and we keep dancing. I think she´s the one who told me the rumors about Kai.

I glance in his direction while moving. *He´s still there.*

She whispers into my ear. “He´s been watching you the whole night.” She grins. “So, stop looking. Cause he´s watching anyway.” She chirps. *He watched me dancing.* Now, I feel aware of my body. My skin heats, but it´s thrilling. *I feel good.*

We take another shot and continue to dance.

Three drinks later, I´m dancing with a guy. He spins me around but then some arm blocks me. *It´s Kai´s.*

He stands between us and builds himself up. “Wren, *she`s* off limit.” He threatens and they both glare at each other. *What? Did he just? Off.. limit? What the fuck is that about?*

“Kai” I try to get his attention. But he doesn´t move.

What was that about babysitting again?

This guy is so ambivalent. I can´t figure him out. But I suspect his next move, so I just walk past both toward the stairwell.

I don´t have to turn around to know he´s already behind me. I sit down on the concrete stairs. I imagine him leaning against the door frame. *Silence.*

"Would *Wren* be a guy to put something in my drink?" I ask, directing my gaze out the ceiling high windows. *Silence.*

"No," he admits, but he´s pissed. "Okay?" I ask, confused. "He wouldn´t be the type to put something in your drink, but that doesn´t make him any less of an asshole." His voice comes closer, but he stays behind me. *So, what do you want then? Play with me? Protect me? Has he no clue that people warned me from him?*

"And who says I don´t want an asshole?" I ask.

When he doesn´t answer, I turn around. *But he´s gone.*

For the rest of the evening, I sit on the step and stare into the night. I´m sick of partying. And if I didn´t depend on my friends to get out of here, I would have left a long time ago. My social battery is dead anyway, and I don´t want to see Kai nor Wren or any other guy.

22

Leon is in the hot tub with Nina. *Dry humping.*

Aidan dancing with a girl, or rather making out. And I sit next to Kai. He frowns as he stares at me. "What?" I ask, bracing myself. His eyes narrow. "I was dreaming about you." He accuses me making a face as if it was my fault. "Huh?" I grin-frown. I really wasn´t expecting that. "What were you dreaming?" I ask. Judging by his expression, he hasn´t considered I might ask him about the plot. I can see his mind working. "That.. you piss me off." he finally blurts. *Sure.*

"I´m glad I annoy you even in your dreams" I smile. His jaw flexes. And I try hard not to let my pleasure show too much. *He´s dreaming about me?*

And of course, I don´t tell him that I´ve been dreaming about him, too. But the fact that he´s furious amuses me.

He bites on his lower lip. Then he suddenly grabs my foot and puts it on his lap. "W-what," escapes me. He tightens his grip as I try to pull away. "Hold still," he barks. My bare skin tingles under his touch. I struggle under his grip, but he holds me firm. He takes a black marker from the table and opens it with his teeth. With the cap in his mouth, he guides the pen to my Vans. I squirm, but he tugs on my foot to keep me still.

I finally give in because I don´t want him to let go.

He writes on the white margin. And I watch him, riveted. As if he were Salvador Dali, creating a masterpiece, my eyes follow his hand.

Two words.

"Sex Drive."

Sex Drive?

When he finishes, he leaves his hand on my ankle. And strokes my skin with his thumb, barely noticeable. *But I did.*

The feeling like being on a roller coaster spreads through my stomach.

Soggy and warm. Scary but good.

He clicks the cap back on and tosses the pen on the table. "Are you going to tell me what that means, or what?" I ask. "I´m not going to have a sex education conversation with you." He replies, kicking my leg away from him. I roll my eyes. *So predictable, idiot.*

My body aches for his touch.

Was that supposed to be a hint that he dreamed banging me? Or that he wants to?

He stands up and walks inside.

"Love has many faces."

Reads his back. *I think his love has no face.*

23

Before I forget, I put the clothes I still have from Kai into my bag.

When I arrive, he`s at the grill with Finn. I haven´t seen him in a while. He isn´t often on the parties and not long either.

Aidan, Leon, and Nina sit on the sofa, so I join them. As I observe the two, I ask, "they´re brothers aren´t they?" I don´t know why I ask that only now, and the answer is obvious, but I had to. "Yeah, Finn is twenty-five they´re three years apart." Aidan explains. *I assumed.*

So, I´m not surprised, because apart from the style they look *very* similar. Like twins if Finn wouldn´t look older. Unlike Leon and Aidan, who hardly look alike apart from hair and eye color, which is both brown.

Kai laughs aloud. This is the thirty-second time I´ve heard him laugh.

Why am I counting that?

He laughs tears. And even at that, he looks attractive.

They seem to get along. Whereas the last few weeks I had the impression they had friction every now and then. But now that I know for sure they are siblings, it makes even more sense.

He wears that white shirt which reads.

"What´s a good day?"

Those quotes are my favorites.

When we´re done eating, we smoke shisha and talk. Finn leaves because he must head to the office. *On a Sunday.* Apparently also very busy, like their parents.

As the sun goes down, alcohol flows and we play truth or dare. Mostly because Nina forces us.

After a few rounds, it´s my turn and Aidan sets the task. Between us, it is always a bit spicy but in a humorous way. "Take your clothes off and get in the hot tub." He says with a mischievous grin. Everyone chuckles. Nina cheers with excitement. I shake my head and grin, "I hope you don´t mean *naked*, because that´s not gonna happen" I counter. "Not yet." He smiles. "Dream on" I hiss.

After a deep breath, I stand up. "Alright." Luckily, I´m wearing matching underwear. A black lace bra with a black high rise Brazilian brief. *I look hot in these.* With any other, I would have chickened.

I pull the top over my head. And see Aidan eyeing me, followed by Kai taking a pull from his cup. "Don´t stare at me like that guy´s you come along." I say as I unbutton my jeans and pull them over my butt. Aidan already takes off his shirt. Shortly after, he sits in the whirlpool. Nina and Leon also follow. Kai, who is still leaning back, looks at me with the shisha in his hand. *No pod today?*

His eyes wander to the side of my thigh, where my scorpion tattoo is. When our eyes meet, he stands up and starts to undo his belt. *Why do I think this is hot?*

His gaze is still on me as he unties his jeans. I have to look away. When he pulls his T-shirt off, I can´t help but look. In the daylight, his muscles look even more defined.

This really must stop.

Luckily, the others are busy moving the shisha, lugging drinks, and snacks instead of witnessing our eye fucking. Because that´s what we´re doing. I rip my gaze off his body and help them. But on every move, I feel his eyes on me.

I sit down next to Aidan, and opposite sits Kai. Leon and Nina rather over each other since they start making out.

Aidan seizes the conversation "Do you have someone?" He asks, looking at me. Kai takes a few drags from the shisha looking bored.

I know that Aidan is not a fuckboy. He doesn´t play with the girls, but he always has some around. *But why is he asking me that?*

"No. I wouldn´t have kissed you," I reply. Aidan nods. Kai still shows no reaction.

We change the subject.

Aidan says goodbye. Probably a hook up.

At some point, the two disappear before tearing off their remaining clothes. Kai snapped at them to go fuck somewhere else. I´m surprised they didn´t just have sex next to us. But there was definitely some touching involved. And I know for sure they had sex in here weeks ago on one of the parties. *I could never.*

Now I´m alone with Kai. I think it could be weird. Which is stupid cause I was already alone with him before. And he´s not *that* rude anymore.

"I won´t lend you any underwear today." He says with a cheeky grin. I return it. "Even if I got the impression, you really like dressing up as me." He mocks, thinking of the time he pushed me in the pool.

He lights himself a joint. *There it is.* He smokes. *Again.*

"How come you don´t have a boyfriend?" I blink at him. *So, he did care.*

"I want to focus on me. And I´m happy the way things are right now. I´m not looking for anything." I say. "Aren´t you looking or is just nothing looking for you?" He grins. I roll my eyes. "If it doesn´t blow me away, I don´t waste my time. Simple as that." I say. He nods.

"I think a relationship can only work if you know each other well enough." I tell him. "In what way?" He harps, taking another drag. "These days, most people get together after a month or so and wonder why they´re not right for each other once the butterflies are gone. Because that´s when they realize what bothers them. Cause they didn´t take the time to get to know each other deeply. No one works on relationships anymore; everyone is always looking for something better and more exciting." I shrug. "True," he says, blowing the smoke aside and *not* in my face.

"I just don´t assume anymore that I´ll be with someone forever, at least not in our generation." I say. He nods. "There´s no such thing as *forever*." He agrees.

"I want something real. Someone who challenges me. Someone who understands me and with whom I can be myself. A bond, trust, and communication. I want it to be exciting. And sex. *Good* sex. And if I don´t have that, I´d rather stay single." I´m in the flow, not thinking about *how* honest I am with him right now.

He nods. "*We are all fools in love*," he quotes. I frown at him. Quoting is his thing. He does it rarely but more often than average. Well, *no one* quotes on a daily.

"That means.." He begins to explain, but I cut in. "I *know* what that means. I was just wondering where I heard that, you ass," I say. "Pride and Prejudice," he helps me out. *Pride and Prejudice?* He said he reads classics. But I didn´t think *such*.

Love alone is often just not enough. Friendship and trust. That´s much more important." I shrug.

"But honestly, I don´t want to get attached to anyone anymore." I say. "But whatever, what about you?" I ask. "I don´t date." He says. *Heard that before.*

"Never?" I ask. "It´s just not for me." He shrugs. "I´ve never really been interested in a girl." He says. "Not *beyond* sex." He adds. That girls are into him is not lost on me, but as he says, he hasn´t shown much interest. *Flirted, maybe.* But never made out or something. At least not that I´ve seen. He rather tortures the girls. And it´s now that I realized that I never saw those two girls again after that. *Did he kick them out?*

"Never had feelings?" I quip. He looks tense. "I´ve *had* relationships, if that´s what you want to know. But whether I felt anything for them is something else." He laughs. "I was *horny* but I wasn´t *in love*." The way he said it like he has never known such thing as love.

"I desired girls. But never loved one. Most of the girls I dated eventually wanted a relationship or confessed their feelings. That´s when I always ended things. And it´s not like I didn´t make it clear from the beginning what it was for me." He says.

Just how they told me. Brutally honest.

"But.." I begin and he cuts me off. "You want to know if I have ever been heartbroken? *No.* Normally *I´m the one* who breaks hearts." He says. "Can imagine." I say. We stare at each other.

"If it´s not a fit, it´s not a fit" I conclude. He nods with a grin. "I put myself first." He´s using my words. *He´s messing with me.* But I like that.

"It´s just I don´t *like* love. I think it´s useless. Love is nothing other than your ego. I don´t need to feed *that*." He says and I smile. "What?" He nudges my leg. I shake my head grinning. "No, it´s just I *can* see it." I say. "See what?" He rakes, frowning. "Your ego.." I squint my eyes at him. "It´s *huuge*. You really shouldn´t love anyone, it might burst.." I say and he kicks my leg. "Shut it." He spits but grins. And I crack up.

\- 27 -

"Most people can´t separate sex and love.." He breathes. "So, I don´t. *Mostly*." He says. I raise my eyebrow. "You don´t *fuck*?" I ask. "I do." He says. "But I choose wisely *who* I fuck." He adds. I frown. "Sex connects." He begins. "You exchange energies. Like plugging your phone. You transfer your traumas, fears, and emotions. That´s a bond. You connect emotionally, spiritually, and energetically." He says. I haven´t expected such a mindset of him. I mean I knew he´s spiritual and all but this.. *is different.*

He seemed to me to be the guy who plays with girls. And not the one for deep connections. "I think that, too." I whisper. I get the feeling he´s uncomfortable, like he doesn´t often talk so openly. So, I decide to be vulnerable, too. As if I haven´t already revealed enough.

"To be honest, the opposite has been the problem with me. I was really a burr and way too early head over heels in love. I always gave 100 percent for the other and if they gave less, I gave even more. I always wanted to get the love that I gave and never got it. Now I know what I want and what I don´t." I pause. I hope he doesn´t make mean comments.

"*And now she waits for a love that she cannot deny.*" He quotes amused. "That´s from *JmStorm.*" he adds, his grin wide. I must smile. *He stares at me weirdly.*

"What?" I ask. "*Love is pain*" he says, and I could swear his irises are blood black at this moment. And I think he´s quoting, but I don´t know who. It feels similar. *Somehow. How does his brain come up with these quotes anyway?* Like I would have to memorize them, but he just uses them like his normal vocab.

So, he hasn´t been in love but talks about it like he has?

After a while, he grins to himself. "What´s so funny?" I ask. "I won´t open up and you´re the opposite. Or at least you were. So, we´re kind of fucked the same." He jokes. "I guess you´re right about that." I look at him.

"You know what?" I ask. He looks at me with a smile. "Someday a girl will come along that will change everything. I´m sure." His grin disappears. "I don´t want *anything* to change" he retorts. I fall silent. I shouldn´t have said that. And to be honest, I don´t want that either. I´m doing fine on my own, and I don´t want anyone to mess with the relationship I have with myself. And something tells me he feels the same.

We sit for a while, not talking much, but both enjoying each other`s company. At least, I think. After all, he hasn`t kicked me out, which I wouldn`t put past him. But he´s shut down and his jaw flexes. *He´s in his head.* And I wonder what he´s thinking.

Sometimes we make eye contact.

He puts his arms on the edge of the hot tub and lets his head fall back. His chest rises and falls. As he does so, I stare at his muscles. Looking at his naked torso, I wonder why he only has one tattoo.

- 27 -

When I´m at the gate, he calls my name. *He didn´t say my name before.* I´m so captivated by his voice that I´m almost willing to pretend I didn´t hear, just to hear him say my name again. *But I turn around.*

"Yeah?" I ask but he´s holding my top. *Of course, what would he want?*

"Oh right" I dig his clothes out of my bag. His naked chest, covered in droplets, catches my attention. As he hands me my top, I avert my eyes. "Good night, Sky." He says with a smirk. I lick my lips. "Good night, Dark." Everyone calls him by his last name but bis brother with his forename. *I don´t know why.*

Leon and Aidan are both called Avery. *It´s weird.* But I´m used to it by now.

What is a good day? I remember his shirt. *Today was a good day.*

[NOTEBOOK ENTRIES]

We sat in the rain but didn´t talk. I liked her company. I caught her looking at me. And unfortunately, I had to look at her too. Even though I forced myself not to.
We played Paranoia. But those games were just the tip of the iceberg. There were things we did she didn´t know about. No one did. Some we did with all. Some with the pirates. And some with the close circle. But it was fun because I could mess with her. She called me smart. At least one opinion she´s right about. She eats her birthday cake alone. If she knew about our insulting cakes, we make on every birthday. I wanted to punch me for that. I don´t care about her birthday.
Some girl told her about Neverland. Took long enough. Of course, the Wendy´s quack. The lost boys don´t care. Either they hit on the newies or scare them off. So, she got a whiff of what those parties are about. But she only knows the fairy tale. But there´s a dark side. A twisted, fucked up and bloody one. With scars and pain. She doesn´t know with whom she´s fucking with. But she´ll know soon enough that Pan loves to spill blood. She asked me about Hook. I told her because I was stoned. And if I wanted to play with her, she needed to know what she was on. At least in ways. But she pointed out all the flaws. She´s smart. I liked that. The arguing is annoying but thrilling. I love the games as much as the hurt. Her Hook is losing control. But she doesn´t know, there are many Hooks you´ve got. But she would discover soon enough. Neverland does that to you. Show you your fears. And I knew I would let her lose it. The control she wants so bad. I could tell she always needs a plan. A control freak. But out of fear and not perfectionism. But you must face your Hook to get rid of it. I bet she needs a little stab to reach that and I´m pleased to help. Because she has to understand she has nothing in control. You must rip your wings to fly. And I´m gonna rip her until she´s a flying devil. There´s no liberty without a great pain. The pain makes you fly. Makes you survive. I´m gonna teach her. I´m curious though what game she will come up with to prove herself to our group. If you have a fun idea, you can stay. The riskier, the better. It has to be thrilling and a bit illegal if you´re good.

I'd like to play with her a bit longer because Peter loves to play and so do the lost boys. So, she has to entertain us. Show us who she is. Who she wants to be. Who she can be. She stepped a foot into our world, and she won't leave until I said so. No one leaves Neverland. They die or get stuck. They play or go. She's in my world now. I can make her fly or off her. It's up to her. Is she worthy of staying? To fly?

Peter did not have one Wendy he had many. And they wanted him to grow up, have him, trap him. To play family and play love. Taking him with them. But he wouldn't grow up nor leave. Never. He didn't want any of them. But deep down he knew there was a Tinker. One that could make him fly. With stardust. But he didn't want to find her. He knew he couldn't anyway. He knew well enough that what makes you fly can make you fall. And all he wanted was the now and his lost boys. No Wendy's. No Tinker. No love. No family. No growing up. He wanted the lost ones. The ones like him.

The girls talked to her. They didn't warn her. They wanted to mess with her. Play their own games. Because they noticed she's different. That I mess with her. They saw me staring at her. And got jealous. They knew Nina brought her. They didn't fear any girl before which strung with me. What was so different about her that everyone saw but me? They sensed she had a connection to the inner circle. To the lost ones. No one ever had. That made her special I guess. All the girls want to be Nina's friend. Anyone ever is. The girls never stay because of me. She's just a funnier game. This one is bigger. Just as the fall afterward. The worst is she bought everything they fed her. I was hurt by that. I thought she got it. But she doesn't. She's not different. She's a Wendy. Nothing to stay. Nothing to want.

She's still pisses me off. Still gets in my way. Still gets invited. Still doesn't fit. It became a habit. And it became a habit for me to fuck with her.

She wore that black dress. In which her ass and tits looked stunning. Most of the time she wears oversized. But in that dress you could actually see her body for the first time. No hiding. And everyone looked at her. Gaped at her. That made my blood boil. And that realization made me even madder. Did I have a weird protecting thing for her? I scared off the guys. They knew if I had a girl to play with, it would be mine and mine only. The Wendy's are for all the lost boys or the pirates. Until I claim one. And I claimed her. I was the one breaking her. I walked her home, even if walking made no fucking sense. But she's as stubborn as I am. I couldn't look at her though. I was all in my head thinking what the hell I'm doing. I'm not walking girl's home. I'm not scaring dudes off for a girl. At least not for other reasons but the games. ~~But it wasn't just the game that made me look at her. Or protect her. I wanted to walk her.~~ ~~I felt~~

~~nervous. I never do.~~ ~~I shouldn't be alone with her.~~ I kept kicking stones to keep my eyes off her. After I stared at her the whole night. Like it would make the fact go away. ~~She was fucking beautiful.~~ ~~And not just that night.~~ I even waited for her to enter her room. Like, who the fuck am I? And who the fuck is she? ~~And why did I keep that stupid rock?~~

Looks like I have no choice but to give her the chance they all asked me for. Nina won't stop inviting her over and Aidan seems to really like her. I hope he isn't planning on hitting on her. We don't need her to get involved. But even Leon likes her. He rarely likes people. Me neither. But it doesn't mean I'm going to make it easy for her.

~~I catch myself searching eye contact. But if I'm not mistaken, so does she.~~

I stalked her social media. Fucking drinking game. I didn't want her to think I was into her. ~~She danced with Aidan and I couldn't look away. Why the fuck do I have to look at her all the time? I don't even realize until I snap out of it.~~ Our knees touched. She didn't leave. ~~Neither did I.~~ ~~I felt.. something.~~ It stung me that they get along. He's my best friend. She won't have him. None of us. If he fucks her, which he definitely wants to, we have a problem. She'll fall for him but he's not the relationship guy. None of us is. And Leon and Nina aren't a normal couple. They do lots of things different. We all do. We're messed up. She's not. She doesn't fit.

Some guy poured his beer over her and tried to touch her. I snapped and to his luck, Leon stopped me from polling his face. I have to admit I liked seeing my shirt on her. ~~That pleased me in some fucked up way.~~ It was the first time we talked normally. ~~And I liked it.~~ She wanted to box. ~~Maybe I'll teach her sometime.~~ What the fuck am I talking about?

I texted her. And we kept texting. All night long. Not that I could have slept anyway. It was just some texts. Nothing more. I still hate her. Still don't want her in. It's just part of the game. Getting in her head. Under her skin. Until I stick my knife inside her and twist it until she begs me to kill her. Foreplay I call it.

I have to admit she doesn't get on my nerves as much as in the beginning. She's funny and sarcastic. Our fighting became teasing. And today I threw her into the pool. Because she said my name. She never did that before. ~~I liked how it sounded coming from her lips.~~ ~~Then I thought about her lips on mine and around my dick~~.. ~~I wanted to taste hers~~. ~~I can't fuck her.~~ ~~Not yet.~~ I don't plan to. ~~But my cock clearly has other preferences. That happens sometimes. I look at her. And my cock twitches. Notices her lips, her body. I can't stop it. I'm attracted to her.~~ She was dressed in my clothes from top to bottom. She tried to piss me off. But I thought it was funny. ~~And all I could think of was the fact that she wears my socks. My shirt. My shorts.~~ ~~Fuck, I liked it.~~

~~Way too much. Did she wear underwear?~~ No girl wore my cloths. Went to my room. Sat with me in the rain. Driving with me casually. Nor did I walk any girl home or texted. Ever. ~~She was different.~~ I just knew I wanted it to stop. But the way she kept sticking up to me pleased me. It made me hard. She gets on my nerves so easily. ~~Fuck, and I like that.~~ I need the games to get me going. The pain. The thrill. Sometimes even blood. But no girl wants that. They want ~~love~~. Something I don't have to offer. But she'll learn that soon enough. I took her with me. She loved it. The speed. ~~And I liked her liking it.~~ She smelled like me. ~~That was.. something.~~ ~~No girl ever smelled like me.~~ She showered in my bathroom. ~~Fuck, that.. was too much.~~ ~~I wanted to do that with her. Watch her. Fuck her in my shower.~~ I don't want to like her. ~~But she's not that bad.~~ ~~We fooled around. I liked spending time with her.~~ No, I didn't. It's just the game that keeps me going. It's the excitement for her downfall.

We went to Wren's party. The pirates. She has no idea who he is. Better so. ~~I sought her proximity.~~ I don't know why. I didn't even think about it. ~~I just had to touch her.~~ And the fact that she was annoyed with me by taking up so much space only made it funnier. I watched her dance. ~~The whole night.~~ ~~I couldn't take my eyes off her.~~ She liked me watching. But of course, out of all the guys, she picks fucking Wren. Hook himself. We used to be friends and grew up together. But that changed. We're enemies. And now he fucking danced with her. What's his plan? Trying to stab me? But Hook shouldn't forget that Pan cut his hand off. Hook is no villain. It has always been Pan. And it made me mad.. for many reasons. I knew the risk of stepping in. Of him knowing she is indeed different. But I was a fool to think he wouldn't know that already. There were times he knew me better than myself. But even the closest friends can fall apart. I've changed. I don't know if he knows me anymore. I thought seeing her with Aidan was bad but seeing her with Wren was the worst. She stomped off and said she wants to date assholes. She's so naive. She sat the whole night on that stair. And if I wasn't pissed, I would have sat next to her. ~~I wanted to.~~ But I knew I shouldn't.

We had that rule between the guys. That if you claimed a girl, it was yours. Of course, if she wanted to be yours too. But the guys wouldn't try to mess with them if you did. We snatched the girls from each other despite those rules sometimes. To piss each other off. If you knew a guy liked a certain girl, they would try to hit on her. We liked the games. When we were teens. But the games had gone too far. Friendships have been broken. People were broken. And rules too. But I didn't want her. I just wanted to be the one to mess with her. When they knew she's important, they wouldn't leave anything untried. They hit on Nina constantly. Even if she's with Leon. They break up *every now and then and if, she´s surrounded by lost boys and Wendy´s. Some guys have been banned from Neverland. Some of them wanted revenge. Wren wants revenge. But that´s on me. If he seeks revenge he should cut off my hand, not hers. So, since the others like her, I scared off every guy. There was never a girl that was that off limits. So maybe they were right, and she is different. But not for the reasons they think. Because different doesn´t mean anything. It doesn´t mean good or better. It just means different.*

She´s always around. ~~And it doesn´t bother me anymore.~~

She gave my hoodie back and it smelled like her. ~~I catch myself smelling it. And not washing it.~~ Fuck, I am an idiot.

I admitted ~~I dreamed about her~~. To confuse her I smeared the name of a song on her Vans. ~~I caught myself thinking of her while listening to it. I catch myself often thinking of her.~~ She probably thought about it all night. The thought amused me. ~~Now, I´m not the only one with sleepless nights. But I kept wondering if she dreamed about me too.~~

No, I didn´t.

Aidan dared her to strip down. She looked stunning. ~~I couldn´t take my eyes off her body.~~ She has a belly piercing and a tattoo on her thigh. A Scorpio. ~~That´s so damn hot.~~ After Aidan left for his side chick, I asked why she has no boyfriend. ~~I was curious.~~ I couldn´t bring myself to ask the others., They would have tried to set me up with her. She told me about her mindset. I was impressed. She said she´s rather alone. There´s nothing worse than people who are in relationships because they can´t be. We´re born alone, and we fucking die alone. Why do we have to try to not be, when all we have is ourselves? But then she talked about "the one" for me. That´s bullshit. Wendy´s are all the same.

She gave my cloths back. Which again smelled like her. ~~She smells like a summer night, the seaside and hot rain.~~ I´m so fucked.

24

The past weeks, we have seen each other almost every day. I can´t remember a time I saw friends that regularly. *But I begin to like it.*

- 27 -

Heat Waves – Slowed - Glass Animals

Kai reaches for his shirt and wipes his face with it. My gaze is glued to his stomach as he undresses. *On the V.*

But Aidan throws me into the pool.

I get out and grab a water gun and chase after him. Then I get a full blast in the face from Kai, who is still *mostly* dry. He aims at Aidan, and I get the opportunity to push him into the water. I catch him off guard and his attempt to pull me with him fails. All laugh, but even before he surfaces, *I know what will happen.*

He pulls himself out of the water with ease. His gaze on me. Armed with water balloons, I stand at the opposite edge of the pool. He fixes me and walks in my direction. His jaw twitches.

"Go away," I warn, with a laugh, but he runs, and I race with a shriek. I try to flee, but he catches up with me. I squeal and run around the sunbeds. Only the beach chairs separate us. "Just give up" he demands. "I´ll get you anyway" he adds smug. "Forget it" I say knowing I´m trapped but show no weakness. I throw him a charge at chest level, but he catches it easily, whereupon I run away. I can´t stop laughing. I feel like a child. That´s how I always feel when I´m with them.

Having fun and be in the now. Living in Neverland.

He runs after me and grabs me by the waist. I squeal and try to get away, but he wrestles me in one motion to the ground. None of the others seem particularly interested in us, let alone coming to my aid, as they wage their own wars. He crouches over me and presses my hands to the ground beside my head. I keep laughing and struggle under his body. His dark eyes pierce me. And I have lost the battle I didn´t know I was fighting. I am defenseless against him. Still, I leave no stone unturned to push him off me. *In vain.*

I can´t ignore the fact I find the situation *very* hot. How he leans over me. Water dripping down my face from his hair. "I told you I´d get you" he says boastfully. We stare at each other. My heart explodes. *He stares at my lips. Frowns.*

But before I could think he would actually kiss me; he grabs both of my hands with one hand. He picks up the water balloons. "No" I screech, laughing. He takes three at a time and pushes his fingers in, so they burst all over my face. I squint my eyes.

He chuckles. I mewl to myself.

He wants to take new ones. "Stop it please" I plead laughing. "We´re even" I call out. He looks at me. *Pretends to be seriously considering.*

Grinning, he pulls back and let´s go of my hands. For a moment I miss his weight on me. "Thanks," I say with a grin. He stands a few steps away from me. "Changed my mind" he says with a grin and lifts me up. "Put me down" I protest. He walks to the pool. "Kai" I admonish playfully, but he takes a running start and jumps into the pool with me.

I surface, followed by him, and try to push him underwater by the shoulders.

Unsuccessful. He´s a wall.

He grabs my waist and pushes me underwater instead. Then he pulls me up again. I cough. He drowns me again and pulls me up cause I didn´t have the time to inhale. I spit water and wrap my arms around his neck, hoping it would stop him. He freezes as I wrap my legs around his back. We lock eyes. He grabs me by the throat and throws me off him.

I give up and escape from the water, hauling myself up on the edge. With my hands, I point timeout in Kai´s direction. Then I sit down on the sofa with my water. That throat grab was.. *fucking hot.*

Kai walks towards me. He has a towel wrapped around his neck. I take a big gulp of the ice-cold drink to kill the butterflies in my stomach. He rubs his hair with the towel and runs his hand through it. They stick out in all directions. *But still looking good.* He wipes his face with the towel and throws it on the backrest. Then he reaches for me.

For a moment, I´m at a loss. He wants my bottle.

I hand it to him; he throws his head back and empties it in one stroke. Without wiping it off. I don´t drink from *anyone*, not even my family. I have a little hygiene tick sometimes, but honestly, I would even let him spit in my mouth. *What*?

"I´ll get you a new one." He says and walks inside.

They both knew they secretly liked each other. *And they both knew they don´t.*

25

September

We come to a stop on a parking lot where several cars are parked. About seventeen are lined up. One is more blatant than the other. Among them BMWs, Audi´s, Mercedes, a Corvette, a Porsche, a Lambo, and others. There are also a few motorcycles. I even spot Leon, Nina, and Finn. Engines are howling, exhausts are popping, and donuts are being pulled. The whole atmosphere makes me feel high. A mixture of excitement and adrenaline runs through me.

A few minutes later, Aidan shows up on his Ducati. And apparently, we are now complete, because as soon as he comes to a stop the Ford GT drives off with spinning tires and blinking three times. All the others follow. This is another "*game*" they do.

When it´s our turn, I get butterflies in my stomach. We drive onto the road in a column. The sounds are music to my ear. His arms are covered in veins. I follow every step, of his hands. He looks fulfilled. *In the flow. Free. In the now.*

We speed of, onto the highway. When the track is clear, Aidan overtakes and rides alongside us. Both exchange a glance. The next moment, he shoots on, and Kai pulls onto the left lane as well. I am pressed to the seat and my heart drops. But unlike on the free fall tower, this feeling is nothing but exhilarating. *Addicting.*

The two of them race to the top and as we pass the others they also sheer out and follow. Kai flicks the finger to the mustang who was at the top. *I smile.*

\- 27 -

We sit at a crowded bar. Kai next to me at the end of the table. I´m facing Kai to follow the conversation of the others. But I hardly can because first, it´s too loud in here and second, there are people I don´t know.

With one hand I play with the paper straw of my cocktail, and with the other I twist my ring and let it wander over my fingers. As I see, Kai stares at them so I stop. He frowns at me. *I place it on the table.*

Instead, I start to pool off the paper of a beer and begin to wiggle with my leg as an outlet. Which I haven´t noticed until his hand on my knee stops me and I freeze. He doesn´t look at me when I look at him. There´s just his hand on my knee under the table.

Grounding me. Calming me.

As he joins the chat with the others, he squeezes slightly. I feel my pulse in every fiber of my body. I´m hyper aware. *Anxiety all gone. Replaced by butterflies.*

My cheeks grow hot. I take a sip of my drink. *But it makes it worse.*

Our knees touch. I think I might faint. *He touched me. On purpose.*

And he moved closer. My heart races. My neck tingles. *I empty my drink.*

\- 27 -

His hand stayed there the *whole* evening. He didn´t look at me nor talk to me. But he didn´t need to. His hand did all the talking, and it screamed, *I want to touch you. I care. I noticed. I´m here. You´re safe.*

I felt high. *Dizzy. Happy. Excited.* But most of all confused.

26

Leon is driving for a change. So, Kai has been drinking and so did I. It´s just the three of us. Kai sits in the passenger seat and I behind him. I direct my gaze out the window. I must try not to watch him in the side mirror. Besides, I´m afraid he might catch me. So, I imagine a giant knife cutting off everything we drive past.

And at that moment I feel ten again.

As fat raindrops patter against the windshield, I stop. And at the same moment I feel *fingers* on my Vans. Kai leans his head against the windowpane and has his arm between the door and the seat, *tapping* my sole.

My eyes shoot to Leon, but he doesn´t notice. Apart from, it´s too dark anyway. My eyes wander back to his fingers, which are resting on the spot he smeared weeks ago. *Sex Drive*. Still don´t know what that was about.

A thick vein sticks out on his forearm. His fingers bob to the beat. I rest my head against the glass, to get a better look. He reaches for my ankle and strokes my skin. I could never have imagined how much such a banal touch could trigger.

This is crazy. My stomach is going crazy. I am crazy.

For a moment, I wonder if this is really happening and if I´m not imagining Kai doing something like this. If I didn´t see it. Or feel it in every part of my body. I would think he was crazy. But he *did* touch my knee last week too. But now there´s no excuse like my anxiety. He *wants* to touch me. *For no reason.*

I´m glad I shaved my legs today, or I´d cut him with my razor-sharp stubble.

Every fiber of my body wants to touch his arm. *To feel his hand.*

His finger slides over my ankle and stops on my vein. He applies pressure. *He feels my pulse.* With that realization, it probably only increases. *Fuck.* I can even feel it pounding through my chest. I wait for a reaction, as if he´s about to make a comment or laugh. *But nothing.* He continues to stroke my skin. *And I love it.*

For the next quarter-hour, he continues. I even took a picture, so I know it really did happen.

Kai apparently had his eyes closed because Leon punches him in the shoulder, "Wake up dickhead. Had too much huh?" He laughs. Whereupon Kai grumbles and chuckles.

Right, he´s plastered. I forgot.

Before pulling away, he tightens his grip for a sec. He stretches and lets out an annoyed growl. My skin tingles for the rest of the car ride, and I wish he never stopped.

27

Kai sits with his legs apart and leans back. Unconsciously, I loop my leg over his while I´m on the phone. His posture changes, and his eyes shoot to mine. I realize what a harmless but intimate gesture that was. Especially considering we don´t do that thing. I can´t interpret his look. *Was that too much?* Of course, it was. *Stupid. I wasn´t thinking.*

Apparently, he noticed my hesitation, because before I can make a retreat, he puts his hand on my knee. And that touch sends warm signals through my body. Especially when his hand wanders towards my thigh. I must pull everything together, not to put my hand on his or to run my fingers along his arm. Instead, I force myself to keep scrolling, trying to look busy. That he can see *exactly* what I´m doing on my phone, I clearly did not consider. I was too distracted. Too aware of his hand gripping my thigh.

But then the garden gate opens, and the others come with more alcohol for the party. Kai not-so-gently takes his hand off my thigh and stands up, pushing my leg off him, before anyone can catch what he was doing. *Or we.*

I take a deep breath to swallow my anger. *Ass remains ass.* Period.

And the line on his shirt makes me rethink my whole life.

"Sorry if I looked interested. I´m not."

Is this some sick joke of the universe?

Clearly, he´s not. He´s just messing with you. *Playing games.*

- 27 -

At the end of the night, I catch myself thinking about him as I fall asleep. I don´t want to think about him, let alone make up fake scenarios because all of *that* is never going to happen. All you get from daydreaming is a headache and heartbreak. That´s one of the mistakes you make when you first meet someone. You imagine situations and conversations. So, you create a version of the person that doesn´t exist. Practically, you fall in love with your *own* thoughts. *Stupid.*

We don´t date. He doesn´t. So, do I.

Then I drift into dreamland haunted by black eyes and thigh touches.

28

It´s pitch dark. The wet asphalt splatters under my shoes. The air is fresh, but not cold. I follow Kai, who walks ahead of me at a fast pace. *I am drunk. Very drunk.* I don´t know *how* that happened.

Every time I stop, he pulls me on annoyed, which amuses me. That´s also why I stop extra often, to tease him and to extend the way a little.

When I called Leon to pick me up, he hung up. *Kai´s not the only moody one.* But not two minutes later he called back. But Kai was on the phone and asked where I was. He was angry right away. I thought it was funny. I imagined him frowning.

He does that all the time.

He insisted on picking me up. I think he´s pissed because he had to leave a party. But he wanted to walk me home, so idk. I would have gone alone if I hadn´t had so much beer.

I hate beer. Why did I have beer? And why is he mad at me?

He called me back. I asked Leon. Seems that the rude version of him is back. It was only a matter of time until he started hating me again. *After the touching.*

We´re walking along the road at four in the morning. In the middle of the street. *Village life,* I call it.

When I stop again, he grabs my upper arm and pulls me behind him. "I can walk by myself." I protest, squirming under his grip. When he let´s go, I regret it immediately because I didn´t think he would. He continues walking ahead. Without a comment. Generally, he hasn´t said much yet. But he isn´t much of a talker most of the time any-way. But other times he seems not able to shut up. I grin to myself. *He´s handsome. If he wants to.*

Otherwise, he´s a pain in the ass.

I try to focus on his hoodie to read the quote but it´s hard when you see the world shiver. After three attempts, I manage to identify the letter chaos.

"Whoever brings you the most peace should get the most time."

I giggle. How he´s right now, he isn´t at peace at all. He´s annoyed. And angry. And stubborn. *And just Kai.*

I strain to get after him. I grab his biceps to keep up with him. But he stops abruptly under my touch, and my heart with him as I slam into his body. I feel his muscles flex, but then he keeps walking. My free hand moves to his forearm. My fingers claw into the fabric of his hoodie. *I can´t walk alone.* Not when I can walk with him.

I count the middle line stripes.

"Are you cold?" he asks for the fourth time since he got to me. I shake my head, "No." I say also for the fourth time.

As we reach the first lanterns, I let go. My hand slides from his biceps down his arm to his hand. *Hoping he´ll take mine.*

Which he doesn´t. Instead, his pinky seeks mine. I hold it. With all my fingers. He has big hands. *I like that.*

I walk two steps close behind him. And after a while, it´s also just my pinky holding his.

And only now I notice we have passed my street a while ago. *He´s taking me to his.* Or he wants to go back to the party. Whatever it is, I´m fine with, because I can keep walking besides him a little longer.

When we arrive at his, I see no trace of a party. There were no cars in the driveway either. Only his BMW.

I lie down on the sofa and cover myself with one of the blankets. Spirit and Moon lie down by my legs. Kai puts a water bottle on the table and sits down on the other end of the sofa. It all turns. He looks straight at me. *Still no talking.*

He turns on the TV on a low volume. And even though I want to keep looking at him, my eyes get heavy, and my mind leads me away.

- 27 -

My throat groans for water. My stomach for relaxation. *I drink and drink.* When water isn´t enough to quench the thirst, you know *Yesterday* you exaggerated. And I clearly did. I have a bad headache. And I need a moment to get my bearings. The sun shines through the panes of the patio doors. And where Kai sat, no one is sitting anymore. Even the dogs are gone.

I can´t remember much of the night. That did *never* happen to me before. I never drink over my border. *Never.* At least I didn´t vomit. *Did I?*

I think we were kind of holding hands.

Nina comes over and tells me the boys have a soccer game since it is Sunday. Even though I don´t feel like it, we go watch them after I have freshened up a bit.

The fresh air did me good, and the whole game my eyes were looking for Kai and Aidan.

But mostly Kai.

And that day I decided to watch every game.

29

Kai makes a plank while biting his shirt. His hair is damp, and his skin covered with sweat. Clothes stick to his skin. He´s struggling. But not giving up. The way he keeps going. *Fighting. Pushing.* The way he´s *pained* is hot. A timer rings and I see he´s been doing it for five minutes. I can´t even hold a minute.

He gets up and hands me his black cap, which he wore backwards. I tie my hair into a low bun and put it on. He lifts his shirt off. He promised to show me kick boxing. I try on the black gloves and fail to close the second one. He grabs my hand and closes it.

He shows me the fighting stance and the right-hand position. Then punching techniques with fists and kicks. I try to focus on his instructions instead of his bare skin.

"Watch your footwork. And most of your power comes from your hips, not your shoulder." He explains.

Then we practice defensive techniques.

"Okay enough, let´s fight" I say to which he laughs. "Come on" I whine. As he still grins, I throw a punch at him, but he blocks me with ease. *Shit. That´s hot.*

Even when I try again, he reacts with lightning speed, to which I only get more frustrated, angry and most of all *turned on*. I´m aware I can´t fight him, but I still leave no stone unturned. "Hit me back," I demand. I want to provoke him. I don´t know what I´m trying to accomplish, but I want him to have a reaction. *Something. Anything.*

"I won´t hit you." He says. "Come on I thought you could take me." I say, but no sooner have the words left my mouth, he grabs my hands and turns me, so my back is to him. His grip tight around my joints. So hard I can´t move but not strong enough to hurt me. "It´s always the *smallest* who bark but can´t fucking bite." He snaps into my ear. His body presses against mine. My breathing is heavy, and my heart racing a mile a second. He breathes hard. My stomach tingles and my center throbs.

Fuck. This is turning me on. Hella turn on.

He loosens his grip. I reposition myself. His gaze hard and wild. His veins stand out on his hands, arms and along his neck. The muscle in his jaw twitches. A bead of sweat runs down his forehead. My body reacts like crazy to him.

"You want to fight? Then hit." He says piercingly.

The first blows he deflects skillfully. But I manage one or the other lucky punch, but I´m sure he lets me, so I have more fun. He hits me not hard, but at least he does *something*. When I try a kick, he grabs my shin and fires it back, making me stumble, but he catches me. Anger and above all frustration boil up.

"Get on nerves, huh?" he grins. "It does," I press between clenched teeth. "You want an outlet?" He asks. *Yeah.*

"Hit my abs." He demands. My eyes widen. "What?" I mean, I´ve seen that before, but he can´t be serious. "It´s just toughening up." He assures me. "And you´re not going to hit as hard as an exercise ball." He adds smug. "All right," I say, and give him a punch and wait for his reaction. But his face is *expressionless*. Hard and cold.

I hit again. Again. And again.

Until I stop counting. *It´s fun.*

At one point, he grabs my wrists with one and pulls me to him. He stares into my eyes. "*Love the pain.*" He says with a rough voice and a smile. I´m only aware of his breath rather than his quoting. His lips are a few inches from mine. Which he also realizes as he looks at them. He licks his lips. Automatically, I open my mouth.

The next moment he lifts me up and slams me against his closet, pressing his body to mine. I draw in a sharp breath and wrap my arms and legs around him. I want to touch him. But the gloves prevent me. His pitch-black eyes lock with mine. Anger, pain, and desire are written over his face. I have the feeling he´s not breathing. So, I hold my breath too, as if I can´t help but mirror him.

His breath hits my face. He leans in but instead of kissing me, his forehead bombs against the wood next to me. *What?*

His chest rises, and he slowly lowers me to the ground. *Snap. Like a kill switch.*

He presses his hand against the door next to my hip. Then wordlessly and without looking at me, he opens my gloves, strips them off and puts them on himself. He uses his teeth to tighten them and turns to his bag. "I have to train." He says coldly, as if whatever *that* was didn´t happen. The lump in my throat kills me, so I leave. *Fuck you.*

Did he want to kiss me?

Did I want to kiss him? Of course, I wanted to.

And did I feel his erection? He was already hardening at my back.

I settle down on the sofa. Even though I hate beer, I open one. Little by little the guests arrive, and the terrace fills up.

As I open my third beer, I notice the look of a girl. "What?" I ask her somewhat passive aggressively and bring the bottle to my mouth. "Is that Kai´s cap?" she asks. He didn´t want it back, so I kept it. "Yep," I reply and take another swig. She raises her eyebrows in surprise and mouths *Oh*. But I´m already too drunk to wonder, how she knows what caps he wears and, why she even cares.

I stand up and face Luca. "Beer?" she asks, knowing I detest it. "Hmm," I mutter. "Finn?" I ask as I notice her watching him from a distance. She grins. "Is it *that* obvious?" she asks, embarrassed. "Yep. I know you, but I´m sure he´s not aware of his luck." I say.

- 27 -

At some point, Kai comes back. I don´t look at him. *I´m mad at him.*

At this whole situation.

We come close and take a step back. *It´s frustrating.*

I take a sip on my beer. Kai looks at me confused. I nod at him with a dead expression. "Who are you?" He asks frowning referring to my drink. "The girl you´d die for." I say dryly, already a bit drunk. He´s as surprised about my answer as I am. He falters and just looks at me. I act like I made a joke and it´s no big deal. I´m *always* like that. I say sarcastic things. *Nothing to feel weird about.*

"You *never* drink beer. I haven´t seen you drink it *once*." He says after a moment, ignoring my statement. *Why does everyone ask me that?*

People can fucking change their mind.

"Yeah." I shrug. "Now you do." I add, lifting it and walk past him.

That day it was their first *almost*. How little did they know how many were to come.

30

:p – La+ch

Kai sits next to me. He licks the blunt paper and looks at me while doing it. His tongue sends shivers through my body. My eyes follow him as he lights his joint. He takes a drag and blows the smoke into the air. Then he leans back and throws his head back.

When his eyes meet mine, he nods in my direction. "Want some?" He holds it to me between his thumb and forefinger. "Nah," I laugh. Whereupon he grins and shakes his head as if he knew I would decline. "I can´t" I begin to explain. "Tried it twice. And almost died on the second attempt." I laugh. "I can´t seem to smoke on lungs. Choked and almost suffocated. Literally near-death experience." He can´t help his grin. "Yeah, I know. *Lost*." I can´t help but grin, either. "If cannabis, it´ll be baked. I wish I could smoke." I whine. "You don´t have to smoke on lung." He says with a grin. But as his eyes explore my face, his expression is hard.

"Come here," he murmurs. As if hypnotized, I scoot closer. His arm on the back of the sofa. My heart does somersaults as his chest approaches mine and his face just inches away. His other hand grabs my cheek, and my heart slips into my pants. "Trust me." He says and pulls from the joint. My stomach sinks and my ears are burning with heat. His thumb strokes my bottom lip, causing my mouth to open. My body is already high from his touch. His lip brushes mine and he lets the smoke into my mouth.

He gives me a headshot.

I fight against pressing my lips to his. Even though, they burn and tingle with the desire to be kissed. When the smoke eventually escapes, he takes another drag and blows it into my mouth. *And again, and again.*

In between, he takes a drag himself. I have stopped counting. And just as I tell myself I feel nothing, *I feel it*. In my cheeks, because I must grin like insane. My clitoris pulses as I eye him. His eyes fall on my lips. And at that moment, I realize I´ve been biting my lower lip. *He stares at it.* Then he adjusts his jeans. *Fuck.*

And with that, the pulsing between my legs becomes a hammering. I am not only happy but also horny on Kai fucking Dark. And I´m pretty sure so is he. His gaze burns on me. I have the feeling every second we fall over each other like predators. My brain is light and heavy, and I wish it would never stop. I am nowhere else but here in the now. *With Kai.*

The seconds pass like hours and hours like seconds. I´m intoxicated by him. Time expands and runs out as we gaze at each other. Our legs touch, and I still sit close to him. His head leans back, facing me. His eyes fix on mine.

We don´t talk but say so much.

I want to touch his chest and sit on his lap. I want his hand on my ass and for him to kiss me. I know for sure he wants that too. Because the wall that usually surrounds him is not gone, but I am no longer outside the fortress. Which doesn´t mean that all the soldiers aren´t pointing their guns at me right now. Because they do, and I know any step can be my death. But I´m high and death-defying.

The next thing I notice is an arm pulling me up and forcing me to my feet. *It´s Aidan.* A very drunk and happy Aidan. *And maybe stoned?* This party became a stoner party; I think. Everybody seems high on something. *Was this another game?*

"Come, *Scar,* let´s dance." He says, dragging me. He leads me onto the dance floor, and I pull Kai with me. And he follows closely.

I don´t care about anything. The music blasts through the speakers and makes my body quiver. Luca, Nina, and the others also join us. We all move in slow motion and I´m sure it looks like the scenes in the movies. I feel like I´m in *Project X.* Free with my friends.

Dancing. Forgetting. Laughing.

We´re raving and jumping and it´s like the floor is a trampoline. Or jiggling pudding. This is a one lifetime moment. When nothing else matters. *Euphoria.* Adrenalin runs through my system.

We all smoke again. Kai gives me another headshot. He takes a drag and passes it to his brother. Then he takes my face in his hand, and I open my mouth for him. His guns drop as his lips crush on mine. Hard as razor blades, they cut me and in the next second he abruptly let´s go of me and passes me by. One of the falling guns fired and hit me. The others didn´t notice anything. I even wonder if I imagined it. As quickly as it happened it was over.

Or am I just high?

Even if the cut on my lips says otherwise. *Pulsating and bleeding. Craving.*

I think it was all a dream. *Once in a lifetime.*

After that he stopped responding to her texts. And she stopped texting. Like it didn´t happen. Like two addicts didn´t just got their first line.

31

One Week later

Stones hitting my window wake me. It´s three in the morning and Kai´s in front of my house, gathering small rocks to throw. I put on some panties, a hoodie that reach mid-thigh, some shoes and hurry downstairs.

Just as he smashes another handful, I round the corner. His eyes shoot to me. Hands now in his front pockets. "You know how late it is?" I whisper-yell. He shrugs. "No watch. Remember?" He asks, mirroring my tone. I fight a smile, but I nod. "But you have a phone." I state. "So?" He shrugs. "I don´t use it for time." He says. "Well, for *normal* people, it´s time to sleep." I say. "I´m not much of a sleeper." He says. "I figured." I say. *And not normal. But who is?*

We look at each other for a moment. *Won´t he talk?*

He looks at me like he has no idea why he´s here either. He looks past me and on the ground between us. I take him in. *He´s fully clothed. Was he on a party?*

Haven´t heard of him since he stopped responding. *The day he kissed me.*

I figure he won´t talk, so I speak up. "You stopped texting." I say quiet, not looking at him, because I don´t want him to know how much it hurt me. But now he knows, it did.

He nods, still not talking. "Why are you here?" I ask staring at his chest. I´d like to fiddle with the ribbons of his sweater. To hug or touch him, even yell at him. *But I don´t.*

"I did." He says ignoring my question. "Cause, I don´t like that stuff." He says, uncomfortable. "No phones rule." I guess. He nods and clears his throat. "I stopped. Cause I rather spend time with you in person than.. having a phone between us." He explains looking past me. The way he couldn´t look at me told me he really meant it. "What you wanna do then?" I ask. He shrugs for the thousand time. It´s his thing besides the frowns. "Talk I guess." His voice husky. *He came to talk?*

"You wanna come up then?" I ask. He bites the inside of his under lip, shaking his head. He tilts his head. "Let´s walk." He suggests. "I have no pants on." I say. "So?" He asks, looking down on me. "Are you cold?" He wants to know. "No but.." I begin and he cuts in. "It´s late, you said, so no one will see ya." He states. "Yeah but.." I say and he interrupts again. "But what? You look good. Now come walk with me." He urges. "Was that a compliment?" I narrow my eyes and grin. "Nah." he says, but I saw the tiny smile on his face before he turned.

"All you need is less."

Colson Herzog

"I like that statement, but I think sleep wasn´t meant by less." I retort. He looks at me. "You can sleep too much, though." He states. I shake my head at him but mirror his grin. "Alright, you have an answer for everything don´t you?" I ask. "I can always find one." He grins. I slap his arm.

We walk on the streets heading nowhere.

"So, have you thought of something for your game yet?" He asks. "Actually, I have. But you have to read." I say. He looks at me curiously. "Read?" He asks with his brows raised as if he hasn´t himself shelves full.

I take out my phone and show him. "Read that series and you´ll know my wish." He eyes it. "Series? You want me to read *three* books?" He asks. "Yep." I reply. "Why don´t you just tell me?" He´s confused. "You wouldn´t understand." I say. "You must read it to get it. It´s a *mindset*." I grin referring to their party culture. He smiles back, seeing it as a challenge. "Then I´ll read that series." He says. "Is it a romance?" He asks. "Yeah, dark romance but it´s so much more. It´s following the call of the void." I say and he nods. "I want a game like those. They play games too, you know." I tell him. "Tell me more." He´s all excited now. "Nah, you´ll have to read yourself." I say. "Alright." He shuts up and we keep walking.

"You know you can throw rocks at my window when the sun´s up too." I say sarcastic. "Where´s the fun to that?" He asks. I smile. "You´re a dick." I say, shaking my head. "And you´re a pain in the arse." He fires back but grins, I punch him, and he shoves me back.

We keep fooling around.

- 27 -

As we say goodbye, I ask him. "Will you still want to talk to me at the party?" He looks at me. "Why do you ask that?" He wants to know. I shrug. He frowns at me.

But says nothing.

"Forget that I asked." I tell him and walk along, but he grabs my elbow, stopping me. "I will." He says and let´s go of me.

The following weeks, he shows up on her street more and more. They sit and talk. Or walk and talk. Or just stand and talk.

And even on the parties they talk more. But sometimes even talking means nothing.

32

It´s just the two of us on the sofa and talking about all kinds of things.

"I think I´m a loner." I say. "Yeah, me too." He says. "You have a lot of friends. You do sports. The boxing and soccer." I say and he shrugs. "You can be lonely with friends, too." He says. "That´s right." I agree. "But you´re more a mix of an introvert and extrovert. I´m an introvert." I say. He looks at me weirdly. "But you know there´s a difference between being silent and being silenced." He says, and it hits deeper than I could have imagined.

He shakes his head. "But you´re both, too." He says sensing my feelings. "You think?" I ask. He nods, looking like he knows. "It totally depends on the people you´re with. You have to feel comfortable to be goofy." He says, and the fact that he noticed makes me blush. "Kind of yeah." I grin. *Exactly like that.*

"But deep down there´s always that loneliness." I say. "Know that." He says absently. "We have more in common than we thought, I guess." I say. "Hm." He agrees, and he has that look on his face. He stares at me like he knows something about me, not even I do.

And I believe he does. He has that way of reading people.

- 27 -

It starts pouring. "Shit" I get up. "I´m here with my bike" I whine. He raises his cup in the air "I´d give you a ride, but I´ve been drinking" he says. "I´ll just ride home quick, it sure stops soon." I say, but there´s a thunderclap. *Great.*

"You can stay here." he walks up behind me. I turn to look at him. "Let´s go inside. When it clears, you can go." He nods towards the door. I follow him as lightning flashes.

"You don´t know me."

His sweater reads. *But I want to know you.* And I think he does too.

He hands me a T-shirt and asks if I need sweatpants, but I decline. It fits like a dress anyway. I would have preferred what he´s wearing now, but I won´t ask him. We change and I get ready in the bathroom. When I come back, he´s in the bed reading. I smile. He lies on his back with one hand behind his head. He wears only black shorts, like the ones he wears during training, and his shorts stick out, also in black.

I lie down on the left side of the bed and turn to him. "Will you read to me?" I ask. He looks from the book to me and back, drawing his eyebrows together. Then he gets back to the first page and begins to read aloud. I get goose bumps. As the rain pelts the windows, I listen to him intently, page after page.

I don´t even know how long he´s been reading to me. The shower mutates into steady rain. The sound of his voice calms me even more than the thunderstorm ever could. And before I notice my mind drifts away.

- 27 -

I am forced out of my sleep. I jolt up. Completely confused in the dark, I grab Kai´s upper arm with both hands. He, too squirms. “Hm,” he grumbles sleepily. I realize I´ve laid down with him. “Sorry” I whisper and want to pull back. *It was just the thunder.*

But before I can pull away, he stops my hand. He reaches for it. Electrified and at the same time surprised, I pause for a moment.

He pulls me to him. I lay my head next to his shoulder. My hand is still in his.

It doesn´t take long to fall asleep again. *Safe and calm.* And not at all lonely.

- 27 -

Awakened by the sun´s rays, I find us in the same position. Only he has turned his head to me. I feel his breath on my face. His eyes still closed. He looks so peaceful. It´s still raining. I still cling to his arm. The book on his chest. Apparently, he fell asleep while reading or he didn´t want to get up to wake me. *I really stayed at his. We slept in one bed.*

I study his face. *He´s so close to me.*

I run my free hand over his skin on his forearm, and as I reach his palm, it twitches from the touch. My fingertips slide between his fingers, and before I can make a retreat, his fall into mine. Like an anaconda snatches its prey. *Dominant. Greedy for me?*

A slight ache runs through my bones. But as quickly as he caught me, he lets me go again. *As always, when we get close.* As if he realized what he just did.

He takes a deep breath and stretches his hands above his head. I sit up and watch him. His biceps are bulging, and his skin is covered with veins. His expression a mix of sleepiness and bad-tempered. *Rather grumpiness.*

But he looks hot as ever. Not even in the morning does he look remotely less perfect. On the contrary, his hair is even better so.

Do I look good? I avert my gaze and run a hand through my hair. He grumbles and stretches again. I push myself to the foot of the bed and stand up. My shirt hangs on my hip and slowly slides down. With his hands behind his head, he watches me as I walk to the window. The streets are still wet. I lean against the windowsill and cross my arms under my chest. Wordlessly, we fix each other. *What is he thinking?*

His irises are menacingly black. Even though they are probably just a very dark brown, I am convinced they are at least a brown, black. His gaze is hard but as inquiring as mine. My eyes travel to his bare chest down to his stomach. A few seconds pass before he stands up with a groan and walks toward me. With a full-on morning wood tightening his shorts wanting to be free. I must pull it together to act normal. A clear rock-hard bulge in the boxers. My heart stops, and my clit takes over the beating. He catches me staring but doesn´t flinch. He just fixes me.

I avert my eyes. He has a print on his arm from the pillow. Which makes me grin. It´s both hot and cute at the same time. He runs his hand through his hair.

"Huh?" he nods to me and stands right in front of me. *Closer than he has to.*

I run my hand over the spot. "You have a pillow print." I whisper and grin. When I lift my gaze, he´s already looking at me instead of his arm. My pulse shoots up, and my ears get red-hot. I wish he had a print on his face so I could touch him there. "Sleep well *Sleepin´ Beauty*?" He asks raspy. *Sleepin´ Beauty*?

He steps closer. If I take a step, we´d touch. We´re so close I think he might kiss me, but instead he looks out the window and I realize I haven´t given an answer. "Do you want me to drive you home?" He asks, but I shake my head. "I´ll ride my bike." I say and for a second, he keeps staring out of the window.

"Okay." He says looking at me.

That night, he could sleep for the first time. And she could sleep calmly again. They became their safe space without even knowing.

33

After that night, we began seeing each other casually. In addition to the days, we saw each other anyway. After partying, I stayed, and we talked. Sometimes we drove somewhere. Other times we just texted. *As now.*

"*Are you up for reading?*" he texts. "*Sure,*" I reply.

After a few minutes he texts "*I´ll pick you up in ten.*"

- 27 -

I grab my book and head downstairs. I get in his car. A song by Machine Gun Kelly plays. Then another. It´s starting to get creepy how alike we are. Yet we couldn´t be more different. And now I realize who he was quoting when we were boxing. "*Love the pain.*" When he looks at me with a furrowed brow, I realize I wasn´t just thinking. "Uhm.." I stumble. "MGK is my favorite artist" I say. "Mine too." He says frowning. Sometimes looking at him feels like looking in a mirror. For good and bad.

"Are you going to his concert?" I ask. "Are *you* going?" He asks me instead. "Yes, in October." I reply. "Alone?" His frown deepens. "Yes, actually, I am." I say. "Isn´t that bit weird alone?" He glances at me. "Not at all. I don´t know anyone who likes him so.." I shrug. "I don´t mind. I like it that way. I do lots of things alone." I point out.

"Like?" He wants to know. "Shopping, watching a movie.. basically, everything." I laugh and look ahead.

Because I have no friends. Or at least had.

"Because you have to? Or because you like to?" He asks with a frown. I stare at him. And shrug. "I can go with you." He states his eyes on the road. "You would join me?" I ask, expecting him to mess with me. "Sure." He says. "Okay." I say.

We drive to the next town. There are meadow fields on the hillside and cherry and apple trees. The view is amazing. You can see the whole city from here.

I watch Kai as he spreads the white picnic blanket.

He wears a white T-shirt with shorts.

"Your energy is your currency."

I like that he´s spiritual. *I never thought he could be like that.*

His silver wristwatch reflects the sunlight. All around us are flowers, bees, and butterflies. The sun is high on, the deep blue sky.

We lie down. He reads *The Portrait of Dorian Gray by Oskar Wild.* I´ve seen him read that one before. *It looks horrible.* Like he read it a hundred times and threw it just as often. It looks used. The spine is cracked and looks like the lifelines of a tree slice. Old with wrinkles and marks. It looks like he loves it. I had to read that in school, but I read two chapters and quit after that. I don´t know how I made it through the lessons. I don´t even know the ending or the main plot. Back then, I hated reading. And now all my money tiles in books. Funny how life works out sometimes. And a month ago he despised me, kicked me out, and now he asked me on a date. Times change.

But I wonder how many times you can read a book until you´re done with it? When does it get boring? When do you remember all the letters? When doesn´t it surprise you anymore?

I blink, trying to regain my focus. He´s supporting himself with his forearm. His veins stick out and his muscles seem more defined. He probably has been training more lately. I force myself to start reading, but I read the same page for the fifth time and have still no clue what the letters want to tell me. It´s hard to concentrate. Especially when I see him looking at me in the corner of my eye. It´s a wonder I don´t grin like a little kid.

I manage to read some pages. But he´s still staring at me. I glance at him. "Hold still," he says. "There´s a butterfly on your book." He whispers. He takes his phone and snaps a picture to show it to me. I grin. "I really like that one." I say. Normally I look like shit when others take pictures of me. They just don´t know the angles. Apparently, he does. Well, *duh,* he´s a hobby photographer.

He´s typing. So, I take him in. Inside the phone cover is a Polaroid. But it´s flipped over, so you can only see the black side. *Weird*. But that´s typical Kai. He has his own head. In every aspect of life. You can´t figure out the things he does.

"Mourning cloak," he says after a while. "I´ve never seen one like that before." I say excitedly. "Neither have I." He opines. "Mourning cloaks have one of the longest lifespans of all butterflies. But one-year isn´t that long if you don´t chose to live it." I look at him, trying to get what he meant.

"Is he still there?" I ask afraid to move. He nods and grins. In such moments with him, I can forget everything. *It all feels simple.* The now feels enough to stay.

Eventually it flies away.

\- 27 -

Kai throws his book on the blanket and leans back. I grin to myself as mine gets spicy. I must pull myself together not to react in any way I usually do.

Commenting and squirreling.

I press my lips together, but I can´t fight the big smile on my face.

"What are you smirking about?" he asks, amused, to which I only smile more. *Fuck.*

"What you´re reading anyway?" he asks, snatching the book. "Heyy," I whine. I can´t stop grinning. "Give me that." I demand, trying to get it back. *In vain.*

He holds it up in the air above and grins at me smug. I hold onto his chest and try to get it. But he dodges me every time I try to reach it. I almost sit on his lap while trying to get it back. His grin only makes me angrier. And he *obviously* enjoys pissing me off. He has that shit grin on his face. It´s handsome and sexy but makes my blood boil.

At the same time, we both realize *how* close we are. How I straddle him. How his hand holds my hip down. And how I hold onto his shoulder and neck reaching. How we look at each other and how close our faces are. *So close.*

And when the eye contact becomes too intense, I sit back.

He reads intently. I probably turn red. His smile grows bigger. In between, he throws me a mischievous sideways glance. Whereupon I bury my face in my hands.

"I didn´t know you read *porn*" he laughs. Then he quotes some parts. And I can´t deny how hot it makes me to hear the lines coming from his mouth. I can´t help but imagine doing those things with him.

"Neither did I know that porn in books is *actually* a thing." He adds. "It´s not porn." I defend myself, knowing it is. *Well, not just.*

"It´s just a bit spice." I say grinning. "*Spice*." He snorts. "That´s what you´re into?" But it sounds more like a statement. I press my lips together. "It´s called smudge." I clarify.

"You got more of those?" He asks, clearly amused, and throws it back to me. "A whole shelf." I say. "I´ll have to check *that* out." He grins. *I return it.*

"When you start the series, I told you about you´ll get more of that too." I say. "That´s porn too?" He asks and I nod. "Even better." I taunt. "Got me. I´ll definitely read it." He retorts. "I told you *days* ago." I point out. "Yeah, I know, but I had others on my tbr list you know." He states with a grin. "But *now* it´s on top." He says. I shake my head.

34

We went to a café in the old town and continued reading after we watched clouds and shared headphones for a while. His eyes are focused on the book. A strand of hair hangs in his face. His forehead wrinkles.

I would have never thought we´d be on an actual date. I mean, I don´t know if it is one but at least he wants to spend time with me. *He doesn´t hate me anymore.*

"You´re staring at me." He says in a rough voice, without lifting his gaze. I don´t answer.

I wonder what series he watched as a child. What has he played with his friends on the street in the summer? What loves he? And what hates he? Why his parents are never home? Why he spends time with me? And why he´s such a pain in the ass? And why sometimes he not? What does he do when no one is watching him? What does he think about me? What does he think about life?

"What are you thinking about?" I ask the dumbest question I could have picked. He looks at me without lifting his head. "I´m reading." He lifts the book. *Yeah, stupid question.*

He turns his attention back to the page.

Why didn´t I ask any of the other questions? And why is he always pissed?

"I think about you." He retorts, not looking up. "Cause.. you´re staring at me." He says. My pulse pounds in my throat. "I can´t concentrate, and I´m rereading the page for the tenth *fucking* time now." Then he finally looks at me. "And I still don´t know what it´s about." My ears are burning. My stomach tingles. "So, if you could stop staring at me like that" he snaps. And the tingling turns to discomfort. *Why are you such an ass? Can´t you just say cute things and not playing them down afterwards?*

You said them. *Own it.*

He turns back to his book. And I, too, continue to read. Actually, I don´t read a single word. I just don´t dare look up again. I just stare at the letters that make no sense and wait to turn the page. A chapter later, I haven´t read a single word. I put the book down and get up.

I need air. My eyes are burning. *For whatever reason.* My throat is crushed by a hand. *Why didn´t I just shut up? Why does he get pissed every time we come close?*

He says something honest, only to undo it in the next. Today was nice until he snapped. Until there was that kill switch again. Until he hated me again. *I feel like an idiot.* The satisfaction he must feel because I left. *I hate it.*

"I paid let´s go." He says from behind. I don´t answer, trying not to burst into tears. I walk along next to him. *Why do I have to cry when I´m angry?*

Fortunately, he doesn´t talk. Neither on the way to the car nor on the way home. Even when I get out, I´m close to tears. But only in my bathroom I allow myself to let them out. Hot tears run down my cheeks. *Why am I reacting so emotionally?*

Cause you want him to like you. Because you like him. But he doesn´t like you. He messes with you.

I´m so confused. I don´t know where I stand with him.

He is definitely someone you fall hard for. But I don´t wanna fall at all. *Not anymore.* But I don´t know if I´m not already slipping.

I wipe away my tears and take a deep breath. *I put me first,* I remind myself.

I chose me. No feelings. No falling. No losing yourself anymore. No more.

I am in control.

35

I haven´t seen Kai in a few days. *We haven´t texted.* And I dodged the invites of the others. But today I decided to come.

Behind the garage is a basket where the boys practice. Finn and Leon play in the team of the city. They have two games a week and lots of training. But they exercise a lot. All the boys practice with them.

I hear the ball hitting the concrete before I put a foot on the property. As I round the corner, I see it´s just Kai alone. For a moment I watch him. *I like those moments.*

When he´s unaware.

He´s in his black shorts and a gray shirt.

"Life is pain."

Colson Herzog

I guess it is.

He´s sweaty but in a hot way. He wears tennis socks. His hair is damp. He´s all handsome. And he lands *every* cast. *Why is he good at everything?*

He makes tricks, some speed and coordination exercises. While doing that, he catches me standing in the corner of his eye and stops midway. My heart jumps. *Shit.*

He looks like I scared or woke him from a dream. He was in the flow and didn´t expect anyone to be there. "I didn´t.." I begin but have no idea what I wanted to say. His hand claws the ball. His chest heaves. He´s just staring at me, breathing hard. I stare back, unable to move. He blinks at me. "You wanna.. throw some?" He asks, his voice pressed from the breathing. "Nah." I decline. "I suck." I add. He stiffs a laugh. "Come on. Try some." He demands tilting his head. I hesitate for a moment but walk towards him. He hands me the ball. "From where?" I ask. He points to a faded dot on the ground. I position myself. Haven´t done *that* in a while. He stands close to the basket, watching me. *No pressure at all.*

I dribble and jump. *I hit the wall.* He catches it with one motion and passes it back to me. I pitch and hit the net. *He hurls it back.* I fling and throw past it. He darts out, catching it with ease. I get annoyed with every time I don´t score. *And I don´t cast at all.* Even after I stepped closer, I keep failing.

He chuckles, watching me with the slightest smile I´ve seen on him. "Come here." He hushes. "Take it." He hands me the ball. Then he steps behind me with his hands at my waist. He lifts me up and his fingers touch my skin. I squeal and reach for the basket to put the ball into the net. He lowers me, still holding me. *Under the shirt.* We breathe in sync. I almost feel his body against mine. *If he just steps closer.*

"Can I sit on the cage?" I ask, wanting him to lift me again. He chuckles and lifts me, sending my body on an emotional rollercoaster. I grab the rim and hurl myself up with his hands pushing my ass and thighs. I adjust myself to not fall over the edge. And when I feel safe, *I look up.*

The sky all reddish mixed with yellow and orange. This is how a summer night should feel like. *It feels not at all like pain.*

He´s watching me closely. Ready to grab me any second. "I´m never coming down." I say with a big smile and eyes on the horizon. "Know that feeling." He says from down. I close my eyes and feel the wind on my arms, giving me chills. He always grounds me. Drags me back to the now. And he doesn´t even try. He just lifts me to watch the sunset. I hope I can bring him the now sometime too.

When I open my eyes, I cling to the basket suddenly afraid to fall. It´s high and woozy. "How should I come down?" I ask panicked. My hands immediately sweat.

"Jump, I´ll catch you." He says, stretching his arms out. I look down on him, shaking my head. My stomach sinks with fear. "I can´t." I laugh. "You can. And I´ll get you. Just let go." He assures me. "I´ve got you." He adds, reaching for me. "Trust me." He goes on. "What if you´ll drop me?" I ask. He looks at me a bit hurt. "Do I look like I´d drop you?" He asks. "No, you don´t." I say. "So, then what?" he presses. "You won´t fall when I´m here to hold you." He argues. "I don´t know how to jump." I stammer. "Like hands first? Or ass first?" I ponder. He chuckles. "Just do it fast, don´t think." His voice calm and sure. The way he said it made me trust him on a deeper level I wasn´t even aware of then.

"What if I´ll knock you over?" I consider. He smiles. "You already have." He says but goes on. "Now jump, Scar, or I´ll drag you down." He jokes. *You already have.*

I let go and jump. *But with my heart first.* And eyes wide open.

He grabs hold on me. Wrapping my arms around his neck, I land on his upper waist. He lowers me to get on eye level. My heart races. I hold his head. Gripping his hair gentle. He searches my eyes, his breath hitting my face. His chest heaves. We´re nose to nose. He leans in until our foreheads touch. He´s warm and a bit sweaty, but I like how he feels. *This isn´t how just being friends should feel like.*

Or how I don´t like you should feel.

We breathe into each other´s faces. His hands tighten around my thighs. My hand holds his neck. He holds me like it´s all he ever wanted. For me to jump and land in his arms. For him to catch me. *Hold me. Have me.*

And I hold onto him, cause deep down I wanted the same.

[NOTEBOOK ENTRIES]

I got used to her being around. ~~At the pool~~ ~~I could think of nothing else but her in my bed.~~ It was a good excuse to get close to her. ~~I almost got rock hard having her under me.~~ I was too close. So, I jumped with her in the pool. The water brought me down. I grabbed her by the throat. I didn´t think straight. My cock twitched, and I had to get her off me. ~~Even if that wasn´t at all what I wanted.~~ I took a sip of her bottle. ~~I liked the thought of her lips on that.~~ ~~Or on my dick.~~ I need to get my head straight. And my dick.

~~She smiled at me. But that´s when I realized how lonely she really is. She didn´t smile a lot. But I made her smile.~~

We took her to our race. She was with me. ~~I liked having her.~~ I just happened to sit next to her at the bar. ~~I didn´t wait for the others to sit, so I could sit next to her.~~ I thought she has anxiety but I wasn´t sure. But today I saw it up close. She started to look around. Touched her jewelry and neck. She spun her ring. But stopped when I caught her. She wobbled with her leg and fiddled with the paper of my beer. She wasn't thinking of it. It was mine. She didn't consider it could piss me off. She didn't do it to mess with me. She did it automatic. Out of unease. I put my hand on her knee. I don't know why I did it. Maybe, because I know anxiety. Know that feeling. ~~Maybe because of something else.~~ She stopped. ~~I kept my hand there, trying to ground her.~~ She wasn't present, but when I touched her, she was. She felt me. And fuck, I felt it too. ~~I felt her. And I wanted to feel more.~~ No one could see. Like it didn't happen. And I pretended it didn't.

Now I can't unsee it. She does particular things to calm her. Like finger counting. I don't do those things. I've got anxiety all my life. Always been there. Like Pans shadow. I do stuff to calm me too but.. other things. Like body scan. Counting to twenty-two or breathwork. I try to come up with as many quotes and lyrics I can. I sing a particular song in my head till the end. But there are other things. Worse things. Bloody things. But sometimes pain is the only thing greater than anxiety. But those are things hidden on the inside. So, no one sees that the anxiety is eating me alive. ~~But she's different.~~ She's confident in doing those things on the outside. Maybe she doesn't think about it. But people who know, know. And she doesn't care. ~~But I do. Too much.~~ It took me a lot of therapy sessions to understand I have anxiety. I always thought I'm angry or self-destructive. But anger covers anxiety. I hid my anxiety. Anger was my blanket to hide. But she doesn't hide. She's better than I am. I'm just covering scars with other scars. Diagnosis with diagnosis. Drugs with drugs. Pain over pain.

~~I was drunk last night.~~ And stoned. And in my intoxication, I touched her ankle. I don't know what got into me. It's a weird thing to do. But it came over me. ~~The urge to touch her. I catch myself wanting to be close to her.~~ I never wanted this. I want to get away from her, ~~but on the other hand as close as I can~~. I'm losing it. ~~She makes me lose it.~~ She didn't kick my hand away or said anything. She let me do it. I shouldn't have. The whole thing is getting out of hand. It has to stop.

She put her leg over mine. I put my hand on her thigh. That threw her off that she switched between apps, and I had to fight a laugh. ~~I need to fucking tangle my hands to not touch her anymore. But even then, I'd fucking crawl to her. When the hell did I stop not liking her? Do I like her?~~ No, I don't.

I had to escort her home from a party. When Leon said she was on the phone, I called her right back. He hung up on her that jackass. I wondered anyway why she wasn't with us. Even Luca was with us. Somehow, she has become part of it too. Even though I never wanted her to be. Or that ash blonde girl. That was never the plan. ~~So many~~

~~things were not planned.~~ She was wasted and tried to mess with me. She found herself very funny. But I was pissed. ~~Like why the hell was she alone?~~ And instead of half an hour, it took us a hole fucking hour because of her strolling ass. What did she do there? Why didn´t she ask anyone to come? And in her condition who knows what would have happen. The thought made me sick. ~~Why didn´t she call me?~~ And if I wouldn´t have been near Leon, would she have walked all by herself? Typical to her that even drunk she´s the responsible one. It´s just too funny. Does she even know Neverland is all about breaking rules? That it´s about everything she´s afraid of? ~~But I enjoyed walking with her~~. I took her with me because I had never been to hers before. ~~And I didn´t want to say goodbye.~~ She held onto my upper arm. ~~That felt nice. I wanted to take her to my bed~~, but I didn´t want to wake her. ~~So, I stayed with her and watched her sleep. I had to make myself stare at her. Because if I wouldn´t I would have touched her hair or face. Or worse lay beside her. I didn´t want any of that. So, I just looked at her.~~ Because I couldn´t sleep. I stayed up until I had to head to the game. But she was there watching. I thought it would distract me, ~~but it pushed me. My mind was off because I had to think of her. But as I saw her, I could focus again. I wanted to impress her.~~ Who is she to make me feel all those things?

~~She gets under my skin~~. ~~She turns me on.~~ ~~I almost kissed her.~~ But I could stop myself. I knew better not to cross that line. I backed off. She got drunk. Did she drink cause of me? Cause I rejected her? Does she like me? Fuck I hope not. This is going in a wrong direction. I don´t date. And I won´t start for anyone. ~~We´re friends.~~ At least I think we are. Nothing more.

I helped her get high. ~~Being close to her lips threw me off.~~ So~~mewhere between the drags and her green eyes I lost track.~~ I gave her headshots. ~~Just to be near her again.~~ It was fucking tempting. Addicting. ~~She was.~~ And I lost control. ~~I crushed my lips on hers.~~ But I pulled away. That was a mistake. ~~But I wanted it. I craved her. Still fucking do.~~ And I hate it. I don´t want all of this. ~~That feeling.~~ I´m disgusted. ~~My chest hurts.~~ It´s creeping inside me like a parasite. Like a virus. ~~It spreads.~~ I can feel it. I want to hurt her. I´ve never felt anything more than lust when it came to women. ~~She made me feel something else. Something different.~~ And I hated it. ~~Hated me for longing her. For kissing her. For wanting to do it again.~~ Fuck I hate her so much. ~~I don´t.~~

I stopped texting her. I need her off my system. I dodged her a whole week. ~~I didn´t want to see the kiss on her. I didn´t want to see it did happen. It would make it real.~~ I rejected her. And I reject me for ~~wanting her~~.

I couldn´t sleep. ~~I was thinking of her. Of our kiss~~. I went to hers. ~~I had to see her.~~ She wore that hoodie ~~I wished was mine.~~ She asked me to come up. ~~I wanted to~~ but I couldn´t. ~~I knew I would have tried to kiss her.~~

It started to storm. I knew she was there by bike. I said I had been drinking. I don´t know if she bought it, but ~~I wanted her to stay~~. ~~I want her around all the time~~. She said she´s lonely. That´s how I feel too. ~~I don´t feel like that with her.~~ She wanted me to read to her. I´ve never did. ~~I liked that she wanted that.~~ She fell asleep with her head on my arm. I didn´t want to wake her, so I stayed. At least some part of my body could sleep. I couldn´t feel it, but I didn´t move. ~~It was worth it.~~ It was a good pain. ~~I watched her. She looked like Sleeping Beauty. Clothed in oversized shirts. In mine.~~ There was never beauty in sleep. ~~But when I looked at her, I saw.~~ I read the fairy tale with my mom all the time. But as I grew older, I realized it isn´t at all a tale. But I fell asleep fast. ~~Haven´t in a long time.~~ She woke from the thunder. I tried to calm her. ~~But it was more her calming me.~~ My insomnia was blown away. Usually, I pull a joint or meditate. Or don´t sleep at all. ~~But with her, I could.~~ ~~I smelled her all night.~~ She stared at my dick. I almost lost it. ~~I would have loved to take her to bed.~~ ~~I could think of nothing but her lips on my cock.~~ ~~Of her hands scratching my back. Of me inside of her. I had to pull everything together not to.~~ I couldn´t lose control. But what I did was even worse. ~~I called her Sleeping Beauty~~. I needed her to go. ~~I jerked off thinking of her.~~ But that made it worse. ~~My bed smelled like her. I smelled like her.~~ ~~My room smelled like her.~~ ~~She was everywhere~~. I showered, but I still smelled her. Even after I aired. Even after I put on new bedding. ~~As if she was still there.~~ ~~And in ways she was.~~ I found her hairband in the sheets. ~~I kept it on me.~~ But I took it off when I knew she´d be there. ~~I fucking hid it.~~ I don´t know what I´m doing anymore.

There was this video of dancing people. But also, just for a few seconds, ~~her, and me~~. She sat next to me. I looked at a friend, ~~and she looked at me~~. ~~That.. fucking look threw me off. It made me feel.. something. I kept replaying the part. I made a screen-shot. And printed it. Kept it in my phone case.~~ I felt stupid. I deleted the video ~~but kept the picture~~. ~~Just in case.~~ I haven´t looked at it since. If I don´t look it´s not real.

~~I asked her out.~~ It wasn´t a real date. But the first time the two of us did something together. ~~I catch myself wanting to spend time with her.~~ ~~There was that butterfly I used as an excuse to take a picture of her. She was more beautiful than that little thing. I catch myself staring at it. I printed that too, but I packed it away. She straddled me. She was so close to my face. Close to my lips. Close to my dick. Close to me.~~ ~~She made me nervous.~~ ~~I couldn´t concentrate.~~ I was an ass again. But I couldn´t handle any of this. ~~I lose control with her, and I never do.~~

I was training, trying to quiet my mind. I was so lost in it, I didn´t notice her watching. She just stood there. ~~That made me proud somehow.~~ It´s dumb. ~~It pleased me.~~ I didn´t know how to act. I helped her score. ~~I couldn´t stop touching her.~~ She asked me to lift her. ~~And fuck that´s all I wanted. To let her see the sunset. Grab the fucking stars. See Neverland. Make her fly.~~ She looked so happy. ~~I was afraid she might fall, but I would catch her. That´s when I knew I would always come to save her from falling.~~ Wendy´s are afraid to jump. Only lost girls want to fall. She fell into my arms. ~~Her body felt like it belonged. I wanted to kiss her. But instead, I leaned against her forehead. Hearts racing. Breathing into each other´s face. Holding onto each other. She didn´t just fall into my arms. She knocked me over. And I realized I liked it. I craved even.~~

36

"Come with me," Kai says to me. "Where to?" I ask. "Just come" he urges and goes inside, dragging me with him. I read his hoodie.

"Lost Boy."

Lost boy. Isn´t there that saying that *nothing is ever really lost?*

We go upstairs to his room. He leads me on his balcony.

"You have a telescope" I gush. Instead of answering, he climbs over the concrete wall onto the roof of the terrace. While the others continue partying downstairs, we lie under the stars waiting for the star shower I read about. *Is that why he brought me up here? Did he know about that?* I wanted to watch it later myself. I often lie on the street gazing at the stars after a night out. *It´s the best feeling.*

"I could lie here for hours." I say. "Same." He says. I hum in agreement.

"There´s the little bear" I say, pointing. "The brightest star of it is the celestial North Pole the pole star." He explains and shows me the bright one. I face him. "The entire starry sky revolves around Polaris. And it *always* stays in the same place." He states. *He knows about stars and constellations?* Another thing I didn´t expect. "The Big Dipper." I point briefly. "From Greek mythology, *actually*, the big bear." He corrects me. I look at him astonished. "You sure know your stuff" I say smiling. "My dad used to come up here with me." I remain silent. *His Dad.* I´m glad to have learned something, even if it´s just a small detail.

"The one that looks like a roof is Cepheus and the *W* there is Cassiopeia. Both are in the Milky Way." The fact that he knows about all that is so attractive.

“That´s the giraffe.” He points somewhere. “Where?” I ask. He leans closer and takes my hand. With mine and his outstretched, he points in the direction. For a moment, I just stare at his hand clasping mine and his finger pointing into the night.

“Giraffe?” I laugh, confused. “A *very* simplified giraffe.” I state. “It´s constellations, what do you expect?” He mocks. “You´re the creative mind studying arts.” He adds. “Aren´t *you*?” I tease, knowing he really is too.

He drops our hands but stays close to me. My ears grow hot. “The bright star in the swan is Deneb. More than three thousand light years away, yet it´s one of the brightest stars in the sky.” He says, and I listen.

“Isn´t it insane that stars are already dead but still shine?” I wonder. “Scars also never fade.” He says, and I don´t know where *that* came from.

Then we fall silent. As we so often do. His hand next to mine radiates a heat. The back of his hand touches mine. *Then one finger. Then two.* It wasn´t by accident. I can´t stop my fingers from groping for his either. He *wants* to touch me. *And I burn myself.*

His fingers stroke the back of my hand. I get goose bumps.

Sometimes it feels like I´ve known him all my life. And at other times, he feels so foreign. Now he feels familiar. *Close enough to get lost in.*

“I think I´ll die young.” I say. He looks at me as I look into the sky. He frowns, I´m sure. “It was just a feeling I´ve always had.” I say into the void. He still takes me in. “Or maybe I don´t want to get old.” I say. “Why´s that?” he asks. “Tell *me*, lost boy.” I smile. “I asked first.” He states. I sigh and shrug. “Cause I´m afraid of living *that* long.” I try to answer, but it´s impossible to name the real issue.

“That´s the problem with people with anxiety.” He says, and I look at him at the mention of my anxiety. I´ve never told him, and he just knows.

“They are too afraid to live.” He says. “Kind of.” I agree. “Who lives with anxiety isn´t living, rather dead.” He points out. “But I rather live fast and die young than waiting for pension.” I say. “Know that feeling.” He agrees. I look at him.

He gets me. And in ways, I get him.

“I´m not scared of death.” He says. “*Everyone* is scared of death.” I state. “It´s the source of every fear.” I add. “I´m not scared of what´s after that. If there´s nothingness I don´t care. I´m scared of the death itself.” He says. “I don´t understand.” I frown. “I´m scared of the way death comes. The *exact* moment. What you´ll feel. Think. See. I don´t care what comes after that, but I care about the way we go.” He explains.

“So, basically, you *are* scared of death.” I say. “No, you don´t get it.” He says, shaking his head once. “Then tell me.” I demand. “Energy never dies, Lia. I don´t worry about the afterlife or hell. Everything is connected. But you still have to *feel* death.” He says. “I mean, we´re not sure about that are we?” I ask with a smile. “It could be numb. Maybe the moment we die or the moment before, we detach form our physical body. Maybe, we just watch. Maybe, we´re out of body before we die.” I ponder. “But *maybe* we *do* feel it.” He insists. “Don´t be so cynic.” I say annoyed. “I´m realistic.” He corrects me.

“Life is the promise of death.” He shrugs. “And a poet.” I add with a snort.

“Do you think we relive our life´s the moment we die?” I ask him. “We already lived.” He says.

“You think we can watch?” I ask. “Like your relatives?” He asks and I nod. “Energy is everywhere. I think. you just become part of the great conscious. So, somehow, I think we can.” He responds.

“And what about spirits?” I want to know. “Spirits are people who couldn´t make peace with death. Unconscious people who can´t let go.” He says. “Would make sense.” I retort. “I mean, we are literally made of stardust. We carry the universe within us.” He shrugs. “So, we all are part of the great consciousness. We´re all one. We´re all awareness. *All conscious.* There´s no such thing as an end. *Death is just a beginning.* It´s the swell to another form of consciousness. It´s all in us.” He says, and I listen.

“To die will be an awfully big adventure.” I quote *Peter Pan*. “I think it should go *to live*.” He says. “I think both, is true.” I say, and we fall silent after that.

- 27 -

I say goodbye to the others and stand up. I hug Luca, who stays longer. I´m sure the reason is named Finn, who still has no idea that she´s into him. He seems to be so focused on his work that he doesn´t notice *anything* besides that and basketball. Or he has just no head for women. Maybe he´s not that much different than his brother.

As we break away, my gaze meets Kai´s and something tells me he doesn´t want me to leave. Often, it´s just the two of us alone talking. Sometimes in silence. And sometimes we philosophize about life and talk shit.

We really have fun together. *When he´s not being a dick.*

But not today, so I walk towards the gate. At the same moment, my phone vibrates. *“Front door.”* He texts. My heart skips a beat.

The door opens and Kai steps out. Without talking, we both know what we want. He eyes me. I dart past him, brushing against him as he leaves no room. *On purpose*. We stand in front of each other. He nods his chin at me. “Go upstairs. I´ll be there in a sec.” He says in a raspy voice. For a moment we look at each other until he walks away. As he does, he casts a glance over his shoulder.

I go to the bathroom, put on one of his hoodies and lie down in his bed.

- 27 -

The yielding mattress and an arm wrapped around me wakes me. He pulls me to him and lays his head against mine. His hair is damp. He smells so good. Fresh, like wet asphalt or the forest after a shower. *Now I know what he smells like.* He smells like rain. Like summer rainy days. Rain, weed, and sunscreen. I like the fact that he seems to be wearing sunscreen.

"You´re wet." I mumble sleepily. "It was raining." He opines. "Why didn´t you wake me?" I ask. "Because you were asleep." He whispers into my hair. That´s when I notice he´s hard. *Rock hard.* He presses against my ass.

"I want you to be here all the time. In my bed. With me." At his words, I wonder if I´m still asleep. *He must be stoned. Or drunk.*

"Hmm," I hum, and in the next moment I drift away.

- 27 -

The next few times, our evenings always end at his front door and in his bed. Nothing more than cuddling and erections happen. We are simply together.

Sleeping. Sometimes talking.

And at some point, I already have a beauty bag in his room. But no clothes, because when I brought my own, he insisted I put on *his* shirt. Anyway, that seems to be our thing, along with rain. Whether we´re at a party, at a friend´s house, or just chilling. When it rains, we both always find ourselves outside. At first, it was coincidences that we ran into each other, but by now, it has become a habit. A routine. *Our thing.*

And he really does smell like rain. Not just because he was drained by it that day. He smells like it. *All days.*

Or maybe I imagine him to. But either way. He smells like rain. And I like rain.

A lot.

37

"*You up?*" I texted. *"Always"* he responded. It´s three in the morning.

"What´s up?" He wanted to know. *"Can you get me?"* I asked. *"Sure."* It came back.

"I'll be there in five."

Five minutes later, I get in his car, and we drive off into the night.

“So, what are you escaping from?” He asks, looking over. “What do you mean?” I ask frowning. He shrugs, looking ahead. “Isn´t there something you want to escape when you call a lost boy for your rescue?” He smirks. “*Rescue*?” I laugh, raising my eyebrows. “You *know* what I mean.” He says. *Yes, I do.*

“So, why should I get you?” He asks, tilting his head. “To escape life, I guess.” I tell him. “Alright then.” He grins. “I know *how*.” He tells me. “But first *music*.” He says. “What´s your tunnel song?” He looks at me briefly. “Tunnel song? Like in *The Perks of Being a Wallflower*?” I ask. He shrugs. “Just a song you would like to hear when you *escape* life.” He clarifies. “When you speed off.” He adds. “I think about it.” I say.

“We´re *really* driving to a tunnel?” I ask. “The next is probably an hour away, isn´t it?” I consider. “Plenty of time for you to think of one.” He says with a grin. I smile, shaking my head. “You´re..” I say, but he cuts in. “What?” he asks. “I don´t know.” I say, because he looks at me in a way that throws me off. “Then start thinking.” He retorts. I sigh and pick up my phone to go through my playlists. *Which song should I choose?*

“What´s yours?” I ask, looking at him. He stares ahead as he speaks. “You´ll see.” He teases. I bite the inside of my lip. “So, just one Song?” I want to know. He nods. “We´ll speed off the first time with yours and then back with mine.” He explains. “Two songs. Yours and mine. Six minutes of escaping life.” He says. “With a lost boy. Isn´t that the dream of every lost one?” He smirks. I shake my head. “Would you shut up about that Neverland thing?” I laugh. “I will if you start to think.” He chuckles. “Alright.” I groan. “But a lot of pressure.” I point out.

“Six minutes aren´t *that* long.” I joke. He looks at me. “They can be.” He smiles. “*With a lost boy.* Let me guess.” I say. He licks his lips. “Don´t you forget that I´m Pan.” He says. I inhale. “Which is the origin of a lost boy.” I point out, raising a brow. “I don´t think he´s lost at all.” He says. *Sometimes I don´t get him.*

“You got yours?” I ask. He nods once.

“You do that often?” I ask. Again, he nods.

“Always the same song?” I ask curiously. “Always the same.” He says, giving me a solid nod. “Now think.” He demands. I laugh.

“Maybe I should clarify. You should think of *your* song. *One* song.” He tells me. “Not thinking about everything else.” He snorts. “Fine.” I say with a laugh-groan. He shakes his head. “What?” I ask irritated. He grins, tilting his head back. “Nothing.” He brushes me off. “Focus.” He insists pointing at my phone. “No tell me. I can´t focus while you´re laughing at me." I wine trying to mess with him. He stiffs a laugh, trying to fight his shit eating grin.

Fuck, I love this. That lost boy.

He clears his throat. "It´s just sometimes. You won´t shut up. Despite your shyness." He says. I look at him, strained. He glances at me. "No, it´s.. *cute.* I like it. It means you´re comfortable around me. With me." He says with a shrug. I bite my lip to suppress my smile.

He said I´m cute. Who would have thought.

I tried to shut up for but the questions wouldn´t stop nagging me. So, I asked questions he wouldn´t answer.

After a while I´ve got one song, and we just drove along in silence.

Before we reach the tunnel, I get the Bluetooth and start *Fearless by Lost Sky*. The streets are clear due to the time. He lets down the windows. I put my hair in a bun. He turns up the volume. I fear the paneling might fall cause of the bass. The car vibrates like I´m inside a subwoofer. The exit lights shine neon green. He accelerates to a hundred and more and the only thing that lights up the car is the ambient light. The yellow lights on the ceiling rush past us as we speed off. There are blue lights on the walls. The engine roars. It feels like a dream. It smells like leather and concrete. *And him.*

He´s concentrated more than I´ve ever seen him. As the bead drops, he pushes the pedal all the way down twice to get a boost, and we shoot through the tunnel. *It´s surreal.*

I have goose bumps. The wind sweeps through the car and sends us flying. The exhaust bangs and the engine howls. I claw my fingers into my thighs. My mid throbs with excitement. I smile and laugh. Adrenaline shoots through me and penetrates my bones. My heart presses in the seat and my life falls over in the back.

The lights flicker, making me high. I close my eyes to take it in just to tear them open in the next, so I won´t miss a second. But before I can process what´s happening there´s the end of the tunnel. We slow down and breathe hard. I can´t keep my smile off.

We don´t talk. Just live. Escape.

My body tingles impatiently as we drive along until we can make a turn to go back. My intuition tells me he´ll speed off faster. And my gut fills with butterflies. His song is *Sparklers by Gemini Club*. I know that song from *Need for speed.*

I smile. He touches my thigh before he speeds up, sending explosions through my system. The number on the speedometer shoots up and doesn´t stop. When the car shifts gears, the exhaust pops. The sound of the engine intoxicates me.

We pass some cars, but it´s three-lanes, so we can race past them.

One split second away from dying is the only moment you feel insanely alive.

I trust him with my heart and soul. *Just as Wendy trusted Pan. He sends me flying. And I never want to land.*

I hold my breath to fill my lungs in the next. I could do this all night.

His hands grip the wheel. His veins bulge. His broken Rolex shines in the lights. Fear and happiness mix. My mind flies and expands. *It´s addictive.*

My brain shuts up, and I just see and feel and sense and hear and breathe.

And despite what he said, we do it again. *Twice.*

The same songs. The same two songs. *Just us.*

Escaping life. For more than just six minutes. *For life.*

38

***"C**ome on down."* He texts.

I look out my window and see Kai standing in the pouring rain.

It´s half past midnight.

My window is open, so I yell-whisper. "What are you doing?" He lifts his arms. "Standing in the rain." I roll my eyes. "Come on." He urges.

I get down and run to him. My hair already sticks to my face. He´s so tall I must look up at him. And somehow, it´s only now that I notice our height difference. Because that´s all I can focus on. How small he makes me feel but in all the good ways. His hair hangs on his forehead. Rain beads off his nose. His white T-shirt sticks to his body like a second skin.

"I like your outfit." He says with a grin. I press my lips together. I´m wearing a gray oversized T-shirt dress with Crocs. "Crocs are the best." I smile. He nods grinning. "So, what are we doing?" I ask excitedly. To which he puts one arm behind his back and holds out his other to me. *Like all handsome.*

"Dancing." He says. "You don´t dance." I state. "You never asked." He shrugs and takes my hand. "Neither did you." I reply, thinking back to all those times I danced with Aidan. Especially those times I caught him watching us.

He turns me spinning, and my shoes squeak. *I almost fall.* But he holds me. And I wouldn´t fear falling with him anyway. Mid-dancing, I slip them off and continue barefoot. Dancing with him is.. *different*. It´s not perfect, like with Aidan. It´s more improvised, loose, and easy. *It´s fun.* We laugh a lot. Slip a lot. Smile a lot. I have no idea *what* we are doing *but isn´t that the point?*

At every moment of our life´s, our playlist should be playing with our favorite songs. Simply because everything is better with music. But this moment doesn´t need music, it´s perfect the way it is. But if I had to pick one, I´d choose *Evergreen by Richy Mitch and The Coal Miners*.

From what I´ve learned about him so far is that he´s like a grab bag, you never know what you're going to get. *Grumpy, funny, stubborn, cute, silent, or angry.* It´s everything but boring. He makes me feel. He makes me live. Because every time I do something with him, I get to know him anew. And with each I fall more him.

Right now, it´s more fooling and playing around instead of real dancing. He gets into position and holds his arms in my direction. "Come." he invites me. "What?" I ask. "Run and jump." He says. "No." I laugh. "I´ll catch you." he assures. "I know." I say. "But.." I start, and he cuts me off. "You know, the whole *Dirty Dancing* thing. Let´s try it." he says, still with his arms in the air. I smile. *He didn´t just offer to do that, did he?*

We *almost* managed the figure. But I didn´t dare to jump. We tried about ten times, and each time I stopped short. And every time he just laughed harder. Which only made me angrier. I had to laugh with him, though, which is why I had no power to jump. And even though he assured me he´d catch me and I should trust him. *I just couldn´t.*

But there´s always that one percent chance I´ll knock my teeth or he cracks his head. And somehow, I loved seeing him laugh. At some point he was just lying on the floor laughing. He loves to make fun of me. *I hoped his belly hurt properly.* He seemed to enjoy himself a lot. And I liked to see him so happy. *Because of me.* And that´s when I realized I made him laugh.

If any of my neighbors were awake, they would have wondered what we were doing. But with him, I just forgot everything around me. And the rain was probably louder than our voices anyway.

In the end, we just laid on the warm asphalt. You often think how nice it would be to lie in the rain. But to really do it is unimaginable. I have never been so happy. And with Kai, you do the things you always dream to do. He makes dreams come true, or rather drag you to act instead of just thinking of how great it would be. With him it is. With him, you just do it. With him, there´s no time. *No sleep. No anxiety.*

After what felt like an eternity, we go inside, even though it hasn´t stopped raining. I feel like fifteen again, sneaking my crush upstairs. Arrived in my room, he stands awkwardly in the middle. Like he´s nervous or something. *Which is funny cause he´s never.* It´s the first time he´s in my rooms, so maybe he is.

"You can put your clothes on the heater and feel free to use the towels." I say and walk towards the hallway. "I´ll put on another shirt quick." I say and leave him in the bathroom. As I change, I realize I wasn´t even wearing a bra. I squeeze my eyes shut. *Shit.* Even though I don´t have a large bust, and you wouldn´t have noticed if I did wear one or not. But I still hope the fabric was thick enough and he didn´t see my hard nipples. *Because they were.* But it´s stupid to think because I slept in his bed without a bra before. We even cuddled a few times. So, he´ll know my breasts by now, at which thought I cringe. I like my small boobs, but I want him to like them.

I go back to the bathroom and Kai stands in front of me in boxers. "Do you need a shirt?" I ask, trying not to stare at his bare body. He shakes his head. His awkwardness from the beginning is clearly gone as he walks past me and looks around. "Are these all your rooms?" he asks as he stands in front of more doors. "I live upstairs from my grandparents." I explain. Without asking, he walks into one of the doors. "My office slash dressing room slash art studio." I comment. He looks at my artwork on the wall. Then he looks at my gamer setup. He nods here and there as if to learn more about me. Unlike expected, he goes back to the bathroom instead of my bedroom. He puts on the hair dryer and blow dry´s his boxers, and I stand there watching him. I take a towel and pat my hair.

When he´s finished, he sits down on my sofa. "So, this is the famous porn collection." He says dryly, whereupon I burst out laughing. "Not *just* porn." I insist. "The top tier is nonfiction, psychology, spiritual. And there are poetry and fantasy books too." I say. "Are only five more rows of porn." He states. "Maybe two rows." I correct him. "Ah sure." he says not at all buying it.

"Your books look awful." He points out, frowning at the shelf. I cross my arms. "I like to see I´ve read them. Give them life. Use them. Make them part of me and not the shelf." I defend. "I think the people who do not dare to touch their books are the real psychos." I add, and he grins as he nods. He pulls out one and the other and examines it, as if he never had a book in his hand before and didn´t have three shelves himself.

"So, we have a lot of romance. It´s the *smudge* for me." He pronounces it wrong on purpose. "Also, some fantasy. Idk, but those are just *huge*." He explains like he has a blog. "Classics, we love." He gushes. "That series was *so good*." He touches some. "But those were *way* too long, so I stopped reading them." He says because I just read the first two. "Thrillers. *Do I have to say more?*" He asks me. "Sci-fi. Not read yet but want to." He goes on and on. "Those were *banger*. I cried on that one." He moves over my shelf like he has a clue what he´s talking about. I can´t help but grin as he makes a tour for me. He´s so childish sometimes. At those moments, I forget what a pain in the ass he can be. Or used to be.

When did he stop, anyway? I mean, he did stop, did he?

“So, what are your favs?” he asks. I list him some, but he cuts me off. “So, pretty much *every* book.” He snorts. “No *not* everyone. But they´re all different and each good.” I say. “Well, then make me a list.” He says. “Of what?” I ask. “From the books I´m supposed to read.” He says as if it were the most natural thing for him to say. I must grin.

He wants to read my books?

“You want to read them?” I ask. “Said so.” He shrugs. “I´m sure it´ll be close to 30.” I warn him. “I´m a fast reader.” He says with a grin. “Okay.” I say.

“Your tbr list is quite long.” He states. “How do you know?” I ask. “Because you can tell. Just by the way *they* look.” He says with a bit judgement in his tone. “Yeah, I know. The spines look bad.” I say. “But that´s how I love reading. I like it *used.* And messy. And *you* don´t say *anything*. Because your shelf looks the same. Maybe even *worse* than mine.” I point out. He grins, not arguing.

We look at each other for a moment. And I think we both realize how different our relationship has become. I mean to read fear on his face. As if he considered the consequences. That I had come into his life and into his space. *Maybe even further.*

He swallows and his jaw tightens. I have a feeling he´ll switch at me any moment. And he´ll be the same rude ass as he was before. But he remains silent. He just keeps looking at me. Now I´m the one standing awkwardly in the room.

Why doesn´t he say anything?

He just looks at me. *Takes me in.* Still a bit shaken, but no talking. I like quiet. But *please* say something.

Yell at me, insult me, make fun of me, but stop staring at me like that.

His mouth opens and closes a few times. *Say it. Own it. Talk to me.*

“Which one should I read first?” He eventually asks. *I wasn´t expecting that.* Even though I don´t know what exactly I was expecting. “Um.” I mumble. “You choose.” I say. He looks at the shelf. His eyes fix on a book. And unlike before, I can finally decide which is my favorite. Not because he picked it. But because I already knew it. And he *reminded* me. *As if we are connected.*

He makes himself comfortable and puts a hand behind his head. “Will you stay there? Or..” he raises his eyebrow at me. “No.” I say and sit down next to him. I put a blanket over us and listen.

I´m glued to his words. *As always.*

I loved for him read to me *his* books. But I love even more him reading mine.

Briefly, I felt uncomfortable because he could see all the underlined parts. But I was lost in his words, so I stopped caring. I wish every book I'll read could be read by him. I know if I'll ask him to, he would. *And maybe I do.*

That was the first time he slept at hers. They slept better with the other around. And they stayed over more and more. They got used to each other. Maybe too quick to realize the impacts.

39

The sun is about to set. "Can you stay up with me?" He asks. "You don't sleep much, do you?" I laugh. "No." He retorts. I look at him. "So, you'll stay?" He urges, trying to sound casual. But there's no hiding the fact that he wants to spend time with me. "Sure." I say. He nods, pressing his lips together like he didn't care if I'd say no. *But he did.*

We went upstairs.

"Not antisocial. Just socially selective."

Says the quote on his hoodie. He selected *me* the past months.

"What do you want to do?" I ask. He looks around, finding something to do. *Cause he just wanted me to stay. He didn't think of anything further.* I fight a smile. "Sit on the roof." He says shrugging. I follow him on his balcony. He gives me his hoodie and we climb up the metal stairs. He sits on top and I on the last stair. It was scary at first. High and I felt woozy. *But then we looked ahead.*

The sun melts on the sky in red, pink, and orange. It's stunning. I feel like when he sat me on the basketball hoop.

We just sit there in silence. *It seems like the sunsets last longer in the summer.*

And somehow, I wasn't mad or upset that we didn't talk. Sometimes I liked it better this way. Maybe, because he couldn't hurt me that way. Maybe, because he said more when he said nothing. Maybe, his silence said it all. Maybe, we were okay in silence. Maybe, we were ourselves when we kept quiet. Maybe, the talking made us fail. Maybe, we didn't needed words to speak.

And sometimes when I look back to that moment, I wished we wouldn't have spoken anything after that. *The silence saved us. The talking broke us.* I broke us because all I wanted was talking when I was being silenced all my life. And all he wanted was to keep shut, since all his life he was forced to talk.

There were times when I loved listening to his silence. To mine and his. And to the dance they created. But there came days I couldn't listen. Where I searched answers in words he would never give. But I should have listened to what he didn't say. But somewhere on the line I forgot. To listen to the silence, I knew all too well. I forgot I loved this silence once. I forgot the thing that brought us together. *I forgot.*

And all I did was seeing what I couldn´t hear.

Silence.

40

"What are you drawing, *Scar*?" He asks, lifting his head to look at my sheet. He caught me off guard, which is why I didn´t react fast enough. "You drew me?" he asks. I put my arm over it. *Shit. He saw.* I can´t tell if he thinks it´s a good or bad thing. He frowns at me. But the frown isn´t always bad. *It´s just a thing he does.*

As I close my sketchbook, he snatches it and scrutinizes the drawing. "That´s strong." He says and keeps turning the pages to looks at the other sketches. I´ve drawn the others too. Portraits and them doing their passions. Aidan playing soccer. Finn playing basketball. Luca reading, and Nina doing yoga. *But Kai mostly.* I drew him *way* too much.

My eyes widen when realization hits. "Give it back." I try to take it out of his hand, but he holds it out of my reach. "Kai." My voice fails in a squeak.

He grins. *Fuck. I know why.*

I keep trying, but he fends off my attacks with one hand. I climb on top of him. He blocks any attempts and grabs my wrists with one hand and pulls my waist down.

Fuck.. the way he holds me down.

I capitulate as he holds me off in a lightness of touch. I sit back and watch him. And I know all too well *what* he is looking at. Kai reading, taking pictures, boxing, smoking weed, playing soccer and more. And if I didn´t know better, I´d think he was blushing.

Did I embarrass him?

He looks at me and grins knowingly. No *actually*, he like I´m a girl who´s into him. *Great.* Now he thinks I have a crush on him. *If he didn´t figure by now.*

Just keep feeding his ego, Lia.

"I must draw people. For college." I try to legitimize. *To no avail.*

"You don´t need to make excuses. I´m honored to be *your* muse." He says. And *how* I push his ego. "Would you like me to model?" He teases. "But no nude sketching." He adds, amused. "I don´t think we are there yet." He jokes.

I grab my sketchbook. "*Fuck you.*" I whine. He just laughs harder.

"You´re really talented." He says after a moment. And I know he means it. "Practice thing. Anyone can learn to draw." I justify with a shrug. "True." He nods. "But everyone has their own style." He points out. This time I nod. "And *yours* is pretty good." He says. "Thanks." I say.

We look at each other for a moment. *I hope he doesn´t see me any different now.* I don´t want this to be weird. Or him to interpret anything.

"Okay. Since you´ve been snooping through *my* stuff, you show me *something* private too." I demand with a grin. "Those were your drawings, not your diary." He replies snippily. "Right, but they´re personal too. Art is something private *and* intimate." I retort. "Is that so, or did you just not want me to see you were drawing me?" He asks challenging. "Maybe both." I admit. "But *still* now is your turn." I insist. He looks directly at me. I´d like to know what he´s thinking. He´s probably pondering about how to talk his way out of this situation.

"I´m writing." He says, but doesn´t look at me. "You write?" I ask, and he nods. "What do you write?" I ask. "Everything that comes to my mind." He shrugs. "I´d really like to read some of it." I say carefully and prepare myself for a rejection. "I don´t have that kind of order in my writing. I have to pick out one first." He says. "I can wait." I grin because I won´t let him off.

And to my surprise, he gets up and goes inside.

"Villain."

Maybe even Pan is aware of his place.

And as I go through my sketches, I see not at all a Villain, but a guy, I did fall for.

- 27 -

I finished my drawing. And as he comes back it starts to dawn. He wears his hood hiding his face. He sits down across me. He leans forward to rest on his knees. His hair hangs on his forehead. He´s holding *a book*. An *actual* book, not a notebook. I can tell he has written in it with a *black sharpie*. All book lovers would freak out now, but I would do the same. The book´s wavy pages indicate that most of the others are written on as well. What I would give to read them. I wonder if he´ll ever let me. *Probably not.*

I still can´t believe he´s doing it.

He clears his throat, licks, and bites his lower lip. He feels vulnerable. Even though he reads to me often, he´s *nervous*. But that´s different. *It´s intimate.* It´s his words.

No quotes. No song texts. No, movie lines.

Just his own thoughts and words. At least I hope I get to hear *his* words.

I remain silent.

After he stared at the page a bit longer, he begins to read aloud. His voice rough and gives me goose bumps.

*"**Rain or just Pain?***

Rain soaks me as I drown. Drown in you. Drown for you.

Rain feels like pain. You'll love the pain. You cause me pain. In the rain.

I fall. I fell. Fell hard. Fell. For you. Fell like the rain. Over and over.

Down. Down, for you.

A lover of rain. Or just pain. Or just you.

Like the clouds lose the rain. I lose you.

Till it starts again. Rain again. Pain again. Again, in the rain.

The smell of rain reminds me. Reminds me of you.

Are those raindrops, or just you?

Do I cry? Cry for you?

Or just die? Die for you?

Lie for you? Just to get high of you?

I break away. Rain could take away. What was locked away.

Blocked away. Knocked away.

Rain was home. Until I was wrong.

Wrong. Wrong about you.

Tron. Torn about you.

Pain. Or just rain? Or just you?

***You.**"*

"Will you read it again?" I whisper and he starts over.

Kai writes poetry. I mean that makes sense because he quotes and reads a lot but I didn´t expect that. And honestly, that´s the most attractive thing I´ve ever had with a guy.

I search for the right words. *But fail.*

"I picked this because you were my muse too." He says all vulnerable, his voice husky. *I´m his muse? Would a Villain write a poem about you?*

"I wrote this the night we were dancing in the rain." He explains. "Honestly it´s great, you should post that somewhere. On a blog or something." I say. "Art is *something intimate,* right?" he refers to my words. "Right." I say.

"Thanks for sharing." I tell him. "Ditto." He says. "It´s not like I had a choice." I protest. He laughs. "Right. But me neither." He points out.

We smile at each other.

"You´re really talented, Kai." I say. "Nah." he says, shaking his head. "Great Art doesn´t come from talent, it comes from hella pain." He explains, but it´s true. "Then you have great Pain." I say. "I do." He agrees. I blink at him.

And right now, I can see it. *The pain he wrote about.*

That pain I see when he looks at me. As if.. *as if I pained him.*

As if I was the pain. *You.*

That day he opened up in a way both of them never expected. *But he did.*

41

October

"You´re drunk." I say. "Am I?" he asks charming. I grin and shake my head. "Why are you here?" I ask as I close my door. "Because.." he slurs. "I´m way too drunk to talk to you. But I *want* to talk to you so." He shrugs. I smile cause, I realize, *he can't stay away.* We saw each other almost every day the past weeks. Either I was at his or he showed up at mine when I didn´t.

"Why?" I ask.. "I can say things I´ll regret saying and tomorrow pretend I didn´t." He tells me. I frown. *He´s honest. He must be plastered.* But he seems okay. Since he could walk here.

"Saying what?" I ask. He shrugs. "Things." He says and lets himself fall on my couch. "K." I grin.

"Why did you drink?" I ask. "Because.. I wanted to." He says. I sigh, annoyed by his answer. He inhales, sensing my anger. "Because my *parents* are home, and I can´t and won´t give me their bullshit any longer." He folds his hands behind his head. *His parents are home?*

"And maybe.. I needed distraction." He says, looking at me.

I hoped he´d say you. But that´s stupid.

"Is that a lost boy searching for an escape?" I grin. "Maybe." He says and I sit down next to him. He lays his head back facing me. I rest my elbow and support my head with my hand.

There is a silence between us.

"What?" He asks husky. "Your voice." I say. "What about it?" He asks, searching for the answer in my eyes. "Love your voice." I whisper and he almost smiles but catches himself. "Like yours too." He replies.

He clears his throat. "So, what do you wanna do?" I ask changing the topic. He shrugs. "What did you do before I came here?" He asks. "I read a bit, and I wanted to make a clay mask. But we can watch something." I shrug and he grins.

Yeah, right? When did we ever just watch something? We don´t do that.

"Clay mask?" He asks confused. "Yeah, it´s good for your skin. It´s natural." I say. He smiles, making fun of me. "Okay, let´s do it." He says as he gets up. "Do what? The mask?" I ask, puckering my face. He nods. "It really must have sucked at home for you to do skin care with me." I joke. He looks at me. "You have *no* idea." He says exhausted and walks towards the bathroom. "Besides, that face needs care to look this good." He states with a chuckle.

"Are who you want to be?"

I´m distracted reading the quote on his back.

"Wait a sec." I say before he enters the room. "What?" He looks at me questioning. "Nothin." I hiss. I must check if there´s a bra or a panty. I take a glance before I let him walk in. He gives me a look. "Afraid I might see something naked?" He grins. I shake my head. He stands there awkwardly. Then he sits on the edge of the bathtub looking at me like he has no idea what to do. I take a bowl and scoop, the mud powder, some honey and add water. As I stir, he´s silent, watching me.

"You want a hairband?" I ask. He grins but puckers his face. "Nah thanks." He says. I put my hair in a loose bun and put on the fluffy black hairband with mini bear ears on. "Shall I?" I ask. "Hm." He murmurs. I dip my finger into the paste and apply it to his skin.

I haven´t touched his face before.

He watches me closely. My skin burns. "You can touch me. I won´t bite." He says. "Not yet. At least." He adds. I feel my mouth twitch. But I bring my hand to his jaw and lift his head a bit. For a second, I´m all lost in his eyes. But I catch myself and continue to smear his face. *His eyes never leave mine.*

"What are your parents like?" He asks. Haven´t expected *that* question. *Or any.*

He wants to know about my family?

"My dad has been very strict school wise. My mom was more chilled. But when it came to in her eye´s *bad friends* or *boyfriends,* she ruined many things for me. Which I´m still mad about." I state. My eyes lose their focus. "Something cracked a long time ago. And it´s not the same since. Won´t ever be." I shrug. "I´m cold towards her. Keep my distance emotionally and physically." I tell him.

"My relationship is now closer with my dad than with my mom." I say. "My dad always makes jokes. *Always.* Sometimes jokes that are not at all funny but hurtful. He doesn´t mean it like that but idk. That´s his way of showing he cares." I shrug. "But sometimes it´s just too much, I guess." I avoid his eyes, but it´s hard when he stares into them.

"My mom was always loving, caring and happy. They allowed me basically *everything.* With my older sister, they were stricter." I explain. "I think my anxiety comes from my childhood. They were overprotective. And I didn´t have to do things on my own. They should have *pushed* me." I say upset. "And on top of that was the mobbing in school because of my weight and shyness." I say, and I don´t know why I´m telling him this because he just asked about my parents, not my life story. But maybe I *want* to tell him. And he listens, so I continue. "Maybe I was just too much as a child. I was always quiet, but many things have contributed to make it worse. So, I think somewhere along the way, I stopped trying." I say. I finished applying the mask, but I kept spreading the clay as I spoke.

"Sorry." I say. He shakes his head. "Don´t apologize." He stands up, looking down at me. "I *want* to hear about you." He says, at which my heart skips his beats.

"Your turn." He says and walks me to the sink. I feel sudden insecure about my breakouts. The week before my period is *always* bad. I look at his chest. My heart pounds. My body tingles. My face heats. *I want to run. Hide. But I stay.*

The mask feels cold against my skin. He uses just one finger. *He´s gentle.*

He moves my chin up. I can´t look at him. I look at the ceiling. He moves closer. Our bodies almost touch. He holds my jaw in place. *Fuck, I like this.*

"My parents were.." he speaks, and my heart sinks at the fact that he tells me on his own because I was too afraid to ask. "Loving." He says soft. "At least that´s what I remember. Or how I like to remember it." He shrugs. "When I was young, I got everything I wanted. I have lacked *nothing*. Toys, money, activities, vacations and all a little shit would want." He smiles lightly. "But they had to work a lot. They have eluded me. It was a back and forth. When they were home it was the best time, but when they had to go it was.. *bad*." He says, but he doesn´t meet my eyes, so I look past him. "As teen, it wasn´t that good anymore. My dad got distant and strict. He had already planned out my life and career. We fought a lot." He says. "I was a lot to handle. Always in trouble." He chuckles and I can see it.

Him as a teen. I wish I met him back then.

"I hated when they got home. I wanted to be alone with my brother and friends." He said, and all I thought was.. *and never grow up*.

"I didn´t want to depend on them or be part of their company. They wanted to bribe me into their legacy. Forced me to study something I didn´t want to. Even though I´m good at it. But IT isn´t what I want." He tells me. I don´t look at him because I want him to feel safe telling me all this.

"Look at me." He hushes pleading. I look at him with a lump in my throat.

How can he look that good now?

"Your eyes." He whispers. "What about them?" I mirror his words. "Love them." He hushes. *Love.*

"Like yours too." I whisper back. He stares at my lips for a second and back at my eyes. But the moment snaps as his phone vibrates. *He answers the call.*

"Sup?" He asks. I turn around and wash the bowl. He talks to Finn, but I don´t pay attention beyond that.

He still stands behind me. *How´s he just standing there?*

When I´m on the phone, I walk. But he keeps standing behind me. *Close.*

Our bodies touch. My lips tingle. *I almost kissed him. Or he almost kissed me.*

The bowl´s already clean, but I keep rinsing. Until I realize he already hung up. I lift my eyes and meet his in the mirror. I turn off the tap and face him. "Was that your brother?" I ask. He nods. "He´s full of shit." He says pissed.

"Can I stay?" he asks. "Sure." I say. "Now, let´s read." He says, and we go back to my living room.

We read and afterwards we washed our faces. We stayed up for hours. We watched some documentary about the ancient Greeks. And at some point, we fell asleep.

They became comfortable with each other and opened up. They made their way into each other´s heads. They didn´t realize then, but it was true.

42

It´s the moment before. Before the main act steps on the stage. Before the adrenaline kicks in. When the air is thick. Mixed with smoke, the smell of cigarettes, weed, and sweat. The moment, I have the feeling I might faint. My hands are sweaty, and mouth dry. Trapped in a sardine can. Feeling like the air is running out. Wanting to run. Heart pounding. Feet and hands tingling. Feeling self-conscious.

It´s the moment before Kai touches my hand. And I look at him. Seeking for something to hold onto. "You okay, *Scar*?" He asks into my ear. He frowns in concern.

I can´t speak.

I wipe my hand on my shirt. I look down on my hands. *They´re shaking.*

I clench them into fists. I look at him. "Is it bad again?" he asks. *I think, I nod.*

"Want me to get you out of here?" he asks. We are in the front rows of the concert I´ve been waiting for all year. I shake my head.

I spin my ring. Trying to focus on my breath. *It won´t help.*

I think I might black out.

Don´t do this to me. Not now.

I think he sees the color disappear on my face. He puts a hand on my hip, taking me close. He takes my hand and sets it on his chest. He takes my cheek. Forcing me to look up. “Focus on me.” He demands. “My heartbeat. Can you feel it?” He asks. I feel it with his hand on mine. Pounding calm but a bit faster than usual. “Feel me.” He says. Digging his hand more in. His fingers. *I feel em.*

“Breathe with me.” He says. *I do.*

And I forget the fifteen thousand people around us. “I´m with you.” He says. And all went quiet except for his voice. “You´re safe.” He assures me. *Breathe.*

“I´m here.” He adds. *You´re alive.*

“You´re in the now, with me. And I´ll protect you.” He says like he does that all the time.

Grounding me.

The feeling will pass. All I see is him. All I feel is him. “You´re safe with me.” He says, kissing my forehead. *He kissed my forehead.*

Hugging him, he wraps an arm around me.

When we part, he drags me in front of him. He stands *closely*. Rather presses himself at my body making me feel him. He hooks an arm around me. I hold onto his. Having the anchor, I needed to keep on floating.

That was the moment before my fav artist came on stage. The moment he saved me from having a panic attack. *From throwing up. Blacking out. Running.*

That moment was fight or flight. *We did fight.*

And the moment after, I decided to always fight. Fight my anxiety instead of avoiding. Cause the moment MGK stepped on the stage, it was worth it.

Fighting. Breathing. Feeling.

He was the shore I tried to reach. But he reached me. With his music. With his presence. With his personality. With more than just an artist. With him as a person. It was amazing.

I cried. And laughed. Screamed. And sung.

Kai sat me on his shoulders. He smoked pod and gave me some headshots to relax. He grabbed my jaw and kissed me. *Kissed me.*

I felt like I pass out but from all the butterflies. *He kissed me. We kissed.*

- 27 -

But it was a once in a lifetime moment. Because the day after it was like it didn´t happen. *Like I dreamed it.* Like it was just some trip from the weed.

And the days after, he ignored me. *Like we didn´t happen. Like nothing ever did.*

And maybe it didn´t.

43

Two weeks later

"What´s your pin code?" I ask annoyed. He looks at me weirdly. "Why?" he frowns. "Cause you´re drunk, and I want to call Finn to get you." I say. "Why don´t you use *your* phone?" he asks irritated. "Cause it´s dead Kai." I say showing him. "Dead?" he repeats, not believing me. I nod. "You *always* have power." He retorts. He knows me too well, because usually I save it. *For no reason.* I hate running out. I´m always prepared. In *every* area of my life. At least I try to keep my anxiety in check.

But of course, he knows that too.

"I know. I forgot to charge." I say annoyed by myself. He bites the inner of his lip. "So?" I press. "What?" he asks. "Your pin." I remind him.

"0308." He says after a moment. "But don´t call Finn." He says. "Why?" I ask. "Just *don´t*." He cuts me off. "Then I´ll call Leon." I say. *He doesn´t pick up.*

I try Aidan. *Same thing.*

"I have to call him." I say. He breathes annoyed. "Can´t we *just* sit here?" he asks. I look at him. He lies on his back. Legs angled. And his one hand behind his head and one over his eyes. *He´s nauseous.*

Because he´s wasted, stoned and on the verge of puking.

"And then what?" I ask. "Wait until the sun´s up?" He asks with a grin, but it fades when his head spins again. I lie next to him. Brushing his arm while doing it. He groans. He feels sick. And I feel for him. "Why did you drink that much?" I ask. I get another tortured sound in response. "I don´t know." he says, putting the hand from under his head on his stomach. "You´re lying." I say. "Maybe." He says. He tries to breathe controlled to reduce the pain. I exhale annoyed. "You can´t even answer questions." I say, mad at him that he ghosted me.

After the kisses.

"Cause I wanted to." He states. He always does what he wants.

Like kissing me. Ignoring me. My gut hurts when I think of that.

I take him in. Even on the verge of throwing up, he looks hot. He could do nothing and would look good.

"Well, hope you´re having a great time trying not to puke." I say pleased by his suffering. *But not really.* I´d like to take the pain away. I want to ruffle his hair or touch his arm. But I don´t because he rejected me or pushed me away. *Again.*

"I´m having a *great* time, Scar." He says, not that convincing.

Scar. Why is everyone calling me like that? And since when anyway? I think Aidan said that to me when we got high. But I´m not sure that day´s a blur.

"You want me to get you a water?" I ask. He shakes his head but stops wincing. "Nah." He declines. I straighten up and try to get up, but he shoots up, grabbing my wrist with a pained scowl. "Don´t go please." He begs. He looks like his world spins faster than mine, and I think that´s *exactly* how it is.

He lies down again, but still holds my wrist. Stopping me from leaving him. "I just want to get you a wet towel or something." I say. "For your dizziness." I explain. He lets out a grumble, which is supposed to be a *no*. "It´ll help." I try to change his mind. "Don´t want one." He says stubbornly like a child. *Well, Pan is.*

"Then *what* do you want me to do?" I ask. "Stay." He says as if it hurts to speak. "I´m here." I say. "Sit with me." He says. "Already doing." I say. "Lie with me." He says instead. So, I lie back. He´s still holding my wrist. I face him. We lie close. We touch. It hurts to be that close after the kiss that meant nothing.

"Sure, you don´t want.." I try to ask, but he cuts me off. "No." He insists. "But what can I do?" I ask helplessly. I watch his chest rise and fall. "You´re *already* helping." He assures me as if I would actually do something to reduce his state instead of just watching him suffer.

"Now stop talking." He demands. He moves his head to look at me. *He wanted to see if I´d be upset about his remark.* I´m not. *I know him by now.* His harsh side. But him checking if he´d hurt me is new.

He keeps looking at me. *Like I slow his world.*

I touch his hand, which rests on his forehead. I take it at side, so I can touch his face. I brush his strands out of his face. He closes his eyes. *My chest hurts at that.*

When I stop and lower my arm, he whispers. "Don´t stop." *So, I don´t.*

I touch his temple. His forehead and play with his hair. I trace his neck and jaw. I want to kiss him. *But I don´t.*

After what feels like an hour, he looks calmer. He enjoys my touches. Especially when I run my fingers through his hair or along his scalp. *He hasn´t let go of my hand.*

We keep going for a bit longer until he opens his eyes again. I watched him. Every stare at my lip. Every jaw twitch. Every gaze. Every hint of him liking me that close. *Liking me.*

Proving the kiss was real. *And there were a lot.*

Like his thumb circling the skin where my pulse hides underneath. The slight smirk he tried to hide. The deep lines between his eyebrows disappearing, showing he relaxed under my touch. *Everything.*

I took it all in. Cause he let me see. And I knew he wouldn´t tell me those things I saw. So, I kept shut and memorized them.

"You feel better?" I ask, already knowing the answer. He looks at me.

"I´ll text my brother." He says. *All right, so now we can talk to his brother? Did he just want me to stay?* Wouldn´t be the first time.

He slowly sits upright. And I lie there reading the white quote on his black hoodie.

"Not your Baby, baby."

Okay baby. Maybe we shouldn´t be more than friends then.

"He´ll be here in twenty." He says. "Okay." I nod. He runs a hand through his hair. I straighten up. We touch as we sit. He´s still drunk but less nauseous. He looks at me frowning. "A penny for your thoughts." I say. "You have one?" he asks, nodding his chin at me. I grin. "No." I say. *Of course, I don´t.*

"Then, no thoughts." He smirks. "Rude." I say. "You called me worse." He replies.

I nudge him with my shoulder. He pretends to fall over to the side, holding his arm like I stabbed him. *He winces.*

"Oh, fuck off." I say laughing, pushing him again. *Now he falls.*

I tug on his arm. "You just killed me." He says. "Dead people don´t speak." I say trying to push him up, but he makes himself extra heavy. I laugh.

"Pan is dead, don´t you know?" He asks melodramatic. I shake my head. I like the way his muscles feel under my fingers. *So, I don´t stop touching him.*

"But I didn´t say I´m dead. I said you killed me." He clarifies. Then he lets me drag him back up. I still hold onto him. His arm is flexing under my touch. "There´s no difference." I say close to his face. "There is." He says, looking at me. *We´re close.*

There should be a kiss right now. I know that cause my throat burns. *I could cry.*

There is that lump that screams for his touch. *Kiss me, it begs. I beg.*

But we just watch the invisible knot grow heavier. *And do nothing.*

Over the past months, they became close. *Almost too close.*

It was something that lingered between them and kept nagging. Begging to be looked at. But she wasn´t the only one with anxiety. He had scars he wouldn´t look at either.

44

Friday

The others are already inside, probably at the bar. I try to look out for Kai or Leon as they are the biggest of our group. If Finn had been there, I could have looked for him.

Since he´s the tallest of them all.

But I don´t have to look for too long because the four of them are coming towards me. Kai pushes a cocktail into my hand. It´s a Mojito. He doesn´t look at me.

He remembered.

But clearly, we´re still ignoring each other around them. At least don´t do the things we do when we´re alone.

"Let´s go to the front" Nina says, heading towards the crowd, pulling Leon behind her. Aidan too, followed by Kai and me. *I hate crowds.* Also, a great side effect of social phobia. I push my way between the people trying to keep up with them. I take a deep breath to calm, me but I´m brought back to reality by a hand on my upper arm. I turn around. In front of me, a guy whose eyes are red like he´s on something. "Heey, hon, a drink?" he gushes. I pull myself from his grasp. "No, thanks. And please don´t touch me." I hiss and quickly turn to get away from this creep. When I bump into someone´s chest, I reply "sorry." But at the same moment I realize it´s Kai. Relief passes through me and the familiar smell of rain, books and weed lulls me in. It calms me immediately.

Apparently, he must have looked after me. He doesn´t budge, just glares at the guy behind me. I look over my shoulder and see him disappearing into the crowd. "I can defend myself" I say. Although I´m grateful he came back, something in me wants to be strong. Wants to stick up. Not to depend on him. In *any* way. And I was in control of the situation anyway.

He looks at me, anger still written all over his face. "Good" he says dryly, as if he just realized I might think he cares about me more than he lets me on.

"Come on" he urges, grabbing my hand and pulling me behind him. He *literally* grabs it, as if he doesn´t even know *how* to, or the thought of holding my hand properly is too repulsive. *Probably the latter.*

The tingling I felt, I suppressed. *Friends.* I remind me.

But despite his brash manner, he seems to have an eye on me.

"I´ll be nicer if you´ll be smarter."

I read his back. *That man.* I shake my head.

As I walk, I catch a glimpse of his arm. My eyes catch *something* black. It´s a hair tie. *It´s my hair tie.* I must have left it in the bathroom. I can tell by the imprint that he´s been wearing it for a while. I can´t help but grin. *He wears my tie. Yeah, friends.*

But before we get to the others, he lets go. *What else.*

I´m sure they would laugh at the way he held my hand anyway. Or would be confused that we´re doing it in the first place. Since everyone thinks we can´t stand each other. Or at least not in *that* way.

I can still feel his hand on my skin, like it´s left a brand. One that feels good.

One I like.

Maybe I refer him as pain too. *Maybe.* Maybe, I like pain as much as he does.

45

I go to the bar across the street in the smaller tent. As I maneuver my way to the exit, it seems like some guys are having an argument. I try to not spill anything. But not a second later, someone trips on me and I fall to the ground. The glass shatters and I cut my hand on the shards.

"Fuck" I curse between clenched teeth. The guy helps me up and apologizes. "I´m so sorry I got pushed." I look up and notice *how* handsome he is. He has brown hair, with a few strands hanging on his forehead. He has dark eyes as far as I can tell in the light. He´s wearing a white shirt and jeans.

But still, my palm is bleeding because of him.

He offers me his hand to stand up. *I take it.*

"I´ll get a tissue, wait here" he says and walks behind the bar. *Is he working here?*

The blood drips to the floor. "May I?" he asks with a sheepish grin, and I nod.

Kai wouldn´t have asked.

He presses the handkerchief to the cut. "I really didn´t mean to." He says worried but a slight smile on his lips. "It´s okay. Wasn´t intentional." I say mirroring his smile. He applies more pressure and keeps his gaze down. I look at him more closely. I get the feeling I know him from somewhere. *But I can´t think of it.*

"I was about to start my shift. You´ll get new drinks, of course." He assures. He lifts his gaze to look me in the eye with a charming smile. "That´s okay, I think I´ll tend my wound first." I decline. "Okay." He says, somehow disappointed. "But you can come later if you want. I´m scheduled till half past twelve." He offers with a smirk. We keep eye contact. He squints his eyes as if he is thinking. *Maybe he knows me too.*

"Can I have your number?" He asks and smiles. And I must grin, too. I bite the inside of my cheek to suppress it, though. *Unsuccessfully.*

He grins more and presses his lips together. "Sure," I agree. I get my phone with one hand and hold my number to him. He takes a pic of the screen. "Okay great. I really like to talk longer, but I need to get started or I´m kicked out." He laughs. "You sure you´re, okay?" He asks. *Kai wouldn´t give a shit about work.*

Why am I comparing? I don´t know that guy.

I shake my head. “Yeah, thanks, all good.” I reply. And he walks past me. I look after him. “What´s your name?” I raise my voice. Behind the bar, he looks at me. “Andi” he calls with wide a grin. But then he´s distracted by a girl, so I leave.

Andi. Where do I know you from?

I text Kai he should bring me his keys.

In the distance I see him coming towards me. I must smile. But it fades as I´m slapped on the ass. *This didn´t happen.*

I stop short. Anger boils up and I turn to push the guy. *I recognize him.* It´s the creep from before that touched my arm. “What the *fuck* are you doing? Don´t you *fucking* touch me!” I yell and shove him. He seems to be our age a little older, maybe.

He raises his hands defensively, as if he were the victim. But before I can say anything, Kai rushes up to him. He grabs him by the shirt, punches him in the face, and he stumbles. “Don´t *fucking* touch her,” he howls. Again, Kai throws his fist at his jaw. He staggers. “You bastard.” he roars and hits him in the gut. The guy takes a few more blows until he falls to the ground. His nose bleeding, and his eye framed red. He´s coughing and spits blood.

I step in front of Kai to stop him from. “Let´s go.” I say, but he doesn´t listen. He looks past me. “Kai.” I try again before he knocks him unconscious. He looks at me. I push him back. But he´s still blazing with anger. “If I see you *bastard* near her again.” he threatens but relents and walks away with me.

“I should kill him.” He says through clenched teeth. *I keep silent.*

“What´s going on anyway?” He asks. “Someone fell on me in the bar, and I´ve cut myself.” I explain, showing the handkerchief that´s by now stained red. He stops. “*Who* fell on you?” He asks, grabs my hand, and takes a look. “He got *pushed*.” I say before he turns back. “Who do you want me to hit?” He looks around as if he could recognize the guy without knowing what he looks like. “No one.” I press. “He was nice. Really, it´s okay” I soothe him. “*Nice*.” He repeats. “Yeah nice.” I agree. *He doesn´t say anything more.*

We walk to his house without talking. I can feel how pissed he is.

He gets the first aid kit, and I sit down on the sofa.

He sits in front of me on the table. *Our knees touch.*

He takes my hand and disinfects the cut, applies a cream, and bandages my hand. His hands feel rough and soft. His touch, however small, electrifies my body. His own wounds, don´t seem to interest him much. Spellbound, I watch him. He´s also, quiet, and concentrated.

When he´s finished, he doesn´t let go of my hand but finally looks at me. “Thank you,” I say so soft I wonder if he heard. “You okay, *Scar*?” he asks. He sounds worried. A strand falls on his forehead. I want to brush it back, but I don´t.

“Yeah, I am.” I tell him. “I just don´t get what some guys get up to.” I say. “Me neither.” He says. “Has anything like that happened to you before?” He asks and I stiff a laugh. “Of course. Whether it´s when you´re partying, and they press up against you as they walk by, touch you, or grab your hips without being asked when you´re hugging. Or when someone out of nowhere *grabs* your ass.” I say zoned out. “I am shocked every time anew. Unfortunately, sometimes you can´t fight back the way you´d like to because you´re in shock.” I fall silent. He lets go of my hand and runs it through his hair.

“It makes me *sick* to even think about it” He confesses. “Perverts like him belong..” He falters, searching for the right words. “No woman deserves to go through that.” He says. I nod. “But you shouldn´t have stopped me.” He says. I noticed his rising anger and reach for his hand, turning it over. I stroke his red knuckles and disinfect the open areas. I try to ignore the way he stares at me.

“I´m not going to let anything happen to you Scar.” He tells me. “You´re not *always* there.” I point out. “Then I´ll give you more lessons in kickboxing.” He shrugs. “Or I´ll talk to Aidan. The police station offers self-defense courses. He can teach you too.” He says.

Then he gets up and we go back to the others.

46

I am thinking about going to see Andi, again.

I still have no idea where I know him from.

But I decided to do it. “I´m off for a while” I say to Luca. She nods and I leave.

I start to get nervous as I walk towards the bar. He spots me and grins. He puts the shots down and comes over to me. I sit down on the stool. “Hey,” I say. “Hi, I´m glad that you came.” He says smiling at me. I smile back. “What do you want to drink?” He asks. “You choose” I answer. “Wow about some shots?” He offers. I nod. “I´ll finish up then we can toast.” He says. “Sure” I agree. He disappears behind the tent.

After a few minutes he sat next to me. In his hand a bottle, two shot glasses and sliced lemons. “This is cheesecake. First the lemon then the shot.” He instructs me. We toast. It´s sweet, and you taste zero alcohol. Which is *always* the problem.

After four or six more shots later, I have completely forgotten my nervousness. “So, Lia you want to dance?” He asks full of charm. “Yes,” I say, and we go. Neither of us can dance though, but we have fun anyway. Unlike with Aidan, I often step on his feet, and he has no sense of tact either. It isn´t at all loose like with Kai but it´s somehow all I need today.

Time flies and soon it´s after three in the morning. We go outside and sit on one of the beer benches. I take a look at my phone and see some messages in our group chat and Luca has called me, probably wondering where I am. *I don´t answer.*

I eye him, as if I can figure out who he is by staring. "Tell me something about yourself Andi, the bartender." I grin, hoping to find out where I know him from. "Well, I´m a bartender." He says and I laugh. "But also, a cook at my family´s five-star restaurant. *Italian*." He looks at me. "I´m Italian. I play basketball. Eventually, I want to play full-time. Or lead our restaurant someday." He tells me.

Doesn´t ring a bell. Maybe I´m just mistaken.

"And what about you?" He asks. "I study to be an elementary school teacher. I love art and psychology; those are my passions." I shrug. "I read a lot. And I want to start my own business someday, I´m just missing the crucial idea." I laugh. "Or emigrate. Or write a book. Or become a coach or something like that." I say. "I just want to help people and inspire them." I tell him and he listens.

Time flies by and I did not once think about Kai. Maybe, that´s why I enjoyed spending time with him. As a distraction from the guy, I couldn´t forget.

47

Next evening, Saturday

"**W**ill you ride bumper cars with me? I still have an old chip that I´ve been wanting to get rid of for years," I ask with a smile. "Sure" he replies.

Kai sits behind the steering wheel and I next to him.

But my face falls, and my heart stops as I see who got into the scooter opposite us.

My ex. Followed by his new girlfriend.

My blood freezes when our eyes meet. For a second, we looked at each other. A painful stab hits me in the heart. It´s the first time I see *them* together.

I jolt up and leave. I had to get out of there, or I would have cried in front of him.

As if I haven´t shamed myself enough with my sudden escape.

I throw the chip away and storm towards the tent. *It´s been two years,* I tell myself. My heart races and tears shoot down my cheek. I push my way through the crowds. Crying girls are normal at fairs, which is why I don´t care right now. Although I usually *do* care what others think of me. Just like Kai accused me months ago.

Why can´t I be around him without breaking? Without feeling that my legs can´t carry me? But the far more important question is *why can he?*

Because he moved on. Cause he has a girlfriend. *He´s happy. I´m not.*

I don´t want to show weakness. *But that´s what I did.*

I squeeze my eyes shut. It still hits me. *After two years.*

Memories overtake me, but my thoughts are interrupted by Kai who suddenly stands in front of me and stops me from walking on. "What´s going on?" he asks, confused.

I say nothing.

"Who´s *that* guy?" He demands but then spots my tears and gets angry. "What did he do?" he snaps, making attempts to storm back. "No please *leave it* Kai." I hold him back by his upper arm. He looks at me pleadingly. Though we both knew he would hit him without my permission. *Because he loves to fight.*

"You don´t have to. It´s okay." I assure him. "Then *who* is this guy?" he insists. I sigh. "That´s my ex." I say. He frowns at me. "It just still hurts sometimes." Is all I can say. "I can still punch him." He offers with a smug grin. The guy just *wants* to hit someone.

I shake my head. "No, it´s fine." I decline. He sighs giving in.

Reading my face and nods his chin at me. "He looked after you.. *if* that does anything for your ego." He tells me. "Whereupon she got mad, and then they left." He explains amused. I can´t hide my satisfaction and grin.

- 27 -

Andi comes up to me and gives me a hug. Behind him is Ryan the guitar guy from the campfire.

"Where´s your brother?" Andi nods at Kai. *Do they know each other?*

"Not here." He snaps. *Rude as ever.* Kai doesn´t seem to like Andi very much. *Andi. Wait.*

He´s the one whose name I lost at the campfire. *Did he recognize me too? Did he know who I was? Is that why he didn´t ask for my name?* Because he knew who I was. He said my name and I haven´t told him. *He knew.*

"He´s the one who cut you?" Kai asks, pissed as he puts the pieces together.

"I didn´t *cut* her. Calm down." Andi says with a slight grin on his face. "Yeah, you idiot *fell.*" Kai spits. "Probably tried to hit on her." He laughs scornfully.

They glared at each other. "Leave it" I snap. Kai gives me a look I can´t read.

Is he mad? At me?

But he backs off before I can say anything and talks to Aidan.

Andi and I dance and talk, trying to get to know each other as much as you can in front of a band. And I don´t miss Kai´s scowls in our direction. Every time I let my eyes wander; I catch his gaze. And every time I look at Andi or smile at him, I still feel Kai´s eyes on me.

Always on me.

48

Sunday

I push past the dancing people and fight my way to the bar. *I need a drink now.*

While I wait, I look around. A few familiar faces here and there. Some lost friends and lovers. I have nothing to do with most of the people in my village. I honestly don´t want to, either. *Not anymore.* There were times I was friends with some. We partied together. *But that time is over.* I´ve come to realize I never fitted in. *Never really.* With some I went to school. And others I just know. Most of them probably don´t even know, I exist. *I´m nobody.* In this suburb, you´re either popular *or* you never exist at all.

I´m the latter.

Suddenly my social anxiety surfaces. I feel watched and judged. Even if I *know* not all eyes are on me, it still feels like I´m in the spotlight. *But not at all in a good way.*

My head is foggy. I ran out of air. *There´s no air in here.* I feel like I´m going to keel over. There´s that tingling in my fingers and the numb feet. A dark spot in my vision.

I have to get out of here.

Without taking the drink with me, I leave the tent.

I hate this village. I hate these people. And I hate how they have a hold on me. Or rather, how I give them the might. *I feel weak.* I thought I was past all this. But it´s catching up on me. *I´m not over it.* They keep going and I´m still living in the past. Where we were friends. Where I had friends. Where things were different. But now they´re strangers. And I´m grieving people who don´t give a shit about me.

It starts to drip, and I try to breathe, but my gaze keeps wandering. And my body reacts before my mind can. *No, it can´t be. No.* In the distance, I recognize my ex´s big brother and his girlfriend. *Please don´t. Not again. Not now.*

Behind them, my ex holding hands with his girlfriend. *No.* I want to sink into the ground. Heat shoots into my cheeks and ears. *It´s been years, pull yourself together.* But apparently even after two years, my blood still freezes. *Because again, I´m not over it.*

Before they could spot me, I once again decide to flee. On an empty bridge away from all, I came to a stop. I hold on to the railing. I didn´t notice I started crying. I always start to cry after a night out. Either way, alcohol makes me tired or crying. But this isn´t just because of the alcohol. *Why him? Why here?* He doesn´t even live nearby.

Why the one person who meant the most and hurt me the most?

I almost have to laugh because it must be the irony of fate. I look up at the dark sky and blink against the rain. I failed the test. *I´m not over it.*

Not over those people, nor over him. Years of telling myself that I´m moving forward all shattered in one moment. *All because of me. Because I let it.*

Maybe I don´t want to be. Maybe, I want to suffer. *Maybe, I´m just stupid.* Anger boils up. At myself for not being able to let go. For crying over this. For having no self-esteem.

It starts to pour, and I sink to the ground. I create my suffering. With my thoughts. *I know I do.* But it hurts so much. It feels like I still have an invisible bond to him. *And to those people.* He´s the one who made me feel not at all lonely almost six years of my life. And that´s gone, and I feel even lonelier than before. I´m not just lonely. *I´m empty.* And seeing him shoots needles into my heart. It reminds me of the things I lost and once had.

I can barely see anything from raindrops mixing with tears and mascara.

I should be stronger. I want him to be happy. *But why am I not?* Because I don´t let myself. I let my happiness depend on others. *What could his new girlfriend fix in him that no one can fix in me? Who´s my person after him? Why was he able to open up again after four months? And I can´t after two years? Because you like to suffer.*

The lump in my throat gets bigger. Overwhelmed by my anxiety, thoughts, and apparently long-lost love sickness I´m slowly losing it. Half soaked, I dug my phone out of my leather jacket and try to unlock it. I call the only person I know can calm me now. The *toot* feels like an eternity. Music blares and voices sound from the other end but it´s muffled as if I´m not in the rain but miles under the ocean. *Maybe I am.*

I can barely make anything out. *I don´t speak.* I can´t get a sound out. “Scar?” I think I hear him saying. *I don´t answer.*

“Where are you?” He asks but I can´t talk. *Am I still crying?* All I perceive is that low buzz in my ear. *I can´t stop crying. I hate that I´m crying. I hate all of this.* Everything feels numb. Like I´m in the void. In a black room. *Alone.*

I hung up and tuck it away on autopilot. But I keep a lookout between the silhouettes for my rescue. It doesn´t take long before I see him. He looks around, pacing. *Searching for me.* When he spots me, he runs towards me. I jump up, surprised I even have the strength. I see his lips move, but I can´t understand anything. I literally crushed against his chest. A feeling of security spreads through me. My eyes go black, and I lose the ground under my feet.

And I fall. But Kai catches me. He lifts me up. *Lifts me above all.* I try to see the sunsets he showed me, but I can´t. *It´s black. Dark.*

My head rests against his chest, and he carries me. I don´t know if I´m still crying or if it´s the rain. His scent clouds me. He didn´t smoke pod today. *He´s here.*

It feels like forever. An eternity of safety in his arms. He carries me all the way to his. The rain never stops, nor do my tears and sobs.

There were thunderstorms reported. *I like thunderstorms.*

- 27 -

I´m only conscious again when he carries me into his bedroom. *Haven´t been in a while.*

He takes off his shoes and sits on the bed with me in his arms. He manages to take off my shoes. He also takes off my jacket. "Your clothes are wet. I´ll give you a sweater." He says and I nod. He sits me down on, goes to his closet and pulls out a black sweater. "I undress you?" He asks me for permission. I nod. But he looks at me. *He wants me to say it.* My mouth forms *yes* but there´s no sound. *But he´s fine with that.*

He helps me strip down and puts it over my head. I dropped my bra. Kai gets changed too but doesn´t take his eyes off me while doing so.

Probably afraid I´d pass out again.

He gets my bag and lifts me up. He takes me to the bathroom. He knows me well enough to know I won´t go to bed without washing my face and removing my mascara. No matter *how* drunk or emotionally broken I am.

After he takes my makeup off, he carries me back to bed and pulls me to his chest. He holds my head and strokes my hair. Everything so natural as if it were the most normal thing for us to do. *Like we´re closer than we actually are.*

"My ex again" I say, though I´m not sure something came out. "The most important yet worst person in my life," I whisper. His grip tightens around my body. "What happened?" He asks into my hair. "My ex for more than six years. My boyfriend and best friend. *My home.*" I say. "Who eventually gave up. *Us. Me.*" I swallow. "Who betrayed me. Cheated on me.. *sort of.*" I choak. "Who no longer loved or wanted me. Who didn´t *fight* anymore. Who said he would always be there for me. *But lied.*" I face the void.

"That´s what happened." I say. "I fell in love with him at thirteen and never stopped since. *But he did.* Even if I don´t want him back. Parts of me still miss parts of him." I shrug. I want to cry, but I´m empty. *I feel so pathetic.*

"I´m sorry. I don´t know why I´m reacting this way, I thought I was doing fine. Apparently, I can´t let go. It was just too much. My social anxiety got worse. And I drank too much and.." I admit, but he cuts me in. "Stop apologizing for your feelings Scar." He tells me. And I know him well enough to know he´s about to quote.

"*Don`t cover your scars, let them bleed.*" He refers to a song by MGK and I want to smile but can`t. But he sings *my* scars and not *yours*.

"Six years is a long time.." he sighs. "Even if I don´t believe in time." He whispers. "But it is okay how you feel." He tells me. Then he reaches into his pocket and pulls something out. He holds a chip. *The one I had thrown away.* He picked it up.

He picked it up.

"You still mustn´t forget that you create your suffering" he says, handing it back to me. I hate how right he always is. Well, I don´t *hate* that. *It´s what I love.*

"*Remember the past only insofar as you enjoy it.*" Before I can ask, he replies. "*Pride and Prejudice.*" He says. "I have one too from that film" I whisper. "*Men are either eaten up with arrogance..*" I begin, and he finishes. "O*r stupidity.*" I smile.

He knows them all.

"What is he?" He asks. "Undoubtedly arrogance." I manage a laugh.

"He´s a jerk for letting you go." He says quietly. I try not to interpret too much into that cause he probably just wants to cheer me up. *We´re silent for a while.*

"Will you read to me?" I asked him. Without answering, he takes a book from his nightstand and reads to me.

Normally he´s the one who falls asleep first and fast. But now he waits for me to drift away, but my mind can´t shut up. But I want him to sleep, so I close my eyes and pretend. He strokes my head and brushes a strand out of my face. He reads a bit further, but at some point, stops and falls asleep himself. *I stay awake listening to my thoughts.*

I think I can´t love again. Not until I didn´t let go of my past. I don´t say that´s all my ex´s fault because he´d hurt me. I think it is just the way I am. The way I was built. A hopeless romantic who´s too afraid of love. Who wants it as much as denies it. Who loved once too much. And can´t trust to love anyone again. But I would love to love him.

That day he saw how broken she was. How trapped she was in her past. How she was haunted by her mind. And how it affected her. He saw pain; he knew himself all too well.

49

Two weeks later, Ryan´s birthday

Colson Herzog

Since that night, much has changed. I started dating Andi, and Kai and I are back to the start.

I stopped staying over and he stopped coming over. No more dates, dancing or reading.

No texting. He´s back to hating me. *Not hating, but not liking either.*

I sit in the middle between Leon and Nina. Aidan sits on the passenger side and Kai turns around to pull out. He puts his hand on the seat in front of me. And our eyes meet. I lean to the side, so he sees more. *Why does even that look good?* Apparently, everything he does looks good. His arms are covered in veins, as they´re *fucking always* are. I force myself to stare at the console until he´s done.

Music blares through the car. After the first few seconds, I realize it´s by *MGK.* I can´t come up with the name though. So, I look at the display and read the name. *Sex Drive.* My eyes widen and wander to the rearview. Kai´s eyes search mine at he realizes *what* song is playing. He holds my gaze, but I look back at the cockpit. It´s what he wrote on my Vans, months ago. *Sex Drive.*

I look up the lyrics. My heart beats all the way to my ears at that line. *Problem?* Of course, he thinks *I´m* the issue. *Prick.*

He can´t sleep because of me? I´m confused.

When I look up, his gaze is already on me, as if he *knows* exactly what I did. *Was he indirectly admitting he´s lying awake because of me? Is he thinking about me? Why else would he have written the title on my shoe?* That he doesn´t sleep much I noticed over the past months. *But because of me?* No. *Right?*

Maybe it´s just his favorite song. But still.. *weird.*

During the drive, our eyes meet a few more times. *For milliseconds.* The others are already drunk, and don´t seem to notice. After all, he must keep an eye on the traffic, I tell myself. *Not on me.* I just happened to sit there. *In his way.* He wouldn´t look at me when I sat at the window. *He wouldn´t.*

- 27 -

Andi lifts me onto the dresser. His hands on my hips. Then he leans in and kisses me. It´s our first kiss, and he tastes like *beer.* By the way he looks and dresses, you could assume he likes wine. *But no. He likes beer. As every guy. Which I don´t like.* But he´s a good kisser and a distraction from Kai and his death stares I got all night.

I put my hands on his collar and pull him to me. His tongue forces itself into my mouth. He pushes himself between my legs. *It´s not the best kiss but I like it.*

I feel his phone vibrating on my thigh. He stops kissing and takes it out. He´s distracted, so I look to my left and meet Kai´s gaze. Somehow, I feel a twinge. His jaw tenses. *Dead eyes. Mad eyes.* He takes a bottle and drinks from it while staring at me, Stoic. *He hates you.*

Why do you care to save me but not to like me? He scowls at me. *I look away.*

Andi´s hand is still on my thigh. I slide down from the dresser. He doesn´t move, so we stand close to each other. His hand has moved to my hip. I can feel the slight bulge in his pants. He puts his phone away but let´s go of me cause Ryan approaches us.

They start talking.

I look to the left, but he´s gone. *He´s nowhere to be seen.*

The two of them are lost in their conversation, so I search for Kai. I spy on him alone on the terrace. He leans against the glass fence smoking pod and looking down on the illuminated city. We´re at Andi´s and he´s rich too. This house has ceiling high windows and it´s all modern, clean, and expensive.

I step outside.

"Get off my dick."

Says the lettering on his back. *No, this time I won´t.*

In one hand he has the bottle and in the other the blunt.

"I suppose I´m the driver now," I say. He glances over his shoulder. "Looks like it." He says indifferently and stabs his joint.

"I´ve always wanted to drive your M4." I say happily. He turns and points one finger at me while holding the Vodka in the same hand. "You´re *not* driving *my* car" he howls. "Well, I am because I´m the only who hasn´t been drinking." I retort, pointing to the bottle in his hand.

"I *can* drive" he says. "*You can´t*" I say sourly and take it out of his hand. "*I can´t.*" He repeats in agreement. He rubs his forehead. "*Fuck*" He curses. "You.." he starts but says nothing more. He just opens his mouth just to shut it again.

"Then you should have thought before drinking *idiot*." I snap. He steps towards me, getting in my face. "Then *you* should have thought before *kissing* him in front of *me*." He spits and snatches the bottle out of my grip. *Wha..?* My eyes widen.

"So, I´m the reason you drank?" I laugh. He says nothing. *Wait, he says nothing.*

"Are you jealous?" I ask. "*Jealous..?*" He starts and laughs. Then he points back and forth between us. "There is *nothing* between us and never will be." He laughs and walks past me. I shut my eyes, exhaling. "Kai" I beg exhausted, but he walks on. "That´s not fair!" I yell and he stops. "Not *now*, Scar" he says beat and pushes the patio door.

I don´t understand him. He´s fucking confusing. What´s his problem? Why doesn´t he ever want to talk? Why does he kiss me and then back off? Why does he switch up on me all the time? Does he hate or like me? Can´t he just admit it?

If he didn´t want me to kiss Andi, he should have kissed me. Enough chances he had. But I think it´s more about Andi than me, but I don´t know why.

It takes me a moment to contain my rage before I go back inside. Just to see Andi and Kai build up in front of each other. I don´t know what´s going on, but it doesn´t look good. Their faces are only a few inches in front of each other, glaring. Before I realize what´s going on, Aidan has already taken Kai aside. Leon comes up to me. "We´re leaving" he states, and I don´t argue with him. "Sorry" I say to Andi and Ryan and follow my friends.

The others get to the car. "I sit front" Kai tells them. *They listen. Pan has spoken.*

We stand in front of each other.

He reaches into his pants and hands me his keys. *No arguing.*

Before we get in, he gives me a look over the car. *No anger. There´s assurance.*

During the whole drive, Kai doesn´t let off a single remark, which surprises me. In front of the house, Kai tells the others to get out. *Friendly as ever.*

Again, they do as he told.

We´re sitting silent for a while. *Afraid to speak, afraid not to.*

"Coming up?" He asks, audibly drunk. As an answer, I get out of the car.

We stand at his front door while he´s rummaging in his pocket. He must have forgotten that I have the keys. I grin to myself and wait for him to notice. At some point he stills and throws his head back, realizing.

I hand him the keys as he turns. He looks down. "I know you don´t like driving other cars." He starts. I look at the ground. "Drives fine" I say. "But I prefer to see *you* behind the wheel" I add and look at him. He grins. *Briefly.* Until his lips pull into a thin line because his lips *always* remember hating me, but his eyes never do.

"It was kinda hot watching you drive my car" he says with a rough voice. *I like drunken Kai.* Or this *version* of drunk. *He´s softer. Honest.*

But I just wait for him to play it down again. *But nothing.*

"Are you coming up?" He asks again. "I think I´ll walk home." I say. His jaw tightens, but he nods. "Well then," I say walking away.

"You like him, don´t you?" He asks. I turn to face him. He´s already holding the door handle but is facing me. "Yeah," I admit. *At least, I think, I like him.* I know I like Kai more.

But maybe I shouldn´t.

"How can you like *that* asshole?" He slurs. "Kai," I warn. He nods a few times. "Then for his sake, I hope he doesn´t break your heart. Or I´ll break his neck." He says and opens the front door.

A sunshine as always. *My sunshine.*

Or rather rain shower.

[NOTEBOOK ENTRIES]

~~I looked at the stars with her. I couldn´t help but reach for her hand. I want to touch her all the time.~~ It´s becoming a problem. ~~It wasn´t no longer enough that our fingers touched, or I brushed my arm against her or our legs touching. Something drew me to her. And I could no longer resist. And when she left, something told me to get her back.~~ She went upstairs. And I sat outside. ~~I didn´t want to leave her alone, but I was afraid of what would happen. Because this time I wanted to have her with me. I fucking asked her to. There was no excuse anymore.~~ She knew. ~~And that scared the shit out of me. I couldn´t stop thinking of her in my bed in my shirt with no bra. Not that I would have laid hands on her. But I wrecked my head about what it would mean.~~ I never wanted any girl in my bed longer than for sex. Not even for that. I preferred doing it anywhere else. How did it come so far? From I don´t want her near me to ~~I want her to fall asleep next to me.~~ So, I sat in the rain. Thinking. Smoking weed. Fighting that inner battle. ~~Those feelings. Those thoughts. Her. But I've lost the battle I knew I couldn't win. I laid down with her. I watched her. She wore one of my hoodies. I tugged her to me. I had an erection. But I just wanted to hold her.~~ I fell asleep. Slept like a goddess. ~~She makes me sleep. She calms me. If magic is real. It's her. I didn´t wash my sheets after. I didn´t shower for a day or two. I wore the hoodie she slept in.~~ I´m so fucked.

I came across a quote from Heath Ledger which says: "The most common cause of insomnia is simple; it´s loneliness" And I fear I might believe it´s true. ~~With her, I don´t feel loneliness. I'm myself with her. Like fully.~~ I never feel that way. Just when I´m alone. People make me feel lonely. She knows that side of me most girls hate, and she wants to get to know me despite it. ~~Maybe, she is like me.~~ Like Leon said, we would get along. ~~And we kind of do. More than I'd like to.~~

She´s been awake at that time, which was unusual. I know why I´m wide awake but her? So, I knew I had to cheer her up. Distract her. Make her feel alive. In the now. So, I showed her something I used to do with Finn when I was little. We speed trough that tunnel with our favorite songs. Hers was fearless. Which is ironic since she struggles with anxiety. I wished I could experience that feeling for the first time again, too.

Colson Herzog

But she did. And I was with her. ~~I wanted to show her all.~~ The highs. And the lows. The lows are the best. They lift you even more.

I couldn't sleep. I walked and found myself in front of her house. She came down in just a shirt. ~~I would have preferred to see her in mine~~, but she looked hot anyway. Any other girl would have been getting ready. But she came straight out of bed. I liked that she didn't worry about how she looked. ~~Not in front of me.~~ She trusts me. ~~Which felt good.~~ I could see her nipples. Luckily, the rain brought me down. ~~Otherwise, I would have sucked the rain off her skin and fucked her right on the warm asphalt.~~ We were fooling around. I laughed tears. My belly fucking hurt. ~~Sometimes my body hurts because of another reason.~~ We lay in the rain. ~~This was better than any sleepless night could have been.~~ I liked her art and the bookshelves. I haven't looked at her bedroom, though. ~~That's for another day.~~ I realized ~~I stopped hating her. I didn't even try anymore. I liked her. I wanted to spend time with her. To get to know her.~~ But instead of snapping. I kept my shit together. I liked her. So what? She's friends with my friends. I'm just being nice. She's part of it now. Maybe they were right, and she did fit in. She is different. I tried hard not to like her. Not to think of her. Not to want her. But fuck, I want to get to know her. I think of her. I want to kiss her. Talk to her. Fuck her. Sleep next to her. So what? But I won't tell her. I stayed up and read. I ate it up. Mostly because I wanted to see her marks. And I wouldn't admit, but the story was good and the porn too. I definitely have to check her other books. ~~Something.. changed.~~ I think I accepted her. I didn't fight anymore. ~~I let her in.~~

I watched the sunset with her. The silence said it all. I felt okay. I felt peace. I wanna do the same to her.

I caught her drawing me. I was pleased. She was embarrassed. But there was no need to because she's talented. I told her about my writings. She made me. And read to her. She's so stubborn. It's exhausting and funny at the same time. I'm the same. I didn't know what to show her. Everything I write is messy, raw, honest, and personal. I didn't want to scare her. So, I picked one about her. Since I was her muse too. And she inspired me. I wrote it after we spent the night in the rain. I realized I often write after I see her. I wrote a lot about her too. She brings creativity. I felt vulnerable. I wanted her to hear. Because she wanted to listen. ~~Because for a while no one listened.~~

I was way too drunk to talk to her. I said some stuff I hoped I'd forget. But I didn't. We talked about our parents. I liked being touched by her. ~~And I liked touching her. I almost kissed her.~~ But Finn called. It was a waking call. ~~I didn't want to go home.~~ I sleep better when she's around.

She was on the verge of a panic attack. I tried to calm her. She let me. ~~I kissed her.~~

We were high and it just happened. I made it happen. ~~More than once.~~

I ignored her for two weeks. But it didn't help. ~~She was everywhere.~~

I was drunk and tried to fuck a girl after I ran into her. But I threw up as she tried to kiss me~~. I couldn't if I thought of Sear.~~ She wanted to call Finn, but I knew he was home, so I told her not to. ~~I didn't want to leave~~. She asked for my Pin code. But she hasn't noticed. The world was spinning too fast to kiss. ~~I wanted it.~~ But I couldn't. Literally. Not with puke left in my mouth. If I wouldn't have been wasted, I would have gotten a hard on. She knew all the right places. She stroked my head for hours. At least it felt like. ~~I forgot long ago; how long hours were.~~

I held her hand like an idiot. I wasn't sure if I should do that, cause that's not what we do. She disappeared. I wanted to look for her. My mind was racing. ~~My heart too.~~ I knew something was off. This sick fuck grabbed her ass. I thought I'd lose it. She stopped me. Even if she said he fell. I bet he didn't. If I hadn't had to tend to her wound, I would have gone to seek that piece of shit. I forgot to take off her hair tie. She probably saw it. I hope she thinks it was from another girl. I want to protect her. She must be able to defend herself. I'm sure Aiden can show her some things. She took care of my scratches, because that's all they were. Nothing I'm not used to. My fists have looked worse. But I didn't want her to stop. I should hurt myself more often. We went back but she disappeared again. I panicked and searched for her. Saw her dancing with fucking Andi. I can't stand that son of a bitch.

She ran into her ex. By the way he looked at her, I knew he still felt for her. I would have loved to punch him. But I knew she would be mad. That was the first time she cried in front of me.

They hugged each other. Like, what the fuck? They have known each other for five minutes. But it didn't took me long to figure he was the one who pushed her. The bastard had planned this. He got a whiff I liked her. Now he wants to play games we stopped long ago. I stopped. So, they all did. But some invented new ones. But he wants to play old ones. They danced. I thought I might throw up. But she kept looking at me. And I kept looking at her. She wants me. My dick. Me. What is a lost boy next to Pan? A boy. Nothing.

When she called, I heard her sobbing. My hands shook. She hung up. I panicked. I searched for her. She sat on a bridge in the rain. She looked broken. ~~And seeing her like that made me think of myself. I sat there too. Not that place but in the rain. Panicking. And because no one took me out of it,~~ I had to take her out. Shield her from herself. I didn't want her to feel like I did. When she saw me, she looked relieved. My chest ached for her. My soul hurt for her. She crashed into my arms. I would never let her go. She blacked out. I would carry her anywhere. She wouldn´t stop crying. She had a breakdown. She held onto me like I was her strength. I saved her. She wanted it to be me. No one fucking else. ~~I realized she wasn´t Wendy. She was lost girl.~~ She told me it was about her ex. She mourns him. Heartbroken. She can´t let go. But it wasn´t her demons that hunt her it was his. She lives in the past. But I want to show her the present. And I will.

I made her be okay. But she started dating him. It´s a bit off between us. She stopped staying over. And we´re back to arguing and ignoring.

They made out in front of me. She wanted to talk about it, but I panicked. I acted out of jealousy. I´m such an idiot. I snapped at her. But what did she expect? She messed up. He won´t save her. A lost boy can´t fly. Only I can. Andi wanted to make a point. But I told him to keep his hands off her. That those games are over. But he just laughed. I broke the rules once but not for her. And with that it all went down. Because of me. I let Neverland become hunted by pirates. I made this. I made the games that I fucked up in the end. But he wants to fuck with me for different reasons. Out of pleasure. For things in the past. Nothing has changed. He knew it wasn´t a game. But life is a game. Just smart ones know how to play it. And he wasn´t one of them. Only Pan and Hook knew. Then because of me she had to drive a car with 431 hp. She was nervous about it. But she did pretty well. Maybe I´ll let her drive it sometime. Show her. Cause I know she likes my car. And I liked seeing her in it. ~~I would teach her the world if she wanted me to.~~

He likes playing games. Games of life and death. But little did he know he started playing with the flying devil itself. And the demon always wins.

50

Finns´ birthday, Kai

"Why did Nina even bring her in the first place." I groan and Finn chuckles. "I think the real reason why she pisses you off that much is cause she´s a lot like you." He smiles *that fucker*. I scoff. "She´s *nothing* like me." I retort. "She is." He nods. "And I think.. you like her." He assumes like he knows *shit*.

"Could you just shut up." I snap.

"Her and Andi? I mean *really*. You want *him* to have her?" He asks. "I don´t want *anything* from her." I bark. He gives me a look. "She slept over the past weeks." He tells me like I didn´t know. "Don´t play her." He warns me. "I don´t.." I cut myself off. "He´s the one playing." I say irritated. "He´s after her since the campfires." I shout. He frowns at me confused. “The second time she was over?” He asks with a smile. I nod. “When I gave her my hoodie.” I remind him. His head tilts back like he had an *aha* moment. “That´s when he laid eyes on her. Cause he thought I want her. Which I *don´t.*” I state. His mouth twitches. “But *now* you do.” He guesses. I exhale annoyed. “No, you don´t get it. He doesn´t *actually* wants her. He wants to mess with me.” I rage.

“So, you still do those games.” He sighs. “Thought that had stopped since *you* fucked..” I cut him off. “It *did* stop after that.” I bark. “But apparently, he just waited for something to piss me off. And if you didn´t realize the party developed their own games.” I say. He nods looking around. There were times the Lost boy´s got out of hand. When Pan did. It all went down.

“So, you are upset.” He grins. “I am upset cause he´s not the one in charge. I mess with her and no one else.” I say. He just grins to which I punch him in the gut. He laughs.

“Okay fine. *Little shit.*” He calls me that way since I am well, *a little shit.*

“You don´t like her. But he can´t have her cause he´s playing with her to fuck you up. And you´re her personal bully.” He snorts. I glare at him. “You´re not really friends cause you don´t like her. But she sleeps over and you´re walking over to her in the middle of the night. But on the parties, you just fuck around and scream at each other. Cause that´s what you´re doing. Just making sarcastic remarks and fun of each other. *Nothing more.*” He goes on and my blood boils. *I hate that he knows.*

“Until you´re alone and can stop pretending to not like each other. But you won´t talk about all of this. Because it´s *nothing*. Right?” He grins, and I kick him, but he dodges me. “So, what I´m saying *little shit* is.. you should make a move.” He tells me. I still mid-punch and frown at him. “You heard right.” He looks at me. “Tell her.” He demands. “Or show her. Whatever but do it because *she likes you.*” He says and it´s like I´m just realizing it now. I watch her talk to her friend.

“And she is a lot like you.” He says again. “I bet she doesn´t even want him. Because I think *she wants you.*” He shrugs. “But just in the stolen moments because, on the parties, she hates you. Because no one knows how alike you are. And how you don´t at all hate her.” He says and I zone out.

“Just do it.” He says and I look at him. “What are you afraid of?” He asks the one-million-dollar question. My throat hurts. He punches my shoulder and walks by.

What are you afraid of? Her. *What are you afraid of?* Everything.

What are you afraid of? Nothing. *What are you afraid of?* Just do it.

\- 27 -

Bored – Billie Eilish, Lia

Colson Herzog

Finn and I are standing on the patio. "You think I didn´t notice you sleeping over all the time?" He asks with a grin. I look at him, not sure if I should feel embarrassed. "I don´t know. I assumed." I say and he nods. "Don´t you talk?" I ask. "We *do* talk." He says. "And we have cameras." He adds with a smirk. *Right. I forgot.*

There is a silence.

"You´re doing him good." He nods toward the living room where Kai sits on the sofa.

The question is, is he good for me, too?

I look back at him, confused. "I mean it." He nods. "You give him counter which he needs and you´re important to him." He tells me and I laugh. "Yeah, he just doesn´t show it that often." I say. He looks at me. "You sure?" He asks, raising an eyebrow.

I consider. *Does he?*

"He shows you." He assures me. "In his own way." He clarifies and I look to Kai.

His own way. Yeah, you could say that.

"Can I ask you something?" I ask. "Is it about your friend?" He asks, knowing *exactly* what I had in mind. "She really likes you." I smile. He nods once. "Thought so." He says. I look at him, studying his face. *But I come up with nothing.*

"In ways, my brother and I are the same. I contain distance from women for similar reasons he does." He says and I frown. *I don´t really know Kai´s reasonings.*

"Look, I don´t have time for any sort of relationship." He says, and I get it he trains a lot and works as much as he´s breathing, but I never thought it wasn´t even an option.

Maybe they aren´t that different in the end.

"That´s a pity." I say. He shrugs and clears his throat. "So go talk. He doesn´t want a relationship, but he clearly wants you." He adds. Finn walks away before I can say anything. *He wants you. We do talk. In his own way. You´re important to him. He clearly wants you.*

I know Andi is Finn´s best friend. And instead of putting in a good word for him, he talks me back to his brother. *Which made me think.* Maybe, he wants me. Maybe, he does me good. Maybe, I am important to him. *Maybe..*

As I open the door, Kai looks at me. I sit down next to him. *Closely*. His gaze pierces me. "I thought you don´t drink?" I ask, amused, and reach for the glass.

But lately he drinks a lot more than nothing.

My fingers touch his. I take a big gulp and lick the juice off my lips. His eyes fix my mouth. His jaw tightens. Our knees touch. His chest rises and falls.

"You can always change your mind." He says, still looking at my lips. He swallows. "Besides, I *always* do what I feel like doing, Scar." His voice sounds a lot like trouble.

"And what do you feel like doing?" I ask. He grins smug. "Getting high." *And we get high.*

Countless headshots later, he takes my hand and leads me up the stairs. He pulls me into his room and shuts the door. He steps in front of me, caging me in. I´m with my back to the door. We breathe in unison. *He wants you.*

"I want you." I tell him. My stomach sinks at the look on his face that tells me he does too. We walk to his bed, and I push him down. I sit on top of him, and he grabs my hips. "I´ve been thinking about you." I say. His eyes pierce me. "When?" He asks, his voice all husky. *All. The. Time.*

"When I´m doing it." I tell him, my head in the clouds. His grip tightens and I rub against him. "*Fuck.*" He moans and grabs my ass to guide me. I can feel him getting hard. His fingers dig into my skin, causing a cry to escape. He digs in, leaving marks. His breathing grows heavy. He stands up with me. We keep eye contact. He slides me down slowly. His hand moves to his belt. I swallow. He undoes it and I reach for his hand and look at him. His jaw tenses. He presses his lips together. I undo the rest of his belt. He looks at me hungrily.

He wants me.

He grabs me and lifts me up. Our gazes are full of lust. I wrap my arms around his neck. He grabs my ass, and I run my hand through his hair and down his neck. His eyes tell me *he wants me*. I pull his hair, whereupon he throws his head back and murmurs. He lets out a pained groan, but *not* from my touch. *He´s frustrated.*

"I *want* to kiss you." He breathes on my mouth.

Almost touching me. Almost kissing me.

Almost.

I feel tingling in my stomach and arousal at the same time. My clit pounds against my jeans. *I bet he feels it too.*

The hard on pressing at me tells me *he wants me.*

But nothing happens. Which tells me *he doesn´t.*

"Why don´t you?" I breathe back. He takes a deep breath. "Because.." He begins and I feel him backing off. "Then I want to *fuck* you." He says coldly and puts me down.

Puts me down.

I stand there. *Not able to move.* He walks over to the punching bag.

Doesn´t want you.

For a moment I don´t know what to say.

"What would be so outlandish about that?" I ask. He holds the bag and turns to me. "Of course, I want to *fuck* you." He raises his voice scowling. "I just don´t want a *meaningless* fuck." He spits and whatever all this was, it snapped. *Cause he just cut it.* Now I know where I´m at. *Not even worth a fuck.* I didn´t even want to go there.

I get all woozy and want to cry. *But I don´t.* I won´t give him that.

"Me neither." Is all I can get out. *Asshole.*

I have to get out of here. I walk out and storm to the front door. Hastily, I dial Andi´s number. He picks up *almost* instantly.

"Can you come get me?" I ask without greeting. "Sure, where are you?" He returns. "Still at Kai´s." I say and we hang up.

Just as I want to open the gate the front door opens behind me. I shut my eyes. "Where are you going?" Kai asks, as if *this* hadn´t just happened. *He can´t be serious. I´m sick of his shit. It´s all just a game for him. Lost boy plays but never loves. Not even able to feel.*

"Away from here.. from you." I say as I type in the code. "I´ll drive you" he says annoyed. *Why´s he annoyed with me?*

"Don´t bother." I wave him off. "Andi´s coming to get me." I say and hurry onto the street. I hear him scoff. "Hoping he´ll fuck you meaningfully?" He provokes. *He wants to hurt me. He doesn´t want me. He wants to play me. Hurt me.*

He made me fall for him to push me like the girl he *"didn´t"* kick out of his car. But I won´t be left bleeding with nothing.

"At least he has the balls to.." I begin but he cuts me off. "To *what*?" He rages. "Nothing." I snap. "*Fuck you.*" I yell and walk faster. I don´t want to feed his ego or games anymore. But I stop and face him. "At least for him Kai.. I am *not* a game." I say and he laughs. "You think you´re no game to him?" He raises his eyebrows. I frown confused. He shakes his head. "You´re nothing." He scoffs. ~~He wants you.~~

You´re nothing.

A tear runs down my lip. *I bite it.*

"You´re a sick fuck." I growl and walk along. But he catches up with me. I fight more tears. *You´re nothing.*

"Don´t go." He says his voice rough. *He can´t be serious. He´s insane.*

I turn and get in his face. "Why should I?" I spit. "Give me one reason!" I yell. "Because I don´t believe you don´t care about me." I say. "I´m not *nothing* to you." I shout all tears gone now. "Just say it. Fucking say something!" I yell.

"You know I *can´t* do any of that" he says. *I was hoping for something else. But there´s no hope for a lost boy. I had to learn it the hard way.*

"I know." I say dryly. Some switch has flipped in me. Maybe the same he used. "But he can," I say resignedly and leave. And he doesn´t follow me.

I wished he would. But he didn´t.

I saw the hurt in his face. It was brief, but it was there and that was enough for me to walk away. *I´m meaningless to him. A game. Nothing. He can´t.* There I have my answer. No matter what he feels for me. It doesn´t matter if he can´t show it.

"I could easily forgive his pride, if he had not mortified mine."

Pride and Prejudice is the first thing that pops into my head as I pace down the street. And the fact that I´m quoting like he does make me even madder.

He resented me once, and he won´t twice.

I run away my anger until Andi´s headlights blind me. I get in and even though I feel like crying, his presence calms me or rather distracts me.

From the lost boy that lost part of me today.

Arriving at his apartment, he offers me his sofa and gives me one of his sweaters. I can´t help but think that Kai wouldn´t have let me sleep on his couch.

Stop thinking about him.

"If you need something you know where to find me." He says and leaves me.

I grab my phone and go onto the terrace and dial Leon´s number.

"What is it?" he asks instead of saying *Hi. That´s so him.*

The music in the background booms through the speaker. "I wanted to ask you something" I say. "Wait" he says. Then he´s silent for a while and goes to a different place because the bass gets quieter until it´s just a low buzzing.

"Shoot" He demands. I know Kai won´t talk to anyone about whatever was between us, so I ask. "If a guy won´t sleep with you, what does that mean?" I hear him laugh. "Either you´re ugly aka not his type *or* he´s serious about you." He tells me. "And for what I can tell you´re not ugly so.." He chuckles. I chew on the inside of my cheeks.

I don´t think any of it would fit. Even if I wished the latter were true.

"I read once that guys only want three things from women *support, loyalty, and sex.*" I tell him and I can hear the smirk as he speaks. "Yeah, something like that." He agrees. "Just don´t make it too easy. Let him hunt his prey." He explains laughing. I roll my eyes.

"You always want what you can´t have" I say more to myself. "It´s supposed to be exciting." He adds. *I say nothing. I don´t think Kai just wants to keep it exciting.*

"Any other questions?" He grins audibly. "No" I must grin. "Then good luck getting that guy laid." He says. "Thanks" I laugh, and we hang up. I´m grateful for his gruff manner. I mean, I´ve always wanted to wait a bit before sleeping with someone. At least when it goes beyond friends with benefits. But Kai doesn´t want anything serious.

Doesn´t he? Doesn´t matter. He can´t. And he won´t either.

For a while I try to imagine that Kai doesn´t want to break anything.

But it doesn't work.

I think of his words. He didn´t deny the playing part. So, he did.

He's cruel. Corrupt.

I go inside and without thinking, I go to Andi´s room.

"Can I come in?" I ask. "Sure" he grins. "I'll get your blanket" he says trying to get up. "No, it´s okay" I start. "Well, if it´s okay with you." I laugh to how pushy that sounded. "No yeah sure" he says. So, I lay under his covers with him. In his arms. And I don´t imagine it´s anyone else. I don´t wonder if *nobody* regrets letting me go. And I don´t ask myself if he´s lying awake thinking about me. *I don't.*

- 27 -

I´ve learned to keep things to myself. Not only because I barely had anyone to share things with but also because some things you should protect and keep. Kai and I were one of those things. *Share your successes but not your plans.* Just like you shouldn´t share your fights with your partner. Not even with your closest friends, because you forget, but they have a negative image that *remains*. Especially since it´s none of other people´s business anyway.

Share the highs not the lows. Otherwise, your people will hate your boyfriend instead of liking him. This is also a reason why I didn´t talk about what happened between us.

What should I tell them? That he plays with me? That we're playing hide and seek? Pushing around but never becoming clear?

However, I don´t want an opinion about that anyway. I want them to know, but I don´t want them to *actually* know. I don´t want to be vulnerable. *Maintain control.* Because control is all I have.

Maybe If I had told them things would have been different. *But I didn't.*

So, things went down the rabbit hole.

51

Andi pushes me against the wall and kisses me gently. And I ignore Kai´s scowls. He has no right to do that anymore. *Never did.*

When my gaze wanders to Kai again, he stands with a girl talking.

Andi excuses himself, so I kinda have to stare at Kai and her. They smile at each other. *Why is he smiling?* He doesn´t smile. *Especially not at girls.* Anger bubbles up, becoming a knot in my throat. How long I waited for him to actually smile at me.

He can´t be serious. He doesn´t like that girl. He doesn´t like any girls.

He takes his phone and hands it to her. He doesn´t smile at girls. *Ever.*

I turn away before he sees me stalking. I go inside to find Andi and the others. They´re gambling, so I sit down on his lap and try not to let on that I´m about to explode. I haven´t seen Kai with any girl. In the beginning maybe but that wasn´t serious. He said it himself he doesn´t date. *Maybe, he just fucks her?* But that thought bothers me too. *Maybe, even more than the smiling.* Aidan is the type who fucks a lot. But Kai has many options but doesn´t seem to care. At least until now.

I still sit on Andi´s lap. But now Kai sits there with her. I don´t look at him.

But I snap out of it. That song played the first time I saw him. *It´s not the pictures that remind you. It´s the music that reminds you.* It brings you back. It makes you feel all you felt back then. Feel the uncertainty I felt back then. The cold gaze he gave me. The chills he gave me. Those black eyes. *Him.*

As I zoom back my eyes wander to Kai who searches my gaze too. *That look.* That´s when I know he remembers too. He *remembered* the song he first saw me. Back then he hated me. When we were strangers. When nothing of it all happened.

But what did happen? I´m not sure of that anymore.

I look away. He does too.

\- 27 -

Andi wanted to drive me home, but to sober up I insisted on walking. *He let me. Someone* would have insisted on driving or walking with me. But we don´t think of that one anymore.

So, I walk. *Alone.*

I´m still pissed off. *For whatever reason.* Well, I *know* why. But we don´t think of that too so. *Whatever.*

My phone rings as I´ve almost made it home. *It´s Finn.* He has never called me let alone texted me outside the group chat.

"Hey" I say unsure. "Hi Scar," he replies. So, everyone calls me that way now.

"Can you come back? Like.. uhm *Now*?" He asks. "Yeah uhm what´s up?" I ask. "Kai.. is drunk and.." He begins, and my heart races. "He wants to see you." He says and I frown. "Did he say that?" I ask skeptically. He breathes. "No.. uhm he won´t talk to me, he´s trashing the kitchen and I thought you could.." He breaks off the sentence.

Glass clinking can be heard in the background. I shut my eyes. "So, you´re coming?" He urges. "*Please.*" He begs and I sigh. "Be right there." I agree and he hangs up.

I probably set a record as I run back to the other end of the village. I´ve forgotten how angry I was with him minutes ago. *Why was he drinking? He never drinks.* Okay lately he *always* drinks. In the beginning he drank barely anything and just smoked lots of Pod. But that has changed.

I ring the bell. The music is still booming loudly. Finn opens the door. Remnants of the party are scattered everywhere. All the reasons I wouldn´t want to have a house party. But I´m sure the Dark´s have a cleaning service anyway.

"Please try to get him up upstairs. In bed or into the shower or something." He says. "I´ll clean up. If you need anything, I´ll be outside." He tells me. I nod and he leaves. I don´t even know why I´m here. If Kai had asked me, I wouldn´t have come. But because I like Finn, I couldn´t refuse. *Okay, I would have come.* I´m still mad and hurt, but I would have come no matter what.

I go into the kitchen and see him sitting on the floor. He´s leaning against the cabinet. His legs bent, and his arms rest on them. I walk towards him. Beside him shards of broken liquor and plates. I kneel down in front of him. In the red, fluorescent light, he looks menacing. *Broken somehow.* Like a fallen angel. His jaw tightens. But he stares right through me.

Like I´m a ghost.

I look at his hands, which are open, bloodied and bruised. *How long was I gone?* A quarter of an hour, maybe. *What happened and who did he hit? Or what? And above all, why? What happened to that girl he flirted with?*

His face looks prettier with all the blood. *Like it belongs to him.*

I reach for his hand. He flinches, as if he had awakened from a dream or fallen out of one. I pull my hand back. He looks at me. His pupils´ large black circles.

He seems toneless as he speaks. "What are you doing here Scar?" I don´t answer but consider how to proceed. No matter what I say, he certainly won´t remember tomorrow, so I don´t even try to argue with him.

"Liia," he slurs my name as I don´t say anything. "I asked you a question." He snaps. I take a breath and look at him. "What is it?" He asks, somehow soft. He runs his hand over his face and through his hair. Ignoring all the blood like he´s used to bleed.

Pan was supposed to heal. But he´s bleeding. No healing.

I get up and walk towards the living room. My plan works because I can hear the crunch of broken glass as he gets up. "Hey," he slurs sourly. I fight a smile and turn to face him. He props himself up against the island and looks at me strained. "Come back." He demands. "Talk to me." He begs with his voice raspy.

I walk to him. His chest falls in relief. He leans on the countertop and grips the edge, so his torn knuckles turn white. He must be dizzy, so I run my hand along the back of his neck to his hairline. His shoulders relax, and he closes his eyes. He straightens up to look at me and I know he´s sorry for what happened the other day.

But he doesn´t apologize.

I see the purple circles around his eye. *He was beaten.*

Even his drunken look makes me faint. Judging by his expression, he feels the same. I swallow the longing and try to support him as he swayed. I lay my arm around his back, and he puts his around my neck. I navigate him up the stairs.

Even though he leans against the wall or sits down a few times, we reach his room after what feels like an eternity. Showering would have been impossible in his condition, which is why I maneuver him to his bed. Besides, I couldn´t stand him naked because I´m still pissed.

He drops onto his bed without letting go of me and pulls me with him. He lets out a tortured grumble like the room is spinning or he´s in pain.

I want to get a bucket or something, but he gives another growl and holds me back. "Don´t. Lia, please." He whines and tries to pull me back. *He said Lia. Twice today. He never says my name. Mostly Scar.* My *new* nickname.

Capitulating, kick off my shoes and try to take off his. Then I get up and close the door. I text Finn that Kai´s in bed. And I´ll help him clean up later when he´s asleep. He texts I don´t need to help.

Kai lies there and watches me. I go to his desk to get the trash can. "Leave that." He grumbles. "I´m not throwing up." He retorts. "And come here now." He demands. So, I leave it and stand in front of him. He grabs my hip and hoists me to him. I make myself comfortable on the headboard, and he pulls himself on my lap. He wraps both arms around my waist, laying his head down. I stroke his hair and the back of his neck. When I stop, he brings my hand back. I have to grin. *He´s cute. Fuck.*

Wasn´t I pissed off?

"Thanks," he says, for more than just today. And if I hadn´t heard him say it a few times, I wouldn´t have understood what he´s muttering.

"Night Sleepin´ Beauty." He mumbles. Not a minute later, his body gets heavier and his breathing lighter. *He sleeps.* He always sleeps so fast next to me. And when he´s not with me, he´s wide awake. Even though I would have liked to ask him what happened, I didn´t. And maybe it´s better not to know. *This tonight was an exception.*

I stayed because of Finn.

As the first rays of sunlight found their way into Kai´s room, I left. And as expected, it was as if nothing had happened, or maybe he didn´t remember I was there at all.

Either way, I decided to forget too.

It´s better this way. We´re just friends helping each other out. *That´s all.*

52

Again, my anxiety creeps up on me. I feel like all eyes are on me, even though I *know* that´s not the case. *Because it´s never the case.* And after all, the tent is filled with hundreds of people who have anything else on their minds but me.

I try to control my breathing. To focus on my friends. And Andi next to me. I turn my ring and let it travel back and forth. I do this whenever my anxiety kicks. In general, my social phobia is weird. It doesn´t always manifest itself and to different degrees. At countless concerts or festivals this year I was good. But every now and then, when I´m casually book shopping, it suddenly kicks in. I feel like I need to cough, run, and have no air. I don´t know what it depends on and why sometimes I have it under control and other times not.

But now is one of those moments when I *can´t* breathe it away. It´s like I´ve fallen over a cliff and there´s no way back. And in those moments, I know I have to go. Run and escape. In my head I search for some excuse to leave. But just then Kai searches my gaze. Somehow, he *always* senses how I´m doing. *Why can´t Andi?*

He nods to me, asking if everything is okay. I don´t know what to answer so, I just shrug and force a smile. Which, *of course*, he doesn´t buy and tilts his head to the side, signaling me to go outside. *I follow him.*

"Worse again?" he asks as we sit down on the ground behind the tent. "Hmm." I nod. "Want me to take you home?" He asks but I shake my head. "I just need some air I think." I say and he nods.

"Fear is not failure. It´s an emotion. You have to feel it. Instead of repressing it. It must be felt in order to pass." He shrugs. "Yeah, I know." I nod. "It´s just hard and sometimes you can´t walk it out." I say. He nods.

"Body scan." He says and I look at him. "Sit with your back to mine." He directs. *Kai Dark wants me to do a mindfulness exercise?* I mean the concert was an extreme situation. He basically had no other choice as to calm me. And at that bar he grounded me too. But *here* I could *easily* leave. *But he wants to help me.*

Even though the thought alone calms me, I sit against him. He sits up straighter to give me support. *Like his presence doesn´t already.*

"Close your eyes." He says in a raspy voice. I do and cross my arms over my knees. "Take a few deep breaths." He tells me. Although I know *how* to do it, I don´t stop him. Especially since his voice is already reassuring me. I feel him breathe in unison with me. "Find a steady rhythm." He says. *We´ve already got that.*

"Perceive the underground." He tells me. But all I perceive is his back against mine. I try to concentrate in earnest. *In vain.*

"Direct your attention to different parts of your body. Notice them consciously." His voice puts me in a meditative state. Which is kind of crazy next to a beer tent. But only those who can meditate anywhere are really meditating. So, I start at my toes and move up to my belly, to my chest, to my fingers and to my head.

We sit there for a while. He doesn´t give instructions any further. So, we just sit and breathe together. In these minutes I feel more grounded and present than anywhere else. Kai calms me in a way that not even I could evoke.

I focus all my attention on him. On his back, his muscles, and the way his body presses against mine. We give each other support.

My fingers *crave* his. I rest my head against his back and place my hand in the grass. He breathes uneven for a moment. His body shifts. I open my eyes, and my breathing quickens as I *feel* him. He places his hand on top of mine. Butterflies explode in my body.

But in the next moment, it´s over. As a ringtone snaps me out of my bliss and Kai´s hand moves away, to rummage in his pants.

"Avery?" he answers. "Where are you? Is Scar with you?" I hear Aiden. "Outside. We´re coming." Kai replies. Then he hangs up. *Silence.*

My perception decenters again, and I notice the loud music.

Kai stands up first and holds his hand to me. *I take it.*

We walk to the others who are already in a mood to leave. Turns out we´ve been sitting there for almost an hour. And the fact that Andi didn´t seem to notice says a lot.

53

The cold air hits me. I should have brought my jacket.

I just stand there and listen to someone´s conversations, considering saying something. But I rather stay silent because I don´t feel much like talking right now.

So, I just listen.

I realized I´ve zoned out a bit. My eyes try to find their focus again. Focusing on Kai who sits across me. He stares back. *Have I zoned out on him?* Great.

He watches me closely. I don´t know where to look.

Should I do something? Say something?

He pinches his eyes. *I look away.*

In my peripheral vision, I see him stand up. I look after him as he walks inside.

"Silence is better than bullshit."

I guess that´s right.

A few minutes later I see him coming towards me. He wordlessly hands me a black hoodie with a white quote on the back.

"Your anxiety is lying to you."

I blink hard at the letters. *My eyes burn.*

I kind of want to cry. I look at him. He plays it off like it´s no big deal. But it is *very* considerate. Not just because he noticed that I´m cold, but that he gave me *this* specific one. I put it over my head, and he sits back down. Not even waiting on me to thank him. I lock eyes with him. He leans back, taking a sip of his cup.

We keep looking at each other.

Over the past week, we´ve sort of managed to get along again. I can´t explain it. I think neither does he. But we do. *Mostly. Get along.*

54

Kai answers the call. "Did you send me that red rose?" I ask. "What rose?" He asks offended. "The one on in front of my steps." I say. "No." he says irritated. *Silence.*

"If I wanted to send you flowers, I wouldn´t have sent you red roses." He retorts. I sigh. "Rose." I say. "It was just one." I correct him. "Whatever." He responds. I inhale annoyed. *Why did I call him? And why the hell did I think he would have sent me one?*

Maybe I wished?

"I wouldn´t buy you a flower." He states. "Of course, you wouldn´t." I scoff.

Silence.

"I would have sent you.. *white ones*." He says his voice clear. *What?*

"I would have bought you a bouquet of white roses." He repeats. My heart stops and my face falls. "And I would have given you them in person." He adds his voice soft. *Silence.*

"So, no I didn´t send you that red rose." He tells me. "Because I wouldn´t." He states. I blink my confusion away. I can´t speak. *Silence.*

"Probably your boyfriend." He states. *Wha..?*

As I don´t say anything he clears his throat. "Well since you have lost your voice I´m gonna hang up now." He informs me. *Silence.*

He waits a sec before he ends the call. *What did just happen?*

55

Why are you here - Machine Gun Kelly

Kai stands at the other end of the room with a girl. I try not to look but can´t help it. I can´t even follow the conversation of the others. The two of them are just talking. And I realize I´m getting jealous. I´s not a girl I´ve seen before, though I don´t know if that makes me feel better or not. Otherwise, it would mean he had a bond with her. And I don´t want him to bond with someone else. *But me.*

When his gaze meets mine, I manage not to look again. Especially since I have no right to feel that way.

Andi dances with me. We kiss and for a moment I can ban the image of them out of my mind. But his gaze often falls over my shoulder.

And after a few songs he finally speaks up. "He´s staring at you." He says scrutinizing my face. Even though I know what he means, I try to hide it. "Who?" I ask. "Kai" he nods in his direction. "He doesn´t." I lie. He lets out a laugh and stops dancing. "He does all the time." He snaps. I say nothing, just inhale annoyed.

"Who´s the girl?" He harps. I cast a glance, as if the image of that girl I with him hadn´t already burned itself into my brain along with all the other girls over the past days. Kai talks to her, but as if he senses my gaze, he looks at me.

"I don´t know. She must have been to one of the parties." I say truthfully. "Probably banging her." I add. Even though the thought makes me want to throw up. *I just don´t want a meaningless fuck.* I remember his words. *And what is that then? He lied. Surprise Peter lied. He doesn´t want a meaningful fuck. What the one-night stands prove.*

When my eyes find their focus again, I have no idea what Andi just said.

"He just doesn´t like you. I mean you two can´t stand each other for whatever reason, and even if he stares at me, he wouldn´t admit it. But apparently, he kind of cares about who dates me." I say and he laughs. "You´re right we´ve never gotten along Scar. But the only question is what his intentions with *you* are?" He says. I frown. "He´s playing you." He tells me. "No one plays someone." I say even though I´m not sure. Ignoring what I just said he glares at him. "Eyes talk Lia." He tells me. "What do you mean?" I ask. He laughs throwing his head back. "He wants you." He says. I shake my head. "Bullshit." I say. He groans. "Come on Lia he was already pissing me off on Ryan´s birthday." He barks.

Why is he mad at me then?

They both maintain eye contact. I can see the anger in his eyes. They despise each other.

"What the fuck was going on, anyways?" I ask, because to this day I have no idea what Kai said to him. Or why they almost came to blows.

"What?" He asks not having paid attention. "Between you two on the party." I clarify. They exchange a look I can´t read. "Not that important." He brushes me off now not only annoyed by him. He lifts his not at all empty beer as an excuse to leave.

What the hell?

Kai leans against the wall and gives me a challenging look. He grins, as if he *knows* we´ve been arguing about him. He smirks. His ego *clearly* needs a sting.

- 27 -

When I step out of the toilet truck, Kai stands a few meters in front of me.

This guy is giving me a hard time.

"Now you´re stalking me?" I scoff. He smiles. "I´m smoking." He holds up his joint. "Back to stoner then?" I comment. "Fighting in love paradise?" he counters. I roll my eyes. "When did you start *fucking* again?" I blurt before I can stop myself. He grins self-satisfied. "I never said I *ever* stopped." He replies even more pleased because now he knows I care. I clench my teeth. *I want to punch him in the face.*

"Jealous Scar?" He nods fighting a smile. I bite my tongue. "You have a boyfriend." He can´t hide his grin. "He´s not my boyfriend.." I begin, but he takes a step towards me towering over me. "I don´t want him to get close to you." He tells me. My chest rises and falls.

"Kai" I warn not meeting his eyes. He comes closer as he speaks into my ear. "I can´t stop thinking about you." He says and I stopped breathing. He flicks the joint stabbing it.

"You turn me on. 24/7." He adds his voice hoarse. My eyes widen and my clit responds to his words. His gaze full of lust. Pain and anger. He says he doesn´t want me *but he looks at me like that? Like he wants me.*

"I don´t care." I lie and press my lips together. His mouth twitches taking me in. "So, you don´t care.. but you do care enough to say you don´t. So, you *do* care." He says grinning.

He´s so convinced of himself.

I shake my head. "You don´t get to decide who comes close to me." I scowl. He glares at me. "Sorry for your dick but you won´t fuck me." I bark even if that´s all I want. “Already do.” He spits. I shake my head. “You´ve had your chance.” I snap. “But you want something *meaningful* right?” I add. His jaw flexes. “What´s her name?” I ask. “Jenny? Laura? Sarah? I´m sure you don´t even know yourself.” I tilt my head. He takes a deep breath. *Right, that pisses you off.*

“Or the other girls the past week? I can´t wait for *them* to fall hard for you. So, push em away, cause you have *no* balls. But *that´s* meaningful right.” I nod and he glares at me.

I ignore the fact that I admitted I fell for him.

“Fuck you.” He barks and I smile. “You´re driving me crazy.” He rages. “You´re so fucking confusing.” He rages. I throw my hands in the air. “Dito,” I yell.

We´re silently looking at each other for a moment.

Suddenly his voice is all rough and low. “I know the others don´t understand us. Our friendship and all..” But I cut him off. “Because all *this* is ambivalent.” I point back and forth. “*Toxic*. And I don´t know if that´s how *friendship* is supposed to be.” I add.

“But I guess we´re not friends. Never really were, right?” I stiff a laugh. “All just games. Nothing. Meaningless.” I go on. He shakes his head. “You´re right we´re not friends.” He spits. “But you know you´re wrong.” He presses. “What?” I ask. He shakes his head. I look at him waiting. *But nothing. Nothing. Of course.*

“What?” he asks reading me. I stiff a laugh. “Nothing.” I nod. He looks at me questioning. “You really *can´t* don´t you?” I shake my head. “Can what?” He rakes. “Admit it.” I yell. “Admit what?” He looks at me strained. *As If he doesn´t know.*

“Nothing just forget it, Kai.” I say. “Why?” He asks. “Because *fuck you* that´s why. I date Andi and you have to stop all this.” I gesture. “All what?” He snaps. I shut my eyes. “Nothing Kai I´m tired of this.” I say beat.

When he doesn´t say anything, I walk past him indifferent.

“I can´t get enough of you. Okay?!” He shouts almost pained. *I stop.*

It sounded more like an accusation rather than a declaration of his feelings. But the way he said it, feels like I´m causing him physical or mental pain. *Am I?* He referred to me as pain in his poet weeks ago. *Maybe I am.* But he pains me too.

I turn to face him, but before I can respond he rushes up to me. “I know you Scar. You think he makes you happy. But you *know* that´s not true. I know you don´t want him. Not as much as you *want* me. I know how you feel. And I know you feel the same way.” He says and I stare at him shocked. He speaks into my hair. “*Lonely even when the room is full.*” He refers to *Lonley by Machine Gun Kelly*. But then he storms past me. Leaving me. *Lonely.*

I know you. And I know you feel the same way. Which way?

He knows how I feel about him. I mean of course he does. But him telling me makes it real. I´m so confused. *Did he admit he feels for me?*

But it felt more like an insult. Which is *exactly* the way he would put it.

56

When I come home after spending the day with Andi, Kai sits on my bed. He stands up as I open the door. "What are you doing here?" I ask. "I had to see you." He says and I sit down. "Okay" I say questioningly. "Okay" he repeats. *He´s nervous.*

"Just thinking about him getting close to you or touching you.." He trails off. "It´s killing me." He admits not meeting my eyes. "Not talking to you like we used to.. Not having you next to me at night.. Not texting you *kills me*. Not spending time with you *kills me*." He looks at me. He´s all vulnerable and *that* kills me. I don´t know what to think. I didn´t expect him to say those things.

Is he trying to apologize? Or confess his feelings?

And even though part of me wished he felt that way, it comes a little too late.

He paces the room. "I´m not the dating or relationship type of guy." He says.

Okay I have no idea where this is going.

"I know. You already said that more than once. And *yet* here you are." I say, and he looks like he realizes the same thing. Like he´s thinking about leaving.

But not this time. Not until I get rid of this.

"I don´t know what this is but I´ve been thinking about what you said at Finn´s birthday." I say but he cuts in. "I didn´t mean it," he says, and I nod. "I know." I stand up. "It wouldn´t be a *meaningless* fuck. But you know *that* right?" I ask. He´s silent telling me it´s true.

"Because that´s *why* you said it." I shrug. "You can´t say something nice, so you say something that hurts." I conclude. *He´s silent.*

"I´ve been so many times at this point. Friendship or more?" I tell him. "I have already lost many people. You *are* important to me. Our friendship. Even though I don´t even know if you see me as one." I say, and he listens. "I met Andi under different circumstances. It was good you rejected me. Especially since you made it clear you weren´t interested anyway." He wants to reply, but I cut him off again. "*The definition of insanity is doing the same thing over and over again and expecting different results*." I quote Albert Einstein.

He´s silent for a few moments.

"Of course, *I care* about you." He tells me. "If I didn´t, I wouldn´t have been protecting you. You wouldn´t have been lying in bed. No girl ever did." He says. "I wouldn´t be *here* right now." He raises his hand to stop me from saying anything. *Even though I didn´t want to.* But he knows I usually trip everyone up.

"I´m having a hard time with *all* this. And you *know* that." He says, and he´s right. "Trusting someone and open up. *I'm trying.*" He gets angrier. "I mean, why else couldn´t I trust *anyone* until now? And why can´t *you* trust since your ex, who happened to be your *best friend*?" He asks. *I say nothing.*

"Because there´s no friendship. You always say it yourself that you have to know each other well enough. Trust each other." He adds. *And yes, I did say that.*

"And Lia, *madness* would be to go against your *own* principles you always preach." He points at me. "It´s not that simple Kai," I say. *But actually, it is.*

"*Nietzsche* once said *not the lack of love, but the lack of friendship, makes unhappy marriages*." He says, and despite being impressed, I must laugh. I don´t know why. I think some switch flipped because all I get is angry. *And why does he keep quoting?* As if he´s too gutless to find his own.

"You throw around words like relationships, love and marriage, but still won´t open up?" I scoff. I mean to see pain in his expression before it becomes a dark wall. "If you think I haven´t opened up to you, then *you're* insane," he snaps.

"Then tell me what you want, Kai." I bark. "Sex? Friendship? Nothing?" I yell, and I know it´s unfair, but I can´t stop myself. "Tell me and I´ll be fine with it." I shout. "Because that´s not fair." I tell him. "I like Andi." I howl. He gapes at me. He wants to say something but doesn´t. Instead, he stays silent and lowers his eyes.

"That´s what I thought." I stiff a laugh. *Cowardly asshole.*

"You know, *trying* is not good enough to reach your goals." I snap. "Take actions or fucking stop." I rage. He looks like he´s about to explode.

"Fuck you, Lia. *Fuck you.*" He spits and shakes his head. "Maybe I`m insane but you're the *fucking* same." He states, and with that he walks away.

"Dead inside."

Says his back. And right now, I feel anything but that. *I feel it all.* The weight of my words. His echo in my thoughts.

Tears well up. Every time I try to push him off me, I hope it doesn´t work.

The question is, does he hope the same when he pushes me?

I spend the next hours trying to make sense of what he´s been telling me. It´s like he´s throwing breadcrumbs, all different kinds. *Nice ones. Venomous ones.*

But there´s no bigger picture, there are just fragments of different paintings. And I can´t figure out what it´s about. *It´s hate and affection. Ambivalent. Toxic.*

The roles have switched. This time she stabbed him. And sometimes a little blood soothes the pain. *But sometimes it boosts it.*

57

Few days later

I´m already in bed when I get a message from Kai.

"Can you come? Please." We haven´t talked much since our argument last weekend. *But he needs me.* And he´s been there for me, too. So, I put my confusion aside and do what feels right.

"I´ll be there in five." I send. I feel sick because I don´t know what´s up with him. I open the gate and there´s Kai sitting on the steps. He has his black sweater on and his hood up. His forearms rest on his thighs. *He always sits like that.*

He looks up at me. His eyes are fiery red. I am stung by his look. Maybe he´s been crying or smoking pot. *Probably both.*

He never cried in front of me. *Why did he cry?*

I sat next to him. I don´t know how long, but he needs me. *So, I´m here.*

When it starts to drizzle. Even when it pours, and it thunders and flashes in the distance.

Nothing smells better than rain on asphalt.

And it´s when I realize he´s right just like no one understands us I don´t understand us either, but I can´t help but wanting to be with him. Or ending up with him. Just as we can bring each other down, we bring each other back up.

He is my storm. My rain. My snow. All in one.

And here on this staircase, I feel like we must go through the natural disasters that we create ourselves to get to Nirvana. We hurt each other to heal. Which is a beautiful and painful truth.

I can´t tell if we end up with each other, or if we just keep destroying until there´s nothing left. But what I know for sure is that we´ll always find your ways to one another.

And that´s enough to stay.

He´s crying. *Because the thing that woke Wendy was Peter sobbing.*

I can see his body shaking. And his attempts to suppress it. I wish he didn´t have the need to do that in front of me.

I lean against him. Whereupon he trembles even more. I wrap my arms around him, and he lays his head on them. *He broken. And he called me. He wanted me.* That I put his broken pieces together. Like he did for me. I don´t know who or what broke him, but I know I can heal at least a bit of it, so I´ll be there for him. I think he knows that too. Like the past weeks have proven, we´ll always come back. If it´s for good or bad. And if that´s all we´re sure about each other, then that´s okay.

At some point he gets up and we go inside. He sits down on the sofa. And I kneel between his legs. His bloodshot eyes search mine. I put my hand to his cheek, and he flinches, as if he hadn´t expected that or my touch has hurt him.

Both hurt me even more.

But whatever it was he pulls me up anyway so I´m sitting on top of him. He puts his hands around me and drags me against him. I wrap my arms around his neck and rest my head on his. We haven´t exchanged a single word since I got here. It doesn´t feel strange, though. *Familiar even.*

He smells like rain again. *But he always does.*

We lie down. He´s lying on my stomach with his arms wrapped around me. I run my fingers through his hair until he falls asleep.

I don´t know what´s wrong with him, but even in his sleep he looks like he´s in a lot of pain and can´t turn off what´s hurting him. I´ve been giving him space. I assumed he wouldn´t want to talk about it. *He just needs me.*

But seeing him like that hurts. He hasn´t said it, but me being here shows it. He can´t show it. Not the way I might like him to, but he opens in *his own way*. Like Finn said. He´s just different.

And we both need to learn to trust. *To let go. To communicate. To love.* If the latter is even an option for that lost boy. But for me, I know it´s inevitable to love him.

Even when he doesn´t tell me what´s wrong, he lets me reassure him. We trust each other. But we are also afraid to trust. When something comes close, we run or push it away.

We are insane. Insanely broken. Insane about each other.

We know it. *We´re the same.* But somehow, we both resist it.

His body rises and falls. He´s deeply asleep. Yet his firm grip does not slacken. I let my eyes wander through the living room. The patter of rain is like therapy. The dogs sleep on the floor. And I spy Kai´s cell phone next to me in the crack of the sofa. I fish it out.

The lock screen is all black with a white quote.

"This moment will never come again."

I don´t know what I had in mind for his wallpaper, but somehow it fits even more than his BMW. *Always in the now than man.*

I don´t plan on snooping, though. That´s a mistake I would never dare to make again. No, I want *something* else.

My gaze falls on the still sleeping Kai. I notice my heartbeat quickening, as if I´m about to go through his phone instead of *lifting* his phone case. I´m afraid he might wake up from my breathing or heart thumping. So, I hold my breath, as if that will make a difference, and turn the polaroid around. My eyes widen. *And my heart stops.*

This is a picture of me. *Why is that a picture of me?*

Rather, it´s a picture of me *and* Kai. We´re sitting outside on the couch and I look at him. He looks in another direction.

I don´t know *when* it´s from or *who* took it. It´s a little blurry, so it could be a screenshot from a video. But one thing is for sure, it was printed.

He printed it. And has it in his sleeve. All this time?

I try hard to think of when I noticed the picture. But I don´t know. Mostly because he´s hardly on his phone anyway. So, I barely see it. *The picknick maybe?*

I can´t make out anything from our clothes either. Especially since we saw each other almost daily. *So, it could have been on any day.*

I study it. The way I look at him. I understand why he likes that one. Kai looks sexy as always. He´s not smiling though. *Co*ld but hot. His cheekbones. His arms. His veins.

Beautiful. And I look good too.

He has a picture of me looking at him.

The way I gaze at him tells *how* I feel about him. *And the fact that he keeps it that close does that too? Doesn´t it?*

My heart slips again, as if I´m sitting on a free fall tower, plummeting into the depths. *Deep abysses.* Abysses filled with black butterflies and rain.

All that he makes me feel.

I don´t know how long I look at the photo. But at some point, I took a picture and squeezed his phone back where I found it. I won´t miss the opportunity to take a picture of him too. With his arms wrapped around me.

I look at the pic on my cell. Then I go through my gallery looking at all the pictures I secretly took of him. And the ones of our group.

I know something connects us. *I feel it.* And I know he feels it too, or I wouldn´t be here right now. Or he wouldn´t have *that* picture in his sleeve. Or wrapped his arms around me. Or not wanting me to get closer to Andi.

And that´s when I´m struck by the realization. *Kai is into me. He must be.*

And maybe he´s been even longer into me than I would have thought. Because I just found the proof of it. The proof that he does care. *He does want me.*

I know for sure now. But he didn´t say it yet. *Well not exactly.*

He said other things that may be a hint. *In his own way.*

Maybe he will say it. Maybe, he wanted to tell me the other day.

And I turned him down.

Maybe, it is how he said. You must get to know each other first. But that´s what I´ve told, but somehow, I forgot. But maybe that´s what he wants, to get to know me.

He said he misses me. He misses spending time with me.

He wants me. Kai is into me.

[NOTEBOOK ENTRIES]

We got close. I felt her throbbing. ~~I wanted to kiss her. Fuck her. Claim her.~~ But I knew there was no going back. Feelings ruin people. And I was already ruined before. I just couldn´t. ~~Even if it was all I wanted.~~ I told her she´s meaningless. ~~She´s anything but that.~~ I know I hurt her. Besides, she´s with Andi. I wanted to explain. But she´s right. He´s better for her. I would ruin her. ~~And she would ruin me.~~ I told her she´s a game. ~~But she´s anything but that.~~ I don´t want her. I hate her. ~~Fuck I don´t.~~ She´s nothing like me. And I didn´t lie awake at night thinking of her in his arms. I fucked the girl after she left with him. ~~I did think of her to get off.~~ I felt sick thinking that son of a bitch will take her. So, I threw up. I don´t know why I´m so overprotective. Why I even care that much. ~~I hate her.~~ Don´t I? I picked up a fight with some dude. It was an unspoken agreement. I wanted to feel something. To suffer. I wanted pain, it to stop. I lost control. ~~A year ago, I was worse. It´s a wonder I´m still breathing. But I barely survived.~~ ~~She was the one thing I couldn´t control.~~ I did everything to keep the upper hand. I needed a valve. I found one. Alcohol. I slept worse without her. But I was used to that. Finn told me to act on it or leave her alone. Because his best friend is starting something with her. But I´m his brother for fucks´s sake. Why did he switch up on me? I told him I already fucked up and that I don´t want her. He didn´t buy shit but I can do without the advice of my brother. He has no idea anyway. He doesn´t even know that Luca wants to fuck him. Any dumbass could see that. So, where the hell does he get off giving me advice on women? He doesn´t know her. ~~Not how I got to know her.~~ I have made a mess. I was mostly angry at myself. I couldn´t admit why. He called her. Because he can´t fucking handle me. Never did. At least not until Pan became a teen. But Peter didn´t grow up. He stayed the same. And in ways he got worse than a broken kid. Because a lost child loves the whispers of devils. As a child you need anyone to care. And for me, it was the demons. But then she was there when I felt nothing. When I listened to the hellbent. Like an angel she was there. But no angel exists in hell. Only fallen ones. But she was still pissed. So was I but I was too exhausted to fight. I liked the idea of an angel walking through hell for me. I didn't let her go. She didn't argue. I just wanted sleep. And forget for a night, I fucked up. That I'm a monster of my own nightmares. I wanted to have her before I'll lose her again. Before I burn her with my sins. And when I woke, she was gone. Like a dream. Never happened. Never really yours to keep. Not for longer than it lasts. Before her, all I had were nightmares. And I thought they were real. And some say they were.

The whole evening, I knew that she wasn't doing well. I bet she would have preferred to stay home. And that asshole didn't give a damn. I notice everything about her. I was on the verge of grabbing her and driving her fucking home. I took her outside and helped her relax. I was hoping, she wouldn't want to go back in. But when I reached for her hand, Avery called.

I had a hoodie that was made for her. But I never dared to give it to her. But today she was freezing and Andi didn't gave her his jacket. So, I handed it to her. She liked it. But then she left with him.

Andi knew I was right. She didn't want him. She's into me. He doesn't have a chance. But he started a game I mastered, played through and beyond. *They argued about me. He was pissed cause he couldn't fuck with me. They never can.* ~~*There's just Hook who stabs, Pan.*~~ *But she plays with my mind without even knowing. I kept dating those girls to show him I don't care. And to numb her.* ~~*To numb that part of me that does care.*~~ *She was pissed off. Just how I wanted her. She's hot when she's angry. It turns me on. I have her rather mad at me than indifferent. I wanted her to yell at me. That she'd go as crazy as I was over her. But I said some things I shouldn't have. And she wanted me to give it out. My feelings. But every time she pushes, I shut down. But no matter what I tell her, it's not enough. I told her* ~~*I feel the same about her*~~*. What am I doing? She's dating another guy.*

I told her that I care. I wanted to explain. But she friend zoned me. It's like she didn't let anything I said, get to her. I even told her about my trust issues. But she shut me down. I tried to tell her I wanted to be good enough for her. But apparently that's not what she wants. ~~*I never tried for any girl.*~~ *I made a fool of myself. She gave shit about what I had to say. Shit about me. I opened up for fucks's sake. And she kicked me in the balls. I'll never do that again. I hope he breaks her heart. Cause she fucking spit on mine. And if he won't break her I fucking will.*

I can't sleep anymore. Not that I did before. ~~*I miss her next to me. Miss holding her. Talking to her like we used to.*~~ ~~*No day has passed without thinking of her. I can't bare*~~

~~how I feel about her.~~ I drown my thoughts. But it doesn´t help. I´m a mess. She made me.

I couldn´t stop myself. I needed to see her. I needed her. I knew she would come. I hoped she would. And she did. Cause she does care. And fuck I care about her. She sat with me for hours. I started crying. Tears I haven´t shed in years. There were only few that saw Pan cry. They think he can´t. That his body has no tears. But all he has is tears. But they are black and bloody. She made me feel okay. ~~She let me cry not knowing it´s about her. It´s all about her.~~ I never cried over a girl. I fell asleep in her arms. ~~I dreamed about her.~~ And that night. I just knew. I´m fucked. ~~I´m into her.~~ I knew.

58

Few days later, Kai

Since that night. I can´t get her out of my head. No matter how many times, I pound my fists in my punching bag. Beat my knuckles bloody. I cut myself. No feeling is stronger to resound over the existing one. *The feeling for her.*

No matter how loud the music thunders into my skull or the bass flows through my body. Joints I smoke and puffs I take from the bottle. I can´t get her out of my head. Her and Andi´s fucking hands on her.

As someone who has never thought about anything but themselves, it sucks to share those thoughts. *Especially with her.*

But I´m possessed. *I´m sane.* It makes me sick. *It´s exhausting.*

I´m smiling when I think about her. I think about her when I smile. I lost control.

Her fucking green grayish eyes won´t leave my thoughts. They haunt me, farther than I´d like. How they seem green when her eyes are red from crying. And gray when she´s angry. They look blue when it rains. The mirror of her soul. As if I could see how she´s doing by the color. As if she had a mood ring but in her eyes.

I knew she was going to be a problem the moment I saw her, and my dick twitched at the sight of her lips. I just didn´t know the *extent* it would all take. And it has become more than just a problem. *This is no game. This is not nothing.*

But not enough that she has control over my thoughts, she also has my dick. I can´t jerk off on *anything* but her. I don´t even know how many women I´ve had around my cock the last days, but no pussy, mouth or deep throat could suck the thoughts of her out. I haven´t even touched her but she´s in my bones. She´s in my scull like a bullet. And I don´t want it to move.

It´s addicting. A drug implanted. I´ve never had anything like that. I don´t understand how *anyone* can like this feeling. Because I hate it. I don´t want it. I don´t want to be dependent on anyone. Especially when it comes to my orgasms. But I could get hard just by seeing her.

But what is worse than all that is the feeling I had before, during and after I hooked up with those girls. Everything in me resisted, as if I had to be faithful to her or some shit. *It made me sick.* Like I could throw up. *Well, I did. Every time.* Just at the thought of hurting her. *I mean, what the hell?* She's not my girlfriend or anything. *She's nothing.* Just a template to jerk off to. *Bile rises*. I'm sick of myself. I'm full of shit. And while I feel like this, she probably fucks him. Without any problems.

No guilt. No vomit. Nothing. Why can't I?

She should never have become part of us. I knew she would mess everything up. I just never thought it would include me. *Or my dick.* But she's different. Even if I didn't want to believe it. *She proved it.* ~~*And let me fall.*~~

The feeling that has been trying to surface only makes me angrier. It didn't come gradually, but I wasn't getting it intravenous either. It was just there before I could notice.

Before I could stop it.

She is part of my system. Like a virus, she infected me. Like brainwashing, she has twisted my mind. Like the flames of a fire, she has burned into my skin. Like ink, she is under my skin. *Permanent.* Like weed, she makes me high. Like rain, she pours me down. Like darkness, she engulfs me. Like a cartridge she sticks in me. Like a wound she makes me bleed. Like pain, she feeds me. Like the devil she tricks me.

And I play cards with death. Because I let her take me. *Completely.*

She has me in the palm of her hand. Me and my cock.

She takes my breath away. She sucks me dry.

I'm into her. I hear a voice saying. *No. No.* I'm not. *Fuck no.*

I don't even know her at all. *I don't want to know her.* I sure as hell don't want to think about that she smells like white roses and hot summer rain.

A white rose means silence. *That's her. Silence. Beautiful. A white rose.*

What the hell?

I reach into my jeans. I need distraction. *Now.*

Raindrops bead off my display. I wipe it with my hoodie.

I catch me grinning as I stare at the screen. "*Ash blonde.*" That's how I saved her. I should re-save her. *Should I?*

Sleepin' Beauty, I type and delete it giving me an inner slap. *Scar* I use instead. I switch between apps and end up on her profile picture. *Fuck.*

I put my phone in my pocket, annoyed with myself.

Something is growing inside me. Every time she´s with me. And when she´s not. She haunts me. And the worst thing is *I like it.* Which I fight against. *Hard.*

- 27 -

By now it´s after three in the morning and I find myself on the street of the girl I´ve been trying to forget for hours. *Months to be exact.*

I should turn around. I should leave. I shouldn´t stand in front of her fence. I shouldn´t stare at her window. I shouldn´t imagine what she´s wearing.

If she wears my hoodie? The one I gave her?

Is she alone? Is she even here? Is she´s still awake? Does she think of me?

I should go. I should leave. I should forget about her. *I should.. Fuck it.*

My next move I blame on the weed.

I push open the gate and do *anything* but forget about her.

That day he gave in. He accepted that he wanted her. That he´s into her. That he feels for her. He couldn´t stay away. *So, he didn´t.*

59

Lia

I startle as the lights go on and almost scream as I see someone standing next to my bed. *It´s Kai.* Drunk. Or stoned. Or both. *Again.* This is getting out of hand.

"What the hell, Kai?" I yell-whisper. "Are you crazy? I almost pissed myself." I say breathless. "Sorry Scar." He grins before it turns into an awkward smile.

"What are you doing here?" I ask. Without answering, he kicks off his shoes and lies down next to me. *How did he even come in? How did he the last time?*

And why the heck didn´t I question it then?

For a moment, he´s silent, as if he himself has no idea why he´s here. *I think it´s always that way.* He just doesn´t think about it. *Like on autopilot.*

"I couldn´t sleep." He says, lost in thought, staring at the ceiling. He uses that as an excuse a lot. But I think it´s more than that. *He likes me. He´s into me.*

But he has to say it.

He puts his hands behind his head, and I eye him. No matter how much we bump heads, he always comes back. *And I to him.*

He says nothing. *So, neither do I.*

When a low thunder sounds from my direction, he looks at me confused. *Shit.* I still have my sleeping noise on. I quickly closed it.

"What was that?" He asks. "Thunderstorm," I say, hoping he´ll let go of it. "Thunderstorm?" He repeats, raising an eyebrow in amusement. "I listen to that to fall asleep." I say and he grins. I threw a pillow at him. "Don`t judge. I need that. I love rain, as you should know by now." I told him. "And hairdryer." I add, and he laughs. "Or dryer noises. White noise." I go on, embarrassed but laughing too. "It´s good for anxiety. You should try that instead of coming over." I say sarcastically because I like him coming over.

For a few minutes we just lie there. He´s staring into space and I at him.

"Tell me something. About yourself. Something.. *painful.*" He says. *I ponder.* More about what it means that he´s asking me something like that, than about what I could say.

Something painful. I repeat his words.

I say the first thing that comes to mind. "I used to get bullied in school because of my body." I say. "They said I was too skinny. Anorexic they called me." I chuckled sadly. He blinks his eyes on my wall. "I was hurt. Being called out on my weight by strangers and friends. Skinny shaming is just as bad. Just not perceived as that by society." I say. He nods. "Kids are the worst." He sighs.

"So that´s something painful." I say. *He´s silent.*

"Now´s your turn." I look at him. "Tell me something painful." I demand. "I need to think about that." He says to get off-topic.

Minutes pass. *But he knows I wait.*

"Tell me about yourself. Like what you want to do in the future." He says instead of what I asked for. "Like a bucket list?" I ask. He shrugs and nods.

I like that he asked me that.

"Going out to dinner alone. Going to an art museum. Going to the movies alone. Going to Paris alone. Emigrating, scuba diving, kickboxing, lying on a soccer field looking at the stars. Lying in the rain or dancing." I told him. I go down my list and realize I already experienced one or two things with him.

"Where?" he asks. "Where what?" I echo. "Emigrate," he clarifies. "I want to go to Bali." I say. "I didn´t think you were the emigrating type" he says, eyeing me as if he could read my intentions. "I never thought of myself either, but I want to do this. I´m up for meditating, diving, doing workshops and all. Just being on my own and overcoming my fears." I shrug. He grins. "What?" I ask. "Bali´s on my list, too." He says. "For similar reasons as you. But also, self-discovery, culture, photography, writing, surfing, and touring on a scooter. Maybe build something there. Business wise." He tells me, and I watch him. And see enthusiasm in his black eyes.

A burning that makes my heartbeat faster.

“What else is on your bucket list?” I ask him, wanting to hear more before he pulls back up the wall, he has so often around him. “Swimming with sharks. Swimming by a waterfall. Festivals. Starting a business. Flying a plane. Having a threesome. Becoming a father. Buying a one-way ticket. Skydiving. Writing a book. Traveling. Sex on the beach..” He tells me, and I hang on his lips with every word.

We talk like that for hours. Finally talking about all the things in person we texted about months ago.

- 27 -

“If money was no object, what job would you have?” I asked him. He runs a hand through his hair thinking. “Photographer, I guess or.. an Author.” He shrugs. “With you?” He looks to the side. “Artist.” I respond. The brief twitch of his mouth, doesn´t escape me like he knew I would say that.

“And why don´t you?” I asked him. “Hmh?” He hums. “Do it I mean.” I say. “Why don´t *you*?” He throws the question back. *He often does that.* Something I grew to love.

“Because I´m realistic. And I´m becoming an art teacher so..” Now I´m the one who shrugs. “Good point.” He says. “But you should work on your dream.” He adds and I nod.

“So why don´t you?” I ask again. He inhales annoyed. “Because.. I must work for my parents´ company.” He says. I frown. *He must?*

“But Finn already does, isn´t it more important to be fulfilled?” I ask. He stiffs a laugh looking at the ceiling. “If I had a choice,” he says, and I know him well enough that that´s the end of the topic. “You *always* have a choice.” I point out.

I don´t know how much time has passed until he speaks up again.

“I hate my parents.” He admits. *Silence.*

He hates his parents. I mean it kind of make sense *but hate?* I haven´t seen them once. Leon and Aidan´s parents I know, but his.. *I don´t even know what they look like.* There are no pictures. *Maybe Kai took em off?*

The whole house doesn´t look like a home. It´s cold and sterile and minimalistic. Only Kai´s room is lively, with pictures on the walls. It´s dark and elegant, but it´s him. I have never been to Finns room. *Probably never will.* But in my imagination there´s just a desk. More than work he doesn´t seem to need. *And basketball.*

I always thought they were just working a lot. I never thought about it. He´s always short-tempered when I ask about them. He never talks about them.

I don´t know if I should say anything. *Do I want to know?*

And would he even tell me?

I decided against it.

"My childhood never sucked. But I can barely remember anything." I say. "My childhood sucked. And I can remember *everything*." He says in return and it´s like I can feel his pain. "Memory loss is a sign of trauma." I say into the void. "We all have no matter how good or bad our childhood was." He opines nodding. "They say that suppressing emotions can lead to memory loss." I add. "That explains a lot." He responds.

Yes, it does.

More moments of silence pass.

"I hate my mom," I confess, and he looks at me. Astonished, like he didn´t expect something like that coming from me. I give him the, *you hate your parents too* look, but he looks back at the ceiling knowing, *I´m right*. I mean not hate, hate but you know, it´s complicated. Having a broken relationship and stuff.

"Sometimes it feels like my parents are dead." He says and I hold my breath.

Like Pans.

"As rarely as I see them, it doesn´t make any difference. They were never there. They didn´t raise me. My brother did." He adds. So, it has always been like that. My chest hurts.

Finn raised him. I can imagine. But Finn was a teen himself. And before that a kid. No kid or teen should have to raise his sibling. But I guess, he had no other option.

"At least *you* have parents who care." He whispers. And I shut my eyes, but the pain won´t go away. But yes, he is right. And I am grateful.

We´re silent for a moment.

"Sometimes it feels like my mother had died." I hear myself say and as soon as I say it, I´m shocked. Hot tears shot down my cheeks. *I said it.* And I´ll go to hell for it.

Maybe I will.

He looks at me in shock. I have never told this to *any* of my friends. That´s why I´m often with them instead of home. Because home is no longer what it honestly *never* was.

"My mom almost died a year ago." I told him. "She was in an induced coma and had a life-threatening brain hemorrhage. Now she´s back, but she´s not my mom." I must control my breathing. "Honestly she never was." I say. "She hasn´t been the same for a long time. I´m more of a parent than my mother is. She´s handicapped. She can´t drive. Can´t cook. I must clean the house." I stop. "From one to the next moment I had to grow up." Tears burn my eyes.

Pan had a choice to not grow up. She hadn´t she was forced.

But in ways he was too. *Forced.*

"I didn´t want to." I say. "I wasn´t ready." I sob. He looks at me and I know what he thinks. *Like Peter, I didn´t want to grow up. Like himself.*

"She has depression. And it´s unimaginable how she feels. But I have feelings too." I say. "And I don´t resent her for that.. *no*. Sometimes I wish that were the reason but it isn´t." I told him. "It happened years before. And now the opportunity to make it up.. to become clear.. All that was taken away from me. And I must go on with that anger. With that broken thing that probably won´t be fixed." I nod biting my trembling lip. "Because who would I be if I blamed her in that condition for things that have hurt me in the past?" I shrug. "For things that weren´t bad in her eyes. But the worst in mine." I choak.

"And that´s unfair." I shake my head. "Because life always takes what you want the most." I say. "Because you wanted it too much." I nod and I blink to focus. "I don´t want to be at home. I never wanted that. Back then with my ex.. I was *always* with him. I didn´t want to be home even when she was healthy. And now I want to escape even more." I told him. "Because for me home was never a place it was *always* a person. Maybe not the greatest love. But my first." I say. "And ever since he abandoned me, it feels like I´m homeless. Like I don´t even know who I am without him. I´m still looking for myself." I gasped. "*Home..*" I trail off.

"We didn´t always have such a broken relationship. At some point it was just there." I shrug and bite my cheeks. "On my part." I say. "She broke a lot of my friendships and relationships as I told you.. if you remember." I say but he cuts in. "I *do* remember." And he says it as if he´d never forget anything I say. And something tells me he doesn´t.

Forget what I say.

"There´s just a resentment I can´t forget. That I hold onto because I have no idea how to get rid of it. Without telling her." I nod. "How to do it on my own." I add. "And I don´t let people in. I don´t let my family in. I don´t have friends. And I´m constantly between not being completely excluded and not being seen. I open to feel less lonely but close up to hide.. *to feel safe*. It´s hard to let people in." I cry. And he wraps his arms around me and lets me cry until I`m empty.

"You will heal." He tells me in a hush. "You can still fix it." He adds. "I can´t. My parents aren´t around like yours." He says. "It is okay how you feel." He assures me. "It takes time. Take it." He tells me and I nod.

"I`m loyal to the ones I love. But my family is not my home." As awful as that may sound, that´s how I feel. He nods before he speaks. "Home is my friends. *Neverland.* Hook and the lost boys. The Avery´s. And my brother." I look at him. "But not my parents." He confesses. *And it turns out he's not the only lost one. I am too. A lost girl. And Pan took me to Neverland where I was okay for not having the parents I wanted. Where I was okay. And not at all lost. Where I was at home.* And right now, I never want to grow up. To stay where we're both home and never land. *Never.*

Maybe I need that hurt. To have something. Like he holds onto the hate he has. The only thing left. Until we're ready to heal. To forgive. To move on. Or to finally grow up.

"They are more than neighbors or friends they are family." He says. "I've felt more at home with *you* guys than anywhere else." I whisper. He swallows.

"*You* feel like home too." He says barely audibly into my hair, making me cry even harder. My chest tightens with pain and joy at the same time. He draws me into his arms, and I lie on top of him. He holds me and kisses my hair. *You feel like home, too.*

He came through her window and took her with him.

Because Pan only chose lost girls. And she was as lost as Pan was.

60

Since Kai came over the other day, we're closer. *That* brought us closer. It was the second time he held me while I was crying. *Like I held him.*

And it changed something. *Maybe everything.*

- 27 -

I woke up confused. I've must have fallen asleep on the couch.

Why didn't anyone wake me?

I haven't taken off my makeup. So, I went upstairs to the bathroom. But as I wash my face. I startle and bump my face on the faucet.

Screams and pounding come from the hallway.

I turn it off and wipe my face with the towel and step into the hallway. The sounds come from Kai's room. I open the door and see him tangled in his bedding. He's rolling around in panic and clinging to the sheet. *He looks in pain.* Like his dream hurts him physically.

His fists grip the blanket. *He's still asleep.*

I think he's having a nightmare. He lets out a few agonized whimpers. And I kneel beside him. His face is drenched in sweat. His hair sticking to his forehead. I don't know what's worse, waking someone or letting them continue to suffer.

I take his face in my hands and his body shoots up with a scream. *I rare back.* He tears his eyes open, breathes uncontrollably and looks around in panic. For a moment he´s completely disoriented. Like he first woke up to this world. *Like he was in another.*

He looks like a child. *Scared. Lost.* I´ve seen him hurt before, but *this* is a different kind of pain. I reach for his cheeks, trying to bring him back to reality. His eyes shot to mine. His pupils are huge. He looks like a broken devil. Menacingly scary but only hurt. He just looks at me. I ran my fingers over his face. He lets me as he slowly finds his breathing again. He trembles and eventually drops his head against me. He wraps his arms around my body, realizing he isn´t dreaming anymore. His wet hands clasp me. I held his head and ran my hand through his hair. The way he holds on to me makes something die in me. I don´t ask him what he dreamed about. I only caress him.

He falls asleep leaning on me.

When my legs and feet start to tingle from kneeling, I lie back with him still on top of me. This was not a normal nightmare. This was horror. *Torture. Terror. Pain. Hurt.*

A lost child.

- 27 -

When I wake up, we´re no longer tangled. One of us must have moved. We still lie with our heads at the foot of the bed, but next to each other. He lies on his back and his one arm under me.

I look at him. His hair is disheveled and somewhat greasy from sweat. His chest rises slightly. His palms have bloody marks from his nails.

His boxer hangs far down. I can see his hip bone and more. *His V.* And cuts. *Cuts.*

They are no longer fresh. The red is dried. Some deep white faded lines catch my eye. Goose bumps ran through me. *No. Please don´t.*

I take a closer look. And I noticed the scars on his body. *He cuts himself.*

Once again, a shiver runs down my spine. *This does not feel real.*

I might get sick. *I feel dizzy.*

I mean I did that too. Or still do now and then. But only when it gets worse. But seeing that he does that makes my stomach hurt. *My chest hurts. My eyeballs burn.*

I´ve seen his cuts before. *He always has some.* Injuries, bruises, and cuts from kick-boxing and beating. I think I just got used to it. *I got used to it.*

He gets into fights all the time. *That´s how he is.* His hands are open most of the time. *I didn´t question it.* Like everyone.

I feel bad. Disgusted by myself. *How could I not see?* I did see but didn´t. Probably because unlike others he doesn´t bother to hide his wounds. Everyone knows he´s the one on parties, who picks up a fight and gets into trouble. *He's fearless.* Rather careless on getting hurt. He smashes liquor. Punches walls and jaws. He does that. But I think I didn't notice because the scars and wounds from fighting are *somehow* justified. But *those* on his hip aren't. He did it on purpose. With a blade or a knife. *It hurts me.* I want to scream and cry. *I hurt for him.* Even if I don't know for what. I want to help him. *Understand him.* I want to take the darkness away. But deep down I know well enough that that's not my job and not in my might. It's not my burden to take and not my responsibility. *Not my business.* Not my war he's fighting. You must accept that you can't heal others. They need to do it on their own. But my stupid selfish self would love the idea of healing him. *To be his cure.* Or rather my toxic self wants that.

Apparently, he caught me staring. "Don't even start." He snaps and I flinch. "I've seen your scars too." He says sharply and I look at him. "I'm not judging." I say. "I know I'm not innocent. That doesn't make it any less painful." I told him.

"Why do you do it?" I ask. He laughs. "Why you?" He shoots back. *Touché.*

Why do I do it?

"To control something." I say. "When it gets bad, and I don't have an outlet. Because I don't know any other way." I shrug. "And because I like it. To see blood. It feels good. It numbs my brain." I say.

"See?" He says confidently. "No difference." He shrugs. "The only difference is that you care about me more than you care about yourself. That's why you think it's worse when I do it." He tells me and he has a point.

"The only time pain feels good is when it's caused by yourself." He says. "Pain numbs pain." He says and the fact that I can relate to this is sad.

"It's constantly the battle of you against you every fucking day. And the question is which version wins?" He asks as he stares at the ceiling.

"You have no idea of the pain that runs through my system. I'm fucked up in so many ways Lia. But I'm okay." He says as he looks at me.

I'm okay is a way of saying I'm not.

But I nodded, not knowing what to say.

"Thanks for.. coming up tonight." He says hesitantly. We locked eyes and he drags me towards him. *I let him.*

And since then, she started sleeping regularly at his again. She knew he slept better, and she did too.

61

Halloween

Colson Herzog

I wear a black corset with lace and skinny jeans. I smeared black eye shadow, and lipstick. Fake blood runs down on my neck. And there´s a handprint on my arm. My murder weapon a baseball bat, which is also drained with blood.

The windows are fogged up, but I can see red LED light and silhouettes. There are fan heaters on the terrace which makes it pleasantly warm. I spot girls sitting in the hot tub.

Panic Room by Au/Ra blares through the speakers.

My gaze meets Kai´s as he approaches me. He hides his grin by sipping from his drink. When he stands in front of me, he can´t hide it anymore. *It suits him.*

As much as his frowns.

His face looks even more striking in the red light. He wears black Jeans and a matching hoodie. His hair is messier than usual, and he has blood on his face and hands. Around his upper body he has an Ak-74 in black. *He looks hot.*

He eyes me. "*Fuck*" he says wordless and presses his lips to a thin line. The energy between us is undeniable. "You look.." he starts, but I wrap my arms around his neck. Because I was nervous about the way he looked at me.

Touching him overwhelmed me. His body tenses for a second. But then returns my embrace and pulls me in. I don´t know if we´ve hugged before. I think this is the first time. I had the urge to be closer. *I always have that.* But now I gave in.

His smell intoxicates me. *He breathes me in.*

"Stunning." He finishes by my ear. The hug is not long but intimate. *It´s firm.*

"I guess we´re both killers?" I ask as we break away. He immediately puts his hand in his pocket, and I smirk as I notice but look away.

"Looks like it." He says but avoids my gaze. *Blushing.*

"Take a picture of us." He tells a guy and hands him his cell. We stand close. He takes a picture and leaves after they fist bump.

I look around. "Where are the others?" I ask. *No answer.*

When I look at him, he shrugs and turns away suddenly.

"I´ll take a look" I say, but he already joined another conversation.

Sometimes he´s weird. Like there are two versions of him.

For a moment I stared at his back.

"When god sends me to hell, I want the devil to hesitate."

I must grin. *I bet you do.*

The living room is lit with red LED lights. There are creepy decorations everywhere, from spider webs, to skulls, to masks from horror movies, fake knives, and weapons. The house is crowded today. I don´t know what is going on, but there are a lot more people than usual. *Are those people invited?* I laugh to myself.

I spotted Nina and the others. She has dressed up as a dead bride and Leon the counterpart in a suit. Aidan wears the robe from *Money Heist*.

I hugged her. "You look so hot." She smiles. "You too" I grin.

"Very creative." I tease Aidan. He holds his HK MP5 in my direction. "Watch your mouth." He warns us and we laugh.

"And.. *what* are you?" He asks checking me out. "A killer" I say, but I flinch as someone grabs me by the hips. I turn. *It´s Andi.*

Disappointment washes over me. It´s not Kai. *Of course, it´s not.* He wouldn´t touch me like that in front of them.

"Hey," I say with a forced smile. He hugs me. *It doesn´t overwhelm me.*

"Hey, love." He hushes and kisses me on the cheek.

- 27 -

Kai appears next to me. I haven´t seen him for a while.

"Want something to drink?" He asks, nodding toward the kitchen. I follow him. We stand with our backs to the living room. We stare at the spirits and juices. But neither of us does anything. Nor say anything. Somehow it´s weird. Because we´re so intimate and close. But not when everyone is around. We´re not dating but staying over all the time. And I have no idea what to feel anymorc. *What is this? What are we?*

Am I still dating Andi?

I guess, I do. *But what am I doing with Kai then? What does he want?*

Why can´t we just talk about it? What holds us back?

I don´t really want to drink anything. My cup is still full. But we continued to stare at the bottles. "Want me to mix you something?" He breaks the situation. "Hmh," I murmur in agreement. He grabs some of the liquors and with the things he has chosen, it can´t taste good at all. I think he doesn´t even pay attention to what he´s doing.

He hands me the cup without looking at me. We both stare at our hands touching. Which is *very* overwhelming.

I bring the cup to my lips, and his gaze follows. It burns disgustingly and I clear my throat. *It tastes like acid.* But I take deep draughts trying to drown the confusion.

He steps closer but takes it and just looks at me. *I think he wanted to kiss me.*

Instead, he drinks the rest. *Silence.*

"We should get back to the others." I say and he nods. But neither of us moves.

Why don´t we?

Suddenly everything goes dark. Girl´s shriek. Guys howl. I reached out to Kai and touched his chest. And he grasps my hip. *Power failure?*

Even though I can´t see anything, I feel him so close to me. I know he´s looking at me. I feel his breath on my face. His chest rises and falls, and my breathing quickens. And for a moment I wish the light would never come back on. But some phone screens and flashlights come on. We still stand rooted to the spot.

"Kai?" Finn calls across the room. "I´ll take care of it." He calls back. He digs his fingers into my skin and pulls me toward him. My heart sinks and butterfly´s swarm. My hands find his sides, but he lets go of me and leaves. The spot burns with pain. I can still feel his hand on me. My body´s on edge.

The lights are still off as Aidan speaks up on a speaker. "It´s almost midnight. And we have a new game from one of your members." He says. "Let´s play hide and seek." He howls. Girls cheer and the guy´s grunt.

"There are the ones who hide. And the ones who hunt." He goes on and someone lights him with a flashlight. "If you have been caught. You mess around." He adds with a grin. "When you hear the blast. The seekers go on to the street. The hiders will have 15 minutes." He says. "You can hide inside and outside at the Dark´s and the Avery´s house. There will be a countdown." He explains. "Then the blast will go off again. And we will come for you." He says smiling.

"What?" I whisper to myself. But the red lights came back on, and I spotted the boys. They´re now wearing masks and hand more to other seekers.

I lock eyes with Kai, who already stares at me. He takes his phone out and types. I look at my screen, waiting for his message.

"You always wanted to follow the call of the void, right Scar?"

He remembered. I told him I loved to experience such a vibe in real life. My eyes shot back up to him. He just stares at me. My heart races. He wants to hunt me. And I want him to chase me.

The seekers have formed themselves and head outside. Girl´s giggle. Some shriek. Some start to hide. The countdown on the TV is red. I stare at it for a moment. I try to think of a hiding place. Now I get *why* there are so many people here and why the Avery´s are out of town this weekend. *Because of the game.*

We´ve played some games the past months, but this one excites me the most.

This is my game. And it depends on me staying on Neverland.

Nina told me they used to play more games and sicker stuff but that was back when they were teens. A lot of shit happened over the years, and they got older. They do it occasionally. To some just certain people are invited. But things changed over the years. But today we´ll play.

It starts to thunder as I go through every room in my head. *I´ll go to the garage.*

I grab Kai´s keys from the dresser and rush outside. Some girls ran around trying to find a place to hide. They placed speakers around the house, so you can hear the countdown and the creepy music.

I try to open the door as quietly as I can and step in. I keep the lights off, so I try to orientate in the darkness. I hear the boys outside whispering and laughing, growling, and making weird noises. I even think I hear chains. They are loud.

I hear firecrackers pop. *They´re making a real show.*

With my arms outstretched, I try to spot Kai´s car. With hesitant and small steps, I feel my way forward until I bump into the hood. I´m sure no one heard me over the noise outside. I open the back door and close it slowly. I lie down. The shouting from outside are now muffled. *Glass shatters.* They shoot with their fake guns.

But suddenly everything is quiet. No more noise. No more talking. *Nothing.*

My breath seems so loud. *So, I hold it.*

I concentrate on hearing something. *Nothing.*

The blast goes off. *And the game begins.*

My heart hammers in my chest and I´m rethinking my decision. I´m almost completely cut off from everything. I get nothing of what happens in the house. But if I go outside now, I´m about to get caught. I must wait. But it´s so quiet. *Too quiet.* That right now, the silence scares me even more than the guys´ drama earlier. I´m trying hard to hear but all I can make out is the static in my earlobes. Now and then I hear girls screaming or laughing, which tells me they have started. Several run past the garage. Every sound sends shivers down my spine.

I start to sweat. *I´m trapped.*

I don´t know how long I´ll be in the car. But I don´t dare to take out my cell phone. So, I just wait in the dark.

When the door creaks open. I close my eyes. The breath gets stuck in my throat. I see a slight light from the outside. *Shit. Fuck. Shit. I´m scared.*

I want to sink into the floor. I hold my breath but can´t hold my heartbeat.

The door slams shut.

Every hair on my body sticks up. I don´t hear anything. *No movement. Silence.*

But even if there were any sounds, I wouldn´t hear because all I perceive is my hammering heart. *My whole body is beating.*

Suddenly, a hand bangs on the window opposite me. *A scream escapes me.*

The car door opens. And a large black figure grabs my feet. *Hard.*

And pulls me. *I scream.*

62

I grab hold of the door handle above me and kick my feet, and the guy lets go of me. He tries to climb into the back seat.

I pushed open the door and ran toward the terrace. There are people making out, running, and chasing. *They even fuck.*

I dart between them. Looking back, he doesn´t run after me. *He lets me escape.* And that´s when I know. *That was Kai. Was he?*

I got goosebumps as I stepped in. The light inside is off. Of course, they have the fuse out again. I´m afraid to run into some random guy. I don´t want anyone but Kai to find me.

What if Andi finds me first? Shit.

Think.. *where would Kai look for me? Or rather, where not?*

His father´s office.

It´s so quiet here, it´s weird. *Where are they all?* Maybe next door. Or in the garden. Or already in the rooms messing around. *But I hear nothing.* I hold my breath as I slowly walk around, trying to hear or see anything, *But nothing.*

As I pass the stairs, I stop as I see in the corner of my eye something on top.

I turn and freeze. There´s someone staring down. Dressed in all black. Wearing one of those scream masks. *Who is this? Is this Kai? But who was the other one?*

But that guy is way taller than Kai.. *I don´t breathe.*

And just as I wonder if he can see me, he tilts his head. *He sees me.*

Suddenly he paces down the stairs, taking three at once. I shriek and run past the front door, down the hall to the office. But before I can open the door, he reaches me and slams his fist to the door, shutting it. His body at my back, pinning me in. His hand around my neck holding me. I feel my pulse hammering against his fingers.

I don´t dare to move. To breathe.

He smells good, that´s what stings me. *But it´s not Kai´s scent.*

Nor Andi´s or the others.

I don´t know that guy. *I don´t know who this is.*

His hand wanders to my throat, choking me. I swallow hard. He bends my head to make me look at him. His mask is crystallized. And he has *green eyes,* but that´s all I can make out. I know no guy with those eyes. They all have brown ones.

He doesn´t say a thing, just stares at me. His grip tightens, taking my breath. And somehow.. *I´m enjoying this. I´m throbbing.*

But then he kicks the door open and pushes me inside. The door slams shut and I´m alone in the room. I try to catch my breath as I shine with my screen around. Lots of closets and bookshelves. In the middle a large desk. I haven´t been here before, but I seem to be alone. The masked guy is gone. And I´m not sure if I should be glad or not. I stand behind the door, hiding. So, if someone comes in, I could run.

A few minutes pass.

Until I hear footsteps. My senses sharpened. The person stands in front of the door.

Silence. Silence.

Pushes it open. Unlike I had hoped, he *closes* the door behind him. I am without cover and can´t run without him noticing. *I stay rooted.*

He slowly strides around the room. Closet doors creak. The office chair rolls. He pulls at the curtains. *Shit.*

Before the lantern illuminates the room, I try to escape. I reached for the door handle, opened it, and ran back to the living room. *But this time I am chased.* I scream. Instead of running further, I turn left and pace up the stairs, not really thinking about the scream mask guy who was up there before.

He grabs me midway from behind. I squeal. He lifts me up. My scream sticks in my throat. "Kai." I shout even if I´m not sure if it´s him. "Who`s that?" He whispers, and I hear the grin. He throws me over his shoulder and carries me back to the office. He locks the door and pulls out the key, throwing it. The drawn curtains somewhat lighten the room. But it´s still mostly dark. He drops me on the desk. My heart stops as he looks at me. He wears a black mask with scars and blood all over it. This is him. *Right?* He must be.

He reaches for my neck. His hand wraps under my jaw, like a bruise around its prey. He pulls me to him. Looks down at me. Forces me to the edge and pushes himself between my legs. I sucked in a breath as I feel him.

Black eyes.

Then I feel *something* cold on my arm. *Something sharp.* Like.. *a knife.*

He pulls it along my arm. Over my collarbone to my neck. He exerts some pressure.

Maybe cutting me.

I don´t move an inch. "Have I told you I´m into knife play?" He whispers his voice husky. *I know it´s Kai, but I´m scared.* And.. *turned on.*

The blade presses into my skin. I feel his chest against mine and my heartbeat at the blade.

"*I love the pain*." I quote *MGK*. His grip tightens and I imagine him grinning. The knife digs in my skin. His breathing heavy and violent.

"I feel u throbbing." He murmurs into my ear. My ears grow hot. *I am wet.*

I press closer to him and come almost instant when I feel his rock-hard dick through his jeans. As I do so he claws my skin. He grinds his length between my legs, and I close my eyes as a moan escapes me.

"Shh." he hums, holding the flip knife to my lower lip. I licked the blade. And taste blood. Not sure if it´s from my neck or my tongue. *Maybe both.*

I lift my hips to tease him. He groans in response. He drops the knife and covers my mouth with his hand.

We grind each other. "Ah fuck, *Scar*." He growls. *Scar*. It´s him. *It´s Kai.*

His hand catch my moans, and he murmurs into my ear. His touches are *anything* but gentle. He choaks me. Takes my breath. He´s violent. *But I love it.* I want him to crave his name on me. I want the knife in my skin if he digs it.

I smell him. It´s him. He found me. He chased me. He caught me. *He is intoxicating.*

"My favorite girl to play with." He grunts. *And I want him to play with me.*

I held onto his shoulder and clawed at his neck. He strips off his mask and bites the spot between my collarbone and neck. But the pain only turns me on more. I scratch his back wanting him to bleed as well. He sucks on my neck, breasts, and shoulders.

I suck on him.

I bite him when he bites me. We mark each other´s skins. *Like the pain fuels us.*

He grunts in response. Hearing him losing it sends me over the edge. I cry out as I come and run my fingers through his hair scratching his scalp. Not a second later he grabs my ass with both hands and dry fucks me to climax. He aggressively takes my hair and again bites hard into my skin as he ejaculates in his pants.

We hold on to each other until we get our breathing under control.

His black eyes glare at me like the devil at his sins. "It was never my plan to like you, Scar." He says. "But you know I can´t *hate* you either." He says with a raspy voice. "So, you finally tolerate me then?" I asked with a smile. *He smiles back.* But not for too long. Because I could get the impression he likes me. *But I already know he does.*

And as we look at each other a bit too long he whispers in my ear. "Don´t get too close Scar. It´s dark. It´s where the devils hide." He grins and then he leaves.

My favorite girl to play with. My favorite lost boy to get played by.

That day their physical bond tightened. They licked each other´s blood. And it hit em like a drug.

63

Next day

We sit on the couch with the boys. "What´s that on your neck?" Aidan asks with narrowed eyes. Kai looks at him rubbing his neck. Where the hickeys and scratches are, that I gave him last night. Kai´s eyes catch mine for a second, but I look down, pretending to do something on my phone. My face heats. Mine are hidden under my turtleneck dress. But it feels like they can see just by looking at me.

But I know they don´t. No one knows.

"Who did you get laid?" He asks him excitedly. "Finally got back in game?" Leon joins in grinning. *Back in the game.*

"Haven´t fucked in a while." Leon adds, but Kai cuts him off. "Some girl." He mutters not meeting my eyes as I lift my gaze at Leon´s comment. Has he been faithful.. *to me?* But there were those girls in the past weeks. *Or did he just pretend?*

"Spit it." Aidan urges him. *Yeah, spit it.*

"Nah." Kai says, stretching his neck until it cracks a few times. "Who was the girl?" He nods his chin at him. "Must have been hot. The way she left you *like this*. Bite marks and all." He inspects his jaw. "*Bleeding*." He adds with a smirk. Kai just shakes his head, stubborn as ever. "Come on, tell us." Leon presses. "Forgot." Kai shrugs. *I flinch on the inside.* Of course, he wouldn´t tell. *I knew.* But still.. *why did it hurt then?* Because I thought it had changed anything. But nothing changed. I just got hurt and more Invested.

"Stone head." Aidan chuckles, shaking his head. "Completely wasted." Kai nods, brushing them off.

"Don´t believe you a single word." He says, shaking his head. "Yeah bullshit." Leon agrees. Kai shrugs with one shoulder. "But she must be worth the hiding." Aidan says padding his shoulder. That´s when Kai finally looks at me. Not long enough for the others to notice, *but I did.*

Kai licks his lip and nods once. *Worth hiding.*

"Alright, *fucker* won´t tell." Aidan says, annoyed with a grin. "Did *you* at least get laid?" He asks me and catches me off guard. My eyes widen. "What?" I laugh.

All eyes on me.

I catch Kai´s black eyes. *His face blank.*

"No. Uhm.. no one.. Andi didn´t find me." I say. "What a dumbass." He laughs. "Yep." I nod. *And it wasn´t a lie.* No one got laid. *Just bruised.* In ways. *Hidden ways.*

They liked each other and secrets were exciting. *But they don´t feel real.* Because you lock them away and pretend, they don´t exist. But that´s what they did.

64

Two days later

"Fuck," I hear Kai curse.

The door to the bathroom is slightly open. He groans and throws something, whereupon glass is knocked over. I peek through the crack. His left-hand grips the edge of the sink. Our eyes meet in the mirror. His hair wet, and he´s only in black shorts. His cheeks and neck are covered with shaving cream. There´s a cut on his jaw and blood running down his neck.

He has cut himself. *I like him bleeding.*

I wonder what his blood tastes like. *Well, I did taste it.*

Since the fight, his hand is sort of broken. He´s not wearing a bandage or anything. But it looks bad. Wounded, bloody and covered with dark purplish and yellowish spots. It looks hurtfully swollen. He probably tried to shave with his left hand. *He´s right-handed.* Or he tried it with the right and failed.

"What?" He harps. I suppress a smile. "Need help?" I asked him and closed the door behind me. He straightens up and makes room for me. I stand between him and the sink. He looks down at me, breathing calmly. His black eyes pierce me as if he would tell me at any moment how much he hates me. I´m still mad at him, too. *He broke Andi´s nose.*

They got into a fight yesterday. And I don´t know why. But it´s kind of normal for them.

They do that often.

But I have no idea why he´s mad at me. But I swallow my anger because *when did we ever talk about what happened?*

I turn around and bend over, reaching for the razor. It´s made of metal and has a sharp blade. I would cut myself with it, even without an injured hand. He stares at me as I wash the blade. Blood and foam flow in the basin. I don´t even know how to hold it properly, but I don´t let on. I hold my hand to his cheek, but he grabs my wrist before I can touch him. He glares at me. I know he doesn´t like to give up control. *So, do I.*

"Careful." He warns, his voice rough. I look up at him. He lets go of me and puts his hand back on the edge, bringing us closer. I get nervous. Suddenly, the air in the bathroom gets thin. He steps closer as I bring a hand to his cheek. My tailbone bumps against the panel. For a moment, I hesitated. Staring at his face, unable to move.

Trapped between his body. “The angle between the blade and the skin has to be about 30 to 40 degrees.” He says because he guessed my uncertainty. I am sure he sees my skin pulsating by my heartbeat. I can only perceive him and not the space around us.

“Off the cuff and *don´t* push up.” He instructs, his voice hoarse. I nod and carefully, I place it on his cheek as he said and slowly move down. I wash off the lather and draw the next line. He´s silent and watches me. He´s tense and calm. He lets me hold his face. He lifts his head up, so I can get to his neck. I pull him closer, so I can get a better grip. But he lifts me up and sits me on the edge. My clit throbs as his *erection* grazes me. He looks down on me. His left hand is on my hip now. And his right on the flow next to my ass. His chest rises and falls. Even though he doesn´t want to give up control, it turns him on. I slide closer, and he positions himself between my legs. I thrum against his length. I clench my thighs around his body. I lift his chin and continue shaving.

I cut him, but he makes no sound. His hands claw into my skin. And he presses his boner against my now drumming clit. *I know he can feel it.*

His hand holds my ass as far as his injury allows. But I´m sure too hard for his good. With each cut he pushes himself closer. And I am almost willing to cut him on purpose that he continues to rub against me. *But he does anyway.*

Shaving the neck and jaw is much more difficult. My body moves, barely visible on autopilot. I breathe loudly and he´s almost moaning by now.

When I´m done, he reaches behind me and wets a towel without changing our position. He hands it to me, and I wash his face with the cold towel. Then he warms it up and again I wash his skin. I take my time. And he enjoys watching me. After that, he gives me a bottle. I put the liquid in my palm and spread it in my hands. I press it on his neck, his jaw, his cheeks, I´m intoxicated by his aftershave. His jaw tightens. The bathroom is still warm and steamy. My head is dizzy. His veins stand out. One on his forehead, his temple, and one on his neck. His skin is so soft. Even after it´s pulled in, I run my hands over his features. I can´t help but rub against him. The pleasure is too great. One hand holds his cheek, and the other the spot between his bare shoulder and neck. His left hand my back. And his right claws into my ass. He pulls me to the edge, so I sit on his cock. He groans, closing his eyes. He begins to dry fuck me. I wrap my legs around him. My hips slide up and down his length. He´s hard as a metal rod. I am sure it hurts. *It has to hurt. But he likes to hurt. So, it´s good.*

He leans forward and forces me backward. Bottles fall over and Kai throws them to the side with a wipe. We don´t kiss as if *that* would be our death sentence. No turning back then.

And I think that´s true.

He breathes hard and moans in my ear, making me shiver. *I love hearing him.* There is nothing hotter than hearing them, especially *hearing him*.

We just lie there, forehead to forehead, and ride each other into Nirvana. He pulls me back up before he comes to look at me while he does. He looks pained. I know he wants to kiss me. He *knows* I want to kiss him too. *But we don´t.* And at this point I don´t know why.

But I don´t care. Because I want everything of it. *Him.*

"Bite me Scar." he murmurs on the verge of orgasm. I kiss him along his neck to his shoulder and bite his muscles. "Harder." he moans. I do, and he comes. He grabs my hair and throws his head back, moaning in relief. *I come with him.*

65

It is 3:42 and Kai´s sits on the sofa smoking weed. He looks tired and seems surprised to see me. *Well, so am I.* I was with Andi but somehow, I wanted to go home instead of sleeping at his. And at home I couldn´t sleep, cause I was thinking of Kai. Who kissed me and dry-humped me pretending it didn´t happen. *So here I am.*

"You´re awake?" I ask. "I was just about to text you." I add and sit down. "Who said nights were for sleep?" He laughs. *He jokes a lot about his sleep.*

He´s acting weird somehow. *Like he is uncomfortable?*

I look closely at him. The dark circles under his eyes. The red in his eyes. The drained look. And I can´t help but think of all the times he texted or showed up outside my house in the middle of the night. Or the times he watched me sleep, woke up in a cold sweat, had nightmares, or I caught him not sleeping at all. How he *always* wanted me to sleep at his and how we did meet *mostly* at night. It´s like all at once the pieces fall into place. And I see the scars I couldn´t before.

"You can´t don´t you?" I ask carefully. "*Sleep* I mean." I clarify. He looks down. "No." he says, barely audible. *He can´t.*

"I´ve had sleeping disorders for as long as I can remember. Early childhood." He reveals. "Shit." I say. "And.. the nightmares?" I ask to which he nods. "The weed is prescription medication. *So medical.* I´m not an addict." He points out. I shut my eyes.

I called him a stoner. I feel so stupid.

"Does the weed help?" I ask. "Most of the time." He nods to himself. "But other times it seems like *nothing* does." I remain silent. "Neither any shitty herbal teas, pills, meditations, or therapy. I drink little to no alcohol and no coffee. I´m physically active. But still.." He´s angry. He leans forward on his knees.

"I think what a reason may be is inner peace." I say afraid to upset him. He nods. "Yeah." He laughs as if he *knows exactly.* "Got none of that." He says and falls silent.

"The only thing that seems to help is *you*." He says without daring to look at me. I don´t know what to say. *I help him?* I mean, he falls asleep fast with me. But I didn´t really think it was *because* of me.

"Let´s get you some sleep." I say in a whisper and pull him up. He stands up and looks down at me. He looks broken and healed at the same time. And tonight I´m the one who stays awake to make sure he´s asleep.

66

November

Since I started dating Andi it´s been the same. I sit on top of him. He grabs my ass. I run my hands through his hair. We kiss. He takes off his shirt. I ride his lap. He kneads my breasts and pulls me closer. He takes off my shirt.

But then it starts. I can´t turn my head off. I feel uncomfortable. I think about Kai sometimes. And I´m afraid to strip down. Farid for him to see me. *Just afraid.*

We haven´t gone any further than making out and the slightest foreplay. First, I thought that I just need time. But it turned out this is a problem that remains. I know Andi wants more from me than *just* sex. *But still.*

We have been on tons of dates, and I like him. I´m also into him *somehow*. But my brain won´t shut up. Maybe I´m just insecure. *Maybe, more.*

As he tries to undo my bra, I back away from him.

"Wait" I press out. "I can´t" I admit not for the first time, the past weeks. And not for the first time he´s a gentleman. "Hey," he says, handing me back my shirt. "It´s okay Scar. We´ll wait." He says. "Okay" I say. He kisses me on the forehead and takes me in his arms. For a while we just cuddle and talk. He he´s been understanding so far. But I know it does not pass him by without a trace. And he´s a Leo. *Do I have to say more?*

"I think I´ll go." I say and we get up. "Drive safe. And don´t worry that was too rash.. I would never pressure you." He assures me. "I know." I say and kiss him. And as soon as I walked out the door, I started to cry. The closer I get to Andi, the more I´m getting away from Kai. It feels like I´m betraying him, which is bullshit. Because it´s the other way around. *I betray Andi.* Especially after the dry humping. I had to make excuses not to meet him for almost a week, otherwise he would have seen Kai´s bite marks. I liked the wounds. At home, I looked at them all the time. I had lots. He even cut me on my neck. Which I liked as well.

There´s definitely something wrong with me. But as it seems, I´m into knife play.

Luckily, it´s cold outside, so I can wear turtlenecks. Even if we both know exactly what is hiding underneath. I often caught him looking at the place where he had marked me. His look full of lust, pride, and obsession. But as expected, we did not talk about it. It´s just the same as always. Confusing, charged, and ambivalent.

So, I let myself continue to get involved with Andi, since Kai had nothing to say. *Since I´m something to play with.* And as long as he doesn´t admit anything or fights for me, I save myself the headache. *But it finds me anyway.*

- 27 -

Kai opens the door with a towel over his shoulder. He walks back to the kitchen as if he expected me. I follow him after I have undressed.

"Love yourself, not me."

I try hard Kai. Not to fall for *you,* but for Andi.

"You were right" I say as I walk up to him. He turns away from the stove to face me. "With what?" He asks. "Trust" I say. "*What* did he do?" He asks and takes a step toward me. "*Nothing.* Calm down." I soothe him.

"We.." I start but hesitate. "I don´t know why I came here. *To you..* with this. I´m sorry." I say. "Tell me." He urges.

"We were making out.. and it got heated" I say, and his jaw tightens. "And that´s all that happened for over a month. I couldn´t turn it off. Just thinking about what was going to happen next.. I felt uncomfortable. *Insecure.* I couldn´t. I didn´t want to.." I can´t put my thoughts into words. He searches my face.

"You don´t trust him." He says carefully like he just realized. "How could I?" I gape at him. "We barely know each other. I mean, I like him, and we get along. He´s understanding and wants to take it slow." I say, and he turns to swirl the pan. "I can´t relax. I don´t know if it´s going away. That was the exact problem with my friends with benefits. Maybe I´m too insecure or something. I mean I am horny but.. I can´t." I say upset. He faces me. "You can´t sleep with him because you don´t *feel* for him." He says and when I don´t answer he continues. "It isn´t always just *fucking.* Sometimes it´s spiritual. It´s your souls connecting. Bonding. Emotional and physical." He tells me. "I don´t know if I´ll be able to open up to him in that way." I admit. "You have to tell him that." He says. "Yeah, but I need to figure out what´s going on first. I don´t know what or what I *could* feel for him." I respond. "You´re afraid of intimacy with him. *That shows.* It´s not for no reason that.." He began, and I think, he almost said something about us. Because so far, I could trust him. And I would trust him further. Probably more than I should.

He looks uneasy. "I haven´t told you that about me.. actually no one knows." He says. "But sometimes I throw up after I slept with someone." He tells me but won´t look at me.

Did he throw up after us?

"Cause you know the other person has expectations. Those kinds you can´t or don´t want to fulfill. You´re overwhelmed.." He explains. "You think *he* expects sex from you. And I think *girls* expect more than *that* from me. Closeness, love, relationships, attachment." He adds. "So, you shut down and *I* throw up. I get it out. You cage it in." He analyses. He still avoids my gaze. I don´t know what to say.

Why does he throw up after sex?

He sees my worry and without saying a word, he tells me. *Not with you.*

"Or maybe.." He clears his throat. "You don´t trust him cause you´re afraid he´ll leave you. Self-protection and stuff." He shrugs. "You´re looking for excuses to not get hurt." He says. "I´m not saying your thinking makes sense or anything." He walks toward me. "But you close yourself up.. for *good* things." He tells me. And it makes me wonder if he´s talking about himself as *good* things. And something tells me he does. Or I wish he does.

"But you can´t avoid getting hurt. Even if you don´t let *anyone* get to you, you still get hurt. *By you.* Your past. The story you keep telling yourself." He says and he *always* knows the right things to say to cheer me up or analyze me. As if he knows me and my motives.

Maybe he does.

And I know he´s right about the things he says. *But does he even listen to himself for once?* He gives the best advice, but he doesn´t take it into account. He´s the one who does not open up. And if I didn´t know better, I´d think he was talking from experience.

"And what story do you tell yourself?" Before I think about it, it´s out. He seems absent and turns away. *That was too far.*

"Several," he says. "Well, thanks for listening and the pep talk. I´ll go." I say and leave.

I think about what he said to me. I destroy things that could be beautiful out of fear. Something tells me Kai is the same.

I say I´m not looking for a relationship. I want to know someone well first, best to be friends. But at the same time, I am afraid of losing people. Which is why I close myself off and don´t let anyone get close. *Well, I let him in.*

And for some reasons I trust Kai even if it´s confusing and hurtful.

But now it´s not about Kai. Most of all I think, I can´t have sex with him because I´m insecure. Shortly after my breakup I was confident but then I got back to the way I used to feel about myself. Not sexy not pretty enough.

But I´ve come closer to Kai than to Andi. And if Kai wanted me the way I want him I wouldn´t even think about Andi at all. Maybe I´m not *that* into him. Maybe I just want to get Kai out of my head. *Maybe.*

[NOTEBOOK ENTRIES]

She told me about her past, and I told her about mine. She told me her dreams. And all I could think of was wanting for her to accomplish those. Something in me wanted to make them possible for her. She said she feels like home with us. But I knew that she meant me.

I could not sleep because I knew she was with him. And every night she´s not with me, she´s with him. I know they still date, but I´m the one she ends up in bed with at the end of the day. At least, most of the days. Today it´s not one of those.

She fell asleep on the sofa. I told the others not to wake her. I didn´t want her to go. I didn´t want to wake her either, just to sleep better myself. I did sleep knowing she´s downstairs, but I had a nightmare. I can´t remember exactly. There were my parents, and I was a toddler. I was alone in the house. My brother was gone. There were these figures. Shadows. Grimaces. Who whispered to me. There was no light. But I woke up. And Lia was there. I thought I was still dreaming. I was relieved to see her. She held me. With her, I could finally sleep. But she saw my cuts. Or rather, finally got it. I already told her that I love pain. I make no effort to be secretive about it. I crack my knuckles. Start fights. I hurt myself. That´s the way it´s always been. I was the one of the two of us who had to go to the principal weekly. Who had a year´s detention, got suspended, reprimands, and more. I was always troubled. With that, at least I was something for my parents. I wanted them to rip their heads over me. Just not, nothing. No silence. Any reaction, I craved. They had flown in when I got into trouble. And I did it a lot. It´s not that I´m not intelligent, I just made stupid decisions. Always straight A´s average. I just needed bad things. The thrill. I never cared about rules. Rules who made no sense. But she cuts herself, too. I´ve seen the scars on her thigh. She has some on her arms too. But she hasn´t done it for a long time. I notice everything, I just pretend I don´t. Like the way she can´t hold eye contact for too long. How she looks around when she´s talking to you. I wish I didn´t notice all this. But I start liking those details. Like I know her better than anyone. Which makes me feel good in a way. Probably more than it should.

Colson Herzog

Sometimes I smile to myself. Until I realize I'm thinking of her.

I noticed that she won't really talk unless she's spoken to, but once she does, she can talk for hours. She's shy when she's not comfortable with you. When she is, she bubbles and is goofy. She's often quiet. But a good quiet. Enjoying silence. I don't know how I know those things because she never told me.

We aren't together on parties. We're with our friends but we're not together, together. I fight the urge to grab her and take her with me. So, I keep mocking her to have an excuse to talk to her. We might have played dumb, but we knew exactly what was going on. We are a secret we both hold.

We always end up by each other. Like sitting on the sidewalk talking, lying in bed, walking her home in the rain, driving her, or waiting for everyone to fuck off, so we can be together for a few hours. I don't know why we don't hang out in front of our friends. Maybe I want to have her by myself. To protect her. From whatever. Maybe, myself. But if they knew, it would be real. And I wasn't ready for real. If it keeps you happy. Keep it quiet.

When it's just our friends, we talk a lot more and hang out. Mostly arguing and teasing. With Aidan, she's all fooling around and flirty which pisses me off. Leon and she challenge each other. It's a weird dynamic. Like, they can't decide if they like each other. We aren't easy to understand either. We throw some insults there and have laugh flashes after.

She hugged me. We've never done that. She was too close. She smelled good. And I got a boner. I can't remember the last time that happened. I think she noticed. I was happy to see her until I remembered Andi. I organized the game for her. That book brought me on a lot of ideas. Aidan and Leon were easily convinced. We haven't done something funny in a long time. But I had to get her away from Andi. She was already scared when the lights went out. That made my dick twitch. I wanted to kiss her. But the look on her face when she understood was fucking worth it. The thought of scaring her gave me pleasure. My mission was to find her before anyone else. But I knew her better and knew exactly where she was going to hide. Some girls practically let me catch them. But I wasn't interested. I had only one prey. Only one sin. That she took my keys, I saw immediately. Blood rushed to my cock at the thought of her lying in my car. Ready for me. Waiting. Hoping I'll catch her. I didn't know how much this cat and mouse game could turn me on. Turns out I have a new kink. And I think she has too. I let her run. She hid in the office. Of course, she would go there. My veins pulsed as I chased after her. She called my name. But I was not Kai. The demand to take her on the table was immense. But I wanted to make it the right way. The slow way.

Maybe the hard way. But an addicting way. The control I had over her drove me insane. I cut her with the blade. Held the flip knife to her lips. I wanted her to suck my cock as bad as the blade. I felt her clit pulsing. I could feel her wetness through her jeans. I had to grip her harder, so I didn't lose control and free my cock to fuck her. I went crazy when she moaned into my hand. My dick pressed against my jeans, begging to bury itself in her. I wanted to crawl inside of her and never come back. She clawed into my skin. Pulled my hair. Bit me. Pain was never as good as coming from her. She was my new source of pain. I made her bleed. And she bled for me. She likes pain as much as I do. I am the devil, and she's the angel. Forbidden. But inevitable. She came on my dick. No one else's. I came in my pants. The last time that happened was when I was in sixth grade. I knew she would be my downfall or salvation. Somehow, I liked both thoughts. I just wanted her. Whatever that would mean. It was delicious to see them together afterward. Knowing she just came for me. How she wore my bite marks. She was mine that night. My secret to keep. But I had a problem. I tasted blood. Now I wanted more. So much more.

Aidan saw my hickeys and scratches. And the bite on my jaw. You could not miss them. Every time I looked in the mirror, I hardened. And they asked me when she was there. I tried to brush them off, but they kept asking. The jackass even revealed I haven't fucked. Now she knew I pretended I did. She was with Andi, and it would be a shitty way to do it. I said I couldn't remember, but they called bullshit. They know me. But I kept shut. I knew what she hid underneath her dress. But that was mine to keep. After spraining my hand, I cut myself shaving. She was there to help. I knew she was mad at me for beating the dick head she's dating. He figured she was the one who was with me. He was mad. We fought. He lost. As always. But I couldn't kiss her. Even if we wanted to.

I told her about my sleeping disorder. She's the only thing that helps lately.

I just like talking to her, even if I have nothing to say. I'm always angry or numb. With her, all those emotions silence. Like they don't matter anymore. I feel those tingles, and my heart flutters and beats harder for no reason. But it feels good. I can't focus. I catch me searching for those itches. For those black butterflies she gives me. I hate how it feels when she's not there. How my mind sometimes works when I have to listen to the demons in my head. When I have to deal with things. Things I can't shut out. Weed helps. Pain. And her. But she's not the solution. She'll leave eventually. But the pain stays.

I catch my mind wandering to her. I think of her name. Her face pops in my head. Her laughter. Her smile. The things she said. Her scent. Her body. I want to stick a knife into my gut. Because I feel high and dizzy. Even turned on sometimes. Why her? What's different about her? I'm drawn to her. Like a bad curse, I can't elude. I don't know why I can't let myself admit those things. Pretending I'm in control while I'm totally losing it.

She told me she can't get involved with Andi. Physically and emotionally. I knew. I could tell by the way she looks at me. The way she acts around him vs. around me. I hope she'll cut him off. I told her about my throwing up. I saw the worry. She thought I did too after.. us. But I didn't. That's something new. Maybe that's the thing that makes her different. She doesn't make me vomit.

Sometimes I can read her well and other times she's a mystery. She's quiet because she's annoyed. Or when she's tired. Or uncomfortable. Sometimes she's quiet because she enjoys it. I like that I know the difference.

She looks at me, thinking I wouldn't pay attention. But I do. When I don't look, she's confident staring. Sometimes I have that feeling. That knowing she's there. And when I look. She is. Like we're bond or some shit.

She always has to do something with her hands. She tries to spin her ring out of habit when she's not wearing it. I have no idea what she's so insecure about. I picked up that she hates to make calls. I couldn't care less, what people think of me. I wish I could take that feeling for her. I want to assure her. It's silly. The other day we decided to order food, and no one wanted to call. So, I said I'd do. Because I knew she didn't want to. Or when we're partying, and I sense she's uncomfortable, I talk to her to distract her and bring her to the now. Even if I just make fun of her or insult her. Last time I asked her if she wanted something to drink. But she just got a new one. I pretend like I didn't pay attention. I went to the bar despite the fact that my bottle was also untouched. Maybe she has no idea what I'm doing, maybe she knows. I don't care. Well, that's not true. All I do is care. I think, I have a fucking problem.

67

I walk on the train-snowed road. I always insist that Andi lets me out, so I can walk home. No matter what the weather is. And *sometimes* I walk to Kai. Lately, I rarely stay over at Andi's anymore. *But today I walked home.*

The thick snowflakes make me happy. I like snow because it's gentle and noisy. But I like rain the most because it can be quiet and loud. *Like me.*

I walk up to my car and stop. *It's snowed in.*

On the windshield is *something* written.

"This is not you."

I smile to myself. *That was Kai.*

And I´m sure with *this* he means Andi. *Andi and me.*

I watch the flakes fall, as if someone slowed down time and space.

The last few days we were on dates and did something with our friends. Kai looked at me. Probably thinking what it´s all about. Why I´m dating the guy I obviously don´t want. Maybe, I don´t want to admit it, but can´t open up. It´s been *days* and I haven´t gotten myself to tell Andi what I in fact already know. *This won´t work.* It´s like Kai said. *I can´t trust him.* Maybe I didn´t want him to be right. But I can´t lie to myself nor to Andi anymore. I´m not going to feel for Andi the way I feel for *him*.

I take a picture of Kai´s message, clear the windows, and get in the car.

By the way he looked at me when I stood at his door again, *he knew* what was going on. He´s not stupid. He caught me staring at Kai often enough, or him staring at me.

He knew all along.

"It´s only fair to tell you this. And I´m sorry for waiting so long." I begin. "I can imagine falling for you. But I realized that I´m very insecure, and not ready for anything serious. I want to know someone well. And there are so many things in my way. Fears I must understand and overcome first." I shrug. "I don´t want to hurt you *or* myself. Above all, I don´t want to lose you." I say and he´s looking at me, nodding. "Thank you for being so open. I understand and fully respect that. You´re important to me too. And I don´t want to lose that either." He says. *I´m relieved.* But something tells me he´s holding back. The way he spoke was weird. I stare into the void.

"It´s about Kai, right?" He asks after a while. "We´re just friends." I say, but it feels like I´m lying. *Am I?*

He´s laughing. *He´s laughing*?!

"Friends" he repeats, with raised brows. "You´re *not* just friends." He shakes his head laughing. *What?*

"It´s okay, Lia. I mean, it´s natural that you have feelings for each other." I look at him, questioning. *What is he talking about?*

"You have to admit your relationship is ambivalent." He points out. "Ambivalent?" I gape at him sneakier than intended. "You behave like best friends, sometimes lovers, and other times enemies." He retorts. "It´s just hard to understand your relationship. Do you hate each other? Love each other? I don´t know, or maybe both." He says with a shrug. "It´s complicated." I say. "Everyone knows you´re not *just friends*, except you two." He says. "I don´t think *anyone* thinks that." I retort. Because no one knows except his brother and apparently Andi too.

“Well, but I do, and a man knows his rival. I think I just underestimated your.. *connection.*” He responds. A short smile flushes across his mouth. “What?” I ask. “I know you say it´s not because of him, but I´ve known for a long time that I didn´t stand a chance against him.” He says and sees the confusion and goes on. “Look, I know what happened between you two.” He says and my eyes widen. *He knew? Like everything?*

“You knew.” I say perplex and he nods. “If you knew all along, why did you date me?” I ask. He laughs a bit. “Because it´s part of the game.” He says. *Game? No.* I try to swallow his statement but choke on it.

“He played well enough.” He nods. “Had no chance.” He shrugs. *What is going on?*

My stomach hurts. My heart turns. *No.*

“I have to admit, at some point, I knew it wouldn´t work. Maybe it was just a duel. Ego trip. A turf fight. It´s always like that between us, you know. Always played games. But not just on those parties.” He hints and I look at him in shock considering slapping him.

“I know it´s not fair. But I really wanted it to work between us. I like you, but it´s probably not more than friendship.” He says. I´m so confused. I can´t think straight. *How did he switch up on me like that?* Hours ago, we kissed, and all was normal. *No games.* I feel stupid. *He just wanted to beat him? Win? Was it just a game for the two?* They were often on the verge of fighting, and I must think back to Ryan´s birthday when Andi didn´t want to tell me what Kai said to him. *Now I know.* And Kai spraying his hand after he broke Andi´s nose after Halloween.

Halloween. Was that why? Did he brag about dry fucking me? Kai was upset from the start that I met Andi, maybe it was just a bet. And tricked me, and Kai won. *Would he be so cruel?* Of course, he would. He hated me all along. *But all the things we talked about? The times we shared secrets? The holding and saving each other? Was that all a lie? A game?*

But maybe Andi says all this because his pride is hurt.

“Look, I hate that fucker. And I think you shouldn´t trust him. He never wanted you around. He despises all Nina´s girls.” He tells me. *I don´t believe it.*

“But apparently, he likes you. Cares about you, even. *Obviously.*” He stiffs a laugh. “So, I hope it works out the way you want. Just be careful.” He says.

So now he´s caring about me? What the fuck is going on? I don´t know what to think or to believe anymore. I fell for it. *For both of them.*

“And I know about Halloween, by the way.” He says.

There it is. He knows. *He fucking knew.* Kai bragged.

Maybe they made a bet who would fuck me first.

"Fuck you." I scoff and stand up. "Scar I´m sorry." He says. "You´re *sorry*?" I spit. "You tricked me." I say upset. "You two are sick." I scowl. "You and your *games*." I yell. "*Sick*." I repeat. "Lia." He comes close but I back away.

"I know you want him. Just own it." He says and I frown at him. "What the fuck are you talking about?" I ask. "I just think you both are too afraid of what would happen if you were *honest* with each other." He says. "About what?" I ask irritated. "Your feelings." He clarifies. "What feelings?" I yell. "You played me." I shoot. "There are *no* feelings." I say. He smiles like I don´t understand something.

"There *are* feelings." He says sure. I look at him speechless. "You like him, don´t you?" He asks, all calm. It´s the same question Kai asked me weeks ago about him.

I don´t get it. Not at all.

But I nod, looking down. "And he likes you too." He tells me.

I´m not sure about that.

"It´s not that easy." I say. "It´s *just* not easy because you two make it hard, and maybe you don´t want it to be easy." He says and maybe he´s right. Kai loves trouble. Pain and games. *Clearly.*

"You know sometimes you´re not sure if you´re playing anymore." He smirks. "Lines blur." He adds and I frown. "I didn´t sign up for *any* play." I retort. "You went to the parties, didn´t you?" He smirks. "And you *knew*.. they warned you." He adds and I blink, unable to speak. "You both are pretty much alike, actually." He says, and it feels more like an insult. I shake my head.

"You´re sick. Leave me the fuck alone." I spit. "No wonder I couldn´t let me fall with you." I scoff and turn to walk away. *He lets me leave.*

He didn´t have to say it. *I knew.* It all made sense now. But I wanted to hear it from Kai.

I´m glad he never laid hands on me. *Both of them.*

At least not more than they already did. *More than I let them.*

68

I´ve been driving around for a while. *Thinking.*

Trying to convince myself it´s not just a game.

Not a lie. Not a bet. Not a cock battle.

Trying to remember and recall every conversation we had. Trying to find sings.

And I find them.

The way the girls warned me. They said he plays games. He *and* the guys here.

I was warned. These parties. About the guys. About all. The hurt. Him.

They told me he´s the worst. *And he is.*

He even told me he always ended it when the girls fell for him. And I idiot didn´t listen. I did fall too, like all the other girls.

He said, I don´t fit. I knew he hates Nina´s friends.

He asked my greatest fear, which was *losing control*. And he made me lose it.

He literally told me I´m his favorite girl to play with. *How could I be so stupid?*

Andi told me weeks ago Kai plays with me.

And maybe that´s why Kai hid me around all those nights. All the times he brought me back instead of asking me in front of our friends. Because I was a bet. Not something worth hiding, but something that *had to be hidden*. Something not to be proud of. Something you conceal from your closest friends.

He played with me. That´s why he always said, he didn´t want me to be with Andi. But he never really said I should be with him instead. *How could I not see?*

Maybe I didn´t want to see.

Kai accused Andi of having pushed me on purpose. Maybe, that was right too. He knew who I was. That´s why he smirked as he asked for my name. *He remembered me.* I didn´t remember him at first. *He did.* I´m angry, feel ashamed and humiliated. He told him what we did. *The kisses? The dry humping?*

Neither Kai *nor* Andi wanted me. They wanted to play and win.

I drive straight to his house. No matter what time it is. This piece of shit doesn´t sleep anyway. *Hopefully* because I have a lot to say. *But what will I tell him?*

I can´t just have him win. *I need a plan.*

And then it occurs to me. *He left a message. And so, will I.*

Fortunately, his car is outside, so I have the chance to leave him *something*.

I write with my finger on the slightly snowed car hood.

"I forgot I´m a bet. I´m sorry, but you lost."

Then I drove away.

"Left you a message (:"

I texted him.

And crawl into my bed. *And cry.*

69

Not ten minutes later, the door flies open and makes me jump. Kai stands in the room.

Deja Vu.

"What the fuck was that about?" he shouts. I jolt up. I hope I don´t look like I´ve cried. But that disappears as soon as I remember. My blood boils.

"Like you don´t know." I say straightening up. "No, I don´t. So, talk." He demands, walking towards me. *He really wants me to say it.* Inside, I have to laugh.

"It was just a bet. Wasn´t it? Between you and Andi." I snap, shaking my head. "What did he say to you, Scar?" He asks in anger. "Nothing. And don´t call me that." I rage. "He didn´t *need* to say it. Did you make a bet? On getting me laid?" I ask. "You told him about Halloween. Didn´t you? That´s *why* you fight. Right?" I ask.

"What else?" I rake further. He hesitates. "No. I haven´t told him." He tells me. "He figured. And no not a bet. That was never mentioned." He says. I laugh. "You´re lying." I accuse him. "No, I don´t." He defends himself.

"You said it yourself. You like to play. Those girls told me. *You* told me I´m *yours to play with*." I growl. "You sick fuck." I yell. He shakes his head.

"It was a bet. Be honest once." I shout. He shakes his head. "No, it wasn´t." He yells. "But.. I can´t say.. it was *nothing*, either." He admits. "So what?" I laugh but it gets stuck in my throat. "You two did a cock comparison. Who wins her over? Who plays her the best?" I push further. "It wasn´t like that." He says, shaking his head. "Then *how* was it?" I ask upset. "I mean it *was* a competition somewhere, but that´s how it goes between us, it wasn´t about you." He says and I burst out laughing. "Wasn´t about *me*. Huh?" I ask shaking my head in disbelief. *I was naive.*

"I didn´t mean it that way." He says. "Yeah, seems like you don´t mean a lot you say and do." I say and take a deep breath. "Now get the fuck out. I´m sick of you." I say. "Let me explain.." He begs, but I cut him off. "There´s *nothing* you could say." I tell him. "I´m not one of your Wendy´s you can fuck with." I scoff. "I don´t care about your rules." I bark. "Now get the fuck out." I repeat. For a moment, he stares at me helplessly. The way he looks at me gives me the impression he didn´t lie. *That he´s hurt. And sorry.* And there´s fear too.

But right now, I can´t see it. I can´t feel it. Don´t want to. He played with me, and I need him to fuck off.

"Get out." I yell. And he finally leaves me the fuck alone. And this time I´m glad he does. I´m glad I´m alone. *For once. I´m glad.*

70

November 3rd

My alarm clock brings me back to reality. And my memory to the truth. *It was not a dream.* The good dreams end, only the bad ones never stop.

Maybe Neverland was never a dream but a nightmare.

The group chat brings me back to earth. To the fact that today is Kai´s birthday.

Fuck. Great timing. I don´t want to see him or Andi. But I have no chance.

For a split second, I felt sorry that I yelled at him on his birthday. Because when he showed up it was shortly after midnight.

And I kicked him out. But deserved, I remind myself.

The bad thing is, I have no excuse not to go to the party. *Because nobody knows.* Besides, knowing Nina, she´d drag me herself if she had to. She doesn´t take a no when it comes to partying. *Not ever.*

So, I´m going to go willy-nilly. And right now, alcohol sounds pretty good.

My eyes fall on the black notebook I wanted to give him. So that he doesn´t have to write in his books like a psychopath. *How could I forget that it´s his birthday?* After all, I´ve been racking my brains for the last weeks about *what* to get him.

But now he won´t get that.

Throughout the day, I pass different emotions. Sometimes I´m angry. Sometimes sad. Sometimes, ashamed. Sometimes, I could laugh. And sometimes I´m even glad it happened. I don´t know what to believe. Everything that was between us felt real. But also, *didn´t.* I never knew where I stood. We were ambivalent. But when he opened, it felt honest.

Maybe the lines of the game and reality really became blurry. *Like Andi said.* Or maybe he´s just a good liar. *I stiff a laugh.* The way he said he thought better of me when I believed those girls talking shit about him. Whereas in reality, those rumors were all true.

Pan wants to play but it´s only ever for his pleasure.

Between all the back and forth, I came to the decision not to let it get to me. Whether it was a bet or not. I´m not going to show him how much it hurt me.

Even if he saw my eyes tonight.

He will have no control over me or my emotions. *Not anymore.*

Ignorance and kindness are what confuse people. *So that´s the plan for today.*

- 27 -

Some guy I don´t know opens the door. The house is packed. *Those can´t all be his friends.* He doesn´t *deserve* any. *But who am I to judge with no friends at all?*

Kai is popular. *I´m not.*

With the carton in my hand, I go to the kitchen. On the counter are already tons of other cakes in different sizes and colors. The group has such a tradition of gifting cakes with funny quotes and sayings. And I made him a cake. *A good one.* It´s round and glazed in black cream. With bloodred color I wrote.

"I POISONED THIS (:"

I must grin. *It´s perfect.*

I place it and read the others.

"Little shit."

"Let´s make out."

"Daddy?"

"Thanks for the sex."

"Miss your dick."

"See you in hell."

"My therapist hates you."

"If you´ll go to hell, at least you´ll be with your friends."

"Best dick ever."

"No Psychopath. Rather creative."

"Your sarcasm isn´t an attitude. It´s an art."

"Eat shit."

"Satan was born today."

"Devil, seduce me"

"Goddess."

"Love me"

"Weeed be good together."

Seems like some hate him and others love him. But I know it´s sarcastic.

I zone out and think about the friends I made.

Aidan is the popular one. *The sunshine boy.*

Kai´s the loner. Someone who fights a lot. Sho´s sarcastic, silent, and rude. But somehow, he´s still the most popular of the group. *Well, he´s Pan. Of course, he is.* Girls practically throw themselves at him. He doesn´t give a fuck, though. Everyone wants to be friends with him or fight with him. Because he is someone you even want to be hated by. You want his attention. *But he gives nothing. Not to everyone.*

Leon is the grumpy punk with the guitar. Nina is the bad bitch and the party girl. Finn the gentleman, the rich boy, aka the dad. Aidan is the athlete, the funny one and the hottie. *The flirt.* And Kai is the mysterious stubborn guy who´s athletic and creative. He has that aura that tells you to *fuck off.* But it draws you in. Like you want to be the one he likes. To be different. *I wanted that too.* But I ended up with shame and anger.

In ways girls are pathetic. We search for our hearts in guys′ bodies instead of our own.

I have the feeling I′m being watched. My face burns. And when I look up, I see *Kai*. He′s opposite the island, staring at me. My heart sinks painfully. Even though I saw him a few hours ago, it feels like ages. *It feels so far away. Everything.*

We lock eyes. "Thought you wouldn′t come." He says. *Me neither.*

"It′s your birthday." I say, trying to sound normal. He eyes me and comes over. He′s dressed all black. And stands an arm length from me. It would be so easy to reach for him.

But I don′t. I can′t.

"Like your cakes." I say instead of touching him. He nods once. "I bet you do." He responds, hiding his smirk.

I took the box and hand it to him. "I′ve got you a gift." I say with a forced smile. He takes it and opens it. He frowns but then he grins slightly. "I like it." He says, looking at me. He means it, which pisses me off. *He can′t be serious.*

"Happy birthday, *lost boy*." I say, but my voice is weird. His smile fades, and mine too. I feel a stab in my chest as his eyes beg mine to stay.

"I′ll go." I say and walk past him. *So much for behaving normally.*

- 27 -

He stands across the room with his back to me.

As often his shirt has a quote on it.

"Watch me take a good thing and fuck it all up in one night. – MGK"

My chest hurts. *At least he knows he fucked up.*

But that doesn′t hurt less. It hurts even more. *That he knows. That he knew.*

But it did hurt anyway. *Hurt me.* Because he wanted to. *Hurt me.*

And he did. *He won.*

71

We sit on the sofa and play a drinking game.

Kai sits across me. *Somehow, he′s always in my view.* Andi′s to my left. We haven′t talked a word which I′m glad about. He just got wasted the minute he came. And ignored me just as I ignored him.

When it′s my turn, I wish I hadn′t played in the first place. Nina snatches the phone as I do nothing and reads aloud. "Lia has to sit on Kai′s lap for the rest of the game." She announces excitedly.

His eyes wander to mine. Of course, that´s my task.

The universe wants to mess with me.

I inhaled annoyed. His jaw twitches. He hasn´t let me out of sight all night long.

On purpose, he´s always next to me.

Andi laughs muttering "*of course*" under his breath. I shoot him a look as I stand up. Kai straightens and leans back to make room for me. I sat down. His arm rests on the backrest. My face heats. I avoid Andi´s eyes. But I see him empty his cup.

We continued to play more rounds. Kai´s one hand has moved to my waist.

It´s my turn again. Nina, who has declared herself the game leader *(as always)*, reads. "Lia has to spend seven minutes in heaven with Andi." She chirps, smiling at both of us. I feel Kai´s body tense. Andi and I exchanged glances.

"We´re not dating anymore." I point out. He nods agreeing. Nina looks confused. "Yeah, no more grinding on my dick for her." He spits. Kai´s grip tightens. I feel his bones working making the mental decision to stand up, but I speak up. "Get over yourself." I retort. He smiles. He´s plastered. *This isn´t good.*

"That´s the game." Nina says. *And you must play and follow the rules.*

"I´ll go with her." Kai speaks up from behind before I can argue. My heart sinks as he tries to stand up. He grabs my hips, lifting me with him, not letting go for a second too long.

"Sure." Andi comments. "Fuck you." I mouth. "Perfect. Into the washroom then." Nina beams. The room is small, and they lock up and turn off the lights. I exhale annoyed. "What else." I say but Kai turns on a different light above the mirror by the sink. It´s not bright but better than being in complete dark with him.

We stand opposite each other. He leans against the washing machine and I against the dryer. For a moment we just stare at each other until I can´t stand his black eyes and lower my gaze.

"Look.." he begins, but I cut him off. "Kai." I try to stop him, but he interrupts me. "Just listen to me. Let me explain." He begs. I look at him. *He won´t let go.*

"Okay, then go ahead." I say gesturing with my hand, still not looking at him. "I know I fucked up." He says, and I join in "You do?" I ask, raising a brow. "I know I did." He states.

"But it *wasn´t* a bet. I swear. You must believe me." He says and I smile like the devil. "How should I believe *anything* you say?" I ask him. "Just listen." He begs and I press my mouth shut. "Yes, we hate each other but it *wasn´t* a bet. We did fuck around with girls in the past. We did those games and messed with the others crushes. We were never friends. It was always battling between us. I´ve grown up with that pisser. We are like that. Always been." He shrugs. "And I know him well enough. To know his intentions with you. I mean, I think, he really liked you but realized it won´t happen." He says. "But it started with a game for him. He wanted to piss me off. Since he saw me giving you that sweater at the campfire. And then at his birthday when I took you home.." He trails off. "He wanted to get back at me. For things.. *in the past.* Many of the guys try to fuck with me. Because I used to fuck with them. I was the best. The worst.." He says, and I can imagine. "But he never could." He explains.

"Until me." I say, not sure if that´s what he´s telling me. He nods slightly. "But I didn´t mess with you. Yeah, I didn´t like you in the beginning and I wanted you to fuck off. But I didn´t plan to play with you. Not like that." He says.

"Then like what?" I ask. "I didn´t want you near me. Until.. *I didn´t.* But when I realized I didn´t really hate you, he showed up." He looks at me. "And I told you he didn´t fell. He pushed you on purpose. But I didn´t want to show him I care. I knew he would try to hurt me by hurting you. So, I pretended to not care and dated. But he wasn´t stupid. *He knew.* You were different. There were never girls they could have messed with me." He admits. I look at him. *You were different.*

"Never until me?" I ask. He nods. "I couldn´t admit that I care. That I like you. Because I don´t want to." He tells me. "I knew he would with you to piss me off. But I couldn´t tell you. Or him. It´s been fucked. It´s complicated there´s a lot more to what happened in the past. Things got fucked with all our games. But some didn´t want to stop." He says, but I don´t get it. "I know I fucked up. *I know.* But I swear this wasn´t a bet for me. You´re.. more. I.. I can´t explain *how..* I feel.. about you. I´m not good with that. With.. words, but I´m good at stealing them." He struggles to be vulnerable.

As always.

"Songs explain what I can´t say." He nods. "So just listen." He says soft and takes his phone out and turns on a song.

Body bag - Machine Gun Kelly feat. Yungblood

While we were listening, I tried hard not to look at him, touch him, kiss him, cry, or anything. I took in the text I´ve heard before. But now I listened differently.

Line for line. Like he sang em to me.

I don´t think because the song mentions *love* that he loves me. But I think he´s into me. And this.. *was his own way of telling me.*

The others have probably forgotten us. Or gave us some extra minutes.

I still don´t look up. I want to cry. I want to scream. I want to give in and fall into his arms. But I think about the way he left me in the dark. The way he *did* play me.

Maybe without intending to, but he still kept up with Andi. He could have told me, make a move or anything. *But he didn´t. But he had his reasons.*

"It wasn´t a bet." He whispers voice shaking. *Telling me it´s true.*

"It wasn´t." He repeats as I stare at his legs. I swallow. "When you had the chance to sleep with me.. you didn´t." I say and lock eyes with him. "Whereas Andi kept trying. He might have said it was okay, but he kept pushing me. For him, it was a game. He wanted to get on your nerves. He even said that to me. That he knew he had no chance." I say my heart up my chest. But before he can return something, the lock turns, and the door opens.

We head back to the living room.

As I sit down, Nina turns to me. "You still have to sit on Kai´s lap, Scar." She reminds me and I roll my eyes. I sit down, he wraps his arm around me and pulls me close. "Like he didn´t just *fuck* her in there." Andi scoffs. "What the hell?" I gape at him, followed by Kai. "Shut the fuck up." His grip tightens around me in anger. Andi laughs spitefully. "I bet her pussy was tight. You like it tight, don´t you?" He growls and my jaw drops. *What the fuck?*

And with that Kai loses it.

"Bro, what the fuck?" Ryan asks. "Yeah, Ry is right. You can´t talk like that to her." Nina yells at him. Others mutter shocked too. But Kai gets up. "Something you´ll never find out, bastard." He snaps between clenched teeth. Andi stands up too. "Already did." He says with a smug grin. *He didn´t.*

"Wasn´t *that* good." He provokes with a grin. "Son of a bitch." Kai roars and punches him right in the face. Andi laughs like he´s enjoying the whole thing. And something tells me he does. *But I don´t get it.*

People step back, trying not to get pushed by their bodies. Kai collects a few punches but fires back double. Andi lunges at him and they both slam into the glass table, which shatters under their weight along with bottles and glasses.

Kai throws him to the floor and comes on top of him, slamming his fist at his jaw repeatedly. Andi´s face is bleeding, but he keeps laughing.

"You´re right, it´s no game." Andi tells him, and Kai hits his nose until it cracks.

The boys finally manage to part them. Ryan and Finn pull Andi away, and Aidan and Leon drag Kai away. Andi´s teeth are stained red. Kai´s face is equally bloodshot.

"Get the fuck out, piece of shit." Kai yells but Ryan drags Andi outside.

Kai wipes his face and spits blood on the floor. Without looking at me, he walks straight up the stairs. *What..?*

"You okay, Lia?" Nina asks, still shocked. "Yeah." I say, but I´m not sure. Finn faces me. "I´ll handle Andi. I´m sorry. He´s a total dick. I don´t know what got into him." He tells me, but I know he knows. *Finn knew all along.*

"He´s pretty wasted. Are you going to check on him, please?" He asks, looking after Kai. I nod and go after him.

Kai leans over the sink, filling with droplets of blood. When he sees me, he walks towards me. He takes my cheeks with both hands, searching my face. "You, okay?" he asks as if I had been attacked not just verbally but physically too. Like I´m the one bleeding. And that´s when I know he wasn´t lying. *It wasn´t a bet. No game.* He cared about me. *Wanted me. Felt for me.* And he wanted to protect me. I see it in his gaze. *I see it. No hiding. He shows me. He wants me. And it is the truth.* And he doesn´t have to say it.

I nod and he lets go of me. I take his right hand and look at his crushed knuckles. His arms have tons of cuts from the shards. He´s bleeding from his eyebrow, nose, and the corner of his mouth. His lip is split, and his cheek purple red. I touch his face. He comes closer, takes my waist.

"I should kill him." He whispers, clenching his jaw. His hot breath brushes my lips. I step closer. *My heart in my soul.*

"Kiss me." I whisper in desperate. His chest rises and falls violently. And a second later, his lips crash down on mine. He pushes me against the bathroom door and takes my cheek in his hand. I whimper in relief as I taste metallic blood, and it gets me high like a drug.

It tastes good.

He kisses me possessively, as if he were afraid, I would disappear. I reach for his side and hold onto him. I press him to me as hard as I can, and he too comes closer, leaving no space between us. *I can´t breathe, but I breathe him.*

He pulls away, and his red-rimmed dark eyes stare at me. "*Kissed by an angel. Touched by the devil.*" He quotes MGK, and I smile. *Pretty accurate.*

"Wanna get out of here?" He asks with a grin. "I hate birthdays anyway." He adds. I grin. "Me too." I say. "What do you have in mind?" I ask. He smiles. "There´s a rave." He grins and I beam. *How do I know this isn´t another game?* I don´t. But I believe him it´s not.

We sneak out and drive to the coordinates.

Hardstyle drones through the basement. When you listen to music, you feel like the main character. That´s what life doesn´t do to you. It doesn´t give you the main character feeling. That´s why we do art, sport, listen to music, read, or write. We want to feel like the main character we think we aren´t, but we are, we just can´t feel. Can´t see what music lets us feel. But in this moment, we felt like it. *The main characters.* And I believe we were. *In some story, we were.* But I wasn´t sure if it was ours.

I´m high from the headshots and the sight of Kai´s neon red skin. Especially the handprint on his neck, which stretches all the way down to his neck, keeps catching my attention. *My handprint.* My vision blurs and my thoughts too. Flashbacks of Kai putting his hand on my neck. Firm enough to make me horny, but not enough to hurt.

Or just a bit.

My fingers touch the spot on my throat. And after an hour of raving, I still feel it.

His hand. His kiss. Him.

After I branded him with the blood-red paint, he too has left his light blue marks on me. *Marks I never want to get rid of. Never.*

As my eyes focus, the black silhouette in front of me becomes Kai. Kai, who stares at my neck. *At my hand on his mark. Close.* So close that our bodies almost touch. *Almost. Almost close.* So close that I have to lift my head, and he has to look down at me. I think I might pass out from the way he looks at me. His chest rises and falls. And I too feel my skin too tight, taking my breath away. I breathe and choke at the same time. His eyes burn through me. His jaw flexes and his face just inches from mine.

My head is forced to him. And only then do I realize his hand on my throat. I felt him the whole time, like he never let go. *He never did.*

He pushes me to him. I swallow hard as his lips brush mine. His grip tightens as my hands seek his chest. My hand digs into the fabric, his hand under my jaw and our lips collide. We kiss wildly. Full of affection and venom. I bite down on his lower lip, whereupon his hand moves down my back. He kneads my ass and sucks on my tongue. I run my hand through his hair and scratch his neck.

We rave until the morning hours. *Never letting go. Never.*

What they didn´t know back then was that words mean no actions. But actions don´t mean words either.

72

I lie in my bed on a Friday afternoon, the day before my birthday and I pleasantly would like to do the same thing tomorrow. I want to order food and never leave my bed. In fact, I don´t even want to see my family. Not that I´ve done much in the past. The last time I celebrated was in fifth grade. Just one of my friends that I´ve invited came, and after that I just stopped. I prefer to go to birthdays instead of celebrating my own anyway. Maybe it´s because I didn´t have enough people I could have invited. Or I was scared no one would come. Now I do have friends, but I still rather do nothing. *Having no friends is a choice.* And in the past, I have chosen to have none. Now it could be different, but I never liked the attention.

I´m torn out of my nap by my phone. *It´s Kai.*

"Hmh?" I answer. "Pack your stuff. Tonight´s our plane." He says. "What?" I ask, still in dreamland. "I´m not telling you where we´re going. But we´ll be away for the weekend. The two of us." He says. Still drowsy, I don´t really understand. "What?" I repeat. He chuckles and tells me again.

"You´ve already booked?" I ask. "Yes." He replies. "You´re crazy" I laugh.

"What makes you so sure I´m coming with you?" I ask. *Silence.*

He breathes deeply. "You´re going to regret not coming. Besides, you said you didn´t want to see anyone." He says. *I´m glad he remembered.*

"You won´t see anyone you know but me. We both hate birthdays, and you´ve spent mine with me too, so I owe you one." He says. "Good point," I say.

"So, pack your bags." He says. "Hand luggage only." He adds. "You´re crazy." I say again. "I never said otherwise." I hear his grin.

"I´ll be there in an hour." He says and hangs up. *You kidding me?*

I hold my phone to my chest. I must grin. *He´s completely insane.*

I text him that I don´t know what to pack. He writes that the weather is like ours.

I take out my black suitcase and pack everything I think I need. I ask him about the price, but he won´t let me pay. *We´re still discussing that.*

But I have to tell my parents. *Or not?* Maybe it´s better this way.

I wear my jeans with a black long-sleeved top. Along with my black boots and a black coat. I wear my hair curled. I put on Kai´s black cap and sneak out. It´s dark outside and Kai´s already waiting in his car. He gets out and takes the suitcase and puts it in the trunk. He comes up to me and hugs me. He wears jeans with a black sweater, a black coat, and black vans. In terms of style, we have the same taste.

We get in the car. *It smells like him.* And I feel good near him. Even though I didn´t want to admit that to myself but I think he feels the same way. We haven´t talked about his birthday yet, and I don´t know if we´ll do. But I want to spend time with him. I can´t believe we´re doing this. *He spends my birthday with me.*

- 27 -

We walk toward the entrance.

"How do you imagine that I won´t know where we´re going?" I ask. "On the plane, I hear it anyway." I say and stop. He faces me. "I thought I was gagging you." He says wryly. I smile, but I´m annoyed.

"Come on, where are we going?" I beg. He rubs his neck. "Alright" he starts. "My parents´ company has several locations, mainly in Europe. We have apartments or offices to stay in. For employees and directors." He explains. "And we´re spending the weekend in one of those." He says. "That´s impressive. Are they all condos?" I ask and he nods. "They run through the company. One of the few advantages of having busy parents who don´t give a damn about their family." He laughs until he´s not.

"Well, it doesn´t matter" he says and won´t meet my gaze. We´re silent for a while, and he stares on the ground. *He does care.* But it´s worse to want something you know you´ll never have, so better not to want it. *Right?*

"Paris," he says and seeks my eyes. I have to grin. "Really?" I ask. He nods slowly. "You´re crazy." I say, and but beam. "You already said that." He points out. I nudge him.

At the gate we sit at the window watching the planes, and he reads to me. After I showed him my bookshelf, I had to lend him *every* book. He bought another shelf for my books. After he read mine, he bought them. But he insisted on reading mine first. He wanted to see my highlighted parts. And at the beginning I felt unease of him seeing all the thoughts I shared with fictional characters. It was like a piece of my mind, or like a diary. Secrets he now knew. You can get to know someone well by looking at their annotations.

He doesn´t annotate. He practically writes between and over lines. His books are full of his writings. I tried to read them, but they´re way too messy. Like he tries to rewrite the book or to write his own onto the pages of others. He has so much to say but writes instead of saying. Books are his second brain. They are part of him. Maybe even part of his soul. I really tried to read, but it´s like trying to understand the smearing of a professor. Just like I can´t figure him out, I can´t find the code for his scribble. It´s just words, but it´s so much more. Like he has his own way to use letters. So, I stopped reading but let him read them to me, because he had a perspective in his chaos. We even read books in sync and talked about them afterward. Like our own book club.

On the plane, I sit by the window, and he next to me. We listen to music and look at the lights of the cities. He reads his book, and I watch him.

As I try to sleep, he pulls me to him, and I lay my head against his shoulder. Eventually he lays his against mine as well.

And we drift away over the clouds of Europe.

73

The apartment is modernly furnished with a Parisian touché. It has two floors. Upstairs is the bedroom and an office, along with a huge bathroom with a freestanding bathtub. The lower level has an open kitchen, a living room and dining room. A fire escape leads to the roof terrace where are flowerpots an old gazebo with fairy lights and a daybed. From up there, you can see the Eiffel Tower.

"Why don´t you always live here?" I ask, enjoying the view. "This is not our home" he says as and leans on his forearms.

"We used to come here more often, though. When I was younger." He says. "It´s amazing" I look to him. "I really appreciate all of this." I assure him. He nods.

"So, what do you want to do?" He asks. "Let's get something to eat and take a walk?" I suggest and he nod. "I´m just going to put on a dress" I say.

- 27 -

We make our way home, as it´s shortly before midnight. Kai plays hobby photographer and makes pictures of me, as I walk along the street.

When we reach the building, it starts to pour. But I head into the other direction.

"What are you doing?" He calls out. I turn to face him, walking backwards. "See the Eiffel Tower" I shout back. "It´s pouring." He yells. I beam at him. "Has that ever stopped us?" I retort. He looks at me and grins. He shakes his head and joins me.

He knows the answer to that.

We walk towards the Tower and after a while, he reaches for my hand and stops. He turns me to face him. "Dance with me." He begs, his voice rough like he´s nervous. He hands me one of his pods. The song *Devil like me by Dexter and the moon rocks* plays. There are people around us hurrying with their umbrellas, as we start to dance. He takes away my tension by spinning and pulling me into his arms. With one, he holds my hand and with the other around the waist. His forehead touches mine. Our cloths are drenched and the asphalt fills with puddles. Everything splashes around us as we move in the middle of the endless sea of the streets. He sings the lines along, and I laugh cause of the high I feel. We drank wine and, he got weed from some friends, so we´re actually a bit high of it all.

I stopped counting how many times the song repeated. How many times the devil sang to me, and I listened.

Again, he turns me. *Back and forth.* But this time he doesn´t pull me back to his arms but let´s go of me. Blinking, I try to look at him through the rain.

"Happy Birthday, *lost girl.*" His voice husky through the rain.

I totally forgot my birthday. I forgot the time. *I forgot it all.*

"I don´t think much of presents, but I think much of you, Scar." He says and I smile at him. I fall into his arms, and he holds me. For a while we just stand there. Holding each other while the rain does the kissing, that we don´t need at all.

As we part, he asks me what I want to do. Partying or going home. But I just smile and let myself fall backwards into the puddle that became a sea.

He tried to reach for me to stop me from falling, but I caught him off guard, so he had to let me fall. *Watch me fall.*

I laugh and he looks down on me. "You okay?" He asks and I beam. "Always wanted to do that." I say and let my hand through the rainwater. He chuckles and lets himself fall next to me, splashing.

We look the sky and blink at the drops to see the stars. I smile because I feel like seven.

But before the cold sweeps into our bones, we get up and hurry back.

74

We hung up the jackets and shoes to dry after we wrung them out.

"We should take a shower" he says. "Definitely" I agree. "Wait a minute" he says and disappears into the bathroom.

When he comes back, he takes my hand and leads me. *It´s pitch dark.*

"Do you trust me?" He asks. His voice sounds sexy and smoky with a hint of strain. "Yes," I reply. "Okay." He whispers. I hear him taking his T-shirt off and his pants and the rest. He walks into the rain shower and turns on the water.

He left the lights off for me? He remembered I couldn´t take that step with Andi. He wants me to feel comfortable.

It´s even more exciting to see nothing. My heart races as I take off my clothes and get into the shower. I stand behind him and sense him. The hot water runs over my body. He stands facing me, because even though I can´t see, I feel his gaze on me.

I always do.

He keeps his distance. But I want him to be close. I reach for his chest. He takes shallow breaths. *He´s so warm.*

His hand finds mine and holds it tight. "Turn around," he murmurs. *I do.*

He brushes my hair aside. My body tingles. Lust and goosebumps mix. He kisses my shoulder, down my collarbone to my neck. His hand holds my waist. I can´t help but put my head in the neck. And as I do so, I bump into his chest and his cock grazes me. He sucks in a breath. Then he kisses me under the ear and a moan escapes me. My heart beats all the way to my fingertips. I press against him and feel his full length against my back.

"Fuck," he growls. *He feels big.*

He grabs both of my hips, steadying himself. We breathe louder. He claws into my skin.

Scratching me.

He keeps trailing kisses.

But before more can happen, he backs away.

Breathlessly, I stare into the dark. He kisses me on the forehead and gets out of the shower. He hands me a towel. He disappears and lets me get dressed.

I tried hard not to touch myself after. He had another chance. *But he didn´t.*

Sex is something spiritual. It´s a bond. That´s why he waits. Because he knows it´s more. Or to make you fall more, a voice told me. *But I didn´t listen.*

75

In bed, I lie at the foot and watch the rain pattering against the ceiling-high windows. I imagine him and Finn with his parents here years ago.

I wonder how everything changed?

"Want me to read something?" He offers taking me back. "That you´d even ask," I say offended and he chuckles. I hear him turn the pages. *I close my eyes.* And concentrate on the rain and wait for his voice. Hearing him is like drinking lavender tea before going to bed. Or waking up in a warm bed before you have to get up. It´s like watching the starry sky. It´s the tranquility of snorkeling. The soothing sound of the hairdryer. Like a thunderstorm. The air after rain in the summer. *It´s like a night in Paris.*

His voice has such an effect on me that I´m peacefully tired and wide awake. His voice is deep, raspy, and sexy. It´s how I imagine dying peacefully. Where it is warm. And raining constantly. You hear the voice you love, and you fall asleep.

He stops reading and stands up.

"Come on." He urges. "Now?" I ask. "Yes now."

It´s not raining anymore. We sit by the river across us, the Eiffel Tower. It´s kind of chills, but we brought a blanket. "You want to tell me what we´re doing here?" I ask impatiently. "Just wait." He laughs. "Fine." I say.

Moment´s pass, and then the tower lights in white and blinks like a diamond in the sun. I grin and I feel him staring at me, watching my reaction. Or maybe he has seen it many times. *Either way, he´s watching me.*

"It´s beautiful." I say. "Hmm." He hums and after a moment he looks ahead too.

"I feel bad that I yelled at you on your birthday." I say quietly. "No, you don´t." He laughs. "No, I don´t." I admit. "I deserved." He states. "You did." I agree.

- 27 -

The rest of my birthday we spend eating, reading, and visiting an art museum. Finn told Kai that Nina has organized a party, so we flew back. I´m sad, *but sometimes things have to end when they feel the best.*

The party was nothing special compared to Paris, but it was the best birthday. I got cakes from the group. Andi made me one for apologies. *I forgave him.*

"Cute but Scorpio."

"One year closer to becoming a milf."

"For you, I would."

"Small boobs big heart"

"Lost girl"

"Another love"

"Small tits for big dick"

I wondered which one was from Kai. *Or if he even made me one.*

76

December

Kai opens the door. I´m in my pajamas. He´s too. *For a change.*

He looks calm, as if he *actually* slept for once. "Hi." He says. "Can I come in?" I ask. "Sure. " He says, making room for me. We go upstairs.

He gets back into his bed, watching me standing there. "You okay?" He asks frowning. "Yeah." I nod and lay next to him. He reads my face. We snug under the bedding, and he flips the light. We´re on the side facing each other. The lantern outside illuminates the room slightly.

"You´re okay?" He asks again, voice soft. My throat burns. "No." I choak feeling my face heating. He pulls me to him and under his blanket. I grab his shirt. He holds me tight. I feel our hearts beating too fast to be friends. *As they always do.*

But hearts can´t speak. So, they keep beating the words we can´t say.

He pushes his knee between my legs to get me closer. He kisses my forehead. I look up at him. Our noses touch. Our breaths sync, brushing each other on the face like rain carried away from the wind.

"I feel safe with you." I whisper. He looks like that was the best compliment he ever got. And then he kisses me. But slow and soft. For the first time it´s not violently or possessive.

It´s gentle and intently.

"I feel okay with you." He says, and my heart shatters into a billion butterflies. "When I´m with you. I like myself." He adds in a whisper.

I melt into his lips. He touches me like he never made me feel confused. It´s overwhelming. Like *everything* when it comes to him.

It´s so good I might die. I might cry. *I might fly.*

- 27 -

I wake up and we switched positions. He spoons me. His hard on pokes my ass. His arm is underneath my shirt. He holds my hand while grazing my naked tits with his arm. His head is against mine. And his other hand is under my head outstretched. I hold his other hand too.

How did we end up in that intimate position?

But I´ll give anything to wake up like this every day.

We lie like that for hours. *Even after he woke up.*

That kiss was different. It wasn´t like the first, too quick to be real. It wasn´t like the second, full of affection, neediness, or sadness. It wasn´t like the third, wildly, drunk, and high or the others.

It was honest and full of rare emotions. *It was conscious.*

77

Christmas

I know Kai and his brother had to spend most of their Christmas´s with the Avery´s. Although I can´t imagine their parents are as rarely as Kai told me at home but I haven´t met them.

I haven´t seen Kai in a few days. *Life got busy.* But I had to see him today.

The light of the lanterns illuminate the thick flakes falling from the night sky. I wear a tight, black, long-sleeved dress with a beige-brown coat and high black boots. The door opens, Finn who´s dressed in a shirt and suit pants. *As always. I barely see him in leisure clothes.* Mostly when he trains. His shirt is unbuttoned the first four, exposing his chest. And there is a dishtowel around his shoulder.

"Lia," he says, surprised. "Hi, come in. Kai´s next door. I´m sure he´ll be back when he knows you´re here. Or you can go over if you want." He continues.

"I should have let you know I was coming. I just thought.." I try to explain, but he interrupts me. "I´m sure he´s happy to see you." He assures me. "I´ll be in the kitchen. If you want something to eat or drink. Help yourself." He says and with that he closes the door and heads to the kitchen. I follow him. *Silence.*

He looks to the side. "I suppose you want to know if they were here." He assumes. "Yeah, I know, he doesn´t like to talk about them. So, I thought you could if you want, tell a little." I stammer and he nods. "They were. For a few hours. We had lunch, and they were planning to stay over the holidays." He begins. "But they pushed Kai. Talked about the company. And it got out of hand. He yelled at them. And freaked out. He threw the presents on the street and left." He says and leans against the counter.

"There were times when at least one of them was with us. When we were younger. At least.. for Kai." He runs his hand through his hair, Kai does that too when he´s thinking. I take off my coat and put it over the bar stool and sit down.

"That must have been hard for you. I mean now you are older but back then." I say and he sighs. "I had to grow up early. Taking care of Kai, manage school, basketball, the house, relationships, and friends at once." He tells me. "He was just nine when they went on their first business trip for longer to London. I was thirteen, and it was easier for me. They always worked a lot, but before they were at least at home. They were away a lot, but it got more." He says. "There were other times, of course. Kai always had hope they would stay. But they kept jetting between here and there." He trails off as he talks. "I think the worst thing for him was not knowing when they would fuck off again." He looks through me.

"Nobody deserves to grow up like that. For Kai, you were the safe haven. You can be proud of yourself." I say, but I know I can´t find the right words. "I had no other choice. When I hit puberty, I had him on my leg. I always took him with me when I went out. All my friends knew him. He loved to play Neverland." He slightly grins. "He would play or sleep there while we were partying. We often stayed here so he didn´t have to be alone, or I asked the Avery´s if he could spend the night with them." He tells me.

"They were like a second family, weren´t they?" I ask. He looks off, and it seems like he´s reliving old times. "Yes, especially for Kai." He says, and we´re silent for a while.

"He told me about the insomnia." I say softly. He looks at me in surprise. "He did?" he asks, and I nod. "How long?" I ask. "Since they left. But also, before." He says. "All his life, actually. It came creeping. Started with nightmares and sleeping paralysis. But then it got worse as he grew older. The dreams got vivid. He couldn´t sleep at all or didn´t want to, anymore. I couldn´t calm him. He wouldn´t let me. Even as a kid." He says, and I can imagine. "He always wanted to do things alone. I think, he had the feeling he had to." He says quietly. *Because he was left alone.*

"His anxiety was bad, but therapy didn´t help. Then he got prescribed cannabis, and it got better. For a while." He explains. "But as a teen, he stopped sleeping. Sometimes he slept during the days." He nods but trails off.

"He has a quite different relationship with our parents than I had. We had in general such different childhoods. But I´ve been responsible for him." He says and I listen silently. "It was important for them to leave us *something*. A name and a company. They always been workaholics. It was their dream to become successful. Never to be good parents." He says.

"I grew up lovingly. But with Kai, they seemed to have other priorities. I´m mad at them for him, but I can´t feel what he went through. Even if I wished I could take away the pain." He says. "I could only be more for him than just his brother. But no one can replace parents." He says and I nod. "Maybe someday they will regret their decisions. But that doesn´t undo anything." He says. "I was a teen but had to be a parent. Even as a Kid, I had to." He says.

"I don´t know what to say. Why didn´t they hire a nanny?" I ask. He grins. "They did." He nods. "But I´ve sent them away." He tells me. "I did not want any strangers to raise him. He didn´t need more people in his life who would leave." He says, shaking his head and I nod.

"It´s remarkable what you did. That you have mastered all this." I say. "Sometimes I wonder how I managed." He smiles weakly.

I can´t imagine what they´ve been through.

"It certainly took away part of your youth, but you became a stronger person. For you and your brother. You have each other, and that´s the most important thing. Your relationship." I say and he stiffs a laugh. "I would have traded my childhood for him." He tells me. "I know." I whisper.

Finn pulls out two wine glasses and pours for us.

"I´m glad because we´re close, but on the other hand I hate them for taking away the chance of a normal childhood. And it´s no fun doing teen things when there´s no one to punish you. Even though Addison and Logan did that part well." He chuckles.

Aidan and Leon´s parents. You could think the four are brothers as they behave. And in ways they are.

Pan had never siblings, he made him ones. The lost ones.

"I tried but I was a teen myself." He says. "Understandable," I counter, sipping the wine. He drinks his glass in one go and refills.

"Thank you for trusting me. It´s not a matter of course." I profess. "It feels good to talk about it, and maybe it will help you understand him." He says and smiles at me. I stare at his dimples. He´s always serious Like Kai. *But in a different way.*

"Yes, it does." I nod. "I don´t want to push him to talk. Sometimes he just wants me to be with him, I guess." I say and he grins. "He has never let a girl get to him like you." He´s studying me. I can´t hide my grin, and I´m probably beaming.

"But don´t tell him I said that. He´ll kill me." He adds, pointing his glass at me. I have to laugh. "He would deny it." I retort. "Yeah, he definitely would." He matches my smile.

We stare at each other. He blinks twice and clears his throat. "I´m going to take a shower. I need to get out of these clothes." He says, tugging at his collar. "Make yourself comfortable." He says and puts the glass on the counter. "I will, thanks." I say and he disappears.

I go to the front door, take off my boots and hang up my jacket.

The door to the terrace opens and I turn to see Kai in the living room. He wears a black shirt, which is rolled up. He looks chic and casual. His wispy dark brown hair is full of individual snowflakes. He wears a ring on his right index finger. He wears it seldom.

But it´s always the same.

He looks at me and for a second, I can´t breathe. We haven´t seen each other for a while.

It feels like lifetimes.

In his eyes I see despair and longing. He drops the coat he´s holding and walks towards me. My heart sinks as he wraps his arms around me and buries his head in my neck. I can feel his heartbeat and for a second it seems as if our hearts beat in the same rhythm.

"You´re here?" He asks breathlessly into my hair. "I wanted to see you." I say against his chest. "Me too." He admits.

We break away and he eyes me. "You look beautiful." He whispers as if afraid of what his words will do.

His eyes are red. *Always black and Red. He cried.*

"Thanks. You too. Should wear it more often." I say, smiling and grab his shirt by his chest. He holds my hand before I can pull away and presses it to his heart, so I feel it thumping. I love how he shows me what I am to him. He doesn´t say it with his words. But much more beautifully through quotes, looks, touches, and actions. Even though it hurts that he doesn´t open up the way I want him to. That he pushes me away and runs. But I´m grateful for every second. *For all he can give.*

"Thank you," he says. "For coming." He clarifies. His voice is brittle.

Always full of meaning. Full of pain.

Only now I notice his purple knuckles. I take his hands and stare at his wounds.

Did he punch his father? Finn would have mentioned it. *Right?*

When I look at him, his eyes are glassy. I have rarely seen him as broken as at this very moment. But this time, I´m the one breaking down his walls and press my lips to his. His hands clasp my cheeks, trembling, and our bodies press against each other. Salt paired with bitter vodka makes its way into my mouth. And I know that I belong to him. Even if we don´t quite have each other, we do. Those moments when we push our fears aside and let our hearts win. When we shut our brains and feel the moment. When Kai falls and I catch him. When I fall and he catches me. *When we live. When we dare. When we care.*

We break away, and I see traces of hot tears on his cheeks. "Kiss me again." He hushes with a need I´ve never seen on him.

I kiss him again. He kisses me.

"Again Scar." He begs me to kiss the pain away.

We part, and he kisses my forehead. He looks a lot calmer. My heart flutters at the thought I did that.

His head leans against mine, and we breathe each other in.

"Wanna dance in the snow?" he grins staring down at me. As an answer, I get dressed.

The snowed-in street sparkles like diamonds. And now I discover the presents in the snow. He spins me around, and we drop into the cold snow. I do a snow angel, and he watches. We lie down and look up at the starry sky. Thick flakes fall into my face, which makes me grin. Snow is like rain, only silent. Like when you cry, but no sound comes out.

"Did you have a nice Christmas?" he asks. "I think so." I say. "You?" I ask, regretting it in the same moment. *Why did I ask that?*

"I do *now*." He says, his voice soft. But before I can say anything back, a snowball hits Kai in the face. Not a second later, I too get a charge.

We jump up. Aidan and Leon are at the fence and throw more in our direction. Screeching, I save myself behind one of the cars. Kai fires back.

Aidan grabs me from behind and wrestles me to the ground, dumping snow down my neckline. I cry out. When he releases me, I chase after him.

I put snow in Leon´s pants and polish Aidan´s face. The two of them pin me to the ground so Kai can pour snow on me. *Burying me.*

Later, even Finn joins us, and we form teams. We fight and build snowmen. And have one of the best Christmas we ever had. With our real home. *Our friends.*

The lost boys. *In Neverland.*

But just as a snowflake melts, the moments pass. *And they never come again.*

78

December 31st, One More Light (Originally Performed by Linkin Park) – Instrumental – Covered up

We spend New Year´s in a disco with the usual clique. It´s been seven days since I last saw Kai. But only seven seconds since I thought about him.

Only a few minutes until midnight.

I´m standing on the roof between people dancing and the starry sky above me. Fireworks are already being set off, illuminating the black night.

Since neither Kai nor I drink alcohol, we stand there without champagne. We wanted to meet up here, but there are only Kai and me. Maybe we should have drunk.

Only a few seconds left.

Our eyes roam and meet again, which makes us smile.

We have a conversation. *I just don´t know about what.*

Some start counting. Kai lights a sparkler. I hold mine up to him to light it.

Ten... Nine... Eight...

He looks at me while I tell something. *I just don´t know what.*

Five... Four... Three...

He steps closer and grabs my cheek. But he stops in front of my face. As if it occurs to him that we are not alone. That we´re not doing this. Kissing each other in front of everyone. But not even our friends are here right now. *Or not yet.*

But still. *Nothing.*

Two... One...

"Happy New Year, Scar." He says his voice rough releasing my cheek and taking a step back. *Away from me.*

Zero...

Not a second later, Nina and Leon come up followed by Aidan, Andi, Finn, Luca, and Ryan.

Happy New Year.

We look at each other. *My heart on the line.*

Nothing.

My heart on the ground.

And that´s the moment I realize nothing has changed. And it probably won´t either. He had the chance to kiss me in front our friends. He had those chances in the past, but today it could have been official. I´m no longer with Andi.

But he didn´t. He stepped away from me. *No hug. Nothing.*

I didn´t kiss him either, but he´s the one in charge. It´s his step. *But he refused.*

I thought after Andi, he would realize what he has in me. I thought he just needed time. But I was wrong. I was still a secret. *Still nothing.*

I chose him. He chose to change nothing. I thought Christmas had changed something. But it didn´t turn out the way I hoped. *Even hope dies in the end.*

And because no one knows. No one noticed, either. They didn´t see how close I was to cry. How we just looked at each other like oceans got between us. Like he knew he drew that line.

So, they didn´t see how I was breaking. *But he did. He saw.* And again, he did nothing. I wanted to jump and let the wind take me away. *Away from Peter and his empty promises.* Away from nothing. *But I didn´t.*

Maybe I didn´t told anyone because they would have talked me out of it. And I didn´t want to hear that. I wanted him even if I shouldn´t. And that´s where it got me.

Nowhere.

Wanting to be wanted is the saddest and loneliest feeling ever. I just want to be loved by someone else than myself.

My eyes burn like hell, and I must pull myself together not to cry. Because no heartbreak is worse than unrequited love. *Then hope. Then unfulfilled wishes.*

We all hugged and wished each other *Happy New Year*. We watched the fireworks. But all I could see was a firecracker that didn´t ignite. Every time we tried to light the string, it didn´t work. The flame went out before it could reach the fireworks.

Is that what we are? A broken firecracker? Something that you know would be beautiful, but out of fear it would be ephemeral, you leave it untried?

But maybe it´s a good thing. Because fireworks are only breathtaking for a moment, until they disappear. Something beautiful can turn into nothing in seconds.

A theory pops into my head. *Murphy`s law.*

Anything that can happen will happen. And anything that can go wrong will go wrong. *So why not leave it the way it is?* Kai and I are friends. We finally managed to get along, and I don`t want to jeopardize that. We don´t hate each other, and we know that now. He can´t open up, and I don´t want to open up. *Period.*

I don´t run after potential fireworks anymore. *Especially not duds.*

And sometimes it´s best to just leave things as they are.

At least nothing changes. For better and worse.

Because sometimes being lonely is better. But those who rather stay lonely are the loneliest people. But most of the time they won´t admit that, so things stay as they are.

Which is funny. Isn´t it?

That day, nothing changed. Nothing on the outside but everything on the inside. She made peace or rather accepted that and he didn´t dare to change at all.

79

5 months later, May 2021

For the past months, we´ve spent every weekend together. We studied for exams, had reading dates, painted, boxed, and took pictures together. And I´d be lying if I said situations like the one on New Year´s didn´t happen more, but still nothing has changed.

Something did.

But certainly not what I wanted to. So, we´re just friends. And at some point, I stopped expecting things.

- 27 -

Death – White Lies

It´s dark outside. The sky is clear and magically shines on earth. Kai leans against his car. He grins as I walk toward him. I do the same.

"What are you doing here?" I ask the same thing as always. "Kidnapping you, Scar." He says, into my hair as we hug. And by now I´ve gotten used to that nickname.

I kinda like it.

He steps aside, opening the passenger side. *What? That´s new.*

I frown-smile at him. He waits for me and tilts his head. "Get in the fucking car, Scar *please.*" He snaps as he sees my smile. I laugh and get in. Then he walks over to his side and gets in too. I guess he´s not going to tell me what we´re doing or where we´re heading, so I keep shut for the ride.

We stop in a gravel parking lot next to the clubhouse. He jumps out and opens the door for me again. *Who are you?*

"Hurry the fuck up, *please*." He barks, but he can't hide his twitching mouth. I get out, rolling my eyes.

We're at the soccer field where Kai, Aidan, and Ryan have games. I was here a lot last year watching them with Luca and Nina. I looked for number seven, that belonged to Aidan, and number thirteen, which was Ryan's. But somehow my eyes were always searching for number twenty-one. *Which was Kai's.*

Now, in the dark, the pitch has something different. We walk across the field. "What *exactly* are we doing here?" I ask as I stare at his back. "Being a small part of the universe." He says and lies down. I realize he does *once again* something from my list. Even though he won't admit it, he's doing it on purpose. He did the past months and still does. I have to smile that he has made a mental note of all the things I want to do.

And maybe I'll fulfill some of his wishes too. Maybe.

I lie down next to him. And as he said, with the endless black above me, I feel like a tiny, insignificant unit of the universe. *In a positive sense.*

He stands up. "Wait here. I'll be right back." He says and walks across the square to the house and disappears. For a few minutes I lie alone on the damp moan, and I couldn't be happier. *It smells like summer. Like childhood. Like joy.*

A strange noise makes me listen. I lift my head to locate it, but the next second, cold drops trickle down on me. I screech. *The sprinklers.*

My screaming turns into squealing. But I remain lying there laughing.

Kai's chuckle rings out a few feet to my left. I stand up. He walks towards me, all chill. "Did you know they were going on now?" I yell, but still must laugh. "No, I didn't." He says and raises his hands defensively. "I really didn't." He adds. He stands now in front of me. "I just turned them on." He shrugs and grins.

Before I can say anything, he grabs and drags me toward the beam. I squeal and tear myself away to run but he grabs me immediately. After he gave my head a shower, we chase each other across the meadow. Dancing under the rays, slipping and messing up our clothes with stains, giving no fucks. Laughing and smiling like there's no tomorrow.

And it feels like there isn't.

He lifts me up and spins with me. I hold onto him with my legs, spread my arms, and lean back. He's steadying me and I fly. He brings me back up before I get dizzy. He smiles at me making the stars seem useless. He lifts me up, and I feel like I can touch the sky and bring down all the magic. He lowers me and our faces are inches apart. His face all wet. *Hair damp. Clothes drained. Chest heaving. Eyes locking.*

He speaks up breathlessly. “Who needs Wendy when Tinker knows how to make him fly?” He asks the night. “She´s the magic.” He tells the void.

But in reality, tells me.

I lean against his forehead. His breath hitting me like Novocain. There´s that moment again. When we´re *that* close. When the quiet twinge creeps up on us. When we´re supposed to kiss or say something. Plagued by the same feeling, he slowly lowers me, and we stand in front of each other. Overwhelmed with elation and drowning in pain.

He feels it too. I know.

We felt it since we stopped coming close. He looks like he´s in pain. A bit sad and heart racing. A bit of something between nothing. We look at each other. *No talking.* Being quiet is a way for us to talk. *Always been.*

So, we just let the silence say what we are dying to since months. *Screaming, please talk to me. What is this? What are we? Why, don´t we just let it happen? I want to be close to you. Don´t you?* But seemingly the screaming is too loud to hear.

Such things happened before. We would search each other´s hands. *Knees. Legs. Hair.* But we never kiss. *Never grind.*

I would fall asleep on the couch and with his hands in my hair or mine on his neck. We would move to each other while sleeping. *But we never stayed the night.* We never crossed the line he drew on New Year´s. And as in the past months, *we let it pass.*

Soaking wet, full of grass and emotions, we stand there. After not just friends dancing romantically in the shower. *But still nothing. Cowards. That´s what we are.*

“I´ll turn off the water.” He says, pointing over his shoulder. I nod and watch him move away. *Away from me.* Every muscle in my body wants to move. To run after him. To kiss that jackass. *But I don´t.*

I just stand there and watch him leave. Most of our conversations end with him walking away. *Of him leaving me.*

I run my hands over my face and through my hair.

Everything in me wants to scream. Beg him and to break down his walls for good and disarm the dud or destroy it altogether. *But I can´t.*

He walked away first. He backed away. It´s his step, not mine.

I don´t know if it´s our egos or fears, but whatever it is, it´s holding us back.

And it´s annoying. And mostly painful.

We´re in between. Between friendship and more. Needing and wanting. Complete fusion and deep chasms. Between, the run and the hide.

The sprinklers are off and suddenly I freeze. *I wasn´t cold before.* I didn´t even think about anything but him. But now it´s over and I feel it. *The ice in my bones.*

"We´d better get out of here." He says as he reaches me but walks straight on to pass me by. I follow him wordlessly. I keep reminding myself not to give in. Not to show weakness.

We´re friends. That´s okay.

I imagine saying something like. *Why, don´t you just love me? Why, don´t you just say it? Why, don´t you ask me to be yours? Why, aren´t you kissing me if you want to, so bad? Because I feel that too. What happened?* But then I remember that not even I have an answer for those questions. *So, I don´t.*

He drives me home and doesn´t get out to open the door again. I haven´t slept over since Christmas. But I know that´s what we´ve been craving. But it seems like we´re as stubborn as self-disciplined. *Deadly combination.*

Just because Tink makes him fly doesn´t mean he chooses to be with her. On the contrary even, that´s why, he rejects her. *He never knew how to fly.*

Now he was scared of finding out.

80

"Wtf," I say out loud. "Huh?" asks Kai, looking in my direction. "Lol" I say, still looking at my phone screen. "What is it?" he prompts. "My ex.." I trail off. "Texted me." I finish.

A beat of silence.

"What does he want?" he asks harder. He doesn´t look at me but keeps his eyes on the road. I didn´t miss the way his grip tightened around the steering wheel as I said it. "I don´t know." I admit. He texted me on social media.

"Hey"

For years, I waited for *that* hey. Not that we didn´t keep in touch, because we did. We were still friends for the first months. That´s what we had always sworn. But at some point we both had feelings for someone new and we lost contact. And then he was in a relationship, but I stayed single. He kept texting here and there but never consistently. Cause after all, he had a girlfriend. And I was still single. I understood. But it did hurt. I was never really over losing him. I always hoped. *I always wondered what if?* I kept that door open. But at some point, I stopped looking. *Until he looked.* Until he texted me. *And surely not for nothing.*

Months ago, I saw he was back on the market. My ego and still broken heart loved that. But I wanted him to be happy even if it meant I wasn´t part of it anymore.

And now he´s texting me. Kind of funny. And the timing pretty sus. They *always* get back eventually. That´s the way it´s been so far. And I had already given up that he ever would. But now he did. And I couldn´t believe it.

I stare at that *hey*. The *hey* I waited, dreamed of, and hoped for. I smile unconscious and my body shakes. I´m nervous and more pleased than I should be and like to.

I answer and want to throw up. *Anxious.*

Not three seconds later, *he´s writing* again.

"And?" harps Kai, ripping me out of my thoughts and my smile. "We´re texting." I reply. "About what?" He spits but I shrug. He remains silent.

He´s pissed. But I ignore him.

He asked me how I´m doing. *Well, how am I doing?* I´m still single. I can´t open up, but I can´t stop wanting to fall for the first guy I lay eyes on. I still dream about him once a week. Which is annoying and confusing as hell. Because every time I open my eyes, I realize he´s still gone and we´re not back together. But somehow my brain loves to play with me. Telling me he wants me back. *Torture me.*

I do dream about Kai too. And it´s as tricky as the ones about my ex. In my dreams they want me and we´re together. *But dreams are dreams.* And those you have at nighttime are harder to achieve than those in your heart.

He does small talk. *What does he want? Just checking in?*

Shortly after I announced who texted to me, Kai headed home. Otherwise, our drives *always* take longer. He was clearly pissed, and I get why, but I couldn´t ignore my ex.

We sit down on the terrace with the others. "Guess who texted me." I grin at Luca. "No way." She returns my smile, *knowing* who I´m talking about. I hand her my phone, and she eyes the chat. "Didn´t I just say that the other day?" I begin. She nods, understanding. "Was so obvious, right?" she asks, shaking her head.

Aidan, visibly following our conversation, cuts in. "Who?" he asks, nodding toward me. "Her ex." Answers Luca triumphantly. "Did you answer?" He asks intently. "Yeah, we´re good with each other." I shrug. His eyes squint in suspicion. "Define *good*." He rakes further. "Well, nothing bad happened between us. We´re friends. Not the closest, but every now, and then we hang out, gamble, or go out partying." I explain and he blinks at me. "Friends with the ex." He nods with a grin. I tilt my head, annoyed. "What? You don´t think that´s possible?" I ask. "*You*?" He cocks an eyebrow. "Obviously." I state. He just looks at me.

"And are you going to meet up with him?" Asks Luca as she hands me my cell. Now it´s not only Aidan that looks at me expectantly, but also Kai, who finally raised his gaze. I know he has been following our conversation. *Even though he pretended not to.*

"Yes, I think so." I say, biting my lip. "It´s been months since I´ve seen him." I justify. And Kai gives me a look *knowing* when. "Doesn´t he has a girlfriend Scar?" Kai asks and I inhale. "Yes. He *did*." I exhale. "But they broke up." I correct him. He frowns at me, irritated. "And he asked you right away if you wanted to see him?" Aiden inquires skeptically. Kai exhales a mocking laugh. And Aidan grins, too. "I know what you´re thinking." I say. "Do you?" Kai asks a bit too angrily and plays it off afterward with a laugh. I sigh annoyed but ignore him.

"And yes, I´ll meet him.. actually, today." I announce. Kai´s eyebrows raise, Aidan nods a few times and Luca smile beams. "*Now* to be exact." I say as I check the time and stand up. "Keep me posted." Luca chirps. "Me too." Aiden raises his hand with a grin. I smack his shoulder, rolling my eyes and I give him the middle finger as I turn away.

But just as I reach my car, the gate opens and Kai walks towards me. *He can´t be serious.* I try to hurry fiddling my keys, but when I open the door, he blocks me. His hand reaches between the car roof and the door slams shut. Neither the door nor Kai bulge. I close my eyes, taking a breath. "Kai" I warn without looking at him. "Do you really want to run after that asshole?" He asks, not hiding his anger anymore. *But to run after you?* But I won´t say that.

I face him. We stare each other down.

"Who *cheated* on you." he insists, and I gape at him. "I´m not *running* after him, Kai." I clarify and he laughs. "We´re friends. And he *didn´t* cheat. Well, kinda. But it wasn´t that simple" I shake my head. "We were not even together anymore at that time. And it was on and off long before that.. *so*." I explain, but he won´t give up. "I just need to know.." I say, but he cuts in. "*Know* what?" he barks. "I need certainty." I say upset. "*Certainty*." He repeats, laughing, as if it´s the most ridiculous thing he´s ever heard. "What kind of certainty?" He puckers his face. "Whether we still understand each other." Is say and he laughs soundlessly. "That´s so stupid Scar." He shakes his head at me.

"He dumped his girlfriend *when*?" He begins. "Yesterday and *now*, he´s coming on to you. All of a sudden. Ask yourself *why*." He snaps. "He just wants to know if he can still mess with you." He tells me. "And *you* fall for it." He accuses me.

Like that isn´t what Kai´s been doing last year.

"You´re on his ass like back then." He shakes his head. "I thought you *never* wanted to be dependent again?" He asks spitefully. I gape at him but swallow my anger to stay calm.

Can´t he see that I am already? Dependent.. *on him.*

He´s jealous. *I get it.* And I like that for once he shows that he cares.

But it´s my ex.

It´s him. My lost home, I tried to find for years. *I can´t miss that. I just can´t.*

"It´s been almost three years, and I *still* dream about him. I´m still processing a lot. There are things unasked. Things I *need* to know. Things we need to talk about." I say. "I´m curious. Who he is now." I tell him. "You might not understand because you didn´t love before, but he´s been an important part of my life for over six years and still is." He looks like I´ve slapped him. *Almost pale.*

But I go on. "We´ve always had a bond. We grew up together. He used to be the most important person in my life." I say and he stares at me without emotion, like he tuned out somewhere. "I´ve wondered all these years what it´ll be like when he´s single again. I *need* to do this. I need to *know.*" I say but he doesn´t budge, so I continue. "I need closure. Okay?" I search his gaze, and he looks at me. "To let go." I add, begging him with my eyes. He stares at me for a moment, jaw set.

But then, wordlessly, he backs away and lets me get in my car. In the rearview, I see him hitting the roof of his own car. My heart sinks. *I hurt him.*

I understand that he is angry. And I understand that he doesn´t understand. And fuck yes, maybe I´m stupid and naive, but at least then I´ll finally know. And can answer the questions that nagged me for years.

Are you ready to let go? Or to hold on?

Kai has seen me break because of my ex. But maybe my ex is the person who can fix what was broken in me since. Because of him, I can´t get involved with others. *With Kai.* But all I know is that I need answers, peace, and closure. I want him to set me free.

Because the minute he texted me, all I felt was hope. *Excitement and Love.* The love I grew up with. *The love I know.* I still feel in my dreams. That haunts me. That broke me. That made me a home. The love I lost and the love I now need to find or loose for good.

We can´t let go of someone because we still hope. Maybe that feeling will never go away with him. The feeling of your first love. *It stays.*

That day he lost her to her first love. That day, he realized she lived more in the past than in the present. *Where his home was.*

He realized how much she craved love. He saw it in her eyes. All he never wanted. *Love.* Love he couldn´t give. *Love she looked for in another.*

81

It was okay. We still get along. It was the way I always wanted it to be. But still different. I realized I don´t find him attractive anymore. I mean, he is beautiful. But I don´t feel attraction towards him. There´s not that feeling he caused years ago. It´s weird.

A blue feeling.

It´s like remembering a childhood friend. It´s blurry and faded. You recognize and remember. *But it´s different.*

Somehow familiar but foreign. It´s like a past life. Like you can´t believe, it did happen. You really lived that life. Because your life now is so different. It feels like it never happened.

Who were we? Do I know these people?

It´s close but so far away. You know each other but in the same you don´t. You have no idea if the other is still the way they were.

How did they change? How did I change?

Years seem like nothing but meeting your lost love shows it´s lifetimes. I still feel our bond. But there are no feelings. I don´t know why I´m surprised.

What did I expect? That he wouldn´t have changed? I changed too.

Why wouldn´t he?

We´re both different people now. It doesn´t fit anymore.

How could we change so much? How could we grow up without the other?

We were it. Inseparable. I´m gonna marry him. He´s my home. My life.

But it wouldn´t fit anymore. And realizing that hits you like nothing else. Somehow, it feels like I can breathe for the first time.

I have certainty. But it feels like I can´t breathe any more ever.

I have my answer. I missed my best Friend and not the relationship. I missed not being alone. I missed having a home. A home that was not me. *It was Love. His love.* But it´s gone for good. *It´s gone.* And I need to find a home in myself.

I´ve always had the assumption that my ex took something from me. Like a piece of my soul. *My personality. My happiness. My spark. Myself.*

But I realized he didn´t. I just caged those parts of me. Because they reminded me of him. My brain linked them to him. But I forgot they were mine. Like those parts didn´t belong to me but him. *So, I rejected them.* Abounded and locked them.

Because it was too hurtful. I identified more with him than with me. My focus was on him. My world evolved around him. *I lost me. Not him.*

But I don´t know where I put those pieces nor how to find them.

Maybe I don´t even remember those parts of me anymore. All I know is the feeling that the loss left behind. *The home I lost. Myself.*

Maybe, in a heartbreak, you´re not murmuring the other but yourself. Maybe, what you love about love is the love you give. Maybe, you love yourself, but don´t notice. You just tell yourself it´s the others love. *It´s never you.*

You lift them high above. You forget to let yourself fly. You can fly by yourself, not because of them. You just think they let you fly. But your own love does.

It all hit me like a punch in my eyes. *In my gut, my heart, my face. On my brain.*

It did hurt every second. Knowing I did this to me. That I didn´t allow myself to be myself. *For a long time.* Such a long time that I don´t even know that version of myself anymore. Probably wouldn´t recognize her.

Is she even there, or did I outgrow her too? Like him. *Like my first love.*

Myself. *Outgrown.* She´s alienated. She´s foreign.

I was always sad and angry because he changed. *But I did too.* I was just too stubborn to admit it. I´ve chosen to hold onto him. *To us and my old version.*

That I no longer want to be. *No longer can be.*

I´ve let myself in pain, believing if he´ll come back it would be gone. *I was wrong. It´s not gone. It´s worse.* Going through a heartbreak is bad. But after you let go. After, you realize it´s over. *It hurts more.* And you´re going through another heartbreak. *You´re lovesick. You feel alone.* And you realize love is not good. Love makes you believe you need others to be happy. *To love.* To feel whole. To feel loved. *But it´s all lies. It´s a lie.*

The love sickness you feel after losing someone isn´t because you loved them. It´s because you realize you didn´t love yourself. Because if you loved yourself and would have known your worth. *You wouldn´t feel loneliness.*

Unless you love yourself. *But who does that?*

You grieve your own love. *You grieve yourself.*

When you hold onto such a pain over years. And then suddenly it´s unjustified. *It´s useless.* It´s like losing part of your identity. That versions of us didn´t exist anymore. *But in my head, they did.* The love I still remember and feel in the depths of my heart.

It´s gone.

And realizing that is another heartbreak. *It´s the purest form of pain.*

So, I grieve. *Myself.* And the love I can´t give myself.

Colson Herzog

- 27 -

I didn´t go to the others. I went home to bed and slept.

The next week I didn´t go to the Dark´s either I went home to bed and slept.

I slept. And slept. Like sleeping beauty, I couldn´t wake up. *I had to sleep.*

82

Two weeks later

I get in my car because, it´s drizzling and, I want to see Kai.

A burden has been lifted from me. But it doesn´t feel any lighter. To be honest, it felt even heavier. Having certainty is not easier. Because now I have no excuse for my commitment and trust issues. I´m attached to an old idea of love. *Of me.*

I am the problem. *I´m creating it.*

But I´m sure I can finally let go. *At least, I hope so.*

I always wondered if I´m over him. But the second I saw him, I knew it. Even if my heart still clings onto him. *I´m over it.* And fuck, I thought that might feel less world shattering than it does. And just like Sullivan in *Monsters INC.* freaked out when the door didn´t lead back to Boo. I freaked out, realizing the door won´t lead back to *him* anymore. It was just a door leading nowhere. A door without function.

A dead end. Our end.

I realized your first love is the worst that can happen.

But I was wrong about that too.

As expected, everyone sits on the terrace. *All except Kai.*

“Lia” Luca calls out joyfully. *She´s the only who didn´t pick up that nickname.*

The others also seem happy to see me again. “We thought you had written us off.” Jokes Aidan. “Sorry guys.” I say with a weak grin and sit down.

“So, how did your date go?” he asks. *There it is.*

“It wasn´t a date.” I clarify. “But it was.. okay.” I sigh. “We hit it off.” I add. “And?” He asks cautiously. “And nothing.” I shrug. “There was a reason we broke up.” I tell them. “And what about him? Doesn´t *he* want anything from you?” he asks, and I swallow the lump in my throat. “I don´t know, honestly.” I lie. “What´s your impression?” asks Luca and I shrug once more. “It doesn´t matter anyway. That´s through we´re friends.” I say and with that the topic´s done. That he asked me if we want to have friendship with benefits, *I do not tell.* I know we decided back when we were together that if we split up, we would continue to sleep with each other, but we had no idea how it would be. *We had no idea.*

It felt like he slapped me. *He wanted me for sex.* That´s what he wanted. Not me as a person. *Sex.* And all I wanted was him. But clearly, he didn´t want me in return. Maybe he wanted to get close again through sex. *But I don´t think so.* It showed me how he felt about me. No missing, dreaming, hoping like I did. No leaving the door open just in case. Well, he did keep it open but for sex. He doesn´t want me but my body. *I felt disgusting. Worthless.* As if everything that was between us was gone. Like the love didn´t mean *anything.*

So, he asked me, and I turned him down. Of all the things I expected him to want, *that* hurt the most by far.

"Where´s Kai?" I glance around pretending it´s a normal question, which *is* but also *isn´t. But they don´t know.* They just know we don´t hate each other that much anymore.

"Well, where?" replies Leon, knocking on the post of the canopy behind him. Aidan grins. *On the roof. I could have thought of that myself. It´s raining, after all.*

"I´ll say hi." I say and stand up. *No one seems to care.* Because it´s normal to look for your friends. Because that´s what we are. *Friends.*

I spot him on the terrace. He sits on the concrete wall, leaning against the house. He smokes pod. He looks off into nothingness. His hair is damp but in a perfect mess. When his eyes wander to mine, I push open the door. I sit down on the wall across him and a few minutes of silence pass. *He looks off.*

"Where have you been?" he asks. "Needed time for myself." I say and hug my legs. "Have phases where I don´t want to see anyone." I say. "Sometimes I just disappear and need to be alone" I explain. *And I haven´t been alone for months.*

He nods like he knows what I´m talking about, or he thinks I´m talking shit. I´m not sure because he´s acting weird. *Distant. Indifferent, maybe. Cold.*

I wait. Wait for him to ask, but he doesn´t. *Why doesn´t he ask?*

"I realized I wasn´t mourning our relationship; I was grieving my best friend." I begin. "It was never about having a relationship, but having someone I can tell everything to, someone who knows me as I really am, who understands me without words and whom I trust." I say and he doesn´t look at me. He looks like he doesn´t even listen.

Even like he´s amused?

"But I stopped letting people in. I´m not afraid to be alone anymore. I´m afraid not to be." I say. His eyebrows are drawn together and now he´s holding eye contact. "Falling in love is like being on cocaine. But I don´t ever want to be high again. I don´t want to be addicted anymore." I say. My eyes lose their focus as I speak. "Before, being in love was what I craved. But now it just means loss of control." I shrug. "And I know it´s not better from one extreme to the other. But this extreme feels less wrong." I say and again, he nods slightly but he´s really silent. I don´t think he gets what I´m saying. *Maybe I don´t either.*

He looks at me like he saw me for the first time. But he looks confused, as if he doesn´t know me. "Not all drugs work like cocaine Scar." He says dryly after taking the last drag and stabbing the stub between his legs.

There is more meaning behind his words, but I can´t make it out yet.

He looks at me differently. I can see the wall between us. *The distance.*

"You think what you had with him was love, but he was your drug, and you were addicted. And I´m not your new drug to get high on." He says and stands up. *What?* I blink at him in shock. *He´s hurt.* That´s why he says something like that.

But he´s not my drug.

"How am I supposed to get high on something I´ve never had?" I retort. But he stiffs a laugh and walks past me kicking the door open.

What just happened? Did I miss something? Why´s he pissed at me?

If she knew what would come, she would have left. *But she went after him.*

83

"What´s your problem?" I snap. "I don´t know what you´re talking about." He says. "Bullshit." I bark. "You know *exactly.*" I say. He sits on his bed, looking stoically.

"What is with you?" I ask. "Why are you like this?" I gesture. He just stares at me. I sigh. "Can we just for *once* talk?" I ask. "We do, don´t we?" He says with a spiteful grin. "You *know* what I mean." I say. He shakes his head, flattening his lips. "Enlighten me." He demands with a grin. "Can we discuss what was between us the last months?" I beg. "There was nothing." He says, surely but he lies.

He could have as well as hit me in the gut.

"Kai." I plead. "No Scar, please *enlighten* me.. what *exactly* was between us?" He asks, rising to his feet. I look at him, unable to speak. "Thought so." He spits and laughs. "After Christmas.." I begin, but he cuts me off. "What?" He gets in my face. "We need to talk about it." I repeat. He stiffs laugh, shaking his head. "For what?" he wants to know. *He´s angry.*

"That you run after the next dumbass? Just to be *loved*?" He asks scornfully.

He slapped me but in the throat.

"You´re pathetic Scar." He spits and hits me in the heart. I look at him, trying to understand why he switched up on me. "Is this about my ex?" I ask confused. He shakes his head in disbelief. His nostrils flare. "No Lia it´s about you." He points at me. "You *want* to be loved." He states. *I think I´m lost on something.*

"What is this about?" I ask, still not knowing why he´s suddenly so harsh. "It´s about you." He tells me and I frown. His mouth opens and shuts a few times.

"About you being *fucking* confusing." He snaps instead. *Like he isn´t.*

"Kai, just call it." I say. "I took a step back for you." He yells. "You said you can´t trust. You want to know someone first. A best friend." He says. "But friendship is more important to you than relationships. And you don´t want to depend on others." He adds. "But you run after attention as soon as it occurs." He says and I blink. "How am *I* supposed to know what *you* want?" He asks. "You change your mind every three seconds." He states. "And I´m not the only one who has complexes or fears." He says. "So, don´t tell me *I´m* the problem. You don´t know what *you* want. That´s the problem." He rages. *What is happening?*

"So, we´re back to accusing?" I ask. "Seems." He shrugs and I exhale. "I know what I want. I want you." I say. "I don´t want to lose you. And if that means we stay friends, then so be it." I tell him. "And I´m not saying it´s all *your* fault. But you´re giving me mixed signals *since* we met." I accuse him. "I want to open up, but I´m scared." I admit. "It´s taken me *years* to be okay on my own. I don´t want *anyone* to take that away from me." I say.

He says nothing.

"You hid me. Us." I tell him. He shakes his head, and I sigh. "But you´re right, I don´t want to be dependent or lose control." I shrug. "What *my* problem is, is that you get close just to push me away." I yell. "I don´t know what *you* want, and I´m not sure, you even know." I retort and he gapes at me. "I want the same things as you." He yells back.

Not sure about that.

"But it´s not so easy to open up when everyone has left you." He snaps. "I never knew it any other way." He justifies. "And your behavior is just as ambivalent as mine. One moment you´re close and the next pulling away." He says gesturing. "Out of self-protection." I shout. "I´m just waiting for you to do or say something to get rid of me." I hiss. "I´m *trying* Lia." He yells back. "I don´t have that for *any* girl. And I´m here." He steps closer.

"*You tried?*" I laugh. "Saw you trying on New Year´s." I say stepping back. He shakes his head. I know it´s not fair but it´s the truth. "Yeah, because you tried?" He laughs.

I say nothing.

"This is new to me, Lia." He justifies. "I know." I say. He holds my eyes and minutes pass between chest heaving and silence.

"But you feel for me." I whisper, and his eyes go weak for a moment. "Don´t tell me otherwise." I add before he backs off again. "I´ve.. seen the Polaroid you´ve been carrying around." I say quietly. His jaw tightens and he blinks once. My eyes burn as I speak. "So, don´t tell me.. you´re not into me." I whisper and he lowers his gaze.

I´m right. He is. He´s into me. There´s my answer.

"I did fall for you." I say to assure him. But he stares at the space between us. Finally, he lifts his gaze, but I see anger in his features. "I didn´t fall for you, you *fucking* tripped me Scar." He spits.

Why is he doing that?

I just told him I feel the same. And he has to turn me down again.

"This isn´t some sort of game, Kai." I snap. "It is." He retorts.

"I didn´t made you fall for me." I say. "Not like I had any choice." He says but goes on because it almost sounded like a compliment. "It makes me *sick* how much I want you." He choaks. *That´s a compliment pared with an insult.*

"Sounds." I lift my chin, and he inhales. "I just.. *hate* the idea of anyone having you. And I fucking hate that I feel like that." He continues. That was honesty and playing it down afterward. *Like he always does.*

"Shower me with compliments." I say. *He just can´t don´t he?*

"I don´t want to get hurt either." I say. "I just want to hear what you feel or think for once, Kai." I pray him. "I *fucking* told you seconds ago." He snaps furiously. "No, you didn´t you played it down. An *insult* is no honesty." I point out. "No." He barks. "The problem Lia.. is *whatever* I give or say to you is not enough for you. That´s your problem." He calls me out. *Maybe he´s right.*

"Fucking own it." He scowls and I bite my tongue, trying to numb the pain.

"Just because it´s not what society dictates doesn´t mean *it´s* not real. That *it* isn´t honest." He adds and I have to laugh. "What is *it*?" I ask. His jaw set. *Nothing.*

"Of course, Kai." I snap. "We´re not together. We don´t have friends with benefits. But we´re *not* just friends, either." I point out. *Silence. Yeah, right.*

"And you know that you´d be a born bad boy according to the industry´s *false image.*" I laugh. "Besides, you keep quoting books. *Romances.* So how can you not believe in love?" I ask. "Love means nothing Lia." He says and I roll my eyes.

"I see you. I respect you. I care about you. I support you. All *those* things mean *something.*" He adds. "But love means nothing. Love is all bullshit." He spits.

"I don´t believe you." I say, although he has a point. "Love doesn´t exist. At least the way love is sold to us." He says. "Love is just pain and nothing more. It´s in your head. It´s a trick. And as you said, it is like an addiction. Like a drug. Love acts similarly to a drug in your brain. Your reward center is stimulated. I mean, don´t people get what that means?" He´s furious. "It´s a fucking drug. Addictions are never good. So why acting like it´s not as bad as alcohol, pills, or cigarettes? Because it is." He nods.

"They act like it´s the best thing in the world.. *because it numbs you*. Just as every other drug. It´s not healthy. *Never.*" He rages. "Addiction is the memory of pleasure. And drugs work like that. You chase the feeling of the high. The rush and not the person. *That´s not love.*" He shrugs. "That´s not how it should be. *It´s wrong.* Something so pure shouldn´t destroy you. It shouldn´t be the reason to be alive for people." He goes on. "*Love is weakness.*" He says. "Love is losing control by thinking you remain in control. *But you don´t.* There´s no control in drug use." He shrugs. "Never." He nods.

"And people are stupid to think otherwise." He barks. "And I already have *enough* addictions and drugs." He tells me and shakes his head.

"But I do believe in love. But not the kind everyone thinks they have. It´s not called love, it´s peace and enlightenment. It´s something higher than just a feeling. It´s greater than love. Then everything. It´s energy. Awareness. Consciousness." He lists.

"But people forget that love is just a feeling, and it passes." He nods. "It´s an emotion. And all emotions you hold onto make you sick." He snarls. "But people hold onto all of their emotions. They don´t let it go. Flow. Pass." He throws his hands up.

"But that´s what you have to do. Let the love *fucking* pass." He growls. "Because it means nothing." He says. "It´s a trick to your brain." He states.

"What do you mean?" I ask. "In short. *To define is to limit.*" He quotes Oscar Wilde. "And love is defining. And I don´t want any limits." He says. *I say nothing.*

"I mean, why do people have to label everything?" He asks fed up. "You don´t have to *label* everything, but you can be honest for a change." I retort. "I don´t ask you to be my boyfriend. I ask you for honesty." I reply wearily. "I *am* honest." He states. "But you can *show* it." I say. "We had this conversation months ago." I point out. "Call it." I push him. "How about *you* being honest?" He asks instead. I inhale on edge. *Fine.*

"I want you. *You hear me?*" I yell. "I´m into you. And I´m confused about what´s going on since Christmas. But I want this. You. Whatever the hell *it* is." I look at him. "I don´t want to label. But I want to hear it." I say, my voice weak. "But what about you?" I whisper breathlessly, begging him to come clear.

Just say it once. Just say it. I´ll pretend I don´t listen. But please just say it.

He reads me but squeezes his eyes shut as if he´s in pain. He´s quiet for a while.

Because he´s thinking. He´s weighing things up. *He fights. I see it.* I feel it, the fucking energy. I feel his mind reaching for mine, but his stubbornness blocking him.

I´m quiet watching. To see if he runs again. *Or if I run. Or both of us.*

Silence as his eyes meet mine. *Nothing.*

"But you´ll never say it." I whisper with resignation. "Scar.." He begins but, I cut him off. "What are we?" I yell, voice breaking. *I don´t want to cry.*

"Addicts." He whispers as if it were less true then. *Addicts?*

"Addicts Scar. *Addicts.* That´s all we are." He hushes, his voice thin. A single tear escapes, and I tighten every muscle on my face to keep me from falling apart. He reads my expression like he always does, and his eyes soften instantly. He wipes his mouth. "Fuck" he ruffles his hair. His eyes are full of it all. And that´s when I know he´ll tell me.

He swallows hard and opens his mouth. "I wanted.. to kiss you. All those months. And fuck the hell out of you." He yells upset. "But I didn´t because I wanted you to trust me. To feel safe with me." He says, pausing to gulp the lump that I feel too. "I don´t want to be just a phase. To be your next high or low." He admits.

"I was annoyed, by you, because we were as similar as Leon told me." He tells me. "I hated you. I didn´t want you in. Because I knew you were my downfall." He reveals. "You sparked interest in me. Which drove me crazy." He says.

"I hated that my eyes were looking for yours. I hated that I looked at you when I told a joke to see if you were laughing. And fuck, I hated that I dreamed about you when I was awake. I hate that I only get a boner on you. And I hate what you do to me. I hate that my body wants you. I hate how I feel when you´re with me. And even more so when you´re gone." He continues.

"What I feel then, kills. And I don´t want to write about you in my books anymore." He tells me upset. "I always had the girls and my feelings under control, but with you, it all went down. You dragged me down. And I don´t want this. I don´t want it." He shakes his head. "But I want you." He whispers.

"I hated it all and those feelings, and at the same time I wanted more of it. More from you." He locks eyes with me. "And most of all, I fucking hate that I don´t hate all those things. Or you. Because I don´t. *Fucking don´t.*" he spits. "It makes me crazy. I´m losing my mind over you. I´m losing it. I don´t want to think about you or have the need to kiss you every time I look at you." He says, and his voice cracks. *I might cry.*

But I´m too speechless to spill them. He steps closer, reaching for my hand and presses it to his chest. His heart beating like crazy. And it feels like it misses some beats or doesn´t remember how to work. It pulses and makes somersaults. "*This* is scaring me" he says, his voice heavy. "It´s okay to be scared." I tell him. "I am too." I say. "But what is not okay is that you didn´t tell me all that. And left me wondering." I say, but he cuts in. "You didn´t either Scar." He whispers and I know he´s right. *I didn´t.*

He lets go of my hand. "But I´m not gonna say it." He says. "Do you hear me?" He looks at me. "I´ll *never* say it. That I´m in love with you." He tells me. *My heart stops.*

"I want to open up, but I can´t." He says. *He can´t.*

"I´d like to be the man you need and deserve. *I tried.* But I´m not." He says honestly. *But I don´t know if he tried.* And I don´t know why I´m disappointed, either. Because it´s not like I didn´t know from the beginning, that he didn´t want a relationship. *That he can´t.* But after what he just confessed to me.. *I start to cry.*

He´s an emotional wreck, but so am I.

He wipes my hot tears with his thumbs holing my jaw. "I can´t promise you I won´t push you away again. The only thing I *can* promise is that I´ll do. Again, and again." He says.

"But I´m not doing it, cause I want to or to hurt you, but because I can´t help it. I´ve never learned any other way." He tells me, and the fucking truth hurts. "I´m crazy about you. I really am. I can´t deny *that.* Not anymore. But I´m broken." He says and I don´t know if his words are supposed to make me happy, sad, or angry.

"I don´t want to hurt you, but those of your green eyes look so damn pretty when you cry." He hushes and the white of his eye has turned into red. "*I know* I hurt you." He hums. "I´m self-destructive and selfish. I´m not made for what you want." He tells me.

For what I want.

My face is wet against his hands, who can´t hold my tears. *He can´t hold them.*

And I can´t be mad that his honesty is hurting me. *The honesty I asked for.* Everyone always says honesty is the most important thing. But the truth is honesty hurts the most. Honesty isn´t always to protect others but to hurt them. He didn´t intended to, but he did. And in a way it was necessary. *Hurt.*

"Maybe I´m a masochist or just self-destructive. Maybe, I´m even a bit of a sadist too. Or maybe I´m just not right for you. Or you´re not right for me either." He says.

Maybe, we´re too much alike. *Same fears. Same desires. Same all.*

It´s too scary to look, even if you want to.

At this moment, I just want to go back to the in between we had moments ago. Back to confused instead of broken. *Back. Just back.*

"I won´t get close to you when I know I´ll break you. Because I don´t know how not to." He tells me as he strokes my hair behind my ear and holds the back of my head.

“I don´t know if being broken together is such a good thing.” He says softly, and I give him a weak smile and taste my bitter tears. “You can only heal yourself.” He whispers. And again he´s right with that.

“I think my problem is that I´m afraid that if it´ll start, it´ll end.” I tell him no voice left. An almost soundless laugh escapes him. He gives me a tight smile.

“As different as we may be, Scar, we´re pretty much the same.” He says his voice all husky. *And that sums it up perfectly.*

It´s far from easy, it´s hard and confusing. As he says, we have traumas and need to heal. An outsider would call us toxic and yes, maybe we are ambivalent, but I feel we are the only one who can heal the other after we licked our wounds by ourselves. We bring out each other´s deepest fears and are forced to deal. That´s as precious as frightening. But necessary and in ways a good thing.

“So, if I tell you that I can´t give you what you want from me. Then I mean it.” He says, trying to look through my tear-shot eyes. “I am not capable of love. I´m not made for love. I wasn´t even build from love.” He says his words full of pain. I bite my lips, trying to stop them from trebling. “You can´t love someone who´s already dead inside.” He takes my face in his hands and kisses my forehead. I shut my eyes from the aching. A gesture that usually triggers butterflies, which now tears me into a thousand pieces. No one tells you that butterflies die at some point. Some last not even a day. Some only months. *A few a year.*

But they die in the end. *They die.*

Maybe it was too much honesty, too late. Maybe, if he would have told me sooner, we could have figured it. If we would have talked more. But maybe it would have been the same.

Maybe, it would have been killed either way. That butterfly.

“Are you still coming to the wedding with me?” I ask, not knowing what all this means for us. “I do.” He says, into my hair. *I do.*

I always thought I´d never get over my ex. I got attached to my ex at a young age. I was thirteen. And I was eighteen when I lost him. But part of my soul stuck to him. And maybe I´ll always stick with him. Murmuring him is a part of me. I grew into it. *It´s always there.* Mostly unconscious. *But it´s there.*

And I can feel the way Kai takes a similar significance. It scares me that, he´ll be a bond I can´t outrun. *I´ll never get rid of. I´ll never let go of. No matter what.*

But I do this to me. *To myself.* I make me suffer. I let myself get attached. Because I am an addict. *An addict of love. Addicts that´s all we are.*

84

One week later, the Wedding

My dress is black, and it has a mermaid neckline. It´s short in the front and long in the back. I wear same-colored high heels and a small clutch. My hair curled and tied in a low-set braid.

I walk into Kai´s room. He stands there, looking down at his phone. I take him in. He wears a suit in black, matching me. And there´s a white rose on his chest. He looks handsome. He looks up at me for a moment. *Doing a double take.* He shoves his cell away and grins. I do too. He holds his hands in front of his mouth. "Fuuck" he says into his hands. He puts them down and walks toward me. "You look.. *incredible*." He says, looking down on me. Even though my heels are high, he´s still taller.

He takes my hand to turn me. Then he pulls me to him by my waist and I lock my hands around his neck. "You look incredible yourself." I smile at him. There is *that* moment again when a kiss would fall for normal people, but with us, *it doesn´t.* Since we´re not dating and anything but normal. *We don´t kiss.* We just look at each other. And it feels even more intimate than any kiss could be.

His grip tightens, pulling me closer. The energy between us is painful. From overwhelming last year to painful now.

His jaw tightens. *Like he´s in pain. And I bet he is.* Sometimes he seems like that when I´m around. *Like I pain him. Like he referred to me in his poem.*

The past days have been different. We´ve been different. But also, the same. I could tell that we´re closer now. *More intimate.* That fight brought us closer somehow.

But it also didn´t. It pushed us further away and I have no idea what we are now.

Maybe we´ll figure today.

"I need to go." I stammer. "I have duty." I say breathless and he nods once. "Maid of honor." He agrees and I hug him. He wraps his arms around me. I breathe him in. Our hearts pounding on each other. *Until we break away.*

I give him a tight smile and he waves at me as I turn to leave.

"Wait." He bursts and I turn to face him. He walks over to his drawer and takes a box. He opens the lit and it´s a white rose as his own. With a white ribbon.

I would have sent you white roses.

He takes it and lifts my right arm to put it on. He holds my wrist, and I look at him, but his eyes are fixed on the rose. *Not red a white one.*

"Now we match." He hushes. I smile. *But we did already.*

- 27 -

Kai´s already at the location with the other guests and family. I help my sister get ready, curl her hair, help her into the dress and hold the train while she walks down the aisle. But instead of looking at my sister as she walks toward her fiancé, Kai´s eyes are on me. I felt it even before I saw him sitting there. Maybe I´ll walk that aisle down for you.

Maybe, someday.

As her maid of honor, I am constantly busy. But Kai never leaves my side. And it´s hard to ignore the confusing mood, but I´m glad he´s here today. The whole week was a bit weird between us. I haven´t seen the others, and haven´t stayed over. Kai and I just texted.

But mostly about the wedding.

He seems odd now. He behaves differently. *Like, he´s tense or something.*

Maybe, he´s uncomfortable because a wedding is very personal. *And after all, we´re just friends.* Well, I don´t know *exactly* what we are. And I stopped wanting to label it myself. But I´ve given up telling relatives he´s not my boyfriend because it seems *impossible* for that generation us to be just friends. *So, he´s my boyfriend today.* Although he´s *clearly* not. And probably won´t ever be.

Maybe, that´s what´s bothering him. Or why he´s so nervous. *Maybe, not.*

When I finally have a quiet minute, he takes me outside to the garden. Fairy lights hang between the trees. There are flowers everywhere. Inside, the band is playing some love song.

"Dance with me," he says and takes my hand. He holds me by the waist and spins me around. We dance through at least three songs. The sun low by now, that the golden hour makes the garden seem magical.

I can´t help but wish things were different. That we didn´t need to pretend to be together. *Well, we don´t, but everyone thinks we are.* I wish we could kiss and try to do it without the labels. But there are still so many unspoken things between us. And right now, I see it on his face. *On his posture. On his muscles tensing.*

And the energy that shifts. Because he looks at me like he´s going to blurt it at any moment. And I have to brace myself for whatever the hell it is.

[NOTEBOOK ENTRIES]

I hoped she would text me. Maybe I even hoped she would show up. Well, she did, but not to wish me happy birthday. She came to insult me. I had no idea what the hell was going on. But I knew this fucker, said something to her. I went over to her, heart racing. She was talking about some bet. I don't know what this prick told her. But it apparently worked. She kicked me out. I can't blame her. Happy birthday fucker. You fucking lost. But not a bet. You lost her.

I didn't think she would show up, but I was glad to see her. I racked my brain all night over what to say to her. I had no idea how to explain the dynamic between Andi and me. Or the games we used to play. We did try to fuck the same girl. We did such bets. To prove a point. Back then it was fun. With her, it wasn't. I told him to fuck off. I tried not to let show, I liked her. All I wanted was to protect her. But I failed. I wanted him to be bored by her. I tried to not care. But I did. And he noticed. That's what's different with her. That she's my pressure point. But he kind of liked her. But not how I did. But it wasn't a bet. I wished it were. That she was just like the other chicks. She's so much more. She tried to avoid me, but luckily fate was on my side. I liked the cake she made. It was something. Any reaction was good. She sat on my lap. She couldn't get away. She relaxed into me. Cause on contrast to him, she felt safe with me. When she was supposed to do seven minutes in heaven with him my stomach turned. I went with her. I wanted to be alone with her anyway. She had to play. And for that game, she knew the rules. But there's no rules for my life. Sometimes I don't even know the rules myself anymore. I let the lines speak. I felt that she believed me. But after we got out, this wanker talked about her like she was a whore. I polished his face. That was more than overdue anyway. It blew all my fuses. I regret not stopping him from ever laying hands on her in the first place. He said it was no game. He meant that I feel for her. He was just mad he lost. But he had no chance in the first place. Cause she was no bet. She was anything else. She begged me to kiss her. We snuck out. Haven't had a good birthday in a long time.

I took her to France. I liked seeing her happy. We showered in the dark. I had to keep everything straight to not go further. The others didn't know about our trip. And I wanted her to eat her cake and not alone. Because other than she still thinks she wasn't alone anymore. She has the lost boys. She has me.

She seemed down. She snug into my bed. I want her always with me. She said she's not okay. And that hurt me more than it should. She said I make her feel safe. I felt proud. That was.. something. ~~Everything.~~ Something that made my heartbeat faster. I let myself fall. Be vulnerable. Show her I care. But I couldn't bring myself to tell her more than that. We stayed in bed. We didn't want it to end. I know that kiss changed something.

I knew it would escalate. It always does. They should have stayed away. Like they did all my life. What difference does it make if they're here on the holidays? None. Their crappy Rolex or whatever useless gift they brought is ridiculous. They always do that. Pretend to care. It's always about the company, future, and work. I had to get high to put up with any of their hypocritic talk. I drank, but they wouldn't shut up. They're disappointed in me, I know that. It's not like it's not the other way around. They asked whether I still go to therapy. I have a girlfriend. How my studies are going. Do I know which department I want to work in? If I'm still thinking I'll be a photographer or author? If I still want to waste my time by traveling around the world? If I get, what is at stake? I'm sick of talking. Of telling them about my life. They never cared anyway. I stopped long ago sharing my dreams. And when I gave them nothing but dead looks, they focused on their loving son, who never let them down. Just three years apart but lifetimes away. I bit my lip so hard it bled while they played family. I couldn't help but start laughing. My dad said if I had a problem, I should stand my ground. I laughed even harder. And I did. Stand my fucking ground. I told him to ask my therapist about it. The one they hired to fix me. To fix what they made wrong. He muttered he wished I were more like Finn. He really said what I knew all along. How I felt growing up. Wrong. Unworthy. Burden. I saw red. And lost it. I punched him. I have never hit my dad. I almost threw up after. I told him he should have raised me then. And that a child without parents simply becomes a disappointment. Tears threatened to spill, but I drowned them. He said nothing. As if I were not even there. As always. They just continued to eat. I'm invisible to them. He did not even hit me back. I fucking wish he had. I'm not even a reaction worthy. Like I proved who he thought I am. Pathetic. Maybe I'm acting like a child, but that's not how family should be. That's not how a dad should be. Life was better without them. I cried for an hour outside in the snow. It didn't made me feel better. Not the way I hoped it to be. Growing up, all I wanted was to hit back. But I was not strong enough to strike. I went to my real family. The Avery's. They were not surprised to see me. I knew I'll end up spending Christmas with them. And I would have moved years ago if they weren't our neighbors. Because these people who used to live there don't feel like home. When they're around it doesn't feel like Neverland, it feels like prison. Even if part of my childhood was beautiful, I repressed those memories. But no pain can cover over that kind of pain, it's primal. They raised not a child; they raised a devil. When Finn joined us, I knew they were gone. I am no longer the little boy who spends his birthdays waiting. Who hopes to find his parents in the basket instead of chocolate eggs that his elder brother hid. Who tries to do everything to be enough for them, so they won't leave anymore. I have played through that game. I know the shortcuts and cheats. But there is no other ending. No end where I don't lose. No end where I have no parents. Where I'm not alone.

Colson Herzog

Not in pain. So, Christmas was a shitshow. Until it was not. When I saw her, I felt like a kid. The weight on my chest disappeared the second I hugged her. She kissed me and took the pain away. I knew she could save me. But I wasn't sure if I could save her other than destroy her. Because what she made me feel was her soul. And she tasted just like mine.

I don't know what happened after, but I blocked completely. I knew she wanted me to kiss her on New Year's. I should have. But I didn't. And that felt like I missed something big. I can't forgive me. But I can't take it back. I lost her. And I don't know if I'll find my way back. But she expected me to do it in front of everyone. That would have been a step I'd never take. I can't even accept myself, that I want her. How the fuck should I tell them then? I don't even want this. I don't want a girlfriend. I don't want them to know. I don't even want to know myself.

It's a constant struggle. I want to kiss her. But I do nothing. When I kissed her, I could feel the next fucking years of my life. And that scared the shit out of me. I never think of the future. Of growing old. No one has ever meant as much to me as she does. Neither could anyone made me feel. I don't know how to deal with this. With her, I feel peaceful. But I can't let me feel that way. I just can't.

There's a fine line between wanting and not wanting. I fall back and forth on it. Fear paralyzes. When she comes close, I panic, but also when she's gone.

At this point, I'm no longer sure what would hurt more. Not kissing her or kissing her. Cause it kills me. Hope at least it kills her too. But I know it does.

There is that voice that tells me we want different things. So, I shut down.

Mom called. They never do. Dad apologized. They want to spend time with me. They want me to come. Fuck no. When I went to London, it was for my friends or the drugs. But not for them. They can fuck themselves.

I promised her to take her to her sister's wedding. I don't know if I should.

Her shitty ex reached out. She said she needs clarity. She's naive. I thought better of her. Fucking again. He just wants to get her laid. He's not done with her. She runs after every spark of attention. I snapped at her. Acted like her fucking boyfriend. She went to see him. I'm glad I didn't kiss her again. Fucking glad.

After radio silence, she came back. I knew she would eventually. I wasn't surprised to hear she didn't want anything from him. I realized she doesn't know what she wants. She's totally ambivalent. She uses love to make herself feel better. Probably to distract herself from her own problems. She's dependent on other people. I never was. Never will be, and she won't be from me. She ran after him the minute the opportunity of love came up. But after she realized that won't happen, she came back to me.

Colson Herzog

Wanting my love. And of course, she pushed me to talk. She just wants the highs. But all I can give are lows. She knows about the polaroid. How the fuck did she find out? But I made it clear I'm not capable of having a relationship. It's almost like she wants me to push her away, so she can chase after me. She fell into her old patterns. But I'm new to this kind of addiction. I do everything I can to not relapse because I tasted her, and I know what'll happen if I do again. If I'll get close to her, I'll be gone. And the only thing that helps is cold turkey. You could die. Sounds tempting to me.

85

Kai

She looks incredibly beautiful and sad. Like she *knows* something's going to happen. Like we're connected. She can read me as much as I can read her. *So, I know she knows.* Maybe not *exactly* what, but she knows I'm going to say something lifechanging.

And she's right.

There's that tightness in my chest all day. Since I saw her in that fucking dress.

She's an angel. But that feeling drains me.

I know she can feel my tension. She always does. And I want to be the person for her. The one who kisses her and doesn't let go. The one who kisses her on fucking New Year's Eve in front of their friends. *But I'm not.* ~~*Although I want to be.*~~

That all is so far away. *I am so far away.* Not in my body. *Numb.* And there are only two ways this can end, and I know neither of them will lead to a relationship. But that's what she wants. What I cannot give. What I am not capable of.

But I see it in her eyes. She's not just into me, there's more. I don't think I can take.. *more.* We've been on this edge for months. Knowing either we'll start or end. *So, we did nothing.* To prevent something good and horrible. Our communication is great in so many ways but sucks at the same time. I know that as much as she does. Because even if it doesn't seem that way, we're pretty aware of our issues.

We just pretend we're not.

And I know I like her. *Even more than that.* And I do fucking know she does too but still I can't. *Because how can you know how a healthy relationship works if your parents have never been there?* The relationship they obviously have that I've never been a part of. I grew up thinking relationships or marriage mean business. Love and work go together. It's a contract, something formal, ugly, and impersonal. An outward appearance. Something I never wanted. Something I never had. I mean, my parents aren't unhappily on the contrary even. But family for them meant only their marriage.

The two of them. Plus, Finn. Except me.

Finn was more part of their love than I was. As if my birth had prevented them from becoming more successful. I was a burden. So, they left me alone. *They lived their own life.* And I was on the other side looking in. They took vacations without us.

Without me.

That´s not family. Not one I want. For me, family is something negative and sad. My friends are my family. How family should be. And in many ways, she´s too. *Family.* Maybe she´s the only I´ll ever have to myself. *Maybe.*

But how are you supposed to know how to love when you have never experienced the love your own brother had?

Where´s the difference? I have asked myself all my life. As a child, everything your parents do, you think you´re the one at fault. And even though you now know you are not to blame; these beliefs are so deep that you can´t get them out. You can´t cut them out, scream them out or cry them out. You can only choke on it. *Choke and die.* On the fact that you´re not lovable. *Not worthy of love. Alone.*

Those beliefs have become your identity, and you die under it.

As a child, I was helpless and sad. As a teenager, angry and self-destructive. And now in my early twenties, I´m just numb and cold. *I hate them for that.* For rubbing me the ability to love that girl. *To love her. To love Scar. My scars.*

My brother´s been more of a parent to me than my producers ever were. They got Finn because they *wanted* him. They got me because they thought they *had to* have me. Or that Finn wouldn´t be an only child. They wanted a sibling for him, but they didn´t want me.

Not the way they wanted him.

I´m born for the love of my brother, not the love of my parents. I am envious of the childhood he had. He´s not broken. He doesn´t hate himself. He can love. *He would know how to love her.* He doesn´t hurt himself or others to feel anything. *He wouldn´t hurt her.* He doesn´t destroy everything around him out of self-protection.

He wouldn´t destroy her. He can do everything better.

And maybe that´s why I reject myself. *Cause they did.* Because he can and I can´t. *Because they made me like this.* But I can´t blame me anymore or I´ll die on it. *I have hurt myself enough.* I´m a masochist. *They made me.* So, I blame them. In order to survive.

In order not to die.

All my life, I wanted to be the villain. Because I never had a hero as a father. I know my parents love me. But because of *the way* they love and *the way* I have learned to love, I don´t want to do that to anyone. *Not to her. Not Scar. Not anymore.* That´s not how love should be. *But for me, it was.* Love was taken away from me all my life. I had to be my own role model. *My own hero.* But I was sick of it and became the villain. *My brother's the hero.* I like to be the dark side of us. *The villain.* Instead of love, I hurt. I've hurt before, I wouldn't hurt her. *Not more than I already did.*

Unlike Finn, I didn't get my act together. He became successful, I only broke.

But what if I like the pain of the break? What if I need it? To hold on. *What then?*

And it's not that I hate my parents but it's just that I don't feel anything. Except a broken relationship. An invisible wall that *they* have built. *To shut me out.* They raised a demon, a monster, or the devil itself.

So, no, I do not love. I am not made for that. *I won't love her. Never.* I can't treat her the way she deserves. *Even if I want to.* I can only destroy her. So, the only way to save her and me is to keep myself away from her. *As far as I can.* Before I take her down with me. And the truth is I don't want to be the hero in her story.

Why should I pretend to be someone different? It's who I am. And I think it's time for her to meet me. *The devil.* The other side of the fairy tale. *The darker one. Where Pan is the villain.* Because sometimes it's not the villain with the bloodiest hands. *Sometimes it's the victim.* And I want to be the villain in her story because she was in mine. She forced me to fall for her. To let her into our group. *Into everything.*

Into every raindrop that falls and hits the ground like a meteorite. *Extinguishing.*

She's the villain in my story. *And I'll be in hers.*

I look down on her knowing I'll do the ~~wrong~~ right thing. *Push her away.*

I told her I would. *I can't help myself.* Because sometimes you have that voice in the back of your head that says. *This action has consequences.* Or maybe it's just the devil I'm friends with telling me lies I like to believe.

Because what else should I believe when all my life I heard his screams?

And cause I'm doomed, I have two of them. There is no angel but two devils. And I like how they talk to me right now. I listen and take the blue pill.

As I look at her now seemingly ice blue eyes, I can only think of one thing.

A butterfly.

86

Kai

A deep blue butterfly trapped inside of her eyes. She might have said her eyes were green but for me they always been blue. *The Butterfly Effect.*

If a butterfly flutters in Brazil, it can become a hurricane in Texas. *Chaos Theory.*

Something snaps in me, and I can´t help but think of the phone call I had with my mom last month. When she´s been pleading me to come to England and take the job that had been set aside for me since I was born. After all, even my shitty father did call apologizing for idk, *maybe everything.*

She wanted me to look at it and then decide what to do. *We could spend time together,* she said. Even though I don´t really want that, the way my mom begged made me hesitate. And right now, it sounds better than being here with her. With her heart in her eyes. That butterfly that can change everything.

Looking at me, already breaking before I even said a thing. Because she fucking knows me better than I want her to.

I´d be away from my friends. *But also, away from her.* Which seems to be the better option than to be *that* close. And lately we seem to come even closer. And *that* without any kisses or dry humping.

This has to stop now.

I hate how much control she has over me. My thoughts, feelings, and body.

Everything.

I need to get aways as far from her as I can. She makes me weak.

It is better that way, I decide. So whatever creature just whispered to me, saved me from the sin right in front of me. Those fragile wings tricking you into believing they don´t cause hurricanes. But the truth is, butterflies will keep flapping their wings and cause hurricanes.

So, I do the only thing I´ve ever could and cause a few hurricanes. And because I´m not her hero but her villain, I rip that fucking butterfly. I rip until it´s gone.

Until the butterfly died. ~~And something in me, too.~~

87

Lia, Songs about roses – Owl Jhon

I can see his mind working. And feel myself slowly leaving my body. I´m afraid of what he will do or say next. So, I zone out and watch it happen.

At some point, he stops dancing, freezes in place, and we break away. He looks at the ground and I stopped breathing since his body did.

It feels like an eternity until he speaks up. "I have to leave soon" he says. "Where to?" I ask, my voice raspy and heart racing. *And I know he doesn´t mean just leave the wedding.*

He presses his lips into a thin line and looks past me. "I´m going to move in with my parents for now." He admits. *I step away.*

"What?" I ask with my heart in my throat. "They need my support at the company. And I can study from there, too." He simply says like it´s no big deal. "There as.. *London*?" I ask breathlessly. My brain couldn´t process.

He nods, looking at me. "When?" I ask, feeling dizzy. "My plane leaves today." He says. "Today?" I burst. I don´t believe what I´m hearing. I try to blink away the situation, but I won´t wake up. *It´s happening.*

I stare at his chest. *At the white rose.* At the fact that we match. That he indeed bought me those roses he talked about. But it´s not a bouquet but a single one.

Maybe there´s the error.

"And how long will you be gone?" My voice breaks. His jaw tenses and he looks past me. "Can´t say yet." He says, quiet as if he´s lost his breath and I fall silent. Our silence has always been good. But this.. *this hurts.*

For a moment, we just look at each other. I wait for him to tell me it´s a joke.

Because it has to be. He can´t be serious. *On my sister´s wedding?*

Kai, who hates his parents´ *plans to move in with them?* This must be a joke.

I have such a lump in my throat, I couldn´t even make a sound without crying. He´s been acting weird since our talk. *Did he know? Was this planned? When did he decide that?*

My throat tightens with each passing second. Each second, he won´t speak and won´t look at me. *Can´t you look at me?*

I feel out of body. *Disconnected.* But I´m here and it´s over. *All at once.*

I don´t recognize the guy in front of me. I know his cold and hard way. *But this..* the way he looks at me. *There´s nothing.* Like he made that choice a long time ago. *Dump me. End it.* Like he has a switch for it all. *To kill it.* All that was. All we were or could be. *Gone.*

I feel dizzy as I speak, trying not to faint. "Did you have a *choice*, or do you *have* to go?" I ask. His eyes move from the point he´s been staring at to the gravel on the ground and then back past me. *I know the answer before he says it.*

"I had a choice." He confirms. My chin tilts back. I can´t hold it together anymore.

It was his choice. The knife in my throat digs to my chest.

"Okay," I choak and walk past him. There are black dots in my view. My legs are weak, and I can´t feel my body anymore. *It´s gone.*

"I never wanted anything to change, Lia." he justifies. His words cut into my back, eating me from the inside. *It rips me.*

And the fact that he uses my name *now* makes me want to throw up. He rarely uses it and each time I love it, but now I hate it. *I fucking hate it.* Use that fucking nickname *they* call me. *That you call me.* I´m Scar. *Don´t say my name.* Don´t make it real.

I want to yell at him, but I can´t. I just walk onto the street. I want to beg him to stay.

But I can´t. I´m tired of begging people to love me.

Even though I´m outside, the fresh air won´t reach me. I feel like I´m suffocating. My tight dress only supports this feeling. *I need more air. Where´s the air?* Here´s supposed to be air. *He took it. All of it.* He took the air I need. He choked me.

Give it back. Take it back.

I can´t cry. *Even if I want to.* I just stand there and try to remember how my body functions. *I forgot it all.* When you try to focus on such normal things as breathing, your brain can´t do it anymore. *It´s supposed to be automatic.* No one taught you how to breathe.

How to think. Or how to bring your heart to beat it´s beat. How to work after it´s broken.

I never wanted anything to change, Lia.

Something breaks as I realize the day in the jacuzzi. He remembered what I said, and he used it against me. *He killed me with it.*

I hear a car unlock and my eyes shoot across the street. *It´s Kai´s BMW.*

A few meters away, parked on the sidewalk. Kai walks across the street.

And I watch him. Unable to move. Unable to breathe.

And I wait. Wait for him to look at me. For him to see the pain. *That he stays.* That I see pain on his face. Not the coldness from seconds ago.

But he doesn´t look at me. *Instead, he gets in.*

His engine roars and he drives away. *He drives away.*

His exhaust pops. An otherwise familiar sound, which now gives me the biggest sting. I stand there and watch his car disappear into the sunset. *He dives away.*

And I know he´s not coming back.

88

I´ve lost all sense of space and time. I could have been standing here for five minutes or an hour. *But it´s my sister´s wedding*, I remind myself. The most beautiful day of her life. *And the worst in mine.*

I can´t break down. I have to function and to go back in. But as much as I try to ignore the knife in my chest, I can´t the pain in my throat and in every cell of my body. *It doesn´t feel real. I don´t feel real.* I´m looking onto my life from the outside. *This is not my life.* It must be the wrong dimension. *Where did I go wrong? Where did we go wrong?* I haven't been out of my body in months. Kai made that disappear. I felt wide awake with him. *And in the now. Present.* But now I´m gone and he drowned me.

The rain I loved. Choked me. To death. It drained me.

I can´t take it anymore and sneak out. I take off my shoes and run barefoot across the asphalt. I unlock the car and get in. I drive as fast as I can to the Dark´s. Once there, I unlock the front door with the spare key Kai showed me. I pace up the stairs to his room.

He is not there. I look around. His cameras are gone, and even on the bookshelves are empty spaces. I rip open his closet, and it looks emptier, too. *No.*

My heart pounds to my ears. *No.* I sit down on his bed. *No.*

Tears are finally streaming down my face. *He knew all day and didn´t say anything.*

I get cold and goose bumps all over my body. *Tinnitus.* I stare into space. He left like I was no reason to stay. Like he never wanted to stay.

Never wanted anything to change.

I am torn out of my paralysis by the engine of Kai´s car. I could never forget that sound. I jolt up and pace down the stairs. But when the door opens, my heart sinks as Finn stands in the hallway. *I stop.*

He looks up at me, frozen, searches my face and a deep frown appears as he realizes. After a moment, he speaks. "He.. didn´t tell you." He assumes. "No," I say, barely audible. Because the words are cut off by the knife, he stabbed me with.

The knife that still kills.

He curses under his breath and rubs the back of his head. I get down and take the key from him and walk outside. *He follows.*

"Where you going?" He asks. "Find him." I say. "You can´t drive like this. And he might be already gone by the time you get there." He tries to stop me, but I keep walking. "I´ll drive you." he says, closing the door behind him.

I flinch at the memory of Kai offering me to drive.

I hand him the keys and get in the car. We don´t speak during the ride.

While Finn parks the car, I make my way to the scoreboard. The fact that I´m in my dress, barefoot, with my shoes in hands running past the people disturbs me little. And that I do not care about the looks of the people is due to the adrenaline. Otherwise, my anxiety would overtake the situation quickly. *But it keeps shut.*

When I find the flight number on the display, I compare the departure time with the actual time. *Shit.*

Finn is meanwhile next to me and spares the *told you so* speech since he knows better.

We push our way up the escalators to get to the viewpoint. I stand by the window front and stare at the runway. I scan the planes for the airline and spot the right one in the distance. Tears try to surface, but I slam them down.

I have to see this. See him leaving. I need to picture it and never forget it.

I know I won´t.

The plane shoots across the stage and takes off. A tear slips and I fall to the ground and cry. Even though I always wanted my life to be like the movies, I certainly hadn´t had *that* in mind.

Finn sits down next to me. *I give him credit for keeping quiet.*

We sit there and watch the planes taking off and landing, while I try to calm my thoughts.

Why didn´t he say anything? Why did he just leave? Why today?

He didn´t even look at me. He didn´t even say goodbye. He left for people he didn´t even consider as family. For those, he never talks about. *For those he hates.* He left to get away from me. *And with that the dud was defused.*

"Come" he says softly at some point. I have no sense of time anymore, but I stand up and try to look at him. *He looks so much like him.* I look away.

"You have a wedding to go to." He adds and takes my hand to pull me with him. He picks up my shoes with his free hand and doesn´t let go of me the whole time.

Nor do I.

In the car, he breaks the silence. "He´s an idiot." *I say nothing.*

"He told the other." He tells me but after I say nothing, he continues. "I assumed you knew. I should have known him better." He says and I sigh. "The thing is, I can´t be mad at him. We´re nothing." I say trying not to cry. "You´re not *nothing*." He says upset. *I´m silent.*

"You´re *not* nothing, to him." He repeats making sure I know.

And fuck I do know, but still he left.

"But that doesn´t seem to stop him from being a *giant* asshole." He adds and I bite my lip. "All the confusion aside, he´s my best friend and he doesn´t tell me that?" I rage. "I wouldn´t have stopped him." I whisper in frustration, and he nods. "But you have to remember, he´s not just a jerk running away from his *feelings*, but a boy hoping to spend time with his parents." He says carefully. *And then it clicks.* I hadn´t thought of that. *How I related.*

My ego wants him to stay because of me and thinks he´s leaving just because of me.

I´m so stupid. The thought of nine-year-old Kai makes it hurt less. I hope he gets what he´s looking for.

"How long do you think he´ll be gone?" I ask him quietly and he looks over at me. "It´s hard to say." He says. "If it goes like Christmas, he´ll be back in a few hours." He jokes but stops, apologizing instantly. "But if they´re not selfish egomaniacs for *once*.. who knows." He shrugs. *Who knows.*

"He always runs away from everything. When things get tough. He just does. Hurts and lashes out." He says and it seems like he has shown me a new side of himself.

One I´ll never want to meet again.

"But sometimes you just have to stop long enough for things to find you." I say more to myself and the universe than to him. *But I don´t stop.* Not anymore.

Like he did, I´ll move on. *At least I hope.*

"But that´s hard when you´re a runner." He adds.

When he´s a runner, what am I? A chaser? Or just a fool?

89

After missing almost two hours of the wedding, I got back.

"Are you coming with me?" I ask as I´m fixing my mascara in the mirror. "Of course, I won´t let you go alone" he says. "Thanks Finn." I give him a weak smile. "Always, Scar." He answers and a soft smile plays on his lips. As always, Finn wears a white shirt and suit pants. From his trunk, he gets the matching jacket. He takes my hand in his and we walk back inside. I get my purse and go to the bathroom. I still look like I cried but it´s a wedding so no one will ask.

He waited for me, and we go dance. And it turns out that he´s a real pro. He dances better than Aidan. He sure has taken a course. *He´s good in everything.*

I take some drinks to loosen up, and we have fun once I´ve reached a level. And thanks to their similar looks, no one noticed I switched brothers. Or they just thought they were insane by thinking I did.

I can really forget for a few hours what happened. He´s a gentleman and a good distraction.

"Finn?" I ask him before we get out of the car. "Yeah?" He faces me. "Please don´t tell him I went after.." I say and he nods. "Sure." He agrees.

After telling him I need a few minutes, I sit down on the sidewalk and look at the starry sky. He said he´s going to push me away. *Repeatedly.*

I was prepared for that. *For push away.* But not almost 800 km airline distance. I hoped I would find him at the airport changing his mind like in the movies. *But this is no movie.*

God, I miss him already. *How can I feel like that even if we´re not together?* Maybe I´m sick. Lovesick like a disease, not a heartbreak. *Sick of longing love.*

And Kai was right after the letdown of my ex, I chased *his* love. I was sad and lost and wanted *something*. And now I lost both. I´m lovesick by two guys. And no one knows.

Except for Finn.

I want to open up and then realize I can´t. Another time I consciously don´t want to open up and keep my distance. And another time I lose myself completely. *Why am I like that? And why do women always think that they can change guys? And why do guys think she´s different?* If *madness is doing the same thing over and over*, like Albert Einstein said. *What is it to be aware of it and still choose insanity?* Doomed.

People think that true love is forever. And if it´s not forever, then it wasn´t the right person. *But forever never happens.* And sometimes forever doesn´t even last a sec. *Ours never begun.* The only forever is the now. You´re always in the now. And our now is over.

I don`t chase anyone. *I tell myself.* And I don`t beg anyone to stay. *I tell myself.*

But it still hurts. And somehow, I love that pain. *Like he does.*

In that way, he is still here with me. *Through the pain.* Cause it´s not at all hell if you fucking like how, it burns. And in a sick way, I like it.

- 27 -

After I have removed my makeup and opened my hair, I go to Kai´s room and stand there with one of his T-shirts that he left in his bed. *It smells like him.*

I sense that Finn´s here. And when I turn around, he leans against the door, like Kai used to do. *They have the same frown too.* He looks worried, waiting for me to say anything.

But I don´t. He unbuttoned the first two knobs and rolled up his sleeves. He watches me closely. I know he´s concerned.

"Will you unzip my dress?" I ask and he looks at me for a second. As an answer, he pushes himself off and walks towards me in two strides. I turn around and he unzips it, carefully. I drop the dress to the floor and pull Kai´s shirt over my head. It reaches mid-thigh.

He´s still behind me.

"Do you want me to stay?" he asks, voice raspy. *I don´t answer. I want him to stay.*

My eyes lose their focus and well up. "I´ve been waiting to wake up." I say with a sob. He pulls my hair out of the shirt. *I loved that gesture.*

"Don´t give him up." He whispers. "Not *you*." He says, barely audible. Tears roll. "It´s the last thing I want to do." I choak and another sob escapes me. He wraps an arm around my neck and pulls me in. I reach for his arm to gain a foothold. He lays his head on mine and stops me from falling. But in ways mentally too.

Eventually I turn around and he takes me in his arms. We stand there for a while. He lets me cry, and I let him hold me.

"Stay." I beg and we break away. He walks to the bed and lies on top of the bedding. I lay my head on his chest, and he wraps his arm around me. He lifts the sheet to cover me and tugs me in.

"They burned witches, but showed magic exists." He says and I frown. "He burned all that what was between you just to show how much it was real." He tells me and I blink. That sounds a lot like something Kai would say.

But is he right? Was he simply scared? Maybe.

His other hand caresses my hair, and I close my eyes. We don´t speak anymore but I can´t sleep right away.

90

When I woke up, I thought it had been a dream.

It smells like him. I´m in his bed. And for a moment I pretend he´ll be there when I open my eyes. But he´s not here when I open them.

You can´t wake up. This is not a dream. A voice in my head tells me.

I look at my phone. *He hasn´t texted me.* My stubbornness won´t allow me to reach out first. But I know him well enough to know he´ll do the same.

Finn isn´t holding me anymore nor lying next to me. He´s probably working.

Even if it´s Saturday.

I stare at the ceiling and press my face into the pillow that catches my soundless cry. This physical pain that you feel in every cell is louder than a scream could ever be.

My heart contracts and my organs too. As if I would be eaten from the inside out. It sucks the life out of me and drags me into a black hole. *But there´s no bottom.*

I cry tears that won´t spill anymore.

I punch the pillow and claw at my skin. *It hurts. Hurts. Like hell.* And then it hits me. *I´m hooked.* This *is* cold turkey. *I am addicted.* Like he said. *We´re Addicts.* Kai´s words feel like poison to my system. *I´m high.* And lost access of my drug. I´ve lost sight of myself. *Again.* I´ve let myself get infected. Maybe he didn´t left just for him but also for me. *Maybe.*

But I was addicted before I pulled the first line. Before I jammed the needle into my veins. *I was into deep.* Now he´s inside of me. *Get it out.* Suddenly I don´t want to be in this room anymore nor in his clothes. *I can´t breathe. It´s too tight. It hurts.* I jump to my feet and almost faint cause I´m dizzy. I stumble into the shower.

I need ice-cold. But my body won´t feel. *It feels him.*

I try to imagine washing everything off. *Letting go of everything. The pain. The dependence. The longing. The missing. The loving. The self-doubt.*

And everything that keeps me from losing sight of myself again.

I don´t use the lotion. *I don´t want to smell like him.*

I wrap myself in a towel and walk down the corridor to Finn´s room. The door is ajar, so I slip through. It´s refreshingly bright decorated. A complete contrast to his brother´s room. But different to how I thought he has more furniture than just a desk. He has a basketball hoop. On a shelf are trophies and signed basketballs. Some signed jerseys adorn his white walls. It´s all clean and his bed is made. So, either he stayed with me the whole night or made it. *But I think he never left. He wouldn´t.*

I go to his closet, not knowing if I´ll find anything to wear. I´ve seen him in sweat-pants and a T-shirt, but mostly when he´s training or in the gym.

He´s always dressed. Always working. Always in check.

Behind the first set of double doors are only shirts and suit pants. In the next, I find jeans, sweaters, and jackets. Behind the last door, finally, loose clothing. I take a plain white shirt and pull it over. Fortunately, the fabric is thick enough, so my nipples aren´t visible. It reaches below my knees. He´s the tallest of em all. *The tallest lost boy.*

But I´m not sure if he´s lost at all.

Downstairs, I find him at the kitchen island. He´s on his laptop, drinking a green smoothie. Completely immersed in his work. He always seems to have his life under control. *Always hustling. Always fit, and productive.*

And not just at work, his basketball is his next possession. *His discipline.*

Next to him is covered. Lots of fruit and veggies. Pancakes and a second smoothie. He hastily taps away on the keys, and I sit down next to him. “Morning,” he hums without averting his eyes. “Vegan pancakes.” He adds, still not looking up. “Thanks.” I say.

After I drink the juice and take a few bites, he pushes the laptop to the side and turns to me. He grins softly and looks down at me. *At his cloths.*

“Already outgrown my brother´s shirts?” he jokes, and I give him a weak smile. He curses and apologizes. “Too soon.” He says, shaking his head at himself. “It´s fine.” I assure. He looks at me reading my face.

“Thanks really for the food and all, but.. I can´t get a bite down and I can´t be here any second longer, either.” I admit. “Understandable.” He nods. “Don´t worry about it Scar.” He assures me and I stand up. “I´ll bring your shirt back in a few days.” I say. “No worries.” He waves me off. “You can have it.” He says with a soft smile. I hug him goodbye and pack my things.

I start my car, and some love song starts to play. I put the volume up and listen.

I skip the song. A lot of songs to be honest. Because *everything* reminds me of him. And I don´t want to be reminded. So, I drive the rest in silence. Which is also torture.

Maybe it´s time to find myself.

- 27 -

A butterfly never knows how beautiful it is. And some of them don´t even last a day. We get to live up to ninety years and probably *never* know how beautiful we are. We get *lifetimes* to realize but refuse to see. And it´s the butterfly´s that die without even having a chance of knowing. We can look, and we should.

At the beauty of the butterflies. *Even the dead ones.* Especially them.

91

Weeks later

I stopped counting how many times I wanted to text or call him. But I also stopped hoping he would come back. Because I knew at some point, *he wouldn´t.*

From I don´t care, to, you hurt me. From I never want to see you again, to come back to me. From I didn´t want anything to change either, to I hoped *something* would have changed.

I felt it all.

I wish I could tell anyone. But I can´t.

I grew up in a loving environment. It just seems that the love I received was never enough. I always craved more. And I still do. More I can´t have. More of him. So, I´ve come to realize that maybe I needed him more than he needed me. And others just move on. They sleep around and find someone else. They´re open to love. And I just stay broken.

But in ways, I always knew he didn´t really hate me. But that hurts even more because in the end it wasn´t enough to stay. He left because he didn´t hate me. His stubbornness might have been the art of self-destruction. But it turned out it´s my artistry too.

And the thing I learned from all this is that I still get attached. And the one who cares less has the upper hand. That´s just the way it is. And in our case, he did.

And I lost.

Not just him, but myself. And I don´t want any of that anymore. I´m happy to have my friends and nothing has to change about that. I didn´t want a relationship a year ago.

When did that change anyway?

When I met him.

- 27 -

Since Kai left, I´ve spend a lot of time with Finn. We understand each other better than ever. And since he´s the only one who knows what was between me and his brother, he sort of understands me. He´s there for me and somehow through him, it´s like a part of Kai is still here. He distracts me. But also listens if I want to talk. He talks when I need him to and he´s silent when I need it. He´s working and I sit next to him reading books. I´m at all of his games. He´s the captain. He´s a legend. He could play professionally easily. I like to watch him. And I grew to love basketball. I watch him train and we work out together. He helps me to get rid of those feelings I can´t express.

I do more art since Kai´s gone too. Okay *more* is wrong I do *different* paintings.

It´s darker. But it´s real and raw. I try to work on myself. Get to know me. And figure out what I need and want in life. I try but it´s hard.

The boys were able to distract me throughout the afternoon. Even if they were not aware of *how* much. We were in the pool. Played ping pong. Then beer pong. And then we played games.

Now I sit on the couch with five guys watching trash TV and gossiping. They make me laugh so easily. But when the conversation comes to Kai, I feel that sting in my chest. I pretended that he told me too, that he would leave. They made bets on how long he´ll stand his parents. I understood that it´s always like that with him.

On some days, I can´t turn off my thoughts. I can try to push them away, stuff them into a drawer throughout the day, but eventually it overflows, and everything pours. And that moment has *now* come, and I go upstairs.

On the way to the bathroom, I´m drawn to Kai´s room. So, I slip inside closing the door behind me. The smell that wants to make me believe he´s still here makes my eyes blur. I close em and try to imagine him being here. *On his bed. Between the sheets. Reading his book.* But this only makes it worse, so I walk over to the bookshelf. My fingers slide across the spines. I can´t help thinking about the night he told me he writes.

I don´t know if I should do that. It´s not his diary, but neither is it just a notebook. *Art is something intimate*. But I need this now. A part of him here. Especially since he left them behind, so they can´t be *too* personal, I try to justify. I can have the guilt later, so I pull out the copy of *The Great Gatsby*. I flip through, and a few pages catch my attention. Most of them are smeared with sharpie, markers, fine liners, and ballpoint pens. *It´s a total mess.*

But *his* mess. *I really should have gifted him that notebook back then.*

Sometimes it´s text and sometimes just sentences or only single words. On other pages there are quotes. I think these are from Oscar Wilde. He writes quotes of other books in books. *He´s weird. But I like it.*

And it calms me to read his thoughts. His poems. And for a moment I can forget he left. I even find ones he quoted to me *and ones I wished he would have.*

But at some point, I remember he´s gone. *And stop reading.*

92

It´s not just Finn who saved me those weeks. *It´s been Aidan too.* His goofiness his smile and his charm. I danced a lot of nights away with him. I also drank them away. Smoked them away. Cried them away. But also laughed them away. And all those laughs caused Aidan. It was a mix of fox trot, tight dancing and fooling around. We sang along and slow danced. Then we danced over the top, as if we were on *Greace* or *Dirty Dancing*. It felt like we were the main character. And I think to the people around us, we were. *We definitely were.*

It was fun to dance in front of others. And I didn´t care about the fact that one or the other even filmed us. Because with him, I could forget. *Or shut it out.*

And at some point, the people around us joined us dancing. It was like a flash mob. *It was thrilling. I was happy. I could forget. Him.*

We were a dancing crowd losing shit and forgot all the things we needed to forget. Aidan didn´t really help me forget but he made it so much easier. With him, I can enjoy every moment. And I don´t have to think about Kai every second. *Just every third.*

I´ve never partied so much as in the last weeks. I´ve rarely been so drunk and stoned, too. Ever since I´ve seen Kai out and about in the clubs of London, seemingly fucking everything, I´ve started to distract myself too. I couldn´t be alone anymore. I love being alone. But since he left, I´ve been more with the others than in my own four walls. I´ve been more in his bed then mine. I feel less alone there. Even though I know *his* isn´t at all empty. He´s a lot with girls. *Partying.* Out with friends. It´s like he´s having a different life over there. *Like, we don´t exist.* The guys say it´s no big deal. *He´ll come around.* He´s off more than once a year. But they don´t know that I might be a reason why he left in the first place. And why he won´t come back. But I´m glad they are as much of in a partying mood as I am. Well, except Finn, who´s worried about me. But right now, I don´t wat to deal with the fact that I lost once again my first love and Kai at once. *So, I won´t deal.* Because it seemed to be easier to swallow fucking acid than the fact that he left and probably won´t be back.

I feel alone since he left. Even though I have my friends around. *But they´re not him.* And don´t even get me started on *home*. I don´t have anyone at university either. At least no one who stays. *Like anyone ever did.* I don´t even know how to make friends anymore. I´m too lazy to talk and introverted too. And if it were like in the movies, I would just approach someone. Someone who´s also alone, and we´d be friends. *But it never works that way.* I´m in my second semester and I haven´t made any friends and that´s probably how it will stay.

Because I chose this. And there is nothing wrong to sit alone in the Mensa.

Cause it´s a choice. But sometimes it´s not.

And the thing is life is full of sudden goodbyes. And *that* goodbye was foreseeable. *But I couldn´t see.* Because he´s always been distant and cold sometimes. But it was different then. And I know I should deal with my grief differently, but nothing helps but to turn up the bass so that it controls my heartbeat. Numbs the pain and the brain. Because the longer he doesn´t check in, the more my heart breaks.

The heart of an addict. And those tend to break too.

But music is the best medicine for ~~broken hearts,~~ *addicted hearts*.

So that´s what I do.

But I have to admit, I miss what we almost had. And that *almost* hurts more than any *having* could have.

Even though I´m mad at him, I wonder if his insomnia has gotten worse. Because I stayed over often. Sometimes he texted or called me. *I knew it was because he couldn´t sleep.* Even if he never really said it. *I knew.*

He knew that I knew at some point too. But we didn´t talk about us knowing. Like about anything else we knew and we didn´t mention until it was too late.

He came over or I went to his. *Mostly the latter.* And we talked about everything and nothing. *Literally. Nothing.* Sometimes we just laid in silence together. Looked at each other or stared into the void. And sometimes we stayed online, *not texting*. Just knowing the other´s there. *We did some silly things.* But some would call it romantic.

I bet he sleeps well enough with other girls. While I sleep *every* night in his. Thinking about whether he can sleep without me. *Because I can´t.*

93

June, When the parties over - Billie Eilish

Leon and Nina had an off phase so she wasn´t around anymore for days. And Luca went on vacation with her brother during the semester break, so I didn´t saw her either. It was just me and the lost boys. *The ones who saved me without knowing.*

The truth is, I´m a mess. *It´s worse.* I don´t deal with my emotions.

I just drown them. Distract myself. Not daring to be in silence.

I did this for a month. And somehow, I snapped. *And I knew I would.* I just hoped it would last longer. *But it didn´t.*

My vision burrs from the alcohol. And my brain is foggy from the weed. But neither helped to forget those *black eyes*. None of the things I did. Nothing helped to shut him out completely. I try hard to silence the thoughts. *Thoughts of him. Those eyes.*

Of the lack of light in them. Of the promises buried behind them. Of the memories that come with them. *The emotions. The loss. Everything.*

I stand with my back to the pool. *I just need it to stop.*

I empty my cup. *Make it stop.*

I smash it in my hands. *Shut him out.*

And I let me fall. *Backwards.*

And I stop and fall in slow motion. Like when they fall off the building. *It´s long.*

Longer than a moment. *It´s slow falling.*

And falling at the speed of light. *Falling, falling, and falling.*

Down the rabbit whole. *Will I ever get out?*

I fall as if I could never land and shatter a hundred times.

I hit the water, cutting me. *It´s good.*

I land in the water. It is hot and cold. It´s loud and quiet. It´s light and heavy. It´s soft and hard. Knives in my back and throat. I sink and sink. *Sink.*

I shut my eyes; I rip them open. I see the cup on the surface and the silhouettes of people. I close my eyes. *It´s so quiet. It´s peace.*

My lip´s part. Like I forget I don´t live like this, I fill my lungs. I breathe and I choke. It burns and soothes. I stare and blink. I touch the ground. I hit the ground. *Is there a ground?*

I feel upside down. I hurt and feel nothing. *Nothing.*

I don´t know how much time passes, but eventually *someone* grabs me and ~~pulls~~ *rips* me to the surface. *I choke. I spit. I breathe. It hurts.*

I´m forced to breathe. I´m forced to deal. I´m forced to feel. Finn got me out.

Black eyes.

The same as his. *I look away.*

"I´m fine" I snap as he carries me through the water to sit on the edge. I jolt and stand up. I walk past the people staring at me. *I don´t care.*

Completely drenched, I drag a trail behind me.

Like I did when he had thrown me in.

Like, I did on my own now. *Make it stop.*

"Scar wait." He yells. "I´m fine Finn." I bark, hurrying onto the street. "I just wanted to *rest.*" I say, trying not to sound toneless. "You´re *not* fine." He says somewhere behind me. But I keep quiet because I know I´ll say something I regret later.

I don´t know if I breathe. *If my heart beats. I just blink.*

It´s the only thing I notice. *And I walk.*

But I know he´s following me. He doesn´t try to do it silently, but he doesn´t talk to his luck. *He´s just there. Always there.*

Making sure I´m okay and don´t lose it. *But I already did.*

He´s there. Guarding me from whatever is on the outside. Making sure I´ll surface again. He saw me fall. *Of course, he did.* He got me out. *Of course, he would.*

He stays because his brother didn´t. He won´t leave my side until he´s back again.

And that is enough. It´s everything.

I left without my phone. *That never happened to me before.* I will have to get it tomorrow. *Well, I don´t really need it.* Cause I don´t get notifications. *No one I care about.* Surely the others will know by then that I tried to drown myself.

Now´s not just the rumor about Kai´s attempt but mine too. But he didn´t and neither did I. I wanted peace and not to off me. *That´s all.*

Finn came all the way to my house and even upstairs. He insisted on staying in the bathroom and while I showered. He turned around covering his eyes. He didn´t even leave when I wanted to pee. Instead, he covered his ears and turned on the faucet.

If I wanted to kill myself, I would have done it.

Someone who wants to do die does it.

Without a fuss. Without witnesses. And I won´t kill myself for a guy. Especially not since he already killed me. *Kinda.*

I had to stay in there too when he showered because he jumped for me. So, I stood there facing the door. Then I gave him clothes I still had from Kai, and we laid down. It was weird seeing him in Kai´s clothes. They were a bit tight but not too much. He´s always dressed up so this was.. *unusual.*

We stared at the ceiling. "He hasn´t called yet, has he?" he whispered, as if he didn´t want to scare me off. *I didn´t answer. I didn´t cry. I couldn´t.*

I closed my eyes. *Black.*

"No." I whisper. *But he´s already asleep.*

I lie down on his chest. *And cry.*

Until he wakes up wrapping his arms around me. So yes, he saved me.

More than once.

- 27 -

After I cried the whole night, Finn took me with him. I stayed in Kai´s bed till the sun set. And now it´s just the boys and me. No one cared or noticed about my pool drowning thing.

Or they didn´t want to mention it.

Maybe no one paid attention. *Maybe, they did.* I´m glad and sad about it.

They´re doing their best to cheer me up. *I know they do.* They won´t mention it, but they do. Because even though they might haven´t gotten a whiff on yesterday, but they saw my puffy red eyes today. They don´t know what is off but they know *something* is going on.

They would never guess.

They tried hard to make me laugh. And I did, but it didn´t reach the right place. *My heart.* But what did reach that part was the song that came on. *It did send me over.* There´s nothing I could do about it. Blame it on the booze I´ve had. Or the weed in my lungs. *But I started to cry. Like ugly cry.* Like that kind of cry, you hide behind closed doors and sheets.

As I said before, I was a mess.

Hot tears shoot down my cheeks. I was crying and I don´t in front of others. *Not like this. Not ever. But I couldn´t stop. Couldn´t shame enough to care.*

Aidan got up immediately, cupped the back of my head and dragged me into his arms. "Guys." He demanded and shortly after, I felt Finn hugging me from behind. And then more arms from Leon, Andi, and Ryan joined in. *All of them hugging me.*

While I cried like I lost it. They didn´t say much. *Just held me. Let me cry.*

That made me only cry harder. And after a few minutes, we parted. I apologized and blamed it on a bad trip. After that, I felt better. And they pretended it didn´t happen.

I love them for that.

Aidan even made me laugh then. *He always did.*

94

One Week later

Leon is at my front door. "Come on, let´s go." He says and runs down the stairs.

Always short-tempered that guy.

"Where to?" I ask and his head snaps back, annoyed. "Listen.." he begins walking a few meters back. "I don´t know what´s going on with you or which guy you´re on about at the moment." He tells me. "But I *don´t* care, because I want the old Scar back." He shrugs. "And I *know* what helps, so come with me." He says. "I don´t feel like doing *anything* right now." I try to brush him off but it´s true since the pool thingy I´ve isolated myself.

He glares at me. I know it´s a big step for him to come here wanting to help me, but I´ll rather stay in bed. "Either you´ll tell me or whoever of us what the fuck is the matter with you. Or which guy we should beat." He spits.

"Or you´ll get your *fucking* ass down and deal with your shit." He points at me. "You have to get it out to get over it. Don´t give it the power to overpower you. Let it give you the strength to fight it. *Face it.*" He demands. I know he doesn´t want to talk about my problems. He didn´t came to talk or let me cry. He came to help with whatever he has on his mind. And that´s what I love about him and our friendship.

He´s straight on.

"Tell me at least what we´re doing." I insist. "Am I even dressed right?" I ask, looking down at myself in jogger, and a top. "Yes, you are." He states.

"We´re going to relieve *stress*. Now move your ass or I´ll drag you down by myself." He barks, I smile and give in. Because stress relief is *exactly* what I need. And knowing the situation between Leon and Nina, I´m sure he´ll need this more than myself. He does this for himself. *And who would I be to refuse him?*

- 27 -

We´re in a lost place, an old factory or something similar. It´s at that small, abandoned city where no one goes to anymore except those lost place dudes. And apparently the lost ones and pirates too. *Or used to go.*

We entered through a back door. It´s a concrete hall; the ceilings are as high as those of a gymnasium. Electrical equipment lies around everywhere. Some old cars are parked in front of the big gates too.

"Here," he says, handing me a pair of goggles from his backpack. Then he pulls out baseball bats, golf clubs, batons from a closet and throws them on the floor. "Pick your baby" he grins and turns on music over the speaker. *Since U been gone by a day to remember* resounds through the hall. *It seems to come from everywhere.*

He puts on the glasses, jogs to the other end of the hall and starts crushing. I watch him for a moment destroying everything. I fucking love it. *A private rage room.*

I chose the baseball bat, press my glasses into my face and scan the room for *something* to destroy. I catch sight of a flat screen that appears to be intact except for dirt and concrete dust. I take a swing and hit it. Again and again, until the display is cracked. Then I kick it, grab it, and throw it across the room. When I can´t get any more dopamine out of that junk, I look for the next. A PC. Then a game console. A washing machine. And other stuff.

I moved over to the cars. My choice fell on an old model of a BMW. I push off the mirror with my foot. I knock it off and smash it into a thousand pieces. I don´t think about whom these things belong to and whether they would still be functional. I don´t worry about whether this is legal or not. I hammer on the hood and let it all out.

All the times, I´ve been silent instead of raising my voice. *I rip off the license plate.* All the times, I didn´t stand up for myself. *I smash the windshield.* All the times, I´ve been hurt, screwed over, cheated, lied to, or ignored. *I take a big shard and stab the tires. Cutting myself in the process.* All the times, I´ve acted according to my role instead of breaking out of it.

I climb on the hood, onto the roof, bounce, and stomp as hard as I can.

Every time I said no instead of yes and every time I said yes instead of no. Every time I´ve lost myself for a guy. Every time I gave more than I got. Every time I wanted too much love. Every time I chased others love instead of choosing mine.

With my hopping, I seem to have caught Leon´s attention because he stopped his crushing and ran over to me. He climbed up and we continued dancing. Leon uses his golf club as an electric guitar, and I sing along loudly. I haven´t had that much fun in a long time. The adrenaline makes me think I´m drunk. *And suddenly I have the urge to drink.*

"Do you have any booze?" I yell in his ear. He nods with a grin and jumps off the car. He keeps playing air guitar and jogs dancing across the junk to his backpack. He pulls out a beer, a bottle of cherry liquor and holds them in the air. *I cheer.* I have to grin at the fact that he remembered *I loathe beer*.

I help him get on the roof and our private concert continues and gets better and better. I´m glad I came here. Talking is really the *last thing* I want to do right now. He´s not like Finn, who wants to talk all the time. Or Aidan, who just cheers me up and makes me laugh. *But sometimes I can´t laugh.* Sometimes I *need* to scream and beat it out. And Leon has the right sensitivity.

And the smashing is like therapy. Screw therapeutic writing, I´ve tried that. *Didn´t work.* I wrote him a four-page letter. *Pathetic.*

But this is a thousand times more effective and liberating. And if at the moment property damage is the only way out of the hell in my head, I accept that. Because if I allow myself to think about how much I miss him, or how much he has hurt me, or how emotionally involved I already was, I will go crazy. So, when this is how I cope.

Then I´m okay with it.

I can suffer later. *So, I cope.*

We sing along and smash all around us. I drown the bottle more than half, and we keep dancing, kicking, throwing, punching, slicing, raging, singing until we´re exhilarated.

It´s intoxicating. I feel like we´re Damon Salvatore and Vicky Donovan dancing around the house trashing everything. But I can do without the scene where they dance arm in arm, and she cries to him. *And I´m sure Leon can too.*

He throws me a spray can. "Now one last one." He smirks and I didn´t miss the graffiti. "You have to immortalize yourself" he says and disappears somewhere with a can. I stand in front of the wall and look at the writings. I think about what I should spray. A thousand quotes shoot through my head. Rage builds up. Because of him, my brain starts to search for quotes all the time. *I hate that. It reminds me of him. All does.*

But I would give anything to hear him quote. *He would think of something.*

I play his words back in my mind, searching for something I could use. I never heard him quote anything in front of the others. It was how he expressed his feelings and thoughts to me. Which makes me happy *and* sad. He did it through poetry, lyrics, and quotes. You might think it would have been worth less but somewhere, everyone has already said, sung, or written everything. *And they are just words.* Only he gave them more meaning.

He managed to sneak back into my thoughts. *Shut it out. Get it out. Express it.*

"He´s not hell if you like how he burns."

I spray on the brick walls in black paint. *Black as his fucking eyes.*

The ones I´d like to forget. *But can´t.*

If I´m broken, then at least I´ll make art out of it.

- 27 -

After that I got my shit together. I still cried a lot, but I got better. I dealt with it and got it out. *It helped.* And the boys knew it was about some guy. They didn´t know who. But they knew how to make me better.

Aidan brought back my smile. He was responsible for my laughter. Leon brought me down and helped me with my anger. Finn was the one saving me the most because he saw me the lowest. Ryan was just Ryan stoned and basically, helping with not talking at all. And Andi boosted my ego by bashing him when no one was listening. And the cooking and cocktails he made. Those were great.

Nina distracted me with partying and Luca with book shopping. They didn´t know, but they saved me all. They made it hurt less. And in ways hurt more.

95

Two weeks later, Off My Mind – Joe P

My social battery is lacking, so as in the past I escape to Kai´s room. To hide between the sheets that can cover the pain. The sheets I didn´t change once since he left. It´s gross, but it smells like him. *I can´t change them.*

But as I make my way through the party, I spot Aidan sitting on the stairs with a cup in his hand. *He looks off.*

When he sees me, his gaze lifts. He doesn´t seem cheerful. He´s always in a good mood and up for fun. *Always smiling. Except for now.*

"Sup fucker?" I ask, trying to make him smile, and sit down next to him. "Pretty nothing," a faint attempt of a grin flicks across the corner of his mouth. "Everything good?" I ask, nudging his shoulder with mine. "Yeah" he says, not very convincingly and takes a sip from his cup. I consider how to get through to him but before I can expand on my plan, he speaks up. "I think you´re the only girl I know who doesn´t want a relationship." He says and looks at me. *He´s wrong about that.*

“I´m not saying I don´t *want* a relationship; I´m saying I´m not looking.” I clarify. “I don´t *need* one to be happy.” I explain, trying to convince not only him, but myself as well. That´s what I´ve been trying the past weeks. *That I don´t need him.*

“Every girl I´ve dated wanted more, though.” He says. “Aidan the heartthrob.” I joke.

“*How do I get rid of them in ten days?*” I laugh referring to the movie. He chimes in, pushing me with his body and I´m glad I made him smile. *Like genuine.*

He smiled the minute he first saw me. Kai on the other hand.. *stop it.*

“I´m serious.” He says, facing me. “Even if I make it clear from the start that I don´t want anything serious, they still sleep with me, *knowing* they want more. And then they get pissed when I close up, when they start with jealousy, etc.” He complains. “Guys are then considered as *fuckboys*, even though we´ve openly communicated what´s going on. Unlike them, who weren´t honest at all.” He continues. *And he has a point.*

“They keep quiet about their feelings. But at that point, you should end it and not continue trying to change him.” He brags and I nod along. “They hope they´ll be the one he´ll change for.” I say *knowing* that feeling myself.

“Yet men can keep a much greater distance from emotions than women. And through sex, the emotional bond is strengthened, which makes it hard. So, they sleep with them, hoping they would get feelings and fall for them. *And stay.*” I try to analyze, and he listens. “Makes sense.” He smiles. “But I´m tired of it.” He groans and I smile. “Hard to fuck when all they want is your heart.” I say and he smacks my knee taking another sip.

We´re silent for a beat. *He eyes me.*

“And.. all is well with you?” He asks, leaning onto his knees. He waves the cup in a circle lowering his gaze. *There´s the question.* The one they all avoided the past month watching me losing my shit. And I was glad they didn´t rake further because I couldn´t tell them. But no one asked, so I had not to talk about it. *Until now.*

“Honestly?” I ask and he glances over his shoulder nodding. “Always.” He straightens up and watches me closely. “That I don´t want a relationship..” I begin. “I forget that sometimes.” I admit and he squints his eyes at me frowning. “*I knew* a guy was responsible for your mood.” He says proud of his detective skills.

If you only knew he´s your best friend.

“That obvious?” I ask knowing the answer. “Kinda.” He gives me a half smile, but it fades as he speaks. “Hoped you would have told me though.” He says softly. “I could have given you advice.” He grins. “Yeah no.” I shake my head. “I know I mean. *Thanks.*

But no there was no help." I stammer. "We weren´t good at *figuring* things out. And it didn´t work.. so." I shrug and he nods.

"You don´t have to tell me anything if you don´t want to talk about it." He assures me and I know he means it. "It´s just it creeps up on me that I don´t even realize." I say frustrated. "I want to focus on myself, but then I fall for some guy and get lost." I complain. "I don´t even want it. But I can´t help it. I want love but I´m afraid of it." I tell him. "Then I get to the point where I wonder *when* it happened? And how I forgot that I am the most important person in my life?" I zone out. "I´m a control freak who´s afraid of losing control, commitment, trust and losing people. Yet a freak who wants love with all his heart." I say and almost laugh. He doesn´t answer and just looks at me. But not because he doesn´t *know* what to say, but because he actually listens.

When he realizes I´m really done, he begins, "I´d like to know what my problem is too." he leans forward. "Why do you think you don´t want relationships?" I ask and watch his wrist circle the liquor. "Don´t want to take responsibility." He mutters. "I panic when it comes to feelings. It narrows me down. I like it loosen." He shrugs.

Seems to be a lost boy thing.

"With all those girls. Have you never been in love?" I ask. "Don´t exaggerate. There aren´t *that* many." He points out, knowing there are. "Not for a long time." He says looking in the void. "Be glad. I´ve always fallen in love way too fast." I say and he looks at me. "Watch out or you´ll fall in love with me, Scar." He grins making his dimples appear. I don´t mention that he *definitely* has the potential. And I would have tried to hit on him if we wouldn´t have become friends that quickly, and the other reason is now gone anyway.

So, I never considered us as that.

I have to laugh. "Sure." I say. "I´d rather think *you´re* falling in love." I say. "With *you*?" He raises his brow and laughs cheekily. "I bet you fall in love faster." He lifts his chin challengingly. "No," I shake my head.

"*Bet*" he nods. "Whoever falls in love *first* loses." He says. "But no others. *Just us.*" He holds out a hand to me. "You´re up?" He asks. "That´s stupid." I laugh. "No. Look.. You and I don´t want a relationship. Right?" He asks. "Right." I agree, smiling confused. He´s still holding his hand in the air gesturing with the other while he talks. "You fall in love too fast, and you want to know *when* it´s happening. And I don´t want to fall in love, or at least think I *can* have sex without feelings." He explains. "It´s like an experiment. Psychology is your thing anyway, right? For research." He grins, convinced of his idea.

"That´s crazy. You´re crazy." I say. "Come on Scar. It´s all worked out. We have sex, go on dates and everything. Make out. Have fun. It´ll be great. Friends who fuck for research." He teases and I shake my head. "And if one of us gets feelings, we stop. We just end things. No one gets hurt." He says with conviction, but I frown at him. "Where are feelings, there´s *always* hurt." I say and he looks at me for a moment, realizing. *Blinks twice.* Then puts his hand down that he still held out to me.

His expression changes. He nods once.

"You´re right." He shakes his head at himself. "You´re my best friend.. and I should not jeopardize that. I´m sorry Scar." He apologizes. "Really, I don´t know what got into me." He ruffles his hair. "I drank too much.. I guess." He says, lifting his cup. "That was really stupid. Just forget.. I said anything." He says, drinks and leans on his knees. Somehow, I feel guilty that I rejected his offer like that.

I look at his back. *And see him. My best friend.* The one who makes me laugh. The one I feel safe with and myself. And distraction is still something I can use. And if it might make me understand myself and my motives better. *Why not?*

And he is incredibly hot, and we do function so.. *maybe*.

"On one condition." I say and his head turns to me. "We communicate." I demand, reaching for the cup. As I do so, my hand rests on his. His gaze falls on our hands.

By the tingling I feel, I´m afraid to lose before it even started.

I take a sip before he takes it back and straightens up. "Then I hereby communicate, that I want to kiss you really fucking bad." He says, looking straight into my eyes before his gaze lingers on my lips. *Fuck.* His eyes *literally* undress me.

"No." I say, and he looks at me, a frown building. "You want to kiss me *again*. Remember?" I grin. The worry disappears and his jaw sets. "I haven´t forgotten *that* kiss Scar." He says intently, causing my pulse to skyrocket. *I lean in.*

Our legs touch, my chest explodes. He grabs my cheek and presses his lips to mine. A taste of cherry liquor spreads. A familiar taste, even though I only tasted him once, but it´s trusted as if we never stopped. I put my hand on his chest and his moves to my thigh. A heat spreads from my face, radiating throughout my body. His tongue teases mine and he bites my lip, and I bite his. I sit between his legs, and he leans against the wall. We make out like teens on the stairs of a party, like we´ve just met.

When we break away, we grin at each other. "So?" He asks, "in love yet?" He smiles and it reaches my heart. "Worse." I joke. "*I love you.*" I say, to which he chuckles. "Will you marry me, Scar?" he grins, and I kiss him.

We smile at each other. “Come.” He eyes me. “I want to dance with my date.” He says and stands up. And I´m glad I didn´t go to Kai´s room and slept in his empty bed like I´ve been doing the last weeks.

Aidan insisted on walking me home. He blamed it on *girls being into that sort of thing*, but I know he would have walked me home regardless of our bet. He knows the sidewalk rule. *A gentleman.* Too bad, that he doesn´t want a relationship.

It´s a thing all the lost boys have in common. No love. *Shit.* First weakness noted.

We phone until he´s home. *I insisted on that one.*

“I have one more condition” I say. “Let´s hear” he means. “We´re always honest. We can tell each other anything, okay?” I ask. “Of course,” I can hear him grinning. “I mean it. I really don´t want to lose you, Aiden. If that breaks anything..” I lament worriedly, but he interrupts me. “Scar it won´t.” He assures me. “If we´re both honest.” He adds. “Okay,” I say. “I don´t want to lose you either.” He says, and my stomach tickles at his words.

If she only knew that her lies would mess everything up.

She would have stopped right there.

96

When I woke up, a good morning message was already waiting for me. He´s really putting in the effort. *Point for him.* He texted to pick me up at 8:30 pm and to put on something comfortable. *Direct, but that´s how I like it.*

This will be our first date and he´s already in front of my house on his motorcycle. I put on the black helmet and watch as Aidan swings himself onto his machine. He starts it up and plays with the gas. He looks over his shoulder tilting his head, signaling me to hop on. I hold onto his back to get on and wrap my arms around his stomach.

“Hold on.” He says, even if I already do.

With a jerk, he pushes the bike forward and heads down the road. The exhaust of the Ducati pops, giving me chills. We race through the streets. And for the first time in a long time, *I can breathe.*

At the traffic light, he puts his hand on mine. Another time he puts it on my thigh. At every opportunity he touches me. And every time I get butterflies.

This whole bet thing will be hard.

We drive onto a dirt road away from everything. Only meadow, wheat, rape fields and the sunset. And his Audi. He must have driven the car here first. The fresh country air brakes on me as I take off my helmet.

"Close your eyes for a minute." he tells me, walking toward his car. "Okay" I laugh and turn away from him. I hear the trunk open. Then the wind blows my hair and takes away my attention. I hear birds singing. And feel the warm summer air on my skin.

"Okay," I hear him from behind me and I turn. The sun´s rays blind me before the car comes in view. The back seats are folded down and a mattress is in the trunk with pillows and blankets. A string of lights hangs in the car. On the white blanket a bouquet of sunflowers. And next to it chocolate strawberries and other fruits. I can´t help but grin. It looks beautiful. *He´s good.*

He grins at me. "You like it?" he asks. "I didn´t make anything like this for any girl." He brags. *The typical statement of a fuckboy.*

You are different. You are the only one.

"Sure, you did." I say with a broad grin. "And yes, I like it." I say truthfully. "I didn´t know you were romantic." I add piercing my eyes at him. "There´s a lot you don´t know about me." He states with a smile. *I believe there is.*

Actually it´s the nicest date I´ve had so far. *Paris was not a date.* And those reading dates were between two friends. *All we ever did was between friends.* Well, I´m not even sure about the friends part anymore.

"It hasn´t even started. I can still screw up." He warns me with a laugh, but I shake my head. He kicks off his shoes and gets in. I do the same and settle down next to him. He takes the laptop, and we watch some movie. And as you would expect, he puts his arm around me and pulls me to his chest. *He smells so good.*

I pop one of the strawberries into my mouth, and he watches me closely.

We finished all the fruits and the movie, though we talked, laughed and didn´t even pay attention to the plot. His hand is on my waist, stroking the skin. We hold hands and our fingers caress each other. Such simple touches are intoxicating. *I love that. Focus.*

Note to myself first dates already trigger feelings. Great. How bad do you want to fall? Yes. *How needy you are for love?* Yes. *It´s a sickness. Craving love.*

Get your shit together. Happy hormones. Dopamine. The same areas of drug use. Addicts. My chest hurts. My jaw clenches. My mind does that sometimes. Wandering to Kai and the things he said to me. And every time I get stabbed anew.

Stop thinking of him. You´re here with Aidan.

He lets go of my hand and brings my chin to his mouth. *We kiss.* A cocktail of butterflies and pleasure shoots through my body. *Shit, shit, shit.* That.. *feels way too good.* Way too much like I´ll fall for you. *But I can´t stop either.* So, I put my leg over his and his hand travels down my thigh to my ass. He kneads it, whereupon a low moan escapes me.

Fuck he´s good.

He grins as he kisses me.

"Are you trying to get me laid on the first date?" I tease him breaking the kiss. "I would never" he lies and grins leaning back in. All men want is *support, loyalty, and sex.* I read that in a book. I´ll give him the former, but the latter can wait. Because I´m not going to lose. Even if the butterflies announce otherwise. *I will stay strong. Not losing control. No falling in love head over heels again. We know well enough how that ended last time. In him leaving.*

"I have to pee," I say to avoid the temptation, and hop out of the car. I have to leave before I break my resolution. I walk along the path for a few meters until I can no longer see the car. I go into one of the cornfields and try to empty my bladder without peeing on any part of me.

If this bet distracts me from Kai, and it does most of the time, I put my focus on winning. *I stay busy. Too busy to think of him. Busy with Aidan in the now. Cause all I have is the now. I just hoped the now would bring Kai with it. Stop it.* I´ll learn a lot about myself. And I get to know him better. And get laid. *Just not today.*

I go back and Aidan walks toward me and kisses me. *I forget how to breathe.*

When he lets go of me, he says "Need to piss" with a smug grin and passes me by. I sit down on the edge of the trunk staring at his back. But unlike me, he makes no effort to get away. He merely stands with his back to me a few meters in by the field. I watch him as he holds his arms in front of him. His veins stand out on his forearms. And my gaze wanders to his defined upper arms. As he begins to pee, he throws his head back in satisfaction. *Why the hell am I turned on by the way he pees? I´m completely fucked up. Crazy about him and what he has to offer. This is going to be harder than I thought.*

I press my lips together, ignoring my pulsing clit. He shakes off, sips himself up and turns around. *I´m hypnotized.* His boxers stick out. *Shit.* He catches me staring. *At his crotch.* I swallow, and he grins slightly *knowing* what´s on my mind. I try not to avert my gaze. And fix him as he walks toward me. There had always been *that* chemistry and affection between us. *And it seems even stronger now.*

"What you´re looking at Scar?" He asks nodding his chin at me and I fight a smile. He grabs my cheeks and presses his lips greedy to mine. He pushes me backwards, and I tug him with me. He presses his hips against mine and makes himself room between my legs. I scratch his head to which he sucks on my neck. I feel him harden under me.

"Like that." He murmurs. We change position, and now I sit on top and kiss along his jaw. We´re not having sex but there´s nothing against making him horny. He grabs my ass and pushes his boner against me. He grunts and I whimper. Adrenaline rushes through my veins.

"We should stop" he hushes into my hair his breath hot on my ear.

No. Yes. Fuck. We should.

"You´re right." I say straighten up. His cheeks are flushed, his lips are bit swollen and pink. *Bedroom eyes.* His hair´s a mess. *A great mess.*

"I don´t want you to lose within 24 hours." I say trying to hide my grin. "Words," he laughs and grabs me by the hips, throwing me off his lap and I giggle. He braces himself on his hands next to my face. "If then *you´re* the one who falls once you´ve felt my dick inside you." His voice all raspy. My mouth falls open. Shocked and turned on, I look at him.

He bites my lip.

The golden hour makes his eyes brighten. He lays his forehead against mine and takes a deep breath. He stays like that for a moment, and I feel his chest as he breathes steady breaths. Then he gives me a kiss on the forehead and slides out of the car.

He adjusts his pants.

"I´ll get the net before we get stung to death." He says as he rubs his neck not meeting my eyes for a sec. He goes around to the passenger side. He really thought of a mosquito net. *Genius.*

He stretches it across the trunk and secures it. "Smart," I counter as he slips back in. "Me?" he asks pointing at his chest. "Always," he gives with a grin. *I love how much he smiles.* Probably because I hardly ever do. He´s simply happy. And I love his dimples. And the faint lines that have already formed from laughing. I love how he lightens my mood.

He makes me happy. No matter what.

We watch the sunset and fool around and laugh till our stomach hurts.

- 27 -

When I wake up, we lie in spoon position his arms wrapped around me. His erection against my ass. I carefully turn around so that I can watch him sleep and study his face. He has some light freckles. Even when he sleeps, he has a faint smile on the corner of his lips. And only now I notice a scar on his nose. He has lots of scars along his back. I´ve seen those back in the summer. But I never asked about them.

Maybe he had an accident or something.

But those on his face I didn´t see. Maybe, cause I´ve never been *that* close to him. Not longer than a kiss. I´m taking in every detail. He had a cut in his lip. On his forehead a pit. And next to his eyebrow another pale mark. Without thinking, I run my finger over his faded seams. His grumble makes me wince and I quickly lift my hand.

"Go on." He mumbles, so, I continue. A slight smirk plays his mouth as I wander over his nose and to his mouth. I graze his lower lip, and he bites my finger. I flinch and he chuckles. I cup his jaw and kiss him softly as he explores my mouth with his forcing tongue.

- 27 -

"Leave your phone in the car." Aidan says as he gets out. So, I put it in the console and close the door behind me. I walk over to the concrete wall and watch him lather up his car. Luckily, my sunglasses are tinted, which allows me to stalk him.

Even though I know he knows.

As he starts to rinse it off, he nods to me. "You want a turn?" He asks and holds the hose to me. I stand up, but as I reach for it, he sprays me right in the face. I squeal, laughing and try to take it from him. *In vain.*

I run around the car to hide. Just as unsuccessfully because the spray hits me. I run towards him for another attempt. He holds the jet in the air and makes it rain over our heads. I squint my eyes and as I try to reach for it, he kisses me hard. I wrap my arms around his neck. He drops the hose and walks me toward the hood of his car.

The next moment, I´m sitting.

Everything is so easy with him. *Fun and light.* Even a simple car wash.

97

Three weeks later

The past weeks we went to play paint ball and laser tag. We did rock climbing, go-karting and went to the trampoline park. He took me out for sushi and burgers. And we even went to concerts and a festival with the others. He also took me book shopping, which was my personal highlight and with that he had my heart. And I already catch my stomach making somersaults. I can feel the tingling. *The excitement.* Because the tricky thing is by telling the other which things cause butterflies, we give the key to our hearts. And we use the lock to challenge each other. Keep pushing the right buttons to make the other give in.

Or to fall first.

And Kai was right. Love is a fucking drug. *It´s a sickness. It´s addicting. It´s fogging your brain. It´s a fucking game you play to get happiness.*

But right now, I can´t stop playing. And I´m not sure if I ever can.

"Put on a skirt." Aidan texted before he picked me up. *So, I did.*

He paid for both the tickets and the popcorn. *He never lets me pay.*

After twenty minutes into some action movie, he gets up and pulls me with him. "Where are we going?" I whisper. "That movie´s fucking boring." He mutters. "We´re going into that horror movie." He adds, in a whisper and I follow him up the stairs, trying not to trip in the dark. "You´re serious?" I whisper yell. "You´re just going to sit in another movie?" I laugh uncomfortable. "We paid." He points out. "Does it make a difference which movie we see?" he asks. *He has a point.*

"See?" He says as I say nothing. "But I *hate* breaking rules." I tell him. "I know." He whispers, though no one is around. "But we break no rules. Despite, we all are rule breakers if you didn´t notice." He says. "What if someone catches us?" I ask, still whispering. He shakes his head at me with a grin. "No one will." He says. "But what if?" I insist. "Then we´ll run from security like in the movies. And go hide in some closet. And I get in your pants." He laughs. "But.." I try to go on, but he cuts me off. "What if you´d stop worrying? Or thinking? For once?" He asks. I bite my lip. "Now shut it. Sometimes you have to *ignore* the rules. Especially unnecessary ones." He says and I look at him not convinced. "Sorry but I´m a bad influence and I´ll ruin you." He grins. "Should have put that into my dating profile." He jokes in a whisper, and I grin. He knows he got me with that one.

"But aren´t there cameras?" I ask looking to the ceilings. "There *are* but by staring *into* them, you won´t make it better." He states with a snort. "Fine but if we get caught.." I begin. "Then I forced you. Now shut up Scar." He hushes into my ear walking me along. "If you can´t jump yourself, you need to be pushed." He opens the door to theater, and we slip through. The movie has already started.

I really hate this. There´ll be people staring at us.

We sit down in the upper middle. The auditorium is not full, but not empty either. The movie is not far yet. We missed the boring part. It´s a movie about a psychiatric institution. And since we have already eaten our popcorn, we have to spend the rest of the movie without it. He has one arm wrapped around me. His other hand moves to my knee and slowly slides it under my skirt. I give him the side eye.

Now I understand what he´s up to with the skirt.

But I stop his hand and look at him, shaking my head. "What?" he asks innocently. "You know they can see *everything*, right?" I whisper. "That´s the kink Scar." He forces my hand away and I get chills when he calls me that way. I try not to look at him, hoping that *if* a security guy is watching, there will be less suspicion that we are groping.

He caresses my skin for a while. *I´m tense.* Because the movie actually seems to be a good one and my clitoris pulsates with excitement. He strokes my pants with his middle finger. *Up and down.* So light that you wouldn´t normally feel it, but at this moment my body is on alert. *I feel it all.*

Aidan builds tension along with the film. *I think I might go crazy.* The protagonist walks around the asylum in the dark. We hear strange noises of inmates screaming. I´m scared and aroused. The last time I felt this was.. *Whatever.*

She´s now in the children´s ward. A girl sings somewhere and with each degree of tension, Aidan rubs me harder. When I flinch from a jump scare Aidan´s fingers slide under my junk. *Fuck.*

He circles my clit, twisting it between his fingers as she runs away. "You like it?" he murmurs in my ear, and I press my lips together trying hard not to make any sound. I nod slightly and grab his thigh as he slides two fingers inside me.

My pants already soaked.

I must pull it all together not to moan. Fortunately, the movie is loud enough. His thumb continues to work my clit and his fingers pump in luring motions. He palms me and I throb against his hand. I guide my hand up his jeans and squeeze. I can´t hold a second longer and open my mouth slightly as the orgasm sweeps through me. Aidan looks at me as I do so whispering things to me.

After I have recovered, we exchange a look, and he doesn´t have to say anything for me to know what´s going on in his mind. He stands up and pulls me with him. We hurry up the stairs, he close behind me. Before we leave the hall, he presses his boner against my ass greedy for what will come. He takes my hand and leads me down the endless hall. My center still pulsating.

Then he pushes me to the left into the toilets. Before I can see in which sex, we went he crushes his lips to mine. He lifts me up and walks backwards with me on his arm. He kicks open the door with his foot and throws us against the door in the cubicle. His hands hold my bare bottom. I rub against his hard-on. We´re not loud but not trying to be quiet either. I don´t even know if anyone is in the room with us.

I don´t even care either.

My hands move to his belt. "Fuck," he groans as he breaks our kiss. "What?" I ask breathlessly. His head bombs against the door. *Deja Vu. Kai did that too when..*

"I don´t have a *fucking* condom," he spits, putting me down. "Oh." I mouth. We haven´t had sex yet. And somehow, I assumed he would have some on him.

But I need him. Now. In some way.

So, I push him against the wall and get down on my knees. At that moment, the door opens, and some guys come in laughing. “Wha..?” escapes him but he keeps shut letting me unbuckle his belt. The guys are in the next room by the sink talking. His gaze lies on me. I grab his groan on top of the boxers and his breathing becomes more violent. I push them down and his length hits me in the face.

“Fuck” he murmurs in a whisper. I take him in my hand and look up. He looks down at me and presses his lips together. I lick his pre-cum and his cock twitches in response. The guys walk into the room and stand at the pissoir.

“You can´t.” Aiden whispers above their voices. But I take him in my mouth to which he rests his head against the door and closes his eyes. *The boys piss.* My tongue slides along his shaft and I hold onto his hip. My other hand slides under his shirt along his six-pack. His hand lies on top of mine on his shirt, and he grabs my hair guiding me along. He fights not to make a sound and pushes towards me. *I want to drive him crazy like he did to me.* So, I take him deep throat. He´s pushed backward as an intricate moan escapes him. He slams his fist against the door. Chuckles and some talking I don´t really pay attention to comes from the guys. *They probably figured.*

He grips the edge of the wall looking down on me. As they leave, he starts moaning softly. I watch him how he bangs his head against the door and his chest heaves violently. He looks at me as he thrusts into me faster.

“Is it... okay if...” he tries to ask between thrusts. I nod and he grabs my hair like he´s trying to make a braid and pumps into me. “Oh... fuck. Scar.” He grunts as he goes rigid for a sec and comes in the next down my throat.

- 27 -

“**S**o, you guys are dating now?” Leon asks with a confused look. “No, I just fuck her.” Aidan shrugs. My eyes widen at his response. All of us exchange looks. I burst out in a chuckle, to which Aidan cracks up too. *So, they have noticed.* As if it wasn´t obvious. Because we don´t hide. Not like Kai did. *They know.* Not all of it but they know, and that´s enough. That´s more than Kai ever gave me.

“Come on guys, are you two together?” Nina asks curiously. “Not exactly.” I say and look at Aidan. “Kinda.” He says to them but looks at me grinning widely.

“Alright guys.” Leon says annoyed by us. “Whatever.” He exhales. “What´s up tonight?” He asks, changing the subject. *And that´s it.* We didn´t talk about it anymore.

So easy can it be. Kai never knew. *How easy things can be.*

Mid July

We almost had sex in a locker room, on a park bench, in the swimming pool, in a sauna and our list is getting longer. So far, we just make out and have petting. We want to wait.

On what I don´t know.

But we take it slow. Maybe to build feelings. *It´s weird.* The lines and rules blur and I lose sight of what´s real. *Are we still playing? Or already falling?*

The feeling creeps up on me. The voice that whispers *this was no good idea.* But I don´t listen. I´m already into deep. And I want to see if he´s too.

And the whole bet thing has become more of a *who gives in first.* We both know that we have a crush on each other, only neither of us wants to be the first to admit. Maybe we don´t want it to end. We´re afraid of saying it.

Because what then? Do we end? Do we start?

We said we would end things. But I think at this point, neither of us want things to end.

- 27 -

I sit on the sofa with one leg over Finn´s, and he has his hand on my thigh. He´s on his phone busy with work, and I´m talking to Aidan who sits across from me. Finn lightly strokes my thigh tapping on it to the beat of the music. It´s just one of our little jealousy games. We flirt with others to provoke each other. Try to get the other to admit it bothers them. *To show you care.* But mostly that just turns us on more.

What I would never have expected.

But it´s our new kink after we had sex in almost every place imaginable. In short, we lost sight of the bet a little. *Well, a lot.* We haven´t kept in touch about our feelings, because it came to the point where it´s been obvious that we have a thing for each other. But we don´t address it. *Cause then it would end. Or wouldn´t it?*

So, whatever it is we avoid that bet thing and do this new game instead.

I feel something I haven´t felt in a long time. *Eyes on me.* A familiar burn on my skin. *Tingling. A draw.* Something that forces me to look up. And as I lift my eyes, I meet them. The black eyes I tried so hard to escape. *Fate wants to play a trick on me.* Because Kai stands a few feet away. *My heart sinks.*

Even between the dancing people I recognized him right away. He looks me right in the eyes. He seems relieved, maybe even longing. But then his gaze falls down. *On the hand on my thigh.* And then on Finn. His jaw tightens and his look changes to pure rage. He doesn´t meet my eyes and lets a bouquet fall at his side. *A bouquet?* White roses. *Those were for me.* My stomach turns.

He manages his way past the people and comes straight at us. When Finn sees him, he gets up to greet him. But Kai hits him in the face and Finn falls to the ground grabbing his nose. *He caught his brother off guard.*

Kai doesn´t even look at me, but calmly heads inside as if he hadn´t just given his big brother a right. Still in shock, I look at Finn, who has sat up. *His nose is bleeding.*

Aidan chuckles and I face him. "Big dick is back in town." He snorts amused. "That was some hell of a comeback." He adds excited. "I´ll go talk to him." I tell them and go after him. He stands in the kitchen and his hands clutch the counter. He looks at me with such hate I´ve never seen on him. *He´s here. I must dream. But this is a nightmare. This isn´t how I imagined him to return. Not at all. I didn´t think that he ever would. He looks different but the same. He´s back. He beat his brother. And he hates me. I don´t think he ever stopped.*

The muscles in his jaw play. Contrary to my expectation, he says *nothing* and goes upstairs. Well, actually, to say nothing is *exactly* what he would do.

As always. But not now. He owes me.

So, I go after him. "Kai," I call. "Lia, just fuck off" he growls and with that he slams the door behind him. I go back to the kitchen as Finn comes in. I take his face in my hand to look at his nose. "Was *that* my brother who almost broke my nose as a greet?" he asks, perplexed but laughing and I nod. "After what? Three months?" He adds confused.

My heart aches. It´s been a while. Now I realize how long.

I inspect his wound and it´s weird cause I haven´t done that in a while. I always tended Kai´s wounds. *No one else´s.* He´s been the only picking up fights or punching holes in the walls on a weekly basis.

"We saw the same ghost." I say. "I honestly didn´t know he was coming." He says with a frown. *He told no one. Not even his brother.*

I take a handkerchief and dab the blood off. He takes it, wipes once and throws it in the trashcan. "I´ll talk to him." He tells me and goes upstairs. I take some breaths that are not deep enough to calm me. *How can he be mad?*

Why is he here? And what about those roses?

Did he want to surprise me or something?

He wouldn´t have given me them in front of everyone. *Right?* That´s not what he does. *He hid me.* He didn´t gave me flowers. Or anything other than insults or teasing. We were friends and that´s all he let them know.

I hate that he's back. Why now? Now that I'm falling for.. *his best friend.* He freaked out seeing Finn's hand on me.

What will he do if he finds out that Aidan and I.. Fuck. I shut my eyes.

He was happy to see me until he saw his brothers' hand on my body. *He hit him. Bought me flowers.* He can't just buy me flowers after months of no talking. *He just can't.* And all that is not the way I imagined his arrival to be. *Not at all.*

Finn snaps me out of my thoughts. "You go talk to him." He says not looking at me and walks past me. *That doesn't mean any good.*

I take a deep breath knowing nothing can prepare me for that. *For him being back.*

The moment I've spent months imagining. *All the scenarios.*

But none of them considered *this.*

99

He's sitting on the bed when I close the door behind me. He won't look at me and it fucking hurts. *Him being here.* How I've pretended him to be the past months. Where I wished to find him telling me it was a mistake. *But that never happened.*

He can't just come back like that.

So, I push my sadness away and gather my anger. Because that what happens, sadness turns into rage. "You're back?" I ask, crossing my arms. He nods slight. "Yeah, seems." He hisses still not looking at me.

We fall silent. If he only *knew* how many times I've been in his room. My eyes burn. I wonder if his bedding smells like me instead of him by now. *And if he noticed. Stop it. Focus.*

"Was that necessary?" I ask, forcing me to think clearly. His head snaps in my direction. Finally, he looks at me. *Like you refused to when you left me.* It hurts him as much as me as our eyes meet.

But he catches himself glaring at me. "When my *brother* screws my best friend?" He asks furiously as he gets up. *Best friend, huh?*

"Fucking yes. It is." He barks, coming toward me. If he only knew *who* fucks me. "It was just a hand on my leg.." I try to tell him, but he snaps at me. "My brothers hand." I inhale. "And we're *not* fucking." I add. "Besides, what do *you* care?" I ask and I wait. He opens his mouth to say something but lets it go. *Of course. As if it was ever different.*

"It doesn't." He plays it off. "Hmh." I let out a laugh shaking my head.

Fucking coward. He shouldn't have come back.

I turn to leave, but he grabs my wrist holding me back. “Scar,” his voice breaks pulling me to him. My throat hurts. *Fuck I don´t want to cry.*

“You left!” I yell at him and jerk away. “Not me.” My voice weak. “You can´t just come back after months of radio silence. Buying flowers, we both know you´d be too much of a coward to give them to me in front of them.” I snap. “And you can´t punch the first person who´s near me.” I shout. “Especially since he´s *your* brother.” I say shaking my head.

Especially since he´s the one who put me back together. Who was there when you weren´t. But I don´t say that. I don´t want him to *actually* break his nose.

“Besides you have no right to do that, you´ve *never* had, and you *know* it.” I say and I have no idea where I get the strength but I´m glad.

He remains silent. Of course, he would.

“Those weren´t for you.” He whispers and I frown. “What?” I ask confused. “The roses.” He tells me. “Those weren´t yours.” He lies lifting his chin and I give him a venomous smile cause I´m fucking over his shit. “I figured.” I say stiffing a laugh and leave. *And he lets me.* And for the first time I´m glad he does.

I sit back down next to Finn. “How did it go?” He asks just for me to hear. “Lousy asshole as usual” I smile fake and that´s all I say, because I don´t feel like talking. I´m too mad right now to think straight.

Andi looks at me, reading my face but I just look at him. He´s is the only one besides Finn who *knows* what went down last year. And without me saying anything, he *knows* he fucked up again. That´s the thing he does. *Mess things up.* And leave you with nothing but blood. And not at all with roses. *Maybe black ones.*

And just now I realize that when he left me on that street. I really ended up like that girl they told me about. With nothing but a bleeding heart. Because that´s what he did. *Break me.* And now I´ve decided to break him too.

“Did the others?” I ask. “I told them we had something to sort out.” He tells me. “Thanks,” I say just as Aiden sits down beside me wrapping his arm around my neck. “So, he´s really back?” He asks, smiling. “Apparently,” I say, trying hard to grin genuinely. “About time,” he says, returning my grin. *Sort of.*

I nod and he kisses my hair. “Missed that fucker.” He says and tears threaten, but I bite my tongue as hard as I can. “Me too.” I say. *And it kills me.*

Even though I always hoped he´d come back, I never thought he *actually* would. And now that I date Aidan, I hoped he would never come back. Because I knew it would mess everything up. And it did. But it did before. *By him making us a secret.*

And by me not telling Aidan.

[NOTEBOOK ENTRIES]

I told everyone but her. I just didn't know how to. When I saw her in that beautiful dress. It felt too good to stay. And way too painful to stay. I waited until the last minute. It was fucked up. But I knew she would have stopped me, and a stupid part of me would have stayed. The pain in her eyes burned into my memory forever. I couldn't look at her. I couldn't say goodbye. I had to pull everything together not to run to her. Not to kiss her. Or hug her. Because I knew If I did, I would have stayed. But I needed to go, and she needed to let me go. I felt sick. I had to hurt her. ~~Before she could hurt me any further.~~ I turned the rear mirror so I wouldn't look at her. She stood there. That hurt enough. But not enough to stay. On the plane, I had to drown the pain with alcohol and pills. Until I felt nothing. Until I forgot she existed. ~~Like I could ever forget.~~ Until it all went quiet and dark again. How it was before. Before her.

At my apartment I slept through the night. Two days to be exact. Not because I was that tired, but bc I had to. I just wanted to shut it out. I could sleep. I took enough pills to make sure I would. I thought I might never wake up. And that was tempting. I forced it all away. I didn't want to deal. Feel. Think. Breathe. I wanted her out. ~~But I knew she was into deep.~~

After the first week of "sleeping." I went to my parents. Even though they wanted me to live in their loft, I wanted my own place. Because having my room wasn't a fucking option. No matter how big it would have been, it wouldn't have been enough distance. Part of me didn't want them to see me like that. How I dealt with shit. Dealt with me leaving her. But my mom saw.

I ignored the calls from Finn. But what I couldn't ignore were the missing ones from her. I didn't text either. I would have bet on it that she would call me until I came back. But she didn't. Because I was wrong about her. She wasn't pathetic as I called her. I was.

Still no message. If we have something in common, it's our stubbornness.

I spent the first days with my parents. But I'm just waiting for the rake. We haven't had that much contact in years. Even though I hardly talk to my dad. He knows better not to address me. But they tried. For once.

I can't remember the last time they took a week off. They did for Finn. Never for me. They walked me through each department. Shared their visions and revealed their strategies. They have a life-plan. So much in the future. Did they ever spend their now's? But at least they let me choose where I wanted to be involved. They showed me my job and office. I'm a professional in programming, and it would be stupid not to accept this high position. But I never wanted to follow their footsteps. And certainly not to work for them. Finn is made for this world. But just because you're good at something doesn't mean it's the right thing. But I have no idea what else I want. I don't care about money. Well, that's easy to say if you have a lot. I probably wouldn't have to work for the rest of my life. But I want to be passionate about my work, not simply perfect. I want to write, travel, and take some balls-ass photos. I want to mean something. To change something. To inspire. But I give it a chance. Not that they deserve it, but I have to give it to myself. I haven't left for nothing.

With everyday life came the thoughts. It's like Peter thinks your thoughts make you fly. But they can make you fall even more. So, I smoke more weed than usual. I drink a lot more too. But what's new are the pills. Mostly to reduce anxiety. But also, to numb the pain. The anger. The guilt. And to sleep. I know that I'll become addicted. Instead of treating the symptom, one should find the cause. But I know the reason. And that's exactly what I try to numb. Her. ~~And other stuff that happened over the years.~~ I never claimed to be good. Neither to make good decisions. So, I'm swallowing those pills until they come up or make my heart stop. I kept the number of my dealer. I knew the day would come. The day had come. He's my savior. Feeding me with all I need and even more. Some snow falls too in London. Even in the summer.

I made new friends. And met my old ones. My friends here are different. They are even worse than all the lost boys. It's more like I'm around devils here. But all I need. We go to clubs. And I fuck girls. But I avoid the blond ones. But that one time I slept with a girl who looked quite like her. At least I told myself. ~~She didn't look at all like her.~~ But instead of coming, I threw up on her. I was in a bad place. I knew. ~~But I didn't admit to myself why.~~ But with that girl underneath me. I knew. I fucking knew. So, I puked her all over her chest. Because she wasn't her. And I was sick of myself pretending otherwise. I grabbed her clothes and kicked her out. Just like that. I haven't said anything. I never saw her again. As I said, I was a fucking mess. I couldn't pretend it was her. Because no one is. Cause the most dangerous drug I took had ash blond hair and green eyes. And I knew it would destroy me. And that night I realized how fucking much; Scar had scarred me.

I stopped sleeping with girls, but I started to cut myself. Haven't done that in a while. Not because of her. But because of who I am. Because of whom I can't be. I tried to be better for her. Well, I didn't really try. But something broken doesn't get less broken if you don't treat it for what it is. It was good to leave her. She's better without me. But I'm worse without her. But once in my life, I have to be selfless and let her fucking go.

I'm on sleeping pills, painkillers, and narcotics. I know I have a problem. I called her an addict and in reality, I'm the junkie. I still go to therapy. But I haven't mentioned her. I can't even tell him, who has a duty of confidentiality. How the fuck should I tell her then? That's why I left. ~~Because I had to run from the girl, I don't hate at all.~~ I don't want to hear that I'm bad for her. That I should stay away from her. I already know all that.

Work is fun, and I missed London and some of my old friends. I like the weather as much as it hurts me. ~~The rain reminds me of her.~~ But not a day goes by that I don't spend drunk, stoned, high or bleeding. Maybe that's why I like it. I pass out a lot. Write a lot. Train a lot. Take pictures. And try to go on. Emphasis on trying.

I watch their stories. It's like it makes no difference to them. They seem to do even more together. In the beginning I had contact with Leon and Aidan, but now we don't even text anymore. I know it's my fault. Cause I left again. But these fuckers could reach out too. But no way, I'll text first. They know me. I disappear from time to time. I like to travel and that's just who I am. How I deal with shit. They know I come back. But they don't get it. They don't get me. So as the time passed, and the weeks went by, the contact faded, and I lost the grip on my old life. Lost the grip of them. Of her. Of me. Of all.

At this point, I don't even know if it's worse if I'm clean or on drugs. I'm over myself. I'm homesick, but not because of my home. It's cause of my friends. And because of her. I'm dying to talk to her, but I refused to call her. I'm sad, numb, and tired. But the sleep left me. Now I'm wide awake. Counting hours. Counting now's. Now's without her. I'm not present anymore. I'm just gone.

"Never let her know how much you love her or she'll kill you with it." Oxygen thief once wrote. And for me, he was an old friend reminding me I'll hurt her, so I let go of her. But with that, I'd hurt myself more. But she already hurt me too.

I stopped the drugs. I still do weed, but none of the pills. No snow. No opium. No parties. Just me and my thoughts. It kills me. But it kills me more to shut it out. So, I let it in. Let her in. With that, guilt comes. But I take it. Crave it even. I want it to hit me. I want to feel. I'm sick of the numbness. I need to feel what I've done.

It feels like she has cut herself into my skin. She's everywhere and I hate it. I think about how she made me laugh even if I didn't let her see. I think about the way she looked at me at parties thinking I won't see. How she saved me, although she knew nothing about it. I think about how I started to write about her the day I first saw her without even thinking about it. How all the lines were written, because of her. Still are. How every poem I make is about her. How I take pictures of things or places that remind me of her. That as Oscar Wilde wrote she "is all my art to me now." Because she is now. My Art. All of it.

I don´t want her to go down with me. I´ve always been the architect of my own destruction. I won´t be hers too. But I know it´s all I can do. Because I´m not the guy she needs. I´m not like my brother who´s a gentleman. I´m the toxic one. But somehow, she fell for me. She wasn´t even scared to fall. Little did she know I wouldn´t hold her. Not the way she expected me to. I had knife´s in the hands she fell in. She just didn´t realize.

Some goodbyes set you free. But this one just sat me on fire. I sat myself on fire. There´s no rain to stop it. Not even in London.

Pan without Tinker is just a boy. She made me fly. I let her fall.

They were right Peter´s just selfish.

How do you run from what´s inside your head?

With each passing day, I realize what mistake I made. I can´t stop thinking about her. And if I´m not thinking of her, I dream about her. I see her everywhere. I lose my mind. I see ash blond hair. She´s in every bookstore I pass. In every raindrop. In every step. In every breath. She´s here but she´s not. It haunts me. Her face when I told her. How she stood there in her fucking beautiful dress watching me leave. But what haunts me the most is how I didn´t text her once. And how she never texted too. How many times I dialed her number and hung up because I had too big a lump in my throat.

All those months. There was no moving on. Just running away. But you can´t outrun the things that haunt you. That are in your head. I can´t take it any longer. I fucking miss her. I need to see her. I regret leaving her. Not reaching out. And I need to tell her. I booked a flight. I´ll buy white roses. Fifteen for every week since I left her.

100

Kai

I lost it as I saw the hand of my brother on her thigh casually gripping. *Like what the fuck? That´s what they´ve been doing? Trying to fuck my brother?*

They say it wasn´t like that. *But what the hell was it then? Did they bond or some shit? Did she move on?* It seemed like it. Well, she looked relived to see me. But she´s been shocked and angry too. I mean I get why she´s mad. I´m mad at me too. But still I think it was the right decision to leave. *I needed it. She did too.* Even if it killed me. *Like, actually. I had to.* But if I knew she´d move on I wouldn´t have left. Because I did everything but move on. *I didn´t go past her.* I just shoved her away. But I dragged her with me. Through all the highs and fucking lows. But I don´t know if she did too.

And she´s right I have no right to be jealous. But she moved on and I didn´t. It fucking hit me like a meteor.. And I made a fool of myself by thinking otherwise.

As I sit back down with my friends, my mood gets better. I decided to deal with that later and spend time with them. And I really missed those fuckers.

Especially two of them.

But that´s gone when I start to realize. It happens in slow-motion. I stand still watching the scene. Aidan sits next to her. Nothing odd cause, they´re over each other all the time but they are close. *Very fucking close.* Closer than normally. Closer than before.

Closer than ever. A different kind of close.

His arm around her on the backrest. Her hand on his leg and they look.. *intimate.*

He leans in saying something into her hair. *She smiles in response.* A thousand needles slice my neck. My fucking eyeballs burn like hell. My jaw cracks with every second of realization. I clench my teeth until they might fall out or I´ll break my jaw.

His hand moves from the rest to her thigh squeezing. *Way too far up. Much too familiar.* And fucking way too touchy for friends. He kisses her hair while holding her head and I bite my tongue. My eye flinches and her eyes shoot to mine. *And that´s when I know.* The glimpse of guilt in her eyes tells me. I lift my chin and flex my jaw as realization sets in. It´s *not* my brother fucking her, it´s my *best friend* who fucks her. I taste blood and suck it. *They fuck.* I want to puke, although my stomach is empty.

She looks away quickly.

The scene is over and I´m back in the play. I avert my gaze. And *something* crushes inside me, cracks open and lets out hell. I never want to feel like that again. *Ever.* Anger boils inside me. I want to rip his hands off her body and push him off her. I want to yell at them. *But I don´t. Because I can´t. He doesn´t know.* If he did he wouldn´t touch her.

She didn´t tell him. Neither did anyone tell me about them. *No one.*

I empty my glass to get a reason to fuck off. I get up. And walk in.

When She Smiles – Gigi Perez

I feel dizzy and nauseous as I stumble and the world spins ripping me apart. I bought her roses and came back for her. Cause I couldn´t forget her. Cause she haunts me. Cause I wanted her. But she..*forgot me already.* While I couldn´t fuck without thinking of her. *Without vomiting.* She fucked..

I pace up the stairs trying not to fall and get into the bathroom. *I vomit. Even if it´s nothing.* Because nothing comes out. But I want it out of me. *All of it. Out. Get her out.*

My face is sweaty. *It´s wet. Why is it wet?*

I´m choking on it. *I shiver. It´s hot and cold.*

Acid runs through my system. *Intoxicating me.*

I puke and fucking pray, she´s in with it. I finally feel the shit rise my throat and vomit until nothing, but bile comes out. Until there is nothing in me but pain.

She fucking broke me into pieces. Pieces I never knew existed and never wanted. I got it out, but it came right back at me. *Why the fuck did I let her have so much influence on me?* She ripped me apart. *I let her.* I gave her the power.

She fucked my best Friend. Fucks. I correct myself. *And he fucks her.* ~~My girl.~~

I thought I knew pain. Because I felt it every day. I was seeking it in every possible way. *But I never knew. Not until now.*

Until she held my heart and burned it, with me watching. *I fucking hate her.*

Why didn´t he fucking tell me? That he fucks our best friend? That he fucks Scar? Why didn´t Finn? I know why Andi kept his mouth shut. *But my brother?* Fuck..

My whole life I´ve been the architect of my destruction. *Now she is.* My throat burns from the acid. My face is wet, and my eyes burn. *Why the fuck?*

I look in the mirror to see that I´m crying. *Crying.* I don´t *fucking* cry over her. My fist slams against the reflection of the guy with bloodshot eyes. The guy who let *that* girl rip him apart. The guy who let himself love that girl just to lose her. The guy who fucking shatters just as the mirror into pieces. *Because of her. Because of me.* Pieces I feel now inside of me.

Cutting me. Ripping me open. Bleeding me out. Fuck her. Fuck him. Fuck you all.

- 27 -

When I got back, she already left. *They all did.*

So, I got back inside to find Finn in the bathroom. *Standing on my shreds. On my blood spilled for her. On my heart everywhere. On the evidence of me losing her.* Right after that I blacked out. *I can´t remember it all. I saw red. I was raging. I lunged at him.* And slammed his head somewhere. *He let me.* But then he hit me back. I knew he´s stronger than me. *He always was. In every way.* But that didn´t stop me. *Never did.*

So, he hit me. *And I deserved it. All of it. But so did he.*

We spilled more blood. *Until he stopped.*

We both knew that wasn´t just for what happened the last months. This fight was so much more.. *It was overdue. For years.*

Then we sat there across the other. *Defeated.*

At least on the outside. I looked at him.

I was broken. And I didn´t hide it. *Not anymore.*

"You didn´t tell me." I choak trying to find my voice. "I know. I didn´t." He at least admits. "Why?" I ask him on the edge of fucking crying. "Because she deserved it." He says locking eyes with me. *And that´s it. That simple it was. Because she deserved it.*

I slammed the balls of my hand to my eyes, growled and cried. *Because he was right. He always was. She deserved it. To move on. For me to let go. To let her go.*

He didn´t move. *Nor did I.* We stayed there. *I cried.* He watched me. *I felt it all. And I let him see.* That at least someone knew how fucking much I love her. *Even if I can´t say it. Nor tell her. Or tell them. Or my therapist. Or me. Because I can´t.* I can't express it. I can´t feel it right. *I can´t.* ~~It happened before and it did again.~~

He knew I fucked up. I´m not able to love. *My love destroys. I destroy. I can´t love..* I couldn´t love before and I fucking can´t now. I just hurt the ones I love.

Especially those.

And he saw before.. *what my love did.* He knew how it ended the last time.

Peter loved to hurt Hook, but now he just hated that he can´t even love her.

I love her. But not the way she loves. It´s the way I love. *Deadly.* She deserves to never hear that. Or her world would become what mine is. *Shards and blood.*

So, I decide to let her go. At least on the outside. *Because she deserves.* As my brother said. *She deserves all.* But not my love. No one deserves that. *Not even me.*

Maybe I should finally accept that I´m not capable of.. *Love.*

101

Later that night, Lia

I went for a long walk after I left. *Hours to be exact.* I couldn´t go home right away. I had to walk and think it out. Even if I came up with nothing. The look on his face when he realized made me only now realize.. *what I did.*

I wanted him to hurt as much as he did to me. But it didn´t feel how I hoped it would. And I´ve hurt him. Maybe even worse than he has hurt me. *I know I did.*

As I turn into my street, I catch sight of Kai and my heart sinks.

What is he doing here? But when did he not show up?

My heart races. I don´t know what will happen or in what mood he is. He just left and didn´t show up anymore. And it was easy to suppress my feelings when he wasn´t around. But now, it´s *anything* but easy to forget. Especially when he´s in front of my house leaning against his BMW, like he did only months ago. *How things change.* And also, don´t.

Only when I´m a few meters in front of him, he finally looks at me. And my stomach sinks. *He´s all beaten up.* Bruises and blood all over his face. He looks horrible. It´s the worst I´ve seen him. My insides cries, thinking I did this. And just hours ago, I thought about how long I haven´t touched his wounds. *Well, that didn´t last long.* But I won´t touch him now, even if I want to.

He walks up to me. His lip split on each side and as I look at his hands, I see his open knuckles. *There are cuts too.* Please tell me he didn´t cut himself like that on his hands. I hope it wasn´t Aidan he beat. He hasn´t told him, *has he?* Well, I know the answer to that.

He definitely would not. So, it wasn´t him he had a fight with, but *someone* did.

We walk towards each other, and I don´t even try to hide my worry. I hug him as he´s in arm reach. Cause I might slap him if I wouldn´t. He holds me firm and lays his head on mine.

It hurts. That´s all I know. The hurt. Always the hurt.

"What happened?" I ask on the verge of crying. "Had a fight to lose." He tells me. "With whom?" I rake further as we move away from each other. *Which hurts.*

"My brother." He tells me and my eyes widen. *Finn did beat him like that? Why?*

But I don´t ask. He won´t tell me. I bet on it.

We avert our gazes. Probably scared of the pain we´ll see in the other faces. So, we look *anywhere* but at each other.

"Are we looking at the stars?" He asks. I nod and we lie down on the hood of his car. After going over all the constellations, he breaks the silence. "So, you and Aidan?" He begins. "Yeah," I reply. *I´m still not sure in which mood he´s in.*

"How.. did *that* happen?" He follows up and I blink, but the stars won´t fade. I don´t know and I never asked myself why. *I guess it just did.*

"Since you left, we got along better. We all did." I shrug. "And eventually we got closer too." I explain. "So, you guys are..?" He asks. "No." I shake my head. "We´re just friends. Friends with benefits.. kind of." I say. "It´s not *that* simple." I try to put into words and I deliberately don´t mention the bet. "Okay." He replies, stands up and I sit up as well.

That´s all he has to say? After he beat up his brother? After he bought me roses?

"Okay?" I ask and he´s with his back to me. He nods. "I´m happy for you guys." He says. "You´re my best friends and I want you to be happy." He faces me. I nod still confused but slide off the car. We stare at each other for moments of nothingness till I turn to get inside. "Scar?" He asks at his car door. He has *that* look on his face I know all too well.

He´s sorry. But I don´t want to hear it anymore.

"Listen.." he tries to apologize, but I interrupt him. "I know." I say and push the gate open, and he gets in his car. *And that´s it.* It´s not what I expected or hoped he would do after *everything*. Maybe it´s worse to sleep with his brother than his best friend. But whatever it is, it makes it easier. *I least hope so.*

102

One week later

Things are back to normal. *Normal* as it can be after everything. Kai´s somehow the same as months ago. We´re the same but different. *We´re friends.* Or at least we try to be *just* that. And I think this could work. Us as friends. Although it still hurts and there is an awkwardness still but not like before he left. There isn´t that *waiting* anymore.

That almost. It´s gone.

Maybe, we´re good at being friends. The one thing we can.

So, we´re back to friends and I´m dating his best friend. Everything normal. And today we´re the first time alone. And I hope that state of *normal* can last.

He picked me up when the sun set and drove to some forest. And I know how that sounds. Every horror movie begins with that. But spoiler we didn´t die.

Because we already did.

We laid down on a picknick blanket on a clearing and talked. He told me about London and how it went with his parents. I was surprised by him opening up. He told me how much time he spent with his mom. He also showed me his new tattoo and told me about his friends. I told him about the partying, the concerts, and the festivals. And how Aidan and I got to the point where we at. But of course, I left out the parts where I lost my mind, cried, and slept in his bed for weeks. And the bet I made with Aidan. Or the part where I ran after him to the airport. So, in short things are normal.

But different. He´s different. But so am I.

There is that faint ripple of a stream somewhere. And the howl of an owl deep into the forest and the crickets chirping around us. Wood cracking and animals I can´t place. It´s peaceful. Above us the infinite night sky in the deepest of blue almost black. The stars bright and the moon wide awake.

We lay there as next to us appear small yellow-green dots. They make the meadow glow like little fairies flying by. "Omg, fireflies?" I marvel. "I haven´t seen one in years." I say and I look around. "I used to catch them with my hands when I was a kid." I laugh as they surround us. "There was always *something* magical about them." I say happy.

He props himself up on his elbows and watches one in the air between us. "To me, they always had something poetic." He says as he tracks one with his eyes. "Why´s that?" I ask and he straightens up. "All *that..*" he begins, catching one with his hands. "Is their farewell glow, so to speak." He says leaving space between his thumbs and the inside of his palms are shining neon green. "As a larvae, they eat for years, in order to glow for just a few days, hoping to mate before they die." He explains, releasing it. It rises above us, and I watch his every move. How it disappears between the grass and the flowers. *Searching for love.* I look at all the hundreds of glows around us, and all at once, sadness mixes with the enchanted feeling. All these fireflies searching, looking for love in their last hours before they die. There´s something *tragic* about it.

I look at him and he reads me grinning. "And if they don´t find anyone, they die alone?" I ask, half laughing and half crying and he shrugs. My eyes wander from light to light among the grasses and his gaze burns on me as he speaks. "Sometimes things are just beautiful because they end." He says and I search his face, not sure if I can place what his words mean.

My face falls. "Just that you know, you´ve completely destroyed my image of them." I laugh upset slapping him on the chest. "Won´t be the last thing." He jokes with a hint of truth. *Yeah it wasn´t.*

"I´ll never be able to see them any other way." I tell him angry.

"That´s so sad." I whine. "I don´t think so." He shrugs and I frown at him. "How? You just told me their sad love story." I retort. "Please enlighten me. How´s that *not* sad?" I ask pissed but he smiles. And I know he likes telling me how he sees the world. And he knows I like hearing about it. *So, I smile too.*

"So? In what way?" I ask impatiently. *I´ve missed this.*

"You can learn from them." He says making a dramatic pause. "They devote their whole larval life´s to hustle with *only* one goal in mind, to find someone. To find love." He speaks poetically and I love him that way. "We humans do the same." He shrugs. "Rush blindly through our lives in search of *the great love*." He quotes in the air. "And forget the most important thing." He makes a pause again, and my grin widens. "To live." He tells the fireflies. "We should shine not only for love or once in our lifetime, but for ourselves and every fucking day." He says and I get chills. My eyes well up.

"If we do *that* we shine forever even after death." He hushes and I love his view on everything. He always opens new perspectives.

"I see it as a reminder to be in the now." He adds and I watch him. Simply look at him. Take in the guy in front of me. See him as a person. As my best friend. As someone who says so many right things. He should write about all that.

I smile and he nods at me. "What?" He asks with a frown. "Something poetic." I say to which he grins. "Yeah, something like that." He agrees and smiles till his dimples show.

I really missed having him around. Maybe, we work as friends. Maybe, this is the only way we'll ever work. Maybe, it's okay how it is. Even if I still feel about him. But maybe I should let that go. Maybe I should focus on Aidan and me. Maybe.

103

I sit on the terrace with Kai as Aidan comes home from patrol. He greets us giving me a kiss. Then he hits it with Kai and goes over to his to change for the hot tub.

I take off my top and shoes. Kai still sits leaning forward on his knees. I pull down my jeans and look to Nina and Leon as they come over. Looking back, I see Kai's eyebrows shoot up for a second as I step out of my pants. His gaze hardens. I frown and take off my socks. He walks past me, undresses, and joins Leon and Finn in the jacuzzi.

Aidan now no longer in his uniform but dressed in his red swim trunks gets in too. And just as I was about to do the same Nina screams from behind. "*Someone* had some hell of a night." She chuckles and climbs in giving Aidan a knowing look. I look down at myself and my eyes widen.

There are red scratch marks and bruises all over my ass. *Fuck*. That's *why* Kai was looking like that. I shut my eyes for a sec before I get in. "Huh?" Aiden asks, grinning. "You branded me." I say, trying to hide mine. I half turn so he can see, and he runs his fingers over the sore marks and grins proudly at his handiwork.

"*Branded*? You massacred her." Nina points out and Aidan and Leon chuckle. He grabs my waist and pulls me onto his lap. "I did." He says pleased with his work, and I don't meet Kai's eyes because I know he does the same.

Aidan kisses my hair. "Sorry Scar" he whispers and grins. I return it and he wraps one arm around my stomach and caresses the side of my ass. His other rests on the edge of the pool. Kai clears his throat. "So, what's new besides Avery fucking Scar now?" he asks, and they laugh. But only three of us know that wasn't a joke.

- 27 -

Kai's the first to say goodbye shortly followed by Finn. Normally he's the one who stays the longest, including me. But times have changed and now he's the first.

I miss the nights we chatted. But I date Aidan now, I remind myself.

So, it´s just Leon and Nina with Aidan and me making out. We´ve been on double dates the past weeks and it´s nice to spend time with them. It´s different to the past year where I spent most of my nights with Kai. *Stop it.*

"Bro." Aidan interrupts our kiss and slaps Leon´s shoulder with the back of his hand. "Fuck off." He demands and Leon just grins as they exchange looks. He lifts her up and gets out of the water. *Now we´re alone.*

He changes the song to *Quick Musical doodles by Two Feet*. I sit on top of him and the hardness between his legs rubs against my center as I ride him. "I want you to brand me," he murmurs in my ear, and I claw at his hair. He throws his head back and puts his arms on the edge, letting me lead. I kiss along his neck, suck, and bite at his skin. When I get to his ear, his hand grabs me and guides me over his length. He struggles to keep his breathing and his hand travels up my spine to my clasp. In a flick of his wrist, he opens it and my top falls in the water. I lean against his chest to cover my breasts and wrap my arms around his neck.

He lifts his head and grins. "What?" I ask. "And don´t say *boobs*." I laugh and he shakes his head, grinning. "I knew I was right" he says, amused. "Knew what?" I ask, not stopping. He looks at me with a smug grin. "*This*." He hushes, pushing up. "That you´re going to end up here *naked* with me." He says proudly and I frown at him, but then I remember and must grin. "Indeed." I agree. *He was right.*

As he speaks, he pushes my bottom to the side and inserts his middle finger.

"So much for *that* never happening." He says as I cling to his shoulders, and he inserts another finger and kisses me. For a moment I wonder, *what if he plays games too*?

They said they all do.

But I push that thought away. I don´t think *anyone* plays games as much as Pan..

Stop.

I moan into his mouth on the third finger. He lifts his body and pushes his trunks down and I clasp him. *Condom. I´m not on the pill.*

"Did you?" I ask and he nods, grinning. He slips it on, and I realize the song is on loop. He holds himself as I lower onto it and press my lips together to keep me from moaning. He leans back and lets me take control. He bites the back of his hand and grips the edge; his knuckles stand out white. We try hard to be quiet, but he slams his fist against the paneling. The next moment he turns me around and I´m kneeling where he sat. I lean on the edge as he takes me from behind. His one hand covers my breasts, and the other holds my hip. I take his hand off my bust and bring it to my neck. He takes the hint and holds me by the throat and his other hand moves to my clit. His grip tightens, showing me, he´s almost ready. I let a moan escape to give him the rest. He holds my moans with his hand, letting me chase my orgasm too. He moans low into my ear, knowing it´s what sends me, and he can´t keep it either as I shudder underneath him and he pours himself into me. He collapses on top of me, and we lie on the edge breathing heavily.

I love the feeling of his weight. It´s a good weight. A weight I love to bear.

He brushes my hair to the side and kisses along my neck, and shoulders to my back. Then he wraps me in his towel and carries me over to his. Setting me down in the shower just to finish me a second time. *And a third in his bed.*

104

Before Aidan left for work, he said into my ear, "Keep your dress on." And I heard his smirk. "Keep your uniform on," I replied and then I´ve spent the day with the others on the couch gambling.

My cell phone vibrates with a message from Aidan. "*Come out, I want you in the car.*" I try not to grin like a lunatic. "I´m out of here guys." I say and get up. "Greets to Aidan." Laughs Andi to which the others chuckle *except* Kai pretending to be busy on his phone. He´s *never* on his phone.

I give them the middle finger. *They salute with theirs.*

I shake my head at them with a grin. *I love them.* But I don´t dare look at Kai, even though I can *feel* his gaze, so I head out. The sun has already set and it´s raining. And it´s just now that I realize we haven´t been in the rain since he´s back.

It can´t stay everything how it was, I guess.

His Audi is parked outside, and I get into the passenger side. He lets down the window. "Don´t you want to drive *into* the garage?" I ask with a smile. "That would be boring." He grins and for a moment, we just look at each other. Me pondering and he´s trying to wordlessly persuade me to give in. His gaze is full of lust before he gets out to sit in the middle of the back seat.

"Come here," he murmurs, and I climb on his lap. He holds my back and kisses me as I run my hands through his hair, and he slides his hands under my dress. He breathes loudly between kisses, and I do the same. I stroke his neck; cause I know it turns him on as I ride his lap.

He unbuckles his belt impatiently. "Put it on" he demands, handing me the condom. So, I pull it over, slowly roll it down and enjoy having him in my hand. We keep eye contact, and he presses his lips together. His jaw tenses as he holds his shaft and pushes my panties aside. I crouch over him, and he strokes my v with it. I feel like I´m going to swoon with pleasure and hold onto his chest moaning into his mouth.

"I want you" I gasp against his neck as I kiss him there. "Huh?" He asks. "What was that?" He grins smug. "I want you to *fuck* me" I tell him. He takes my face in his hand and pushes hard up to enter me. Our lips collide as he pumps inside of me. I take the lead and his head snaps back. He holds my hips and claws into my ass.

"Fuck" he presses. He straightens up and kisses me hard.

He lets go of me and looks at me. "Tell me you love me, Scar." he demands. That look on his face makes my whole-body shiver. "I love you." I say without hesitation. Then he kisses me wildly and holds me hostage against him. I put my arms around his neck, and his move around my body like a snake trying to eat me.

"I love you, Scar." He groans. And moments later, we climax. The windows have started, and the air is a mixture of sex and love avowals. *And lost bets.*

Both having lost. Given in. Ended it.

It´s the first time we told each other what we feel. And we said we´d end it then. But now we´re *clearly* past those butterflies. *There is more. There is love.*

- 27 -

Aidan walks into the bathroom in boxers and I still wear my dress, which he strips off taking his time. Kissing, we rush into the shower. The water is ice-cold, which makes me squeal, whereupon he laughs. I stare at him washing the foam off his body ad he holds my gaze *knowing* I have something to say.

He tilts his chin gesturing me to spit it. "What.. was that about?" I ask and he runs his hands over his face and through his hair.

He inhales before he speaks. "The truth." He says exhaling trying to hold my gaze.

"I guess.. we both lost the bet." I say quietly and he looks at me for a sec trying to read me. He stops mid-headshake. "It hasn´t.. for me, it hasn´t been a bet. Not for a long time." He admits and a frown builds on my face. "More accurately, it was *never* about the bet for me. It was about you." He confesses and my heart flutters like a bird trying to fly.

"Back on the stairs.. I already had a crush on you." He tells me and my eyes want to fall out. *What?*

He licks his lips nodding. "I had a crush on you *since..* I first saw you and kissed you that day." He says and my legs won´t carry me anymore. *Since the day we met?*

I step forward trying to hold onto him before I fall, and he steadies me. I don´t know what to say but can only grin ear to ear and kiss him. I don´t know if I can let him get to me like that. And even less so do I know if *he* can. When I think about it, I get scared and want to push him away. I don´t know if I´m ready for *something.* I liked it the way it was light, easy, and fun. *No responsibilities. No confusion. Just Sex.* But now.. *what does this mean? I mean sure we loved each other before. We´re best friends. You love them.* But this now.. *is this more? More than friendship? Because love is serious. Love is a lot. But I do love him? Like I love someone else? Like I should love him?*

There´s that feeling again, what I had with Andi too. *Is this the right decision? I feel naked. And yeah, I am. And he saw me naked before. But I feel vulnerable and anxious. Because now I can lose him. And that´s the last thing I want.*

He recognizes my change of mood and lifts my chin to make me look at him. "No rush we will figure out." He assures me and I nod. He kisses my forehead.

"I just don´t know what *this* means." I say and he nods wrapping his arms around me. "Me neither Scar." He whispers and he´s as scared as I am. Scared of love.

105

Chance with you - mehro

It´s been a few days and I told him I need some time to think. *And he did too.*

It somehow felt like I´ve betrayed Kai which is dumb because I´m not. *But I can´t help it. I don´t know what to do.* But I know that I should talk to Kai about it. I´ve lied about a lot of things. *The bet for example.* But before anything more can happen between Aidan and me, I owe Kai to know. And I need to know If it´s okay for him. It´s been easy for me or fall for Aidan because I pushed my feelings for Kai aside. *He distracted me. He makes me happy.*

But I know I just suppress things. And maybe I need this conversation.

About everything.

I´m scared because the last time we talked, things ended. But he came back and there are still things unsaid. *And those roses..*

I just know I can´t let Aidan in if I still hope on Kai and on to those almost´s.

"It´s been a year." Nina says taking me back to reality. "Hmh?" I ask absently. "One year ago, you partied with us for the *first* time." She chirps. "And *now* you´re with Aidan. Took you long enough." She adds and shows me her throwback. It´s a video of me kissing Aidan. I look so different. *I look happy. We look happy.*

A year from now things were so different. I didn´t think I´d come back and now I´m here daily. Kai hated me and now.. *idk.* And Aidan and I are where we started.

It´s crazy how things work out.

My eyes catch the date. The third of August. Time has passed so fast. I can´t believe it´s been a year. The video replays over and over. So much happened. My eyes wander again to the date. *03.08.20. Wait. That can´t be. 0308. That´s..*

I look at Kai. *Who´s already looking at me.* Kinda pale so he´s nervous I can tell. My heart sinks. *That´s his pin code.* I know because I typed it tons of times before. I never asked what those numbers meant. *Or that date.* But I always wondered.

It´s the day we met. The third of August. A year ago.

I don´t know if he still has but it´s something. Like the picture in his phone case, which is still there, I saw. But for no one to see. Just like his feelings for me. Hidden.

That broke me. Again.

I don´t have to ask him to know bc his face tells me. His cheeks are pink. He knows what I´m thinking about. I tilt my chin and a slight smile on my face as I give it to her back. He averts his gaze. *That douchebag.* He had that pin a long time ago.

Back when he hated me.

Now we must talk.

"Didn´t thought she would stay didn´t you?" Nina shoots at Kai and his eyes flicker to mine but jaw all set. There´s that hate again. *But more hurt.* He shakes his head and keeps shut. *No, he didn´t think I would stay that long. Nor that I would have end up with Aidan.*

But, neither did I.

- 27 -

It´s been hours and I already left, but I came back to talk to him.

As he opens the door, he´s surprised. Because of course we haven´t done *that* in a long time. But it´s time to talk so I push past him.

"What?." He asks, frowning. "Is Finn home?" I ask and his frown deepens. "Office." He says and I nod. "We need to talk." I say. "Okay." He nods. "Stop frowning." I tell him and he almost smiles to that.

"So where do you want to talk?" His tongue clicks and I look around. My heart starts beating, my face heats and my confidence slips away. He senses rubs his neck. "Uhm.. my room?" He asks. *He´s nervous too.*

I nod and we go upstairs silently. Then we stand there looking anywhere but at the other.

Fuck, this is weird. Why did I want to talk to him? Can´t remember.

We look at each other and I feel my hands start to shake. I open and close them. *Don´t cry now.* He looks down at my hand. *Says nothing. We stopped calming each other, too.* He sits down on the floor at the end of his bed, looking up to me. He pats the spot besides him and I sit down. At least, I don´t have to look at him when I tell him.

"When it´s about the Pin.." He begins, but I interrupt him. "It´s not." I whisper. He nods.

What do I say? I want to cry.

"You can tell me." He hushes, knowing I´m anxious. "Aidan said he loves me." I say, and the air feels thin. *Silence.*

"And you tell me because..?" He asks carefully, voice on edge.

I hoped you had to say something to that. I swallow a pill named venom. Named hurt. Named rejection. Named him.

"Just so you´d know." I whisper and he nods again. "I´m happy for you." He says.

Not what I wanted to hear.

I nod and tears I didn´t allowed to escape, so I jolt up before he sees. But he´s on his feet, holding me back. I´m still with my back to him. "Scar." His voice soft. It´s a plea but an empty one. "You love him?" He asks, his voice all raspy. "I don´t know." I admit. "What do you mean, you don´t know?" He asks. "Of course, I love him. But we´re friends and I.." I stammer. "Do you want to be with him?" He asks, cutting the air between us.

I want to be with you.

"I guess." I say instead and I bite the inside of my cheeks so hard I hope I die. "Then I guess you should." He tells me, letting my arm go. *And with that letting me go.*

And I go and don´t look back. I might have seen the lie or the truth behind his eyes.

But what does it matter when he doesn´t say em? When he doesn´t change anything?

It changes nothing.

I close the door behind me and meet Finns eyes down the hallway. He sees me cry but he saw me in the past. And now he sees me again. But I walk away. And no one follows because nothing has changed. *Nothing.*

106

One week later

Aidan and I decided to slow down. *To remove the pressure.* To which I´m grateful.

But I feel worse. I lie to Aidan and to my friends. I lie to Kai. I lie to myself. I mean, I love Aidan, but I love him too. But he doesn´t want me, but Aidan does. I just can´t let go of it. He let go of me, so I know now it´s my turn. *But I can´t.* Maybe because I don´t believe him. *Maybe, because I can´t accept it.*

It´s just one of those days when everything feels huge. Like you can´t breathe. Like you can´t see the reason. Like you can´t but cry about everything and Nothing. Today is one of those days. Where everything falls apart.

And who´s the one person you go to when everything falls apart?

I scroll through my contacts and stop at Kai Dark. I swipe to the right and put the phone to my ear. Hearing it ring not even twice. I end the call. *Why did I do that? Why didn´t I call Aidan? Why him? Because you want it to be him.*

My whole-body shakes. *I´m nervous. Anxious. I cry it all out.*

I can´t control my muscles. Just shake, stare, and try to feel it in order to let it pass. I put on the hairdryer, warming me. Another weird habit of mine but it calms me and drowns it all out. I just sit it out. *I can do this. Just breathe and feel. Tomorrow it´ll be okay. You don´t die. You´re in the now. You don´t have to worry about things that are in the future. Or in the past or never happening.*

I count my fingers and breathe. *How are people not mentally unstable?*

I don´t know what is worse. Going blindly through everyday life or being aware of all the mechanics and coping mechanism of your brain. Knowing it´s all in your head makes it worse. Because you feel guilty of feeling like that when you know it´s your brain. But you can´t just stop because it isn´t that simple. *Because it´s never, isn´t it?*

I let the tears spill until it´s all out and a honk wakes me. My head snaps up. *Another honk.* I jump out of bed and look out of the window. *He´s here. He is here. Kai´s here.*

I quickly put on my crocs and walk outside.

It´s raining. Doesn´t it always when he´s around? Like he´s the God of rain.

I get into the heated car.

His wipers are on, the engine runs, and I don´t meet his eyes. "What´s wrong?" I ask trying not to sound like I cried due to a mental breakdown, but I probably look like it, *so why am I trying*? I can *feel* the swell of my skin. I can´t imagine *how* I look.

"Bc you called me." He simply says. "It didn´t even ring." I say but he cuts in. "It *did*." He insists. "Well.. it was mistaken." I lie. "That´s why I hung up." I add. I don´t know why I must lie about that. *I really don´t.*

The thing is I want people to know but in the same moment I don´t. That´s why I panicked when I called him. I rather shut down than open up. Maybe we´re not that different. We´re pretty the same. And I don´t know what´s wrong. But I don´t want to be alone. Maybe, that´s a Scorpio thing. *Keeping secrets.*

Fear of being vulnerable. Fear of letting people in.

But he´s the same I´ve come to learn. Not just because of our sings.

It´s our personality. Our fears. We are very alike.

And that makes it all difficult. But we understand each other. We can read moods and energy shifts. *But somehow, we fucked up anyways. Didn´t we?* Despite it all.

"Okay." He nods after I say nothing and drives off. *I don´t argue.*

We drive along and he doesn´t speak. *He´s just there.*

After a while, I realize he heads to a drive through. *I´d really like fries now.*

I´m starving. But sometimes hunger is better than to feel nothing at all.

That´s another way of self-punishment.

He rolls his window down and orders. He drives ahead, hands his card and pays. *Then we wait.* His elbow on the car door and his chin on his hand. His forefinger brushes his lip absently staring off and I watch him wondering what he´s thinking. He doesn´t care that his arm and his car get wet.

"What are you thinking about?" I ask and after a sec, his head snaps in my direction. "I´m just thinking I´m not the monster you think I am." He says and I´m completely caught off guard by that and keep shut. *What does he mean?*

"I´m worse." He breathes as we get our food and places it on his legs. *I´m quiet.*

He parks on an empty lot of a long-closed market. We´ve been here before many times. The railroad tracks are nearby and there are lots of trees.

It´s a vibe with the faint rain.

We unpack our bags, and the music plays on a low volume, so you can still hear the pattering. I watch him mix ketchup with the mayo and I grin. "Haven´t done *that* in a while." I say with a smile. "What?" He asks, focused on his dip. "Mix *those* together." I say. "I did that as a kid all the time." I tell him. "Same." He nods. "Haven´t stopped since." He says glancing at me before he dips the fries. "You haven´t stopped or haven´t grown up?" I grin and he rolls his eyes. "You know the answer to that lost one." He smiles.

We eat silently.

"So why did you call?" He asks, mid-eating. I take a breath and hold it.

"Because.." I begin, but don´t continue for a long pause. I look ahead as I speak. "I don´t know if I´m made for *anything*." I say truthfully and he frowns at me, I know that. "Living. Working.." I laugh despite the lump in my throat. "My anxiety gets *worse*." I manage to say without a sob. "I hate responsibility. Unknown situations." I go on. "Even *talking* to people, I don´t know.." I say in a whisper in order not to cry.

"Sometimes it´s just the daily stuff you do. Like standing in a line at the grocery store and panicking on the inside. Because there are people watching you." I tell him. "But you know it´s unjustified because no one cares about you." I whisper, knowing it´s true. "But maybe that´s the problem." I nod to myself. "That nobody does." My voice cracks and I try to hide it by clearing my throat just to cough, almost choking on whatever.. *myself,* I guess.

Can you do anything?

"I know it´s all in my head and I let my fears block me, but I can´t.." I fight not to cry. "I have no idea what job I´m good at. I don´t know if I´ll manage my studies. I have the urge to quit. Before it even started." I yell, upset with myself.

"I´m a mess." I say now crying. "I hate my parents for it because I´ve never had *anything* to do on my own. I was *always* isolated. And now I have anxiety." I rage, swiping away the tears. "And I think I won´t be able to bare it. To make it on my own. Maybe I don´t want to do it. *Anything. Alone.*

"So, I rather do nothing. I simply avoid things and control everything." I add irritated. "It´s like I can´t make mistakes because *then* I proved I failed." I continue and he just listens.

"I know I have to face my fears and overcome them. But.." I cry again. *Fuck.*

"*I* hate it. I feel helpless. Stupid. It is eating me alive." I slam the balls of my hand into my running eyes. "Sometimes it feels like I´m on the edge. And there are just two ways things to play out." I say, staring ahead. "Either I slip and fall but catch myself, *or* I slip and fall but won´t get out of it." I try to explain how it feels. "My mental state is fragile. I mean, I´m healthy and I´m good and grateful. But I´m also not okay." I admit.

"*I mean, how are we supposed to know all that stuff?* Like, what you want to do with your life and stuff.." I go on furious. "I´m just afraid I can´t work like a *normal* person, because of my anxiety. *Like what if I start working as a teacher and it blocks me?* I want to help people and inspire them. *But what if I fail?*" I ask and I close my eyes because my eyeballs burn. *Tears run.*

"But what if not?" He hushes and I feel my eyes swell. "Let me tell you, you won´t." He says softly and reaches for my hands, taking them off my face. He pulls my head to his chest and holds me. I cry and for the first time in months, something actually helps me to stop. *To feel better. And it´s him. He helps. He makes me okay.*

"You can *always* talk to me." He soothes me. "I´m *not* nobody." He says intently. "I care." He tells me. "I see you." He says all the things that mean more than *I love you.*

At least for him.

"And you´re not alone." He whispers into my hair. "I´m here. Always Scar, *always.*" He promises and I cry until I´m over it.

He lets go of me, I straighten up and we look at each other. “The only constant in life is change. And our brain hates that.” He says with a small grin. I nod, chuckling cause he´s *always* right.

He gets his phone and checks the screen. A smile on his lips as he holds it to me. “*22:22*.” He grins pleased. “*Alignment*.” I say. “Right place, right time.” He adds, locking eyes with me. *Right person* says the voice in my head. *Wrong time.*

I must grin, *angel numbers*. *Has he planned that?*

“Did you just check the clock?” I cock an eyebrow. *He never does that.* Every time I asked him about the time he *always* pretended to check just so say something like *“Uhm.. wait it is exactly.. Now Scar, now.”* Cracked up about it and I smacked him. But at some point, I stopped asking. Because I knew he wouldn´t say anything other than that. He would never tell the time. Just showed me his tattoo *“Now”* on his wrist. Telling me there is no time. *Because in Neverland there is no such thing.*

Because in Never is always a Now.

I shake my head, remembering. He looks at me, fighting a grin. “I guess I did.” He nods. “Sometimes all you need is time.” He says and now I´m confused.

“*No tree, it´s said, can grow to heaven unless its roots reach down to hell.*” He quotes *Carl Jung* pretending to be Socrates on the marketplace in Athens, announcing his glorious knowledge. “Fear is just the memory of pain.” He says gesturing in the air, and I laugh. “Shall I continue?” He asks and sips from the Water. I shake my head but can´t stop smiling.

He´s like a search engine for quotes.

“You´re insane.” I tell him, but with all the admiration I have for him.

He´s such a clown sometimes and I love it.

“If it´s just that.” He shrugs and I look at him. He really cheered me up.

He reads my face and breathes through his nose. *And sudden he´s nervous.*

His cheeks grow pink, but I´m not sure why but he looks past me for a moment until he looks back at me. “I have anxiety too.” He says. “When I think about my future. When I think of *time*.” His voice small. *Time. His Hook. His greatest fear.*

“Like, what if it runs out? Before I did the things, I wanted to do so bad?” He asks, life but not me. “What if things *end* before you lived?” He asks and he seems so vulnerable right now. He zones out for a minute.

He blinks once, twice regaining his attention. “But why thinking scary things if you can think happy thoughts?” He refers to Pan. “That´s why it´s so important to stay present.” He looks me in the eyes. “In the moment.” He nods. “That´s the *only* place you ever are.” He says, showing me his wrist tapping on his tattoo. *Now.*

And I have to smile weak. "I wish I could be more like you." I hush and he smiles softly. "No, you don´t want that." He says.

"But I can show you how." He says and I look at him, questioning. "I´ll teach you." he says. "How to be in the now." He tells me, I nod, and he smiles.

"Thanks." I whisper. "That you came." I clarify. "*Everything*." I say and his jaw flexes at my words. "Always Scar." He tells me.

We look at each other for seconds.

"You´re eyes are green." He states. "They *always* are." I say with a grin, thinking back at our argument a year ago. He stops mid head shaking. "But they´re greener when you cry." He says, quietly, like he speaks more to himself than to me. Some far Deja-vu washes over me, but I can´t put a finger on it. "Your eyes are black." I say. "But they´re darker when you look at me." I add without thinking. His muscle twitch in respond.

Who´s the person you go to when your world falls apart?

What says that about you and the other?

107

August

He sits on the edge of the bed and his eyes are bright red. *Never seen him like that. Broken.*

In his hand, he holds a letter.

"Aidan?" I ask, kneeling in front of him. He props his face in his palms.

Minutes pass until he speaks up. "This is from my father," he says but I don´t understand. Tears are running down his cheek. *His gaze hurts.*

I take his head to my chest, and he clings to me. Seeing him like this makes me shed tears myself. "What do you want me to do?" I ask helplessly and we break away. He wipes his nose with the back of his hand and looks at me but lowers his eyes because tears are coming. I take his face in my hands to make him look at me.

"It´s okay how you feel." I assure him my voice softer than a snowflake.

He presses his lips together, stopping them from trembling. His mouth opens and closes four times before he can bring himself to say it. "I´m adopted." His voice breaks with his revelation. *This can´t be. Can it? I can´t help but think about the fact that he doesn´t look much like Leon. But so do a lot of siblings. I don´t look much like my sister either.*

"My mom died when I was born." He tells me, seeing my confusion. "And my birth father blamed me." He struggles. "He beat me a lot. Hurt me a lot." He tells me and I shut my eyes. *His scars. No.*

"Hated me, the asshole." He spits. "The more I ran away from home, the more I got it." He nods, remembering everything. "Addie and Logan were my mother´s best friends. And I was often with Leon when things went bad." He says and grips his hair. "When I was thirteen, I left for good. Tey adopted me later." He´s not crying anymore seems cold now. "He even beat me when I smiled. When I cried. When I did nothing. He just beat me. Got drunk and into drug use and beat me." He stares into the void.

"I don´t know what to say, Aidan. I´m so sorry." I cry. "He had no right to do that. It´s not your fault. You were a child. And you lost your mom too." I stop myself *because what can I say to make it okay? Nothing.*

"If there´s *anything* I can do." I say and he holds the back of my head kissing my forehead. "You´re *here* and that´s so much." He says, and I know he means it with his heart. "I just want you to know, I´m not pushing you to say anything if you don´t want t." I tell him and he nods. "I know." He says, looking at me. "But I want to talk about it." He tells me. "Okay," I whisper.

And he tells me about his childhood and his teenage years. About Leon and his friendship or more brotherhood. And about Finn and Kai. How they started to play those games to escape. How Kai invented them. How *he* made them watch Peter Pan all the time. How *he* became Peter to their Lost boys. How *he* taught them how to fly. How to have fun and think about nothing else but the now and their friends. How they became family, and I realized how much more those games are to them or were. *Neverland. The lost boys and girls. This is family.* And I get for the first time why Kai didn´t want any randoms in.

He told me about all the stuff they did. How they sneaked into the outdoor pools as preteens and hid until they locked up. How they stole candy as kids and beer as teens. And how they stayed overnight in their school and in furniture stores to play hide and seek all night. How they made bets and dares, and how they became a group. How they met Andi, Ryan, and Nina. How they grew together. How Kai became his best friend. How the Dark´s house became their Neverland. How it became their home.

Their escape.

And I listen and like how his eyes light up as he talks about their adventures and stupid shit they did. How they´ve run from the cops´ tons of times. How they started to invite other people as they grew older. How their playing became partying. How their water became liquor. How their gum cigarettes became real ones, weed and other drugs.

How they invented other games to have fun with. Bets and dares and all and even worse things. How it got out of hand at some point. And how they formed some rules. How they had their first loves and fights and all. And most importantly, how they all found their *Hook.* And how he realized his was *love. His fear was love.* Because he never got it. At least not from the only person he had left. *His dad.* But he got the love he lacked here. *In Neverland.* With the Lost boys. *And Peters smile. That damn smile.* And I begin to realize that that´s why, he has no relationships. *He fears love.*

And with me, he found it. *Love.*

"And now he wrote you?" I ask and he nods a few times. "Did you had any contact after you left?" I ask. "He wanted to go to court and get me back, but Logan spared him *a visit* and after that he relented." He tells me. "The years after that we had no contact. And now, after *seven* years, he writes." He scoffs.

"Logan and Addie.. your parents are such sweethearts. They took care of Finn and Kai, too. *Of all of you.* And you deserve this family." I tell him as he draws stars in my palm with his finger.

"Are you going to open it?" I ask carefully. "I don´t know." He admits descending the lines on my palm. "I don´t have anything to say to that guy." He scowls. "Understandable." I nod. "But it´s okay to be curious." I assure him. "I know." He licks his lip, and I look at his face. *And it klicks.* The scars on his face, chest, back actually all over his body are from his father. I want to scream so much it aches. At the thought of how he must feel, I get nauseous. Infinite pain spreads through my chest. *I never asked him.* Not because I didn´t care, but I thought if he wanted to tell me, he would. And there are people who laugh to cover their scars. Aidan is one of them. I just couldn´t see. I wish I saw sooner.

"Your scars." I whisper, my voice shattering in the air between us. "Yes" he says and again his voice breaks. Tears spill and we lie down, and he cries.

And I cry with him. *For him.*

After hours, he gets up and goes to the bathroom to read the letter on his own. I wipe my face. *He doesn´t want a relationship because he thinks he´s not worth loving.*

Tears fall again and my heart breaks into a thousand pieces at the thought of younger Aiden, who has been beaten into believing *he* is to blame for the death of his biological mother. *I cry so hard I might pass out.*

I swallow some water to hydrate and then I stare at the ceiling as I wait for him.

Not after five minutes he comes back, and I jolt up facing him. The paper in his hand. His eyes swollen to death and he bites his under lip to suppress more tears. He wipes over his chin. *Over his mouth. Over his face.*

He lets his arm fall and breathes hard before he speaks. “He went to therapy.” His voice breaks. “He apologized for..” he struggles for air. “Failing me. As a father. For blaming me. For the abuse.” His face´s wet now. “For not loving me. For despising me.” He goes on and then he shakes his head. “He.. he did that not for me.” He states. “He did it for therapy. He *had* to do it. For himself. For his guilt. His conscience. His peace.” He shakes his head again. “He doesn´t want to see me.” He choaks. “Not that I want to see that fucker. But..” his jaw flexes painfully.

“You wanted him to want to.” I say and he bites his lip nodding. I get up and run towards him, and he hugs me so tight he´s hurting me. *But I´ll take it. All of it and more if I can take away at least some of his pain. But I know I can´t.*

After we held each other for another hour, he talked to his parents and Leon. I waited in his room and when he got back, he looked less shattered. He held me tight and told me about what they said. He didn´t cry anymore and told me that he went to therapy his whole life. But he stopped when he was eighteen.

Now he´ll take some sessions again. *And he won´t answer him.*

108

It´s been a few days since Aidan told me everything. And I´ve had a few days to think about whether I should just go and tell him because part of me feels guilty. We lie to him. Not just to him but to them all. And after what Aidan told me about their friendship. I can´t believe why Kai didn´t tell him about me. But somehow, I think it´s not my place to tell.

So, I decided to talk to Kai.

We´re partying at the regular and I´ve quite had a bit. Not too much, but enough to feel bolt to do this. And just by looking at Kai now, I know he had too some drinks. *Since he´s back, he drinks a lot. A lot more than before.* He seems less high and more drunk. I don´t know what´s with him. *But when do I ever know that? Right? Never.*

I use the moment of Aidan being gone with some of his buddies to talk to him. He went to the garage to get some liquor, and I slipped in, shutting the door behind me. His head snaps to me as the door slams.

Mid grabbing the bottle, he straightens up. “Sup?” He nods his chin at me.

That frown tells me he knows I´m up to something, or that he has no clue what I want.

Both I´m okay with.

"Do you have a sec?" I ask and it´s still a bit weird to be alone. We used to be so easy and spontaneous about that. It was like we ran into each other and just stayed.

We just did. Hung around and did stuff together. *It was no question. It just was.* And now it´s that. *Weird.*

"I have them all." He says with a half-smile.

So, he´s in a good mood. That´s something.

How can I do this without us coming to blows or him leaving?

He comes up to me. "So?" He asks, cocking an eyebrow at me. "What you´ve got on your mind?" He asks slurry. *Why´s he so happy?*

"Uhm. So, Aidan and the adoption.." I begin and he frowns at me, not knowing where I want to go, but he nods slowly. "He told me about his childhood and teen years with you all. How it all started and told me *some* stories." I continue carefully. "*What* did he tell you?" He asks slowly. *He thinks he told me some secrets.*

I laugh. "Nothing bad." I calm him. "It´s just I´ve realized *how* close you all are, especially *you* two." I try to go on. "And you´re telling me this *because*?" He asks. "I just.." I begin and he cuts in. "You *what*?" He snaps. "I wondered why.." I trail off feeling unsure if I should have talked to him drunk.

"Why *what* Scar?" He rakes, glaring down at me. "Why you didn´t tell him." I say, locking eyes with him and he blinks at me. "*What*?" He asks loudly. "What do you mean? Tell *him* what?" He barks.

And I think somewhere he knows. But he wants me to say it.

"What was between us." I say and he gapes at me. "There wasn´t *anything*." He shuts down again and looks at me like I´m pathetic. *And now I feel like it.*

"We lie to him." I say upset but he shakes his head. "We don´t *lie* to him." He tells me, grinning like I´m insane. "Kai come on." I plead. "Can´t we just once have a normal conversation? We owe him. I can´t keep *this* anymore." I say and he scoffs. "Don´t you fucking *dare* saying anything to him about the *bullshit* in your head about us." He gets in my face.

And he could have just stabbed me, and it would have felt the same.

"We´re *friends* Lia." He barks and it sounds like an insult. *Maybe at this point it is.*

"And friends don´t *fuck* each other in the hot tub." He spits and my eyes widen.

He knows?

"Yeah, I know." He tells me venomous. "You *fucked* him in that.." He doesn´t finish shaking his head. "You two are *more*. And *we*?" He points between us. "We´re just friends." He says again. "That´s it. And I didn´t want *anything* to change. I´ve told you so before." He growls, his breath hitting my face. "You´re with him." He throws his arms in the air. "Now *fucking* let go of it." He snaps and I look at him in disbelief. "You don´t get it, right?" His smile filled with venom, and I swallow. "Then let me put it this way." He tilts his head. "Remember when you asked if it was all a bet?" He asks and I know what he´s doing, but I don´t believe it. I nod slowly wanting it to hear anyway.

Wanting to know if he´ll play that card.

"I lied." He says. *And he does.*

"It was a bet. It was all just a game." He says. "You were right about me. I played with you. But that´s what we do. What *I* do." He goes on. "They warned you about me. I warned you. Andi warned you. But you didn´t listen. Because you´re pathetic and naïve." He spits. "I played you and Wendy´s are to play. To break." He says all the things I was scared of hearing last year that now, just stab me.

Just to push me away. Just to shut down. Just to hurt.

"I wanted you to fall for me. I wanted you to *fall*." He says intently. "And you did." He nods. "Now let it go." He growls and pushes past me.

I flinch at the door slamming shut and I blink three times before I sit down and take the vodka he left and drown deep strokes.

So, there it is, I have my answer. *To him, it was nothing.*

I´m just self-pity that I´ve held onto *nothing* for so long. *So, I let nothing go.*

109

The next evening

The boys play some game before the party starts and I sit on Aidan´s lap. Kai´s on the armchair and plays against him.

Kai lost the game and tossed the controller to Leon. When I want to get up, Aidan holds me by my waist back. "Give me a sec, Scar." He murmurs into my ear, but Kai caught it and looks at me for a moment but then looks away.

His grip tightens and he kisses my cheek. A thousand butterflies shoot through my body. But as I see Kai´s scowl, all the butterflies *die out*. And instead, a Butterfly knife stabs my abdominal wall up to my heart and along my throat.

He quickly averts his gaze, but the pain remains. *That always stays.*

I want to get up and leave because I cry any second. But Kai gets up to leave. If he doesn´t want things to change and wants me to be happy with Aidan.

Why can´t he stop looking at me in those moments, like I´m the one who stabbed him? Like I´m the one placing black butterflies into his gut that rip him from the inside?

Because he does the same to me. I have the same plague in my body.

They eat me too.

But he won't admit it. Because it was nothing.

Then fucking start acting like it's been nothing. Because those looks you give me don't tell me nothing. They say it all. That you hate me.

And maybe I begin to hate you, too.

[NOTEBOOK ENTRIES]

First thing for me to see when I got back was her with my fucking brother's hand on her thigh. He tried to talk to me, said it was nothing and stuff, but they were close. Like they've bonded or some shit. But they were not fucking. It was Aidan. My best friend. ~~And I came back for her. I fucking bought her white roses.~~ Just to see her already moved on. And the worst is there's no bro code if you didn't even know about the girl. I couldn't even tell my closest friend. Who's been fucking her while I was gone, missing her, and losing my mind.

For a second, I thought about giving her those roses I told her were not for her. Who am I even lying to? Everyone. But I've thrown them into that box under my bed, where I collect all the stupid stuff that remind me of her. Like some hairbands she left back when she stayed over. What seems like lifetimes ago. I like to collect those things and never look at them. Like ever. Once I've put them inside, they stay. Untouched. Locked away. Out of reach. But not as far as I like them to be. Cause in my head they show up. Like the note of our pizza order where she drew those faces. Or the stab of the first joint I shared with her. All those kinds of things. Stupid things. Things like my pin code and that Polaroid. And now there are those roses too. And the rose of the wedding. In a box where I can't see em. So, I went to her. I didn't really say those things I wanted to but that's no surprise. When do I ever say what I intend to when it comes to her? She worried about my bruises. She didn't touch em though. It's been a long time since she touched my wounds. Now she just touches scars. Holding her after those months made me realize how much I missed her. They have friends with benefits. But I'm afraid there are feelings involved. He liked her the day they kissed. I always wondered why he didn't hit on her. I told her I'm happy for them. Even if it ripped me. But when did something not? Kill me.

I wish I never fucking left. I wasn't in a good state there, but right now anything is better than seeing her with my best friend. And the worst part? She's happy. I mean objectively, it's a good thing. I never thought that something could tear me apart and make me happy at the same time. I had to come back. But maybe I should just leave. They would kill me. But being back kills me more. I couldn't make her happy. He can. Seems like everyone else can but me. I should accept that. I knew it all along that's why I left. I'm still not able to love. Seeing her already moved on is hell. Because I didn't. Don't know if I'll ever can. I can't even let it snow here because the others would know, so my other buddy alc has to do his best to hold me together. I stopped the weed. I don't know why. I just did.

It doesn't hurt less to see them, but it gets easier. I'm walking around with knives in my body. If you remove them, you'll die. And since I love a good pain, I take what I can get. I think I'll never get used to seeing her with anyone else. But I have a feeling I must.

We saw fireflies. I knew they'd be there, and I wanted to show her. And fuck I missed her. But I can't have her. Not the way I want her. My eyes touch her where my hands can't. Cause we don't do this anymore. Cause his hands are on her now, not mine. How should I fucking get past that?

She had scratch marks of him all over her. With that, she punched me in the chest. But what punched me in my fucking soul was that she fucked him in my jacuzzi. Like, what the hell? Is she serious? She can't be. I sat on the roof, drowning my liquor till I heard that fuck song on repeat. And then.. I heard her. Them. Really, she could have just killed me. How could she fuck him there? She knew I could have easily run into them. I wanted to fucking rip my ears out. And my heart. But that's what she already did anyway so.. fuck her. That night, she simply became my deepest scar and I've had quite a lot. And she got me one I could never forget. The sounds of her with another. With my best friend.

They fucked in the car. I mean, can they make it any more obvious they fuck around? For God's sake, I hate this. I need to leave soon.

He's into her. I can tell by the way he looks at her. I know him. And how she acts with him. She's into him too. It's been only months. What did I miss? I mean they have always been close and flirty, but this is different. This is more than just friends with benefits. They don't know yet, but it fucking is. And the worst part is that it makes sense. They do. They're easy, healthy, and light. They're good for each other. We never had that. When I left like a coward, I fucked up. When I told her to be with him. When I could have told her not to.

She figured what my pin was about. She knew my code. But now she knows. I never wanted her to know. Never the Polaroid never that fucking Pin. If she'll ever find that box, I'll kill myself. That day changed a lot and now she knows.

When I opened the door to find her, it was like we used a time machine. It felt so familiar but foreign. She told me to stop frowning. I almost laughed at that. I knew she wanted to tell me that tons of times. Probably the first time she saw me. She was all confident. But then, she wasn't. Her hands shook and I wanted to touch her, but I wasn't sure if we did that anymore. I wasn't prepared for love. Time stood still. I could hear my heartbeat. It stopped. Maybe it never worked since. I couldn't think of anything to say. I wanted her to say it. I didn't dare to look at her. I knew she was crying. If I had faced her, I would have kissed her tears away. I would have told her. I would have looked into her green, green, red eyes and would have never left. She would have seen the lies. The regret, the hurt, and the love. Finn yelled at me why I made her cry. He told me it's fucking obvious that she's in love with me, and I told him that's bullshit. Or she wouldn't have fucked him. She wouldn't have moved on. They fuck all the time. I hate being back. Maybe I should do my trip to Bali. I can't stand seeing them. Being the gentlemen and letting her go. Is not fucking generous. It's pretentious. It's a lie. It hurts.

I got in my car after pondering if she really called or if I just imagined it. I did that a lot in London. When I was on it. High and low. I hallucinated about her. One of the reasons I dumped the pills. I didn't even have to look at her to know how puffy and red her eyes were. Pretty but sad. Her crying eyes are the greenest in a deep blue sky. She opened up about her fears. Is it sadistic to think she's fucking beautiful when she's sad? But fuck she looked so pretty. How are you so pretty when you cried out all, what's left in you? Until the only hydrated part were her eyes. Those green eyes. They get me all the time. Shining bright like you just threw acid in them. Too beautiful to be sad. She called me. She trusts me. She even made me check the time. Just to see an angel number. Right person, right time. But with us, it always feels like the wrong. She's the only person I ever showed my heart to. ~~I know I haven't really.~~ And she's the person, why no one fucking else will ever see it again. She's another reason ~~besides the other one~~. But my heart claimed hers and it won't settle for less. Nothing but hers.

She wanted to talk. That killed my mood. She asked why I never told him. Like, I fucking knew. I saw red and told her I knew about the jacuzzi. The way she was clueless. Like didn't she fucking think? Did she ever think about how it fucking felt for me? Him and her? She never told me, either. I had to find out. Did she ever think about hurting me with that? No, she didn't. She just thought about her own ass. Because the only reason she wants to tell him is because she feels guilty.

And in the end, it was like they never cared I left. Aidan has now a girlfriend. Leon and Nina are good without me. Finn doesn't care. Andi and Ryan are not close enough for me to care. And she never cared. That's why she didn't stop me. I should have stayed away. Maybe I'll just go.

Colson Herzog

I´ve booked a flight. They can continue to move on. And this time I´ll do the same. Move the fuck on. Because you know what? I deserve too.

110

Kai

I storm into the kitchen, grab the vodka, and slam it down on the countertop.

Finn walks in with a shit-eating grin. "You´re really bothered, by *that* between them." he states, and I scoff. *Bothered is an understatement. It kills, it fucks, it rips me. No, I´m not bothered I´m just utterly pissed off by them. But not bothered, no.*

Without responding, I twist open the cap with a snap of my finger and let the burning stuff flow down my throat. *Hoping it´ll take her with it, or at least kill anything left of her that I didn´t throw up weeks ago.*

The burning warms my stomach and displaces the feeling that until now was screaming to be heard. *It´s gone. She´s gone.*

I scowl at him. "What makes you think that?" I ask and he laughs. "You´re boozing. Drinking in excess since you got back. You haven´t touched your weed. And I´m sure London was pretty *snowed in* wasn´t it?" He crosses his arms.

Why does he know me so well?

"And I know you." He adds but I stiff a laugh. *There it is.*

"No, you don´t." I bark. "If you would, you would have fucking stopped whatever the hell this is between them." I say, looking past his shoulder to them making out on my fucking couch. *My best friend´s making out. My Scar.*

I shut my eyes for a sec, breathing. Then I rip em off them and back to him. "Or at least you would have told me. *If you knew me.*" I say. "You would have fucking told me that she moved on while I was a fucking wreck." I yell just as loud for him to get my point, but not enough for them to hear. I get in his face. "I took E and coke and numbed myself with *anything* I could get, so if you fucking knew, that *this* would happen.. then why didn´t you tell me?" I bite my tongue craving the blood I can´t spill on his face again.

He says nothing. I raise my chin. *Fucking knew.*

"Did you try to get into her pants or what?" I snap. "Don´t come at me like that. We talked about that." He snaps. "I know *how* you feel about her." He says, to which I close my eyes, trying to tame my rising anger.

I point at him. "You don´t know shit." I growl.

The party has started, and the music is loud enough for us to fight.

"I think, you finally realized you care about her. And then you came back. But now she´s dating Avery. But she´s still attached to you. But you´re too scared.." He analyzes me, but I cut in. "Shut the fuck up."

I drown another few strokes while he keeps talking, but I don´t listen to his bullshit and zone out. The vodka hits my system in all the right places. And all I can sense is the feeling of throwing up as I watch her starting to dance with him.

So, I drink some more because *anything* is better than feeling what she´s doing with her ass at his dick right now. I rip my gaze off zoning in on my brother.

He´s so fucking perfect. Of course, he knows everything better but he´s not my fucking parent. No one is. Peter never had parents. That´s why he´s in Neverland. There were way too many never´s in his life. Never growing up. Never leaving. Never. And most of all never loving a girl. Girls are trouble. Never. But then came that girl along and tried to change the boy. That didn´t end well. It never does. Never.

I blink too many times trying to forget that firefly. *Or was it a fairy or just a girl*? *Did I really stop taking drugs or? Am I just insane*?

I shake my head, looking at my brother. "Of course, it fucks me up that my best friends fuck." I yell. "And that no one, not even my brother told me." I look at him. "You knew." I growl and he looks at me, sorry. *You better be fucker.*

"I know and I´m sorry. But also, I´m not. You hid her too and you left her. On her sister´s wedding." He accuses me. "Don´t start on that." I bark.

"I´m no good guy. Why the hell are all of you *that* surprised if I mess up? I always do. Always did. And yes, *that* was messed up." I go on. "Don´t you think I know? You know *why* I left." I shout and he breathes hard saying something, but I don´t listen anymore.

I know it´s my fault. I shouldn´t have left in the first place. Or shouldn´t have cut the contact to them but people make fucking mistakes.

But he did it on purpose. Why did no one tell me? Don´t they care about me? Why hasn´t she stopped me? Why didn´t she fight for me? Why does the guy have to do that all the fucking time? Why didn´t I just tell them? You know fucking why.

"Look, I´m only telling you this because I want you to feel better." He explains rubbing his neck and my attention turns back to him. *I didn´t listen.*

"Say what?" I ask confused, not having followed his sermon. "She´s after you." He says. Something presses against my heart. It might just smack. *She what?*

I feel all sober now. "What?" I snap sharply and feel my pulse in every inch of my body about to implode. "She was here looking for you." He says slowly and I shake my head just as slowly. *Looking for me.*

My jaw tightens. "When I got back from the airport." He continues carefully. My neck heats and a shiver I can´t shake of runs through my spine. *I taste blood.*

"The wedding." He says and I shake my head. *My eyes burn.*

"No." I say, not wanting to believe what he tells me. "She was upset and wanted to go after you. So, I drove her." He says, looking all guilty. "Although I knew you were already boarding." He tells me. "She ran through the airport to find you." He says. My stomach tightens I´m cold and my mouth dry.

"What are you talking about?" I ask angrily. *I don´t believe what´s coming out of his sickening mouth. She went after you. She did care. She wanted me to stay.*

I blink the thoughts away before I snap his neck right here. "I sat there with her for over an hour." He says quietly. "And watched the planes take off." He adds and I bite back the tears that want to shatter. My mouth fills with blood. A dull roar offers itself from my ears into my brain and a sharp pain makes itself known in my chest area, but I don´t allow it to surface. *Tinnitus. A low buzz.*

I rear and grab him by the collar. "You say that *now*?!" I bark. "I promised her not to." He justifies himself. *Fucking what?*

I shake him, raging. "*Promised her?*" I yell glad she left with Aidan minutes ago probably for a quicky in the bathroom. Some tears escape, but gladly they just hit the ground instead of rolling down my fucking face for everyone to see.

"You´re my *brother*," I growl, shoving him and I almost slap my face by wiping the tears. "She went after me? And you didn´t fucking tell me?" I ask and shake my head. This can´t.. *She was there. While I drugged and numbed myself.*

"I would have.." I begin but stop myself cause my eyeballs burn like hell does for sure. "You would have come back?" he asks, not believing me. "I would." I say and my hands twitch with the ache to get his blood on them. "I would have stayed if she asked me to." I say upset but he shakes his head. "What?" I snap. "You should have stayed in the first place." He says, and I hit his nose in response.

"You *fucking* should have told me. You could have texted me. She could have texted me." I hit him again and want to move past him, but he holds me back. "I told you to make you feel better. Not that you´re going to her and ruin things for them." I bite my teeth together. *I could kill him.*

"I promised her not to tell you. And Aiden is *your* best friend. *And so is she.* Don´t mess that up." He warns me. *What the fuck?*

We glare at each other.

"How the fuck is *that* supposed to make me feel better?" I yell and heads turn, so I lower my voice. "Now take your *fucking* hands off of me before I break them." I threaten, but he just grabs my T-shirt yanking me in.

I know he'll can knock out me easily. But right now, I feel like I'd win.

He gets in my face. "You *know* I'm right. You *love* her." My eyes twitch at that comment. "But she *deserves* to be happy. And you had your shot *little shit* and lost it. You didn't act on it. More than once." He tells me the mistakes I can't forget myself and I suck my blood off my teeth to soothe the crave for pain.

"Now leave her alone. And get your shit together. You've told her often enough you're just friends now act like one. Be a friend to her. Let her go." He tells me what I know, I can't.

He protects her. From me? What the fuck? He's on her side?

I want to smash his face on the counter he deserved it after keeping all that from me. *He promised her.* Inside, I must laugh. *I have no words.*

"For once, if you're honest with yourself and admit how you feel about her, let her be happy." He looks into the living room. *So, they're back.*

I hope no one got a whiff on anything but I say nothing and don't look at her either. "You never thought you'd get that attached, did you?" He asks, looking at her and then let's go patting my chest, pushing me away, so I stumble. *No, I didn't.*

"Be a man and let her go." And with that, the *big brother* sermon is through. I grab the vodka and head to my room and ignore the looks of the others, and especially the look of her. I just shoot her a glare that tells her *I fucking hate you and I don't want you here* before I spat blood. They didn't intervene cause first they know better not to and second, they're used to us arguing. *Especially since I'm back. We're constantly fighting.*

So, they have no idea why. Since I made it a secret in the first place.

My greatest mistake.

Hiding her. *No idea..*

111

I punch the bag, pretending it's me. *But it doesn't work.*

After sweating and letting off steam, I still feel little of the alcohol. On top of that, thoughts about her at the airport and her with Aidan fucking earlier haunt me. So, I take my copy of *The Picture of Dorian Gray*, along with a pencil, a joint and climb onto the patio roof.

The thought of her makes me light the joint. And the image of her kissing my best friend to smoke it. With each puff, her silhouette blurs out of my mind and a bit of my soul too. Until she´s gone and only endless silence and numbness are perceptible. *Just how I like it.*

I open to a blank page and write.

I rip the page and begin anew.

"How can you love if you´d never had sex with her? How can you give the freedom without caging yourself?"

I rip it and start again.

"How can you be selfless when all you want is to be selfish? How can you watch her with someone else without breaking? Without wanting to be him?"

I rip more pages in rage.

"How can she feel for you and still chose not to be with you?"

Well, how you did. A voice tells me.

I stare at the lines. At those damn lines. *Does she love me? And do I love her?*

I close my eyes. *I know the answer.*

A lump spreads in my throat and wetness wants to fight its way through my eyelids. I squeeze them shut tighter as anger boils inside me. *This is bullshit.*

I rip out the page and crumple it. Then I pick it back up and look at the lines.

My eyeballs are on fire. *Fuck.*

I reach in my back pocket, pull out the lighter and hold the flame under it.

What did I think would happen when I come back?

That she´ll wait for me for months?

She´s not someone who waits for others. I´ve learned that the hard way. What on the one hand impresses me, but also hits me. I underestimated her, for which I hate myself.

For which I adore her more.

I had to and wanted to go. It was easier to leave. I thought she would say something to stop me. *But nothing. She let me go. Just like I wanted to.*

And she didn´t contact me all this time. *Just like I did.*

But *she went after you,* a voice tells me and I´m willing to stick my hands inside my mouth to fucking find that voice and snap it´s neck between my fingers.

When I ran away to London, I found it easier not to think about her. And when I did, I looked for women to fuck to forget about her. *Until I forgot her.*

But at some point, even that didn´t help. My cock wanted to be faithful to a girl that it didn´t even have yet. And I didn´t want her for her body. I wanted everything else *and* her body. But I didn´t even think about getting her laid. *I mean, I did.* But mostly I wanted her to be near me. *Talk to her. See her. Feel her. Have her.*

But I couldn´t and no matter what pussy or mouth I buried myself in, there was only her. *So, I had to come back. I wanted to.*

But now seeing her is killing me. Seeing her with him is literally killing me in ways, I never knew could happen. And as all I had to think about was her, while I fucked the living daylights out of women in Londoner clubs, trying to forget her, she has already forgotten me. *Worse, she fucked my best friend.*

And worst of all this is all my fault. Cause I couldn´t tell her.

Still can´t. Now even more.

After I told her that it´s okay what´s between them. *That I´m happy.*

That they should be together. And that between us is nothing but friends.

So how could I mess the luck and happiness of my two best friends?

Yeah, I just couldn´t.

112

My head snaps to the left as someone opens the patio door but I growl as I see my brother and not her.

I close the book and face him. He rubs his neck. "Look Kai I´m sorry." He says, and I listen mostly cause I´m high and I have no energy to throw him off the roof.

"I should have told you. Maybe I shouldn´t. But.." He cuts himself off, starting new. "I just hoped you wouldn´t need me to tell you all this in order to come back. To realize you want *this*." He admits, and he has a point. "I´m not the one to tell you what you should feel." He justifies, and for once I get it. *He´s right.*

"I want to be honest with you. I think she want´s you. They´re more friends than you two are." He shrugs. "Maybe, now it´s her turn to figure that on her own you know. And she´ll come back. Deep down, she knows I´m sure." He considers. *Maybe.*

"Is there anything that happened when I was gone besides the airport?" I ask and he crosses his arms looking like he´s in pain. *Telling me there was.*

"She´s been a mess. She was hurting. *A lot.*" He frowns. "She´s been here every day *and* night." He says and I frown at that statement. *He reads me.*

"She slept in your bed." He tells me quietly and I blink slowly, grinding my jaw.

I thought I imagined that scent. Like my brain wanted to trick me. I smelled her the moment I stepped into my room. She´s been here when I was gone? Alone in my bed.

Fuck.

I shut my eyes. *The sheets. It all smelled like her.*

Not cause I´m insane. Cause it did.

"She couldn´t be alone. Wanted to be around all the time. I took her to training. She sat next to me when I worked and all." He tells me. *He looked after her.*

"She partied a lot. Smoked. Drank.." He trails off. "And what?" I press. "Don´t freak okay." He tells me holding his hands in front of him and I get up ready to throw punches. "If someone says that, *usually* people do." I bark. "Now spit it. What happened?" I snap. "That one night at the party, she let herself fall in the pool." He says carefully and I frown. "What do you mean? *Let herself fall..*" I ask.

"Do you think she?" I cut myself off as he shakes his head. "No, I don´t. But she wasn´t in a good place. She missed you. And she had no one to talk to. Since no one knew. And she didn´t really want to talk about it, but I was there." He says and I nod.

He looks at me stunned. "You´re not mad?" He asks, assuming I would throw him off that roof, but I shake my head. "I´m not." I say. "She needed someone." I say quietly. "So, thank you." I tell him. "For caring about her. For.. being there for her when I couldn´t." I say and his frown deepens, not used to hearing those words coming from me.

He nods after realizing I really won´t punch him. "And after that?" I ask. "Leon took her to our rage room." He grins soft "He did?" I smile. *Bet she loved it.*

He nods. "Yeah, he and Nina had their monthly breakup, and they knew something was off with her, so he took her with him." He tells me.

I wanted to show her, but there wasn´t the opportunity. But I´m glad he did.

"She really needed that because after she got better. She dealt with it." He nods.

What I never did.

"And then her and Aidan got the idea they could be fuck buddies." He says. "I couldn´t stop this. As we noticed what was going on.. they.. already.. you know." He says and I nod.

She found her distraction just as I did.

But hers wasn´t white but a person. It was Aidan.

"Then you came back." He says. *And then I came back.*

"Thank you for telling me." I say calmly. He nods and leaves me with that alone.

So, she suffered as much as I did. In different ways but for the same reason.

Me leaving.

I rip another page and write again. Write what I couldn´t admit nor pronounce. Not to me, not to her. *Not anyone.*

"I thought she loved me. And all the weeks and months I told myself that I don´t need her, want her, or even care about her. I told myself and her so many lies. And you know you´re a good liar when you start to believe your own lies. Until you don´t.

I didn´t want to love her, but over time I grew into it. There was no way out but to love her. I know that now. I fucking love her. And I have to tell her. I have to be honest once in my life. About the fact that I indeed love her. No matter if it´s good or bad love."

Again, I light it, watching it disappear. And if only those feelings could do the same, I would set my heart on fire. I would choose to forget and not to feel.

But I do. And I can´t run from that. *Not anymore.*

I love her. I do. *How did that happen? I´m fucking scared. I don´t know what to do.*

I think she loves me too. *Does she? But what about him?*

I never thought I might ever get to love anyone but my friends. *Never in my life.* ~~Well once.. *but we know how that went.*~~ But it´s her. She´s the girl that changed it all. She was fucking right about that too. *Not even knowing she´d be the one.*

I pour some more vodka down my throat. *Until she´s gone. Gone for now.*

113

Lia

The Party has been going on for a while as I make my way to the bathroom. Kai wasn´t back since the fight with his brother. Even though the two fight a lot lately, their bond is still close. It´s a weird dynamic between them but considering that Finn was not just his older brother but sort of his parent, it makes sense.

But I can´t stop thinking I might be the reason they fought. Cause the way he looked at me. Rather, the way he´s been looking at us the past weeks has kept me wondering. And the hateful growl he threw at me earlier was like a year ago. Like he hated me with all he had.

It had to be about me. I just feel it. I couldn´t hear though due to the music, but I have a feeling. And I could have asked Finn but idk, maybe it´s better not to know.

But as I reach the stairs, I freeze. *Speaking of the devil.*

He sits on the last step, looking down on me. *Looking* is an understatement, more scornful staring. I´d love to turn and leave, but it´s obvious I wanted to go upstairs. So, I bite my cheeks and walk on. I hold my breath, hoping he´d leave me alone. Which he does until I pass him, and his hand grabs my arm, holding me back. My blood freezes at his touch and I shut my eyes. *Of course, he wouldn´t let me.*

I face him and he looks up at me. His eyes red from weed. And this time I´m sure it´s not from crying. And he´s drunk. *He´s been drinking alone?* I mean I saw him disappear with the bottle but he wasn´t downstairs since.

And since when does he smoke again? And why did he stop anyway?

His eyes lock on mine. "Can we talk?" he asks and my heart aches.

How many times I wanted to hear that.

"Uhm.. Sure." I say and he stands up, towering over me. He rubs his neck, looking unsure about the talking part. *As always, he didn´t think about what to say.*

With him, it´s always like that. He speaks as he goes.

"It´s.. uhm, about us." He says, searching for words and I watch his features. "I´ve thought about it all." He goes on wiping his face with both hands. "What went down the past months. And at the wedding. All before that." He tells me and I frown.

What is this about?

"It´s just.." He breathes. "I can´t stand this.." He trails off, looking lost. "What?" I ask in a whisper. "You and him. Me and you." He says, facing me and his jaw twitches.

There´s something in his eyes. Something different. I can´t tell, though.

"What do you mean?" I ask, not sure what he´s telling me.

He scratches the back of his head and licks his lips before he speaks. "I know I said we´re friends and there was nothing.." He struggles, that I can tell, and he grips his hair. "I know I said I´m okay with this.. with you two together and that I´m happy for you which I am but.." He shakes his head. *He can´t look at me.*

"Kai.." I begin but he cuts in. "Look I know I said I never wanted anything to change.." he begins looking right at me, but I interrupt him. "Kai wait." I stop him. And I see in his eyes that it´s important for him to say whatever he has on his mind. Maybe he´s even *dying* to say that, but he has no right to mess things up. And I know the Lia months ago would kill me if she knew I would reject him right now. Now that he apparently wants to open up.

But I can´t stop myself.

I´m glad he remains silent as I continue, and he just works his jaw. "I´ve waited for you to tell me how you feel the past year. And then we finally talked, and I thought, maybe this will change things for better.." I stiff a laugh, and I don´t know where I got the confidence to play him down.

"But then you left." I say disappointed and he looks down at the floor. That makes it easier for me to keep talking. "And I can´t even blame you because I know you wanted to spend time with your parents." I say, and he shakes his head, probably thinking I´m wrong about that. "But what I *do* hold against you.." I say and he lifts his gaze. "Is that you didn´t check in this whole time. You didn´t even tell me you´ll leave until you did. *Everyone knew.* Everyone but me." I say upset.

"But that was what you wanted, right?" I ask and shake my head. "And the past weeks, you´ve had chances to say *something*. To tell me you care. To tell me.." I stop myself. "But you didn´t. You told me to let go." I accuse him lifting my chin and I take a moment to gain strength to say the following. Because it hurts, but I have to.

I owe myself.

"So, whatever you were going to say." I tell him. "I know that´s not fair, but please don´t say it." He looks hurt and blinks like he´s trying not to cry but just for a second. Because then there´s just coldness, indifference, and anger. Like I told him, he died for me. He closed up within seconds. Like a switch to his feelings. *He killed it all. Maybe even me.*

Because that look on his face right now. It´s worse than any I´ve seen on him. That look earlier I´ve talked about was *nothing* compared to that. And for a second, I feel guilty because he tried to open up, and I turned him down. *But it passes.*

I´ve wanted to hurt him as much as he did to me. *Maybe, this is the hurt.*

He nods and clenches his teeth, so his jawbones work under his skin. In the light, his irises look deep black. Black surrounded by fiery red. *The devils red.*

And I know he´ll say something spiteful. By the way, his features have changed.

"Does he.." he begins, challenging and I scoff, shaking my head *knowing* exactly where this is going. *And hells no this won´t happen again.*

He can´t just switch up on me like he wants. Not this time.

I step closer and raise my chin. "Does he know?" I begin. "That I slept at your place daily? That we sort of dated? That we texted all night? That we met after the parties? That you dry fucked me? That you made it a game for you to keep me away from Andi? That you took me to Paris on my birthday? That we´ve spent yours kissing on that rave? That you were the one I was with on Halloween? That your bite marks and hickeys were mine? That I was worth the fucking hiding?" I spit. "That your Christmas was good just cause of me? That we actually liked each other and not hated?" I ask spitefully. "Or that you hid me? Kept me a secret? Played with me? Pushed me away? Made me fall?" I ask grinning and he just looks like he might choak me. *I dare you even.*

"That you´re a coward? And you fucking ditched me on the wedding? That I.." I have to pause because a lump has formed in my throat, causing me to burst into tears as soon as I utter another word, but I look back up at him. "That I went after you like an idiot to the airport?" My voice breaks and again, he lowers his gaze.

I wait but nothing. *Why isn´t he saying, anything?*

He seems more composed than I would have expected about my revelation.

Well, maybe he doesn´t give a fuck. Maybe, this is just another game trying to mess with me. He stopped me from dating Andi, but he won´t stop me now.

"That you didn´t reach out to me after you left?" I ask, but he still doesn´t look at me. "That you came back for me with those roses that aren´t mine?" I ask and he looks at me, jaw set. "That you´ve hit your brother cause of me? That you had no balls to just say it? That you lied and said it´s okay with you? That it isn´t at all okay that I date him and not you?" I go on until I can´t think of another reason, even though there are tons of more.

"So, if you mean all that." I say gesturing fed up. "No, he *doesn´t* know. Your *best friend* doesn´t know. Because no one did." I say, and right now I feel pity for him. "Because you didn´t tell em." I say. "You didn´t either." He retorts. "It wasn´t *my* place to tell *your* friends." I yell. "And if I did you, would probably have pretended like all that didn´t happen." I say and he shakes his head. "You would have." I tell him.

"You could have told them on New Year´s. But you didn´t. And don´t say you´ve been scared. Because I was too. But I was open about my feelings. You never were." I say beat. "When did *you* tell me about your feelings?" He asks offended. "I did. But I didn´t even had to cause it was obvious I felt about you. But with you, it was never. You gave me mixed signals. And it doesn´t matter what I feel because I´m sick of it." I say and he looks at me like I´m insane.

"You said you weren´t coming back, Kai." I snap. "It was a mistake, okay!" He yells upset and I shake my head. "You don´t get it." I say.

"But maybe you´ll understand if I quote." I say to give him the final push. "*Experience was merely the name men gave to their mistakes.*" I say slowly, enjoying his face twitching with anger and his nostrils flare. "Oscar Wilde." I add knowing it´s his fav.

"I came back." He argues and I give him a weak smile. "I know." I say. "But that doesn´t make it easier, nor does it change the way you treated me." I tell him resigned. "Look, I´m happy the way things are. At least I was until *you* came back." I say, and even I felt the pain for saying that. And for a moment, I think I see a glimpse of hurt in his eyes, maybe even remorse. But then the emotion fades.

Like it didn´t happen. Like all of it. Like us.

He nods. "Then I shouldn´t have come back." He looks me in the eyes. "No, you shouldn´t." I say.

We look at each other. *No one moves.* If we do, *it´s real. It´s over. So, we don´t.*

And just look at each other, letting the pain sink in. Sweep into our souls and bind us forever. *Forever almost. The almost that hurt the most.*

"I thought it is, okay?" I ask quietly and he looks at his feet and then back at me. "Of course, it´s not." He says soft, almost broken. *I think I might cry.*

"I mean my best friend?" He asks on edge and barely shakes his head lips trembling. "Like really? Him? What.." He rubs his hand over his mouth.

"What the fuck?" He adds upset. "I´m sorry." I say defending but he shakes his head. "No." He looks at me like he doesn´t know me anymore. "No." He repeats. "Fuck this." His chin bolts back, and he turns and heads to his room. I watch him leave.

Why´s that he´s always the one leaving? And why the fuck do I watch?

And I swear I hear him say *"hate you"* under his breath. *Yeah, me too.*

My eyes fixed on his back.

When did he stop wearing those quotes? And why didn´t I notice?

The door slams shut, and I flinch even though I saw it coming. But with all in life, it hits you harder if it actually happens. Even if you knew it would. *Especially then.*

How did I do that? Where´s that confidence from? Honestly, I don´t know.

But looking at his closed door, I just know. It´s a gut feeling that he´s not done.

This isn´t over. But am I even prepared for what to come?

114

Black Out Days – Future Islands remix (Slowed) – Phantogram, xxtristanxo, Slowed radio, future Islands

I´ve been dancing with Aidan for a while, but my mind keeps wandering to Kai and our conversation. I try hard not to think of those black eyes that went red when I pushed him away.

Aidan and I fool around as he spins me in his arms as in my purview, I see Kai and freeze. He stands next to us and Aidan smiles at him. But my stomach sinks as I face him and reading his energy. He holds an *almost* empty bottle in his hand, which was *full* when he left after the fight. *He drank that all. Shit.*

We stop dancing. "Sup bro?" Aidan asks grinning, but Kai ignores him and faces me. "Are *you* going to tell him, or should *I*?" Kai asks menacingly, pointing between me and him with the bottle in his hand. *This is bad. He can´t be serious.*

His pupils are dilated and he´s way too drunk now.

"Tell me what?" Aiden harps confused but still grinning. Kai looks at me expectantly and ignoring him. "Kai, what the fuck?" I hiss, stepping closer and he grins smugly enjoying this. *That fucking asshole. He can´t be serious.*

"Can someone cut the shit already?" Aidan demands a bit pissed but Kai merely laughs in amusement. He tilts his head, watching me.

"You tell me?" Kai asks amused. *No. Not like this. This is wrong. This is cruel.*

He can't do this to him. To me.

"You're drunk." I say and he shrugs. "So?" His eyebrow raises and he seems spiteful and not himself. He wraps an arm around my neck, forcing me to him. "We have to tell you *something*." He chirps, pretending to sound happy and I jerk away from his grip. "Cut it Kai." I snap sharp. "Cut what?" Aidan joins in. "What are you talking about? Telling what?" He asks pissed and grabs Kai by his T-shirt as he doesn't answer and glares at him threateningly. Kai returns his gaze but smiles smug, like the devil. *And like before a big bang, I can't look away. I just watch and see his decision before he speaks. The devil deciding to sin.*

He looks briefly at me, glances at Aidan and then he blurts, "she loves me." Aidan loosens his grip and Kai just grins watching his friend react to his words. But then his smile fades, and he looks directly at me all smile gone. *Fuck.*

"And I love her." He tells him but holds my eyes. My heart skips a beat and forgets it has to actually work. *Love? That word coming from him makes it seem wrong.*

A shiver runs through me. *He loves me?*

Aidan lets go of Kai, equally perplexed and Kai's words echo through my head in a continuous loop. *She loves me. And I love her. Love.*

His gaze burns into mine.

I feel like everyone can hear my heartbeat. Like my body is made of glass, and they can see it pounding and my thoughts running. *Everyone stares at us.* My cheeks and ears begin to glow, and I almost forgot that there are people around me.

People like our friends.

I take my eyes off my fallen angel who's become the devil and look at Aidan in panic. Kai then just turns around and heads towards the patio door, but I jolt forward, grabbing his pecs to stop him. "You can't just leave now." I shout but he shakes me off, walking along.

I run after him, but Aidan rushes past me and grabs him by the shoulder, jerking him around. "What the fuck are you talking about? *Love?*" he asks furiously, but Kai pushes him away, to which Aidan shoves him in the chest.

"As I said." Kai says, holding his hands in the air and shrugs whereupon Aidan smacks him in the face. Kai grabs his lip, grins, and takes a swing. Aidan stumbles back, his nose bleeding instantly. They throw some more until they glare at each other holding their wounded faces. Kai holds the bottle to his lip and spits a mixture of blood and vodka onto the floor. Then he looks at me, lifting his chin in victory.

Hurt. Satisfied. Angry.

Telling me *I did this cause you hurt me. Because I'm in love with you.*

But then he turns his back on us and walks inside. Tears threaten, but I fight them away. Out of all the ways we should have told Aidan and the others, this was the worst. *And he knew. He did it to hurt me.* It felt like he sliced my chest to hold my heart. To let me feel him have it. To show them all he has it. That he could have it. And then he'd let go and left me with a hole acing for his touch. Or maybe it wasn't hands but knifes, who knows with him.

"What the fuck is going on, Lia?" Aidan rips my thoughts away. "What was that about? You love each other? What am I missing?" Aidan snaps, stepping into my view. But all I see is Andi looking like he's watching the best movie of his lifetime.

Yeah, I bet it was fun for him. Finn staring off with a frown. Nina in shock but loves the gossip, and Leon really pissed. *Like he might hit me. Even if he won't.*

I blink, focusing on Aidan. *But I can't think straight. I can't do this right now.*

"We'll talk in a minute okay, I promise." I tell him. "I need to talk to him." I say and he looks upset. "You serious?" He gapes and I nod. He takes a deep breath and runs his hand through his hair. But eventually he nods. "Okay." He says, and I run inside and take three flights of stairs at once. The door is ajar. *Always ajar.*

My heart races as I open it just enough to step through. He sits on the bed and looks at me. *Like he expected me to come.*

He stands up and my heart stops. I don't know how long we just look at each other, but it feels like time stands still. *He looks guilty, sad, and hurt. And in love..*

"You love me" I hear myself whisper. "Yes," he hushes hoarsely.

"I had to say it." He adds, voice breaking painfully and I shut my eyes closed. "Why like this?" I ask and open them. His eyes are fixed on his feet. *He's sorry.*

I eye his chapped lip. He punched him not just verbally but emotionally.

I don't know what to say, so I tell him the thing I know. "I love Aiden." I say. And pain flits across his face, to which he lowers his gaze. His hand is covered in blood. He looks at it and balls fists just to unclench them again.

And because I still don't know what to say, I say the other thing I know. "But you're right." I say, and he searches my eyes. "I love you." I tell him, my heart on the line. "Which doesn't make *this* any easier." I admit, voice breaking and he nods but lowers his gaze and bites his lip hard.

"I should talk to Aiden." I say, and he hums in agreement, not daring to meet my eyes again. Just one nod and I leave. I close the door behind me. *And can breathe again.*

Aidan is still where I left him, and the others are chattering.

I walk up to him. "Let´s head over." He says, looking past me and I nod. We head over to his garden. *I can´t read his mood.*

We sit down on the wooden bench in front of the campfire. I´ve often thought about telling him but didn´t know how. *But this wasn´t how it should have been.*

"Talk." He demands. *He´s mad at me.*

"I don´t know where to start." I admit. *He stays silent.*

"Nothing ever really happened between us." I lie and shut my eyes.

How should I explain what I can´t understand myself?

"That´s a lie." I say. "It did happen, *something* between us." I confess and I almost feel him flinch. "Not in the past three months." I clarify but he nods in confusion. "Why do you lie?" He asks. "Because it didn´t feel like it really happened. Cause we never acknowledged it. We did it to hide." I take a deep breath. "It wasn´t real when it happened. It wasn´t real when he left. And now that he said, *that* made it *somehow* real." I say and he nods once.

"What happened *exactly?*" He asks slowly. "Kai and I.." I start, but I don´t know how to describe it. "I suppose it was complicated." He tries to joke, but I can hear that he´s pissed. "Yeah, kinda." I say.

"Um.. so last year I thought he hated me and somehow, he did. But then he kind of didn´t." I say. "He gave me mixed signals. We´ve spent a lot of time together after the parties and sort of dated. He showed up in the middle of the night and I went to his. It was confusing. He was rude and also not." I say and he looks away. "I slept at his a lot. First nothing happened, we just cuddled and talked. And partly because of him, Andi, and I didn´t end up together. He sorts of told me not to. We were in Paris on my birthday. And sneaked out to a rave on his. There were some kisses." I tell him and he blinks. "But we never talked about it like it didn´t happen. Most of the time he acted like it didn´t. And we… uhm dry fucked." I say and feel his body next to me tense.

This wasn´t at all how he should find out.

"But somehow after Christmas it was like it didn´t happen. He didn´t kiss me on New Year´s in front of you all, so I gave up on the idea." I say. "So, we were just friends, but it was weird sometimes. We had a fight after I met with my ex. We tried to talk about everything, but we screamed at each other and made things worse." I explain. "Then he went with me to my sister´s wedding but ditched me and went to England." I say.

"But there was never more. No sex." I tell him and he nods. "It was always back and forth. He never said how he feels about me. He played with me and made me a secret." He looks focused. "He didn´t once reach out to me after he left. And then he came back, and he thought I had a thing with Finn going on.." He looks at me. "That´s why he hit him." He puts the pieces together and I nod.

"I told him about us or rather he noticed. He said he was happy for us. Despite, he was *clearly* not." I pause and press my lips together. "He said we should be together. But other times he screamed at me, why his best friend and all. I tried to make him talk to you, but he shut down." I say.

"I´m sorry I didn´t tell you. And earlier he tried to tell me he´s not okay with us, but I played him down. And then he.." I trail off. *Said he loves me.*

He runs his hand through his hair and wipes his face with his palm, holding his face for a moment. "Okay," he brings out. *Okay?*

I can literally watch his mind working. We´re silent for minutes as he thinks.

"Kisses? Dry fucking? Love?" he harps, shaking his head. There is pain in my chest. "Yeah, but we fought often because the whole situation was very confusing and fucked up. He had trouble to open up. And I pushed him too much." I say and he says nothing and just stares at the floor.

"So.. you we´re that girl on Halloween?" He asks looking at me and it pains me, but I nod. "But you dated Andi at that time." He says frowning. "I did, but he knew." I say and his head tilts back. "The games.." He says annoyed and I nod. "Sort of." I say and he rubs his face. "Fuck." He curses.

"And you were lovesick cause of him? That was all cause of him?" He looks at me in horror and I nod.

"We assumed it was about your ex." He says fed up. "It was, but not just." I shrug. "Mostly it was about him." I sigh.

"I thought you were talking about your ex on the stairs." He whispers. "It was at the same time. Both hit me kind of hard." I say and he shakes his head. "Fuck why didn´t you tell me?" He yells. "I´m sorry I don´t know.. I wanted to forget." I say. "He said he wouldn´t come back and I believed him. I didn´t even know he would move. He told me and left." I tell him. "That sucker." He barks. *I say nothing.*

"So, you love him?" He ask and I nod. "And he loves you?" He asks intently. I nod again and he almost laughs.

"We were not something but.. we were not nothing, either." I say silently and he shakes his head slowly as if he can´t process what I´m saying. "I need to.." He stumbles. "I need to think.. I can´t talk right now." He says and I nod, standing up, but stop in front of him. He leans his head against me almost automatically. As I run my fingers through his hair, he tenses and straightens up, catching himself. He stands up and walks past me.

Why's that everyone walks away from me?

I stare into the dark.

I'm afraid of losing my best friend but I'm even more afraid of losing the boy I love. What did I think was going to happen? That Kai would never come back? That things wouldn't be awkward? That this wouldn't happen?

And have you ever thought, that's not my life? That it can't be the right dimension? That it has to be a mistake? How did it all turn out like that? When did I miss the path?

I think that a lot.

116

Kai

She left after they talked but my head is still foggy and my lip on fire. I blink, recalling the day I came back, remembering the talk I had with Aidan.

...

I let myself fall to the couch besides him and gamble a few rounds.

"So, you're really back man?" He asks with a grin, and I glance at him. "Yeah." I nod, facing the screen. "I'm glad. I've been bored without you fucker." He jokes and I grin but my chest hurts. "Sure, about that?" I ask shooting him a look and he smiles.

Silence.

I clear my throat. "So, you and Scar now, huh?" I ask, trying to sound casual. "Yeah." He smiles wide. "What about that?" I rake further, feeling my neck heating. "We're having fun. It's not serious yet." He tells me and I swallow. "But I like her." He says, and my gut districts. "Good for you, man." I smack his shoulder but smacked myself with that. "Yeah, she's a keeper." He says. *Yeah, she is.*

...

I could have told him. It was the last chance to tell him since I haven't told him the past year. But I couldn't bring myself.

I told her I would never tell her. But I did and I did it in the worst way. I said it to everyone, just not her. I wanted to hurt her and him. *As I always do.*

But this time I fucked it all up.

As I enter the kitchen, I see Aidan already waiting. Leaning on the corner, he stares at me. "Look, that earlier was a shit move.." I say but when I reach him, he gives me a right. I expected him to, so I take it. *Crave it even.* I have to stop myself from smiling, even if I know he´d get angrier. I want him to beat me until I black out. But he stops after a few punches because I don´t fight back.

So, we stand in front of each other. "You´re done?" I ask pretending to sound sad to which he glares at me. *Wrong thing to say.*

But I´m not the only one who messed up. He didn´t tell me either.

My anger boils up. "You´re fucking in love with her." I point at him, almost wanting to throw up. *I don´t know why.*

"Yeah, because *I* dated her." He tells me. "You knew. And you dated her behind *my* back. Our backs." He fires back. "We didn´t date." I retort. *Lying again.*

He stiffs a laugh, knowing it´s bullshit. *That fucker knows me too well.*

"Well, *something* had been going on or you wouldn´t *love* each other." He says.

And he´s right. We didn´t date. But there wasn´t nothing either. We did spend time together. All those times I walked her home, I drove over, or she showed up.

They never knew.

"You didn´t tell me either." I say. "Yeah, sorry, but you moved to your parents." He says. "You know me. I always come around." I tell him but he shakes his head. "Yeah, no, but those were *vacations* not I pack my shit and I´m out. This time was different. And you know it." He spits. "Because she´s been the reason you left, right?" He asks and I nod. "So, we both fucked up." I yell upset. "No, *you* did." He barks. "Fine *I* did." I agree.

"Did you fuck her?" He asks. "No." I shot back. "I thought she told you about.." I add. "She did." He says. *But he wanted to know if she lied. Can´t blame him.*

A moment of silence passes, and I know he calmed down a bit.

"I may have fucked her head, but not.. *actually* her." I say and he nods. "You never mentioned that man. I mean, that you thought she was hot, I knew. We all did.. but.." he trails off, and I rub the back of my neck. "I just couldn´t.. handle it. She was driving me insane." I tell him.

"I didn´t know what was going on myself. I couldn´t tell you. No one." I say.

"That girl on Halloween?" He asks absent. "Was it her? The girl you hid?" He asks and I nod. "Fuck." He curses.

"Look.." I begin, but he cuts me off. "I love her," he interrupts me. *I know.*

"I do.. love her too." I admit again, even though I swore I would never say those words. I said them twice now. *And again, not to her.*

"*Shit*," he groans. "*Fuck*." He curses some more. "Yeah," I growl, and he sits down. "Why didn´t you say something? We *always* talk about girls. You could have told me." He says and I lower my eyes. "I know." I rub my face. "Well, you didn´t tell me either."

I say. "Because I was mad you left again. You're my mate. You can't leave me with the shit show we call Neverland." He says and I smile.

"I'm sorry I stopped reaching out but.. idk I needed time." I explain and he nods. "You came back for *her* then." He says, and it's not a question. "I did." I say. "Shit." He hisses. "This is so fucked up." He shakes his head, and I nod. "It is." I say.

He raises his glass in the air. "Booze?" And even though I feel like throwing up, I accept his offer. *Because we need this. Cause I can't lose him.*

~~*I lost my best friend once, I won't twice. Not another.*~~

117

Four days later, Lia

I didn't hear from Aidan for days, which I respect, and I also needed time to process.

Did he really say he loves me? In front of all our friends? After he said he wouldn't. After he pushed me into Aidan's arms more than once.

I haven't talked to Kai. *To none of them.*

So, I'm nervous for today. Cause I'll see both of them. *All of them.*

We're in the backyard having BBQ and the mood is somewhat tense. We ate the first minutes in complete silence.

"So.. uhm you're back for good or didn't you like *move*?" Andi asks Kai to start a conversation. *But more to provoke this.*

Kai's eyes snap to him and all our eyes too. "Yep," he says dryly. "For now." He adds, shoving a fork of pasta salad into his mouth.

Finn looks at him. "What do you mean for *now*?" He asks and our heads wander between them. Kai takes a sip from his drink, taking his time before he speaks. "Just a stopover." He grumbles, clearing his throat. "Now that we're all here and that *jackass* mentioned it." He shoots Andi a look. "I can tell you about my plans." He says, rubbing his neck. "Plans?" asks Nina curiously. "As if you were planning more than your next joint." Shoots Aidan, who's been staring at his beer the whole dinner. To which Kai gives him the middle finger and Aidan fights a smile. *So, it's still loaded between the two. But they will work it out. They always do. At least, I hope so. I don't want to be the reason their bond breaks.*

"Spit it already Dark." Leon barks and Kai nods. "As you know, I've always wanted to travel for a while." He begins, but Aidan cuts in. "You *always* travel." Kai glances at him but keeps talking. "And *now* I think is the best time." He says, and Aidan snorts.

"You just got back, didn't you?" I ask more accusing than I planned.

Now all eyes are on me.

"True." Leon agrees. "I need to figure some things.." he begins. "Didn´t you already *figure* who you love?" Mumbles Nina but Kai ignores her. "What I´ll do with my life." He says. "*Messing other life´s*." Aidan hisses, but again Kai ignores. Leon nods in agreement. "Like that." He says. "Yeah." Ryan joins in.

"Do our parents know about your *plans* yet?" Finn asks. "They will soon enough." He brushes him off. "Besides, they won´t know because I can work from anywhere so.." Kai shrugs.

"Where you´re going?" Ryan asks and Kai scratches his neck before he speaks. "Thailand," He replies, and my eyes fix his, but he won´t look at me. "Didn´t *you* want to go to Bali too, Scar?" Andi asks me. "Yes" I say slowly, but my gaze never leaves Kai. He hasn´t forgotten either, which is why he won´t look at me now. That was a thing on my bucket list a*nd* on his.

"Anyway, I´m leaving next week." He announces. *All heads snap to him.*

"Already?" Nina blurts. "After you told her you love her?" Andi mumbles with a cough and Aidan shoots him a look. Kai nods, ignoring him. "Yep." He nods.

"You can´t be serious." Nina says irritated. "How long?" asks Finn and he shrugs. "Don´t know." He admits and I shake my head. *Aidan looks at me.*

"One way ticket for now. And then I´ll see." He shrugs. "Got until October before college starts again, but even then, I could stay there." He tells us, and I feel like I´ve been transported back. *He leaves. Again. Unclear how long. Again.*

"You´ve been away for three months with dead silence. And you´ve been back for a month, and you want to move on right away?" I ask and I know it sounded like, moved on from me. *I didn´t really think.* But everyone looks at Kai instead of me. Because it´s what we all think. He looks at me. Aidan between us. Kai averts his gaze but it hasn´t been short enough to hurt.

"That´s the way it is, though." He cracks his neck. "You´re all welcome to come along." He grins, but it fades and anger boils inside me. "Why *now*?" I snap and is eyes meet mine. His chin tilts back but he doesn´t say a thing. "You´ve already booked didn´t you?" I ask with a spiteful grin. *All eyes on him.*

He stops mid-nod. "Guys, I know it sucks. But I must do this for me. Take pictures. Write. Be alone and stuff." He justifies and we´re silent for a moment, taking in the news.

Or more repeating history. And I understand where he´s coming from. I want to go there for similar reasons. But still, I´m mad and his timing.

"I´m sure it´ll be great." Nina opines. "Yeah, it´ll be the right thing." Leon nods but I frown. Ryan chats with Kai about surfing so I zone out.

They all except Aidan and Finn are okay with it. They are used to it.

To him leaving. *Again.*

118

Aiden gives me a look across the table that tells me to follow him. So, I stand up as the others get all hyped up about that trip. *All except Finn and us two.*

We sit again on the bench in the Averys´ backyard. It´s been just a few days, but it feels like all has changed. *And maybe it did.*

"Why didn´t you tell me?" He asks right away now clearly ready to talk. "I don´t know.. I was.. confused. I know that´s no excuse. And I know I should have one." I say. "I should have told you right away. I think I wanted to forget." I admit. "And I thought he wasn´t coming back. Or at some point hoped he wouldn´t. I guess I thought we´re done." I say knowing it´s stupid.

He just nods, staring at the yard. "Kai and I talk about women all the time." He tells me. "But the fact that he didn´t mention you *once*.." He trails off. "That *shows* he´s serious." He faces me. *I wonder if there´s something to that. A year ago, Leon told me something similar.*

His head in his hands now. "I´d be lying if I said it didn´t throw me off." I admit and he nods, feeling the same. "Yeah, it was the *loving* part for me." He says half joking. "And the *dry fucking*." He adds and I lower my gaze. "I´m sorry." I whisper. He nods, but it´s more of a shrug.

"You love him don´t you?" he asks after a while and I just look at him, not knowing what to say. He takes it as an answer. *It´s the silence that holds the truth.*

"It all makes sense now." He speaks like he replayed everything that went down last year. *Like now, he can see it.*

"How he´s been acting last year." He looks lost in thoughts. "How *you* have been acting." He shakes his head, gripping his hair. "I mean, we knew he was kind of possessed over you. But we thought because of the games. That he just liked to mess with you." He shrugs. "I mean, *how* did we not figure?" He raises his voice. "It´s been so obvious and right in front of us." He almost laughs.

"Well Andi knew.. and Finn." I say quiet and he looks at me. "Ya´ll my best friends, I wish you would have told me." He says and the hurt in his voice kills me. "I´m sorry. I wished too; he told you. But when this between us started, I should have. *I know that.* I´m sorry we lied." I tell him and he nods. And we fall silent.

"I´m fighting for what I love Scar." He says, looking me in the eyes. "But he´s my best friend." He adds. "*Fuck*," he groans, gripping his hair. "If I had known about you, I never would have.." he stops and I give him a weak smile, telling him to just say it. "I would have never started *anything* with you." He confesses and fuck, *I want to cry and scream.*

But I keep quiet.

That was so honest it hurts. And the worst is that I understand him, but his words make me feel less worthy.

"I just don´t understand why he would drop that *now* that he´s planning to leave." He opines and I nod. *Me neither.*

"Because he tends to run from things." He says, rubbing his face. *Exactly what Finn told me. I should listen more to the things they say.*

But Kai can´t just say *I love her* and then disappear. *Not this time. Not after he broke me again. But does he run from me? Does he want me to join him? Should I join? Do I want to? Of course, I want to go. But I can´t. Right?*

"Maybe he leaves *because* he said it." I say and he nods. "Thought so too." He agrees. "But he can´t just leave now after he messed it all up." I say fed up and he nods.

But we know he already did.

After a while, I hear myself say. "I want to go with him." And it pains me. He looks at me, bit surprised but mostly hurt. "This has been my dream for a long time. And.." I fall silent. But the look on his face rips me as he realizes.

He looks ahead. "You can figure what is between you." He concludes and I shut my eyes for a moment.

"I´m not going to be *with* him, Aidan." I say. "I´m not choosing against you." I say. "I´m choosing me." I explain and my throat swells.

"Our friendship is important to me, Scar." He locks eyes with me. "I love you and him. But I want *me* to be happy. And you two." He pauses, swallowing down emotions. "We both lost that bet anyway." He shrugs. "And the agreement was that we would end it then." I can hear that this is not at all easy for him. *Nor is it for me.*

"No one gets hurt." I whisper his words from back then but stare past him. "Where are feelings, there´s *always* hurt Scar." He mirrors mine, and with that my heart breaks and shatters. It´s like at once it all crushes down on me. Breaking through the layers of skin. Cracking my bones and reaching my thrumming muscle and breaks it. Breaks because already broken hearts don´t heal, they break even more. *Over and over.* Until they open again. *I hope they open someday.*

But how can something heal you that broke you in ways you can´t name?

He gives me a sad smile and I break into pieces at the sight of him smiling at me. *At this moment. When I broke him, and he broke me. He smiles. Genuine.*

It´s hurting but it´s selfless. Aidan is selfless. Kai is selfish.

And what am I? Heartless?

"You won Scar." He says. "I´ve lost the bet before I started it." He admits as he catches my tears that won´t stop falling. But they fall, and with them, I do too. *Fall.*

And there´s no one to catch me but myself.

119

Almost one week later

Kai packs his suitcase and I help him pick out books, swim trunks and T-shirts while I try to figure out how to tell him I´m coming with him. He leaves tomorrow.

He´s on his phone checking his list or something when I decide to speak up. At least I don´t have to look at him when I say it. "I want to come with you." I blurt and he looks up from his phone. Confusion is written all over his face. His eyebrows draw together, and slight lines appear on his forehead.

"What?" He asks. "With you.. to Bali," I reply, stepping closer. He frowns at me a second longer and then his features soften, and he grins. He doesn´t say anything, so I add. "If you *want* me along."

He looks at me for a beat, then grabs me and throws himself backwards on his bed. I squeal caught off guard by his move.

I sit up. *We grin at each other.*

"You´re coming with me?" He asks and I nod.

His smile widens and he crosses his arms behind his head and stares at me with a serious expression. "You´re the only person I want with me, Scar." He tells me and my heart sinks, but I must grin. *I´ve missed that. Him. Us.*

He straightens up and I lose balance, but his hand holds my back as mine grabs his shirt steadying me. *Suddenly we´re so close we haven´t been in months.*

Our faces inches apart.

My fingers dig into the fabric. "You´re coming." He whispers more to himself than to me. "How could I not?" I hush and he smiles but lays his head between my neck and shoulder. *I feel his smile on my skin.*

He holds me tight, and I hold onto him.

He doesn´t know about what Aidan and I talked. But they know we ended things.

Now he knows why. Cause I come with him. Tomorrow.

120

Next day

"I´ll miss you" Luca says into my hair. "I´ll miss you too" I sigh.

Leon hugs me briefly but tight, and Finn doesn´t want to let go of me at all. Nina asks me to bring her a present. And Ryan and Andi hug me both at once, almost choaking me.

As Kai carries the suitcases to his car, the others leave me and Aidan alone. With his hands in his pockets, he takes me in.

I hug him and his hands shoot to my back. My eyes are burning. "I shouldn´t let you go." He says painfully and I squeeze tighter. And I can feel his body doesn´t want to let me go, but he lets me go and I quickly turn around to make it easier for both of us and walk toward the gate. But with each step, the desire to fall back into his arms grows stronger. I squeeze my eyes shot, turn around and run into his arms, he meets me halfway and buries his hand in my hair. I wrap my arms around his neck, and he takes my face in his and presses his lips onto mine. *It´s as if part of me wants to leave and the other desperately wants to stay.*

Because my heart has been cut in two, loving them both.

We pull away, and I turn leave, to see Kai leaning against the wall watching us with a slight frown. But he´s not mad, he looks worried. "Ready?" He asks, but his gaze is on Aidan. I nod and force myself to smile. They both nod to each other.

I have to get out of here fast.

As I walk away, I hear them smack. They hug and a pat on the back. "Take care of her." Aidan tells him. "Always." Kai answers and my throat tightens. *I love them.*

I get in the car shortly followed by Kai and we drive off. Leaving everything behind. Hot tears fall down my cheek as I look out the window, so he won´t notice.

But he does. Of course, he does. He always does.

He reaches for my hand and doesn´t say anything but holds my hand. He takes it away only to shift.

Eventually my tears dry and the sun sets. And with it goes the lump in my throat.

At the gate, I rest my head on his shoulder while he reads to me. On the plane, I sit by the window, and he next to me. We share headphones and listen to music.

We fly first class, and he insisted on paying. Even though I know that won´t be the only thing he will pay for. My feminist wants to be independent, but I understand why it´s important to him. He takes care of me, protects me, shows he cares and pleases me.

So, I let him.

- 27 -

It´s a large bungalow in white. Loud tropical plants and flowers decorate the stone path to the entrance. We have a small kitchenette with an old wooden dining table. It relates to the living room. A white sofa is aligned with the floor-to-ceiling window wall. Small palm trees make the light marble floor look less cold. Through an arched frame, you enter the bedroom. Against the wall is a white bed with wooden frame. By the window front is a freestanding bathtub made of a light beige stone.

The view is breathtaking. The sea. The palm trees. The green rice terraces that extend into the valley. The beginning sunset reflects on the infinity pool in blood orange. A swing hangs near the pool and to the left on the porch is a daybed made of pallets with a white curtain. There are two bathrooms, to my relief. A small one with a toilet and a larger with a rain shower, two sinks and another toilet. *It´s perfect.*

- 27 -

Calling – Vin Bogart

We went with a scooter to the beach.

Once we get there, we run to the ocean and, without hesitation, take off our clothes to get in. I wear my black Brazilian briefs and a black lace balconette bra. Kai, a pair of black boxers.

The sun has almost disappeared, and the beach is empty except for a few people. He grabs me midway and sprints into the ocean with me on his arm. *It is refreshing.*

He lets himself fall into the sea with me and I feel free. The last time I fell in water, I fell alone. *Haunted by him.*

Now I fell with him. *Safe.*

And the only way I want to fall. Him to do it with me or him to catch me.

I forget everything around me.

For a while we fool around in the waves and watch the sun disappear on the horizon. I close my eyes and listen. *The sea roaring. My heart pounding.*

My thoughts disappearing.

When I open my eyes, I catch sight of Kai, who´s watching me.

He does that all the time.

I missed that. Missed him. Whatever we are. I missed it.

His wet hair hangs in his face. He runs through and tousles it once and waits to the beach. I follow him swimming because I want to stay in as long as I can. As he watches me, he grins and sits down at the water´s edge resting his forearms on his knees. He doesn´t take his eyes off me and his gaze wanders down my body.

I stay on my stomach and come to a halt next to him in the sand. I prop myself up on my forearms and let the sand run through my fingers. His gaze burns hot on me as I search for stones.

"I used to collect rocks when I was a kid." I say, grinning to myself. "Rocks?" he asks, amused. I bet there´s that frown on his face.

"Yeah, I have shoeboxes full of them." I admit. "Plural?" He asks and a slight Deja-vu hits me in the back of my mind and I can´t help but think of the day I first saw him. I never imagined how close we would become. *Or Aidan and me.*

Lost in thought, I nod. "You´ll have to show me that collection." He says sarcastic and tries hard to suppress his laughter. "I´ll take your word for it; I´ll show you every single one." I announce with a laugh. "Hm." He hums in agreement. "I mean it." I warn him and he chuckles.

I lay my finds next to us as I make my way through the sand. Kai takes the rocks and places them somewhere else.

As I gain a look, I see he wrote "*Scar*" with them. I smile and keep going.

After a while, he holds his hand out to me. *In his hand a stone.*

"For your collection." He says with a broad grin. It is a small white one, smooth and with a lot of imagination it looks like a deformed heart.

Rather deformed than broken, right?

I smile to myself. "Thank you." I say. "I don´t have one of *those* yet." I try to sound as serious as I can, but he bursts out in laughter but catches himself. "Thought so." He nods. "Your collection isn´t complete without it." He says, trying to suppress his grin.

And he´s right about that. That stone has been missing.

I tuck it into my bra and straighten up to sit down next to him.

"Have *you* collected anything as a kid?" I ask curiously but he shakes his head.

I tilt my chin back, frowning. "Football stickers? *Pokémon* cards? Matchbox?" I list and he shrugs. "Nah." He says. "I´ve never had anything I wanted to collect." He tells me.

That´s sad.

We´re silent for a while.

"What did Aidan say about..?" he asks at one point. His gaze fixed on the horizon and mine too. The water is lit by the moon shimmering. *Didn´t they talk?*

"He wants me to be happy." I answer. "Did you..?" He asks. *Broke up*?

"We weren´t together." I say softly. "I know." He says nodding. "Kinda." I add.

"I´m sorry" he finally says, meeting my eyes. "I know" I say.

We get up and head to our new home for the next month.

"You´re probably the only person who prefers bringing rocks from the beach instead of shells." He opines. "Weirdo." I agree with a smile, as I lay them out on the wooden floor of the patio. My back is turned to him, but I know he´s still standing there watching me do it.

\- 27 -

Kai is taking a shower, and I sit on the swing and stare into the darkness.

We had agreed to have no contact, to gain distance from everything except in the group chat. But now I´m sitting here not even 48 hours later and dial Aidan´s number. After the fifth ring, he picks up. *He wasn´t sure to pick up. And I can´t blame him.*

Silence. No one dares to speak first. So, we´re on the line quietly.

"I shouldn´t have let you go." He says eventually, and I close my eyes at the sound of his voice. "I miss you." I whisper. "I miss you too." He replies.

"Is it nice?" he asks, changing the subject, which I´m grateful for. "Yeah, we went to the beach earlier." I begin to narrate.

I let the cold water run down my body and try to numb my thoughts. I brace my palms against the wall and hang my head.

They broke up. Kinda. Cause they weren´t together. That´s what she said. Aidan told the same. But we weren´t together either. I don´t know what all that means. But I just wanna have a great time while we´re here.

I turn off the water, wrap a towel around my waist and take another to rub my hair. I put on some deodorant and leave the bathroom. She´s not in bed, so I check the living room and kitchen. *She is not there either.*

But when I turn around, I spot her on the swing. She sits with her back to me, so I walk toward door, to see that she´s holding her phone to her ear. I wonder who she´s talking to.

Which I know the answer to.

For a moment, I watch her in pain. *Cause she called him.*

But I force myself away and put on a pair of shorts and lie down in bed.

Our bed for the month. We´re going to share. Right? Or does she want me to move to the couch? I hope not. But I will if I have to.

I cross my arms behind my head and fix my eyes on the ceiling. My vision blurs as my eyes lose their focus.

Does she miss him? Of course, she does dickhead. Does she regret coming along? I don't know. I don't think so. At least, I hope so. Is she homesick? Like after him?

I shut my eyes at the pain and my throat grows heavy. *Fuck. I hope not.*

She told me *we* feel like home. She didn´t say *you.* I told her *she* feels like that.

She didn't. I just thought she meant me. But maybe we feel different about each other. But she's with me here, and I must stop fucking worrying about shit I have no control over. Be in the now.

I push the thoughts away and grab my book from the nightstand, but it´s hers.

Ugh. Whatever. That'll have to do. I need distraction. Now.

So, I flip through the pages and get stuck on the highlighted parts. Underlined with a blue highlighter matching the cover. I smile to myself. *Such a control freak.*

My eyes are glued to the lines. *Page after page.*

Seems like the guy can´t give her the love she wants from him. And the girl wants more from him than he can give. So, she keeps pushing and he shuts down.

Is this a joke? This is about us. I mean on the surface.

Did she choose that on purpose?

Does she like to read sad things? Like, does she want to hurt?

The guy thinks if he could open up, it would be for her. And it fucking hits like nothing else. Because for her, I would. *For her, I did.*

Maybe not willingly, but I did. First, I fell for her. Second, I loved her. Then I broke for her. *Now I'll heal for her?*

It feels like I´m reading her mind or her diary. *Which is bullshit.*

But I can't stop. I love reading her books. Especially searching the lines, she marked. It tells a lot about you, what you highlight in a book.

I read everything she has marked. Devour every bit that tells me more about her thoughts and perhaps feelings. Because she´s not that open about her feelings too.

It's not just me.

But when I hear her footsteps, I throw the book back on the table and stay lying across the bed, pretending I´m already asleep as the sliding door opens.

- 27 -

Lia

It felt good to talk to Aidan, but I promised not to call again. And he promised not to answer again. *See how that goes.*

But I know we need that. *It was the last time.*

Kai lies in bed, and I smile at the sight of him. He´s taking up the whole wingspan. I roll my eyes and quickly hop into the shower.

When I come back, he´s still in the same position. He´s lying on his stomach with his head buried in the pillow *on my side*. His arm hangs off the edge of the bed. He just passed out and I too sense now how Jetlag kicks in.

I take the opportunity to grab his T-shirt and pull it over. *I haven´t smelled him in a long time. Since I´ve stopped sleeping at his. I don´t even remember when.*

I stop in front of Kai, looking down on him thinking about *how* or rather *where* I should lie down. At the foot end is too little space and at the headboard it seems to me too uncomfortable to lie over the pillows.

So, I decide to sleep on the sofa. Since maybe, it´s better not to sleep in one bed. Even though I want to. *Another thing I´ve missed. I can´t even remember the last time we slept next to each other. I want to touch him so bad. I want to be near him. But maybe I shouldn´t.*

But as I turn around, his hand grabs my thigh. *He´s awake?*

He lets out a low grumble and pulls me back. I hear the blanket roll under him, and he makes room for me. *I have to grin. Did he wake up, or did he just lie there consciously all this time? It could be both.*

But I lie down, and he wraps an arm around me pulling me closer. *Into his arms.* And I let him, cause it´s the only place I want to be. *Finally, home.*

122

Two weeks later

He offered to give me space. If I want to be alone. *But I don´t.*

I mean, we do things alone but we´re also here to figure out what is between us. Even if we didn´t talk about doing that we both know that´s one of the reasons we do this. And I know at some point we have to talk about stuff and all, but we need to enjoy our time here too. And I know those weeks will pass in a rush. And then there´ll be the day we leave and I´ll see Aidan again. *But I can´t think of that now. I need to focus on myself and the feelings I have or not have towards him.*

The first days, Kai and I have done workshops. We meditated for almost three hours one morning in one of the most beautiful gardens I have ever seen. Besides that, we took a Balinese cooking class, we also did a sunset tour, swung on a swing above the treetops of the jungle. Collected trash on the beach. We saw elephants, went quad biking, and saw various temples.

The other day we did yoga classes and looked at Balinese art. Kai fulfilled his wish and took a surfing course. As to be expected, he was an ace in contrast to me. I preferred to stay with the standup paddle. But I also can cross something off my list, because we went diving at the wreck of the USS Liberty, where we actually saw baby sharks and turtles.

We both considered getting a tattoo, but we decided to leave it for now.

In sum we had an amazing time. It was light and funny. And we never left the now. We could forget the things that went down, and it was like a year ago when things were different. When we were friends. *Or maybe a bit more.*

But we´ve spent time alone. I was at the beach reading and snorkel the whole day. And he went on a tour making connections and photographing. I went hiking, ended up meditating and collecting stones by a waterfall, and he surfed with guys he made friends with. He wrote a lot in the nature, and I drew a bit.

We also partied with the people we met. *Round about it was a bliss.*

123

Kai

We´re at the butterfly park.

And she looks so happy. I haven´t seen her that much smiling, the past year I´ve known her. It makes me happy to know she´s happy here. *With me.*

She really fucking blooms. She isn´t anxious, she´s free and in the now. We should come here more often. *Maybe every semester break.*

I take pictures of her with my camera. How she´s covered with tiny and huge butterflies.

All different ones.

How disgusted she looks at the spiders in the terrariums (*which amuses me the most*). And she shoots photos with her Polaroid camera of basically everything she finds aesthetic. And I watch her doing it. I like watching her.

Make Art. Draw. Read. Swim. Sleep. Everything. Just her.

I stop at taxidermized exhibits of various insects and my eyes fall on a glass case with blue butterflies.

If a butterfly flutters here, it can become a hurricane somewhere else.

Deja Vu hits me right in the face, the gut, and every fiber of my body.

The day I left I thought about that. I got anxious, thinking about what would happen if I´ll open up to her. So, I left her.

Back then I told myself the day I´ll stop hating myself, I´ll love her. *So, never. I thought.* But now I know the day I stopped hating me, I loved her. I did what I never wanted, or thought I could, and it happened anyway. I don´t say I love her right, but I don´t act like I don´t. *Not anymore.*

Maybe it all had to go down like that in order to be here with her. And maybe if I knew, she went after me. *Maybe I wouldn´t have come back.* Maybe if I would have known she and Aidan started dating. And if I had stayed, maybe I would have never told her I love her.

I wouldn´t have been forced to.

So maybe all *that* was meant to happen. Maybe I was meant to rip those wings. To snap the butterfly in order to see this one. *The blue one.*

To see the value in it. To see her and what I feel for her.

They say you grow the most by destruction. *And maybe I needed it.*

Maybe I needed to destroy it all for us to have it. *For me to have her.*

"*Butterfly Effect*," I hear her say behind me, and I wince. "What?" I turn around far too quickly, seeing it all spin.

She smiles having scared me. "Those blue butterflies remind me of the *Butterfly Effect*." She says, pointing to them and I blink at her shaking my head.

"What?" I repeat, not believing what she just said. *Was I talking out loud?*

I frown, still confused. "The movie?" she asks with a grin. *How did she?*

"Sci-fi thriller starring Ashton Kutcher." She explains as I´m still staring at her like an alien. She must think I´m bonkers. *But right now, I feel like I´m nuts.*

"One of the best movies." She says. "You just have to know that one." She harps in disbelief. *What?*

"I *know* that movie" I stammer, still wondering if she can read my mind. She looks at me frowning, probably thinking *I´m weird.*

We just look at each other for a moment.

"Do you believe in it?" I ask her, still irritated. "*Chaos theory*?" She asks, facing the butterflies. "A flap of wings?" She adds and I hum. "Yes" she says. "Don´t you?" She faces me. "I do." I tell her. *Really fucking do.*

It was one of the reasons I left. *A silly butterfly.*

Masked as a thought. Masked as the future. Masked as a fear. *Masked as Hook.*

It was a butterfly for time. Something not significant. Something I don´t do. Something I don´t pay attention to. *But something that caught mine.*

That dragged me down the rabbit hole. Something that showed me Hook. ~~A Hook I knew years ago, that looked right back at me.~~

Something that made me run. *Something like a butterfly.*

One time I saw the beauty in it. And the other time the horror. *In a butterfly.*

The figuration of beauty.

Something like love. Something like a butterfly. *Something blue. A butterfly.*

"A wing beat of a mourning cloak." I whisper absently, thinking of that picture I took of her at the picknick. "You´re being weird." She says with a half grin, and I shake my head, facing her. "Yeah, no I know." I stammer, scratching my neck. "It´s just.. I thought the same thing.. and then you just.." I stutter stunned. She just grins. And all I see is a butterfly. It´s a beautiful one and it throws me off. *She´s beautiful.*

"*I don´t need stuff to remind me who I am.*" She quotes and suddenly two more of that movie pop in my head.

"I´ll come back for you."

"I´ve already lost you once, I´m not gonna lose you again."

I came back. *Now I won´t lose you again.*

And if a butterfly can cause a tornado, it can also prevent one. *At least, I hope.*

So, this time I don´t snap the wings between my fingers. I hold my hands out for it to land. To let it come to me. *A butterfly. Her.*

124

Days later, Lia

Kai walks out of the bathroom with a towel around his waist. And it hangs way too low to not stare and see the beginning of his dick or the V and his new tattoo.

And the cuts. They´re healed, but new ones since I last saw them.

He grabs a boxer and lets the cloth fall. I quickly turn away, even if his ass is as fine as any other part of his body. But this shouldn´t be the way how I see his dick.

When he changed, I face him as he rumors in the dresser. "You´re still cutting." I say in pain and e stops. *Please don´t explode.*

"Lia," he pleads me. *He´s always using my name and not Scar if he´s serious.*

"Why?" I continue and he breathes annoyed turning to face me, leaning against the sideboard. "Just tell me why you do it, and I won´t ask again." I rake further. "What do you always have with the why´s?" He asks and I just look at him. He grips the sides of the wood and his nostrils flare to control his temper. *I look at him, waiting.*

His head falls back. "Cause, I like to Scar." He says bugged but I still watch him, expectantly *knowing* that wasn´t even the tip of the iceberg. His head snaps back. And his chin tilts up when he knows I won´t let go. "Cause I can." He says, raising his eyebrows.

Why can´t he just tell me?

"Come on." I beg, fed up and his arms twitch in the air. "I don´t know Scar." He yells upset and I narrow my eyes. "I call bullshit." I tell him and he stares at me. "You won´t stop?" he asks. "No." I shake my head, and he inhales. "And you won´t bring it up again if I´ll tell you?" he wants to know, and I nod. "I won´t." I promise.

He runs a hand through his hair. *Once. Twice.*

Rubs his neck and stares off. *Completely zoned out.*

Minutes pass.

"Because not even the only women who was supposed to love me stayed." He states, as his eyes won´t find their focus. "They could have worked less. They could even have taken early retirement if they wanted to. Or pass it to someone else." He shrugs. "But they didn´t want to." He nods to himself. "They didn´t want me." He corrects. "And so, do I." He blinks and my eyes well up.

"I´m not mad at my mother. But she didn´t show me how love is supposed to be." He says, trapped in the void that calls him to keep staring. "I´m mad at my dad, who didn´t show me how to love a woman properly." He says anger rising, cutting his voice. "They didn´t show me how to love myself. To love others." He trails off. "How to be good. How to be okay. How to.." He shakes his head absently.

And then suddenly snaps out of it. His head twists in my direction. "They showed me pain." He tells me, pointing at his chest and I blink the tears away. "That´s all they taught me." He grins almost. But it´s like the devil smiles about something.

Almost like a grimace.

I´ve never seen him like this before.

"That love comes through pain. That love means pain. That love causes pain." He spits like he´s talking to them, not me.

"All I´ve ever known is that, so I need it. I cut to feel it. The love. The pain." He explains. "And if I don´t cut, I get the pain otherwise." He adds. "Because that´s better than all they ever gave me." He stiffs a laugh. "In that way, it is *my* pain. My love. *Mine.*" He says, and the vein on his forehead bobs.

He laughs mad. "And you know the fact that I expect love to hurt shows just how fucked up I am, Lia. I know that. That´s why I kept my distance. At least I tried to. That´s a reason why I left." He tells me.

He grins like a maniac, and it hurts me to see him like that. "Because I love through pain." He says, and his eyes look as if all the cores have burst, dying it bloody red. "And that´s not love." He zoned out again. "That´s just sad." He says lost. "Just pain." He nods.

He shrugs a few times. "So, I don´t know if.. if that´s the reason why I do it." He looks at me. "Maybe it´s some sick way of showing myself love. Cause I´m a masochist." He shakes his head but smiles to stop the tears threatening to spill.

“Or maybe..” He raises his voice. “I just do it, cause I got used to it.” He throws his hands in the air. “Because when they left, I craved the pain they caused.” He says, and tears steam down. “Maybe that´s why I don´t tell those things, to my therapist. Cause I don´t want things to get better. Getting better is scary. Sometimes even scarier than staying the way you are. Cause what if that´s the only pain.. the only love I can get?” He asks and I can´t see for a moment due to tears.

“I´m sick in the head.” He taps his temples, raising his voice fiercely. “I wish to be different. But being okay is scary.” He says, and he´s right it is. Tears run down his face and mine fall too as I´m watching him losing it.

“Maybe I punish myself. Maybe I free myself. Maybe I *hate* myself. Maybe I don´t love myself. Maybe I don´t want myself either.” He yells. “And maybe I do it to stop fucking hurting others. Cause if I hurt me. I hurt less others.” He bites his lip. “Cause it´s a way of coping. A way of dealing. A way of surviving.” His hand comes to his chest. “Cause I don´t know how to love. I just *know* how to show pain.” He says beat, not even fighting the urge to wipe his tears or hide any emotion that shows up. He just bites down on his teeth, causing his jaw work.

I´m unable to speak nor to breathe. We just stand there and watch each other´s motions. I haven´t expected he would open up *that* much but I´m glad he did even if it really hurt.

I don´t know if he wants´ me to say anything. So, I wait for something.

After a moment, his hand reaches for me, and I take it, and he drags me in his arms. His body shakes as he cries, and I hold him.

He kisses my temple as we break away.

He never did that before. Maybe he wanted to kiss me but decided against it.

We lock eyes. “I´ll show you.” I whisper softly and he looks at me in a way I can´t place.

Maybe glad? Hopeful? Sad? Maybe everything. Or nothing.

And part of me *knows* I would take *any* love he can give, even if it´s just his pain.

So, maybe I´m as fucked as he is. Or maybe I just love him with all the pain I have. Because pain attracts pain.

“Pain covers pain. Just as love covers love. Loneliness covers loneliness. So, you cover and add pain and pain and pain. Until there is nothing else but pain. All you´ve ever felt. All you´ve ever used to was pain and loneliness.” He explains, and another sick part of me thinks it´s poetic. “Love isn´t always pain.” I point out and he smiles weakly. “It is Lia.” He tells me with such a conviction I might believe him. “Pain evolutionary shows us that *something* is wrong and bad for us. Pain is *never* good. And all you get from me is pain." He looks at me. "You shouldn´t want this." His voice breaks and I shake my head not believing.

But I should have.

"You think you deserve the pain you let you go through. But you don´t." I say. "Believe me, I do." He tells me. "And even if I don´t. I still need it." He shakes his head slightly and I could scream. It´s like he has already given up on the love others know. Like he accepted that´s really all he can get. *I wish I could do anything.*

He reads my face and speaks up. "You know, sometimes it´s just better to feel the physical pain instead of the psychological." He says. "And for me, the cutting isn´t about suicide, it´s about control. About staying present." He tells me. "*That a burned child loves the fire*, Scar." He quotes and something hurts deep in my chest like he revealed his secret. In ways, I think he did, I just couldn´t see it back then.

"At least that´s what Oscar Wilde thought." He adds and I blink away the tears that won´t stop coming.

"You can´t be poisoned when you´re the venom. So, you become what hurt you." He whispers as if it would hurt less then and I close my eyes.

"Love." He whispers. "I never wanted any of that, and then I met you." He says. "And now I want it all, just to realize I can´t give you any of that without hurting you." He hushes and I know all that is no excuse for how he acted or treated me, but even the devil itself had a parent. And there are *always* reasons why people act the way they do. Lucifer itself was never evil, he just had a free will. His own head and own plans. And today I met him and he´s *everything* but evil. *Just hurt.*

Because what I saw was a broken angel in the devil´s eyes. And he looked like he wanted love. *And not at all pain.*

It´s being said that your eyes hold everything your soul tries to hide.

And his hide love. Not pain.

All I wonder is why he calls me Scar when his body is covered with them. And not just his body but his soul. His laugh, tears, love, and pain. *Covered in scars.*

I hold his eyes as I speak. "*Sometimes even a monster is no monster. Sometimes it´s beautiful and we fall in love with.*" I quote Stephen King, to which he grins.

He loves when I come up with one.

"A monster you love is none." I tell him and he looks at me for long seconds before he speaks. "No. When you love a monster, you´re one too." He simply says. "Then I´ll be one." I say. "Because I´d love to get all your pain." I tell him with a small smile, and I don´t know why but we´re whispering. "Don´t let me feed you pain you confused with love." He tells me softly and I look at him. *Why can´t he left me in?*

"I don´t care. I want it." I tell him, to which he shakes his head slightly. "I want all you have to offer." I say. "It may be deadly." He warns with a faint chuckle. "Then it´ll be worth it." I counter but he´s not convinced. "Pain soothes pain. But love soothes pain too. So let me soothe some of yours." I hush, my breath hitting his lips. His eyes lay on them for a split second before he wraps his arms around me, holding me to his chest.

We lie down in silence.

"But I know it´s bad. You know." He whispers. "Training helps a lot. And weed. Writing. Music. You." He tells me.

"I used to do it *worse*." He says. *Should that help?*

"Believe me, I´d like to stop." He assures me. "I try." He adds and I sigh relieved closing my eyes. "Thanks for telling me." I whisper and he kisses my hair. "Thanks for caring." He tells me as I drift away.

125

We sit on the terrace.

Kai has bought a guitar at the market and I didn´t even know, he could play until he came home with it the other day. He tunes it and I watch him as I scrabble in my sketchbook.

I must grin because I recognize the song, and his voice blows me away. Goose bumps and butterflies´ ways. I thought Leon and Ryan had kick-ass voices but hearing the person you love sing to you is something else.

It´s *Songs for you by Vin Bogart.* I know that because I listened to it months ago, all the time. *Before he left.*

So, he must have remembered that song. I mean, he had no other choice but to listen to my songs just as I had to listen to his. Every time we drove somewhere we listened to my music mostly. We have the same taste overall. But when I listened to different type of songs like this one, he had to listen to them too, even if he groaned or complained. But I know even if he wouldn´t have admitted back then he actually liked most of them. I caught him sing along before turning away, coughing, clearing his throat or covering it. He tapped his hand along on the wheel or bobbed his leg to the beat or his head absently.

The other time he had a catchy tune all day long. He had no idea which song it was. Then he hummed, and I smiled because it was one of mine. He raged and blamed it on me cause I´m blaring and torturing him with all my songs.

But he liked them and that he sings one to me now is the proof. Or maybe just because I listened to them. *Either way, it shows he cares.*

My heart does flips, and my vessels release butterflies. Even though it´s just a song I know it´s another way for him to tell me how he feels. *Just like his quoting´s.*

He hides behind them. But they say so much about what he has to keep.

There are different times when you fall in love with someone. And this is one of those when I fall on my knees for him, and he craves all of him inside of me.

"You shouldn´t have done that." I say as he finished, and he looks at me confused. "Because now you don´t just have to read to me but sing." I tell with a grin, and he suppresses a smile biting his lip, nodding.

"Why didn´t you sing to me before?" I ask and he shrugs. "Never got around to it." He tells me. "And you never asked." He grins. "How should I have known?" I gape at him, but he just smiles and sings another song.

Afterward, we sat in silence for what felt like hours. The sun started to set, and we listened to the sound of the moment. *Trying to hear the others´ heartbeat.*

Until he turned to me and asked. "You wanna know what I.. adore the most about you?" I look at him and I think he wanted to say *love* but decided not to.

He doesn´t speak for a moment.

"You understand my silence." He says quietly. "Because sometimes I do not understand it myself either." His gaze fixed on the horizon. "But you do." He nods. "Like silence´s your language or some shit." He smiles shrugging. "It´s okay to be quiet around you. And it doesn´t feel weird. It feels like peace. It feels right and good. Like trust." He adds and my heart aches. *I never adored a compliment more.*

"I feel the same way about you." I tell him and he´s right, sometimes silence became our way to speak. *Like it was our love language.*

Maybe the only we spoke. Maybe the only we understood.

126

Next evening

"Why did you leave?" I ask him what I´ve been dying to ask. He frowns at me from where he lies on the daybed. "Why are you asking me that?" He avoids answering me. "Cause I wondered." I say as I push myself up from the floor.

"Can we just stop asking questions?" he tries to evade, and I walk up to him. "I know it´s hard for you to talk and all, but I need answers." I tell him. "And you owe me." I remind him and he´s silently looking at me.

"You know I´m right." I say and he in and exhales, *knowing* I have a point. "How about that." I say as I sit down beside him. "Just one question a day." I say and he puts his hands behind his head, watching me intently. "You ask me whatever you want to know. And I must answer." I say. "Then I ask *you* a question, and you have to answer in return." I shrug.

"One question a day." I offer and he considers frowning. "Alright." He says giving in. "So why did you leave?" I ask again, not knowing if I even want an answer now that I might get one. I asked that myself for weeks racking my brains over this. So much that I was at a point where I had already gone through every possible answer.

At least I thought.

He groans at my question as if he hoped I´d forgotten I´ve asked that. "I think.. I left because I got scared of what would happen if I wouldn´t." He admits and I blink at him. "I wasn´t ready to find out. I couldn´t handle. Couldn´t admit." He says and keeps thinking. "It felt right.. so, I panicked. And I thought it would be easier to leave but it wasn´t. It was worse." He tells me and I nod. He left, cause of his feelings for me.

So, Finn was right he´s a runner.

Just as I expected him to not ask me anything, he speaks. "Why, Aidan?" he asks the question I never expected, and my heart misses some beats.

"Why we started dating?" I ask but he shakes his head. "No. Why him?" He clarifies and I press my lips together. "Because.. he made me feel good." I say. "He made me smile and forget." I say, and I almost see him flinch at the last one.

"We were both down for different reasons." I say. "He cause of some girl, and I cause of you. He didn´t know that at that time." I tell him. "It just happened." I shrug. "We kissed. Then dated casually. We were both down for it.. the whole friends with benefits stuff. It wasn´t planned to catch feelings neither to fall in love. We wanted to end it when.. it gets complicated.. but ya know." I explain and he nods. "But why him?" He asks again but I shake my head and shrug, telling him I don´t know what he wants to hear.

He looks at me expecting.

"Because he wasn´t you." I say. To that he seems satisfied and keeps shut. I can´t tell him about the bet, though. I mean, it wouldn´t make a difference, I guess. But I think that´s just between the two of us. *Aidan and me.*

- 27 -

After that it became a habit. Every day we asked our questions.

Sometimes they were lame as *"What superpower would you want to have?"* I said being invisible. Because I could go anywhere without notice. And Kai wanted to stop time while you sleep. Because he learned how to lucid dream and when he did that, he had less nightmares and could be anywhere. That way he would spend endless time dreaming.

I liked that one.

Other times we asked deeper questions. "W*hat´s about the Polaroid?*" I asked and he said he liked how I looked at him. It was a look on my face he would never be able to see cause that´s how I look at him when he isn´t watching. It made him feel special and pleased him. He wanted to have it with him. It showed him how I felt. And he hid it cause he couldn´t admit his feelings for me.

"*Why the pin code?*" I asked, and he *knew* that one would come at some point. He shrugged and said *cause it was the day I met you*. He didn´t say anything further, and I didn´t push him to explain. Cause it´s been the date we met. *As easy as that.*

A day we both seem to never forget.

Another day, I asked, "*Why did you kiss me when we got high?*" And he said he couldn´t not to. But he didn´t say why he backed up after.

Often, he gave one sentence answers. Sometimes just words. But I didn´t say anything, cause I was glad he´d agreed to the thing in the first place.

The other day he asked me, "*Why did you date Andi?*"

Because he was nice to me, I told him.

And I wanted distraction and to make him jealous in a way.

Once I asked what had nagged me the most. "*Why was New Years different?*" *You tell me, h*e said. *He said he wasn´t that sure either why or what was different. It just was. He panicked a lot. He wanted to be near me but couldn´t. Like his head said kiss her idiot, but his body did nothing. Like in sleeping paralysis. You want to move and scream, but you can´t. You can just freeze and watch it happen. So, he did nothing. It scared him how I made him feel. And there was that barbwire around his throat every time he wanted to tell me.*

And then his smart ass asked me with a grin, "*Why was New Year´s different?*" I laughed but he had all right to ask me. *I said I was afraid too. And that I thought it was his turn, so I did nothing. I thought maybe it´s better this way. We´re friends and I don´t want to lose all that*. He just nodded with a grin.

Next day, he asked, "*Why did you go after me at the wedding?*"

I froze and asked *what's that for a stupid question?* And he asked *if that was my question*. I just laughed and then I told him *I couldn't believe he left. I wanted to see him one last time.*

For him to see what that did to me. I wanted him to stay.

I asked, "*Why did you tell me it was okay dating Aidan?*" He shrugged and said *cause it was, but it also wasn't. He wanted us to be happy, but he knew it would kill him.* I wanted to cry as he told me.

"*Why did you join me?*" he asked. *Here?* I asked and he nodded. *Cause I wanted to,* I shrugged. *I wanted to be with you.* I told him.

"*It wasn't a bet?*" I had to ask him. *He told me no, it wasn't.*

"*Why did you break up?*" He asked me. *We didn't,* I said. *I know*, he said.

But you know what I mean, he added.

Because I love you, I said, and he bit his lip and nodded. *Good reason, h*e said.

"*What are you most afraid of?*" I asked him. *You*, he said, and I know he meant it in a way, but I rolled my eyes at him. *No really.* I raked further. *You know my Hook.* He told me. *Yeah, I know, but I mean what are you afraid of?* I asked him. *Myself.* He said and I frowned but didn't asked further.

You? He asked and I didn't call him out on his second question there. *Spiders*. I said and he smiled at me. But I knew he meant something deeper than that.

"*What cake was yours?*" I asked him, squinting my eyes. He grinned, pressing his lips together. *What do you think?* He asked, licking his lip. *Is that your question, then?* I asked him challenging. He shook his head grinning but then his face fell. *For you I would.* He said softly and my heart stopped.

"*Why was it a secret?*" I asked quietly. *What?* He frowned. *Us?* I whispered. He looked at me lost and pained. *Because.. I knew how it would end.* He told me. *I think it was easier to hide in the dark,* he said.

"*Why did you hate me?*" I asked. *I didn't hate you.* He said. *But you were a dick.* I told him and he smiled for a sec. *I was. But you liked our insults, didn't you?* He asked.

I did.

I knew if others made fun of you in a way that hurt you, you shut down. You're silent. But you wouldn't say a thing. He told me and read me like a book. *But with me, you would say those things. You would speak up for yourself if I hurt you. So, I made fun of you. And made sure no one besides me would.* He said and I smiled.

"*Why did you stop with those quotes on your Shirts?*" I asked and he looked at me considering. *Cause, you made me speak.* He said after a moment.

"*What's that tattoo about?*" I asked and he looked at me questioning. *The "scar" above your scar.* I clarified, referring to his new tattoo at his waist. Next to the word *Hook*. His face went pale. "Nah." He shook his head. "Won't tell ya." He brushed me off. "You have to answer." I reminded him and he groaned annoyed. "Well.." he shrugged. "It's about a scar." He grinned and I shook my head. "Fuck u." I scoffed. "You first." He smiled smug and I smacked him. "I see Pan still makes his own rules." I said and he smiled smug. "I'll tell you.. *someday*." He said, and I gave in. *Someday.*

We got used to the questions and opened up easier. We always gave an answer, even if it was just a cryptic respond, but we did not *once* skip one or chickened out. But he wouldn't be Kai if he wouldn't have quoted occasionally instead of using his own words. But every time he steals the words, they fit like his own. And it made me smile even more.

Sometimes, we waited for the other to finally come up with a question. It was my favorite part of the day, besides the cuddling at night and the other touches throughout the day.

When we had no questions left, we asked stupid things like "*What are you thinking about?*" And other times things like. "*How are you?*" or "*What made your day?*" The latter I asked him, and he told me *talking to you*. And that made my day.

But Nothing happened between us yet. And it's okay, but I feel the tension growing with each minute.

Maybe things would have been different if they had continued to ask those questions.

But they stopped. And with that, the issues came along soon.

127

Two weeks later, To You Alone – Tom Rosenthal

I sit on the wooden terrace enjoying the rain on the surface of the infinity pool.

It rains a lot here. It's what I like about it the most. *It's our weather.*

Because when others get out when the sun shines, we go when it rains and storms. Like we need the rain on our skin to survive. And just like others need the sunrays kissing their skin, the rain kisses ours.

We sit a lot in the rain and meditate. *It's what we do and what we are.*

The sound of the pattering along the roof and down the banana leaves soothe me. Like the waves, it makes me sleepy.

But I´m brought back when Kai sits down next to me. He rests his arms on his knees and in the corner of my eye, I see that he´s holding *something*. He runs his fingers over it.

But I can´t see what.

"I´m darkness." He says, looking ahead. *So, cryptic Kai today,* I smile. "Black is the absence of light. The absorption of all color." He tells me.

Okay, now we have an art lesson?

"How can you love something that´s not even a color?" He asks, still letting whatever *it* is wander between his fingers.

"Yin and Yang are two dual forces that oppose yet relate to each other, not fighting but complementing each other." He says and pauses holding *the thing* in a fist.

A moment of silence passes and thunder rumbles in the distance.

"I promise I´ll try for you." He says painfully and finally looks at me. I´m a bit confused what he´s talking about though. "You changed it." He adds almost in a whisper. *What?*

He looks away again. *Changed what?*

His voice is small when he speaks. "I think I love you, Scar, but I don´t know how to do it." He admits looking down on what he held before. My eyes lower to his hands to see it´s a ring. *A silver ring. With yin and yang on it.*

"I bought it at the market today." He says quietly. "Handmade." He adds. "I didn´t know what size you were. But it didn´t even fit on my pinky, so I thought it should fit you." He turns it between his fingers, and I watch him. "It´s a promise ring." He says and looks at me.

I promise I´ll try for you.

He holds it out to me between his thumb and forefinger and I look at it. It´s an old silver. It has scratches and dents. In some places, it´s tarnished black. It´s thin and a little bent at the bottom. I take it and try it on the index, middle, and ring finger.

I try the other hand.

"My fingers are too thick." I whine and he looks at it with a smirk. "Give me your hand." He demands as softly as he manages and takes the ring and my hand in his other. Then he slips the ring onto my pinky, where it fits perfectly.

"It´s a promise. It should be on the right finger." He says, still holding my hand. My organs melt and my eyes burn. *I never wear rings there, but I kinda like it.*

"Thank you." I whisper and clench my fingers into a fist, causing his to grip mine and a moment of silence passes.

He´s the brightest black I´ve ever seen. He might be dark and broken. But he´s glowing. And I´m drawn to him. *Hypnotized.*

"You can love it because not any other color could ever be more beautiful than black." I tell him and I know it´s not a color but it´s the dye of his eyes.

Black. The absence of light. The absorption of all color.

He looks at me. "And.. *your beauty never ever scared me.*" I quote the song *Mary On A Cross by Ghost.* And without letting go of my hand, he holds the side of my head to kiss my forehead. He rests his chin on my head, and I lean into him. Even though I wanted him to kiss me, I know that gesture meant much more than our lips touching.

It was meant as a promise.

That day he promised her to try.

But somewhere along the line she stopped looking, he did.

[NOTEBOOK ENTRIES]

She didn´t try to drown herself, but I bet the people made that out of it. Just like they did to me. She wanted to drown the things inside of her head. She wanted silence.

I wanted to tell her how those months have been for me. But she turned me down. She´s right I kept her a secret. But she kept me, too. I´m not the only one to blame.

They all heard what I said. I wanted to hurt her. But that was low. We never fought over a girl. I never wanted to tell her those words. And now I used them against her. Aidan knows me and my struggles. But I stepped back. I´ll leave anyway. I´m glad I got it out, but it was a fucked-up way. Now they at least know why I´ll leave. Or what adds to the never-ending list. I told Aidan I was drunk and stoned when I said those things. I meant them, but I don´t want to ruin things for them, even if I already did. I don´t care about my happiness. I´m happy when they are. But I can´t stay and watch them.

He said they got to a hold. I feel like shit. I did that. I´m not a good friend.

I haven´t talked to her. I didn´t want to make things worse. But she came over telling me she would come. I don´t know what it means, but she had chosen me. At least in a way.. I guess they need space. And I´ll give her space if she needs. I wanted to kiss her. But I can´t mess up again. But I´m afraid I eventually will.

I never wanted to believe she loves him, but when I saw them saying goodbye, I knew. I don´t know what happened between them when I was away, but it had to be a lot.

She´s weird but I love it. Because at a beach full of shells, she picks up stones. That´s why I adore her. She´s herself.

If she´ll chose him, I don´t know if I´ll can let go of her.

I make her smile and it's the best feeling ever.

Opening up gets easier. She's patient. But she came up with those questions. I thought it would annoy me, but it was my fav part of the day. And I noticed she started quoting. One of the things she adopted from me. I fucking adore it. I always think in quotes, but I kept them to myself. Even around my friends, but around her, I have to share them. Because I know she gets it. She makes me creative and write. Like my thoughts matter. Like all I do does. She makes me proud. Maybe I'll read to her. Maybe I'll show her. Someday.

Before I might lose her again before I even had her once. I need her.

128

September, One Week left, Kai

Only the light of the moon illuminates the room and through the speaker, drones *Work Song by Hoizer.*

Scar and I are dancing. Because her question of the day was, "*Will you dance with me?*" So, I hold her hand and body close to mine and dance as my other hand rests on her lower back and move in time to the music.

Actually, I hate dancing like this. I've never really danced with a girl like that before. Not more than grinding. But with her, I've danced more than *once* and every time it felt more like just dancing. *It felt like something I don't hate at all.*

Because feeling her forehead against mine, her hand in mine and her fingers on my bare chest makes me resist ever stopping. And for the first in a long time, I feel at home.

I always feel like that with her.

All I notice is her warmth and the beat of the music in my chest. And right now, I believe the myth of Zeus splitting humans in two for them to find each other.

Because I might have found mine.

I spin her again and again, making her black dress spin. *She looks stunning.*

Our eyes are on each other, and I sing along softly but exaggeratedly to make her smile and laugh. *Successfully. I love her giggle or hearing her laugh.*

It turned into a show of me dancing and singing overacting and her watching me in amusement. She shakes her head at my goofiness, but it just fires me. My skin burns from her gaze, and her eyes seem gray today.

I hold her close to me and softly sing to her the words I can't say and feel every line.

And I know she does too.

I hold her to my chest and stare into her eyes. Her arms around my neck, grazing my hair and my sculp and when the refrain comes on, I spin her, and she twists like a merry-go-round. And I watch that smile on her face. Her eyes are closed until they fix mine again.

Then I turn her one last time, and she falls into my arms. The tension between us is hellish and I´m totally and utterly consumed by her. Every cell in my body screams for her and if I´m honest, they have been ever since I first saw her. So, I finally give in before the time runs out. *Before Hook gets to us and in our way.*

And reach for her cheek and press my lips to hers. *And let go.*

And this time I won´t pretend it didn´t happen. *Because it did. It happened.*

- 27 -

Lia

Relief spreads throughout my body. *And pain.*

Pain I have carried with me for over a year. Every time we´ve argued and kept silent. Every time, we got closer and moved away.

It hurts so much. I feel it in my bones. It runs through my veins like venom and spreads making my heartbeat unsteady, my knees buckle, and legs give in.

I´ve never kissed anyone whose kiss was so painful. Not even the kiss, after my ex´s breakup, and we had a one last time together, knowing it´s still over, hurt as much as this one. I can´t even tell you why it hurts so much. *Only that it does.*

Maybe because the last kiss was months ago. Maybe because my body tells me to cry in relieve. *Whatever it is, it is painful.*

Just like the love he promised to give. Pain. But a good one.

One you crave more of it. One you don´t want to end. It´s a kiss of him.

Usually when you kiss, it feels like finally but we didn´t have that. *I didn´t.*

It didn´t feel relieving. It felt heavy. It isn´t supposed to be like that. Right?

My throat tightens and my eyes burn. While in my stomach, *everything dies.*

Our love is not a rainbow, but the rain shower. *The storm.* No colorful butterflies, but black ones. Not a sunrise, but a sunset. Not inspiring but crushing. Not lukewarm, but intense. *Bleeding. Dark. Black. Pain. Is that what love feels like?*

The feeling of not being able to breathe. The feeling that a kiss isn´t close enough. The feeling of kissing Kai for the first time in what feels like a lifetime.

Or is it just him that makes me hurt? Is his love pain?

The song changes to *I wanna be your girlfriend by girl in red* as Kai lifts me by my thighs and carries me to bed. I wrap my arms around his neck, and he slowly lowers me onto the sheets without breaking our kiss.

Now it stopped hurting at all. Maybe it was like burning a wound. Hurting like hell, but after it heals. Maybe we needed the pain and hell to reach for heaven.

His body crouches over mine as he supports himself with his forearms. His groin presses against my pulsing clit as his hand travels up my thigh to my butt and pushes my dress a little higher. I wrap my legs around his waist to bring him closer and claw the muscles of his back.

He lifts me again and stands up. "*Do you trust me?*" he asks his question of the day. "Yes" I whisper against his lips. "Good." He hushes and kisses me carrying me to the bathroom.

Leaving the lights off, he walks into the shower and frees one hand to turn on the spray. Warm water drenches my dress.

Next, he slides me down and pulls the wet fabric over my head. I feel his breath on the crook of my neck as goosebumps spread down my arms to my breasts. He kisses the spot behind my ear, and I lean against his swelling, breathing heavily.

Deja-vu hits me. Hoping silently this time, he doesn´t stop. And I know he won´t.

His chest rises and falls violently as he lays his head on my shoulder and his weight rests on me for a moment. He lets himself be vulnerable with me.

The next moment I feel him strip off his shorts, and now only our underwear separates us. The thought of his naked body against mine makes me inhale sharp.

He moves his hands from my neck down my sides to my briefs and slides his fingers up and down. He kisses my neck and turns my cheek to kiss me. With pressure, he strokes over the fabric, and I stretch my ass against him. Whereupon he throws his head back and we bump against the wall. I moan with every circling movement, and he murmurs in my ear. With his other hand, he grabs my hip to give himself support. And the second before the next song starts, there´s only Kai´s groans and the water running.

I reach behind me, tug his boxers down and I let out a moan as his cock grazes my back. He unfastens the clasp of my bra and tosses it away, yanking my panties down. Next, he presses his dick against my ass and reaches for my breasts. Longing for his thumb on my swell, I touch myself.

As his hand finds mine, he moans and guides mine and I melt under his touch. His fingers play with my nipple as he inserts two fingers inside me, and I explode with pleasure.

I reach for his length and encircle it, and he twitches in my hand. Slowly I slide over his shaft enjoying what effect I have on him. Then he inserts my fingers with his and his other rests over mine on his erection and we climax together.

We´re still leaning against the wall as we let our breathing come to a rest.

Kai brings me one of his black T-shirts, and we lie down in bed. He lies facing me and I lie on my side.

I get goose bumps when his fingers run over my tattoo on the side of my hip. From the Scorpio to my butt and the beginning of my thigh.

"Love your scars." he whispers. *The scratches that turned into scars are from my ex. Three years apparently aren´t log enough for the red to fade away.* And maybe he has left me like that song says with his marks, "*reminding me to forget*."

Or reminding me not to. Because they, won´t vanish.

"Even though I know they´re from him.. I kind of love them." He says after a moment.

So, do I.

"Is that weird?" he asks, and I shake my head. "No, it´s not." I say.

It´s not. It´s love. And not pain.

130

The last days we´ve spent between the sheets. The constant rain shower was one of the reasons but not only.

We haven´t had sex yet but *anything* else. We can´t keep our hands off each other and it´s good we did get to that point at the end of our trip or we wouldn´t have left the house once.

We made the emotional bond over the past year and now we´re making the physical one. Mapping out and Memorizing every curve, every muscle, and every scar. We´re like teenager exploring it all as if it´s our first time. And it feels like the back and forth was worth it. Waiting was worth it. *Hurting was worth it.*

- 27 -

Sometimes (Backwood) – Gigi Perez

Like the past days we end up kissing in bed.

He hovers over me. *Skin on skin. But it´s too far away. As always.*

I bite his jaw because I figured his love language is biting. Or pain as a whole. It turns him on, and he likes biting or scratching me. *I like it too.*

I mean he told me before he likes pain but it´s really a thing. *A thing I like a lot.*

He groans in pleasure as I bite his lip. Then his neck and his shoulder.

He slips on a condom as in the past days. *Even if we just had heavy petting.*

He holds himself up with one hand and slides his groan over my wetness. Every time he slides over my clit I bite down, and he shivers. He groans and keeps up his pace. His chest and neck are covered in marks and hickeys. *I have them too.*

He really loves through pain.

But is it justified if you love it? At least right now it feels like it. Like it´s love.

His eyes close in pleasure and his jaw works. I drag him down on me because I need him closer. I wrap my arms around his neck, and we moan in sync as our bodies rub together. I open my legs making room for his body.

He straightens up a bit to look at me and guides himself to my entrance teasing me.

Watching me.

And my eyes beg him to connect us not just physically but spiritually. It´s the last bond we need. *After that there´s no return and we both know.*

He stares down on me his eyes holding mine as he slowly pushes inside me, enjoying every inch. He takes his time and our eyes lower watching him enter me. Not wanting to miss any second.

Our lips part and he groans as he reaches deep, and our skins touch with a slap. He repeats the motion still watching me and slowly taunting. Torturing both of us.

But I need him close.

So, I reach for his back and neck and make him kiss me. Then I force his ass with my legs toward me. But we break the kisses almost every push cause our lips part in moans. I grab his hair; he holds my head. He speeds up a bit and his balls slap me causing an electric tingling to my clit.

He lowers himself on me fully and I love his weight. Love suffocating under him as he chokes me while pacing and hitting deep my consciousness with every thrust. I hold onto his arms scratching his back.

He holds himself up searching for my eyes again. And his black ones filled with pleasure swallow me. "Bite me." He begs needing me to finish him. So, I meet him and bite down over his collarbone. He holds the back of my head as he crushes down on me climaxing. He spills in the condom breathing hard and I come undone at his sounds.

His weight hugs me as we lay there for minutes, breathing each other in. Calming our racing hearts that won´t stop beating for the other.

He´s still inside me when he kisses me, and we fall asleep.

And as we wake up, we´re still lost in each other.

He finishes me again and I come twice after I gave him head.

- 27 -

We had sex just that one time. But it was enough for me to know this had changed everything. *What that everything was I would find out soon enough.*

131

The flight was tense. He´s been nervous and all in his head but I was too. Trying to figure out what I feel. *Because honestly, I don´t know.*

But when I see Aidan and the others at the exit. I can´t help but run to him. Jumping, I wrap my arms around his neck, he lifts me and spins us. And suddenly it´s as if I hadn´t been gone for a month. As if I haven´t slept with his best friend. At that moment it was just us. We didn´t kiss, but I know he wanted to.

He sets me down and I hug the others. After that, Kai brings me home. But not three hours later, I´m at the Dark´s again because I must talk to Aidan before the party starts.

I sit down at the edge of the pool, and he gives me a sideways glance. "So, between you two?" he starts, and I don´t know if he has talked to Kai, but I nod. "We kissed and had sex, on the last evening." I admit. "*Fuck.*" He wipes his mouth and nods a few times. He curses and I know we *knew* the answer. *But now it´s real.*

"At least now you have certainty." He says absently. *Do I?*

I say nothing and he groans, cupping his mouth. "I´m a complete idiot." He says, gripping his hair. "Aidan," I counter. "No Lia." He looks at me. "I was stupid to lose my best friend by falling in love with her." He yells and my face heats. "You didn´t lose me." I try to calm him. *But I´m not just lying to him; but to myself.*

He shakes his head. "I don´t think.. I can just be friends with you." He tells me quiet, and my throat tightens and heart breaks. And again I´m losing people.

How did it get so far? I let it happen. Feelings, *sex, and love. Ruin everything.*

We just look at each other, trying to think of a way how things can be normal again. But we come up with nothing. *We can´t change what happened.*

"All I know.." he begins, looking ahead. "Is I care about you. And would it be anyone else.." He shrugs and looks at me. "Then I´d take what I want." He tells me. "What do you want?" I ask before I can stop myself. "To be with you." He says the words Kai never got around. Words that make my heartbeat faster. I don´t even know what Kai wants. Or what I want. But he knows and he´s the only one who´s honest. Kai acts out of intuition. *Emotions.*

But Aidan knows exactly why and what. *And he tells me.*

He shakes his head. “But he´s my best friend Scar.” He says looking up the sky. He´s silent for a while. *Thinking.*

“Fuck, I don´t know.” He hisses. “I need to talk to him.” He gets up and I stay rooted. He didn´t ask me what it all means. Maybe because it´s obvious. But not for me.

Not at that time.

I was confused and couldn´t see. I just saw I loved them both for different reasons. I didn´t want to lose them. And deep down, we all knew but it scared us too much to face reality and to stop before things would get confusing. To face that this would change everything. *Our friendships. It would change it all.*

- 27 -

The party has been going for a while and Aidan and Kai talked. They said we should talk later, and I guess we should. *The three of us.*

“So, you love them both?” Andi asks curiously but I´m quiet. “It´s okay.” He tells me, breaking my silence. “Is it?” I ask, facing him. “I guess so.” He shrugs considering. “Kind of.” He adds, tilting his head. “At least it makes sense.” He says and I look at him questioning. “That you feel for them.” He clarifies when he sees my expression and I sigh. “Well, but it feels *anything* but okay.” I tell him.

“What´s not okay is leaving the situation the way it is.” He shrugs. “Sit down and talk.” He says. “Yeah, we´ve planned on that.” I tell him. “Good.” He nods.

“Why can´t it be easy?” I complain, rubbing my forehead but he smirks at me. “What?” I ask. “Is it *that* hard? Or are you just not ready to stick up for your feelings?” he asks me. “To fight for what you *really* want?” He adds. “Face the truth?” He continues and I groan cause he´s right. “I think you already know the answer, just like back then with me.” He shrugs. “Now is no difference. You may love both. But you know you love *him* more.” He tells me what I indeed already know. But I don´t listen to that part of me. Because if I would admit that to myself now, then all that happened between Aidan and me would be a lie. *But it wasn´t.*

“You know I´m right. Otherwise, you wouldn´t have hesitated to reject Kai when he told *everyone* he loves you.” He says. “And you wouldn´t have gone with him.” He calls me out before he leaves me with that and my third cup of vodka.

He has a point. The guilt I feel shows it, but I drown it. *I can´t feel that now.*

And deciding would mean changes and losing both. It would mean losing control. And that´s the last thing I want. *Facing my Hook.* But she was about to face it.

Hours later, Affection - BETWEEN FRIENDS

Kai, Aidan, and I sit on the sofa. *Drunk.*

The party is over and we´re the only ones left. And we *wanted* to talk.

About everything.

But the boys had the glorious idea of having a drink first. And one drink became *many* drinks. *Lots of shots.*

And now we had *enough* to forget about how shitty this triangle situation is. Pretending things are normal. *Even if they aren´t.* That this isn´t a crossroad or messing with our heads.

Just for a few hours we pretend to be best friends that party to forget. And that´s what we do. *Party and forget.* We dance, sing, smoke weed and get wasted. I know it would be better to leave or say something that will stop us from or making it worse. Because that´s exactly what we´re doing right now.

But Kai holds my cheek and pours liquor into my mouth, and I kinda forget why we´re here in the first place. And they grin and I get lost in them. *In those lost boys.*

I grab the bottle from his hand and do the same to him. Next, I kneel over Aidan´s lap and let the drink flow down his throat. His hand moves from my thighs up to my hip as I hold his neck, making him swallow.

We look at each other. His gaze heated and my clit starts pumping, and he licks his lip.

I know that look. He´s horny. Fuck me eyes. Hungry eyes.

I feel the urge to kiss him. *Now.* In front of Kai. *What am I thinking?*

Aidan gives him a look, but I don´t dare facing Kai. Then he grins, and before I can think further, he reaches for my cheek and presses his lips onto mine. His hand slides down and kneads my ass as a relieved moan escapes me. His wild kisses force me all the way down onto his lap. *He´s already hard.*

His tongue forces mine to play with his, and he rocks my ass on his length. I moan into his mouth as he groans, satisfied and I run my hand through his hair. *What am I doing?*

Kai sits not even an arm length away from me. And I kiss his best friend. But why doesn´t he do anything? Like ripping me from his lap or beating Aidan´s ass?

I pull back and see Kai watching us. *And there is no anger.* There is just.. *lust.*

His arm is on the backrest, his chest rises and falls but that´s the only sign he´s pissed. His jaw clenches and his eyes burn into us. *Maybe liking it? That can´t be.*

I´m afraid Aiden might feel how much I´m throbbing, so I stand up.

I don´t know what I´m doing anymore.

But Kai gets up too, looking down on me.

I am wet. Throbbing. Anxious but excited. And wanting more.

When he slams his lips down on mine and lifts me up, I just want one thing.

Sex. With Kai and Aidan.

I feel his boner through his jeans and have the final proof of how much he liked what he saw. He kneads my ass, and I grind on his erection moaning as he bites my lip. He murmurs too as I bite him, but he sets me down, and I feel Aidan´s chest blocking me. His crotch at my back, caging me in. My heart pounds in my chest. The two of them lock eyes over my head. *I always knew I´d like to have a threesome, but I´ve only now realized how much.*

They exchange looks I can´t place and they talk without talking. But then Kai moves to get another joint as Aidan´s hands find my waist, holding me in place. He lights it and they share it as they sandwich me. Kai takes a deep puff, blows the smoke in my mouth, and passes the Jibbit to Aidan. He does the same, holding my jaw to bend my head back to kiss me. They both take turns, and I let them spit the booze into my mouth. And not two minutes after that, we´re in Kai´s room, and I´m sitting on the edge of the bed. In front of me, the two men I´ve grown to love. Both I want right now.

Aidan reaches for his T-shirt and pulls it over his head. Kai begins to undo his belt, and I watch. Then they come for me and undress me, taking their time. I lie between them. Aidan in front of me and Kai behind me. I slide them the condom on. I push Kai´s with a firm grip and he watches me closely gasping with a groan. His lip´s part to which I kiss him, and he hardens further under my touch. Aidan´s I push slowly in a teasing way, so he moans with pleasure, closing his eyes throwing his head back pressing his lips together. *I like to watch their reactions. And to have control over them. But I also like to give them control over me.*

My head is foggy, and my knees shake. They both take turns guiding and sliding their erections over my pussy. I´m so wet they bump against each other.

But they don´t stop. They just keep going. Pacing up and going rigid.

Aidan moans in my mouth and Kai in my ear as they once again grind onto each other.

They liked it.

And hearing them sends me over the edge, and I come. Kai kisses my neck and bites teasingly. Aidan kisses my nipple, licks, nibbles while his hand caresses the other. He runs circles with his finger, rubs and pinches lightly.

Sensory overload. My whole-body tingles.

We sweat on each other and Kai kneads my ass biting my neck and back, giving me goose bumps. He circles his length over my entrance before he pushes inside of me, with a grunt. When he pulls out Aidan slides right inside and Kai smacks his tip against my ass, waiting for his take. They keep going like that, torturing all of us. And my heart beats not only in my chest but in my throat and pussy. They take turns thrusting into me and I gasp very time they enter and push back. They groan in satisfaction.

It´s addicting.

They feel so different. Aidan´s cock is thin whereas Kai´s is thick. Both long and rock hard. They keep pushing and grinding until they lose temper. Lost in rhythm, they start to thrust uncontrollably into me. Both at the same time.

Fuck. That feels.. like pure affection between friends, lovers and more.

They´re moaning, groaning, breathing hard, as they move closer to sandwich me and I wrap my leg around Aidan´s back, dragging him closer as Kai´s fingers rub my clit from behind. His chest presses against me and our bodies melt skin on skin. Until not just our bodies collide, but something else. *Part of us.*

Kai forces my face to kiss me while Aidan sucks my neck, leaving marks for sure. Then I grab hold on Aidan´s neck and pull him towards my lips sticking my ass towards Kai who grabs my cheeks and rocks harder, slapping me between thrusts. He bites my shoulder hard as Aidan and I kiss.

The room is filled with us panting. "Fuck did I miss your pussy" Aidan moans into my mouth and in response, Kai grabs me by my throat and pulls me back to his chest.

Away from him.

He holds my neck tight, hitting me deeper. *I love his possessiveness.*

He chokes me as I watch the expression on Aidan´s face that I know all too well telling me he´s ready. "I´m close, let me finish." he breathes between clenched teeth´s to which Kai lets go of me and slides out. I whimper due to his absence, but Aidan pulls me onto him. He lets me take control and grabs my hip digging his finger into my skin, helping me move. I make eight circles knowing he likes that the most and hold onto his chest, trying to keep up pace.

When I look over to Kai, he locks eyes with me as I ride his buddy.

He touches himself. Watching closely.

Never taking his eyes off me as he fists himself.

My lips part as I watch him. His veiny hands and his twitching muscles send me almost over the edge again. But I tear my eyes off meeting Aidan´s.

They burn on me. He watched me watching Kai.

His body shoots up and he holds my back tight as I wrap my arms around his neck and rock my hips meeting his. I grip a handful of his hair, scratching his neck and he moans in my mouth as he thrusts a few more times and comes inside of me.

As he recovers, Kai grabs hold of me and lifts me easily in his arms. Our eyes lock as he lowers me on my back and forces himself between my legs. He thrusts into me till our bodies slap, and we watch him enter before he lowers his body to mine and our foreheads touch. He kisses me and buries his head in my neck biting me, kissing me, and sucking on my skin. He´s holding my throat as I scratch his back and fist his hair between my fingers. First, he´s slowly and then solid. His skin covered with a thin layer of sweat, and mine too.

I feel my orgasm build up, so I bite his neck to muffle my noise and hold onto his biceps afraid to fall. But he steadies me, holding me as firm as his thrusts are.

He collapses onto me as we both climax. *And with that, we lost control.*

133

Rays of sunlight wake me.

I lie on Kai´s chest for a few seconds, watching him until I realize that my legs are not only intertwined with his, but also with Aidan´s.

And then reality hits me. That wasn´t a wet dream. This did happen.

And it crushes down on me. I had sex with both and instead of talking, we got drunk. Instead of me being honest, I messed up even more. And all at once, I realize what we´ve done. *What we´ve done.*

Maybe this was the end. Maybe this was what they both wanted. The end. It was their idea to get wasted. Did they plan this? They suggested to wait for the party to end. For them all to leave. For us to be alone.

My face heats and my stomach turns. I can´t help but think of the way they exchanged looks before Aidan kissed me. He grinned and Kai didn´t budge.

Did they know? Did they want this?

I feel dizzy. *Was this a game? Was this planned? Did they..?*

They said they fucked the same girls. They messed with each other. Did they mess with me? Their friendship would be saved, and they could dump me now. Was this all a game?

No, this was no game. It was a mistake. It was a goodbye. It was a way for them to save their friendship by sealing it with getting me laid. And I´m the disruptive force in our relationship. They both wanted it.

Aidan told me he doesn´t know if he can be friends with me. And the last thing he told me was *he´s my best friend Scar*. And then they vanished for hours talking. And at the party they boozed. And Kai, idk what he thinks. He´s usually protective over me. He wouldn´t let *anyone* get close to me let alone touch me or fuck me.

Would he? Well, but he did. He fucking did.

But I think they liked it. *Did they? Of course, they did. They´re guys. No guy would decline a threesome. Not even the ones you love. Especially them.*

Why did I let this happen? Because you wanted to, a voice in my head tells me, but I shut it out. *They were drunk. I was drunk. That´s why. Drunk and stoned people do stupid things. Things like sleeping with both of your best friends. Things that should have never happened. Things that´ll destroy everything and end things.*

It´s either the best thing I´ve ever done or the worst. *My gut tells me the latter.*

I feel sick thinking about last night and scurry out of bed as silently as I can and get dressed quickly. Before I go out, I take one last look at the two of them buried naked in the covers. *I love them.*

But I was selfish coming between their friendship, and for letting me love them both. I was naïve to let them have me. *Both of them.*

Maybe that´s why Aidan let me go with Kai to Bali.

Because they knew this would happen? Whatever it was *I need to get out now.*

I was selfish, but now I must be the responsible one and leave. Maybe their choice was the right one. *To end things.*

For them to stay friends cause they´ve known each other all their life´s and for me to return to my life. *My life without them. To my life before them.*

I take Kai´s Polaroid from the dresser and snap a photo.

A reminder. To let go and to forget. To move on.

The shutter is so loud that I throw the camera back and run down the stairs shoving the Polaroid into my jeans as I pace down the stairs. Hastily, I put on my shoes and rush out the front door.

But if she knew what would come, she would have stayed.

134

I*t must be the end.* I tell myself as I walk away. *This is the end.* I tell myself to keep going.

This couldn´t end well. I convince myself as I put one foot in front of the other.

And more steps away from both. It was fucked up before but now I messed it up. Tears run down my cheeks as I hurry across the turning area towards the main road.

But as I stand on the pavement waiting to cross the road, I hear Kai calling after me. "Scar." He yells and I freeze as I hear his voice. My heart sinks and I cast a glance over my shoulder. He has put on a pair of shorts and walks after me as he puts on a shirt.

And he´s fast.

I turn to walk along, but I hesitate due to the cars. "Scar wait" he yells but I ignore him. But when I again look at his direction. *He runs after me.*

And as he almost reached me, I take my chance and race across the road to get distance between us. *I can´t. Can´t see him. Can´t talk to him.*

But just when I passed the street and put on to run, I hear it. It´s loud and time stops for a moment. Like some higher might tried to show me, this is a life-changing moment. And it is because when I turn around, my life has changed.

135

Everything happened really fast.

I don´t know what happened in what order. Some of it is black. Some of it people talking. Some of it lights flashing. Some of it crying. Some of it screaming. Some of it, blood. Some of it numb. Some of it loud. Some of it quiet. *Some of it, Kai almost dying.*

Time expands and contracts. Kai called after me.

I should wait and talk to him. But that was before.

I hear a car bump *something*. Hitting *something*.

Car tires screech. There are a lot of cars. Brakes are heard after *something* bangs the ground and I turn around. *No, I´m already turned.*

Someone is screaming. *No, I´m screaming.*

People talk. Car doors open and close. *Tinnitus. I want to throw up.*

Aidan sprints to the road. "Call an ambulance," someone yells.

Something lies on the street. *Something* is covered in blood. *Something.*

I blink and *something* turns into *everything*. And everything into Kai.

He is lying on the ground. Kai got hit. *Kai.*

The hood and windshield show the impact. *Shards.* The bonnet dented. *Blood.*

"Can you hear me?" Someone asks. There´s more talking. *But I can´t focus.*

My brain shut me out. It switched that thing for you to be safe, when ~~things like that~~ *things like the love of your life getting hit by a car* happen.

So, you´re not there anymore.

Why am I not here anymore? What if he´s dying and I´m not here? I need to be with him. I need to see him. To hold his hand. To see if he´s still there. But I can´t.

And I can´t come back. I don´t know how. I don´t even know where I am or how to get out of it. *I´m just gone.*

I hope he´s not gone. But if he´s in pain I hope he´s gone to hide until he can come back.

I look up and the sun is shining. *Why is it shining?*

My perception has focused on my inner self. It´s like I´m covering my ears. Or *someone is* covering them. Or, as if I´m diving underwater. It´s all foggy and long gone.

"Hello?" Someone asks. *All sounds are muffled.*

My whole-body shakes as people give him first aid. I don´t know how I am even standing anymore. *I can´t help him. How are we supposed to help?*

He´s across the street. *After me.*

He didn´t pay attention to the cars. *There were cars.*

There were cars coming. *Why didn´t he see them? Hear them?*

I passed the street between them. *How did he not see?*

Because all he saw was *YOU*. It´s *your* fault he lies there.

I feel like I´m dying. I feel like I throw up. I feel like I´m crying. *I do.*

A quote pops in my head as I straighten up again. *Life is a constant reminder of the death.* And life is crashing down on me. *Life crashed him down.*

Aidan comes to me after he helped him and takes me in his arms. He was able to help him. *I´m grateful.*

I start to pray for whatever higher might there be out there. To send their spirit guides and angels to help him. To watch him. *To save him.*

Tears are streaming. Or it´s raining. It´s not raining the sun shines.

Why does she shine? How can she shine on a day like this?

I bury my head against his chest. But the images in my head don´t go away.

The blood. Him. Kai.

Aidan´s body shivers with mine but he´s steadier than me.

They try to talk to him. He isn´t answering. *Why isn´t he answering?*

He got hit by a car. *It´s my fault.*

He ran after me. *Is he dead?*

He´s unconscious. *Where are the ambulances? Shouldn´t they be here by now? Is around 50 or 60 kilometers per hour fast enough to die? Was the car going faster? Why did he run in front of the car?*

Because of *YOU*.

I shouldn´t have run. I did to him what he did to me all the time. *Run*.

I ran from him, and he followed me. *I never did that.*

Sirens in the distance. *Please come faster.*

They take so long. I can´t look. I must breathe. Aidan helps me breathe. *Aidan*.

His best friend. *Finn*.

His brother. *YOU DID THIS.*

Car doors. More loud voices. The roll of the gurney.

Aidan is talking. *Aidan lets go of me.*

And I´m back here. Everything is so loud. *Sensory overload hits me.*

I blink and focus on my breathing. "Someone can go with him." Says a paramedic. "You go with him Lia, okay? I´ll wake Finn and we´ll go right after you." He tells me and I think, I nod. *But I can´t answer.*

I get into the car. The doors close. The EMTs are doing something to him. They ask me questions. *Some of them I can answer some I can´t.*

I hold his bloody hand. He´s not holding it. He isn´t holding it. *He can´t hold it.*

His hand is warm, I think. *Or is it mine?* But that´s good, *right?*

It´s not cold. *That´s good right?* Cause mine is. *Cold*. His is warm. *He´s there.*

But his eyes are closed. His face is bloody, and I can´t see the wound.

I have to be strong for him. I can´t lose it now. *He needs me.*

They ripped his shirt open. *Everywhere is blood.* His arms, legs, and knees. All over his body. Scratches and blood.

I sob soundless hoping I won´t bother them.

I fix my eyes on his hand. *Maybe he´ll hold it.* In my mind I tell him to hold on.

Just hold on. I´ll never run from you again just please hold on.

I hold onto him hoping I can hold him. Hoping it´s what holds him back from floating away. *Hoping he holds on too.* But it´s just his body. I can´t hold his soul. I only can hold his hand. *The hand that doesn´t hold me back.*

This can´t be the end. *They´ll fix him. He´ll be saved. He´ll be okay. He´ll be.*

My mind constantly reminds me of what just happened. *Like I could ever forget.*

I slipped between two cars to get to the other side. He got between them.

Did he crash between them? I didn´t see.

The ride takes years as if it were my own hell.

But no one said you can´t pray in hell. That you can´t beg to reach heaven.

I prayed and told him he´ll make it.

At the hospital, I am asked to wait. Finn and Aidan arrive shortly after, and Finn went straight to the nurses.

Aidan´s eyes are bright red. *We hold each other and wait.*

"I need to call our parents." Finn tells us and walks a few feet away. *We wait.*

The police questioned us. Aidan got something to drink for us. *No one drunk.*

Finn paced. Aidan and I held each other. *We wait and pray.*

136

I don´t know how much later it is, but you hear heels running down the hall.

Their parents. This is the first time I´ve seen them.

His mom has long brown hair in loose waves shining and looking spotless. She´s dressed fancy all black. *She is beautiful like a model.*

And his father wears a black suit matching his wife. He looks so much like his sons.

It´s surreal. Surreal seeing them. Because somehow it really was like Kai always said to me. It was like they didn´t even exist.

But maybe even Peter Pan has parents. And they´re now here to look for their lost boy. But he´s not in Neverland where they left him with his lost boys and Wendy.

He´s at the hospital. *Because of me.*

I look at his father. *The father of lost boy.*

His hole appearance and aura scream authority figure. But there´s worry in the lines of his frown and I see where they got their beauty from. He has darker hair, but they have the same black eyes. Even his mom has them. *Surreal.*

I´m sure there was a reason why I never met them. And now I´m the reason they had to fly here by jet to see their son in the hospital. He was having surgery. Or still is I´m not sure.

You don´t get much information.

But I´m sure his father can get anything he wants out of people.

Finn wraps his arms around his mother and his father hugs them both.

It looks so familiar. It´s weird. Watching them being affectionate. Being a family.

Why is Kai no part of this? Kai who never got that from them.

I know Finn has always been closer to them. They love him more.

But why? Why did they reject him the way they did and still do?

"I am going to talk to one of the doctors." Says his father and walks down the hall.

I don´t even know their names, my brain tells me. *Never dared to ask.*

Finn joins him and I watch them disappear. I blink once or twice. Then I turn to Aidan and whisper, "I think I should go." And stand up but as I do his mother turns to me. "Lia Sky?" She asks *knowing* my name. *Knowing me?*

And all at once, the fog in my brain is gone. And I´m here at the hospital and Kai´s mom in front of me. "Yes?" I retort not sure what to say or expect. But she just wraps her arms around my upper back politely and squeezes me warmly.

Has he told her? He had to, right?

"I am glad he found you." She tells me. *Found me?*

"I´m so sorry." I try to say but someone cuts in from behind. "He´s in the recovery room." We loosen our embrace and turn. *It´s his father.*

The three of them walk down the hall and I sit down with Aidan. "I saw the cars." I say without expression. "He didn´t. He didn´t see them. He just crossed the street. Following me. I didn´t want him to follow me, that´s why I crossed the street. I didn´t think.." I sob. "That he would.. Why did he cross the street? Why would he cross the street?" I start crying all over again and the fog is back clouding my brain.

"You couldn´t have known he would run across the street." He tells me. "He should have seen the cars." He tells me. "That´s not your fault, Lia." He tries to tell me.

But I can´t listen. Because it´s all my fault. And I hope, pray, and I beg he´s fine.

137

Kai

I have the same dream over and over.

I run after her. *But she runs away from me.*

She runs and I can´t reach her. *And then she gets hit by a car.*

Each time I run after her faster. But each time without success.

Beep..

She wears that pink dress. *Sometimes it´s blue.*

She runs from me. *She hides.*

When I find her, she sleeps. She won´t wake up. *I can´t wake her up.*

She´s gone. She wants to sleep and never wake up. She´s beautiful but gone.

Beep.. Beep..

The other time she fell down a rabbit whole and I couldn´t hold her. Her hand slipped through my fingers. *I watched her fall.*

She followed that white rabbit that told her lies but she didn´t listen to me.

She couldn´t stop, she had no time.

And then she fell and fell and never got out. *I couldn´t hold her.*

Beep.. Beep.. Beep..

Again, she runs away, and I call for her and warn her, *but she keeps running.*

And before I can grab her, *I can´t run anymore.*

I want to scream, but I can´t. *I´m paralyzed.* I try to scream but it´s muffled. *It hurts.*

I watch her die. Every time she slips away.

Beep.. Beep.. Beep.. Beep..

She ran away from me. *She wanted back.* She wanted to leave me. *She wanted out.*

Then Hook caught her. *He killed her.*

I couldn´t save her. *She didn´t want to play anymore.*

She wanted to grow up. *She wanted to leave.*

Beep.. Beep.. Beep..

She runs away from me. *She dies.*

I can´t reach her. *She dies.* I can´t save her. *She dies.* I can´t hold her. *She dies.*

She falls. *She dies.* She´s gone. *She dies.*

...

My eyes are closed, and my limbs are heavy. I´m numb but my head burns. And all I hear is this soft buzzing in my ears.

Beep.. Beep..

It takes me a moment to come to reality. *She runs. Falls. Dies.*

Beep..

I run. I fall. She dies.

I open my eyes. *I blink.*

Beep.. Beep..

The room is dark. The ceiling is white.

My throat is on fire. *I run. She dies.*

Beep.. Beep.. Beep..

I am in a hospital. *She dies.*

I let my eyes wander and see Finn asleep in a chair.

I´m not sure if I´m still dreaming. Flashbacks from the dream hit me. My head is dizzy and mind foggy. *She runs from me. I run after her.* Blank. *She dies. Where is She?*

My eyes search for her ashy dark blond hair. *She´s not here. She dies.*

Panic rises.

I spot my mom next to me in my Dad´s arms. *My parents?*

I have yet to come to my senses. My head pounding like hell against the top of my skull trying to break free. I feel a slight pain somewhere in my gut and chest.

"Kai?" I hear my mom, and she kisses my head and cries. My dad takes my shoulder.

I flinch on the inside.

Finn´s head snaps in my direction. *He jolts up.*

I try to speak but seem to have forgotten how. So, I fix him and hope he understands what I want from him. Frustrated, I try again. "Where is she? Is she okay?" My voice fails and is more like a toneless whisper. But Finn finally understood what I tried to ask. "She´s outside." He tells me and I shut my eyes. *She´s here. She´s okay? She´s alive.*

138

Lia

The first thing Kai said was that he wanted to see me. He could have died because of me and wants to see me.

Aidan leads the way, and as soon as I see him, hot tears run down my cheeks. Kai reaches his hand out to me. *My heart breaks at that.*

With the back of my hand, I cover my sobs as I run towards him before I crush on the ground. He tries to straighten up to meet me, but he stops himself wincing in pain. I put my head on his shoulder because I don´t want to hurt him. He holds my head and presses his against mine.

The others leave the room to give us privacy.

I put my hand on his neck and my feet onto the bed. Kai cries soundlessly and his body shivers. He trembles and holds me for minutes in silence. *I cry too.*

"I´m so sorry." I whimper between tears, and he kisses the top of my head. "I´m so sorry." I repeat. "I´m sorry." I say as a chant over and over. "This is my fault." He whispers not to claim his voice. I shake my head in disagreement, but he grabs my head forcing me to look at him. He shakes his head and kisses my forehead.

"When I was gone.. I thought you died." He says hurtful and his voice is barely there and stricken. "You ran away from me." His says and I cry but nod because I did. "In my dream you always died." He says. "You got hit by a car." He tells me and I shake my head no. "*You* crossed the street because of me." I tell him. "*You* ran after me." I say and his mind works. "You got hit by a car." I tell him again.

He looks off with a frown on his face. "I saw the car." He whispers and my throat hurts. "I thought I was going to make it." He says. "I thought I could reach you." He says and I wipe my eyes trying to see.

"If you saw the cars, why did you cross the street?" I cry upset and he looks at me. "Because I didn´t care about anything." He says quietly. "I just wanted to get to you." He tells me and I shut my eyes at the pain.

"Your life *does* matter." I say strongly. "I know." His hand strokes my hair. "I know." He says like he really knows as his thumb catches my tears. "You could have died." I hush. "For my sake." I sob and his forehead is now on mine. I close my eyes focusing on his breath on my face.

"I held your hand and you didn´t hold it back. I thought.. I thought you´d die. The blood.." I say in panic, but he cuts me in *shh´n* me. "I hold it now." He tells me. "Don´t I?" He asks as he takes my hand in his and I try to catch my breath. "Don´t let go." I choke. "I won´t." He promises and a while we lie there head-to-head my hand in his just breathing. Listening to the sound of thankfulness. Feeling the hand, we´re holding. *Both warm.*

"After tonight.." he begins. "I was afraid I´ve lost you. That you might regret it." He whispers. "And I saw you left so, I panicked." He says softly. "That´s why I ran after you. I wanted you back. I was afraid to lose you. That you might hate me. That you´ll leave me." He says and my heart hurts like hell will.

"Do you regret it?" he asks carefully, and I look at him.

He´s worried. Filled with fear. He really thinks that´s why I left?

I shake my head. *I must admit that to myself.*

I pull the Polaroid out of my jeans. Where Kai lies on his back and Aidan on his stomach. The only space left where I was. Both between the wrinkled white covers.

Tangled in each other.

I show him. "I didn´t regret it for a second." I admit softly as tears threaten to spill.

"I regret leaving." I tell him and he looks at me relieved. And *somehow* in love. And that tells me there were no games. *Never.*

I tuck it back into my pants and lay back down in his arms. "I didn´t regret any of it either." He whispers at my neck, and I stroke his hair.

It wasn´t an end. He wanted it. And so, did I.

Eventually his parents come back in, and the others are here by now too. I stay next to him like that for the rest of the night because neither he wants to let go of me, nor would I have left him alone.

- 27 -

The next four days are the same. Just him with me in bed. *The hospital bed.*

Aidan stayed over too. Sometimes we´ve managed to scoot all three in that bed. And other times he slept on the chair right next to us with his head fallen back or lying on the mattress. *He didn´t want to leave either.*

The others were here every day, and his parents stayed too.

But they didn´t talk much. At least his dad.

He was mostly on his phone or laptop. *All busy.*

One night I couldn´t sleep, so I got up leaving the room. It was cute how they laid there. Aidan fell asleep on that chair again and leaned forward onto Kai´s arm holding it. And Kai´s other hand was on Aidan´s head. Seeing them like that did hurt but also made me happy. The last time I watched them sleep I´ve run away, and we know how that ended.

I won´t run anymore.

I sneaked out to walk a bit and get some snacks. But as I left the room, I stopped short. There was Finn leaning against the wall next to the door. *Sleeping.*

I didn´t wake him and got back in.

When I woke up, I checked the door. *He was gone.*

Later that day he came acting all normal. He left in the evening and that same night I checked the door again. To see him lying there. *Sleeping. Again.*

All dressed and no blanket or a pillow. *How could he sleep like that? Did he sleep like that every night? And why didn´t he come in?*

He could have come in and stayed on the couch. The private room is big enough. But he didn´t want him to know. *Right?*

He wanted to watch him. *Guard him.*

So, I got back in. If he didn´t want him to notice, I´ve decided not to wake him and let him be his big brother.

- 27 -

How bruised he was. *The cuts and all. It was scary.*

And I didn´t wash his blood off. Maybe that´s weird or crazy. *But I let it dry.*

I didn´t wash my hands either. *Despite my germ phobia.*

I don´t know why, but I kept looking at it. At his blood on me and on my cloths. I had his blood on my hands. *It felt good in a sick way.* It´s insane but that´s how I felt. It was part of him. And it was a way of dealing. *I know that now.*

It reminded me that I love pain too. *That I like seeing red.* And it reminded me of my guilt. Because that blood on my hand.. *his blood was there because of me.*

Despite the car was going too fast it was still *my fault*. Despite his choice of running after me, it was *my fault*. His blood on me was *my fault*. The blood on the street was *my fault*. No one else got hurt luckily. But he did and it was *my fault*.

So, I needed to see that blood as a reminder of what I did. As a reminder of him surviving.

Of him not dying.

But I washed it away. *Eventually it washed away.*

They told me to wash it off on the third morning. *I washed it off in the evening.*

It felt like losing him. It felt like washing him off me. *It felt like part of it gone.*

Aidan washed it off the day it happened. *He showered five times.* His skin was shore from the scrubbing. That was for him a way of dealing. *We all dealt.*

After what happened, my whole body was under permanent tension. *We all were.*

I didn´t have a chance to review the night. Not that I allowed myself to think about anything else than Kai´s well-being. *We all were on autopilot.*

But I always knew that I wanted to have a threesome at some point in my life. And also, that it if it should be with two guys. And probably no matter who you would ask, everyone would say the other two or at least the third person should be someone you don´t know. Otherwise, there could be problems. *Well, our combination was even worse.* Three best friends and the girl in love with both. So, we´re pretty fucked and I don´t know what effects our night together will have. But I know I would do it again. *And what about them?*

But I can´t think of that not now. *We´ll deal with that later.*

139

Over a Week later

It´s been almost two weeks since Kai´s home from the hospital, and yet we still haven´t talked about that night. But I know *they* talk. *They talk a lot lately.*

Just like they do *now.*

I sit on the sofa while the party is going around us. They stand across from me in the kitchen and glance at me occasionally. My cheeks grow hot.

Do they talk about me? About that night?

Their grins drive me crazy and Kai´s clearly enjoying this. I would even go so far to say he *loves* it. *Messing with me.* Well, he *always* liked his games. *Didn´t he?*

It just drives me mad how they look at me. And I have no idea what the heck they´re laughing about. *And why am I no part of it anyway?*

We haven´t slept together since. Neither the three of us nor the two of us. But the mood is heated. We´re in withdrawal. Sitting on hot coals. Because now Kai is fine. His cuts have healed, and his bruises faded. But that means we have no excuse to wait any longer to talk about our situation. And talking was never our strength.

I know Kai didn´t regret it *but what about Aidan? And what does it mean? Does he want me? Does Aidan still want me? What do I want? Questions over questions. None of them answered cause we don´t talk.*

We just do *this*. Waiting to see what the other will do. What the next move is. But it´s just a matter of time. Someone will do the first step. *Someone has to.* But somehow no one does. Aidan is waiting for Kai to stop him and claim me. And Kai is waiting for Aidan´s move. But most of all they´re waiting for me to decide. Like it´s just me that fucked up. And not them coming up with the idea in the first place. But I didn´t say *no* either. *None of us did.*

Maybe that´s why. Because somewhere we all know what that means. But no one dares to say it. But I know I must decide. I know I´m the one. *But I can't. I just can't.*

So, I let us do this. We circle around each other like vultures around meat. Not sure what happens when we dare to take a bite. *Is it poisoned? Is it good? Do we like it? Does it taste the same as the last time? Will it kill us? Or set us free? Or in a cage? I don't know.*

But what I do know is that they are constantly horny. I can see it on their faces as they watch me watching them talk. That *indeed* they want that piece of meat. And they know exactly the prey won´t run. *Not this time.* But the scary part is, that means it´s no game anymore. *It's a decision.*

Their eyes burn on me, and I feel it. How my clit is throbbing. I cross my legs. But it gets worse. It feels even better now.

Kai´s eyes lock with mine. His slight grin tells me he knows. He says something without tearing his dark eyes away from me. Then Aidan´s eyes search mine and I stop breathing. They´re just looking at me silently staring, jaws working. A slight grin on Kai´s face. Aidan´s blank. And I know *exactly* how Kai suppresses his shitty grin right now.

They´re looking at me like.. *like at their prey.*

Like they want me, and I can´t breathe. My mouth becomes dry, but I can´t look away. I have the urge to run but I can´t, so I stay rooted. I want them to hunt me.

Come after me. Eat me. Tear me. Touch me.

But they don´t move. They just continue to glare. And that´s when I realize what they´re doing. What *this* is. *They're fucking with me. Messing with my head and playing with me. Trying to edge me. To push me. They want me to do or say it first.*

But hell no. No way. I'm not gonna say it.

My gaze hardens and I tilt my chin. *Because sometimes the prey becomes the hunter. And it's the victims with the bloodiest hands. Not the Villains.*

I fight a smile and then look a bit too long at Kai´s crotch knowing what it´ll do to him and lick my lips. I avert my gaze looking straight into his eyes that are already on mine and Aidan´s too. Then I get up and talk to Wren who stands near me.

I know he hates him. Why I don´t know. I just know he´s off limit. But I don´t care. If he wants to mess with me, I´ll do the same.

And I know I shouldn´t mess with Wren because he´s kind of dangerous. At least that´s what I heard. Their folks are a little different. They do things a little differently. What that means *I don´t know*. I mean I´ve been told that about these parties too, so idk maybe there´s something to all of it. *Maybe not.* I just know they´re drug dealers and stuff I don´t know much about like hacking. I´m not so sure to be honest what *exactly* they do. But they´re always at our parties. But they´re not *really* part of it. It´s like they´re the opponents. *Enemies who party.* They hate each other but they get wasted together and join their games and other stuff they do. But they also fight a lot and come to blows all the time. *It´s weird.*

It´s just that they´re here no matter what. And I know they were friends a long time ago. Wren and Kai. *But not anymore.* I´ve seen a crumbled picture of them on Kai´s wall. Like he had already thrown it away and decided against it. Like having your enemies close to know their moves. Maybe that´s why they´re always around despite the hate. They mostly ignore each other pretending the other doesn´t exist. They just talk about the important stuff. If it´s necessary. *But that´s all.* From best friends to nothing.

I think I´ve heard they were the ones calling the cops on them when they´ve done something not that legal. *I think it was even Wren.*

Maybe that´s why they parted. It was out of revenge or something. I don´t really get what happened. *I won´t ask either.*

Their dynamic is just strange. *Enemies. Leaders of their group.*

They exist near each other. They´re the ones making it all work.

But they tend to break the rules a lot. The parties wouldn´t be the same without them. It´s just a nice mix. They bring people. We do. Some get along some not. It´s the way things are. It´s an unspoken rule they hate but tolerate.

I know they get the drugs and our group the alcohol. It´s two different packs coming together. They do those car races, activities like the rage room and other stuff. Those competitions and sports like paintball matches. They come up with games as we do. And we join their parties too. But sometimes we do things partly. But the parties are always at Wrens just as ours are here at Kai´s. So, he´s the leader of the others. Just as Kai´s the leader of us.

I can´t help but wonder that if Kai is Pan and the guys the lost boys and the girls Wendy´s and this is Neverland.. *then who is Wren and his folks and most of all what are their parties?*

I´ve been told the pirates. *But what does that even mean then?*

But I snap out of it as Wren talks to me with that plain smile, so smile too, but I don´t even pay attention to what he´s saying. I haven´t talked to him since that party a year ago. When he danced with me. *When Kai got between us.*

I say something in response but too quiet on purpose and he leans down to hear me better.

That will drive him crazy.

I rise on my feet repeating what I said near his hear. He nods and smiles at me.

I don´t even know what I said.

He looks down at me leaning against the wall. He´s flirting with me and I flirt back. He makes me smile and I make him smile.

Wren looks at me just how I want him to look at me. Like he would tell me all I would want to hear. Because he would say what he thinks.

He´s no one to hide. No one to run. He´s straight on. He´s an alpha. Intimidating. Stunning beautiful and single. A girl magnet and talking to me. And all I need for Kai to see.

And just as he pushes himself off the wall stepping closer Kai approaches us. And I almost smile because I knew. "Don´t even think about it." Kai spits facing him.

Wren just smiles.

They glare at each other and things are told without really saying.

Then he steps back jaw working. "Now fuck off before I break your fucking neck Fates." He growls and I grin. Wren walks away winking at me when Kai doesn´t look and I think he knew I used him. *And he played along well. Of course, he would, he hates him. He enjoyed to mess with him as much as I did.*

"Déjà-vu." I say meeting Kai´s eyes. "Wasn´t that the guy you scared off last year? And the one when you told me to sit next to you?" I ask. "I probably forgot." I shrug, suppressing my victory grin. He just glares at me for a second.

"Stick your fucking laugh up your ass." He scoffs. "Don´t act like you don´t know who he is." He spits and I shrug.

"Look I´ll share you with Aidan. With him, it´s different. I trust Aidan. He´s my best mate. But with no one fucking else. Especially not fucking Wren Fates." He gets closer to me while talking and shakes his head. "You know he´s off limit Lia." He says.

That´s why I did it, idiot.

"I´ve fucking told you so." He yells at me. "You don´t get to tell me. And you told *him* not me." I shout back but he shakes his head and glares at me ready to explode.

I know flirting with the enemy is bad, but he deserved it.

“Fuck this. Fuck you.” He scoffs and I grin. “You don´t own me.” I tell him. Now he grins like the devil´s brother. “No, I don´t.” He agrees with a solid nod and leans in. “But you know, I do.” He says with *that* voice into my hair that sends goosebumps all over me.

Yes, I do.

“Get over yourself.” I snap instead but he just grins knowing he got to me. And then he just walks past me. *He´ll probably smoke weed to come down.*

The grin on my face never leaves and Aidan shares my smile as I lock eyes with him across the room. *He has seen it all.*

I walk over to him. “You made him jealous.” He faces me and my grin widens, and he narrows his eyes. “Maybe *you´re* the devil.” He says and I chuckle. “Maybe.” I shrug and his dimples show.

“You weren´t jealous.” I justify and he nods once. “Because I knew what you were doing.” He replies instead of saying what is obvious. *That he wasn´t.* Kai feels clearly more for me than he does. *At least, I think.* Kai claims me over others. He´s the possessive and protecting one. But when it comes to Aiden, he seems to have no problem. Maybe with us, it was just about sex and with Kai it was more.

“He knew too.” I retort but he shrugs. “Maybe.” He says. “But he won´t admit that.” He adds. “Yeah, he probably won´t.” I say as I stare off. “He just can´t admit it.” I say resigned and he looks at me for a moment.

“Maybe we have to make him.” He suggests as he throws a chip into his mouth. I look at him and he grins smug. “Maybe we do.” I agree.

140

I take the last ones to the front door and now there´s just the three of us and the remnants of the party.

I go back to the living room. They sit on the couches. Aidan, who´s the DJ, changes the song to *Stalker from Stevie Howie* and as I walk by, he takes my arm. “Sit on my lap.” He demands and pulls me onto him straightening up.

Kai sits on the other couch to our right. His eyes fixed on us as Aidan wraps an arm around me and pulls me closer to his chest. He brushes my hair to the side and speaks into my ear that only I can hear him. “We´ll let him watch and see what he does.” He hushes, and I shiver from his breath on my ear, but I smile. *Kai fixes us.* He´s still pissed from earlier but right now, I can´t read him further. I feel transported back to the moment before I kissed Aidan. Where I didn't know if he was going to yank me off or hit him.

My pulse rises as the tension grows. Aidan's grip gets firmer on my waist, and he starts kissing my neck. I close my eyes for a moment enjoying but as his hand runs down my leg, my eyes fly open. Kai's jaw flexes and his muscle twitches under the skin.

Yes, he's watching.

Aidan kisses my ear and bites at the lobe. I close my eyes again leaning into him. When I open them again, Kai looks angrier than before. His chest rises violently. I just don't know if it's cause out of anger, jealousy, or lust. Or maybe all of it. *But he won't stop looking.*

Aidan's one hand moves to my breast and his other finds my clit on my jeans. I feel his bulge pressing against my ass as I slowly move against him. "She's throbbing." Aidan says. "Stop." Kai demands between clenched teeth, but Aidan keeps rubbing me and kneads my breasts under my top. I moan and start grinding him. And since Kai makes no move to stop him, we continue. *And he continues to glare.*

I buckle my back against him as his fingers twirl my mid. A whimper escapes me, and he breathes on my neck whispering in my ear. "Tell him how I feel." And he lifts his hip to meet my moves. "He's rock hard." I pant. "Get off of her." Kai growls.

But he doesn't move a bit.

"Make me." Aidan taunts grinding his dick on me. "Move your hips faster." Aiden conducts me further. So, I rock my hips on his length and moan at his circling motions now *inside* my panties. He tilts my head and kisses me letting him see our tongues meet. He inserts fingers and I cry out in satisfaction. "Say my name." He whisper-moans. "Aidan." I moan. "Piece of shit." Kai insults whoever of us. But we don't stop and he doesn't stop us either. "Now say his." He hushes. "Kai." I breathe and his eyes hold mine. My lips part as I grind on Aidan's lap and stare at Kai having his hand now on his crotch.

I bet he's hard. But he does not touch himself. He doesn't act on it. On any of it that's happening. He just watches. And throwing insults at us.

"Say you want me to fuck you." Aidan murmurs in my ear. "Fuck me." I beg and I mean both. *And they know.*

The song is on repeat I realize now as Kai gets up and towers over me looking down on me. *He looks menacing. My stalker.*

Aidan's fingers pump inside of me as I hold eye contact with Kai, and I come under Aidan's touch. *Watching him.*

"Take her from behind." Kai demands with a raspy voice and tucks a condom out of his pants handing it to him. Aidan unzips his jeans and puts it on. Kai helps me undress and I lower myself back onto him. Aidan grabs my hip thrusting inside me, and I stretch my ass towards him holding onto Kai still standing in front of us. He opens his belt and frees his cock. "Suck me." He taunts and Aidan slows his pace as I lick Kai´s tip. His groan twitches and I take him in my mouth. He fists my hair and guides me.

As we all find a rhythm, we speed up a bit and I look up at him taking him deep throat. He throws his head back groaning in pleasure. *And then he loses it.*

He tenses and jerks off down my throat and I swallow. Then Aidan lifts me and forces me on my stomach. He takes off his jeans, parts my legs with his knee and pushes himself back inside me. *Kai watches.*

141

Aidan tucked himself back in, and I just finished dressing when Kai grabs him by the shirt and pushes him against the wall. "What the hell do you think you´re doing?" he barks just inches from his face holding him by the throat. *Aidan grins.*

"Nothing we didn´t do before." He smirks to which Kai shoves him, but Aidan chuckles clearly amused by his mood. "You´re mad I get it, but you liked it didn´t you?" Aidan teases with a wicked grin. "I told you to *stop fucking* touch her." Kai growls ignoring his assumption. "Yeah, I heard that." Aidan states. "But you didn´t stop me. And you don´t get a say in it. She´s not yours isn´t she?" He grins knowing he won´t disagree.

Which surprise, *he doesn´t.*

"And you won´t get to tell me or her what to do bro." He tells him and they glare at each other. "Just admit it. You liked what you saw. You wanted her as bad as I did." Aidan goes on but Kai shakes his head. "Shut the fuck up." He spits.

"Oh, come on. Either you fucking admit what´s really going on, claim her and I´ll fuck off. Or you admit to yourself you wanted it, and *we* continue to fuck her." Aidan gets in his face. "Or you fucking coward say nothing as always and I continue to fuck her whenever I want. Because *unlike you,* I´m open about how much I want her. I´ve told her I love her and didn´t use it against her." He spits. "Bastard." Kai grumbles and Aidan´s grin widens with a nod. "But don´t be surprised if she chooses me over you." He laughs.

"It´s up to you." Aidan says threatening and pushes Kai off him. "Well *actually* it´s up to her. And clearly you showed how much you want this." Aidan gestures between us. "Or her." He adds and stands next to me.

Kai looks at us rage in his features. *It´s your move,* I silently tell him.

"Fuck both of you." He scowls and walks off. *He made his.*

We stand there for a moment until Aidan speaks up. "Come let´s head over." He says as he takes my hand. We got ready for bed and stand in his room.

He comes up to me reading my face. "That didn´t work out how we intended." He says with a small laugh, and I sigh. "Yeah, not quite." I agree, and he warps an arm around my head pulling me in for a hug.

"I don´t understand what his problem is." I say into his chest. "I think he doesn´t either." He whispers with a shrug. "I mean he clearly wants you. He just can´t tell you." He says quietly and I close my eyes inhaling his scent. "I´m sorry." He whispers and places a kiss on my head.

We break away. "I think we should go back to him." I suggest and he nods once. "Yeah, I think so too." He agrees.

We don´t knock and walk in because the door was ajar. He lies on his stomach, and we lie down next to him. My head on Aidan´s chest and next to me Kai. *Silence.*

"We love you." I whisper. *Silence. But he´s awake. He won´t sleep. Not alone.*

"We shouldn´t have pushed you." I add. *Silence.*

But then the mattress gives in, and he turns to lie against my back, and I close my eyes in relieve. He wraps his arms around us. His head at my neck, breath hitting me hot and his scent fogging my brain. "I did like it." He admits in a whisper and my heart skips a beat. "But as much as I liked to watch, I also hated it." He confesses.

And I get that.

"Kills me in a way." He says painful and I turn my head, and he meets me to kiss. He holds my cheek, and we make out with Aidan under us.

- 27 -

When I wake up, the three of us are still in the same position. Only I´m lying more on top of Aidan and Kai´s cuddled even closer to me. His arm is around both of us and I´m sure Aidan´s arm holding me is numb.

I caress Aidan´s neck and Kai grumbles behind me. "Stop moving." He whines to which I chuckle. And it´s only *now* I notice his boner at my back. I let my eyes wander down to Aidan´s crotch where´s also a bulge.

I stare at his boxer until Kai´s breath hits my ear. "Touch him." He whispers as he guides my hand on Aidan´s length and I start stroking him on his shorts. He twitches in response and Kai presses his groan at my ass. Aidan´s chest rises heavily, and he begins to moan as Kai starts working on my clit.

"Fuck." Aidan murmurs. "Suck him." Kai demands, so, I push his boxers aside and take him in my mouth. He grabs the sheet and his upper body jerks from my deep throat. Kai fingers me while kneading my ass and Aidan fists my hair guiding my head to his rhythm.

"She´s wet for you." Kai taunts and after that he slips on a condom and pushes into me as I chase mine and Aidan´s orgasm.

142

We´re in the shower. *All three of us.*

Both sandwiching me. Kai with his back to the tiles and Aidan at my front. I kiss them alternately and they touch and kiss me everywhere. But Kai mostly bites.

I take them both in my hands as I gently stroke them. Aidan groans in my mouth and slides his fingers inside of me and Kai sucks on my neck biting down hard in response. "Touch each other." I taunt as we break the kiss, and they exchange a look over my head. Chest´s heaving, they stare at each other. *They hesitate.*

So, I take Aidan´s free hand and place it on Kai´s length behind me. I start to move my hand with his and Kai moans but watching his every move.

Aidan and I lock eyes. Then I take my other hand and bring Kai´s hand to Aidan´s hard on and he lets me but looks in pain.

Aidan steps closer to meet us and after a moment I take my hands off and they keep stroking mutually. Kai´s head falls back hitting the wall with his eyes closed. And I kiss them on their necks, lips, and chests as they work each other. "You like watching him touch me." I taunt Kai and his eyes snap to mine. "You like watching him *fuck* me. You like feeling his dick brushing yours. You like the feel of him. You like claiming me with him. You like when *he* watches." I hush. "And I like watching too." I tell him as he enjoys their hand job.

Kai smacks Aidan´s hand away from his groan and takes both in one hand rubbing them against one another. Aidan´s head falls to Kai´s shoulder to which Kai grips his hair. They grunt in sync and I´m near orgasm watching them get off each other.

Or rather Kai working them.

Aidan´s free hand pumps inside of me as the shower fills with their pants and groans. I watch them as Kai strokes them slowly and then picking up pace. Watching him do it gets me off because he does it differently. He knows what they like, and he looks me straight in the eyes while doing so. *They hold each other.*

"I´m yours and you´re mine." I whisper as his eyes swallow me like a black hole. "I love you and you won´t lose me." I assure him and he kisses me his tongue forcing mine to go along. Telling me without saying that he does, *love me.*

When we break away, I face them. "Kiss." I demand, and they lock eyes but there´s no hesitation just raw emotions. They glare at each other and I´m not sure if they want to *kill or fuck* each other right now. But before I can think more, they crash their lips onto each other.

Kissing.

Kai holds Aidan´s jaw and Aidan throws his hands on the tiles next to Kai, so we slam against each other. Not shortly after they put on condoms, lift me in their arms and glide inside me both filling me up with nothing more than pure love and affection between friends.

And that day he claimed us fully. But they decided not to kiss anymore. They made an agreement that they would stroke each other but no kissing.

So, our triangle is a thing now. No one must understand what we have. *Just us.*

But they were fools to think nothing could go wrong. *Fools they were.*

143

One week later

It´s raining, so I´m at the only place I want to be.

Kai opens the door for me, and he shifts uncomfortable, but I move past him to the living room where *everyone* else is already. *Did I miss something?*

"You´re going for a walk Scar?" Andi asks and I frown-grin. "What?" I ask perplexed. "Doesn´t it like *rain*?" He adds grinning.

They noticed over the year, that that´s our thing. So, he´s messing with me.

"Fuck off." I joke rolling my eyes. "What you´re doing?" I ask.

And why wasn´t I invited? But I don´t say that.

"Watching a movie." Ryan shrugs. "Horror movie, Ry." Nina corrects him, and I nod sitting next to Aidan. There is no room, but I slide between the armrest and his body anyway. I wrap my legs over his and his hand wanders to my thigh as his other to the backrest smiling at me.

And then there is an awkward silence. *What´s up? Did I miss something?*

The others know nothing of our night together. *It´s our secret. The one we like to keep.*

And this time I´m okay with being hidden. But they stopped asking since Kai told them not to. But they don´t understand it and I can´t blame them. They´re already confused about our dynamic and the revelation that Kai loves me so it´s weird. Because the truth is we´re not together. No one made *any* decision besides the fucking. And just as they stopped questioning us, we did that too.

Finn clears his throat breaking the awkward silence and continues the movie. Kai sits diagonally from us and he doesn´t look, but I know he´s burning inside. But the thing is you can burn bright but still don´t say or do anything to change the way you feel.

So, I let him burn. Because he won´t change a thing. He won´t.

And he likes the pain he´s in, so I let him have it.

Despite Aidan and I always were touchy and hung on each other even before the bet, the threesome and all. So that´s normal for us but what isn´t is the fact that Kai and I do those things too but in private. *But no one knew we did.*

Aidan at least isn´t scared to be affectionate in front of others. *So, whatever.*

I laugh when Aidan is frightened, and he digs in my skin when I am as if he could protect me or something. That´s kinda dumb but sweet and I scoot closer to him. His arm wanders to my ass and mine to his neck. I caress his shoulders and the back of his head because I know he likes that a lot. So much he´s turned on every time I do it.

And under my thighs I feel it too.

At some point I look at him instead of the movie, but I haven´t even realized until he whispered. "What you´re staring at?" I blink. "Nothing." I whisper back at the side of his face. He grins and I look back at the TV. *But I can´t focus.*

"Now *you´re* staring." I whisper. "I know." He breathes at my ear, and we look at each other. He grins and licks his lips. "What?" I somewhat yell-whisper with a nod and take his chin. "What´s that grin for?" I wanna know but he shakes his head, and I rest my forehead on his. "Tell me." I beg quiet but he keeps shaking his head. "Nah." He grins, and I look at him. "What?" I yell louder and tug at his collar.

"*Guys.*" Leon snaps and Aidan looks at his brother who sits next to Kai. Aidan mouths *sorry* with a huge grin. I grab his jaw making him look at me. "Tell me." I hush against his lips, and he nibs on mine telling me *no*.

"Get a room we´re watching a movie here." Nina orders. "Words." Leon agrees. We face them but still inches apart. "And take your *puppy* with you." Andi refers to Kai and I let go of his jaw and meet his dead eyes. *My stomach sinks. He looks at me blankly.*

They look at us expectantly. “No.” Aidan grins and I try to suppress a smile, knowing.

Silence.

“You´re having a groan?” Nina asks with a disgusted grin. “Fuck off.” Aidan scoffs. “You have.” She raises her voice to which Aidan´s grin widens. “Gross.” She puckers her face. “We´re watching a horror movie and you´re getting off on it?” She asks offended but the smile on her face never leaves and Ryan chuckles.

Aidan and I share a look suppressing our smiles as soon as they appear cause we´re thinking the same. “Why are you smiling?” Kai snaps. “Nothing.” I say. “That *wasn´t* nothing.” He states. “What was that look for?” He insists and my face heats awfully, but before I can say anything Aidan speaks up. “Not the first time *that* happened.” He says under his breath. *The cinema.*

He frowns at us, and it takes a moment for them to get what we´re referring to. “You did it at the cinema?” Andi asks and we grin but I´m sure I´m bright red. “You´re disgusting.” Nina says laughing. “But it´s kinky.” She considers. “How did you..?” Ryan begins but stops as Leon shoots him a look not wanting to hear about his brother doing it.

“We went to the movies two months ago and..” he begins to explain. “Okay stop.” Nina interrupts him with a laugh. “Yeah, no words needed.” Leon states. “Now stop touching or go fuck.” He snaps. “Right here?” Aidan grins pretending to open his belt. I smack him and he laughs. Ryan snorts.

“Kidding we can wait.” Aidan says. “Love you too bro.” He adds raising his middle finger.

We regain the attention to the Tv. “Not that you two haven´t been in each other´s mouths a thousand times before.” Aidan mumbles. “True man.” Ryan tunes in but Leon glares at him. Ryan lowers his gaze.

“Whatever.” Leon snaps on edge. “Go on.” He waves us off but stands up and walks out. Nina shoots Ryan a look and follows Leon.

We continue to watch without any further interruptions. Andi and Ryan are the firsts to leave. Then Leon and Nina who came back after twenty minutes of guess what *fucking*. Shortly followed by Finn who has work to do.

There is that weird silence when we´re completely alone wordlessly looking at each other. Waiting for someone to say something. Rather for Kai to say something. But he just looks at his best mate and me for minutes.

Then he gets up. “Let´s go to bed.” He says heading upstairs. *And we follow.*

Kai gets me a shirt and boxers for him and Aidan. Then we shower.

Kai hands me the towel. Aidan and I blow-dry our hair, and Kai just ruffles his and helps me afterward.

We get in bed. Aidan on his stomach. Kai on his back. I hold onto Aidan´s arm but lie in Kai´s arms.

It has become a routine. We´re always sharing a bed. And shower together. Just as anything else too. Sometimes we all fuck. Sometimes just one of them fucks me. Other times we just touch, cuddle or make out. *But never alone.*

And today Kai fucks me as I hold his best friend´s hand. *All normal.*

- 27 -

There isn´t always an end to the story. *Good or bad.*

But there´s always a story. And as every summer has a story, every other season too. I just hope the season changes not that quickly. Because this is our summer.

Our story.

So different from last year. But life happens and you never know where you´ll end up.

Even if it´s with your best friends between the sheets.

144

One week later

"Come on." He urges. "Where are we going?" I ask. "Having some fun with our friends." He says with a smirk and puts his hand on my lower back to push me along as if he were in sort of a hurry. *Are we?*

The asphalt is soaking wet. He shoves his hands in his front pockets as we walk along. It´s so quiet out here. We´re heading to the fair I figure. It´s at the end of the village but it doesn´t start until tomorrow afternoon. *What are we doing out here?*

It´s spooky here at night. Most of the stalls are closed, and the covers still hang over the rides. At night and unused the carousel looks like something out of a horror movie.

All here does. Like a Ghost town.

The carnival is not huge but by no means small. So, we walk a few minutes to the main area where he comes to a stop at the huge auto scooter lane. I look around.

We´re alone.

"Where are they?" I ask in a whisper. "They will join us later." He says normally speaking and steps on the stage. "I´ll be right back." He tells me and walks away before I can stop him. *Great. Just leave me alone.*

I look over my shoulder to check if we´re still alone. And indeed there´s no one but I get chills. Every place has a completely different atmosphere when it´s dark. And it´s so quiet it kills me. There´s a black cat in the distance but the only sign of life besides us.

Some switch clicks making my head snap to the left. *Buzzing. Electricity?*

And suddenly the train´s neon lights come on. I turn my head away and squint my eyes at the brightness. I blink some more. The microphone emits noise. *Silence.*

"You smell that?" Sounds from the speaker. *He pauses.*

My heart in my throat trying to rip free. "The smell after rain." Kai´s voice surrounds me. *What is he doing?*

The mic shuts off again. *I look around.*

I can´t make him out behind the glass of the cabin there´s just blackness but then he walks back on the stage. "I think I owe you a ride." He says with a smug grin and memories of last year pop in my head.

"How did you get in there?" I ask suspicious. "I know the owner´s son and I have the money." He shrugs, walks over to the bumper cars, and pulls down the fabric of one of them. He gets in and signals me to come along. In the next moment, the horn signal sounds, and he inserts a chip. I hurry to get in next to him. Not even wondering *who* got them on.

The fog machine covers the track in white and Kai turns circles as we drive in reverse and bang against the empty cars. This right now is what I think feels like to be the main character. Riding with your crush bumper cars when everything is already closed, and you feel like you´re the last people on the whole fucking planet.

And right now, it feels we are. Being like this with him is everything.

I lift my hands in the air and laugh. The wind blows through my hair, and it feels euphoric. But eventually we come to a stop but the smile on my face never vanishes. Kai inserts the next chip as I catch something. *Wait.*

My eyes spot a dark figure in the control room where Kai was minutes ago. He wears a hoodie covering his face. But the fog machine won´t stop producing more smoke, so, I can´t longer see more than our own car. I cough and Kai tenses next to me. The fun all gone now and I really feel like the main character but not in a romance but a horror movie. But before I can question what´s happening, the honk sounds and we drive off. And my heart skips a beat as I spot in the smoke a green neon mask.

Those from the purge. Who´s that?

I look at Kai but he´s focused staring ahead like in trance.

My stomach sinks. What´s going on? Is he trying to mess with me? Scare me?

There´s a beat of silence and Kai keeps driving. Then there´s a noise over the speaker and I get chills. *I know those sounds.*

It´s the *Siren Head Sounds by Bonkers*. It feels like apocalypse and if I wouldn´t sit next to Kai, I would think I´d get murdered every second.

I can´t see. It´s all fogged up and keeps spreading and thickening. My heart races and I frantically look around, but I can´t even spot that neon mask anymore. I look at Kai, but he just keeps driving as if it´s nothing.

I look around as the fog clears slowly. *What the fuck is going on?*

Halloween is next month. I know it´s a game of ours. It is right? It has to.

Not a second later figures appear in the distance. Dark figures dressed in black.

I hold onto Kai´s arm but he doesn´t flinch and just keeps driving with one hand.

The fog machine starts again fogging us in. And everywhere I look people appear.

All wearing the same masks but with different neon lights surrounding us.

145

The metal creaks under their shoes as they jump on the track.

I try to count but fail. There are too many and I keep getting lost because we turn and go backwards. I guess twenty to thirty people. *Maybe more.*

The fog machine stops, and I try to see something as the power to our scooter cuts out and we roll a bit but come to a stand in the middle of the lane. Then they begin to run onto the roadway and get on the bumper cars ripping the sheets off. *They all have chips.* Kai shoves another in the car. And that´s when I notice he has put on his hoodie hiding his face. *But no mask.*

"Don´t let *them* catch you." He whispers into my ear and jumps up. But before I can say anything, he disappears into the fog leaving me alone. *The honk goes off.*

DAYWALKER! (feat. CORPSE) by Machine Gun Kelly plays as I grab hold of the wheel and bump right into someone with a neon red mask. And being surrounded by the guys wearing all different colored masks I feel extremely anxious and dizzy. Those are the friends as Kai called them. *But who are they?*

I look around trying to catch a sight of Kai, but the fog keeps thickening.

Why did he leave me? I thought those guys are friends. Then why shouldn´t I let them catch me? And where are the others?

It´s so loud now. They crash into each other and against the border. They make chains and hunt after each other. *And somehow, it´s fun, thrilling and scary.*

Others run from one to the other side across the track between the cars trying not to get hit. And I shriek as someone jumps on the back of my car and holds on to the bar. I put on my hood as much as I can to hide my face, because they can see *me*, but I can´t see them.

None of them.

And knowing Kai he probably has his own mask on by now. So, I can´t count on him.

As we come to a stop I dare to look up. Goosebumps cover my skin, and a shiver runs through my body. A tall guy is hovering over me and looking down on me but this isn´t Kai and neither Aidan. *He´s so much taller.*

It´s a pink mask. But I can´t make out the color of his eyes. They seem pink due to the light. But they don´t seem dark. Maybe blue or green?

He´s staring down on me and my face tingles. My heart sinks and my throat clogs.

Who´s this?

The mic bumps. And the music stops. *Silence.*

My whole body is on alert face heating under his stare, but I look away and take in the people. *I think those are all guys.*

"It´s been a while." The familiar voice echoes through the night and the guy is still behind me, but I don´t dare to look again. "But we are back. *Hunting*. We have some new players and new rules this year." The voice says and the tuning distortion and my tension prevent my brain from working. *Who is this?*

"Tomorrow the shitshow starts and we´re playing catching on the whole area." He announces. "There are several viewpoints from which we catchers launch, and the hunted spread around the site. Rides allowed." He continues. "The hunters have from midnight till the witching hour to catch *something*." He says and everyone listens in dead silence. "Don´t get caught by security. Stay under the radar. Keep your masks on. Wear black. And if you catch *something* make sure you *mark* it correctly." He warns.

What?

"The prey will wear neon glow bracelets and if something is off you´ll hear the *Siren Head Sounds* over the speakers and then get the hell out of there." He states.

"Now see yall tomorrow and have fun." And then it hits me. *That´s Aidan.*

He´s always the one announcing the games. He announced last year´s hide and seek game on Halloween too. It´s been a while we did something like this big. But Aidan told me they used to do those weekly. Until it all went down, and they grew up a bit. Because even in Neverland they can´t stay young forever. Even if one of them wants to. Kai doesn´t want to talk about the past, so I won´t get much stories out of him. I wished I knew how they were back then. But that way it´s more exciting if we do something like this. Even if it scares me.

Like right now.

The guys start to leave and disappear into the night. And after a moment I feel weight shifted and the guy behind me jumps down and paces after them leaving me as well. But once more he turns, and I stare at the pink neon lights.

All I know it wasn´t Kai nor Aidan.

But I´m not sure Leon would do something like that. Staring at me. Nor Ryan or Andi. And Finn is way too busy anyway. Who are you?

I watch him disappear and then a switch falls out and the lights on the track cut. Every hair on my body stands up. *Silence is scarier than any noise could be.*

And within minutes the area is cleared and I´m alone. *Where the fuck is Kai? He wouldn´t leave me alone, would he? And where did Aidan go?*

No one is here anymore. *They just left.*

"Fuck you guys." I yell into the night. *No answer. Great.*

So, I walk home alone a bit pissed and mostly scared because despite the fact I walk alone I don´t feel alone at all. Like *someone* is following me and *watching me.* But there´s no one. Every time I turn around. *I´m alone.*

What fuckers. Having fun with our friends, he said. *Yeah, fun.*

146

Next day

Neither Kai nor Aidan texted me after last night. There was only this group chat in which all rules where shared.

We should dress in black and wear the glow bracelets so the catchers will recognize us. And there were a lot of players, and I was excited because I´ve always loved the games they play. I´m a bit scared too because of last night. But mostly mad they let me walk alone.

But whatever.

Let´s see who´s going to catch me.

We all wear the black hoodies with *runner* and *catcher* logos someone handed out. And the neon glow sticks on our wrists.

It´s fun and thrilling at the same time. I pace between the people and dodge some hunters as they try to come for me. I watch some guy with a yellow neon mask grabbing a girl by her arm while running. She cries out and he scoops her up and carries her away.

But she looks happy, so I go on.

I spot another blue masked dude throwing two girls at once over his shoulders. And some more getting caught. *They're fast. I have to hide somewhere.*

But we aren't playing hide and seek. So, I must keep running.

And just as I start to run someone grabs me by my hood, but I jerk away in time managing to shake him off. It was the pink masked guy from last night. And as I looked back, he shoved another guy in a black hoodie. *Didn't see that color though.*

I come to a stand at the auto scooter because I can't run anymore taking a breath. As I do, I scope the surroundings. *Aidan wears a grey neon mask.* So, I try to look for him. Orange, Purple, brown and other dyes but not grey. *What color wears Kai?*

I get a bit dizzy from all the neon lights in the pitch-dark night. But I blink and let my gaze wander until I meet someone's who stands in the crowd all still facing me. Although I can't see his eyes I know they rest on me.

147

He just stands there with his hood on. His mask is dark like he let the light off.

He walks up to me. *Slowly.*

On the opposite site of the lane, he comes to a stop. Now I see his neon mask is on. It's just a black one. And that's when I know. *It's him.*

But before I can think further, he shoots towards me. My heart skips a beat, and I shriek in excitement stepping on the track and start rushing between the scooters. He jumps over the cars to get to me. I cry out stopping short quickly changing the direction.

But he bolts after me.

I dash through the people as he chases after me. *This time not letting me escape.*

I pace through the Merry go round, and he follows right on my tracks like he haunted me through life. I pelt between the rides and turn to get rid of him. But then he doesn't follow. *Of course. He likes games. The hunt.*

Leaning against the back of a booth I try to calm my breath. And I know I should keep running, but I need a break. Closing my eyes for a moment but regretting it immediately as I feel an ice-cold *blade* against my neck. *Shit.*

As I open my eyes and look slowly to the left trying not to get my throat cut there's no black mask it's a neon grey mask. *Aidan's mask.*

Relieved I sigh but the fact that it's him doesn't change the knife on my throat. He didn't touch me yet so we're still in the game, but he holds me with that black flip knife I know all too well in place. It's the same Kai had on Halloween. And my pulse drums against the cold edge as I stare into his familiar brown eyes.

"Heard you´re into knife play." He says in a tone I´ve never heard from him before.

It´s like a growl. One that sends my body on edge.

"I like to play too." He taunts in a low voice stepping a bit closer but still not touching me. "I have kinks you don´t know about." His breath brushes my cheek, and my ears grow hot at his words.

He whispers now. "Let´s see who´s worse." I hear a smirk in his tone. And then the coldness leaves my skin, and he too backs away. I step away too and keep pacing but missing the blade on my skin. *What is wrong with me?*

Let´s see who´s worse. Who? Me? Or did he mean Kai?

A sweat pearl runs down my back. I know Kai has kinks like the biting but.. *Aidan?* I mean the cinema was kinky, but that was the only thing I wouldn´t have come up with on my own. In my mind I go through every situation. Once he fucked me on his motorcycle with his helmet on. That was.. *thrilling*. And then another time he wore his uniform and got me in handcuffs. But there weren´t other kinky things. I´ve slept with him for months and he didn´t mentioned kinks once. *Maybe all the lost ones aren´t lost on kinks.*

Mostly I try to outrun other catchers and not the two of them because they just watch me. They come close but not too close. They push me a little, but they don´t track me down. They have an eye on me and keep the other catchers off me.

It´s almost like.. *they don´t want to catch me. They´re not chasing me but playing with me. Cat and mouse. What kink should that be? A boring one if you´d ask me.*

And there´s that dude with the pink mask again. Always watching me and chasing me.

But Kai keeps him off.

It´s a weird feeling not wanting to be chased but still wanting to be caught. But they don´t. *Don´t let them catch you,* he said last night.

Yeah, funny that not even the ones I want to be chased by come at me.

I envy the girl that makes out with some dude on the carousel or the ones having what seems like a threesome in the bumper cars. There are even multiple couples closed in that 3D cinema simulation starship.

And what have I besides, no breath left? Right, nothing.

It´s been an hour and most of the players are gone by now. They didn´t get to me again. Not even when I just stood there. I haven´t seen them either. And it all turned more into me searching for them. *I feel stupid. Where the heck are they? And what game do they think they´re playing with me? Is this a joke? Is it a new way for them to mess with me?*

I stand again by the auto scooter and look around. It´s almost three fucking in the morning and still no sign of them. They didn´t even respond to my texts. *Fuck this. Fuck them.*

I´m sick of it. This is frustrating. Maybe I should have just let someone else catch me and see what they do. But they even took that chance.

Suddenly the music cuts off and the *Siren Head Sounds* play.

This means nothing good. Some of the remaining players start running away, and I do the same. *Something went wrong*. And some were already running from securities all night long. They had three man dragging two guys away from each other as they started rubbing each other on the asphalt. Maybe they finally called the cops on us. But despite the people being creeped out they watched us. And some even joined us. I´m sure tomorrow we´ll be in the newspaper too.

I take a shortcut and head straight home. Not theirs on purpose because they left me. And I won´t run after them.

But I turn around often because I can´t shake the feeling that I´m being followed. But again there´s no one. *Just as last night.*

As I get paranoid I run the rest.

I shower to reduce some of my rage and lie down. *Alone. Thanks assholes.*

They´ve reached a new level of torture. But maybe that was all they wanted.

148

A loud creaking of my parcel floor wakes me.

I move around. *I hate when wood cracks. The ceiling does that all the time.*

Especially in summer.

I try to fall back asleep as it cracks again and suddenly I feel anxious. A shiver runs through my body as I open my eyes to darkness and try to hear something.

Silence. But not dead silence.

My face tickles and my skin burns. *There´s someone watching me. Actually, watching me. I can feel it. And smell it. Cigarettes. The only one I know who smokes normal cigarettes instead of weed, shisha or vapes is Ryan. But Ryan has no idea where I live.*

I hope I´m still dreaming.

My heart beats in my chest and I try to make out *anything* but it´s quiet now. But my gut tells me there´s something off. So, I reach over my head to switch the light on but it doesn´t work. *No electricity.*

My stomach sinks and I try to listen for any movement, but my heartbeat and my ear sounds are too loud. *Silence.*

I hold my breath listening not moving one inch. *There´s someone in my room.*

I heard a bone twitch. Did someone follow me? Did someone break in? What´s with our dogs? They would have barked. Wouldn´t they?

Then there´s a click and in the corner a neon white purge mask light goes on and my breath stuck in my throat.

I haven´t seen one of those the whole night. I think I might die.

But adrenalin makes me think straight so I don´t move and try to feel for my phone on the sheet not taking my eyes of the stalker. *But it isn´t where I left it.*

And in the same moment, I feel the bed yield. My eyes widen in horror. There´s another because the one with the mask still stands in the corner watching me.

But someone´s in my bed.

I can´t move and can´t speak. *I´m frozen. How many are there?*

A second later another klick and the persons mask on my bed lights in the same white and I should shout or something, but I don´t. *I can´t.*

I move to the wall behind me as he comes closer. "What you´re wearing?" The guy to my right whispers so I can´t recognize his voice. *Tears threaten. No.*

"Lace?" He asks taunting and again whispering. "Or nothin?" he adds in a hush. The guy in the corner doesn´t move. He just stares and I can´t make anything out besides that he´s tall and dressed in black as we all were. I can´t see their eyes even if their masks give a faint gleam of a light.

There´s just the cigarette smell. *And I hate it.*

The guy on my bed moves closer. "You showered." He states with a breath. "We like you clean." He tells me. *We? I hope it´s them. Or let it be a nightmare.*

He moves closer until he towers over me, and I think he´s on his knees looking down on me. My throat is blocked, and I bite back tears. *Are they armed?*

"You´re throbbing?" He asks still whispering. *I do. Fuck I do.*

I press my thighs together. *Why am I turned on?*

One single tear escapes. *Maybe scary is my kink. Maybe I´m worse.*

"Bet she does." The one in the corner whispers.

It has to be them. It´s just the two. Please let it be them.

"We´ve come to mark you." The one in front of me whispers. "Deep." The other adds coming closer. I feel dizzy and my stomach turns. My bed is in the corner of my room because I must sleep with the wall at my back.

That way I feel safe. But now I only feel trapped.

He comes to a stand at the end of my bed watching me as the other is to my right. I don´t know where to look so I bite down my teeth to stop myself from crying. *I can´t even scream. I´m paralyzed. This feels like a fever dream. Not real. Too surreal. This isn´t happening. This isn´t real. This is a game. It´s them, right? But they smell like cigarettes and smoke, and they have the wrong mask colors. White, not black, and not grey. White and whispering.*

He snatches my blanket and throws it onto the floor. The cold air hits my exposed legs since I´m only in a black shirt. *Kai´s shirt. And nothing underneath.*

He stares down on me. *That´s Kai. I hope it´s him. I hope it´s them.*

I chant over and over in my mind. *Trying to stay sane.*

If it´s them, I´ll kill them for this. If it´s not, I must find a way to kill those guys.

He grabs my legs and drags me closer to the end of the bed. He holds me by my ankles in place and I notice he wears a ring on his pinky. *It´s him.*

My feet touch his jeans and my breath shallow. "Undress her." He demands not really whispering anymore.

But I stopped paying attention to the voices.

Because I know by now or I just don´t care.

The one to the right moves to my head, and I stretch my neck to look at him. He stares down at me, and I feel my wetness and curse myself for it. *I am sick.*

He grabs my shirt by the collar and rips it apart. Seams tear and my breasts harden as the air hits me. I feel exposed but thrilled and I try to cover myself, but he grabs hold of my wrists and pins them underneath his knee. *They hold me.*

How should I beat two guys?

The guy holding my feet removes one hand and a second later vibration starts.

What the..? They have my dildo. I know the sound. It´s them.

I want to press my thighs together, but his hands force them open holding me in place. He slips it over my entrance and circles my clit as I squint under the vibration. "She´s wet." The one to my back says.

I know those voices. Do I? I´m confused. It´s them. The ring. Their hands.

But the smell?

I move my feet to his crotch, and he lets me. *He´s hard.*

I pant breathing unsteadily as I run my foot over his bulge. Shiver runs through my body as he pushes the vibrator inside me, and I cry out. He twists it and moves it slightly in and out. *Torturing me.*

I bent my body trying to chase the ick and flee when it´s too sensitive. "You like it Scar?" He asks. *Scar. But I´m too dizzy getting hit by my orgasm to notice.*

When I try to chase another, he removes his hand and let´s it inside me. I move, but can´t change the position. *They hold me in place.*

I rub my thighs to guide the direction of the vibrations of the upper part that lies on my clit. Then I grab the jeans of the guy behind me. *He´s hard too.*

I run my hand along his length. He groans and then I know.

It´s Aidan. And it´s Kai who I rub with my feet. It´s them. I know those moans.

Kai sets the vibrator some level higher, and I cry out. "Please." I beg breathless. "What?" Kai asks on edge. "Move it." I beg. "No." He barks, and Aidan grabs me by the throat forcing me to look to him. He chokes me with a firm grip as Kai pushes the vibrator in circle motions, and I rub them as I come undone. The orgasm hits as twice as hard as before.

He presses the button to turn it off but let´s it inside my me and it´s now that I know what Kai meant with *don´t let them catch you*. Because the game wasn´t there. They planned this game here. *Their game. Their kink. But I must admit I miss the knife Aidan had. So, I guess I´m the one who´s kinkier. Of both of them.*

I hear Aidan unzipping his jeans, and he frees his cock stroking it. My mouth gets dry, and I wet my lips. He leans over and taps the tip of his dick on them. They part and I taste his juice. I lick his pre-cum and feel Kai´s grip loosen. He leans forward stroking my breasts as I suck on Aidan´s length. Kai removes the dildo and starts biting my nipples and other parts of my skin. I alternate between sucking and a hand job as Kai licks me driving me insane. He holds my hips in place as he pushes his tongue inside of me while working my clit with his thumb. Aidan finishes in my mouth, just before I come another time. He lies down to catch his breath, and I knee in front of Kai. I bring my hand to his mask, but he grabs my wrist stopping me like my touch would hurt him.

Maybe it does.

I lock eyes with him. *Black eyes white mask. Yin and yang. The absorption of all colors. The lack of light. Black. Him.*

After a moment he loosens his grip but doesn´t let go. I touch his mask, put it over his head and let it fall to the ground. I caress his jawline, the bump over his nose and the cut over his eyebrow. *All of it. Taking him in.*

He stares at me memorizing him. Even if we can´t see much I feel him out. And I take my time. He´s still dressed and he didn´t come but made me come. *Three times.*

For a second, we forget about Aidan, but we don´t kiss and just look at each other. But then he pushes me down and removes his clothes. He thrusts inside me and fucks me hitting deep where my secrets lie.

Aidan next to us, probably watching. But I don´t look, I look at him and feel Aidan´s warm body right next to us as I get lost in Kai. *And I know he´s lost in me.*

We kiss with his forehead against mine and we´re breathing hard trying to find a rhythm. I hold onto him as he holds onto me.

Just holding. As if we could fall any moment. Leastways we would fall together.

He takes his time, and I take mine. The sweat of his body melts with mine and I blur into him. He grunts his breath hitting my face and I moan my breath hitting his. We kiss some more. Tongues dancing as slow as snow falls. And as we climax, he bites my neck, and I bite his. So hard he bleeds, but that sends him. With taste of metal in my mouth mixed with the scent of him in my nose, I fall. And he falls with me pinning me down with his weight of vulnerability and trust.

I have his bite marks on me. *I can feel it.*

And now I know they didn´t mark me. *He did.*

But I don´t know what that means yet. *For us.*

149

One week later, October

The past week I´ve got the impression that Kai tries to avoid us three fucking again. We haven´t been together since the last time. *Since that night.*

We saw each other but not the three of us. And we don´t fuck alone, so, it´s been a while. After he slept with me s*omething* has changed. *But I´m not sure what.*

And today Kai´s trying to avoid us being too close or alone all night. It´s subtle but noticeable. The way he either backs away, talks to some guys, or changes the topic. There are always the others with us, and I noticed he hasn´t drunken all night. He stopped drinking since.. *Bali.* But he smokes so that´s back to normal. *At least his normal.* Although he sleeps well when we´re next to him, he still needs his weed for anxiety.

I sit on Aidan´s lap and Kai disappeared a while ago. *To where no idea.*

I get up and head to the bathroom, take a deep breath and stare into the mirror. Then I hear it. *It rains.*

First, I look at the front door and, on the sidewalk, then on the terrace but no Kai anywhere seen so I walk up the stairs. His room is empty though. But when I turn to leave, I spot him on his balcony. Relieve spreads through me. He sits with the back to me on the concrete wall. His balcony is covered, but he still gets wet there on the edge.

He doesn´t flinch nor look when I open the door.

Like he knows it´s me. Or he doesn´t care. Maybe both.

Numb little bug, slowed + reverb - omgkirby

When I stand next to him he finally looks at me. His eyes are red from the weed and.. *hurt. He cried like a lot. Or he suppressed it until his eyes got like that.*

I knew something was off and I feel the need to be close to him and the wall is wide enough, so I hop onto it and get between his legs. He lets me and moves to make room for me, so I lie against his chest. His arms wrapped around me immediately keeping me warm. It´s a little fresh but endurable. His chin rests on my head and his body begins to shake. I shut my eyes feeling my insides sink. His jaw shivers and his grip tighten. He´s crying and I straighten up to look at him. His one hand on my waist and the other rests on mine. With his finger he´s absently rubbing the place where my ring finger meets my hand. *He used to do that back then. He stopped somewhere along the line.*

Almost forgot he did that.

He stares off and stopped crying. *Just looks broken.*

"Missed you down there." I whisper and his eyes lift to mine.

Now he rubs the ring on my pinky he gave me, and his eyes search mine. "Missed you up here." His voice all husky. My stomach sinks and tickles as he looks down on me.

And then his lips search mine. *Gentle. He never kissed me like that. Like my lips are a snowflake and his fire trying not to hurt. But it melts anyway.*

The kisses are soft and deep, and they taste like salt and rain. He holds my cheek, and I grab hold of his hoodie. I sit on his lap, and we continue to kiss. I no longer feel cold.

Hot tears mix with feelings as he again cries kissing me. Claiming me in a way no one ever did. *Silently. With sobs. So soft barely there. With tears that scream they´re for me. Maybe for us. Maybe for himself. Maybe for everything.*

With his hands shaking trying to be steady for me. With his body holding me and his soul crying to me. With him saying so much by saying nothing. With him kissing me with the tears that cared for me. With tears that want me. With him silently begging me to stay.

Because he speaks the silence no one knows.

Because he chooses me. *Silently. In tears. Shaking. Kissing. Holding. Calming.*

Telling me without the need of words. And that´s when I know. He loves me.

Silently.

And that´s okay. *At least I thought.*

Next night

For the first time in over a week the three of us wanted to have sex but Kai couldn´t get a hard on so we stopped and got dressed.

He said he wasn´t in the mood. *Which I didn´t bought.* Because my gut was telling me it had to do with the other day. When I stayed over without Aidan. We didn´t have sex but we slept alone which we never do. *So, something is off.*

As we come back down Leon, and the others await us blocking our way. "You guys fucking now?" blurts Nina. "Are you?" Leon presses and Finn is silent because he knows. Andi clears his throat playing along. And Ryan looks amused probably proud and a bit envy.

"What the fuck?" I ask and Kai shrugs. "What if?" He responds challenging. "So, you really *do* fuck." Nina chirps excited but also confused. "Like it wasn´t *that* obvious." Andi adds under his breath. "Aidan, what the fuck?" Leon prompts looking at his brother. "None of your business." Kai scoffs in return. "We´re your friends." Nina states. "You could have told us." She says fed up.

"Like the thing between *you* guys." She gestures between me and Kai, and we look at each other. "We know." I say.

"But that doesn´t mean we have to." I add *almost* feeling guilty. *But it´s the truth.*

"How..?" Ryan begins but Nina shoots him a look. "Ry." She hisses and smacks him to which he chuckles. "If you´re asking who´s mouth is where.." Aidan begins but Leon grabs and drags him away before he can explain further. *Luckily.*

Kai walks past them, and Nina and Ryan pester me with questions wanting to know every detail. Finn went after Kai and Andi sat down next to us not really paying attention.

Nina secretly liked to have a threesome too, but Leon would never share her. He´s extremely jealous but they both are. Especially because Leon must compete not only with other guys but also girls. And their relationship is not the healthiest, but they always come back to each other. Even if they hook up or flirt with others during their breaks. *It´s complicated.*

Ryan was as expected down for it as much as Nina. The only one who´s been judgmental was Leon. *It´s his brother. I get it.*

He was probably just waiting for us to screw up on our own. *And we did.*

We just hoped it would last a bit longer.

Leon smokes his joint while playing his electric guitar and I know I must talk to him. He´s mad and he has something to say. *I just know.*

And I know I might have to hear that. Even if I have no idea what he´ll say.

I don´t know how the conversation with his brother went or what is with Kai cause he´s gone for hours. But I sit down next to him preparing myself for nothing other than brutal truth and I wait for him to throw it on me.

"They love you." He begins. "Both of them." He says as if it was anything new.

"But you have to fucking talk about it. All three of you together." He hisses. "Otherwise, it´s going to go wrong at some point. And you *know* that. Maybe the best of all of you." He locks eyes with me. "Aidan is too head over heels and Kai won´t see straight." He tells me. "So, you´re the one who must get a fucking grip. And look at the situation the three of you have going on objectively." He demands. "Because I don´t think so, but correct me if I´m wrong, that you want to have a polyamorous relationship. So, sort it out." He snaps.

If he only knew.

"Aidan would never tell you this because he loves you." He says. "But as his brother, I´m telling you.." He speaks intentionally. "He may say everything is okay, and he probably thinks that. But he´s in love and we both know it *won´t* be okay when you finally fucking own your shit up to your decision that you´ve already made if you´re for *once* honest with yourself and them." He snaps and I look down.

"Believe me I know it´s a fucked up situation. But *this* can´t go on before it´s too late." He shakes his head. "I know." I say. "Do you?" He asks pissed. "Because he´s hoping to win you over. *Do you know that?*" He asks and I say nothing. "Right. Because he does. He doesn´t see that he hasn´t even a *chance* against him. He can´t see. But *you* do. And Kai does too, but he won´t say a thing. So, you´re the one." He tells me.

And he´s right.

"You´re his best friend you *have* to let him go or you´ll lose them both." He tells me. "You´ll lose him." He says quietly. *If I didn´t already.*

"And don´t let me regret having you brought here. I´ve stood by you to stay. Kai *never* wanted you here." He tells me like I don´t know. "Don´t fuck it all up. And most of all don´t ruin their friendship." He warns me with full honesty as always. And it hits me like a heart attack. *Maybe I already did. Maybe I´m the selfish one.*

I´m thankful he doesn´t mince words. *He never does.* Leon addresses things, even when they hurt. *Especially then.*

And it did hurt like hell, but it will hurt more if I don´t change a thing.

So, I go back inside. Trying to fix things I´m not so sure they can be fixed.

Aidan comes toward me. "We need to talk." I say as he tells me the same. We give each other a smile. "To the bonfire?" he suggests, and I follow him, nodding.

We sit down on one of the logs. This is where we *always* sit to talk. Where I broke him once by telling him he´s not the one without really saying it. And I´m about to do the same once again. Because what I´ve realized is that what went down between Aidan and me, was about sex and friendship.

It wasn´t about love. Not like the love I had for Kai. I can see that now and accept that now. I had to face what I knew all along. That with Kai it´s about so much more than sex, friendship, or love. It´s on a deeper and higher level. It´s somehow everything.

"So" he begins his gaze on the fire pit. "You first" I say because he seems to have something on his mind too, and I need to know what.

He nods. "This whole situation is pretty fucked up.. *complicated*." He ruffles his hair. "Kai´s accident.. when you were lying there with him.. in the hospital bed. When I held you.. on the street. The threesome.. when I saw you two.. *That´s when I knew.* I just knew." He´s talking a little jumbled, but I keep shut and listen to what he has to say. "I couldn´t admit that at first because I´m in love with you.. but deep down I knew. *Because I saw it.* Every time he looked at you and every time you looked at him. When he fucked you.." He trails off.

"There´s not just love between you. I can´t tell what it is, but it was more than what was between us." He admits and my stomach sinks.

He looks at me. "I love you. I really do, but maybe we´re just meant to be friends." He shrugs and has that sad smile on his face. "And even though the sex is killer." He chuckles and I smile. "I don´t want to fuck up that between all of us." He tells me. "Maybe it´s already too late for that. Because we fucked *a lot* lately." He chuckles again. "But I don´t regret *anything* that happened." He assures me.

"I´m so grateful. You helped me to get over a shitty time. I trust you with all I have. I can´t lose you. Not when I can have you as a friend. Because I need you. And I need him as my friend." He tells me.

"But what you two have I can´t make up for. I know that. I´ve seen the bond you have.." He shakes his head once more. "It wasn´t easy to ignore. Believe me I *saw.* I just hoped it to be different." His voice filled with hurt.

"I did stick up with it hoping he´ll admit what he deep down, *knows*. That he wants you." He tells me. "So, I helped you." He says quietly. "Even if it was hard, but it was some hella fucks I won´t forget, like ever." He laughs and I join him.

"As you probably realized he has changed too." He looks at me. "Because he did realize." He says and I can breathe and the hand that has been crushing my heart for *months* finally loosens its grip. *Because other to what Leon thinks Aidan knows.*

"I´ve talked with him about this a lot since you two are back. He´s been difficult as always. Either he was closed up or shut down when I asked the wrong questions. Or ignored me completely and got mad at me. But he also told some truth." He says. "I think, he knew exactly what I´ve been doing and why I didn´t backed off. What *we* tried to do. And he was pissed about it but also glad, I think. Because he knew that he needed that. Cause as much as he hates being pushed.. *sometimes* he needs that. Even if he hates you for it. He just needed time." He explains. *Time. The one thing he´s scared of.*

Of time running out. Of time becoming real. His Hook.

And even though his words hurt me I´m glad he sees it that way. Now I know why he did help me all the time with pushing Kai. *He helped him. Us. Me.*

"And what did *you* want?" He asks, and my brain is blank, and I blink at him. I can´t think and have forgotten what I was going to say in the first place. I look at him trying to figure something, but I come up with nothing. *And that´s something.*

"I´m right. Am I?" He smiles weakly. "It´s him. Isn´t it?" he asks, and I inhale. "I´m confused.." I begin. "I love you *and* I love him. I can´t compare. But I didn´t want to mess things up." I tell him and he nods.

"You´re like a soulmate. I´m myself around you." I make a pause.

"But with Kai.. everything is so different. Even if I tried to put it into words.. I can´t." I say upset. "Maybe I knew it all along and I´m sorry I´ve hurt you." I tell him and he laughs.

He laughs?

"When you know why you like someone than it is most likely just some sort of a crush. But when you have no reason or any explanation.. *that´s love Scar*." He says with a genuine grin like he´s *really* happy for us. *And I think he is.*

Because Aidan is that way. Selfless.

"And he seems to feel the same way." He tells me and I look at him questioningly. "Do you want me to tell you how *he* described how he felt about you?" He asks. "But don´t you *dare* telling him. He´ll kill me." He laugh and I nod. *He would.*

He holds out his pinky to me. "Swear." he demands. *So, we make pinky promise.* "*She`s my kink. She`s my heaven and hell. She`s my venom and cure.*" He says.

He refers to me as his kink? In a twisted way, that´s the perfect term for all this. And in my mind, I him saying that to me. *I wish he did. And I hope he does.*

“He was high when he told me all that and he told me some more things but I´m sure he´ll kill me if I did so.. *I won´t do that*. But believe me when I say he´s serious about you.” He tells me and I nod.

“When did he say that?” I ask him and his voice becomes brittle, and he clears his throat. “The day after the accident.” He almost whispers, and pain runs through my chest. “He was still on painkillers, so idk if he even remembers saying *that* specifically. You went to the bathroom, and I talked to him about the threesome. And then he told me how he feels about you. All roses and heartfelt stuff.” He grins weak and my vision blurs, so I close them for a moment. *He told him that day?*

“But after a few days I knew he wouldn´t tell you about it.” He sighs. “He got scared. And he liked our games and the sex of course. And mostly he didn´t because he panicked a lot.” He tells me like Kai told me it was around Christmas. And why he left me at the wedding. *Out of fear. And they all think Pan is fearless. He´s not.*

Maybe he has the most fears. Hooks.

“He may seem cold or a dick, but he feels for you. He adores you.” He says, surely. “It´s kinda funny because never have I thought he would *ever* have actually feelings for a girl. *Any girl.*” He tells me. “So, I thought maybe, I have to force him a bit. But I think he´s simply scared. And maybe you can take him that fear.” He says softly and he´s such a good person. My heart warms and tears run down my cheek.

“I won´t ever stop loving you, Scar, but he loves you harder I´m pretty sure of that.” He says with smile, and I look at him unbelieving what an angel he is.

I shake my head. “You´re too good for this world.” I tell him sniffing my nose.

“And I love you too.” I whisper. “You´re the most selfless person I´ve ever met.” I add, and he smiles at me wrapping an arm around me. “You know what I think?” He asks. “I think we have a *flirtationship*.” He announces. “Because it´s more than just a friendship but less than a relationship. We flirt, cuddle, fool around *and* are friends.” He says and he´s right it´s always been like that.

“And it´s okay that way.” He tells me. “I know you´ll be happy with me. But I know you´ll be happier with him.” He says honest and I could cry.

He´s selfless in a way I could never be. And neither Kai. So maybe that´s another reason, we´re like made for each other because we´re as fucked as the other.

“I told him I´d back off if he wanted me to the day after the accident but he didn´t act on it.” He says and I look at him. *He told him that?*

“He just needs to take that step.” He says. “And I think maybe he´s ready now.” He shrugs. “But I´d still want to fuck you by the way.” He smirks. “But of course, I won´t if you guys´ don´t ask me.” He says grinning and I smile at him. *Silence.*

"It's going to be hard for me Scar. I won't lie about that, but this friendship is worth it." He whispers into my hair and wraps his arms around me. I can't stop the tears from flowing.

He's an angel but I fell for the devil. And devils aren't made for love. They take love and break love. All they can give you is hell.

But maybe that's exactly what I love. Maybe.

151

We agreed to push him one last time.

Aidan leans on the rest of the couch, and I sit on his lap. His hands wrapped around me whispering stupid stuff in my ear making me laugh as Kai approaches us and I get up and kiss him. Aidan's still at my back but Kai pushes me towards him so our chests touch. He grabs my hand, silently leading me upstairs. But Aidan follows as discussed trying to provoke him.

Before we reach his door, he turns to face him. "Don't *fucking* touch her." He growls. "And this time I mean it." He adds. "Touch her and I'll break your neck." He warns, puts his hands on my hips and shoves me into his room, slamming the door behind him. "Wha.." I say but before I can ask, he lifts me, and our lips crush back together. "Shut up." He says against my mouth and bites my lip.

He walks us to his bed, lies me down and puts his shirt over his head. "Undress." He demands and removes his belt as I lift my shirt. He helps me strip down. Then he lies on top of me, and I shiver because his room is somehow cold. He notices and puts the blanket over us and moves closer. He holds my head with both hands and kisses my neck and jawline. He rubs his dick on my clit causing me to moan. We continue kissing and take our time. Our kisses are deep, long, and intentional.

Something's different. *I can't name it.*

I slip on the condom because I know he likes that the most and I like it too.

Having him in my hands. The way he looks at me like I have more than just his length in my hand but and his trust.

He closes his eyes as I stroke him firmly. His chest rises violently, and he moans in my ear sending chills down my body. I kiss his neck and bite down. He drops his weight on me a bit holding himself up. His head on my neck, groaning he kisses me there as I work him and he, me. He takes my hand and leads me to my entrance. He directs my hands fingering me.

His dick twitches and he reads my face. He watches me while licking my fingers and I watch him. We kiss as he slides inside me, and I scratch his back and bite his neck and taste his blood. He holds my head, and I continue craving my nails into his skin until he bleeds. This feels much more intimate. *Like we fuse together.*

He´s making me whole. *Spiritual and physical.* He fills me up with his thrusts so deep I feel his soul. *His soul fits mine.*

And at that moment, I realize he claimed me.

He fucks me alone. He told Aidan to back off. It worked.

He holds eye contact, and his dark eyes pierce me. The look on his face is so much more than lust or affection. *It´s love.*

Although he hasn´t said it again. *Maybe he won´t. But I know he does love me.*

There´s trust and longing. But also fear and pain. Raw emotions all on his face.

And he shows me.

I kiss his face. *His nose. His cheek. His frown. His lips. All of it.*

And as I trail kisses from his jaw to his neck and ear I whisper. "Kai, I love you." And he groans in response, kisses me, and bites the letters in my lips.

I don´t want him to say it back. I want him to know.

And by his reaction I can tell he loves hearing that. And maybe especially because he never heard those words, I have to tell him. Because he *is* loved.

After we climax, he doesn´t move. We breathe and feel each other.

He´s still inside of me as I caress his hair and sculp. And for a while he just looks at me.

Saying so much in nothing.

He kisses my nose, and my forehead.

Then removes the condom, and I lie down on his chest. But he has that frown on his face.

What is he thinking about?

I kiss his jawline and then bite into his skin. I feel his jaw moving as he smiles.

He likes that. I do that all the time. And he always smiles.

I do it when he´s mad to make him break, and it works every time. And this is a happy moment, and I want him to be happy.

But if I would have known what happens next, I would have shut up.

152

His arms wrapped around me holding me tight as I whisper. "Kai?"

He smiles. “Scar.” He whispers back. “I love you.” I say again and I said it just that he knows. *Then* he looks down on me and then kisses me softly.

He never does that. Who´s that guy?

I straighten up to sit on his crouch with my hands on his neck and his on my hips. “Can I ask you something?” I ask. “What you´re *already* doing.” He mocks me. “You can ask me anything. But I don´t know if I´ll answer.” He tells me smug. “Already forgotten about the question of the day?” I ask upset but with a playful smile. He presses his lips together shaking his head no.

We kind of stopped after we got back. I miss Bali. Us there.

I ponder but I have to ask. *I just have to.*

“Spit it.” He reads my face, and I swallow and meet his gaze. “What´s between us?” I ask and he frowns. His fingers dig into my skin. “Why do you ask that?” He wants to know. My heart in my throat choking me and I shrug. “Why not?” I respond. He breathes deep looking at the ceiling.

“Why do you *always* have to push me? Push *this*?” He asks irritated and my face heats. “Because we *never* talk about it.” I say. “We do.” He says annoyed. “No, we don´t.” I counter. “Yes, Lia we do.” He tells me. “When?” I raise my voice. He rubs his eyes annoyed.

“You just can´t let it happen without talking about it.” He says now his hands off me. “Without playing it all through in your head.” He groans.

“I have opened to you way more the past months than *you* did. *You* force me to open up about *my* past, fears, or feelings, but *you* keep your secrets. *That´s* not fair Lia and you won´t even see it.” He lifts me off him and my heart races anxiously as he does. He quickly gets dressed and leaves the room. *And I know it´s over.*

Because I´ve pushed him when I shouldn´t have. And all he wants is not talk. It´s what his parents did. All she wants is talk. It´s what her parents didn´t. *Talk.*

[NOTEBOOK ENTRIES]

I had to kiss her. It felt like we would fall apart. But it healed something. But still, something broke. I felt it. Like the devil kissed an angel. I might have killed her with it.

I´ve seen them hug tons of times. But this time hit me in ways I never knew could. Aidan and I knew our situation didn´t change. Somehow it was up to her. Later he came to me but we didn´t talk and stared at each other in silence. I hate this. If it would be any other girl.. well for me there were never other girls.. but if, I would back off. But with her, I know I can't. So, we decided we'll talk after the party. We'll see how that goes.

We wanted to talk. But I'm not the talker and Aidan neither. I liked watching. And I hated it. But I couldn't look away. We fucked her both. I haven't felt anything like that. I was so possessive over her but still I wanted to share her. It was addicting. Everything about her is I figured. But then she'd ran and I panicked as I heard her bolding down the stairs. I thought I lost her. My head was spinning. We didn't forced her? Did we? She wanted it too, right? Does she regret it? Did she decide against both of us? Is she mad? That all fogged my brain. She ran away from me and that triggered something. Even when she looked at me, she wanted to get away from me. That look on her face.. it fucking scared me. She ran away from me and that was all I could see. So, I ran after her. I wanted to scream that I love her, and I need her to stay, but I got hit by a car and then it's all black. I had some fucked-up dreams. I couldn't tell what was real. I'm afraid of time but not of death. But aren't we too young to not care if we'll die? But there's no time without her and no life where she isn't in it. I realized that. And that day I swore to myself no matter in what way I'll have her in my life. If she chooses Aidan I'll be her friend. If she chooses me I'll be hers. If she chooses no one I'll still be her friend. I couldn't bare being apart from her. It felt like a piece of my soul was ripped out as she died in those dreams. And my parents got here. But I couldn't care less. This wasn't how I've wanted her to meet my parents. Not that I wanted that to ever happen anyway. I think Finn stayed at the hospital too. I know him. He used to sleep in the hallway when I was little. I never wanted him to sleep next to me. I've always wanted to do it on my own. Maybe because I felt like I had to. Even if I didn't. He knew about my nightmares and when I screamed, he came trying to calm me. One time I almost fell over his body as I went to the bathroom. So, I figured what he did. I never mentioned it to him. Just as he never did to me. He wouldn't listen if I would have told him not to. He was stubborn as I am. So, I let him. And somehow, I felt saver knowing he did that. But at some point he stopped because I got older and he too. He would still do it if he didn't know I would beat his ass. But I knew he did that those days. I've seen it on him. His eyes. His posture. His pain filled features. And he knew that I knew. But we both pretended not to. As always, we didn't speak about it. Because we didn't need to. And I wanted him there as much as I wanted Aidan and her. But I knew he wouldn't stay on the sofa, so I let him. Be my brother.

Since I got back, we three are inseparable. Because death is always around the corner, and we realized we can live every day. We stopped worrying. I told him how I feel about her, and he told me too. I know he'd back off if I told him to but I didn't want to think about that yet. He knew but somehow it was like a game to us. Seeing what will happen next. Who would approach her. And who would stop the other? Who's the one she wants? Aidan and I had always the same mindset. We don't like labels. We don't like responsibilities or our freedom to be limited. We want it easy. He's the one who fucks a lot of chicks. And I'm the one who doesn't fuck a lot. We both don't want a relationship though. And that's what she wants. And honestly, I don't think I can give her that. I just know I want her at my side. I want her in my life. Back in Bali I knew I wanted her. I'd chose her no matter what would happen. But now after that night I just want her to be happy.

He tests my limits by tip toeing around the boundaries. I know exactly what he's doing. And I hate but love him at the same breath for it. It's a mind fuck. We enjoy our games a little too much. The excitement. The thrill. She liked the way we looked at her. Until she started talking to fucking Wren. Like why the hell does she pick him all the time? God, I hate whatever fate or karma it might be. I couldn't cut it. ~~Not with him.~~ He tried to touch her. I almost cracked his skull. It was too much. She played all dumb. She fucking knew. He's off limit. That's why she did it. To piss me off. ~~But this was cruel. This was no fair play.~~ We wanted to leave the decision up to her. But again, she forced me to make the first move. As fucking always.

Our games were all fun until they pushed me. Did they gang up on me? It was torture. They wanted me to stop them. But I didn't want her to stop. It made me jealous sure. Even sick. But it made me hard. I was pissed at them, but I liked it. I gave in but afterwards I've almost lost it. He said I should choose. Like what the fuck? Why am I the one who has to say it? Why don't I push her? She needs to make a fucking decision. Not me. She knows I love her, and I told them to fuck off. They did. But they came back. I hoped they would. I told them how I felt. It's like they know I will claim her now or later. But somehow, I like how it is because I know it won't be like that forever. I'll mess up, run, and hurt her again. Even if I want her to myself, he's the one who's going to keep her. I can't give what she wants. So, I take this. Because I won't be the reason to end things. Not this time.

She wanted us to do it for each other. ~~My heart was on my sleeve. Needles poking my chest and throat. It made me feel everything I had forgotten.~~ It was overwhelming. ~~It felt like I could die right there. My chest hurt but filled with thrill and excitement. I didn't want this not with him.. He's my best friend.. I knew how this would end.~~ But it was too fucking good. The way she watched us. ~~I couldn't fight it.~~ But she was right with everything. ~~I couldn't fight anymore. It felt different but familiar. It was how I~~

~~remembered the first line. It made me feel things I haven't felt in a long time. Tears rolled remembering how those kisses have felt.~~

We don't have to label things. We live and fuck. But deep down I'm afraid she'll choose him if we end this. Cause she could have easily chosen me in the first place. And she didn't. She wanted this. I want her so I'll go along. ~~Even if this is a road, I swore to never go down again. But I know it's a different one. The one before is dead. But it won't stop me from remembering it once existed.~~

The others made an intervention about the situation between the three of us. They asked question we didn't answer. It's none of their fucking business. I know they're confused after I declared my love, and she went with me, and they broke up and all. I told them to cut it. But then of course, she came over. Best timing ever. They don't get it. I mean we haven't either a clue what we're doing. But it's our thing. Our mess. We'll have to deal with sooner or later. Rather later. Then fucking Andi called me their puppy I almost lost it. And apparently, they fucked in the theater. It made me feel sick. And it kept me wondering what else they did? But I think, I don't want to know. It made me angry.. the way they are. They do all this in front of them. They don't hide. No secret like we were. Even if it doesn't have to be that way anymore. Somehow it feels like it still is. But I'm not Aidan and she's not the same around me as with him. They're different. It hurts.

We fuck a lot lately. They sleep next to me every night. I can't think straight. It turns me on. But it hurts. I want her to want me. Not him. It's so wrong but right. I can't stop.

I took her to the bumper cars. She was so happy. With me. I didn't want to leave her alone, but it was part of the game. She was scared but I watched her. And then fucking Wren stood behind her. I wanted to smash his brain right there on the lane. But I know why he did it. We left her alone as planned but followed her home. Making sure no one else would. You could never be sure with some of the guys. Especially Wrens shitheads.

We tried to scare the others off her. Wren wandered around her all the time. I almost broke the rules. We made sure she won't be chased. We followed her home. And waited until she went to bed. I've told Aidan what kinks she has. So, we came up with our own game. We wanted to make it even crazier, but Aidan forgot the knife. We come to scare her. Turn her on. I've come to mark her. Even without the knife. I claimed her. But it was so much more. I didn't realize until it was done. Because it changed me.

Somehow that was the start of me realizing I can't do this anymore. The fun has faded and the thrill too. I'm down from my high of I fucking survived and don't want to share her anymore. But I'm scared because what does that mean then? When I can't give what she wants? I couldn't see them anymore. It just hurts. And I catch myself avoiding them. The jealousy and the pain is greater. It was okay when I almost died. But now it's not okay. I'm on edge. I don't want to fall. Not without her in my arms. But what if she wants to fly? With him and not me?

I've avoided them as best I could. I sat in the rain for hours. When did we stop doing this together? When did we stop chasing each other? Why isn't she here? Because she's with him. I cried most of the time. And when I didn't I tried not to. I'm not good at this. It's overwhelming and scary. I felt that I love her. That I want and I miss her. I felt it in every hour that passed without her being next to me. Even if I don't do time. I felt the eternity of those moments in every bone. Like they broke every second without her. For the love for her. Like they broke for her. But when she came it felt like a weight had been lifted. The look on her face told me how I must have looked. Like she saw me break for her. I couldn't hide my shaking nor me crying. We didn't talk. I might have cried as I kissed her. I wanted her so bad, but I couldn't tell her. So many times, I wanted to tell her. So many things. But I couldn't bring myself. There's that paralyzing feeling. I kissed her and tasted my own tears. It occurred to me that she's my biggest desire but my greatest fear. I didn't plan to feel for her the way I do but one day she smiled at me the way she always does, and I thought fuck it. I let her in, but I suppressed the thoughts and locked them away. But I felt it everywhere. My bones cried for her. I'm not a man but a boy unable to deal with emotions. Unable to love. Or rather to show. And I'm scared to fuck up again. I just can't tell her. I wish she wouldn't need the words. I wish she could hear my thoughts. My silent bones braking. My soul begging. My tears pleading. I wish this could be enough. But I know it's not. But she stayed until the rain stopped, but the tears kept falling. My hands shook when I tried to hold her. But she kissed me as soft as a haze. And I know she knew the things I wanted to say. Because even if she wants me to be different, she knows who I am. She knew I loved her silently. I watched her texting Aidan she went home. Then we got up and went to bed. I kissed her how I never did, hoping it'll be enough. Hoping it'll be something. I missed our silence. I missed us and waking up next to her made life seem different. Something worth looking. Worth feeling. And I realized I never want to share her again.

I couldn't avoid us being alone anymore. But I was frozen as they began to do it. My body did the talking. I couldn't get hard. Luckily. So, we stopped. Maybe the fucking was the way all three of us did cope. But the coping is over. The others put the pieces together. But I didn't care. Finn tried to understand why I let this happen. I don't know myself. I just know it won't happen again.

153

Kai

Having slept with her was my downfall. It was on Bali, and it was when I slept with her *without* him. I knew what I was doing, and I thought it would be the right thing but it wasn't. At least not until she tried to push me again.

Sleeping with her alone was scary but all I wanted. I was afraid because she held my heart in her hands as I fucked her. And she held it craving her name with a flip knife. That scared the shit out of me, but I loved it anyway because I did the same to hers.

She makes me anxious sometimes. And I know that's bad. That's not how it should be. You're not rational when you're anxious.

Cause what would you be scared of if you're thoughts are rational? Nothing.

But I'm emotional with her and that's bad. Because fear is no love it's control. It's ego. It's holding instead of letting it come. It's the way I learned it and not the way she did. And I want her in the right way. Even if I'm not sure if I can.. *healthy.*

I want her without the feel of dying. Without wanting to run and I want her to want me without the need to hold onto me. But we're not there and I'm not sure if we'll ever reach that.

Anxiety is why you shut down. You don't let people in. But she's already inside of me.

Choking me. Suffocating me.

Fear shows that you live in the future and not the present. And this isn't where I want to be. I'm home in the now. *Nowhere else.*

And don't get me wrong I'm not anxious when she's with me. Or anything I do with her, I'm calm. But when I think of what will be. I am nervous and feel trapped. I feel like running and avoiding. And she keeps pushing me to feel that way. Pushing me out of the now. And I don't want this. But that's what she does, *push me.* And what I do, *run.*

With our triangle situation I could easily kiss her, touch her, sleep with her without explaining why. Without talking or leaving the now. But now I can't do all those things without thinking about what that that means.

But all she wants is talk. *I don't want to fucking talk.*

Just look at me. Feel me. Love me. Just be.

Maybe I have commitment issues, I mean know I have. But more out of fear and not cause I want to hurt her. I want to be with her, but it is as simple as fucking complicated as that. I just can´t tell her without telling her.

I could write a letter, *but would that ever be enough?*

There is that demon whom I friends with. Who tells me to do stupid things. And I´m used to it. To making the wrong decisions because I don´t care.

But I do care about her.

But you can't just break patterns you've internalized. Like programmed.

And the way I am is not enough for her. I can´t be what she wants me to be. She put me once again in a position where I had to be cruel to her. Cause I started to change because of her. *For her. But again, it wasn't enough.*

She didn't even see me try. She just saw what I didn't. What I still couldn't do. Talk.

I know I should be able to tell her how I feel. *I should be different.*

Because I don´t know how to love neither do I know how to believe I´m loved. And I don´t deserve to love or to be loved. *Never did and never will.*

It´s just every time she tries to talk about what is between us, I panic, shut down, want out and run. I can´t do anything but hurt her. And hurt me for doing it.

I know she´s my twin flame because everything I´ve been running from all my life was all of a sudden in front of me the day I met her. She makes me face my fears even if I seem to not be able to overcome them. Because the silly thing about humans is they tend to run from their problems, pretending they´re not existing. Trying to suppress them. So basically, we suffer because we like it. Because then we have an excuse. We can continue to suffer because it is beyond our power to change our situation, knowing it isn´t. And it feels like you have no might. *But you have it all.* But knowing that changes nothing, it makes it worse. Because our consciousness is our blessing and curse. We are the most intelligent creatures but the fucking stupidest. At least I am, because again I pushed her away.

And I know I'll do it again. I need to get my shit together. But I don't know how.

We are filled with fear and pine for love but are afraid of real attachments. We find what we love and kill it ourselves before it kills us.

We even die for love, *as all shitty poets say.* But I´m already dead and she killed me. Sleeping with her killed me. Because it did the exact opposite of that.

It made me live.

But I think my mind works differently. Cause most of the time I think in quotes, lines, and lyrics. Maybe it´s because I have tons of books and notes in my phone with quotes, I find inspiring. Or maybe I´m just build different. *Or weird.*

My brain just throws those lines at me in situations, and they have an influence on my decisions and emotions. *They always have.*

I hear a word, and my consciousness picks the perfect line of a song or a movie or book, and then I meditate about it. Maybe it´s because I grew up between books and lyrics instead of loving arms. *Or maybe I´m again just weird.*

I can´t even think my own thoughts. Maybe I think mine are worth less.

Maybe they are. Maybe I´m just fucked or broken.

It´s sad thinking even my head thinks what I have to say is unimportant, so it lets others talk. Maybe it´s a way of dissociation. I´m in my head and not in the world. Like I´m floating and watching it happen on autopilot. Thinking those thoughts that aren´t mine and let them lead me. Cause it´s too much and I need them to take me away. Making decisions I can´t on my own. And that happens a lot lately.

Normally, with her, I share those thoughts. Cause I know she wants to hear them, and she understands them. And I even get more because of her. She´s sort of the kick-start to my quote dictionary. *That´s how it´s been.*

But since we´re all the time with Aidan and not that much alone.

I can´t share them. I mean I could, but I won´t.

So, I just write them down and journal about them. *But I want her to hear.*

But right now, I can´t see the point. *I can´t even reach my body.*

Down The Rabbit Hole - Chakaruna

And as I look at her with those blue eyes my brain shoves me right in the gut with a line. Telling me to keep floating and shut down. *So, I do.*

The Matrix is what I have to think about when I look at her. *About when Morpheus talks about the blue pill that will end it all. You can go on with your life and believe whatever you wish. And the red pill that takes you to Wonderland and down the rabbit hole.*

I think about it when she pushes me. When she wants me to open up. Every time I want to kiss her, tell her I love her or that I want her. *The Matrix* is what I think about when I imagine how my life would be with her.

It´s something I want so bad but can´t let myself have it. So, I close my eyes and listen to the next Quote. Also, *Matrix.*

"There is a difference between knowing the path and walking the path."

And that´s how it always is. I know how it would look like being with her. I knew it when I left for London. I knew when we left for Bali. I knew when we came back.

But still, I won´t go there.

Because there is indeed a difference between knowing something and doing it.

So as much as I want to know how Wonderland would feel like with her at my side and see how deep the hole goes, I don´t go down there and don´t let myself fall. Because having her in Neverland is different than running down a rabbit hole.

And all I see is my body from high above. And I keep taking the blue pill. The blue pill I saw in her eyes. *The blue in the butterflies.* The blue that dies.

154

"Stop fucking run for once." She shouts and I snap out of it.

I turn to face her. ~~Blue eyes.~~ *No, they're green.*

"I keep running because you keep pushing." I shot back. "Please don´t run. *Stay.*" She begs with those eyes I have forgotten the color of. "We don´t need to talk about it. But stay. Just stay." She pleads me and her voice shakes with fear I know too well myself. And I look at her but don´t see her. I can´t let myself see her right now. I´m too scared to see. Because I know I fuck up. *But I can´t stop myself.*

"*This* doesn´t work Lia." I tell her and the look on her face almost gets to me.

Almost takes me back. But I keep going.

"You want to talk." I say. "And I fucking can´t." I point at myself. "Now just let it go." I snap. *But of course, she doesn´t.*

"Once you told me it´s Tink that makes Pan fly. But in order to fly you have to keep the fairy with you." She says. "But all you do is push me away." She´s upset. "No wonder you can´t fly anymore." She adds and I shake my head. "Don´t come with Pan now." I warn her.

Knowing I'm the one who refers to that all the time.

"But you should never walk away from connections that touch the deepest parts of your soul." She says and I stop to really look at her.

I can hear her heartbeat. Beating for me. But I need her to stop running after me, so I say something that will hurt her. Because I'll keep hurting her anyway.

She looks at me like she *knows* what I´ll say. "There is a difference between connection and attachment. Connection gives you power, attachment sucks the life out of you. Now guess *who* we are." I say spitefully and I swear I could hear her heart breaking.

And mine too.

I feel sick and there´s that voice screaming and begging me to stop. But the devil tells me to keep going is much louder. *Please let go of me.*

Lia

He broke my heart into pieces.

And not because he was right about what he said, because he wasn´t. He hurt me because he *wanted* to hurt me and get rid of me. I felt it the minute he left the room. He got anxious and shut down. *And he won.*

But he adds one more. "Every time you find yourself giving more energy than you receive, step back." He growls and I shake my head trying not to let this get to me.

He just throws punches, I tell myself. *But they hit deep.*

"You won´t stop running, huh?" I ask indifferently. "Lia the *only* reason why I keep *running* is that *you* keep pushing *this*. You couldn´t just let us be." He stiffs a laugh shaking his head at me. "And the *only* thing I´m running from is the future. *Tomorrow.*" His hands fly in the air. "All I want to be is in the now because I don´t think of a year from now. I think about right now." His voice rises in anger.

"And right now, I want you." He says desperate. "How can´t that be enough for you?" He asks me. "You *just* told me to let it go, and *now* you tell me you want me?" I yell irritated and he shrugs. "Yeah, so why can´t *that* be enough for you?" He asks again but I have no clue. *Why isn´t it?*

I look down and he inhales sharply and speaks slowly. "The only way to be happy is the now." I look up at him. "And there is a huge difference between wanting to live in the now and *actual* living in the now." He tells me.

He´s the latter and I´m the former. Clearly. But what does that mean? What does that make us? Honestly, I don´t know. We´re at the same point we were months ago.

"Another difference is that *you* want love." He goes on. "Need it even. But I don´t Lia." I stare at him my throat closing. "I can be alone and *want* to be alone." I shake my head he´s confusing. "But love makes me feel weak. The power that it gives *you*, takes it from me. It makes me *feel* alone." He says and that stabbed me. "And not the other way around." He says and my heart can´t understand he feels different than I do.

But love is subjective and sometimes we forget that.

"I can want you but still not wanting to be with you." He says and never in my life something hurt that much. Tears spill as I look at him. *How can he say those things?*

I lick the salt of my lips. "You wanna know the saddest part of all this?" I ask him with a blurry vision. "Just as you won´t stop running. I won´t stop chasing after and pushing you." I shrug. "So maybe you´re right." I nod hating that I cry. "I don´t love you. I´m attached to you. I´m sick. An addict." I nod. "That´s not love. That´s toxic. *You´re* toxic." I hiss.

"You should change your therapist because he´s *clearly* doing things wrong." I´m gross for saying that and I feel the bile rise up, but I clench my teeth to stop it.

That look on his face.. What is happening right now? Just a minute ago we were between the sheets saying yes to each other. But then I fucked up. But he can´t always react like that when I want to talk about us.

Is it because of what happened with Aidan? But Aidan told him he would back off. He knew it all along, so what is the problem?

Why can´t he be happy? If he knew from the beginning that he wouldn´t get involved with me wholly, why did he come into my life? Why didn´t he leave me alone? Why did he say he loves me? Why didn´t he let me, and Aidan be? But the most important question is why do I want him so badly despite all that? Why isn´t it Aidan? Why am I doing this to me?

We didn´t last, we didn´t even began. There was never a us the story.

Just him and I but it ended. *Now.*

- 27 -

Kai

Y*es, hurt me. Break me. Hate me. Fight me. Let me go. I crave it. I´m bad. Sick even.*

There is that saying that *if you don´t heal, what hurt you, you´ll bleed on people who didn´t cut you.* And I did even worse than that. I didn´t just bleed on her, I cut her deep. And once I thought I wasn´t her hero but her villain. But what I didn´t know back then was that apparently, she has a kink for villains. *But I can´t.*

We´re too different, I tell myself.

She craves love cause she had it. I despise it cause I´ve never known it.

I just want to cry and rip out of my body. She makes me feel the things I don´t want to face. *I´m not ready. I can´t breathe. I want out. Now.*

I stare into the void as I speak absently not even sure if I really say it or if it´s just the voices in my head talking to me. "When I first saw you.. all the demons inside me stopped. They wanted you.. *like your soul.* I just knew.." I close my eyes. "I´ll hurt you." I whisper and then I look at her. "But it seems like you haven´t had enough."

Just do it, I tell myself.

Stab her. Do it.

"You´re right *you´re* sick. You like being hurt." I say emotionless. "And sometimes emotional abuse.. can feel a lot like love. Believe me I know." I say blinking slowly until I snap out of the void. "But surprise it isn´t." I smile. *And that´s it.*

She breaks into tears and bolts out of the room. *I broke her. But broke me too.*

I stare at the spot where she stood seconds ago and let the anger filled tears steam down my jaw. I inhale and my chest hurts. I grab my shirt wanting to rip my heart instead. *It hurts.*

I pace down the hall and into the bathroom. *I can´t breathe.*

There´s that black spot. Spots I see.

My head spins and my stomach turns. *I throw up.*

But the pill has already made its way into my system.

I made my choice. *I took it. I wanted it.*

I don´t know how much later it is. But I´m still lying over the seat. Waiting for *anything* to get out. *Why am I like that? Why can´t I love her?*

Why am I such a masochist?

She was probably the best thing that *ever* happened to me, and I ripped it apart. I pushed her until she walked away. *Again.* And I know I asked her not to leave me when I do, but she did and I´m glad she did.

Because I don´t deserve.. Because I can´t handle.. Because I´m wrong.

I think I´m sick. Sick of self-hate. Sick of my parents. But mostly sick of me.

She´ll never forgive me for this. *Neither do I.*

I had to push her away. But it would be even more selfish to ask her to wait for me until I get better. *Until I can love. Until I´m not broken. Until I´m not sick.*

But I can´t ask for that and she can´t ask for a future.

I know I´m broken but I never had a problem with it until I met her. I wanted to be strong for her. I didn´t care what happened to me. I almost *died* because of her. *For her.* Because I cared more about her than about me. *This is sick.*

There´s something wrong with me. *It has to be.*

I always liked pain. *Craved it even.*

It´s always been like that. But if I keep destroying myself, I´ll destroy her with me. And even if I´m not worth it, she is.

But how am I supposed to save her if I´m not capable of saving myself?

She doesn´t need to be saved idiot. *You are.*

But the thing is the self-destructive behavior is a way to prove you´re still in control. And control is all I have left. *It´s all I ever had.*

The control I could give myself, that I hadn´t as a child and need to hold on. The control she wants me to let go, and I give up when I´m with her. When I open up.. *I lose control.* I lose part of me when I open up to her. So, if I want her, I need to learn that first.

To lose control.

It´s insane how trauma makes you push people away when all you want is love. When all I want is her forever. *But forever are just many now´s.*

But in the end, you are your worst enemy. Your ego.. *the source of the devil.* So, I told her things I knew would break her. "*You gave her good advice and broke her heart.*" Oscar Wilde once wrote. *I understand that now.*

I broke her heart scared of her touching mine. *But she already held it.*

And I made her walk away with it. But the truth is I don´t have hers. Because I don´t deserve it. *Not yet and maybe not ever.*

155

A few days later, Lia

Finn told me he´ll go back to Bali. *Of course, he would.*

It was foreseeable but I won´t stop him. *I see no point.*

If he wants to leave, he´ll go anyway. But not without answering me one last question. "So back to Bali, huh?" I ask with a plain expression. "Yep." He retorts. I nod.

Silence.

"But I fell in love with you." I say mad at myself for not staying strong.

"Then fall out of it." He snaps throwing his hands in the air.

So, he´s still on defense mode.

I laugh and shake my head. "You said you love me." I say. "I was drunk when I said those things." He says. "And stoned." He adds. "Bullshit." I snap. "I was *completely* wasted Lia." He yells back. "You´re full of shit. And I´m not talking about the drugs." I growl but he stiffs a laugh. "Why did you said it when you *clearly* didn´t mean it?" I ask. "Because *fuck you*, that´s why. You made me love you. I liked being alone." He rages pointing at me. "And now I can´t. So, fuck you, for making me." He says and I grin. "Stop *fucking* smiling. I mean it I hate you." He growls but I keep grinning. "No, you don´t." I say. "No, I don´t." He agrees and I shake my head.

At this point it´s just funny.

"But it doesn´t matter." He shrugs and he´s right. *It doesn´t. Not anymore.*

Silence that slices us.

"You said you´ll try." I whisper. "I know." He says soft and looks pained for a moment. "Guess I lied." His voice cracks as he attempts to shrug.

I nod choking the lump, so I won´t cry. "Can you at least answer me one last question?" I ask him tears begging to spill. "Sure." He manages to say, and the sound of his voice tells me his eyes burn too. Because even if he said all those hurtful things, we both know he didn´t mean them. He said the things to hurt me.

But I´m used to that. It´s about the things he doesn´t say.

“Why couldn´t you let me in?” I ask, knowing he´ll probably shut down and I try to read his face. But it´s hard cause all I can see are his red eyes and a scowl on his face. And eventually he nods looking past me.

He won´t look at me. So, whatever comes is the truth.

“My mom used to tell me that your first love destroys you. That it´ll show you what love isn´t. Because that´s your *first* love.” He says. “You have to learn from *that* love. Hurt and grow. But you´ll lose them and won´t end up with them. Especially in our generation. And my mom´s first love wasn´t my dad either. But she never forgot her first.” He says and looks like he´s in pain.

“You´ll always suffer because of them.” He says. “Because you´re not supposed to keep them.” He whispers. “I never understood that.” He hushes shaking his head. “And to be honest I never wanted that.. love and stuff.” He tells me unable to blink and he frowns as he speaks. “Then I saw how you reacted to your ex. And I think I didn´t want it to be you.” He admits and I look at him. “I never wanted a girlfriend. I thought *some-day..* maybe. But I didn´t care about all that. Because no girl made me feel.” His eyes meet mine. “But you made me.” He says in a hush. *Fuck you, for making me.*

“But I knew. You´re it and it made me mad. For *many* reasons.” He shrugs with a light smile on his face. “I was jealous because *you* had your first love. And I didn´t. At least not..” His voice cracks and he shakes his head, as if he decided to say something different. “Because you´re *my* first love.” He says instead.

“But I don´t want you to be my first. I want you to be the last.” He laughs under his breath looking on the ground. “But you´re *not* my girlfriend. *Never been.* And I fucked up anyway. I always do.” He nods to himself as if he´s doomed.

“But I think *that´s* the reason besides my other issues you already know about.” He says and I nod. “I didn´t want to lose you. So, I kinda never had you.” He locks eyes with me on that last part. “And I know it is stupid.” He says. “But I was mad that *you* mean that to me and *he´s* that for you.” He shrugs.

“You´ll never feel the same about me the way I feel about you.” He says and I think it´s the other way round too.

“I´m sorry I fucked up Scar. But I think I can´t..” He begins but I stop him. “It´s okay.” I tell him even if it´s not. *We both know it´s not.*

I don´t look at him and don´t know how to feel about that either. And I don´t even care anymore if that´s a stupid reasoning or not. I just thank him for answering and let him go. Because I´m exhausted and I need an end. *I need to breathe.*

Why is it that we are so afraid of telling people we love them if that´s the only thing we should be doing?

I´m born to over love and he´s born to love not enough. *But I know it´s not true.* Because if we work on ourselves, we can love the way we won´t push each other. In a way no one will feel the need to run or shut down. *There is a way.*

But I thought we could walk it together. But healing is a lone road, and you have to do it yourself. And I think that´s what we do. *Do it on our own. Heal.*

I look up in the sky ready to cry but instead, I think.

Just a year ago things were so different. And I wanted a summer I would remember, and I got one. One I would never forget.

And I´m grateful but I´m ready for the season to change. *Ready to move on.*

156

This time he didn´t just leave. He actually said goodbye. *Including me.*

"So, he left again." Aidan says as he sits next to me on the asphalt. I nod slowly forcing me not to cry again. I probably won´t have any tears left anyways. "He *always* leaves." I whisper. "Yeah, he does that all the time. He gets on a plane and escapes." He shrugs. "That´s what he does. And the no contact thing.. he does that with us too." He tells me and Finn told me the same.

"I mean if I had the money I would too." He says. *Yeah.*

"He´s like his parents." I say. "He leaves me like they left him. He shuts us out like they did.." I say. *Will that be all I get from him?*

Aidan wraps an arm around me, and I lay my head against him. "I just don´t know if I can wait any longer because it hurts." I admit. *And I´m not sure if I like the burn anymore. Even when he hurts me over and over.. I still try to understand him and his motives. But sometimes love is not enough. And he proved that he can´t deal with that love.*

"We didn´t really say it, but I think we agreed to work on ourselves." I say and he nods. "I think that´s brave." He tells me and I nod. "It just feels like I´m constantly waiting on something that´s just not going to happen." I say and let the tears spill. He hugs me tighter and sighs. "Maybe you should stop waiting." He says into my hair and kisses my head. "Yeah, maybe." I say.

A while we just sit there. *Until he chuckles.*

I move my head from his neck to face him. "What?" I ask and he shakes his head. "It´s just you two are *literally* the definition of idiots to lovers." He says with a grin, and I look at him but then smile. “You just found our trope.” I laugh but my smile fades. “Still waiting on the lover´s part though.” I try to joke before I rest my head back on him.

Sometimes life feels like it´s not yours anymore. Like a book I´m reading. Dramatic and not at all how you wanted it to be. Truth is not all books have happy ends. But sometimes *those* are the best. You can learn from them and grow. And even sad things are beautiful.

But I don´t want our story to be sad or beautiful. I want our story to be.

But it seems like it never will.

We´re broken souls plagued with inner demons, playing a thrilling but destroying game of trust and love. But somehow, we lost a game we hadn´t even started.

And you may think people who are hurting and trying to heal each other would be considered *as love,* but it is just tragic and nothing more. And especially cruel when one of them isn´t healing but hurting you.

“It´s better this way.” I say after a while and get up and go to Kai´s room.

My heart pounds as I walk over to the bed and sit down trying to calm myself. I feel like I´m choking on tears that aren´t even flowing anymore. It hurts even more to know he loves me but won´t be with me anyway.

I walk back and forth and grab a book yanking it off the shelf. Relief spreads through my veins so I throw another. I sweep the whole shelves clean and kick the books across the room. I can´t think of *anything* but getting that anger out. *Just out.*

When I´m done, I realize Leon was standing there watching me losing my mind. *Again.* For a few seconds we just stand there. Me breathing hard and him holding my gaze. Then he strides towards me, puts my head to his chest as I crash into him and cry without tears. The last time Finn held me together. *Now it´s Leon.*

Because now he knows. *They all know.*

And I feel naked. Weak and vulnerable. *Because they know.*

They know he left me. *They know.*

Not five minutes later we´re in his car and I don´t have to ask to know *exactly* where we´re going. He brings me to the same place he took me months ago. Back when he had no clue why I was such a mess. But just like then, he knows how to help me. So, I smash a car while Leon just sits there watching. *No music. Just his silence.* And the sounds of *something* breaking.

How many pains can you take? Until you want to stop.

How many times you would die for love? Forever.

How far will you go? Till I reach him. *Will he ever stay?* Never.

Dozens of questions run through my head as I massacre the hood. And to some of them I have an answer to some not.

I know I´ve felt this for my ex too but the love for Kai is so much more. It´s nothing like I´ve ever had before. I can´t even understand or name it. It´s too much and not enough. And I know we need to work on ourselves. But that doesn´t change the pain.

The hurt. It doesn´t change the now.

He was cruel because he loved me. *He loved me but he left.*

The only difference between him and my ex is that now I´m sure I won´t survive it. Because it´s easy loving someone or falling for them. But it isn´t easy to unlove them.

You can´t stop.

Like a car without brakes. You simply can´t stop. You have to keep driving. But you never come to a halt. *It never stops.*

You always go. *Even if you don´t want to, anymore.*

I carve into the hood pretending it´s his skin. Or mine it doesn´t matter anymore. I´m trying not to cut myself as my vision blurs.

"He is not hell if you like how it burns."

- 27 -

Leon´s car stops in front of my house as the sun has already begun to set.

And the whole drive we didn´t talk. But the unspoken words hung in the air like razor blades. Cutting each of us in different ways.

Now I sit there staring at the footwell. The engine still running but the music off. We won´t hug so we exchange one last look before I get out.

Because this is goodbye. Maybe not forever but for *now.*

157

Six months later, April 2022, Call you tomorrow - Hotel Fish

That goodbye, months ago, was one.

I had no contact with the others. University was stressful, and our lives went on.

Even without each other.

It was different when he left for London but this time I´ve seen none of them.

For different reasons. Because I feel left out, I shut people out. And I´ve shut *them* out because I was hurt.

How easy do you make friends? How easy you lose them? And what says that about you?

The thing with friends is you think you have them. *Until you don´t.*

I was never good at keeping friends. I´ve lost them all. *Eventually.*

Not because I´m not loyal. It was more that I lost the energy to keep in touch. But maybe I am a bad friend because up to a point I can´t open up.

I need space. I´m a loner. And I isolate.

This is what I do. *What Kai did too.*

Or maybe I´m just used to being alone.

I chose to be alone before *they* make me. *What says that about me? That I like to suffer? To be the loner? To be the one no one likes? Is it a way of proving myself that I´m not worth to be liked? A way of self-hate or self-destruction? Or just self-protection?*

Whatever it is. *I lost them in a way.*

And I know I could have reached out to them. But as Leon advised me, I did let go of Aidan and have given him the space we might need to be friends again. And he let me.

They all did.

The contact faded away and at some point, I wasn´t asked to come over anymore. They didn´t reach out and I didn´t respond. I didn´t ask to come over either. I didn´t get invited to the parties. We just lost touch and stopped being friends.

Maybe I lost them because I feared to lose them. Maybe because they lost him too. And I was the reason for all three times he left. Or maybe because I remind them of him. And everything there reminds me of him. Especially his brother.

That he´s not there but 11,741 km crow flies away. And I needed space from it all. And what we realized was that *he* was the center of our friendship, which none of us was really aware of. *Until it changed all.*

I changed their life´s. Their friendships. *I did.*

So, I owed them space. But the only space I didn´t want was the one between him and me. After he finally had chosen me. *But then left again.*

There is only me again. Well not *exactly* because this time it wasn´t just months of radio silence. Unlike expected, *he called me* right after he landed. "*I´m sorry.*" He said as I picked up. But I didn´t say anything and hung up.

Next day, he called again. *I didn´t answer.*

The day after, he called three times. *I ignored it.*

He kept calling for *days*. He didn´t text. *He just called.*

Three weeks in a row. *Until I answered.*

I didn´t speak but he *knew* I wouldn´t. So, after a moment he talked to me. And he kept talking. Told me about his trips. About everything I had missed.

The next day, he called again. *And I listened again.*

He talked to me on the phone every day. Sometimes just a few minutes, sometimes hours. Sometimes we just sat in silence. But it felt like so much more than that. Other times he shared a quote, and he even read to me when I had to sleep listened to me breathing when I dozed off. And sometimes he called to tell me a joke just to hear me laugh. *I didn´t.*

He told me he´s back to therapy. And this time he really wants to change.

He told me lots of stuff. And I listened to every single detail.

I craved it and I loved him talking. *The thing he never could.*

He even sent me post cards and letters. He did all the things I wanted back then when he left. I felt a bit sorry I didn´t spoke but somehow, he deserved it. And I wanted to hear from him so bad. Just as bad when he left the first time.

After weeks of my dead silence, he called me in the middle of the night. And I was half asleep when he spoke. "I read once that in Greek you don´t just say *I miss you;* it is more like *you are missing from me.*" He said and I had my eyes closed. "That´s how I feel about you. *Μου λείπεις.*" He whispered and I cried. *Silently.*

"Talk to me." He begged in pain. "Please, Scar just talk to me. Please I just.." He continued, but I did cut him off. "*Μου λείπεις.*" I said and I almost felt him sigh. For a moment he was silent. *So silent. Like he couldn´t believe I spoke.*

Or he waited for me to say more but I didn´t. Because that was the first, and only time, I spoke to him in all those months. *Last night.*

And that was the last time he called.

[NOTEBOOK ENTRIES]

The minute it happened she wanted to talk. Like seriously can´t she just be in the now? No, she can´t. I didn´t push her I stabbed her. And she fell. ~~Just how I wanted her.~~ The hardest part on walking away from her was knowing she wouldn´t run after me. But this time I called. She didn´t talk. She had all rights to be mad. But she was listening. And that was all I needed. It was something. Maybe it was good for her to listen. And for me to learn to speak. But I really needed to be alone. She knew and that´s why she let me. Maybe she didn´t realize then, but she needed that too. We all did.

I can´t expect her to wait. But I hope she does. I´m in therapy. I´ve grown up with him. He knows me well enough to know that the last three-year sessions where me just telling him about the parties. I haven´t talked openly to him forever. I left the painful stuff out. He knew. But today I told him. ~~Everything I didn´t tell him over years.~~ Of course, he knew I met a girl. He could tell the exact date. He noticed immediately when I changed. ~~*Like he did once before.*~~*. Sometimes I think he knows my brain better than I do. She changed me instantly, isn't that insane? I should have told him sooner. But it's the right time. I finally deal. It's hard but I make progress. But eventually I have to come back.*

She still doesn't talk, but I don't care. As long as she answers, she cares. She fell asleep. I listened for hours to her breathing. Until she moved but I didn't hang up. I wanted her to feel safe. I wrote and read with her on the line. But she hung up in the morning. I hope she saw how long I stayed. I hope she knows that I care.

Sometimes I hear her smile or at least I imagine her to. I hope I make her smile. I have no idea what's going on in her life. I hope she's okay. But there are things we must face on our own. We can't depend on each other. This distance kills me, but we need it.

Sometimes I have that feeling that there is no happy end in this. But I hope I'm wrong. Maybe it's right person wrong time. Maybe we're just bad for each other. But I can work on myself. I can make this work.

I did write a letters. But I haven't gave her one of them. Not those. I've sent her others. But these I'll never show her. It's an exercise in therapy. Therapeutic writing or something. So, this is more for me than for her. But sure, she would like them. Because I'm pretty fucking good at it. But I suck at saying things. But what uses my writing when she wants my voice? And that's the thing I seem not be able to give. My voice.

The first weeks she took her time answering. Probably pretending she didn't stare at my name on the screen. But eventually she answered right away like she was waiting. I called her when I knew she had time. Sometimes I called her twice a day. Sometimes more. But from time to time, I got frustrated and sad that she wouldn't talk. Not even after hours of me talking. I thought maybe she would forgive me. So, I told her everything I experienced, what the weather is like, what I had eaten, which animals I saw, how long I meditated and other stuff. I don't even know what bullshit I told her. There's been a lot, I'm sure of that.

Today she talked to me. I thought I imagined it. But she did and my heart skipped a beat. She sounded sad. As if she had been crying. It meant everything to me.

I booked a flight. One week and I'll be back. And I won't leave her ever again.

158

One week later, Kai

"She threw me off in every aspect of my life. She made me different and the same." I told him. "And you wanna know when I knew I was into deep?" I asked and he nodded. "She made me hard, but not the way I was used to. I knew when I got hard thinking of her. Touching her. Just by seeing her. And I fucking knew when I got rock-hard just by hearing her voice or being close to her." I told him. "I knew I fucked up and I´m on my knees for her crawling like an idiot. That she has my *balls* in her hands. And a knife at my pulse. When I knew, I was hers." I paused.

"I just couldn´t admit that to myself." I said. "All I ever did was fuck and I could never feel. But with her, I did *anything*, but fuck, and felt *everything*." I told him.

"That´s when I knew." I smiled.

…

"I get it you´re closer. But I can´t just forget her. I have to figure.. *how* to get past her." Aidan said.

"I still love her mate." He told me. "But I´ll back up. It´s just seeing you two feels like shit." He said and I nodded. "It felt the same for me." I said.

"For *you*, it was worse." He said. *And he was right, it was.*

…

My vision blurs thinking back to the conversations I had with Aidan months ago. We talked a lot about how that situation made us feel. How it fucked us and how it changed things. And somehow, I could talk to him but not to her. I know that has to change. But I´ve shut down and pushed her because I didn´t want to mess up. *But I did anyway.*

It´s just meeting her was like walking around with a wound bleeding constantly. And coming close to her ripped the wound. But being away felt like phantom pain. Not there but you feel it.

Can love kill you? You can die for love. Out of heartbreak.

And it feels like I might die of loving her.

I don´t know if she´ll talk to me. If she´ll be happy to see me. But I´m back and this time I can´t fuck up again. *I´ve changed. I know I did.*

I just hope she sees that too. *I hope.*

159

Lia

It´s been a week and he didn´t call again. But I couldn´t bring myself to call him.

I´ve seen his posts on social media so he´s okay. *But it hurts.*

Should I have talked to him?

Last month I had my last exams so now I have two months off. And doing nothing is only fun when you have things to do. So, I´m in bed way too early and there´s nothing to watch or read. *Although my tbr list says otherwise.*

So, I just stare at the ceiling trying not to think of why he stopped calling.

Until quiet pattering makes me listen. *It´s raining. It hasn´t in a while.*

I jump up and put on a hoodie from Kai. It´s one I sneaked from him and the back reads.

"In(security)"

I thought it would fit me better because he´s anything but that. *At least in ways.*

I head outside and walk. I´ve been doing that a lot the last months.

At night, *I walked.* If it snowed, *I walked.*

When I missed him, *I walked. Like I used to do with him.*

I put a headphone in one ear, so I can still hear the rain and the surroundings, and I pass empty streets, hiding between the houses whenever a car drives by. I always do that I don´t know why. *Probably only women do that.*

Once I was walking on the country road at night and when a white bus drove by, I jumped down the slope. But other than that, there´s something peaceful about watching the place I grew up sleeping. It´s how I like it the most. *Not being seen but see.*

And I like to see which people can´t sleep wondering what might haunt their dreams. *While I refuse to let mine haunt me.*

Cats roaming around. Broken lanterns. Stars and the moon. Some cars roaring in the distance. It´s when I feel close to Kai. *Doing the things I used to do with him.*

Once he called when I walked. That was my fav call because I could close my eyes pretending having him next to me. *I almost felt him.*

Like two trees separated by a road so the tops can´t touch but underground, the roots are tightly woven and connected. That´s how I feel or have felt without him. Our souls are connected. It´s a bond you can´t see on the surface but it reaches chasms. *Maybe even hell.*

But as much as they scratch the demons, they graze the stars anyway.

He haunts like a ghost. *Always there but not for me to reach.*

You´re sometimes continents apart, but you feel the energy. And our frequencies are on the same station. And only we hear the sound. Like a secret language no one except us speaks. Like a handshake that no one knows except us. Like a song no one has heard before. It´s a connection we can´t escape nor understand.

But it´s real and it´s there. I feel it every day. And over the past months I tried to ignore and deny it, but I know I´ll fail once he´s back. Because I can´t escape and neither does he.

Because we´re bound.

160

No Smoke by Bendigo Fletcher is on repeat. And as often, I turn into the street I know all too well. It´s not even intentional. *It never is.*

It´s a law and my inner compass that *always* leads me back here.

To him. Whether I want to or not.

Sometimes I sit on the side of the road. *Where the accident was.* Other times in front of his house. *Where we used to sit.*

But I never go in because we don´t do that anymore. Because we´re not really friends anymore. But now I´m here and a part of him is with me. *As always.*

Especially when it rains.

I stare at the window, which stayed dark for a long time. And I just had to ring that bell to see my old friends. To see Finn and the dogs or to go to his room. To read his books and to lie in his bed. *But I don´t.*

I just stare and reminisce past moments that I wish had never ended and allow the weakness, nostalgia, self-pity, and sadness. I let them wash over and rip me.

But eventually, I´m back. *Rooted.*

Alive and alone. On the sidewalk. *In the rain.*

But I´m forced back to reality as headlights blind me. A banging exhaust reminds me, and something rings in the back of my heart.

I stand up and blink. *It´s his BMW.*

I try to make out who´s behind the wheel but the wipers race. And then I see him.

It´s Kai.

His gaze meets mine. *And the rain. The world. It. All. Comes. To. A. Halt.*

We´re mirrors for each other. Our faces haunted by a ghost.

Without hesitation, he gets out. Leaves the car door open, and rushes toward me. I fall into his arms, and he lifts me. My hoodie falls and as his hand finds my head. I wrap my legs around him and my arms do the same. *Tears spill instantly.*

"Fuck" he says as his grip tightens and my hand digs into his black sweater taking in his warmth. *His scent. Him.*

I grip his hair stroking the back of his head as he walks a few steps with me. The engine is still running, and the rain soaks us. My eyes burn with joy realizing he came back. And all at once I´m completely at the moment. *At home.*

Doors open and close again. Finn as I suppose pulls the car into the garage and disappears inside. But neither of us lets go or says a word.

It´s all been worth it. The last two years for this feeling. *For this moment.*

"I love you." I almost overhear as softly as he speaks. "I love you." I hear him say again into my hair. His voice is trembling, rough and broken. "Scar, I love you." He repeats once more. *But more to himself than me.*

He looks at me and his eyes are red. *They never lose their hurt.*

He cries, just as I do. But the sight of him hurts. Pain and longing is graved on him.

And I´m sure I look the same.

He takes me in searching my face for idk what. As if I could have changed.

He notices my hoodie. *Or rather his.*

Emotions come and go as he holds my cheek. But he just looks at me. *Why does he hesitate? Because it´s been months? Without me speaking more than two words in total to him? Or because he did hurt me? And he doesn´t know if I have forgiven him? Or he doesn´t know anymore what´s going on in my life? Isn´t he sure I don´t have someone?*

As I realize my heart turns upside down. He waits for my *okay.*

My throat hurts as I speak. "Kiss me." I beg and relief flickers over his face before rain and salt mix together as his lips slam down on mine. I´ve kissed him before while he´s been crying. Somehow, we kiss more with salt than with anything else. But those tears aren´t just hurt or sad. They´re happy and with love. And to be honest those kisses taste the best. It´s rough, honest, and pure. *It´s full of emotions.*

While kissing, he walks to the gate and blindly types the code. Not once do we break the kiss. Not when Finn opens the door and not when we somehow kick off our shoes without putting me down. He carries me up to his room and behind him, he kicks the door shut and leans against it. Still, he won´t let go of me. *Nor do I.*

His head falls back on the door, and he lets his eyes wander in the dark. It´s lit only by the streetlamp and the moon. And a moment of silence passes as I watch him looking around.

I can´t read him.

Then he frowns but before I can ask, he speaks. "You were never here." He states in a low voice and slowly lowers me down. *Don´t let me go.*

I look at him questioningly. His eyes move to mine without lowering his head. "All those months." He clarifies and I blink. *Now it clicks.*

I cast a glance toward the bed, so I don´t have to look at him. The bookshelf is clean. Leon must have cleaned up the mess I left. I bet he notices the difference though.

Even I can tell from here.

But that´s the *only* evidence of me. Because I never was, here. *Not in six months.*

"I haven´t had much contact with the others." I say. "And I didn´t want to be constantly reminded of you." I admit and he nods once. Then he pushes himself off the door and I watch him as he looks around like he´s never seen this place before.

Like it´s dead somehow.

"When I came back from London.. *I knew.*" He grins briefly, remembering. "That you were here a lot." His gaze searches mine and my heart sinks and face heats. "It smelled like you." He whispers. *Shit.*

It never did to me. *It always smelled like him.*

"But now.." He looks over my head to the bed. *The bed I never touched.*

"I was kind of *hoping* you would have been here." He admits quiet and for a moment we´re silent. And I won´t address what he said to me earlier, even though he swore he would never again. *But he did, repeatedly.*

But by not saying he loves me that often, it has even more meaning. And honestly, I think he didn´t mean that he *actually* would never say it, but that he wouldn´t do it carelessly. And I get it because that is how it should be. They say you should tell the people you love. But you should do it when you *really* feel it. Don´t let it be something you just say.

Let it be important.

And now I get him and get more of the things he told me. I can understand him. Now I see it and see him. Maybe we even needed the space to see.

And over the years I´ve come to know *how* he feels about me even without him saying it. *Without the talking.*

And maybe I don´t need him to say it. Because I feel it. Hear it. And now see it too.

"But I understand why you weren´t." He snaps me out of my thoughts, and I give him a weak smile. "I missed you." I say wanting to say the Greek version, but I forgot. "Missed you." He says back and takes me in his arms.

We stand like that for a while until we take off our wet clothes and get into bed as if those six months and the fight didn´t happen. *And somehow it didn´t.*

Because we knew it wasn´t real. It was just a point where we needed space.

"Would you have told me you that you´re back if I hadn´t been on your street?" I ask and he looks at me like that´s the dumbest question. "I would have come to you right away if you hadn´t been here." He says before he kisses me.

The whole night we do not leave each other. Even in the morning I am still in his arm. He buries himself inside of me and I want him to never stop.

And I don´t feel the urge to push him. *I´m only glad he´s back.*

I just want him. *Before everything falls apart.* Because we both know sooner or later it all will. *Fall apart.* We just hope this time we´ll have more time. *More now´s.*

161

The next morning

We go down after Kai has put on a pair of shorts and I left his T-shirt on. We kiss as I walk backwards, tugging him with me. He holds my jaw and grabs my ass under the fabric.

When we break the kiss, he stops and looks past me. His hand moves from my butt to my lower back on top of the shirt and I turn around, *knowing* who I´m about to see.

Aidan and Leon stand in the living room with Finn and my heart stops.

Kai passes me and Aiden hugs him. *They punch.*

"Missed you bro." He says to Kai. "Missed you too." He replies and stabs him in the chest. Then he smacks with Leon, and they hug in the process. "Back again?" He asks. "Yes" He nods. "For how long?" He looks at his imaginary wristwatch. "When´s your plane?" he jokes to which Kai laughs. "Ain´t none booked." He announces and Leon nods a few times. "Good to hear." He says. And as that happens, I´m still standing where Kai left me.

Unable to move or look away.

I blink, watching it like a movie. A movie I´m no longer part of. *Because of me.*

It´s awkward, I´m uneasy and horribly aware of myself even if no one looks at me. I feel myself slipping out of my body, but when I have decided to flee, all eyes fall on me. *Shit.*

There is that moment of dead silence. Like they really just saw him and not me.

And honestly, I can´t blame them.

I don´t know what to say. *Wave? Smile? Cry?*

"Long time." Nods Leon and then Aiden walks up to me, grinning. And fuck, that hurts.

The way he smiles.

I wrap my arms around his neck, and his come around my lower back. "Missed you too." He says into my hair, and I bite my lower lip at the all too familiar pain. I shut my eyes.

I missed him. Missed them.

I nod. “Same.”

We disengage. “We all have.” Speaks Leon behind him. I have to be on my toes to hug him, so my shirt rides up, and I tug it down after.

“Let´s get the others. We´ll have a party tonight.” Aidan announces and they sit down and gamble, talking and laughing and I watch them. *I´m relieved but it´s weird.*

Six months. It´s somehow lifetimes. Somehow like yesterday.

Finn, still standing in the kitchen, grins at me as I finally meet his gaze, and I smile too as he makes his way off the counter. “Come here.” He tells me, and I wrap my arms around his sides, and his come around me. We hug for a long time. It´s been weird without him placing me back together. But I know I needed to do it on my own.

“Been so quiet without you here.” He says into my hair, and I shut my eyes. “Honestly, I was surprised you didn´t come.” He admits. “Me too.” I confess with a sigh.

Silence.

“Although I´ve seen, you´ve been around a lot.” He says, and I freeze. *What?*

I look up at him and we break the hug. He looks down on me and my eyes widen. “You *saw* me?” I ask and he nods once slowly. *He saw me.*

I shut my eyes for a sec. *Fuck.*

“Why..” I ask but he cuts me off. “I thought if you wanted to see us.. you would have come in.” He tells me. “But you never did.. so..” he shrugs. But he´s right, I just wanted to be near. “You never said a thing.” I say quiet. “Neither did you.” He locks eyes with me. “True.” I nod.

“I´m sorry I left.” I say. “Don´t say sorry.” He tells me. “I know why.” He says. And it´s true, he knew from the beginning. It´s sad we lost touch. But there was no other way for me to move on. *But he knew that too.*

“He really wants to change.” He whispers and I frown. “He called you.” Is all he says and all I need to hear. “He did.” I nod and we look at each other for a second. “It is good to have you back.” He says and I smile.

“I gotta put some clothes on.” I say as I walk past the boys and Aiden looks after me. “Better so, *everyone* can see your ass.” He teases. Leon ignores being used to our teasing or he doesn´t want to say something. *Probably both.*

But Kai gives me a sideways glance to check it out. *The shirt covers my ass.*

I flick Aidan the finger. “Fuck you.” I bark. “Kay when?” He asks with an even bigger grin. Whereupon I also must grin but shake my head. And then he and Kai exchange a look I can´t read. And my heart sinks at that reminding me of all the times we.. Leon nudges him to bring back his attention to the game and with that mine too.

After I have changed, I sit down with the others. They stopped playing.

"How was Bali so far?" asks Leon. "Awesome. I´ve been jobbing and took a lot of pictures. Met lots of people and made connections and stuff." He goes on and tells them all I´ve heard before on the phone. And I love the fact that I know all of it.

I wonder if he thinks of that too.

"So, what´s the plan for the rest of the year?" asks Finn piercing him. "May to October is dry season, which is the best for traveling. But I think December to March is better because it´s rain season." He explains. "Meaning?" He raises an eyebrow at his brother, knowing *exactly* what that means. *That he wants to go back.*

Which is something I didn´t know but assumed because I know his heart is there. And if he could, he would live there. But here are his friends, aka his family. And his dogs.

Well and me.

"I think I´ll go twice a year during semester break." He says. "Would be four months a year." He shrugs. "I´ll finish studies first. And then long term no idea." Kai tells us. "Then you´ll never be there on my birthdays." Says Aidan acting upset. "Your birthday is in April *fucker.*" Kai laughs but Aidan shrugs. "But I will on the *important* ones." He assures him. "I hope so." Aidan points at him.

"Okay, guys, I´ll go. See ya tonight." I stand up and Aidan holds his fist to me, but I push his head back instead. He laughs and tries to tackle me, but I dodge him. Leon nods at me and Finn waves goodbye. And out of habit, I cast a glance at Kai and walk to the door.

I slip on my shoes but when I turn, Kai comes into view. I´ve assumed we don´t hug or anything. *Like it´s always been. Us sneaking around and not saying goodbye.*

But the look on his face tells me that is now over.

"Come earlier." He says before pulling me into his arms. "Okay." I say at his chest, and we break away. Then he kisses me, and the dead butterflies awake. *That´s new too.*

162

Kai grabs me by the waist. "Come with me." Nodding towards the stairs, he pulls me a little with him and my stomach tingles under his touch.

We walk into his room. *He looks nervous.*

"Happy birthday." He says. "It´s April." I retort, amused but confused at the same time. "You´re six months late." I add. "I know, but I have something for you." He tells me. "I thought you didn´t think much of gifts?" I counter. "Are you going to take it or keep complaining?" He asks. "Okay." I laugh and he reaches into his pocket and pulls out a rock.

He doesn´t look at me, but at his hand. Like back then when he gave me that ring. "This one´s from Bali." He says and I can´t help but grin. "Got a new spot. I´ll show you in the summer." He adds now looking at me. *He wants me to join? He knows he´s talking about the future right now, doesn´t he? But I won´t say that.*

"Really got into the habit of *that*.. somehow." He rubs his neck, and I narrow my eyes. "Taking a rock in all the places I´ve been." He clears his throat.

"That one was from the nicest place. So.. *that´s* why." He shrugs, holds it up and puts it in my hand and I blink at the stone in my palm. "You have.. *more* rocks?" I ask with a grin, and he blushes. *Blushes. He never does.*

"Yes.. uhm in the shelter." He shrugs not meeting my eyes. "I have a jar full." He rubs the back of his neck, and I squint my eyes at him. "Are you collecting *rocks*?" I grin and he´s embarrassed. *I´ve never seen him like that.*

He avoids my gaze at any costs and is pink as a blossom. I shake my head and can´t fight my grin. *He´s like all shy now.* This is.. *everything*.

I wrap my arms around his neck, and he slowly lifts his gaze biting his lip trying not to let on. "Thank you." I hush and kiss him. He relaxes into me and wraps his arm around me kissing me slowly. But I grin into the kiss.

He collects stones. I´ve never had anything I wanted to collect. I guess that´s another thing that has changed.

"What you´re grinning about?" He asks and I look at him. "When we´re back I want to hear the story about them." I announce. "I´ll show you all the places." He picks me up. "Every single one." I demand and he nods grinning. "Promise." He says as he lowers us onto the bed, and I smile at him.

163

A few days later

"**M**iss your face." His voice husky. "It´s right in front of you." I whisper scooting closer. "No, it´s not." He hushes and pain flicks across his features as if I´m faceless. "It´s miles away." He says and by the way he says it I believe him.

"What do you mean?" I ask sitting up and he does the same. "Look around. Soak it all in." He tells me. "Cause in one year from now *nothing* will be the same." He says and I´m used to his mindset, and poetic side. Even the cryptic one but right now I have no clue what he´s talking about.

He reads my confusion and continues. “Everything changes. Just never the now.” He says. *So, we're on the now topic. I know that one.*

“So, stay here with me. Why being somewhere else?” He asks but it was rhetorical. “I am here.” I tell him, but I know he meant something different.

He shakes his head. “You're not.” He touches my temple. “You're *there*.” He taps and I sigh. “Kai..” I begin. “Please.. let me explain.” He pleads and I nod. “Your problem is you can't stop thinking. Can't you just be in the moment and stay? Because I am here.” He tells me upset and as he speaks, I realize *I've been in my head because I'm still scared he might leave, come to blows and fall apart.*

“Be aware of me holding your hand and kissing you.” He does as he says.

“And be aware of the quietness. *Without* thinking.” He instructs and my lip's part to tell him I do, but his finger shuts me before his kiss gets me.

“So why thinking what if? What if we fail? What if I die?” He goes on. “If you'll die you die *now*. So, don't miss the moment. That would be stupid.” He says. “But people are like that. It happens so fast they miss their own death. Their own wedding or first kiss and first heartbreak. *First everything*.” He's in the flow and this is his passion. He could be a coach or a writer. Maybe on Bali. Photographing and inspiring people.

Telling them about the now.

“They miss it all and don't cherish it. They think of their next day as they live the present one. They're in their heads looking out and sitting on the passenger seat as their life passes by. And before they notice they're old and full of regrets. Full of dreams they never dared.” He continues. “And they think of all the things they could have said and the now's they wasted.” He shrugs.

“Isn't that sad? When all your life you're on that ride to death. And when you reach it, they don't realize because they didn't pay attention. They're just gone.” He ponders.

“Maybe they don't know they're dead until no one sees them or speaks to them. Until they see their bodies lifeless. Until they see their now is gone.” He says, and I wonder why he doesn't write all this down. In a Blog or social media. People should hear him, and he should use his own voice more. But that's when I realize he quotes less than a year ago. He did it all the time. And even his shirts. *That all stopped.*

Because he started talking. *Cause, you made me speak.*

“They call the awaken asleep, that's the issue with people. They tend to not see.” He shakes his head. “But you can't relive your whole fucking life just by thinking of it.” He says and he has a point, but I sigh.

"Just think of it. What problem do you have right now?" He asks. "*You.*" I joke. "Come on which one?" He urges like, this conversation is important. And I guess it is.

So, it is for me too.

"None." I say annoyed cause he´s *always* right. "Right, none." He states and it makes me angry because I´m spiritual too. I meditate, do yoga, and practice mindfulness but he´s different. He internalized all that. He´s living it.

Like Peter, he´s in the now. Pan has no future, but he does.

But still, he chooses to stay.

But I can´t help it. My mind wanders to the past when I´m sad and to the future when I´m scared. But he seems to be able to just stay and I want that too. I really do, but I don´t know how.

"When you focus on your breathing and take in everything around or inside you. There are never *such* things as problems." He quotes in the air. "And I´m not talking about paying bills. Those are things you *must* deal with. But apart from that there´s just now." He shrugs.

"And the reason Lia.." *There it is my name and not Scar. Means he´s all serious. It´s funny I can tell by that. I wonder if he knows.*

"Why we don´t *work* is cause you´re searching for *those* problems. And when you do, you´re not in the now with me." He says and I look down.

"The now is the greatest thing humans can share. It´s the most intimate." He adds. "And I want it to share with you." He looks at me with need.

"Don´t waste your now´s for if's." He whispers and his hand finds the back of my head. "I give you my now´s. There is nothing else I can give." He tells me. "It´s all I have." He shrugs. "It´s all you have too." He hushes his fingers tangled in my hair and his eyes lost in mine. "You´ll decide what you do with yours." He says. "Waste it for your past or future." He shakes his head. "Or invest them in ours." He whispers.

"Don´t be one of the people who miss their death." He swallows. "Don´t miss life." His fingers graze my sculp. "Don´t miss *this*." He kisses me.

"You chose." He shrugs. "You want me to open up." He looks at me indifferently. "This is it." He nods. "I want you now." He pads his chest. "I love you now. I want to be with you now." My heart aches.

"But *don´t* ask me about tomorrow or yesterday. That isn´t what I want in life." He tells me. "It won´t ever be different Scar." He repeats and I relax by that nickname. "Because I´ve changed and do therapy." He assures me.

"But the now´s *stay*. And if you can´t appreciate that.." He shrugs making a pause to think or let *me* think. *But I can´t since I´m here with him. Now.*

"Then I don´t want *you* in my now." He says and my eyes widen at his honesty.

It hurts. But the moment passes.

"That´s why I don´t date or have relationships." He explains.

"Can´t that be enough?" He asks me but doesn´t wait for my answer. "Do you have to *know* that I´m going to marry you *someday* which is *not* now?" He asks and it hurts but the truth always does and the way he mentions marriage so casually strikes me.

As if he would really marry me some day.

And for the first time I understand him and fully get what he means and said to me the past years. And if he said those things two years ago, I would have understood.

But he didn´t.

At least not in that way but I wish he did. ~~Maybe things would have been..~~ *whatever.*

It doesn´t matter now.

"When you worry you´re *miles* away. So, don´t run. *Stay.*" He begs his breath hitting my face. "Don´t waste your now´s for things that didn´t even happen." He adds. "Please stay." He begs again but I kiss him and stay.

I despised him because he sends me over the edge. But maybe it´s what I need.

The free fall. The unknown. Facing fears. The now.

He makes me lose control and I hate it, but I know it´s what I need. It´s why I chased him because in a way he gives me control. The one thing I´m afraid to lose so bad. He takes my fear and shows me it´s gone.

And his fear was time. Not being in the now.

And I decide to take away his fear too and to give him my now´s. Because the whole time I tried to remember time. When all he wanted is forget it existed.

I couldn´t see but now I do.

"Take me to Neverland." I beg and kiss him again and he smiles against my lips.

Just like Pan would.

"You *are* Neverland." He tells me and I smile. *And stay.*

But just like Wendy she never woke.

164

Two months later, June

We strip down to our underwear and wait in the lake.

Stones poke my feet. The sun is almost gone. The sky a purplish-blue with a red transition. In the distance are blackbirds singing and frogs roaring. Swallows fly low and there´s no wind at all. It smells like it´ll rain soon. *Summer air.*

Kai makes a header and reappears a few feet away. I walk slowly to get used to the fresh water on my skin. Coldness runs through me, which disappears, when I notice Kai´s gaze on me. The water is up to his chest and he´s fixating me with the black in his eyes. And only when he waits for me I notice I´ve stopped walking. His eyes eat me up and my nipples get hard. My clit thrums as his gaze lands on my breasts and I´m aware he can see them through the lace. But his expression remains hard as I fight the urge to cross my arms.

Water beads off his torso as he towers over me, grabs me by my waist and lifts me. With a squeak, I brace myself against his chest, whereupon he only lifts me higher, and I´m forced to rest my them on his shoulders. He takes a few steps backwards and unlike what I expected, he doesn´t throw me into the water, but lets me slowly slide down his chest. *Down his body.*

His arms move to my back and the throbbing gets stronger. He´s hard and if we weren´t in the water, I´d still be wet.

I´m so fixated on him that the coldness doesn´t bother me anymore. His eyes search my face as my hand wanders on his chest and the other to his neck. His grip hardens and so does his dick at my belly and we breathe in unison. My pulse against my throat making me fear my artery will burst any moment.

In the distance thunder growls and my desire to rub against his swelling skyrockets. As if mentally connected, he lifts me back up onto his dick and I claw his skin. Relief spreads as I move greedy against him and moan escapes me.

In response, he retorts with a groan, “Fuck.”

I sway my hips as he guides my ass to get closer. Again, I moan, and his lips crash down on mine. He bites my lip, I come and keep riding him as my orgasm carries me away. But his eyes are on me, and they never leave.

There´s no wall. No guns pointed at me. Just desire.

The sky lights up, and I count the seconds to estimate the distance. With his teeth, he pulls the strap of my bra and lets it slide down my shoulder. The fresh air give me goosebumps. He takes my nipple in his mouth and once again, an orgasm is brewing as his tongue plays and nibbles. *Just to bite them.*

I want to feel him inside me, so much that it hurts. “Kai,” I breathe, and he looks at me *knowing*. I open my mouth to ask but remain silent. Desperation is written all over his face too, which only turns me on more. Without letting a second pass, he waits for the land.

I kiss and suck on his neck and under his ear. “Shit.” He growls impatiently and throws me onto his sweater on the floor. The next moment he´s over me, pulling out a condom and holds it with his mouth while pulling his boxers over his butt and my panties off. I stretch my arms back so he can pull my lace over my head. Then he tears open the package with his teeth and even though you shouldn´t do it that way I find the sight incredibly hot.

With one hand he supports himself next to my shoulder and with the other he rolls the condom over. I watch and he too, looks down at himself. He moans as he does, and I feel my moisture running down.

He holds his shaft and guides it to my entrance. His tip slides a few times over driving me insane. He circles my clit and licks his lips, and I pant. He rests his forehead against mine and slides inside me.

The storm gets closer.

Kai slowly moves. *The sky becomes bright.*

He moans in my ear. And I cling to his skin. *I count.*

The weight of his body rests on me as he thrusts into me. He kisses my neck and moans into my hair. I scratch his back and claw into his ass. *It thunders.*

I don´t believe in the G-spot but something inside me, he´s hitting just right as his balls slap against my skin, sending pulses through my body.

Thick drops splash down on us.

He digs his hand into the ground beside us and increases the pace. We moan at the same time. *Rain patters on the water.*

"Scar." He begs and I bite his shoulder. *Lightening.*

Kai thrusts into me one last time and bites my collarbone while he comes.

We breathe, and he lies on top of me with all his weight.

But it´s not crushing, it´s exhilarating because he gives himself to me. *Completely.*

And I feel like I don´t belong anywhere else. *Just with him.*

I kiss his neck and caress his head as he´s still inside me not moving. Breathing uncontrollably, and I enjoy every second. Every beat of his heart is like the air I breathe.

It keeps me going.

When the storm reached us, we detach.

It pours but we take our time getting dressed.

I walk barefoot beside him to his car parked on the gravel and Kai stops in front of the door and leans against it watching me. He grins and pulls me to him. I look up at him as his arms find my lower back returning his grin. He just keeps looking at me with a shit ass grin he can´t wipe off his face. *He´s happy.*

He looks down on me, licks his lips. His smile gone now and just stares at me. And I just *know* what he thinks. Because it´s the same as I do. *He loves me.*

I know exactly that´s what he´s thinking at this very moment. Because I can tell every time, he thinks that. *Every single time.*

Because he has *that* look on his face. He looked at me like that a year ago but I didn´t see it then. *Now I do.*

It´s like he didn´t start collecting stones. More like he started collecting me. Like now, he has found *something* worth keeping. *He has found me.*

But I won´t ask him or push him. Because I know he won´t say it. But he doesn´t need to. Because seeing him like that. Him looking at me like that. *Is enough.*

It tells me more than those meaningless words ever could. And he knows he lets me see it. Because now he wants to open up.

He pinches my ass, and I grab his hoodie pulling him to my mouth. He kisses me like it´s the first time and he gets hard but does nothing. And besides my favorite taste of salt the one of rain on our lips is even better.

Those are the best kisses. Rain and tears. The taste of Pan and Scar.

As the thunderstorm gets worse, he breaks the kiss and opens the car door pulling me onto his lap and closing the door behind us. The car locks up and torrents of rain pelt off the roof. You can´t see anything but black. It´s as if we´re the only alive.

And right now, I think, we are.

I straddle him but we don´t talk. *We don´t need to.*

I never felt the way I feel about him. And I know there´s so much more and I want it all.

He turns on *Nothing inside (feat. Iann Dior) by Machine Gun Kelly* on a low volume.

We can´t take our eyes off each other and the way he looks at me is like every line is directed at me. He sings along in a raspy voice, and I missed him singing.

Especially the refrain he feels the most and I shake my head pressing my forehead to his.

He continues to sing.

I hold his face, and his hand moves to my ass. Midline I cut him off and press my lips to his. He returns the kiss but keeps singing between making me laugh.

I force him to look at me, but he keeps singing like a fool. *My fool.*

He bobs his head and taps on my ass to the beat, and I giggle watching him in amusement. But as the chorus comes on, I lock eyes with him. "She saw *everything* inside." I tell him in a whisper, and he kisses me. And that kiss is full of emotions and unspoken things.

“Sing with me.” He tells me but I shake my head. “Come please.” He begs singing along and I shake my head once more. *He knows how insecure I am.*

He looks at me pondering. And then he reaches out and puts up the volume, but I keep shaking my head.

He just grins pleased. “Now sing with me.” He yells against my lips, and I match his smile rolling my eyes. “Fine.” I shout back but I hold his hands in place, so he won´t put it down to hear me.

It´s like we´re in our own musical. Our own declaration of love. Like my own concert with my new fav artist. *Him.*

He does that air guitar thing and then we´re having a battle Duette. I use his phone as a mic, and he pretends to have one in his hand. We´re totally over the top fooling around but it´s the best thing we ever did. And the way he easily can switch genre and mood is insane. He´s now all cute and gentle.

The car vibrates with not just the thunder around us as he sings to me with all the pain in his voice and my heart breaks and heals. I never thought anything could be more meaningful than hearing an; *I love you*, until now. Until Kai sang to me. And I couldn´t stop the grin on my face. This is the rawest, honest, and most genuine confession of love anyone has ever made to me. *If you can call it that.*

And for the first time, I don´t wish he would tell me, give me jewelry, or anything else. Right now, I wish for nothing else than that he *never* tells me. At least not in the way the norm expects him to. *I want his way. I want this.*

And it´s enough. He is. Enough.

I don´t know how long we´re doing this, but we completely forget that time even exists. Well, *I* do he knows that already but now he teaches me, how a moment can feel.

There are songs where he doesn´t sing and on others more. He also sings parts that are not directed at me, but I can see how much he feels the lines. And I can tell the difference. He opens up to me through those lines and I see him vulnerable.

- 27 -

The storm passed and the only thing you can hear is the prattle rain on the fogged windows. The music is on a low volume almost out. And I lean against the steering wheel looking at his face.

My hair is still a little damp and his all dry messy and hanging on his forehead. His eyes are closed and his fingers trace forms on my body.

“You stare at me.” He whispers smiling slightly. “Do I?” I hush straightening up. “Mhmh.” He murmurs and his hands find my back as I run my hand through his hair on the back of his head. He leans into my touch, and I bite his jaw. He smiles, like I knew he would.

He hardens under me and breathes me in as I begin to rock my hips. He grunts and guides me. Still with his eyes closed his lips find mine and we sway along.

He pulls me closer to him. "Thank you" I whisper on his lips. He kisses me back and whispers. "Sleepin´ Beauty."

I lean back a bit to look at him. "What´s that about, anyway?" I ask years late. He frowns. "What about?" He acts cluelessly. "*Sleepin´ Beauty,*" I quote him with a grin. "The nickname you give me only sometimes." I add and he looks at me pondering.

As if he really has to think about that.

He sighs. "*I know you. I walked with you once upon a dream..*" He quotes and I furrow my brow strained, scrutinizing his face.

Déjà vu hits me in the back of my mind. "*Sleeping.. Beauty* as the movie?" I ask as it occurs to me. "That´s my favorite." I say and he nods. "It´s actually a tale." He says. "She´s beautiful but she´s alone and craves love. But all she ever does is dream about it. About him." He tells me. "That´s all she ever wanted. *Love.*" He tells me what I know.

"And there´s that prince. They have met once upon a dream. But the evil that gets between them is called anxiety. Trauma. Commitment Issues. Fear of abundance. Fear of losing control. Fear of being alone. *Time.* Fear of being loved and not loved at thc same time." He goes on.

"He wanted to save her. But he had to save himself first. He had many demons to fight. He even had to face the devil itself." He says. "But he came for her. He came back and found her. But he found her sleeping." He pauses.

"While he was fighting and facing those demons, she decided to get stung. To be unaware. Unconscious. Dreaming.." He trails off.

"But then he kissed her. *Awake.* And she woke up. And with that her dreams became true." He tells me. "Because the love she dreamed about. The prince she had known was right in front of her." I look at him speechless. "She just needs to stay awake. To Stay." He tells me.

"But if she ever decides to sleep and go back to dream or if he decides to stop fighting those demons.." He trails off and looks at me intently like he tells me something important. But he catches himself shaking his head with a laugh.

"My mom used to make me read that over and over as a child." He says. "And it was my fav too, you know." He looks at me.

"But I didn´t really had a choice." He adds with a chuckle. "She made me read a few..*fairy tales*." He smiles. "And couldn´t escape those movies." He looks past me for a sec.

I wish I would have properly met her. But I don´t know if I ever will. And I´m not sure, I want that either. At least his father.

"Can we listen to it?" I ask. And he digs his phone out of his pants and plays *Once Upon a Dream by Lana Del Ray* and we lie like that in silence for a while, listening to the rain and the song.

"*They say if you dream a thing more than once, it´s sure to come true.*" I quote Aurora and I really believe that. Because I´ve seen it work myself.

"If you keep acting on it and chasing those dreams. And actually, living them." He says in a whisper. *It´s sure to become true, right?*

- 27 -

When we almost fall asleep, we drive home to Kai´s.

And I wonder how it comes that now we work. Maybe what hurt us the past was *not* coming close. It was the not kissing and not saying how we felt or not having sex. We felt early so strongly for each other that we couldn´t handle it. We couldn´t get close. We couldn´t express our feelings. We kept it in and we didn´t even try. We didn´t share those thoughts. Sometimes they leaked but never escaped fully.

And that´s what killed us. That´s what hurt us.

We loved each other but we didn´t show it. Not without the fear lingering or committing fully to the other. Not without the trust we have now. Because back then we forced us to talk instead of getting physically close. We pushed the other to make the first move but never took it ourselves. And there is no one to blame but us. We were so in our heads that we couldn´t let our hearts lead. Because we knew the other had the power to break us. So, we´ve hurt the other before they could hurt us.

But hurt just causes more hurt.

And that´s what we stopped. *Hurting.*

And it´s easy to say that life is too short. And yes, it is but life is scary too. Being vulnerable is and falling hurtful. *And loving is risking.*

And back then we wanted safe because all our life´s we´ve never been safe.

But we didn´t realize we were safe with each other. *But we are. Safe.*

165

I take in the black frame across his bed. It´s a photography in black and white.

Colson Herzog

A carousel.

"Merry go round."

Is the title.

"Why did you take a picture of that?" I ask him over my shoulder.

"Because it´s life." He says as he turns a page in his book. "*Life*?" I ask confused and turn to face him and he nods. Without looking up he speaks. "I like to look at it this way.." he pauses.

"*Merry go round.* It´s life." He shrugs. "It´s your life. You sit on it. You can jump on or run from it. You can even get kicked out or die on it." He says. "But the merry will always keep going round." He tells me. "It keeps spinning. It can light up in flames, or rain on it, but it keeps going." He looks at me for a sec.

"So, go with it. Keep spinning. Keep. *Merry. Go. Round.*" He says as he turns another page. *Is he reading while talking?*

I shake my head. "It`s the purpose of life. It´s how it is." He shrugs once more. "And the best thing.." he taps on his page. "Is you can stop in track and look at everything around you. All those lights, people and the world that burns alive.. you can take it all in while it does his thing. Going round and spinning under you." He says.

"But you´re all still and enjoy. You see and feel it. You can watch it and experience the magic happen. If you only ever stop to look." He says and locks eyes with me. "The *Merry go round.*" He says as his black meet my green eyes.

"*Life.*" I whisper and he nods. "Life." He repeats and continues to read.

I turn and look at his photography. And see it. *Life.*

He really could be a blogger, photographer, or writer. *He has a voice.* One that should be listened to.

"I bet they gonna remember you." I say with my back to him. "I bet they don´t." He whispers. *I bet they do,* I mouth soundless. But I hope he´s wrong because he´s talented. He should bring his creativity, his work, and Art out there.

"You could inspire people." I point out. "I inspire *me*." He retorts. And he´s right that should be enough. *To inspire you.*

166

"You smell like summer." I say with my head in the clouds. "And rain, a bit of weed and sunscreen." I add with a smile, and he smirks at me but frowning too. "Do I?" he asks amused. "Yeah." I say and he grins for a sec until his face is all blank. His mouth a thin line.

"You smell like spring." He says. "And white roses." He adds in a whisper. I frown and grin in confusion. "What does spring smell like?" I ask. "Like you." He says with a seriousness I might believe he knows that exactly.

We stand close and I tug on his shirt, so he comes closer. I grab his jeans and play with the waistband of his black boxer that hangs out. *Always black.*

He presses his lips together watching me. "You´re trouble." He says as I look up at him with *those* eyes. "You´re drunk." His voice husky.

He didn´t drink today but I did. Not too much but enough.

He has bedroom eyes, but I know he won´t act on it cause I´m too drunk and he pretends to be the gentleman we both know he´s not. And he tries, so I guess that´s good. But he doesn´t stop me either, so I enjoy the proximity and keep touching him trying to be close, but I want closer. And the moment I slip a finger under the band he stops my wrist. Glaring at me, he waits, and I know he *feels* my pulse.

"You´re wasted Scar." He says, but his voice is still rough with lust.

I stare at him and shrug. "Plastered." He corrects. "I won´t sleep with you." He states even though he wants to. I sigh.

Why can´t he just get wasted too and take me to his bed?

"I won´t sleep with you, Scar." He says again. "Why?" I whine. "Because I want you to feel every *inch* of my dick." He stares at me. "I want you to be aware of my fingers on your throat. I want you to be present when I kiss and bite your skin. And I want you to be with me and feel all of it." He tells me and I hang on his lips like hypnotized. "Tomorrow, I will fuck you." He murmurs. "But not tonight." He grins and I bite my cheeks.

He stares down on me still holding me in place and all I can think of when I look at him is that I love him. But before I can think the words have left my mouth. "I want your last name." I say. "What?" His eyes widen in panic for a sec before he frowns. "Nothing." I say looking anywhere but him.

I did not just say that to him. I´m way too drunk.

"Say that again." He presses holding me firm. And I look away, but I know he won´t let it down. "I want your name." I say quiet locking eyes with him, and he blinks at me. And frowns. *Silence.*

I wanna die right here. Why did I say that?

"You´re asking me to marry you?" He asks and I say nothing avoiding his eyes. But I don´t know where to look but at him. So, I meet his gaze and.. *he grins.*

Why´s he grinning? He thinks I´m silly.

"That´s *my* part." He says tilting his chin. *What?*

I look at him but there´s no shitty grin and no sarcasm. Nothing but his serious expression and my heart sinks. *Did he just? I´m drunk. He didn´t imply he might one day. I´m drunk and he´s messing with me as always.*

Because this conversation can´t be real.

And being with Kai often feels like I´m dreaming. One time he´s a pain in the ass but other times he´s anything like that. He´s thoughtful and caring and says things like that.

Like wanting to marry me someday.

Which makes me hope. But hope is a tricky one. And just because the last two months have been a dream doesn´t mean he´s going to marry me. He´s still the guy with no labels.

I haven´t forgotten that.

I just decided not to think about it if it´s not a problem now.

"So, if you´re notgonna sleep with me then whatarewedoing then?" I ask a bit extra slurring to change the subject, and he just grins and takes my hand leading me around the house.

We lie in the rain and never have I felt freer. The ground is heated by the sun. My fingers run over the wet asphalt as I breathe in the rainy summer air and feel the wind on my skin.

This smells like childhood. Like playing when the sun starts to set or running over wet grass trying to catch a butterfly. *It smells like joy.*

And we humans go through life asleep most of the time. Only in a few breathtaking moments we´re completely in the here and now. But when I am with Kai, it´s as if time stands still. Like time doesn´t exist. *Because it doesn´t.*

We don´t need it. Because in those moments we last forever. As if we had eternal time and at the same time none.

And then I look at him and I feel whole. *Seen, understood, and heard.*

Maybe we won´t end happy, but we´re in the now and not at the end. And this is all I want. Him stopping time and sharing his now´s. *Him to be happy.*

167

I spot papers on his desk. All over the board to be exact.

As I get closer, I see those are drawings, but Kai enters the room rushing past me before I can reach the mess. He hastily shoves them together, but they slip out of his hands and fall to the floor. “You can draw?” I ask confused. He shrugs scurrying them. “You never showed me.” I accuse him. *He says nothing.*

“Why didn´t you tell me?” I ask upset and he turns to face me the mess in his hands. “Cause, I wanted to see *yours*.” He says on edge shoving them in his drawer, but he missed one, and I snatch it before he can rip it from my hand.

My eyes widen. “You drew *me*?” I gasp. *Not believing what I see.*

He tries to take it back, but I dodge him stepping back and look at him expectantly. “You did this?” I ask again and he nods. “And you´re freaking good at it.” I whine and smack him. “Why did you draw me?” I laugh insecurely and he scratches his head looking nervous. “You never draw yourself.” He shrugs. “I wanted you to see yourself through Art. As Art. As something worth drawing. Something beautiful.” I´m speechless and my jaw dropped.

“Don´t look at me like that.” He says tearing it from my grip. “That´s why I didn´t want to show you.” He says. “Well, how should I react when I showed you *my* drawings but you´re the real Picasso.” I say stunned. “I´m not.” He says puckering his face. “You are.” I shake my head. “This is.. *amazing* and mine look like shit.. you´re a goddess in everything.” I laugh. “Shut up.” He snaps and I sigh giving in. “But you could have showed me sooner.” I point out and he shrugs.

“But I like *your* Art.” He says frowning. “Like yours too.” I retort and we look at each other in silence.

“So, now we can draw together?” I ask excitedly and he pinches his eyes at me shaking his head. “No.” He says. “Yes, we do.” I tell him and his head falls back but he smiles. “And maybe I´ll show you some of my poetry.” I tease and his head snaps back.

That gets him.

“You write?” He asks. “A bit.” I grin. “I *need* to see them.” He demands. “First we paint.” I insist. “Okay.” He agrees and I smile. “But I´ll get to decide what.” He arrogates. “Fine.” I breathe. “What are we doing?” I ask annoyed and he licks his lips trying to fight a smile. *This is no good sign.*

“Body painting.” He grins smug and I nod. “Body painting.” I repeat. “Yeah.” He nods and I shake my head at him. “But we´ll paint with our bodies then. On *actual* paper. We´re not just gonna color each other.” I warn him. “Sure we´ll do.” He smirks and salutes.

But we had sex on that piece of paper after playing Twister paint.

"Now take his fucking shirt off." He growls as he undresses. *What?*

I look down on a plain grey shirt but not his. *It´s Aidan´s.*

There is no big difference. A shirt is a shirt. *But he noticed. Of course, he did.*

"It´s just a shirt." I say. "It is *not*. And you know it." He says slowly. "Now take mine." He demands but I raise my eyebrows at him. He looks at me challenging and I do the same, crossing my arms. "You want me to rip it?" He grins raising his eyebrows like he really loved to do it. *And I´m sure he would.*

But I shake my head with a grin. "No.. still plan on wearing it." I say under my breath and change out of it. "Not when you´re in *my* bed with me without him." He states and I halt.

I face him. "Without?" I ask surprised, and he looks at me blankly. "You would still..?" I ask. "What?" he asks. "Share you?" he wants to know, and I slowly nod, not sure in what mood he is but he reads my face. "Of course, I would." He says and I frown.

"You would share me.. but won´t let me wear his shirt?" I ask amused and he presses his lips together suppressing his shit ass grin because he knows how stupid that is. "You got it." He grins and grabs me by the waist to haul me onto his bed with him. I let out a laugh as his weight drains me.

"As I´ve told you before.." He hushes, biting my ear. "I´d share you with him. But no one else." He tells me. "But I won´t." He says placing a kiss on my temple and I grin. "What?" He asks. "Nothing." I shake my head, but can´t hide my smile. "Tell me what´s that shitty grin for?" He prompts and I squirm under him, but he just presses himself at me searching my gaze.

"What?" he rakes further, and I bite my lip. His eyes widen and darken a bit realizing. "You thought about him. Didn´t you?" He asks and I turn my face.

"You *did*." He says his voice different now. *Husky.*

He takes my chin forcing me to look at him. "Tell me." He demands. "I did." I admit and he grins licking his lips. His irises, two huge dark spots as he glares at me, and I feel him harden. "You want me to call him?" He asks in a tone that tells me he´s turned on. But I know it´s a bit of a threat too. *So, I shake my head.*

"No." I whisper. "What do you want?" He asks and swallows. "*You.*" I hush and feel his breath on my face. His jaw flexes, and I bite it teasing. He lowers himself on me, making him space between my legs. I bite down harder, and he rocks his hips against mine. "You want him?" He breathes and groans as I scratch his back. "I want you." I tell him and he kisses me.

169

As I walk down the corridor, I stop hearing sobs. I hold my breath trying to locate the source.

It´s coming from the guest room. Or rather the Dark´s bedroom but it´s more for guests since they´re never here to use it.

I walk slowly past the bathroom towards Finns room and to the other bedroom in the left corner. *I hear whispering.*

The door is ajar, and I peek through and see Ryan standing across the room looking down on a girl who sits on the floor against the bed. Her hair is dark brown.

But I can´t make her out.

Now he squats down looking at her with a mixture of affection and sadness. He wipes her tears as she continues to cry.

Who´s that girl? Ryan has never girls. Most of the Lost boys have flings but never girlfriends. Does he have a relationship we don´t know about? But why´s he here then?

As his gaze wanders I rare back afraid he´d see me but I listen. He sighs. "You know you could have all you want." He says to her, but she just sniffs her nose crying quietly. "I´d do *anything* for you." He says softly and my heart warms. *That´s all a girl wants to hear.*

And enough for me to snoop around. As I hear them kissing, I back up.

I didn´t know Ryan had a girl. Or problems with girls.

But apparently, we all are tangled in secrets.

Just as I start walking, I hear the girl speak up. "We can´t." She whispers and I stop. My ears poke. "We can." He responds. "Ry." She wines. *No.*

My eyes widen as I recognize her voice pared with the nickname, but I don´t listen further to know. I don´t interrupt them either. All I can think of is the guy she´s crying over.

And it´s not Ryan.

Slowly I go back the hallway and head outside and search all the faces but he´s not here so I go over to the Avery´s, and I keep looking. And I spot him at the campfire.

My heart hurts before I have said a single word. "I need to talk to you." I say standing next to him. "I´ll pass." He brushes me off and I breathe annoyed biting down my frustration. "No, you don´t get it. I need to talk to you.. about *something*." I insist. "As I said." He sighs. "It´s important.." I begin but he glares at me. "Cut it, Scar." He says without looking at me and I bite my tongue.

"But you might need to hear it. It´s about.. *Nina*. It´s kind of.. urgent." I tell him, but Leon cuts me off once again. "Leave it." He snaps and my face heats and I stand there rooted. He won´t look at me and finishes his joint gulping liquor like it´s water.

What´s with him?

They did fight but usually he´s..

My eyes narrow. He´s angry with me without knowing what I´ll..

My mind stops. "You know." I say barely breathing.

"Bingo Sherlock." He scoffs taking another drink. My eyes lose their focus.

He knows.

But I blink it away and he drowns it in one sip as I sit down in the dirt and look at him questioning but he doesn´t spare me a glance and just keeps his gaze on the fire. And I ponder how I can reach him, but I come up with nothing.

He isn´t the talker. Never was. And a rage room won´t help here.

We sit there for a few minutes. He drinking and smoking and me thinking and biting some more of my cheeks.

"How would I *not notice* my best friend wishing for my girl?" He asks with raw acid in his voice and a shiver runs down my spine as I shut my eyes by imagining his pain. "You never said anything." I point out quietly. "What should I say?" He laughs. "Like I´m the sane one in this relationship." He takes another shot.

"I can´t keep my dick in my pants either." He says upset. "I flirt with others after we fight and bury myself inside someone else when she´s crying into him." He says like he hates them instead of loving them. *Cause he does. Love them.*

"Like I have no idea.." he starts and looks at me as he finishes "That every time we fight *he* fucks her to make her better." He says with dead eyes and my eyes hurt and my throat thickens.

He raises the glass, but I stop his hand midway. His eyes are venomous but filled with pain and my chest clenches. He doesn´t push me away but speaks up. "We´re both fucked up. I know that. We both fuck around each other´s back when we hate and end up with each other when we love." He says lost. "He fucks her broken heart whole. And I break it when I fuck other girls." He looks past me.

"But she fucks just him." His chin tilts back. "She might flirt with others but in the end it´s him." He shakes his head slowly.

"She wants me to think she hooks up with the people she´s hanging with. But I know it´s just him. I´ve seen them. I´ve heard them and seen texts." His face red and I still hold his arm.

He leans forward on his knees. “I fuck meaningless. She doesn´t.” He nods and rubs his mouth with his free hand. “But she sticks to me after all.” He shrugs and I lower my hand and let him take his drink.

“How long has it been going on?” I almost choke on my question. He bites his lip and runs a hand through his hair and shrugs. “Long.” He says and that isn´t precise at all but the way he said it told me *everything* I need to know.

“You know..” he starts looking into his glass “I grew up with her. She´s been my first handholding. First, deep look in the eyes. First crush and kiss. My first head and fuck. My first girlfriend. First love and heartbreak. My first *everything*.” He tells me. “She´s been the one I´ve cheated on and I´m the one she has cheated on. We were broken up but what does that even mean in our relationship?” He shrugs and he´s right the two of them are different from *any* couple I know.

“I loved her since I was eleven.” He laughs. “And when you love too hard at that age you can´t just stop.” He states. “You´ve grown into loving her. There´s no way out. You know them like yourself. You did everything with them. You´ve seen them daily for almost all your life. There is no without them.” He shakes his head.

“She saw the first hair on my face, chest, legs, and dick and I saw her breast grow. She made me come and I made her come. I showed her and she showed me. I taught her and she taught me.” He tells me.

“She´s all my firsts. Why shouldn´t she be my lasts then?” He looks at me desperately. “Wouldn´t it be meaningless? All the firsts when she isn´t the lasts too?” He asks me again like I have the answer to that.

“At times I thought my ex would have my lasts too.” I tell him. “But sometimes that just isn´t the case because they already had your firsts, they won´t get your lasts. And maybe the firsts aren´t meant to be the lasts.” I whisper and he puts his head in his hands, and I caress his hair. *I made it worse.*

“But sometimes they are.” I tell him. “Sometimes they are your *everything*.” I say. “But are you hers too?” I ask and he shrugs and a sound that could be a sob escapes him, but he growls straightening up and wipes his eyes fiercely.

“We went from great to toxic and back.” He says. “You haven´t *learned* how to unlove.” He swallows. “You´ve learned to live with that love.” He explains, and I know exactly what he´s talking about I fell in love with my ex at thirteen and never fell out of it completely. I just carry that love with me and deal with it on my own. I store it in a drawer he won´t ever open again. Because he gave the key back since he has no access anymore.

No interests. No love.

“I had no sex life. I had her.” He says. “My teenage years evolved around her.” He grips his hair. “But we *had* to make experience. We were brave enough to cheat and hurt each other but never bold enough to break up properly. Cause we loved each other and couldn´t make a break” He says.

“Maybe that´s our problem. We should have broken up years ago. Before things got tangled.” He goes on. “Maybe she would have dated him even. I would have let her. She would have come back to me.” He shrugs and lets out a frustrated groan taking another shot.

“But he´s your friend.” I say irritated. “And she´s my girl.” He shrugs and nods at once. “How could they..?” I begin but stop myself and he just stiffs a laugh. “Yeah..” He says. “Do they know..?” I begin but he cuts in. “That I know?” He finishes and I nod. He inhales. “No.” He says and searches my gaze. “And that won´t *ever* change Scar.” He threatens and I frown. “What? Why?” I ask but he interrupts me. “If he´s the reason..” he stops himself to say it differently. “If him fucking her, brings her back to me..” He doesn´t complete, but I know.

Then he´ll take it. Cause it would be worse not having her at all.

I know that feeling. It´s the way I feel about Kai. It´s why I don´t push him anymore and don´t ask about the labels. *Because nothing is worse.*

“How?” I ask after a moment, and he looks at me. A small smile plays on his lips. “Love.” He simply says.

“And maybe hate.” He shakes his head. *Maybe.*

I always knew they flirted with others while their breakups, but I never knew there was *fucking* involved. Especially *best friend* fucks.

But now I get it. The way Nina and Ryan are. They´re more than best friends. And I always thought they act like siblings, but I was wrong. They act like they´re in love. And it´s not even unrealistic because they all grew up together. Those games, parties, the lost boys, and Neverland. Even the pirates. They grew to love each other.

And maybe hate.

Was that the reason why he wanted the three of us to stop fucking last year?

Cause he experienced it. But he didn´t get that *we* wanted that at that time. We *wanted* to share until we didn´t. But they don´t share. *They lie.*

“Promise me, Scar.” He demands. “Huh?” I say lost in thoughts. “You won´t say a thing.” He insists and I nod. “Yeah no, I won´t say a thing. I promise.” I tell him. “Right choice.” He says and I nod again.

“Do you think?” I ask, but he knows what I mean. “They do.” He says.

They love each other.

I sigh. "I´m sorry. I hush. "Don´t be." He tells me. "But I am." I say and lean against his legs. "Me too." He says quietly and hands me his cup.

We sit there for a while and get drunk. Or rather I get drunk, and he gets even drunker. He gets his guitar and jams a bit.

"Don´t tell fucked up people they are. *They know.*" He whispers. "Yeah." I agree with him. *They know.*

170

Beige – Yoke Lore

There´s black ink flashing on the right just above his boxers. Leon made him a new tattoo today. I can´t see what the writing says from here. *It´s three words.*

But before I can get a look, he throws his shirt over his head.

What would Kai get tattooed with?

As we lie in bed I´m finally close enough to inspect the ink on his skin.

"Petrichor and Pluviophile."

I frown. *What does that mean?*

I straddle him and run my fingers over the letters. His gaze rests on me as my eyes move to his sore skin. "What is it?" I ask and when he says nothing, I look at him. He just looks at me silently and I give him a look. *Answer.*

"Us." He says with such conviction that I´m almost satisfied with that. The spot between his eyebrow´s wrinkles and I never thought how sexy I would find that. And for a moment, I must grin over the fact that Kai has worry instead of dimple lines like Aidan.

But it fit´s him.

I just wish I could take the weight those have caused on his soul.

But Kai snaps me out of my thoughts as his fingers now want to brush *my* furrows away.

I´m sure that man can read thoughts.

But the gesture brings back my smile and makes one of my worries disappear. "So, what´s this all about?" I ask and he grins. "You´re not letting up, huh?" He asks amused and I press my lips together shaking my head slightly.

He sighs and moves under me. "*Petrichor.* The smell of earth after rain." He searches my eyes. "*Pluviophile.* A lover of rain. Someone who finds joy and peace of mind during rainy days." He tells me and I look at him processing.

But then I smile. "What?" he asks, and again his eyebrows wrinkle. "Us." I repeat his words, and the worry disappears. *He smiles.*

171

"A dream catcher?" He raises his eyebrow. "For your nightmares." I tell him but he frowns. I made it myself out of sticks, light brown string, feathers, and pearls.

"It´s a *sickness* Lia." He says I blink. "I know.. I.." I stammer feeling insensitive. "I´m sorry." I say. "It´s stupid." I add trying to get it back, but he dodges me.

"I *don´t* need one." He tells me and I lower my eyes.

Why did I give him that? I should have given him a bong. Something helpful.

"I have you." He says. *And I freeze wanting to cry.*

"But I´ll hope that *fucker* works." He says and hangs it above his bed, and I bite my lip. Then he tugs me with him, and we lay down. "I saw a quote from Oscar Wilde." He whispers for no reason maybe cause it´s dark. "Yeah? Which one?" I hush. "It threw me completely." He says. "It goes; *the heart was made to be broken.*" He quotes. "Do you think that is true?" He asks but I have no answer.

"That made me question things." He says into the void. "I want an intact love, and I want you. But I fear I have hurt you before. But is it made to be broken then?" He asks and that threw me off. *Completely.*

He´s always fearless talking to me in the darkness. Where I can´t see him or the truth in his eyes. *But I hear it in his voice.*

This way he opens up more to me. He does small steps towards me, and I do the same. We make progress and the *slow* feels even better than the rush we tried to do back then.

"I don´t think hearts are made to be broken." I tell him. "But they can be." I face him but he already fell asleep. But I kept wide awake thinking about life, death, fear, and desire.

Love.

And about hearts that should be broken. And the ones that shouldn´t.

And that was the beginning and the end of *the Now* that she pretended to be in.

172

Kai pushes his knee between my legs, so I can rub against it.

Between kisses, he bites my bottom lip. "Do you have any toys?" He asks against my lips. "As if you don´t know that already." I retort remembering last year. And the smile on his face tells me he does too. He leans over and rummages around in the drawer.

How did they find that without waking me?

With the vibrator in his hand, he now forces both of his knees between my legs to make room for himself. He takes the dildo and runs the tip over my lower lip, causing my mouth to open. His black eyes scrutinize me, and he kneels looking down on me. We keep eye contact as he brushes my lip with his thumb and bites his own as he pushes it slowly into my mouth, and I suck on it. He exhales and claws my thigh with his other hand.

He lets go of my mouth and licks his lips. His boxer tight now, begging to come off. But he holds the vibrator to my entrance. And his cock twitches as he slides it inside of me. Pleasure written all over him as it slowly slides in and out of me.

Then he snaps on the vibration to which I moan as the resting part penetrates my clit and his eyes shoot to mine. Arousal flashes across his face as he reaches for his crotch and kneads it on the fabric with his eyes closed. My mouth drops open as I watch and struggle not to explode immediately.

As he picks up pace he pushes the next level and my upper body shoots forward. His eyes snap open, and he lowers himself onto me guiding my hand on himself as he keeps moving the dildo.

Then he pushes a few more buttons until a pulse-like pattern starts, and I cling to him. He breathes hot on my neck moaning increasing the tempo of his hand holding my orgasm. I claw to the sheets and his hand finds mine.

He watches my orgasm crash over me kissing my cries away.

As I´m done, I reach for his shorts to free his cock and straighten up pushing him over.

- 27 -

Kai

The next moment I´m on my back and Scar sucking my dick like honey.

The dildo still inside her dripping, drives me mad. *Just like the noises she makes.*

Her mouth is warm, and I guide her head grabbing her smooth hair helping her move. When she takes me deep throat, I thrust my hips up with a growl. She wants me to die right here with her mouth on me. *Just the way I would love to go.*

Between thrusts, I let her have control, so she feels comfortable. But she wants my hand on her jaw, neck, and hair and fuck she´s.. *heaven*. Right now, she´s in full control of me and enjoys it. I´ll give her my veins, my eyes, my heart, and fucking mind. She´s got my body, soul, and pounding heart. The heart that has only been alive to pump blood. But right now, it´s pumping for her and pumps those green eyes through my arteries and back into the useless muscle of my heart through my veins. And each time, she takes over more of my body. Like a virus her soul merges with mine. Like she´s mine and I belong to her. And I do and want all of it. *All of her. For. Fucking. Ever.*

She´s gotten used to my movements, so I pump faster. "Fuck." I press my head into the mattress just to bring it back up to watch her taking me all in. "Fuck, Scar I need to come." I pant and her eyes lock with mine and that sends me over as I pound into her hitting the back of her throat and even lower. I grip her sculp and lose it completely. As I come, I black out and reach for her. I see stars and pour down her mouth. I lose sight, time, and control. My body vibrates and tickles as my vision blurs and my head feels loose. I almost lose consciousness but her hands on me save me. *They always do.*

Never have I come so hard or been so lost in my life. Never been in love so hard. Because that´s what I am. *Fucking in love with Lia Sky.*

Because that´s what she does to me. Making me see the stars not only in the night but at any time. She brings the sky down for me. She fucking takes me down. And I love all of it.

All of her.

But just as he realized how much he loves her. She realized how much more she wants. Things she shouldn´t want. Things he couldn´t give. But she thought about it anyway.

173

Lia, By your side – Omar LinX

"You smell like pencil and paint." Kai says into my neck, and I flinch but giggle as his breath hits my skin. He hovers over me, looking at my painting and I frown. "Thanks, I guess." I turn to face him, but the sun blinds me. I squint my eyes, but he kisses me, and I smile to his mouth.

He moves around me, sits down and I scurry my tools and scoot next to him.

How do I do this? Just take it slow. Step by step.

"Don´t freak out, okay." I say and he frowns. "What´s wrong?" He nods at me. "Nothing." I assure him. "Just.. *listen* okay?" I ask, and he moves uncomfortable. "I don´t push, and you don´t have to say anything." I soothe him and he stares at me. "If it´s too much, tell me." I say intently, and I see panic flicker over his face. "I won´t go. And you don´t need to either." I try to get him back and he blinks looking at me for a moment.

But then he nods. "Okay. I´ll try." He says. *This is progress,* I tell myself.

"So, what´s up?" He asks tense. "Can.. we talk?" I ask careful. "The letter thing." He makes a face, and I nod. "Yeah, you know words and stuff." I joke. "Hmh." He hums. “But talking means thinking.” He points out and I laugh. “Yeah, I know Peter *never* thinks and so do you, I get it.” I say and he nods along.

“But a little doesn´t.. *hurt.*” I retort with a smile. “Maybe not *you.*” He says and I sigh. “Kai.” I warn. “Scar.” He mimics my tone, and I smile but shake my head. He straightens up. “Kay then talk.” He clicks his tongue and I didn´t think about him *actually* agreeing to do this.

But I clear my throat. “Uhm.. okay.” I begin and he listens. “So, you know how I feel about you.” I say and his eyes narrow. “Do I?” He asks and I nod. “I love you. And..” I say, but he interrupts me. “And what?” He asks. “I don´t know.” I whine and hold my face feeling tears well up. “*Fuck.*” I curse and Kai scoots closer. “Scar what´s wrong?” He asks and I breathe biting my lip. “Tell me.” He forces. “I don´t know.” I say upset. “Okay, I don´t know.” I yell and face him.

“Did I do something?” He asks and I shake my head. “No.” I say. “Then what is it?” He wants to know. *How should I do this? Without.. pushing this?*

“Maybe I need more.” I whisper. *Silence.*

“More what?” He asks, his voice thin and I meet his eyes. *They´re feared.*

“More *everything.*” My voice breaks and he frowns. “Like what?” He asks helplessly and I groan. “Lia.” He says irritated. “I know sorry.” I yell. “I just.. I don´t want to lose you.” I whisper. “You won´t.” He hushes and pulls a strand out of my face. “Tell me what I can do.” He holds the back of my head, and I search his face. *He´s serious.*

“Write me a letter.” I say and he frowns. “Or a poetry.” I add. “Or whatever.. a sentence.” I shrug. “Write me *something.*” I sob and his eyes mirror my pain. But he nods. “Okay.” He says and tears roll down my cheek. But catches them and leans against my forehead. His breath soothing me. “I´ll write you a letter, a poetry, a sentence.. *something.*” He whispers against my lips, and I close my eyes nodding.

He kisses me gentle and then he gets up and heads inside.

174

An hour later he comes back. With a letter and a sharpie in his hand.

He throws the pen on the table and hands the paper to me and sits down.

“You know I can´t. So, I´m writing you a letter. – Kai”

Reads the envelope.

It´s wrinkled, as if he wanted to throw it away but changed his mind. The page looks like it was torn out of a book. *But it´s a blank one.*

He´s silent as I read.

"It rained that day. And my soul recognized you before my eyes knew who you were. You sat in the rain. Alone. By the campfire. And I`ve never seen anything so fucking perfect. You just sat and didn`t even care. You were peaceful and happy. And at that moment, I saw you and my soul felt you everywhere. I couldn`t get away from you that moment. And ever since."

My eyes burn at his words. The campfire was the second time he saw me. And he didn´t hate me. *He felt me.*

It´s a bit messy and there are things crossed out and scribbled over.

"~~Yes, I love you, Sear.~~"

I grin.

"Nothing happens until something moves. – Albert Einstein"

He quotes.

"You moved me. Nothing happened before. Nothing inside me or around me. And now everything is happening. Everything is moving."

That´s a more cryptic.

"My mind was a dark place, and then I met you. You were the firefly in my life. You were the ever in Neverland. You were the star in my dark. You were the fire in my heart."

This one is more like a poetry.

"We don´t need labels to prove what we already know. I don´t need to give you flowers, buy you jewelry, or marry you to show you how I feel. But I know I will. You know I will. Because for you, I would."

The note is written in different colors and pens, as if he had been writing off and on. Which would explain the whole mess. It´s like an entry from a Notebook or something similar. *It´s mazy. It´s him.*

I look at him his gaze on the floor. "Will you read it to me?" I ask not knowing if that´s too much right now, but I try it anyways and hand it to him. And he doesn´t look at me but takes it silently.

- 27 -

Kai

Even though the lines are already burned into my brain, I fix my gaze on the letter, so I don´t have to look at her while I do it. *Just read it. It´s just words.*

You´ve read to her tons of times.

But no letters. No poetry. No sentence. No something.

I clear my throat, but my voice is annoyingly raspy.

"You wanted more, so this is more.

I tried to run from my feelings. Run from you, but my soul craved you. So, I stopped. But it's scary and new. And everything I want to run from. But I don't. You showed me how to stay. How to be okay and to take a step. How to love."

My gaze still fixed on the crumpled page.

"I wrote this letter, this poetry, this sentence, this something to numb some of your pain."

My throat is clocked, and my eyes burn, and knee bobs up and down. My heart races and skin itches. I sweat and I shiver. I want to get up and leave, but I fist the page and stare at my shaking hands.

I rub my face and take a deep breath.

Then I dare to look up and meet her teary eyes.

She reaches for the sharpie and takes my hand. She bites the cap and writes on my palm.

"You are more. Scar."

I bite my lip so hard I taste blood. *But the tears fall anyway.*

She kisses me and licks my blood as I have licked hers before.

"Thank you." She breathes. *I love you.*

[NOTEBOOK ENTRIES]

I couldn't love her the way she deserved. It was like with your flaws. You know you should love them, but you reject them. That's what I did to her. But I won't anymore. I'll make it right this time. I can love her. I just have to learn to show her.

I thought of a million different things of what to say to her when I get back and how she would react. But I didn't expect her to sit on the sidewalk. In the rain where I want her the most. I thought I lost it. I told her I love her three fucking times. I didn't plan to, but seeing her wearing my hoodie, listening to music. On our spot. Alone. I felt that I love her. The bed was how I left it. Someone rumored around in my bookshelf, but that was all. She wasn't there. That hurt. Even more than when I realized she'd been in my bed back then. I wanted her to sleep in my bed. Read my books. Wear my cloths. But I understood why she didn't. Finn told me he saw her. She's been here at night. When it rained. She sat there. She leaned against my car. Sat on the hood watching the stars. And he thinks she sat on the sidewalk too. Where the accident was. And I'm sure she did. Sometimes I sit there too. She stared at my window. Probably pondering if she should take the step, but she never did.

I kissed her in front of them. No secret. No hiding. I gave her my now's, and she agreed to give me hers.

She said she wants my name. Somehow that.. pleased me. I never thought about marriage. I think it's useless. But her having my name. Fuck that was.. something I never knew I wanted. But now did. Scar Dark. Fits perfect if you ask me. But I'll have to fucking work for it. I need to get my shit together. But first I need to learn how to love her right.

Art is her soul. My soul is my writing and my photos. She wants me to get my voice out there. If she knew I'm already working on that.

She told me about Ryan and Nina. I told her I know. We all have our fucked-up secrets. It's not just us. Everyone has some. We just pretend we don't.

It's still hard to open up, but I'll try for her. I want this to work. I want to be better for her. She told me I'm more. I just hope my more is enough.

175

Weeks later, July, Lia

"I'm in therapy." He states. "I *know*, but you do that for yourself and not me." I retort. "I do it for *us* too." He tells me shaking his head. "What?" I ask. "It's like you can't even see how I've changed." He says. "I do." I argue. "No, you don't. Just let me show you." He offers and I nod.

He takes a deep breath. "My greatest fear is.. losing you but also being with you." He says and looks like he doesn't understand it either. "Okay." I say. "So, you *want*.. to be friends?" I conclude. "I don't know." He shrugs and I sigh. "No." He says. "Then *what* do you want?" I ask. "*Stop* asking me that." He defends and I inhale annoyed.

It's the same as always. We talk more yes, but we're rooted. Circling around the label he tries to avoid. But sometimes you need clarity in life.

"No, you owe me that." I push. "I want *it* to stop." He fires back, and there's a glimpse of regret after he said it. *Like he hurt himself by saying that.*

"What *it*?" I ask. "I don't know. *This* it's too close." He says quietly, looking down and I shake my head confused. "Us?" I rake further. "No. I want closer. But I feel caged in. I can't breathe." He tells me. "Okay." I say and lose focus. "You're sad." He says reading me. "Yeah I am." I tell him. "Don't be." He steps closer. "But I am." I stop him and he sighs.

"You tell me you want me in your life. But not too close. But closer." I shrug. "I don't know what *that* means." I throw my hands in the air. "Do we date? Fuck? Are we friends? More? Less? What am I supposed to feel about this?" I ask him but he can't answer that. "Are we exclusive? But what does that then mean? You can´t just say you want me but not in the way I want and expect me to accept that." I tell him and he stays silent.

But listens. No running. At least some progress.

"How should I know how to act around you? When I don´t know where we´re at? What should I tell guys? That I´m single? Or in sort of a relationship? That I´m with you but not really?" I ask and he shakes his head.

"No, you do that all the time. You *always* push me." He accuses me. "Yeah, I do, but I have to." I shot back but he ignores me. "I should tell you how I feel. That I want you to be my girlfriend and all. But you know how that makes me feel. And I´m still working on it." He tells me upset. "Yes, I´m fucked. But so are you. You´re not better. But you act like you are." He scoffs.

"I´m just not enough for you. Never enough." He looks hurt.

"But instead of trying to change me. Look at your *own* shit." He spits and my face heats. "Because I can´t remember *you* open up to me. I did open more than I *ever* intended to. But you didn´t. You *never* did." He snaps.

"I did every first step. Just think of it." He demands. "I kissed you first, touched you first and even said I love you first." He lists. "But you also took it all back. Acted like it didn´t happen." I counter. "Maybe. But don´t act like you´re the one who´s been open about her feelings because you *never* were." He says. "Not more than I was." He nods and I close my eyes.

"Now it´s your fucking turn. Tell me how you feel about me." He´s angry and maybe he´s right. "But you won´t right?" he stiffs a laugh. "So, don´t force me all the time and expect things that you won´t give me in return either." He rages.

"Okay I´m sorry maybe you´re right I didn´t. I just assumed you knew." I say. "Knew what?" He snaps. "That it´s you." I shrug and he frowns. "That I didn´t want Andi or my ex back. And I didn´t want to be with Aidan. *Never.*" I say. "I wanted it to be you. I just waited.." I stop realizing and he laughs with a nod. "For *me* to say something." He shakes his head. "God Lia." He growls. "You can´t always expect me to fucking read your mind." He tells me. "I know." I say. "No, I think you don´t know." He states.

"We keep doing this. Keep circling. Having those conversations. Coming close, but never too close. I´m so tired of it." I say exhausted. "I know." He inhales sharply. "I know." He repeatedly rubbing his face. "But you have to stop expecting people to love you like you do." He shrugs and I frown. "Well, and *you* can´t expect people to read your mind either. We can´t just *not* talk and expect everything to fall in line." I say.

"Because we do this all the time. Won't talk until we come to blows." I add and he lets out an annoyed grunt.

"I know Scar. I know. But we *do* talk. Don't we?" He asks beat and I nod. "We try." He says quietly and I nod again.

He steps closer speaking softly now. "Can you just stop pushing me into talking?" He searches my face. "Because you push my Buttons. And *then* I shut down. I don't want to do that anymore." He tells me. "I try, but you have to give me time." He begs. "And we're not in a tug of war. We should stop forcing the other over the line." He holds my face. "We can sit there and let the other cross it. Without pushing or running." He says intently and I nod.

"I won't beg you to love me the way I need it." I say and he nods. "But you won't let go of me either." He says and I look at him. "No." I admit shamefully.

"And I do, you know." He says against my lips. "*Love you.*" He mouths before he kisses me and that's how it is with us. Hanging on loose ends. One step away from cutting off and one away from holding on. I don't know which hurts more.

"*You and I, we are what we are and will be what we'll be.*" He shrugs as he quotes his favorite author Oscar Wilde. "And what is that?" I ask with a playful grin. "Stop pushing." He growls low. "Stop avoiding." I counter and he bites my jaw, but I smack him. "*A man can be happy with any woman, as long as he doesn't love her.*" He quotes again and I roll my eyes.

"Oscar Wilde was a wise man." I comment and he smiles. "But you're a coward." I tell him. "I never claimed otherwise Scar." He says, and I nod cause he's right. He never did and maybe I should stop hoping otherwise.

"I'll probably keep running whereas you hide and isolate. But I'll keep trying." He promises, just as he did in the past. *But what are promises made of the devil?* Lies.

"Now done with the quotes. You have a mouth, *use it.*" I snap and a low chuckle leaves his body, and he kisses me.

"I didn't mean *that.*" I say annoyed and he grins. "Then you have to be more *precise.*" He retorts and I roll my eyes. "You have a *heart*, use it." I counter. "Make me." He teases and I hit him playfully. "I already do Scar." He tells me and I smile.

"I promise I'll keep trying too." I tell him and sigh fed up. "Now can we talk about that later? I'm over it." I whine and he nods kissing my forehead.

176

Two weeks later, If you want love - NF

Colson Herzog

We sit at the bar, and I stare at the mirror across me. Stirring absently my mojito with the straw thinking.

He sat with some of the lost boys and watched me talking to a guy. Tall, pretty, charming, and touchy. He came up to me standing close to my back. He scared him off and then he just left. *He did that five times.*

The one time a guy danced with me. The other asked for my number. One gave me a drink. And the other flirted with me from across the room. But all he did was make em fuck off. And he wouldn´t even dance with me he just wanted me to dance alone. Or with my friends.

It made me furious. Because the last time we spoke about whatever the hell we are we said we´d be friends for now. *Because clearly, we can´t be together.*

But this is not just a best friend watching his bestie. He´s making sure I´m not with any guy tonight. While at his table four girls flirt with all of them including him. So, I lost it and when he tried to do it again, I walked off.

He won´t let me get to know someone new but won´t be my boyfriend either.

I´m sick of it. He wants me but not as his girlfriend and doesn´t want to let me go either.

It´s driving me mad. Because the thing with no labels is all funny until you get hit on in a bar. *And then what?* We can´t stand seeing each other with anyone but one another.

Situationships. Yeah, this is really funny.

So that´s why I sit here at the bar alone instead of dancing on the stage like I should.

This whole thing is a shitshow. It´s stupid. It´s..

I´m ripped out of my mind as my chair is being dragged to the right. Towards Kai who now sits next to me. I roll my eyes. *He can´t be serious.*

I close em and swallow my temper as he puts his arm on my backrest. "Stop being mad at me." He says to the side of my face, and I laugh. "Well, but I am Kai." I say. "Well don´t." He retorts playfully and I say nothing, just take another breath.

Then I look at him and he looks as lost as I am. "What are we doing?" I ask and he considers for a moment.

"I don´t know." He admits. Anger boils up. "I hate you." I say not looking at him and a lump in my throat makes me suffer. "I know." He says quietly leaning his head to mine. "Kinda hate me too." He adds in a whisper, and I break and make him look at me. "I don´t.." I try to say, but he cuts me off. "I know." He nods and takes my face in his hands.

All I feel is pain.

"I´m so confused." I whisper almost crying. "Me too." He hushes back resting his forehead to mine and we breathe each other in.

"I don´t want to be just friends." I say upset. "Me neither." He agrees and tears roll down my cheeks. He looks hurt when he sees them. "I´m vulnerable with you. I´m with no one." He tells me and I nod. "I know." I say with our faces just inches apart. I feel his breath on my mouth. "I´m too." I hush and he kisses me softly.

"Wanna dance with me?" He asks trying to cheer me up. "Or home, shower and bed?" He offers. "The latter." I say and he helps me down takes my clutch and guides me to the exit. *But if he actually brought me home is something else.*

177

One week later

I head down the dark hall, searching for a place to hide.

"Wait." He presses as he follows. I exhale, annoyed but keep walking. "Scar." He calls out, but I pace up wanting to be alone for once. "Wait." He grabs my waist, and I try to get him off me, but he drags me to the right pushing a door open with his elbow and tugs me with him.

In one motion he closes the door behind us and it´s pitch dark. "What?" I snap fed up.

No answer.

I try to move past him, but he blocks me. "I don´t want to talk now Kai." I yell, but he still won´t budge. "Can you at least make the lights on?" I groan and try to reach for the wall, but his body moves with mine and I growl annoyed. "No." He grabs my wrist, and I surrender. I take a step back, and I look at him through the darkness. And it´s funny because it´s all I ever see when I look at him.

As if I could see anything else. Because he is.. *the absorption of light.*

I just hoped to find something else when I look at him. But the past weeks I´ve came to realization that there´s *nothing* else. Or at least I can´t see past *that* anymore.

And he knows.

He knows I´m slipping from his grip and that scares him. And yes, it scares me too, but I can´t be in this state of in between any longer. I tried for three months.

But now I can´t.

"Just stay with me." His voice pained and I frown even though he won´t see. "In the dark?" I ask and knowing him, he nods. "Please move closer." He begs and I hesitate for a second before I take a step towards him. His hand finds my waist pulling me in. And just that one hand holding me. *Steadying me.*

And I want to touch him, but I resist. “Did the moment pass already?” I ask actually, hoping it´ll last. “The now´s never over.” He counters and I open my mouth to speak because, I can´t hear that anymore, but he cuts me off sensing my attempt. “Don´t push this now.” He begs. “Please.” He adds filled with emotions.

“I know..” His voice breaks. “Don´t leave now.” He whispers having no voice left.

He knows I want to leave him.

I nod but he doesn´t see. So, I stay, and I try to blink the darkness away, but it won´t fade. And I know he´s crying because I am too. It´s like we know this is going to end. Like he knows I will. *End this.*

But now he´s the one holding on to a *now* that already passed.

“Sometimes it feels like books but the sad ones.” I hush and my fingers itch to touch him, but I don´t. If I do, I´d fall down the abyss but we can´t keep doing this.

“But those are the best ones.” He whispers lowering his forehead onto mine and my lips tremble and a sob escapes me. I feel his hot breath hitting my face like a warm summer breeze. *But it´s winter here.*

His mouth brushes mine and I smell he ate strawberries, so I smile. “What you´re smiling about?” He asks sensing. “You ate strawberries.” I whisper. “Mhm. I did.” He hums. “Want some?” He teases, and my heart makes somersaults, and I nod. His lips brush mine and then he kisses me. *Drowning me with sweetness.*

I suck his tongue, and he moans, digging his fingers in my skin. He brings me closer and bombs against the door. Growling he lifts me and he´s hard but I´m throbbing too. “We can´t keep doing this.” I say between the kisses. “Doing what?” He asks with a smile as he bites my jaw. “Fight, Fuck, Love, Run, Push.” I list. “Sounds like fun to me.” He chuckles at my ear but lowers me to the floor.

“Sounds like *us*.” He says as his hand finds my throat. “Even the love part?” I tease, tip toeing around the pushing topic and his grip tightens. “Even the love part.” He states in a husky voice and my eyes narrow. “Look who´s all confident about his feelings in the dark again.” I whisper venomously. “Dark is my name.” He says and kisses me hard for that remark, but I crave it, and I bite his tongue.

He wines pretending to be hurt. “You *loved* that.” I call him out. “No.” He corrects me. “I love *you*.” He says as if it´s a casual thing for him to say. “Don´t say that just to hold me.” I tell him. “I don´t.” He promises and I keep shut.

He pulls me back into a hug and his heart beats against mine trying to reanimate the half dead butterflies.

We kiss. He lifts me up and we fuck.

178

A few days later, Silver Soul – Beach House

"I hate you." He scoffs but he meant *love.* "I want you to leave me alone." He says, but he meant *please stay.* "I don´t care about you." He says, but he meant *do.*

He said all the things he knew meant nothing. Because he couldn´t say the things that did mean something. We went from heaven to hell in weeks and I wish I could go back to the now we had the first months. *But I can´t find my way back.*

"I´m sick of this." I say. He´s wasted and again, pushing me away from him. Because I got too close to his heart or some shit. *I´m fucking over it.*

"Me too." He slurs. "Now come back to bed." He demands and I gape at him ready to fight, but I know he´s plastered and won´t be able to have a serious conversation, so I shut my mouth and get in.

"You´re drunk. Now sleep." I snap. I gave in because I´m tired since I had to get him from some party he´s been to, alone.

He pulls me to him, and I look at his huge pupils.

The black hole that consumes me every time.

The rabbit hole I fell down thinking I would find love.

"I´m sorry." He whispers against my neck, and I tense. As he notices he starts to shiver, and my eyes fill with tears. *Why can´t we just work?*

I hold him stroking his neck trying to calm him, but tears wet my collar, and his hands claw to my skin like a needle in veins. "I don´t want to do *this* to you." And his voice matches his shaking body. *I stay silent.*

"It´s like something inside of me panics every fucking time you touch me." He says. "Cause it feels too good. Too real. Too everything. Something I´m scared to have but scared to lose." My eyes burn and my vision blurs. "I have this fear of people leaving me. Not loving me or wanting me." He explains and I get it because I trigger all the fears he had growing up. *But still..*

"And it screams when I´m with you." He tells me, his voice breaking all over again and I shut my eyes. I can´t speak even if I wanted to.

"I feel safe with you. Peaceful. Like I belong and I´m loved." He struggles to keep talking. "But it feels as good as scary." He admits. "It´s a constant battle. With the part that wants you in my life and everywhere." He sniffs.

"The part that wants to put a ring on that finger of yours." He whispers and my implodes in a thousand junks. "Against the part that wants to get rid of you, hurt you or leave you.." My skin is soaked of his tears now.

"Before you do that to me." He adds. "And I know it´s all in my head. It´s trauma. Because my parents neglected and left me. Hate me and didn´t love me." He says. "But you know anxiety and the power of it. The weight. It suffocates me." He sobs but clears his throat just to cough again choking on it.

"You know how bad that feels. Wanting and objecting something." He tells me and I nod knowing. "Cause with you the anxiety fades away. But it returns as soon as I linger too long and realize what that means." The lump in his throat makes him stop.

"I don´t deserve you. I know that. I treat you like shit." He says and I cling to him. "Do it with anxiety." I whisper sob. "The fear only tells you something great is ahead." I add my voice unsteady. "I know." His voice cracks painfully as his fingers dig into my flesh.

We mirror our fears.

Maybe it´s a trauma bond. *It probably is.*

We cry while slitting into our skin. Trying to feel, to stay and not leave. *Trying.*

We´re leaving marks, we´ll sure never forget. And as we beat under each other´s skins, a voice in the back of my head tells me, *this is toxic.*

This won´t end well. This needs to stop.

This is bad. This isn´t how it should be. We´re going down. We´re not better. We´re not okay. This isn´t love. This is hurt. This is painful. This isn´t something you should want or need. This is addiction.

It´s a voice so loud, but I can´t listen now. I push it away cause all I can hear is his sobbing and his heart on my skin pounding against mine begging me to let him in, to make it all stop. To make him capable of love. To make him right and make him enough.

And all I can do is listen. To that beat. To those cries. To all he doesn´t say but screams. Because when Wendy – and I certainly am her instead of a lost girl - heard Peter cry she had no other choice but to sooth him. *But who soothed her?*

And I open my heart for his darkness to sweep in. To slice me inside out. To suck all the light out of it. *All the color.*

To write his name on the inside of my skin until there´s just him. Him in my mind, heart, and soul. Hoping to take away some of his pain. Even if causing with that pain in myself.

After he stopped shivering and sobered a bit up, we again tried to talk.

"I´m scared, I´m not good enough." He admits. "You need to be good enough for yourself. That´s the *only* thing that should matter. You." I counter and he nods. "You cause your loneliness and abandonment, to forget and drown out that of your childhood." I say. "I know." He agrees, lowering his gaze. "I know it´s not your fault, Lia. I create the pain. And I´m sorry, I let you down and let myself down." He tells me, still looking at his hands. "I know I need to feel the stuff I´ve been through. I project those feelings on you, on us. I just cover them and make new wounds." He says.

"I´m working on it. Therapy is still a big deal for me. It´s hard." He admits. "And I don´t know if I can face them. Face the fact that my brother loved me more than my parents ever did. That I wasn´t enough. I reject myself for not being enough. For putting myself through the same things as *they* did." He says his voice heavy. "I´m scared I´ll be like that forever." He holds his face. "I want to be a father someday. But I´m scared I would traumatize them. Do them bad. Being like them. Not loving them enough." His voice shakes with fear, and the fact that he just told me he wants children made my eyes burn alive.

"As a child, you experience the bond of your parents as *the love*. That´s the only way you know. The way you think *how* love is supposed to be." He shrugs. "But for me there was no love, no bond, there was just rejection and coldness." He locks eyes with me, and he looks bad.

"You had love and know love. Had *enough* love. And you *assume* to be loved. But you won´t find that with me." His lip trembles with realization. "Cause I assume to be let down. To get nothing and be on my own. Finn loved me because he had to, but my parents chose not to." He shrugs. "And I don´t want to treat you that way but it´s hard to break patterns." His voice quiet.

"I *really* want to change." He tells me. "You just need to understand that it´s too much. Too fast and I need space. Need to breathe and be alone. Because your love *drowns* me. It´s overwhelming." He explains himself. "But I want it. I just need time. And I know I can´t ask you to wait." He shrugs.

"Kai, you *are* worth it." I tell him. "And enough." I say even though maybe I was lying. "You *are* loved." I say all the things he needs to hear. "And you´ll be a great dad. Because you´re different." I tell him and he shakes. "You try and change." I add. "You can run from me, us, your friends, fuck even your parents, but you can´t outrun *yourself*." I tell him.

"No one leaves you alone. Not your friends and not me." I say. "But the one who does.. is yourself. And yourself only." I tell him. "I know." He says, gripping his hair. "I know." He repeats, running his fingers over his scalp. "I know." He says, full of self-hate as a lonely tear drops from his chin.

"I don´t deserve you." He says. "Maybe I do." He shakes his head. "But you deserve so much more. To be loved all the time. Wholly and out loud. Not just in pieces. Not in the dark. In letters, poetry, or quotes. Sentences or something´s." He says, holding my gaze. "You deserve the same." I say and he wipes his face and nods taking my face in his hands. I let the tears escape, but he catches all of them.

He kisses my forehead. "I love you." I whisper and with eyes red, he whispers back. "I love you too." Whereas I cry even more.

179

A few days later, Destroy myself just for you – Montell Fish

It´s just the guys and me before the party starts. *Kai is not here yet.*

So, they use the opportunity to ask questions Kai surely won´t answer. And Andi is the first to speak up. He leans forward and looks at me. "So, what´s going on with you guys lately?" He asks with a grin, and I shrug. "There´s been a switch in the mood." He narrows his eyes, and I nod. "It´s complicated." I say and he winces at that statement. "That´s wary." He tilts his head, and I inhale annoyed. "Yeah, but it is." I shrug. "I never know where we´re at." I tell him and he nods.

"He´s madly in love with you." Leon states and I smile-frown. "Really, that guy´s insane over you." He laughs. "He almost snapped his neck the other day looking at you cause you were laughing about some shit, and he wanted to know *why* and check *who* made you laugh." He says, shaking his head and I give him a weak smile. "I love him but we´re fighting about the same things over and over, and we can´t seem to overcome them." I say and he nods, taking a sip of his beer.

"You say you´re trying to be just friends, but that´s not true. Not anymore." He states and I nod. "I know. We aren´t. But we can´t be together either. It´s been two years." I say. "Yeah." He sighs.

"I know the label thing and shit Scar, but seriously what are you then?" He asks the one-million-dollar question, and all eyes are on me now, but I shrug. "I´d love to know that too." I say. *Maybe we´re not even friends anymore.*

"He really tries Scar." Finn joins in and I look at him. "I know but it´s simply not enough." I tell him. "Lia." He gives me a look. "No, it isn´t." I say. "I mean, *yes*, he tries and it´s different from years ago. He won´t deny or hide *this* anymore. But still, it isn´t enough." I tell them and Ryan agrees. "And I *can* ask for more." I say upset and they nod.

Because I´m right.

A moment of silence passes, and it breaks my heart how they all support him.

"But you´ll always run back to him. You know that, right?" Leon asks and they all look at me thinking the same thing. "Yeah." I breathe and shake my head. "But maybe I can´t stay." I add and Aidan, who´s been oddly silent looks at me irritated.

And maybe sad?

We get up and head over to his garden to talk. Because I know he has something to say. If I want to hear it or not.

"You sure?" He asks. "About what?" I shot back and he gives me a look. "You *know* what I mean." He says. "You want to leave him." He says. "I´m *not* leaving him." I retort. "Yes, you are." He tells me. *I am.*

I inhale annoyed. "Well, maybe I am. But I can´t leave someone I´m not even in a relationship with." I argue and he sighs shaking his head at me. "That´s not true, and you know that." He tells me. "Is it?" I ask shrugging.

Seemingly knows everyone better than we do.

"Because just cause we know that we´re together, and it feels like that and we act like it, doesn´t mean we are." I say. "And he can´t give me more, but I can´t give him less." I say and he frowns at me.

"So, you´re really doing this?" It´s more of a statement than a question and I shrug. "I think." I say and he looks at me hurt. "This isn´t right." He says. "We *need* space." I argue. "You *had* space." He retorts. "Well, it didn´t work." I raise my voice. "That isn´t true." He retorts. "And *you* know that why?" I ask having no patience anymore.

"Because he didn´t gave up." He states and I look at him. "So, don´t you dare give up on him now." He snaps. "Aidan." I warn.

"No Lia, this is a mistake." He says and I look at him stoically. "Then it is. But it´s *my* choice." I state.

"What happened?" He asks, looking at me like I´ve changed. "I realized I deserve more." I say. "*That´s* what happened." I nod.

"He loves you. It´s just *you* for him." He tells me. "I just can´t anymore. This hurts more than it lets me breathe." I say and he considers.

Then he nods. "It´s your decision." He agrees. "But this will kill him." He tells me and my eyes burn. "I know." I say. "But it kills us more to stay at this point." I nod and walk away.

He tried to open up. And I tried to believe it´s enough. But not talking doesn´t solve anything. I need labels and a future. At least the possibility. Maybe that was another way of wanting to control everything, I can´t like him or my future.

I wanted control. He wanted time. Things we couldn´t give.

We aren´t together. And I can´t even tell why. Because there is literally no reason not to be. Maybe because we know it would destroy us. Or we know that won´t be the solution to our problems. A label isn´t the issue. It´s deeper than that. But sometimes there is simply no reason. It´s just the way it is.

Maybe we´re happy, unhappy. Always one step close to having each other and one tripping away to losing each other. And I just waited for the blow. But maybe that way I manifested exactly that. *Us to fuck up.*

The no label rule caught up on us and he choked himself with his own rope and dragged me with him. This isn´t how I want things to be.

It all caught up on us. Until his more and my less wasn´t enough anymore.

[NOTEBOOK ENTRIES]

Does a book mean more than physical contact? More than a kiss? More than sex? More than a feeling? Apparently for her, the words mean more. And I can´t do a thing about it. She´s all in her head and won´t let me in.

She always needed me to tell her how I feel. But she never thought about me needing her to tell me. And she was never satisfied and always wanted more. No matter how much I try. I won´t ever be enough.

We decided to stay friends. That´s bullshit. We´re not friends. She thinks we need space. That´s stupid. I need her to listen. I need her to stay. She acts like it´s all my fault. But it isn´t. She always needs to control. But she can´t control me. She hates that she has no plan and wanders around like the lights are out, but she just has her eyes closed. She won´t work on her issues. I at least try. But she gives a fuck about that. In my mind I told her all the things. That just wasn´t enough.

I can feel her slip. I feel her distancing and drift away from me. She gets angrier, colder, and indifferent. She´s so far way. I can´t reach her. I´m not done. I´m still getting better. I´m getting there. I´ll be the man she needs. I just need more time.

From the day I got back, I knew, and I felt it. I just pretended I didn´t. That she was fine. We were fine. But the truth is I hurt her. And now there is a wall. She´s on guard. Maybe she expects me to leave or to fuck up again. I can´t even blame her. I wouldn´t trust me either. She protects herself. The way I did. Now I´m locked out and she gives less energy into us. Like, somehow, she had given up. Stopped hoping. Like she was in the sea drowning and let herself float or rather sink. Maybe she lowered her expectations on me. Or she has accepted she won´t get more. I really tried. Maybe, all I could do was fail.

When you hurt the one you love, it feels like you hug them, but it hurts them. Like you kiss, but your lips slice them. You say you love them and all they feel is hate. Like what you give isn´t enough. Like I am not enough. Shouldn´t the one you love; make you feel enough?

Colson Herzog

I know she wants to leave me, and I told her how I feel, but I knew it wasn´t enough. She deserves better. We both do. I don´t know how to stop this or to hold her. But where is the sense when the prince keeps fighting if all Aurora wants is sleep?

180

Little Lion Man – Mumford & Sons

"Did you set them up to talk to me?" I ask him. "Who?" He frowns. "The guys." I say. "Did they talk to you?" He asks and I nod. "These *fuckers*. No, I didn´t." He wipes his face. "What did they say?" He wants to know. "It doesn´t matter." I brush him off. "Right." He nods.

"We need to talk." I say and he nods. "Right." He agrees and I inhale. "So, this can´t go on like that." I try to begin but don´t know how. "I know." He says his voice thin. He breathes gripping his hair and his mouth opens but closes a few times. He looks lost and I know I should say something. *Anything but I don´t.*

"I just I don´t know how all this went down.." He trails off shaking his head. "I mean, where did we go wrong?" He asks and talks fiercely. "I just I don´t wanna lose you Scar." He tells me and paces the room.

"I really want us to work." He shrugs. "But it seems like I can´t." He shakes his head with a shrug. "At least not the way it won´t hurt. Or how you want me to love you. I don´t know what to give you differently." He admits and at this point I can´t tell him anymore either.

"If you want to be my girlfriend, then.." He says but I cut in. "It´s not that." I tell him. "Then what is it?" He asks fear in his eyes. *I say nothing.*

"You have no idea how often I wanted to tell you everything, and I almost did." His voice loud and he gestures as he speaks. "But my throat gets tight, and my eyes start to burn. My brain gets foggy and stomach dizzy. And my heart shuts down." He says upset.

"Believe me, I want to. I did a thousand times in my head. I do it every day. Every time I look at you. But the words I want, need to, or should say. Never leave my lips. Cause I´m blocked. *Fucked*." He explains. "And cause you can´t look into my mind or read my thoughts, you get nothing. So, I try to show you in different ways." He says. "In looks, touches or quotes." He shrugs. "I don´t do normal. I do different. You just have to decide if it´s enough." He keeps talking and he doesn´t even realize I don´t say anything to his attempts. He´s hysterical, panicking, full of hurt, and he won´t shut up.

"I know it´s not fair to ask you for time." He says, but I interrupt him. "You´re right." I tell him. "It´s not. And you´ve asked me that before." I say and he nods. "But

I know it´s you. I just have to figure out how to let you in." He begs stepping closer but I back away and he looks like I hit him. *And in a way I did.*

"I don´t care about your promises anymore." I tell him and even I hurt by saying that. He wipes his face and takes deep breaths before he continues. "I´m scared of loving you. It´s ripping me. And at the same time healing me. Because I love you and I´ve never felt anything like that before. It feels like if I´d fall for you completely I´d die." He looks like he´s physically and mentally in pain. And he probably is because emotional pain is processed in the same area as physical pain. So, he is and so am I.

In pain and not in love. And most of all not happy.

"I don´t want *any* girl. I want you, Scar." He says with a lump in his throat making his voice break. "And I´m confused why I´m so afraid of losing you. Cause you were never even mine." He adds, and I nod and shake my head. "We´ve known each other for over two years now." I say and he nods. "There is no progress." I continue and he bites his lip but listens. "You do the same things your parents did to you, to me." I say and his eyes are red now. He looks like he´s about to cry but looks at the ceiling trying to catch himself.

"I don´t want to do that." He says quietly. "I know." I nod. "But you do. You run, refuse to let me in or love you. Or love me." I say and he shakes his head fiercely with his eyes shut, as if he could quiet his thoughts with that.

"I know it´s not intentional. I understand and I´m not mad at you. Okay, you have to get that." He nods. "But I can´t be *that* anymore." I tell him, my own voice shaky and he looks at me, panic all over his face. "Be what?" He manages to ask, and my eyes burn. "Be your maybe. Your almost. Your someday." I say barely breathing. "Because all those years you were my *yes*. Always were." I tell him and his eyes beg me not to continue, but I can´t stop.

"And I was only your someday." I say and he shakes his head. "No, that´s not true." He tells me but I nod. "*It* is." I insist and his eyes fix mine and his chin tilts up. "No Lia, you weren´t my someday. My almost or maybe." He nods and swallows. "You were my *Now*." Tears run down his jaw and my heart want´s to break out and stop beating because it´s too much. It hurts too much to work any longer. And my tears flow too.

"That´s all you ever were. *My Now´s*." He repeats as if I didn´t hear or couldn´t understand what that means. "But you never wanted them." His hand finds his mouth, rubbing over his face, his hair and back and I close my eyes at the pain. At the knife that digs into my skin, heart, scull, soul, and everywhere it can hurt and slice me.

But I shake my head and try to breathe normally. "I don't.." I start. "I can't anymore." I tell him and he starts crying. His cheeks all red, matching his neck and eyes. "Talk to me." He begs, his voice on edge and my face burns. His jaw tight. "Please Scar." He asks but I shake my head. "I'm sorry." I whisper.

He reaches for my cheek to wipe my tears, but I back away. He looks like I hit him in the heart, face, stomach, and balls at the same time. I didn't meant to, but it's better this way. I can't have him close now even if that's all I ever wanted. Because I know, eventually, he'll back off and hurt me again and I'll hurt him.

"Don't." I manage to say but choke on my words. He grips his hair, wipes his face, and shakes his head. "No." He says. "No." He repeats. "Please Scar. I'll do anything." He cries and falls onto his knees in front of me. He holds onto me, and I let him.

But it hurts too much.

He chants that he loves me, that he'll try and he's sorry. But I can't listen because it's too much pain. "Just because you love me doesn't mean I should let you love me." I say and try not to fall as his heart breaks in front of me. He cries for me.

To his first love.

Because that's what I am to him, and I only realize that now that he holds onto me, like I did with my ex when he left me. Not only physically but emotionally.

I showed him love and now I'm taking it. I'm his first heartbreak and he's my greatest.

I hold his head and try to calm him. Stroking his hair and scalp. But the truth is no matter how hard you hold on, at some point you *always* gotta let go. And maybe now is the time for us to let go. Or at least for me. We have to give us space. Loosen the grip and fly the kite instead of holding onto it. Hoping for dear life, it won't fly away without ever letting it go to see how high it gets. But holding is never love. *It's trauma.*

And letting go is healing. *It's love.*

First, we didn't talk about it, and then we talked, but it wasn't good either. And I wish it could be enough, and I could be stronger or more stupid to carry on and endure it.

But I can't. Not any longer.

Not without breaking us or what is left of us. And I need to look at myself and at my needs. He needs that too, even if he can't see that right now. Maybe I'm the one running now but we can't work on it. *Not now.* And I need to put me first and heal by myself. I need to feel whole by myself and loved alone.

And I hate hurting him and leaving him like that. When he tries, begs, and cries. But I can't stay for him. *I just can leave for me.*

And if it hurts more to stay, then you should go. *This needs to stop.*

I want love but what I realized is that I want peace more.

Truth is he always only liked the idea of love but loved the pain more. But I like and love me enough to walk away. To let go and move on. *And I do.*

So, I get on my knees, forcing him face me and his eyes are red like he´s bleeding. His lips shake, and his body does the same. And I know before the words have left my lips that he knows. "We need space." I say into his dark eyes, and he nods but shakes his head afterward biting his lip so hard, he might bleed. "Wounds can´t heal when they get touched constantly. And all we do is stab each other." I add, my voice thin. Again, he nods and wipes his tears before they escape and shakes his head furiously denying what I´m trying so say.

"We need to be okay by ourselves first. I think you can´t get better with me. You can do it yourself. You have therapy and your friends. And me." I tell him.

"Don´t leave me." He chokes. "I won´t. I´m always yours. Your Scar." I whisper. "But I can´t stay." I tell him.

"It´s the highs and lows we like. Because there is no in between." I say. "But there *needs* to be more." I add. "No." He cries. "We can make this work." He states. "I can fix it." He adds. "We can fix it." He says. "Just fix it. Please fix it.." He´s furious. "What?" I ask. "*Me*." He cries, and his weight falls on me. "Kai stop." I soothe him. "You don´t lose me. Okay. We need distance. But I´m not leaving you." I tell him, but little did I know I lied. "This isn´t forever it´s for now." I say and this gets him.

He looks at me. "I´ll stay Kai. I won´t run like you. But that doesn´t mean I´ll be with you. I´ll always stay. But as long as you run, I won´t be with you. Until you chose to stay, too." I tell him. "I did." He whispers but I don´t listen.

"You know it´s you. It´ll always be you." I hush and I´ve never thought I´d walk away from him. *Ever. But I do. I am the one ending things.*

"You asked me once why I couldn´t let it happen." He looks at me pained. "Now I´m asking you why you couldn´t let it happen. And be honest." He says and I ponder staring off.

"Because somehow, I wanted us to stay just friends." I admit what I never even owned up to myself. "That way I would never lose you. Like I lost everybody else." I say.

Like I lost you now.

He barely nods. "Because what we have it´s not love. It´s obsession." I say barely audible. "Addicts that´s what we are." I add quoting him and he can hardly breathe. "But I chose me." I whisper in pain choking on the consequences of my words. "And you need to choose yourself. Do it for yourself, not me or us." I say, and then I try to get up, but he attempts to hold me back and it ripped my heart out and maybe even my soul. *But I walked away.*

I finally did it. Maybe part of me stayed with him on his floor. But I left and he didn't go after me, but I heard him begging me to stay. *But I didn't.*

We all heard him scream as I walked out. But I left like he left me without looking back.

At least I said goodbye.

They saw me leave and they knew I left him. Like I should have in the past. And I don't know where I had the strength to do it, but I did. And in ways I never looked back, until I couldn't anymore.

There is that saying that "*Rome wasn't built in a day, but it burned in one.*" And I've burned us alive. Leaving the boy, I love in ashes. We tried to build it up but it wasn't steady. It was fragile and I just gave the push it would have gotten anyways. Because everything is transient. *How could I think we would not be?*

We tightened and knotted our tie, but we forgot it had holes. *And I've cut it.*

With my ex, I would have done *everything* to keep him because he was my first love. But with Kai, I know *exactly* what will happen. *And that's the thing.*

That now I care enough for myself to know better. *To leave.*

It wasn't a goodbye. It was a maybe someday and another almost. Or maybe a in another lifetime. And that hurt more than any breakup ever could.

The maybe he gave me all along, I gave him back. I was cruel as he was.

Maybe even worse. Maybe.

It was overdue. We just never made the real cut.

The love we denied was real. But just because something is real doesn't mean it's good. Just because a dream feels real doesn't mean you're not asleep. And just because a dream comes true doesn't mean it's right. Dreams can turn into nightmares in seconds.

And it did. It scared me until I woke up.

In order to love you must die a little. But we weren't ready to die yet. At least not for each other. *Or I wasn't.*

He would have. He showed me once. But this isn't how it's supposed to be. You don't die for love. You live for love. And I realized I couldn't.

The now I had was make-believe. His was real. *Mine never was.*

I'll always have feelings for him. I just have to live with it. Everyone has that person and he's mine. And maybe in another lifetime I'm his too.

Scars don't heal, they stay. That's him to me. It's the way we'll have each other.

And in this very moment, to the rain the clouds pleaded; stay. But she didn´t. And some say she never came home again.

181

Two months later, August

When the call came, I knew something was wrong. Finn was making phone terror and showered me with messages I should come immediately. *So, I got there.*

It´s pouring as I get out and run to their house. The place I left behind months ago. *But it feels like a lifetime.*

The Dark´s are here because their Mercedes is parked in front of the gate. No good sign, I learned over the years.

My heart pounding in my throat. I´m not sure what I´m running into, and I haven´t seen him since I left. And his parents since his accident last summer. But since I´m always there for him. *I´m here.*

As I close the front door, I hear the familiar shatter of dishes. "Calm down." I hear a gruff voice say. *Probably their father.* Whom I still don´t know the name of.

"Don´t tell me what to do." Warns Kai and my stomach sinks hearing his voice. I round the corner, walk into the living room, and see Finn standing there. His eyes are red underneath. He´s wearing his suit but his shirt is messed up and his cravat hanging loose.

He looks beat.

More plates crash to the floor, and I wince. Finn, who now saw me, looks at me with relief and pain. But before he can say anything, I turn my attention to Kai. Who stands in the middle of a sea of shards. The kitchen is a mess. Almost like two years ago when he got drunk and smashed liquor. But this is.. *even worse.*

He´s bleeding down his arms and his hands are full of cuts.

It smells like weed and alcohol. He rummages in the drawer and throws cups across the kitchen. His father stands at the counter, watching his son losing his temper. He wears a black suit and there´s a matching suitcase on the island next to him with a cup of coffee on top as if he just came out of a meeting. *Which is probably true.*

Kai grabs a stack of plates and hurls them in every direction. On reflex, I turn my head as the shards fly across the room. With a simple wipe, he clears all the glasses out of the cupboard. His face has bloody fingerprints, his hands are now bloody, and his eyes have the same dark circles as Finn´s. He´s been crying and I think Finn too.

"I am sorry." Says his father whereupon Kai takes liquor off a cupboard and heaves it at him, but he dodges at the right moment, and it blows against the edge. "Stop that son. You´re acting up." He continues. "Don´t call me that." Kai bites and throws another at him, but his father moves again in the right moment and the bottle shatters next to his head and brown liquor runs down the white wall. But he again stays calm. As if he´s used to this behavior. Which is probably true.

But still, why´s he so relaxed? And what is going on anyways?

"Kai." I speak up unable to say anything else and he looks at me briefly as if he hadn´t noticed I was right here in the room with him. But he just fixes his father for a moment and then looks at his brother accusing, probably connecting the dots that he must have called me.

Signaling me, he doesn´t want me here.

I saw immediately he was gone and barely even registered me. He was hysterically losing his mind. And I wasn´t the issue to his meltdown but what was, I was about to find out. As he speaks, he looks at me with dead eyes. "Scar, you must be wondering what´s going on." He says in a weird tone, gesturing with his hands. Like he´s acting on a stage.

Like he´s not even here. He doesn´t seem himself.

He walks over to the fireplace, the shards slicing his feet since he´s barefoot but he doesn´t seem to feel, care or both. He takes out the silverware. A long heavy stick and swings it around as he talks. "Our father.." He points in his direction. "Well, Finn´s father, not *mine*. He´s my producer." He corrects himself laughing like he made the funniest joke.

This feels like a fever dream.

"Well as said let me tell you, that he just came from his business trip to tell us that our mother is dead." He says like his words have no meaning. "She´s dead." He repeats. "De-a-d." He emphasizes and smiles like a maniac. *Not processing what he´s saying.*

"Telling us like the weather or the news. Like it´s a casual thing to say." He hits the table with the stick and the glass cracks. *He´s behaving like a lunatic.*

"Telling us she had *cancer* and *knew* that she was *sick* and *dying*." He hits it a second time causing it to splitter. "But she chose not to spend her last months with her sons." He says, slapping repeatedly causing it to shatter in tiny pieces and I cry hot tears watching him helplessly. "She knew." His voice breaks painfully.

"What were your words?" He addresses his father pointing at him. "That she had obligations she had to follow, and it was her last will to move the company forward. To leave something great.." He yells holding his arms out. "For her sons." He punches the cabinet´s display.

"People call *me* cruel, corrupt, heartless, and worse. That I *can´t* feel. That I.." He cuts off locking eyes with me. "*Can´t love.*" He says and I swallow. He grins mad and rests the stick on his shoulder. He tilts his head venom spilling as he speaks. "Then I wonder.." He pauses dramatically. "What you are? Farther." He asks with a grin that comes straight out of hell. But his father doesn´t answer. To which Kai laughs.

He can´t stop.

He even tears up and we watch.

When he caught himself, he faces his father. "Look, I don´t give *a damn* about your company. Your legacy or money. *Your* love. This house." He yells, looking around like he´s in another dimension. "*This family.* It´s all a lie. And I don´t want *any* of it." He shouts and his father tries to take the stick but Kai growls. "Go to hell." He hits the TV screen. "And *now* get the fuck out of *our* house. Cause it´s no longer yours. *Never been.*" He shouts. But his father again says nothing, and I gape at him unbelieving.

How can he not say anything?

Kai wants to rush outside but stops midway, facing him. "Just tell me one thing." He says on edge. "Why the hell did you piece of shit got your wife *pregnant*, when you knew you would *hate* your child?" He asks and his features are filled with resentment. And I´m bleeding for him.

His father looks like he might faint. And for the first time since I´m here he shows emotions. His jaw twitches and his eyes are filled with something I can´t put a name on. He lowers his gaze for a moment.

When he looks up, he locks eyes with Kai. "We *don´t* hate you son." He answers. "*Didn´t.*" Kai corrects him. "Past tense." He adds and tears run down his cheek because. "I don´t hate you." He says. "I don´t believe you shit." Kai barks. "*I don´t hate you.*" He repeats raising his voice. "But you *reject* me." Kai nods. "Regret me. Don´t you?" He asks but his father doesn´t respond right away.

"You have to calm down. *Then* we can talk." He offers but Kai shakes his head with a laugh. "Now you want to talk." He comments with a smile. "*Fuck off.*" He spits disdainfully and walks out the door and I follow.

182

I know places – Lykke Li

All this doesn´t feel real. Like someone plays a life simulation controlling my character and I can´t do anything except work. *I have to function. For him.*

He rushes on the street with the stick still in his hand, gripping and swinging it. I can imagine what he´s up to. *That´s a bad idea.*

I run to catch up, but he walks straight towards *their* car. But before he gets the chance to hit the hood, I stand up to him and his arm stops as he lunges.

He glares at me. "*Move.*" he demands. "No." I place a hand on his chest, holding him back even though I know if he wanted to get past me, he could.

"*Move Scar.*" He bites. "No Kai. *Listen.*" I tell him. "I *know* you want to do that. Hurt him. And maybe you should. But it won´t *change* anything." I say desperate and he grins fiercely looking up and back down on me.

"Lia, move *now.*" He threats but I shake my head. "You *have* to feel it in order to let go." I say, and he glares at me because I used his own advice against him. "It *won´t* hurt him." I whisper. "He has enough money." I add. "He doesn´t.." I begin but stop, but he finishes my sentence. "*Care.*" And his arm lowers defeated, letting the staff drop. He turns around and walks onto the street. I watch him move out-of-body like I´m watching a movie.

It all just happens.

He looks into the sky that still cries for his mother. *Everything is slow motion.*

He falls to his knees, and I run in front of him. Just in time as he slams into me and painfully wraps his arms around me. The weight of his body all on me. And I hold his head and sink to the ground on the same level. He screams and sobs into me. The pouring rain swallows his painful cries almost completely, but I can´t control my tears either. I hold him tight and lay my head on his trying to protect him. *But I know I can´t.*

My chest hurts at his growls and winces. His body is shaking uncontrollable, and I feel helpless because I haven´t lost anyone yet, so I have no idea what to do or how to help him.

If I even can.

As I look up, I see Finn standing in the doorway watching me holding his brother. And then I realize he has no one to hold on to. *Maybe his father.*

But instead of grieving with him he´s here watching his little brother. My chest rips open and my gut twists at the sight.

I never even met her. In the hospital a year ago she looked *anything* but sick. She seemed nice and knew me. And now she´s gone. *Their mother is gone.*

I wish Finn would come over, but he won´t. Just as in the hospital a year ago, he guards him from afar.

Giving him the space he needs, and he knows *exactly* how to treat him.

I never knew.

He´s just there for him and I´m sure Kai knows. Because somehow Kai lost more than a mother. He lost the *chance* of ever having one. And Finn knows that.

That's why he's there.

I'm torn between looking at Finn trying to give him comfort and focusing on Kai. But since Kai buried his head on my neck, I hold eye contact with his brother. While I caress his hair, and I try to keep his body warm. And I don't let go because I'm afraid what happens if I do. *So, I hold on.*

The last time he fell onto his knees, I left him. *Now I won't.*

I'll hold him regardless of what happened between us. I'll always hold him if he needs me to. And I know he'll do the same for me. *We always will.*

Finn sat down at some point burying his head in his hands and I saw his body shaking. I felt sick but couldn't help. I just could be there.

We sat there until my bones started hurting from the wetness and his muscles mashing my limbs. Until the sun set, and our fingers wrinkled.

Because the rain never vanished.

But as he starts to shiver even worse, I get up. Finn he rises to his feet and walks back in. We get upstairs into the bathroom and help him undress. His eyes red and swollen. And his lips a mix of blue and purple and blood because he drilled his teeth into them. He has the same marks on his arms and thighs. At his sides, and I have them too from his nails craving into my skin.

He leaves his boxers on and sits down in the shower. I turn the water on hot and kneel in front of him. He looks at me, but I know he is looking through me. Because he's not present and not even in there. Something died in him today. *With his mother.*

I'll stay with him as long as he'll let me. *I hope he lets me.*

And I haven't been that close to him in a while. Which is selfish to think right now so I stop, and I focus on him.

I've turned the water out at some point but we continued to sit there until we mostly dried off. And guard him from the demons on the outside. But I'm afraid of what is haunting him on the inside. *At least he lets me lead him.*

And I honestly don't know if he's in control when I'm not here. Because since even Finn called me to calm him, I think we can all agree this is the best.

But I can't save him.

His silence feels like the calm before the storm. He stopped crying and shivering. Now he just stares, and I don't think he has even thoughts at this moment. He just exists as a shell with his soul somewhere else. Like his spirit left his body behind.

Seeking a better place to be.

I cannot imagine how he feels and can only see what is on the outside.

And be there protecting his body as he is somewhere far away.

Finding his way back. Or being gone forever.

How much pain can you bear until you break? Snap and never be, okay?

I want to say something. *Anything.*

But I´m at a loss. *What could I say? Would he even hear me? Would he care?*

I want to take the pain away, but no one can. *I could never ease his pain.*

And I have no idea when he saw her the last time.

Please don´t let it be at the hospital. But he was on Bali for months, so it probably was. Did they even know he was there? I´m not sure if he told them. Maybe Finn did.

But it doesn´t matter since she wanted to be with her husband and let him down.

They let them down.

He didn´t feel loved his whole life and now there is another prove that his parents didn´t gave a shit about him. *Not even to say goodbye.*

Did Finn know?

But he would tell him and he didn´t seem like he has heard this before.

They didn´t even tell him.

After a while, he stands up and we dry off. I sit on the sink with him between my legs and blow-dry his hair as his head rests on me. His hands on the edge to support himself, but his weight is all on me. I caress his hair and his neck to his sculp.

He enjoys it.

His one hand has moved around my waist, holding me. His breathing becomes as normal as it can be now, and his head moves to my neck. But even long after his hair is dry, I continue.

He pulls me down, dries and combs my hair. Then we throw our wet clothes in the bathtub, and he opens the door, and I follow him. But I bump into his back when he stops. "You´re not the only one who lost her. He lost his wife, and I lost my mother too." Finn tells him and Kai´s hand reaches behind searching for my body, so I take his arm. "You´re not the only one who wants to destroy things or lash out." His brother accuses him further. "You at least had a mother." Kai says calm, and his voice is weird after hours not talking, screaming, and crying.

"That´s not fair." Finn says. "Yeah, right?" He responds and pulls me in front of him as if he has to protect me from his own brother. We walk into his room as Finn doesn´t say anything else. Kai closes the door behind him walking towards his closet with me and I forgot I´m still in my underwear. Now I know why he shoved me in front of him.

Not like his brother didn´t see me in a bikini before, but I get it.

He puts on a fresh boxer and hands me one of his black T-shirts.

I put it over my head and get hit by Deja Vu. *I haven´t smelled him in weeks.*

He locks the door, and we lie down. "Don´t leave." He begs, speaking to me for the first time in hours. "I won´t." I promise and hold him until he falls asleep.

Six times he wakes up due to nightmares. He screams, kicks, cries, talks, and sweats. He holds onto me like he could fall into space and never come back. And seeing him suffer hurts more than anything.

I kiss his forehead and caress his hair. And I even read to him while he sleeps, hoping it will calm him. I´ve never read to him before.

183

Kai, In This Shirt – The Irrepressibles

Something snapped that day. My brain shut down. *Completely.*

I can´t remember much of it. I just went out of body. It was like I didn´t exist anymore. It all went quietly and felt like nothing. Everything made no sense. Like there´s no world anymore when people die. *How´s there some kind of God when people die? For what reason do we live if we die? Why do we die? Is death in reality the great mercy and everlasting living would be the real penalty?*

I thought I was numb before, but I was wrong. This was more than numb. This felt scary and calm at once. I never wanted to come back out. *I scared myself.*

I was paralyzed and couldn´t speak. *I just watched. And often I passed out.*

I didn´t know what was real anymore. I think I dreamed a lot. But most of my dreams are nightmares, so I started daydreaming instead. I sat in the rain and flew in the sky. I floated in space and drowned in the sea. I rotted in hell and burned alive.

And I fell.

I didn´t even think anymore. It was just listening to noises. *All muffled and afar.*

Time didn´t exist to me before, but this was a new definition of timeless. Because it felt endless. I´ve been in a place between life and nothingness. *Between space and time.* The world and the great consciousness. The place where you go when your brain shuts it all down. Just barely breathing and working the heart to beat. Swallowing to not die on your own. *Just surviving, resting, and existing.*

Sometimes it feels like you can die without actually dying and I think I did. It wasn´t a bad place but not a good one either. It was saving but numbing. A place you go to when all hurts, and you can´t feel it anymore. A place where I´d love to go to forever.

A place where it rains only.

They never told you that, but it rains a lot in Neverland.

As a difficult teen, you often think you hate your parents, and you want them to die. Well not actually of course, but you know.. *difficult.*

But when they die. *You die with them.*

And you hate yourself for all those times you hated and ignored them. For all the times you could have said sorry, but didn´t. For all the times you could have forgiven but didn´t.

You blame yourself.

Now there is just *nothing.* I´m grieving for someone I have not known anymore for a long time. A mother that never really existed. *Only in my dreams.*

Even if it´s not quite true, I refuse to believe otherwise. I can´t and will not allow myself to be blamed any longer. I didn´t choose my parents, nor did I choose to live. And they had chosen to live without us. To have a life separate from us. And now she had chosen to die without us. And I will never know why she didn´t stay like most mothers do. Why she left me even years before she died. Why I wasn´t enough and not more like Finn. Why she didn´t want me and why she loved her career more than her son. *I´ll never know why.*

And I will never be able to ask my mother for advice for girls. Or introduce my children to their grandma. I will never have her at my wedding, and I can´t introduce *her* to my mother. I´ve told her about her, but she never met her properly. And now she never will. Things I never even wanted were taken away from me within seconds. But she knew more than just a moment she would die.

She left me with the father I didn´t want and that never was one. She didn´t apologize. She´s just gone. No letter no nothing. *Gone.*

The person who should have loved me unconditionally left. And the last time I saw her was when I almost did. *And now I won´t see her ever again until I die.*

- 27 -

My memories since then have gaps. Small and big ones. There are flashes.

But mostly black.

And all I know is that everything went dark, and it keeps getting darker. I kept in that state when you stare into the void, and you can´t break away because it just feels too good. With the only difference that you *can´t* stop. Like in a sleep paralysis you just have to endure it and hope the next demon isn´t standing behind you. Dragging you away. Whispering you things. *Killing you.*

Before, everything was so loud. Now it´s so quiet that it´s scary. I love silence but this isn´t just silence it´s nothingness. You scream but nothing comes out. You talk, but you don´t hear yourself. They talk, but all you see are lips moving.

And I don´t know what time or what day it is, let alone how much time has passed since my father got here. But I know she´s here and never left me once. *Where will I go if she leaves? Because I need her. She´s my family.*

The only I ever wanted and the only I have left.

She´s the light in the black hole I´m trapped in. And if I come out, she´s there. And that is enough for me to bear it.

She left me but now she´s back and I thought I imagined her. Maybe it´s is just my brain giving me the only reason I´ll hold on to my sanity. But I can *feel* her. She´s only thing I perceive. The last string of life is bond, to her.

184

Lia

"Sir." I say as I enter the kitchen. *We haven´t left the room for three days.*

He´s in a suit and drinks from his cup. In front of him the morning paper. His eyes are irritated and dark, but these are the only signs that he´s grieving. That there is *something* other than this perfect authoritarian shell.

"We never had the opportunity to introduce each other." I say and he nods as he reads the news. "The girl from the hospital. Why my son got into *that* accident." He speaks without looking up to me and I gape but ignore that statement.

"I am Lia Sky. I´m.. friends with your son." I say and he locks eyes with me reading my face taking me in. "Which one?" he cocks an eyebrow, and I tilt my chin up.

He can´t be serious. I wear his clothes. Like he didn´t know. Like he didn´t see us on the street.

"Both of them." I tell him and he smiles weak nodding and taking another sip. "I see." He breathes folding the sheet. I clear my throat. "I am sorry for your loss." I continue and he nods. *Silence.*

"You´re not gonna marry my son if you think that´s what you´re doing." He says.

What the fuck?

"Which one?" I counter, he keeps shut and I suppress shaking my head at him. "Only that *you know* he had tons of nightmares tonight." I say on edge, but he just stares at me silently. When he wants to speak his gaze drifts behind me as Kai enters the kitchen.

He stands next to me but so close our bodies touch. Like he *needs* me to be here.

"You´re still here?" He asks somehow indifferently. "No duties, full timeline, meetings or negotiations?" He goes on but his father shakes his head, and I realize he didn´t introduce himself to me. But honestly, I don´t want to know the name of that man.

"Nothing. My assistant handles the schedule. But I have paperwork to do here. For the funeral and everything else that fell on over the year." His father explains, and I feel Kai tense next to me at every word he speaks. "Sure, you have." Kai huffs. "Can´t you handle that from your fucking fiftieth floor?" He asks raging.

"Just get the fuck out of here." He barks. "I´m not going *anywhere* any soon." He intently speaks slowly and Kai´s hand grips the edge of the counter making his wounds cut open again. "Why?" He snaps. "No" he adds furious. "Leave for fucks sake." He demands. "I won´t." He responds sharply and Kai blinks at him.

"I have called Dr. Kunz and made an appointment for you. He´s expecting you at five thirty." He tells him. "And since your nightmares are back.." He implies but stops and I feel him tense next to me. *I shouldn´t have told him that.*

"If you stay I´ll leave." Kai threatens and his father takes a deep breath taking a sip from his cup. "Son, you can´t *always* run." He speaks slowly and this is probably the only thing I would agree with. "Spain or France won´t solve your problems." He adds and again he´s right with that. "Maybe but I can´t stay either." Kai snaps and walks out of the room, and I follow him upstairs.

He sits on his carpet leaning against his bed and I sit down next to him. *Silence.*

I feel him here with me that makes me relax a bit and he plays with my fingers and the ring he gave me. "You wanna know why I´m always in the rain?" He asks, and I hear he´s crying again but I nod even if he can´t see because his eyes are closed.

But he speaks up anyway.

"Because.. when I was younger, I thought least there I had a piece of them." He whispers. "I knew it rains a lot in London. So, I sat in the rain." His voice shaky. "As a kid it made me feel less alone." He says and shakes his head. "But later, it was just painful. A constant reminder of the things I never had. A reminder that I´m worthless and alone." He tells me and something cracks inside me. I try to blink through my tears, but they keep coming. I think he broke me more than he healed me over the years but I´ll take it.

His eyes are still closed as he speaks. "But you showed me that rain isn´t painful. That it´s calming, cleansing, and healing." He whispers his voice husky. "How others looked at the stars you looked at the rain. Like I used to myself.." He trails off.

The campfires. When I sat in the rain.

And his words put some pieces back together. *But the hurt stays.*

He opens his eyes like he faces reality again. “But all I can feel *now* is numbness.” His tone matching his words and face. “I have to grief. But I can´t *here*.” He tells me.

And the pieces break away again.

“So, you really wanna go? Be alone? After.. *what happened*?” I ask. “Just say it Scar.” He scoffs. “After my *mother died*.” He snaps. “She´s dead.” He repeats and I nod. “Yeah but that´s not healthy.” I say. “I think you *should* see your therapist.” I add and he breathes but he´s not annoyed more like he has to remind himself to take breaths. “I can see him over there too. Video calls are not that uncommon in therapy.” He retorts and shrugs. “I´ll come back as soon as *he* leaves.” He assures me but I´m not sure if he really means it or believes that himself.

“And what *if* he stays?” I imply. “He *won´t*.” He answers. “But what if?” I insist and he considers. “Then I´ll make him leave.” He simply says.

“So, you won´t even go to her burial?” I ask and he inhales unsteadily. “Don´t know.” He says as he runs a hand through his hair and back down his face. “I just *know* I have to get out of here.” He adds looking at me. “I can´t breathe in here Lia. I´m not even in this room with you right now.” He says upset.

He´s always on the run. Scared to stop or to settle.

“And what´s with your brother?” I ask. “He´s fine.” He brushes me off. “He has his father and his friends. You.” He says with a shrug. “He needs you.” I tell him. “But I *need* me.” He yells almost. “*I* know I´m selfish. I´ve always been. I´m not the good guy. I´m not my *brother* Scar.” He tells me. “And I don´t want you to save me Lia. I want you to stand by my side as I save myself.” He says his voice filled with pain. “I am Kai. I always was. For years. You know that.” I tell him. “And I´m still after all. I´m here. You´re the one who leaves me all the time.” I say frustrated and he looks at me and that look hurts even more because it says *you left me too*, and I know I did.

But he changes the subject. “I know you can´t come with me. But I´m leaving.” He shrugs and I take a minute to sort my thoughts. *This isn´t a good idea.*

He should deal with it here. He can run from me as long as he wants and deal with that wherever he wants to. But his mother´s death is here, and her funeral is too or at London I´m not sure, but he has to stay. *At least for a while.*

“That´s rush Kai. I think you´ll make a mistake.” I say. “Don´t care.” He says. We sit in silence for a while.

“You´re a liar.” I finally say and he looks at me strained. “You lied to me.” I go on but he looks confused. “About what?” He asks pissed. “You said you would keep pushing me away. But that´s not true. You´re not pushing you´re running away from me.” I say as my vision blurs. “Father, I have sinned.” He scoffs and I shake my head. “I´m here Kai. *Stay.* We´ll do it together." I beg him for the first time in almost three years. "Don´t go. Stay with me and your brother. You can stay at mine if you can´t stand seeing him or being here." I plead and tears roll on both sides.

But that´s when it hits me. For a selfish moment I forgot the last 72 hours. Forgot that this isn´t about me. I left him but he isn´t leaving me. *He leaves them.*

So, I snap out of it the moment I see the loss in his eyes. "I´m sorry." I cry. "I lost my mom." His voice cracking. "Never even had her. I don´t even know who I am. Or want to be. I don´t leave you. I´ll never do. *Never again.* I promise." He tells me. "But I have to go." He whispers and I nod understanding. Tears run down his jaw he´s clenching and I take his face in my hands. "Go find yourself so that you can find me." I reply. "Same." He hushes and kisses my forehead.

I let go of him, and he wraps his arm around my neck and kisses my hair. "You *burned* my soul forever Scar." He tells me and those words burn mine.

He kisses me then. We had more kisses mixed with tears than normal ones.

I love him and I want him to be happy. That´s why I don´t stop him but this time I told him I want him to stay, and he needs to hear that.

It´s not forever, I keep telling myself. *I´ll see him again.*

I realized he didn´t run from me, but from himself. And I´d be cruel to not wait until he found himself. Because he´s worth the waiting and, in the meantime, I might have to find myself too.

I always wanted to be someone´s first choice. But now I want to be his only and last one. But loving someone means wanting the best for them. It means wanting the other person to pursue their destiny, even if that means you´re not a part of it. Letting go means loving and I have to let go. *This time fully.*

My life has been upside down since I met him. He´s all I ever wanted but feared. And I´ve always wondered what it would be like dating another Scorpio. And I think I have an answer to that. It´s like looking in the mirror, but you can see the opposite of you. You bring your best and worst out. *Boon and bane.*

Scorpios are made to understand others. But they aren´t supposed to understand them. Which is a problem when two of them are friends or fall in love.

And we did. Fall hard into dark abysses.

And there was never such thing as running away. *We couldn´t. Even if we did.*

Like hell was our home we had to come back every now and then. Because even hell knows heaven exists. *They just have to reach for it.*

They burn to survive.

185

Heart games - HARLOR

He booked his flight, and I helped him pack. He told me it´s okay if I´ll leave.

It´s easier this way. *So, I left.*

The asphalt is still wet as I walk away.

The past days felt like a fever dream. *More of a nightmare.*

I hope he´ll be okay and he isn´t making a huge mistake.

But sudden, I´m forced to stop as a hand grabs my neck to spin me around. With a cry I crash on Kai´s lips as his tongue forces its way into my mouth.

"I´m sorry." He says and cries. "You asked me to stay." He chokes and his hand finds his face, but I make him look at me. He bites his lips but pulls away.

"All my life I had this feeling." He holds his stomach. "That constant urge to run. To get away and be alone." He yells. "And I realized I don´t have that feeling anymore. I mean I have but what I want is *this* with you." He tells me. "When I run, I want to run with you. When I stay, I want you to stay with me. When I die, I want you to die with me. Not *really* but I want you." It flows out of him.

"Honestly, it was worth it. Being mean, a pain in the ass and a cold bastard to all the girls before you." He says. "And I´m sorry for the pain I caused you. You loved me when I didn´t know how to love myself. When nobody did. At least not the way you do. I´ll need all my life to make it up to you. And I don´t want anyone else to have your heart or fuck you the way I do because that´s only *my* place. And mine only. *You hear me?* Mine." He tells me and then shuts up, looking a bit lost because he doesn´t know what to do or say now. He blinks and looks like he might fall over. Because he actually communicated. And he´s as surprised as I am.

He rubs his neck searching my eyes. "Please come back in. I´ll lose my mind any second." He tells me tears streaming down his face as the loss crushes over him. "But I won´t lose it without you." He tells me beginning to shake. "I can´t do this without you." He adds, and I take his hand in mine, and we walk back.

Maybe our relationship has been confusing, complicated, or even toxic.

But are we fools to want to work on our mistakes? To still try and make promises we try to live up to? To heal something worth saving? Instead of trying to find someone new who isn´t broken? Are we really fools, or are we just bolt enough, to fight?

And a healthy relationship doesn´t define on how long you´re together, or how often you see each other, or tell each other you´re in love. It´s the constant struggle to never stop, to challenge each other and to evolve as a partner and as an individual. And to me, fools are those who run away when things get difficult and think another, better partner is the solution. Humans prefer to run away instead of putting in the effort for real development.

Because it is easier to say it didn´t work out, or you changed.

No, you have given up. Decided it couldn´t work.

And we decided it will work. *Or at least tried.*

But it´s one thing to say we try and another to actually do.

But we would soon enough find that out.

186

I´ve got him to stay. *At least till the funeral.*

And then he´ll go back to Bali. He´s seeing his therapist tomorrow and I made them something to eat while he showered. I left him twenty-five minutes and found him in the bathroom with his flip knife in his shaking hands.

He covers his mouth with the back of his hand, in which he still holds the knife. He cries painfully and falls onto his knees. He tried to cut himself, but he didn´t try to kill himself.

He wouldn´t I know.

But he wanted to feel. *To hurt.*

He won´t end his life. Because that would mean nothing. But he doesn´t want nothing, he wants *something*, so I come down with him. My tears shot down my face as I hug him, not even caring if I cut myself on his blade he still holds. But his hands come around me and I hear the blade crushing on the tiles. And we´re back in the rain on the street holding each other. *In the rain like we never left.*

"It didn´t work." He cries. "My hands won´t stop shaking." He chokes and I nod. "Can you hold me? Like the day you came over?" He asks and I nod. "Can you do this for me?" He asks and I nod again. I kneel and his nails dig into my skin trying to soothe his own pain.

The past days have been like that. Me saving him but somewhere deep down I felt it. Him slipping out if my hold. Drifting towards the darkness and down the rabbit hole. And he wasn´t taking me with him. Maybe he wasn´t aware, but I knew. He won´t let me save him. As he said, he has to do it himself. But I´ll be there for him until he realizes he doesn´t need me. *He needs himself.*

This is all a way to escape and a way of coping. He deals with it yes and therapy helps but someday he´s alone and then it´ll hit him again. But he has to get up alone.

He's stronger than he knows.

I learned that total fusion follows the dark abysses. It's a cycle. There's no end. No beginning. And I know no matter what, I'll love him. But that doesn't mean that I'll wait for him to start my life. Love can't be all I want.

187

Kai

It's hard but writing helps. She does. And smoking pod.

I have a journal. One I don't even acknowledge. Because what I write in there *stays* there. Even if it's bad, weird, psycho, sad, fucked up or about her. In there I allow me to be myself fully. And to feel everything. My darkest secrets, fears, dreams, or desires.

And I won't read it again nor judge myself for feeling or thinking like that. There are things I don't even admit to myself but I allow, to write them down. It's like a dark hole and sometimes I pretend that not even my consciousness knows about that journal. But it's bad, dark, and twisted. It's sick but real. It's who I am.

And now I hand it to her. All my secrets, thoughts, and feelings. Laid out to her cause I want her in. Although though I left some particular pages out, but I showed her some.

...

I hate my parents. I wish I never existed. I hate myself. I want to die. I cut myself. I'm not good enough. I'm jealous of my own brother. Even on my best friends. I want a family. I want parents. I want love. I hate school. I can't even be rebellious and steal money or something like that because they wouldn't care. They never do. My parents don't give a shit about me. Me neither. I wanna die sometimes. A lot sometimes. I speed on the highway at night and fight the feeling of making it stop. But it'll never stop. I don't want to depend on my parents or anyone else. I want my parents to die. I'm lonely. I like pain. It feels good. I hit my brother. I lost my virginity at fourteen. I hated it. Because I didn't feel anything. I'm dead inside. Something is wrong with me. Sometimes I want to run away and never come home. I hope I die. I enjoy fucking girls. I like choking them. I've got slapped in the face by a girl I dumped. It turned me on. I was hard. I told her. She kicked me in the balls. That day I realized I like hurting. I like hurting girls too. Playing with their feelings. Because I can't feel the way they seem to be able to feel. I'm not loveable. I don't want to love. I want to hurt. What if I'm becoming like my parents? I don't love my parents. They don't love me either. I like my mom more than my dad. I wish I'm an only child. I can't sleep. I smoked weed way before I got it prescribed. I tried cocaine once. I won't twice. I lied.

I´m addicted to painkillers. I want to be loved. I wanna feel for a girl when I fuck her. I don´t want to hurt me to feel. I fucked the ex of my brother. He doesn´t know. I wanted to take something from him like he did to me. Something he loves. Something that loves him. I felt sick. I vomited. After I fucked her. It wasn´t the first time that happened to me. I throw up a lot after sex. As I said I think something is wrong with me. I wasn´t abused or something. I don´t know what the issue is. I´m hard when a girl fights with me. I´ve stolen alc. I´ve I fucked a girl without condom because I was that horny. I had to take her to the pharmacy afterward. I tested myself for STDs. Luckily, she didn´t lie. I was clean. I feel useless. I don´t want to work for my parents. I love choking girls during sex. It turns me on when I feel pain. I´m sick. I´m into knife play.

Here I left some years out.

I started therapy again. No one knows. Not even my closest friends. I met a girl. It was the first time I felt. It makes me nervous and anxious. I´m not used to feel stuff when it comes to chicks. She makes me laugh. She calms me, excites me, and turns me on. She´s the prettiest girl I´ve ever seen. And I normally don´t think those type of things. I´m afraid I won´t feel when I fuck her. I don´t want to vomit when I fuck her. But I have a feeling that I won´t. I want to want it. I like her. I feel for her. I kissed her. She slept next to me. I watched her sleep. I dry fucked her. I´m not a good person. I left her. I think of her when I fuck girls. I want to hurt her sometimes. She hurts me some-times. I like it. But it hurts in a bad way. I fuck her with my closest friend. I´m scared of loving her. I´m scared of losing her. I´m scared of having her. I think I might lose her. I lost her.

…

She didn´t say much after she read those pages. She just thanked me.

She doesn´t hate me? She doesn´t think I´m sick?

Maybe I´m not.

188

A few days later, After the funeral, Lia

"Let me show you something." I said "Let´s run away. But together." I told him and he handed me his credit card.

I´ve book us a flight and we packed our stuff and headed to the airport. We flew to Italy and checked into a spa in Milan. *And escaped for a day.*

Storm – Mighty Oaks

"So, what are we doing?" He asks as he follows me inside and I stop to face him. "Either we drown, or we survive." I say and he looks at me. His eyes are red, his face pale and lips dry. He´s drained and just wants to shut down or sleep forever.

I take his hand and round the corner into a dark room. We get in the water holding hands. It´s a small room with square pool. Nothing more, nothing less.

The room is pitch dark. The water is somewhere between cold and warm. The walls are black and so is the ceiling. The water is deep, but I can stand. It reaches Kai´s chest. And it´s quiet not just the room he´s too. Probably thinking what the hell I´m doing in here with him.

Until the rain starts to paddle. The canvases around us light up. The screens show landscapes, lightening, clouds, and darkness. He lifts his head facing the droplets. "What´s that?" He asks. "*Peace.*" I say as the water begins to wave, and it starts pouring and thunder rolls.

- 27 -

Kai

I´m in the middle of a storm. *Drowning.*

I can swim, but for a moment I chose not to, and I let me float. Taking her with me. Even underwater you can hear the tempest. And she´s right. *That´s peace.*

She emerges again but I stay a moment longer. *Letting go.*

I close my eyes and open my mouth, but don´t let the water crush me.

When I surface, she´s there in the middle of all looking at me and I want to cry. Because no single person on this fucking planet would know *exactly* how to handle me.

But she does. Always does.

This is my paradise. *How did she even find that place?*

I take her face in my hands and move her close. "I fucking love you." I say as my voice breaks. And I can´t see because of the rain and my eyes. *Because I´m crying.*

"I think I drowned." I say, trying not to sound stupid because of my shaking voice. "In your green-greyish eyes." I try to smile for the first time since my mom passed away. "In your soul." I manage a chuckle almost choking on my laughter. Because I haven´t laughed since then. "I drowned in you." I say.

"I´ll never run from you. I promise. I´ll rather die." I tell her, and before she can say anything I slam my lips on hers and a beautiful mixture of water and salt mix together as our souls connect for the hundred fucking time since I met her.

I knew I liked her when I saw her in the rain. I knew I´ll tolerate her when she sat with me in the rain. I knew she´d be a problem when I started to dream about her. I had feelings for her when I wanted to touch her ankle. I was into her when she danced with me in the rain with her stupid crocs. I´ll protect her when she had that panic attack. I was possessive over her when she started dating that fucker. I loved her when I saw her at Christmas. I wanted her as she got back to her ex. I couldn´t run from her as I left. I needed her at my side when I saw her at my friend´s side.

I need her in my life as I almost died. I knew she´s mine when I claimed her. I would come back when I left again.

And now I know I´ll marry her. I always believed I´d be alone. Maybe I thought I didn´t deserve better. But she made me want love and not deny it.

I grew up longing love. But it was denied. Then I longed pain instead. Because that was all I ever got from the people I loved. All I could give myself. *Until her.*

Until she drowned me. *With her love.*

A smart girl once told me there will be a girl that will change everything. And that girl was her. And maybe she didn´t heal me, but she helped me to want to heal myself. She´s like water. Powerful enough to drown me but soft enough to cleanse me. Deep enough to swallow me, but shallow enough to save me.

We can´t deny our chemistry. But we can´t deny our issues either. That´s probably why we didn´t work things out.

How can we call something like that love when we keep hurting us?

But I´ll be a better man. I´ll change and I´ll come back for her. *For us.*

She made the pain go away and the love to come. She made me drown on my own beliefs. On my own pain, anxiety, and darkness. And I survived. *We did.*

The devil sat the heaven on fire trying to save her. *But he burned her.*

The angel sat the hell underwater trying to save him. *But she drowned him.*

189

Ten months later, August 2023, Lia

“You know he´ll be there, right?” Luca asks as she flips through a book. “Yeah, I know.” I say biting down the anxiety.

“Will you talk?” She asks and I face her. “No.” I say, and she sighs.

He went alone to her funeral. And then went back to Bali. He decided to push me away. But it wasn´t that hard because there was a cut before. The time stopped for those weeks. But time kept ticking. And we kept drifting apart. Until one day he snapped and shut me out. But I felt it happen long before. So, I knew and that way it was less hard.

All my life I was searching for love I didn´t got back. For love in all the wrong places. But I let him in. And since then, he never came back out. Because the cruel thing about your heart - that no one tells you until it´s too late - is that there is a way in, but no way out.

What is in stays.

Even if you don´t want it in anymore.

After a moment she says. "He has someone." And my heart sinks.

I don´t know how to act.

"What do you mean?" I ask trying to sound casual. "He´s seeing some girl." She says, and something stabs me in the back. "*Seeing*?" I ask even if it´s obvious. "Dating." She tells me carefully and I blink. "Since when?" I ask and she shrugs. "Some weeks, I guess." She says and my face heats. I look at her, unable to say a thing but she reads me. "I know you want me to bash her or tell you she´s ugly. But she´s actually pretty and I kind of like her." She says wincing and I nod.

I haven´t seen him since he left for Bali. I know he´s been there until April. Then he was in Spain for a while. *And since a month he´s back.*

I wasn´t that often at the Dark´s. They still party weekly but I didn´t come. I focused on my studies and myself. And somehow, I got used to it.

Used to not being around anymore.

Luca went without me. She kept me updated, but eventually that faded too.

Mostly because of me.

And now he´s back and one of the parties I go to is up tonight. But right now, I really don´t want to go. *And now he´s dating someone.*

"I don´t know If I´ll come." I say and she gives me a look. "You can´t *not* come." She reminds me and I breathe annoyed. "I know." I say. It´s Andi´s birthday and they´re already mad, I wasn´t there for a month. But he was back and I wasn´t ready. But I can´t chicken.

Not anymore.

I have no excuse left. The exams are over, and semester break began. I can´t avoid seeing him or them. *Even if I want to.*

"But I´ll come late." I tell her. "So, if someone asks tell them you have no idea. We haven´t talked." I say. "As if they would buy that." She laughs but I glare at her. "Just say that." I insist and she nods.

"It isn´t even a lie." She considers. "Since you ghosted me the last months." She pretends to be mad, but I know she knows me. "I know I´m sorry Luca. But it´s hard for me to get back there." I tell her and she waves me off. "I know. I was joking. I wouldn´t have come either." She laughs.

"But I´m glad you´re back and tonight we´ll party like in the beginning." She smiles and I give her a one back, but it isn´t a real one.

Because nothing will ever be like that again.

But if she believes that I try to do the same.

We say goodbye, and she leaves me on my own, trying to find something to wear.

He has someone. Whatever that means. It´s still something I can´t quite picture.

He doesn´t date. Why´s he dating?

I mean, I didn´t expect us to get back to where we left off, but this was the last thing I had on mind. *So that means he´s with her tonight? I don´t think I can survive that.*

My hands shake and I feel sick.

Where did they meet? Is he serious about her? Do I know her? No, Luca would have told me. Why did she tell me just now?

Maybe she´s still a bit mad at me. Can´t blame her.

Are the others mad? I mean, I stayed in contact with them. But it wasn´t like before.. well, I have no idea when it was normal for the last time.

I can´t go in there alone. My anxiety won´t let me I just know. Can´t see him with another girl. *I should have gone with Luca.*

Maybe I need someone too. *A date. A someone. But who?*

I take out my phone and go through my contacts.

I need someone hot. Someone tall. Someone who would play my date.

Someone who..

I smile, but my heart sinks. I feel nervous but in a good way. What I do feels thrilling. Like it´s something forbidden. *Something dirty. A secret.*

"*Hey.*" I text. *He´s online.*

"*Sup.*" Comes back right away. "*You´re at Dark´s later?*" I ask. "*Yep.*" He replies. "*U?*" He adds after a second. "*Yeah, will be.*" I text back. He types long, but just one word comes back. "*Nice.*" He answers and I chew on my lip.

"*Can we talk later?*" I ask after a minute. "*Sure.*" He says. "*K.*" I type. "*Later.*" He states. "*See U there.*" I send. *He´s offline.*

I really do this.

If he dates someone. *I´ll do too.* But not just someone. *Someone off limits.*

Someone who would like to mess with the devil. *And even win if he wants to.*

Because he can. Maybe he´s the only one who can. *Because only Hook hunts Pan.*

Washing Machine Heart - Mitski

Colson Herzog

I´ve put on a black off shoulder top and some shorts. My Vans.

The ones that Kai smeared on. *I really need to buy some new ones.*

My long hair in loose waves. Mascara, bronzer, highlighter, and some Vaseline on my lips. *I look hot. I had to.*

Being back feels weird. It´s familiar but foreign. It´s an emotional roller coaster.

I´m not even in yet.

I want to run and hide. *Or die right here.*

My heart hammers, my ears heat and I feel sick. I mean I have been here since we parted but now he´s here and that feels off.

Someone else opens the door for me. I round the corner, and I see him before he sees me. He´s on the sofa. *But not alone.*

On his lap, a brunette. And just like Luca said, insanely beautiful. *My eyes hurt.*

His hands on her thigh. Her arms around his neck. He´s talking to some guy and she´s listening to them. But somehow, I feel less than I expected to feel.

Somehow it´s numb. Like the knife that tries to split me can´t. It hurts for sure. But it´s not a jealous hurt nor a lovesick one. It´s more of a sad pain.

I take a deep breath and tilt my chin up. *I can do this. It´s okay that he has someone. It´s okay that he moved on. I just didn´t think he would.*

I let my gaze wander and search for my man for tonight. When I spot him, I walk straight up to him.

He takes a sip from his cup while talking to his buddy. But as I come closer his eyes wander to mine and his mate keeps talking. *Like he sensed me.*

He´s taller than I remembered. And so much taller than Kai. Or than *any* of the lost boy´s.

He´s Hook. No lost boy. But I forgot Hook was once a boy too.

His eyes wander slowly down. *He´s checking me out. But that look..*

His eyes come back up and meet mine, but I get on my toes to hug him. He´s caught off guard but hugs me back with the cup in his hand. "Play along." I hush into his ear before we break away.

The last time I saw him was a month ago on some party I went to, knowing *only* him. We talked a bit. Actually, we spent the whole night talking. *Talking to Wren.*

And that night was something I couldn´t forget.

I must lift my head to look him in the eye. He has green eyes. But his are darker than mine. And he must look down on me. I feel so small. And he´s intimidating.

But good.

Like he shields me from everything around us. Because the anxiety I felt a minute ago is now gone.

His buddy walks away and leaves us alone. "Hi." I say and he smirks.

He has dimples.

"So, what game is this?" He asks. "Game?" I ask but his grin widens. "You said *play* along." He smirks. "You´re my date." I say and he frowns. "Yeah?" He asks and I nod.

"Cause tonight I really need a hot date." I explain and his eyebrow arches. "You just called me hot." He states. All the talks I had with him were me mocking him and him shooting back. So *technically* that was my first compliment.

I nod and bite away my grin. "Just for tonight?" He holds his chest, pretending I´ve hurt him. *I like how flirty he is.*

I smack his arm, and he chuckles but then his mouth becomes a thin line.

"Haven´t seen you around in a while." He says, gently kicking against my shoe.

I smile at that.

"Yeah, I know." I say. *I wonder if he thinks of the night we talked.*

"Been hard." I add, not meeting his eyes. He nods, not asking further.

His eyebrows draw together. "For which one?" He asks, tilting his head. "Who?" I pretend to not know. "Which of your lost boys? Or both?" He clarifies and I shake my head. "Not both." I tell him with a laugh. His eyebrows go up and he nods, licking his lips. "Yours." I grin and he nods once.

"So, you´re using me to mess with him?" He cocks a smile. "*Again*?" His eyebrows twitch and I fight a smile. His eyes pinch. "This is becoming a habit of yours." He points with his finger as he holds the cup up to his lips hiding a smirk. I bite my lip, and he shrugs. "But I don´t mind it." He says, locking eyes with me. "It´s a *good* one." He tells me, and his dimples show. *God, he´s beautiful.*

"All right." He says and I look at him. "You don´t even want to know what you get out of it?" I ask and he presses his lips together, shaking his head slowly. "Should I expect something?" he asks. "I don´t know." I shrug. "Well, I don´t." He tells me. "Cause I´ll have you." He adds in a low voice, looking me in the eyes. And my heart trips and stumbles a few times. It me sends me on edge.

"And we had a great time last time, right?" he grins, and I mirror him. "I guess we had." I say. "You guess?" He teases and I nod. "*I know.*" I say and he licks his lips again. Then we share a moment of silence and his gaze wanders.

"Has it something to with that girl he has?" He asks. *I don´t know what to say.*

"Partly." I say slowly. "I see." He nods and I don´t meet his eyes. *Silence.*

"He´s a letdown if you ask me." He tells me. I just look at him and nod. *Silence.*

"What you must know about me is that I´m *always* down to mess with Dark." He grins wide. *I heard.*

"Why?" I ask and now he casts a glance at his direction. His expression hard.

I bet they locked eyes.

"Let´s say I have my reasons." He says holding his chin up, not breaking the exchange.

Those two.

I shake my head, but his focus gets back on me. "You two were friends, right?" I ask. "Sort of." He nods. "But it´s been a long time." He says with a one side shrug.

I don´t rake further. They hate each other and that´s all I need to know.

He holds his cup to me. "Want some?" He asks and I look at his hand. I can´t stop myself thinking of that party when Kai warned me about accepting drinks from others.

It was his party and his apartment.

When I think too long, he speaks up. "You´re afraid I put something in it?" He asks, somehow shocked, but I think he knows *who* started that rumor. "No." I say, shaking my head. "You *just* saw me take a sip as you walked up to me." He reminds me. "And at the party you drank my beer." He adds. *I remember. I really drank beer that night.*

But somehow his tasted just fine. Maybe it was just him. Or maybe I just changed.

"Yeah, I know." I say and take the cup from his hand. Our fingers touch and for a moment we let them linger before he lets go. I take a sip, and he watches closely. He lifts his chin at me. "Let´s get some new." He suggests and nods towards the kitchen. I nod and as I turn, I feel his hand on the back of my neck. My skin on fire sending chills down my spine. I wonder how likely self-inflammation is.

But right now, it seems highly possible.

He walks right behind me guiding me between dancing people. His hand over my hair. Normally I wouldn´t like it if my date whom I barely even know touches me. But this is different. *It´s familiar.* Like he has guided me like that all my life. It feels easy, right, and intimate. Like it´s where his hands belong. *Fuck that´s hot.*

I look up at him and our eyes meet. His jaw clenches as his eyes move to lips and back to my eyes. When I look back his grip tightens, and he holds me back as some guys stumble in our way. I slam into him because he stopped and dragged me back to his body. My heart pounds. And *something else* too. *Fuck.*

My feminism left my body when he did that. Because all I want now is his hand on me holding my neck while fucking me from behind. *Shit.*

191

Me and the Devil (slowed) – Soap&Skin

I lean against the counter and he against the fridge opposite of me. He pours some more liquor as we hold eye contact. *And I take him in.*

His brown hair and thick brows. His lips thin but sharp enough to want to kiss. His prominent chin, and his defined cheeks. His nose ring and a that thin silver wristband. A matching ring and watch. *And it´s ticking.*

Under his Adams apple, the roman number sixteen tattooed. And some writings on his right arm. His collarbone right and left with laurel wreath branches.

He has lots of tats. More than I can see or count. All thin in line art and mostly Greek mythology related.

He takes a sip and hands it to me. I do the same as we lock eyes. *It´s weird.*

The feeling I have with him. I felt it at the party weeks ago. And I feel it now too. Save, calm and right. Different from everything I´ve felt before. It confuses me because I feel like he´s an open book to me but a closed one to the ones around us. He´s totally focused on me right now and is a great listener. He´s sexy, smart, and cocky.

He reaches for the cup, sets it on the counter next to me and steps closer while doing so. He puts his hands on the surface caging me in. He licks his lips. "I´d really like to kiss you." He says, gazing down on me. *He asks for my permission.*

In a way, it´s hot. He tells me what he wants, but he doesn´t just takes it.

Not without my consent. As it should be. He communicates.

Also, something I´m not used to.

I take the cup and press it against his chest. "If you´ll kiss me." I begin and lift my chin to be closer to his face. "Then I want *him* to die." I say without looking in his direction.

Because I feel him watching. I felt him the whole time. But I ignored it. Forgot it almost. Because Wren lets me forget him without any effort.

But right now, having Wren *that* close to me. With his face giving away what he wants to do. *I feel Kai´s glare on us like the devil watching for sins.*

He takes the cup off my hand and looks stoic at Kai´s direction before tossing his head back, finishing in one gulp. He throws the cup, pulls out cigarettes from his jeans and I watch him take one between his lips and light it.

It´s like he´s hypnotizing me. He´s like a myth you didn´t believe until you´ve seen it yourself. Like you know what you do is dangerous but you´ll do it anyway. Cause it´s thrilling. It makes your skin itch and your heart calm and the storm.

Cause he´s off limits. Cause he hates him. Cause they were friends.

And we were too at some point until we weren´t. *But he has someone new now,* my mind reminds me.

You know it´s playing cards with the devil. Maybe even death but you´ll do it anyway because you like the void.

Cause it feels *anything* but wrong.

His eyes hold mine as he takes a drag. He throws his head in the neck and blows smoke. I watch his throat bob, his chest filling with the fume and normally I hate the smell of cigarettes, but they smell good. *Like I might smoke too.*

"Stop smoking jackass." Kai growls from the couch and there´s that glimpse of the sad hurt from before. *But it vanishes.*

Wren turns his head to the right and looks at him indifferent.

That resting bitch face some girls have? He has that too. But way better. He doesn´t even need to scowl or glare he just stares and it´s enough. He´s confidence in person.

He smirks slightly and takes another puff, grinning him off. He blows the smoke up with a challenging look. Lifting his chin, he smirks. *He does a good job.*

Because it´s not just me that want´s to mess with him. *He wants that too.*

Not thinking I grab the collar of his dark grey shirt and drag him towards me. His eyes leave Kai´s late and our lips touch. He moves closer and kisses me softly. His lips twitch, fighting with a smile. *He wanted this. And I did too.*

He takes my face in his hand and throws the stub in a cup. We bang against the counter, and he tastes like mint and ice cigarettes. *And that kiss doesn´t taste like fake dating at all. That kiss makes me already feel for this man and isn´t temporary at all.*

He makes me feel seen. Heard and respected. He makes me confident. Confident about tongue kisses, being watched and giving zero fucks. Confident about owning what I want and who I am. And all that without needing to be drunk.

I barely know him, but I trust him.

Everyone always looks at him as something dangerous. He and his folks mess with our parties. He´s bad, a dealer and an asshole. *Not a good guy.*

But all I see in him is safe. *It´s confidence.*

What I don´t have but get through him.

192

As we head to the terrace, he holds my hand and with him, I haven´t the urge to look or think at Kai anymore.

Wren leans against the pillar and I stand with my back to him, leaning in. His arm around my neck as I hold onto his biceps. *He smokes.*

The others sit on the couches across us. Including Kai and his date. She sits on his lap; his hard gaze meets mine. *I hold it until he breaks it.*

Then Nina sees me and jumps up. "Hey." She smiles. "I´ll be right back." Says Wren, kissing my head and I nod looking after him, followed by Nina. She looks at me with wide eyes. "Omg." She mouths and I nod grinning.

"So, what I haven´t seen you in.. two months and *now* you´re with Wren?" She asks exited. I laugh and shrug. "You´re always so secretive about your love life." She accuses me but it´s more of a whine. "We´re dating for a month or so." I lie with a shrug. She shakes her head, unbelieving but squeals happy. And we´re close enough for Kai to hear. He doesn´t look. *But I know he listens.*

"You two look pretty hot together." She chirps and I smile. "Yeah." I say with a laugh. "Really you make so much sense." She tells me. "And I´m glad you´re over *it*." She says without saying *his* name and my heart stops. Over her shoulder I catch Kai´s eyes for a split second. *Like his did just the same. And I´m sure it did.*

She didn´t mean to be rude or something, she´s just being the noisy ass she´s always been. So, I swallow my hurt, and I nod at her. "Yeah, me too." I say quietly but he´ll hear me anyway. Maybe she did it on purpose. Maybe she´s mad at me. He´s her friend too. More than she´s mine so it would make sense. But she hurt him too with asking that.

"How did you start dating?" She asks. "We ran into each other at parties. It was creepy. Like fate or something." I tell like it really happened. "We started talking. Then texting and then dating." I shrug. "It just happened." I say. And while Nina tried to get every detail out of me Kai has been watching. Staring at me while *she* sat on his lap.

He didn´t even hide his glaring.

"You have to tell me everything sometime." She says at some point, and I nod. She sits down next to Leon, and I take a deep breath. I stand in the middle of the party I´ve gone to many times before. Between the people I´ve been friends with. But it doesn´t feel like were friends anymore. *It feels like I don´t fit.*

I feel awkward and misplaced like an alien. The outsider and creep. Because somehow those people just a length away are still my friends, but somehow it feels foreign. Like we´re not anymore. And I don´t fit in or belong. But maybe that´s just the way I feel. Cause *they* don´t seem to feel weird at all. Ryan smiles at me. Nina waves me over. And even Kai´s *date* looks nice. *It´s always me who feels alienated.*

Because I choose to feel that way before they can make me feel like that. Because all I want is remaining control. *And being here makes me lose it.*

The control I´ve gained over the past ten months. The control that Wren gave me just by being near. Looking at me, touching me or kissing me. All that gone now. Replaced by anxiety and dissociation.

"Sit down Scar." Aidan calls me smiling and I smile back. But before I must say or do anything Wren comes up next to me. *Thank God.*

"Ready to go?" He asks and I look up at him.

Telling him with my eyes, *thank you*, because he understands. I nod and face the others. "Sorry guys." I say. "We´re heading out." I wave. "But have fun. Next time okay." I add and Wren nods his chin at them and hooks an arm around my neck, dragging me away. I hold onto his torso. Feeling in control and inside my body.

He walks me home and tells me he and his friends didn´t want to go, but he saw my unease, so he lied. His buddies stayed and we left. The others might have figured by now that I just wanted to head out.

I told him how I felt towards them or about being back. He listened and asked if I want to hear his thoughts. *Who is that man? How every guy should be.*

I nodded yes, and he waited for me to change my mind. *To change my mind.*

"I think you need to realize you see yourself through other people´s eyes. Try it with *yours* instead." He says but shakes his head right after. "No *actually*, I´m talking bullshit." He says. "You use the assumption of judgment of others to judge yourself. It´s the way *you* see it." He corrects himself.

"Either you own the way you think about yourself, or you change the way you let yourself think of you." He tells me and I look at him astonished. But not cause I´m offended or something because he is right. *Like I said it´s all in my head.*

But I´m startled because at that moment he reminded me of Kai. The way he spoke. And I mean it makes sense they´ve been friends.

They´ve known each other all their life´s.

But he talks clearer in a way. He calls me out. But not hurtful like Leon did. Mocking like Andi, gentle like Aidan or cryptic how Kai used to. He does it like he really considers my point and doesn´t try to give me only *his* opinion.

He works as an air traffic control officer. He smokes rarely. *Mostly at parties.*

He likes gaming and started streaming on twitch. He goes four times a week to the gym and plays piano since he´s seven. *But he stopped years ago.*

He has one younger sister. He´s twenty-six. He´s a Taurus, so that would match. He´s vegan, which I love. He has a dog. Or rather his roommates. They all take care of him. He lives with his buddies in the city. Not where Andi and Ryan live but the next bigger one. He visits his grandmother once a week and brings her flowers and cake just like his grandpa did. He plays tennis and boulders. He likes to play poker, loves darts and billiards. He´s in the basketball team with Finn, Andi, and Leon.

He told me lots of things. I did the same and I really like him. Like way too much for having spent that less time with him. I mean I´ve seen him since years on the parties and occasionally I´ve talked to him too, but we never got around to get to know each other. Mostly because Kai was around, and they barely spoke.

They didn´t even fight. They mostly ignored each other.

Wren gives me butterflies but warm ones. *Not black or dead ones.*

Those that just make you happy and confident. It´s not head-over-heels like I´ve experienced before. *It´s calm and a safeness. It´s just right. It makes sense.*

I told him the story I made up for Nina. And part of it was true because we did bump into each other and talked. But we didn´t text or started hanging.

"I´d like to date you regularly." He says as we reach my house, and I smile. "I´d like that too." I say and he smirks walking slowly backwards with his hands in his pockets. "Lia." His chin lifts and I smile. "Wren." I mimic him. "Good night." He says with a grin and turns to walk down the street, and I look after him. And with that a new player´s on the table.

He has good cards.

But who has the Queen? Who´s the King? And is there a Joker in this game? Who are the players? Has someone already left the table?

Who´s cheating? Who´s winning? Who´s bluffing? Who´s loosing?

And most of all do we still know the rules?

Or do we even play by the rules anymore?

Or has the game changed us? Or did we change the game?

Who has the upper hand? Who am I in this game? And who are they?

193

Two weeks later

We´re at the Avery´s campfire.

We partied the past weekend´s together and I was there with Wren and Kai with that girl.

I sit next to Wren. His hand on my knee playing absently with the strands of my ripped jean. It´s just the others no party. *That starts later.*

Kai sits with his date across us. Her hand around his arms. She´s on her phone. He leans forward, eyes locked on the fire.

Leon and Ryan start singing *Something in the orange by Zach Bryan* with their guitars and my heart aches at the memory. I try hard not to look in Kai´s direction. Because *I* know he´s looking at me right now. Because he used to sing that to me. Back when things we´re different. *When we were different.*

When I look up his gaze is on the fire. But his eyes flicker to mine for a second telling me he *knows,* and I could cry. Sometimes it´s like we can hear each other´s thoughts.

We´re still connected. It´s scary.

I place my hand over Wrens and Kai´s eyes catch it. He stares at my pinky finger. The place where I wore his ring. *It´s gone.*

His expression hardens and he straightens up letting his date lean in. He doesn´t look at me again and we sit there until the party gets going and head back over to the Dark´s.

- 27 -

Wren´s with some of his buddies and I went outside the front door trying to have a minute alone. *But I was naïve to think I could have one.*

The door clicks open behind me, and I turn to see Kai. *It starts to drizzle.*

He gets out and closes the door behind him. We´re alone for the first time since everything and he looks like he wants to talk. *So, I brace myself.*

He lights a joint and clears his throat. "So, Wren, huh?" He asks blowing smoke past me and I nod slowly, not sure where he wants to go.

He stares at me for a moment and then he laughs. "What?" I ask but he shakes his head. "No, it´s just funny because all this time you wanted me to commit to you, but then you first dated Andi, then my best friend, and now you fucking date Wren? Who´s.." He trails off trying to keep his temper. "Like the worst fucking guy, you could have picked. You know I hate him and that we used to be friends." He tells me on edge tilting his head looking like the devil seeing a girl´s first sin.

"Like really Scar what the hell?" He laughs spitefully, but I´m at a loss, so he keeps talking. "Then how should I have opened up or let you in when there was never a chance of having you all by myself?" He asks me. *Why´s he so talkative?*

"Don´t know." I say. He nods with a venomous smile *knowing* I would say that.

This makes me angry.

"Fight." I snap because that was the one thing he couldn´t do. It always felt like an almost. We almost touched, kissed, had sex. Almost said we love each other. Almost been together. Almost worked out. *Almost.*

The past years have been a constant almost. *But there´s been a shift.*

There is no almost anymore. There´s just a fade out. A timer running out. Counting the last moments before the almost vanishes and a *never* appears. Because the almost we had has turned into something that has a limit. And I think we both realized and maybe even accepted that. *That´s why we moved on.*

Why we chose ourselves. Why we´re now with others. *Because we´re done.*

"Fight?" He grins raising his eyebrows. "*Fight*?" He repeats raising his voice. "Like I *didn´t* fight for you." He snaps almost laughing. "All I ever did was fight for you. Trying to get you back. To be good enough for you." He yells and I fight tears. "So, don´t fucking say, I didn´t fight for you. Whereas you never did *anything* to fight for me. You let me leave for London. You fucked my best friend instead of choosing me." His fist hits his chest, and I blink at him.

He takes the last puff and stomps the joint on the wet ground. Then he takes two steps towards me. "Now let me ask you something." He begins demonic enjoying the acid he spreads. "How would *you* feel if I fucked Nina or Luca?" He asks me and my heart sinks.

That came out of nowhere.

But I get what he´s saying.

My eyes burn like hell as he cocks an eyebrow wanting for me to answer.

But I don´t. Because again he´s right.

I look down. "Right." He says and steps closer getting in my face. "So, don´t fucking tell me it´s no big deal that you fucked Aidan, tried to fuck Andi, get back with your ex. Or now fucking Wren.." He stops clenching his jaw so hard I hear it cracking.

"Cause it is Lia. It is a fucking big deal." He growls. "You *fucked* me. Do you know that?" He scoffs his voice shaky. "You fucked *my* best friend´s. And that shit killed me." He tells me and his voice breaks heavily. And for a moment he lets me see behind his mask. But then he grins spitefully and shakes his head. His eyes are red. But maybe it´s just the weed.

Yeah, tell yourself that.

"I wasn´t ready for *this*." He says hurt. "You knew that." He tells me. "But instead of waiting or fighting. You fucked me. You hurt me." He snaps.

"I reflected. But you did nothing like that. You just kept doing *your* shit." He laughs. "And I´m fucking over it." He states. "You fucking gave me *issues*." He gestures with his hands. "And I had already enough." He adds.

"So, go ahead tell me, how should I have trust you?" He asks. "You fucked *many* girls." I try to hit back but fail. Cause he´s right and it´s *not* the same.

"Yeah, I *fucked* them. But have you seen me stick with any girl?" he asks. "There *were* girls." I retort. "I haven´t seen *one* of them longer than two weeks." He says. "But you on the other hand stick to the guys." He shakes his head.

"What about the girl you´re seeing now? You date her longer than two weeks." I say ignoring what he said. "I had her with me cause I knew you´d be there." He says but I don´t know what to counter, so I shut up. "I don´t make bonds Lia. But you on the other hand.." He shakes his head.

"The only real bond I made was with you." I tell him. "Bullshit." He barks.

"No, it´s not." I insist.

"Cause I´m *clearly* always coming back to you." I say upset and his head tilts back. "You didn´t come back." He laughs.

"And you don´t *stay* Scar." He says. "Says *you*?" I ask raising my eyebrows. "I might run. But from my feelings not you. You run from me. To *other* guys." He spits. "How should I feel about *that*?" He scoffs and I shake my head.

"What is *this*, Kai?" I ask not knowing anymore. "It´s about *you* leaving me." He says. "You left me." He tells me and I shake my head. "I never promised you to stay. I don´t say things I don´t mean." I tell him even if it´s a lie.

"You promised me.." I say but he cuts in. "That I´ll try." He finishes. "And I did. And I am here. Lia I never left. I stayed. And waited for you to come back to me. But you *never* did." He accuses me but I don´t get it anymore. Because he did leave and travel, but he clearly means another form of leaving. But at this point I don´t even know to what exactly we´re trying to get back to. *Was there ever something else than this?*

He reads me knowing I have no idea what he´s talking about. "We didn´t broke up Lia." He yells. "We weren´t even together." I say. "Yes, we were." He presses. "No, we weren´t." I insist. "We were Scar." He says again and I look at him. "Well than we had different experiences." I tell him.

"*Fuck you*. You *know* what I mean." He tells me. "We had no labels yes, but we were together." He states. "And you left but you didn´t say were done. You left, for us to get our shit together." He says but I shake my head. "No, to move on." I clarify even if I´m not sure if it´s true because I can´t remember. I can´t even think about the time when things were different. *It seems so far way.*

"I didn´t move on." He says. "You *did*." I correct him. "Maybe But you did too." He agrees. "But we were together Lia. I just couldn´t say it. You knew. They all knew that it was us. You just wanted a reason to end things. To blame me. Because you couldn´t stand that this time *you* were the issue." He calls me out.

Right now, it just hurts looking at him and without Wren, I don´t have the strength to block the emotions. *I feel all of it. It kills me and I don´t want this.*

Memories X Another love – Xist

"You can´t just do that." I tell him. "Do what?" he asks. "Come back." I say upset. He looks at me confused, and I can´t breathe because it hurts. "I let go." I yell and he jerks back as if I hit him.

But he caught himself. "Yeah, did you?" He asks spitefully. "I did." I tell him. His expression hardens again tilting his head. "Then *why* are we talking then?" He asks and I say nothing because I don´t know. He smiles. "Thought so." He nods to himself licking his lips like he tasted blood.

Then he grins like he had a breakthrough. "*You don´t lose me. Okay. We need distance. But I´m not leaving you*." He mimics my voice, and I frown.

"*This isn´t forever it´s for now.*" He says next and Deja Vu hits me like a punch in the face. *He repeats my words.*

"*I´ll stay Kai. I won´t run like you. But that doesn´t mean that I´ll be with you. I´ll always stay. But as long as you run, I won´t be with you. Until you chose to stay too.*" He goes on pretending to whine and I fight the tears that make me see his face blurry. He memorized all the things I´ve said to him as I left. *I wanna die.*

"*You know it´s you. It´ll always be you.*" He adds and my face heats.

"*Go find yourself so that you can find me.*" His voice angry now and I break down tears shedding like spikes. He stops taking me in and liking my tears. No sign of regret. *Just satisfaction.*

Because he likes hurting. *He´s a sadist.*

"I may have broken *promises*." He whispers. "But you broke the worst one." He says and cuts me with it. "*Own it*." He barks. "*Stop*." I shout and he smiles satisfied. "You always promised to stay but you didn´t Lia." He says working his jaw, so his tears won´t shed. And I wipe mine to glare at him. Lifting my chin, I speak up gathering all my strength I have left. "You wanna know why I left you?" I ask in tears. "You really wanna know?" I almost laugh. "I left *you* because you got better. I *made* you better. You grew with me." I rage. "But I didn´t. I got *worse*. You made me." I choke and he looks hurt. *But he did hurt me first.*

"When you left me, I couldn´t *breathe* Scar." He struggles. "Finn had to make me." He says swallowing. "I felt like.. I couldn´t.. *breathe*.." He touches his chest. "And I haven´t since." He shrugs.

I sigh shaking my head. *Stop. Just stop. Stop this. Now.*

"Yes, I didn´t stay. I own it." I yell. "I´m with Wren now." I add. "You´re just with him because he loves you how you want him to. Because I wasn´t enough. My love was never enough. You broke me." He tells me. "That´s not fair." I say upset. "Right, it isn´t." He agrees. "But life isn´t fair." He says. "It never is." He snaps.

"And we´re not in love." I tell him. "We´re dating." I clarify. "But yes." I lock eyes with him. "I´ll fall for him." I nod and he looks like he wants to puke.

"So, *if* you changed then tell me I should leave him." I say and he laughs. "I won´t tell you shit." He bites. "I don´t get you." I snap. "You should leave him cause you *want* to not cause I ask you to." He retorts. "*Fuck this.*" I curse. "Fuck you." He yells back.

"What do you want *then*?" I ask. "What I *want* is you to get it." He grits. "Then tell me." I nod my chin at him. "I made no intimate connection." He says. "But you got *attached* to them. And now to Wren.." He says frowning.

Like this one strikes him the most.

He blinks away. "I never did that. I kept the chicks on distance, cause no one could ever *reach* you." He says and the dying black insects inside of me jolt awake.

But I stab them down.

"I might couldn´t tell you that but I didn´t have to, right?" He asks. "Cause you knew and couldn´t allow it." He narrows his eyes. "Because that thing with staying friends was real. You didn´t want to let me in." He nods and I say nothing because fuck he´s right. He always knows my motives better than I do and I hate it. Because I don´t seem to know his anymore or maybe never did.

"But you blamed me and made me the villain. But you won´t acknowledge that either." He looks at me. "Because you´re *never* the problem, right?" He grins. "I never said otherwise." I say. "That´s a lie and you know it." He shakes his head.

"No one could erase you. But you let *them* have you. You destroyed every piece I gave you." He says. "I tried to make it right. There was just *you* for me. Whereas for you there was never *just* me." He frowns like he just realized that. And I just listen to all the things he has to say. I could counter something, but I don´t. I don´t have the energy. *He´s right.*

"You messed with me my feelings." He yells and I just shrug. *I feel just beat.*

He shakes his head not even realizing I´ve zoned out. "But you know no matter how many guys you date you won´t let *them* in either. Like you did to me. To all of us." He shrugs meaning our friends. And there were times I used to call him out on his issues, but those times have changed. *So, I just shut up.*

"You want to be loved so bad; you chase after *every* possibility to be wanted, but you won´t let it happen. You won´t let *anyone* love or get to you." He says but I don´t listen.

It´s so far away right now.

"You *are* loved Scar, but you won´t allow yourself. Cause the truth is you´re self-destructive and broken. You don´t love yourself enough. And have no sense of self-worth." He tells me, and finally I snap back in my body and look at him.

"Have *what*?" Is all I can ask to the things he just threw at me. He looks at me like I asked the one-million-dollar question. "*Me*." He chokes, and I blink at him.

He´s serious.

This is one of those moments we had many times before. It´s a door or a portal opening up. A path splitting. It´s another almost. *A decision.*

A moment you feel the importance of. And I feel it in every bone. In every beat of my heart. In every breath he takes. In his every move. *I feel it.*

But also, don´t feel enough, to know it´s the last path we can take.

"Don´t do this." I say upset. "Do what?" He asks on edge. "Come back in." I say raising my voice and his chin shots back as if I punched him in the face. But he shot me in the heart minutes ago, and I just go on, cause he can´t do this. *Not again.*

"You *always* come back." I say annoyed. "You always do this when I try to get past you." I say fed up and he stiffs a laugh. "*Trying to get past me*." He repeats my words like scissors slicing my throat. Raising his chin, he grins. It´s scary and dark.

God, why´s he always smiling?

"You don´t get it." He scoffs shaking his head. "Get what?" I ask. "Nothing." He nods. "Go fall in love again. That´s all you can do." He says. *I hurt him.*

"Kai." I say, but he won´t listen shaking his head and nods. "Get past me." He orders and gets back in.

On his back.

"The more you love, the more you suffer. - Van Gogh"

When did he start wearing those again?

But it´s true all you do is suffer. At least that´s how I´ve known it all my life. But with Wren it feels like it´ll stop.

And I can´t help but think about our last kiss in Italy. In the middle of the storm. That day I´ve told him either we drown, or we survive. *And we drowned that day.*

But we thought otherwise and that was our mistake. Thinking we could swim on a planet of endless water.

I blink away the tears as I stand there in the rain. *Alone.*

And for just a moment. A moment of regretting. *Of silence.*

A moment of weakness. A moment of wanting him back.

A moment of an almost. *Almost relapse.*

But that moment passes because we´re never more than a dream.

A daydream. A Déjà-vu. An almost.

Something that might have happened. *But didn´t.*

Maybe in another dimension or a parallel universe. *Or maybe just never.*

We almost happened. *Again.* Like we always do. *Almost.*

- 27 -

I walk up to Wren. He´s with the others on the sofa and *Kai* is nowhere to be seen.

He looks up at me. "What´s wrong?" He asks gentle.

"Can we go?" I ask begging him with my eyes and he nods getting up.

The others frown at me probably putting the pieces together that we happened again. That Kai and Lia came to blows.

"I´ll get the car and tell em we leave." He walks past me and before they can ask anything I turn but slam into a wall. *Kai.*

Behind him *that* girl. His eyes slice mine, but I quickly move around them.

Tears well up as I find Wren and his buddies. He tugs me to his chest and rests his head on mine. "I´ve told you he´s a letdown." He hushes. "But don´t let him get to you." He tells me softly and I nod. And we leave.

I´m glad I left with him and didn´t fell back into those abysses because I never want to go there ever again.

194

We´re at Wrens and his friend´s apartment. We´re in the kitchen drinking tea.

I´ve told him what happened, and he assured me in all the right places. And asked for his opinion where it was needed. And he isn´t judging me nor Kai.

He just understands.

"So, what do you see in him?" He asks. "*You* tell me you´ve been friends with him." I tease, but he looks at me with an annoyed grin. "I asked first." He tells me and I nod with a laugh. "Apparently *everything* others don´t." I say with a shrug, but he nods like he gets what I´m saying. *But no one can.*

"We have a dynamic that is hard to explain." I say and he stiffs a laugh and nods. "Yeah." He agrees, but I don´t know to what. *He reads me.*

"I´ve known you." He tells me like I don´t get the obvious. "The two of you." He clarifies and I frown. "I´ve been to the same parties as you were." He states like I should know that, and I do but didn´t really think of it before.

He knows him all his life. Through friendship and hate ship.

"I know it all." He shrugs. "The back and forth. I´ve seen it." He tells me. "I haven´t *not* seen you those years." He locks eyes with me and shrugs, getting closer. "When he told you to sit in front with him after Andi´s birthday." He steps closer. "The party I talked to you, and he scared me off." I swallow, and he does the space between us. "That flirt game you´ve put on when you had that triangle going on. I saw you." He tells me, and the lump in my throat grows with every word.

He looks down at me. "I´ve seen you the first day you stepped on that party Lia." He tells me. "You just *never* looked." He whispers. "But I did, I looked. Every time. I looked." His voice raspy. "But you only ever saw him." He says.

"You just have to look the other way." He says soft and I nod. "I just don´t know if I ever get past him." I admit. "I can´t unlove him." I say quietly but he makes me look at him. "You *don´t* have to." He states. "I don´t ask you to *unlove* him." He tells me and I frown. "I know.. you can´t." He says with his voice thin.

"I ask you to see me *despite*." He says. "You have to live with it. That love you have for him." He shrugs. *Is that even possible?*

"´m not Aidan who lets you go or hell, even shares you." He shakes his head. "And I´m certainly not Andi who plays with you just to piss him off." He laughs. "I´m with you because I *care* about you. Because I see you and want you." He tells me and I love how he always tells me exactly what he thinks and feels.

"I won´t chase you nor beg you to see me. Cause I´ll show you. I´ll make it the right way. The *only* way." He says stepping closer and his eyes ask me for permission to kiss me and I rise to my toes kissing him. *And that´s it.*

He´s right. Andi was a dead end. Aidan was affection. And Kai was attachment.

But is it more than that? Is this something that can lead to a relationship?

Maybe Kai and I are just for friends. *Or nothing.* And Wren. *He´s so much more.*

He´s trust and I have butterflies but not out of anxiety. Out of a real bond. No traumas, no anything. *Nothing venomous. Just the right way.*

We break our kiss.

"And I get it the toxic is tempting and exciting." He says. "But that´s no base." He tells me what I thought myself. "You feel calm with me, cause I give you *no reason* to feel otherwise. Anxious, how you were when you came back to those lost ones you call friends." He says and I nod. "You´re not used to people not leaving or not making you feel like you don´t belong or are not seen." He says. "Because he *never* saw you." He says with a frown.

And somehow, I believe him.

"And you deserve better than that." He states. "You just have to let yourself. Because you are in your way. Not Kai or anyone else. *Just you.*" He tells me, and again there is that slight parallel to Kai that throws me off. *But it also lulls me in.*

"Happiness is a decision, Lia." He says. "And all in your head." He taps his temple, and I am unable to speak. I always knew Wren was off limit, but I never knew why.

Like Hook is the opponent to Peter.

At least that´s what the lost boys or Wendy´s told me. *But they were wrong.*

He may be to them the villain but not to me. *To me, he´s the hero.*

He nods his chin at me questioning and I shake my head. "It´s just you´re not as bad as everyone says." I smile and he frowns. "You mean like *he* says?" He grins. "No, there are others too." I smile and bob my head. "Nah, I doubt that." He teases. "Yeah?" I ask and he hums in agreement, licking his lips.

"You´re quite convinced of you." I grin and he nods. "I just care if you are." He tells me and my heart flutters. I wrap my arms around his neck. "Everyone thinks you´re the bad guy. But you´re not." I say and he grins weakly.

"Then what am I?" he asks husky over his lips, I say. "The right way." And kiss him. He hums smiling against my lips.

"You´re a good guy." I tell him. "I am not. But I have a sister. And I *know* how to treat women. I´m an asshole, for the fuckers who deserve it." He chuckles. "And he deserves that." He says and I know he´s right.

We all wanted Peter but maybe we should have wanted Hook.

195

One week later

We´re once again at the Darks. *But it´s just us.*

We´re talking and drinking some. Finn has a meeting and Kai isn´t here.

When I get up to get a water, Leon nods me over. And I just know what will happen, but I follow him outside and we sit down. *My heart in my throat.*

"I´m always honest with you Scar you know that." He begins and I nod taking a deep breath because yes, I know *how* honest he is. "I love you and I don´t want to bash you, but you fucked our friend group." He tells me out of the nowhere. I startle and blink a few times, trying to process.

"And believe me, but you're going to fuck up another by getting involved with Wren and his gang." He says, his honesty slicing me open as always. "But you don't want to fuck with his folks." He snaps but I shake my head. "You're wrong." I tell him. I've met the boys and they're *everything* but how they make them out to be.

Somehow, I think it's the other way round.

He sighs with a laugh. "Hope you're right Scar. But I believe you're not." He says and I shrug. "I don't care honestly." I say and he laughs. "Yeah, don't you always?" He scoffs and I gape at him. "Don't look at me like that. You know." He tells me but I say nothing, just frown at him. "We're always having your back Lia but what you did with Wren.." He trails off, shaking his head. "That was a bitch move." He tells me and I lift my chin. *It was.*

"Because they hate each other?" I ask and he looks at me, shaking his head. "I can't tell you. But I don't have to for you to *know* it's been a snitch move." He snarls and I sigh. "You know, I don't have to listen to you anymore." I say and get up. "Yeah, leave." He scoffs. "Get your pirate and fuck off." He growls but I shake my head and get back inside. I know he's really drunk right now and that's why he's even meaner than normally.

But he means the things he said.

I walk to Wren leaning over the couch to ask him to leave.

But as I do so Kai walks in and growls.

196

Damage – Rupert Pope, Giles Palmer

Her hands are around Wren's neck. That close it bothers him. *It always does.*

When he sees her with someone else. It reminds him of the day he saw her with his best friend. *It was a betrayal.*

But what he sees *now* is on a different level, cruel. Cause it cuts him even deeper than anything. *Because it's him.*

And he can tell he's different. *They are.*

They have a connection. *A real one.*

That pisses him off even more. But she doesn't even notice his glares cause her eyes are all on the guy in front of her. "The fuck are you doin here?" Kai snaps, making their heads turn and she straightens up. "We were about to leave." She tells him with her chin high, but he stiffs a laugh. "Yeah, hope you were." He nods.

"Why are you here anyway?" He asks her. "Leon invited us over." She snaps and he frowns. "Well then fuck off." He barks and enters the kitchen, but she ignores the looks of their friends and follows him.

"What are you afraid of?"

Reads the back of his shirt.

Not ever losing that bond of yours, She thinks to herself.

"What´s your problem?" She asks him and he stops on his beer. *Tastes like shit.*

He glares at her. *She knows what´s coming.*

"*You are.*" He tells her and she sighs, fed up. "Why are you here?" He asks. "What do you mean?" She asks frowning. "Him and you." He clarifies. "I don´t know cause we´re friends hanging out." She says irritated.

But they all know they´re not friends anymore.

Not how they used to be. *Maybe never were.*

He nods with a judging grin. "*Friends*." He repeats like it´s an insult. She nods, not sure anymore either. "So, we´re friends now?" he asks with raised eyebrows. "Yeah, I think we should *try* to be friends." She nods. "*What*?" He barks. "*No.*" He adds. "What the fuck are you talking about?" He asks but doesn´t let her speak. "I don´t want to be *friends.*" He scowls. "But we aren´t *more* either." She says, and his jaw clenches.

"Then we´re nothing?" She asks with a shrug. "Is *that* what you want?" she pushes him, but he shakes his head. "Fuck you." He scoffs. "Kai." She calls him. "No, fuck you for that, Lia. Fuck you." He shouts.

"I wanted to be more for years. Maybe we *are* just friends." She defends herself not caring anymore, they hear them. "Don´t act like it´s all *my* fault." He retorts. "It´s *our* fault. But we have to figure things out. We have to stop this." She gestures between them, but he shakes his head. *Walls up. Weapons aimed at her.*

"So, friends, huh?" He scoffs and she nods. "Alright." He nods. "Okay." He nods fiercely. "Then fuck you, *friend*." He says. *And that´s it.*

She looks at him wondering how they got where they are.

"And friends are honest right?" He smiles lunatic. "So, why don´t you just fuck off?" He growls. "What the fuck Kai?" she gapes at him but he just grins. "Why don´t you just say what you gotta say?" She adds challenging and he takes a deep breath to temper his rage, but nods.

"I don´t.. wanna see you. I don´t wanna hear your stupid voice. I don´t want to be near you and *that* piece of shit." He screams completely out of his mind. "And hells no I don´t wanna be *friends* with you." He yells.

"Cause we´ve never been." He spits. *Something breaks.*

But not just in her. *In him too.*

And some even say in their friends too.

Something he broke in Hook long time ago.

"Fuck you." She shoves him, but he snatches her wrists holding her tight. "You too." He gets in her face. "Now fuck off." He adds and pushes her slightly off him. She stumbles but more out of the shock, not his shoving.

Tears run down her cheeks and his face is red. "I hate you." She yells in tears. He bites those down that try to spill. "You too." He repeats cold.

"You know what?" She asks him and the way she speaks tells him she´s about to be brutal. "You say I´ve changed and all. That I am the problem." She tilts her chin up. "But I´m just not in love with you anymore. That´s what has changed." Her voice breaks. "That´s the problem." She wipes her tears.

"You *have* changed." He states ignoring the way his limbs feel like he can´t stand anymore. She just shakes her head in tears. "I didn´t." She smiles weakly. "That´s bullshit." He snaps and she tries to calm herself, but he gets just angrier the minute he looks at her. "Fuck off now." He howls and the others have already snapped their heads at them, witnessing all of it. Seeing them break away. Seeing them pushing each other out of their life´s.

Again, but maybe fully this time.

She stumbles away and Wren jumps to his feet. He gave her the space he thought she needed, even if he wanted to intervene at many points. But just as the others knew, they had to take it out on their own.

"Let´s go." She tells him with a sob not looking at one of her long-lost friends. Without hesitation, he joins her and without saying goodbye, she leaves with the enemy.

With the one they hate. With the pirate. With Wren.

Maybe her angel eyes saw too much kindness in the devil or maybe their time is up now.

197

He walks into the living room. *All eyes on him.*

"What the fuck?" asks Leon. "I don´t wanna hear *anything* from *you.*" Kai scoffs. "You´re the one who invited them over." He snaps and Leon shuts up.

But Nina joins in. "What did you just say to her?" she asks furiously. "As you heard. *To fuck off.*" He growls. "Like she should have in the first place." He yells. She shakes her head at him. “Don´t act innocent. You brought her here.” He accuses her. “Fucking shouldn´t have.” He mutters under his breath.

“I´ve told you I don´t want her here.” He tells her but she shakes her head again. “I call bullshit.” She says. “Yeah, you love her bro.” Aidan says, and his other friends hum in agreement. “Fucking don´t.” He says and looks at all of them. “Fuck *all* of you.” He snaps.

“Fuck you Nina, for bringing her. Fuck you, Leon for telling me she´s like me. Fuck you, Andi for messing with me. And fuck you, Aidan for *fucking* her.” He spits and laughs mad. “Finn isn´t here but fuck him for not telling me how she was when I was gone. Because he *always* knew.” He shakes his head.

“The only ones who did nothing to piss me off are Luca and Ryan.” He looks at them. “So, thank you for doing *nothing*.” He nods. “But fuck her for making me fall for her.” He points to the door. “Fuck *him* for taking her from me.” He yells, and his voice cracks heavily.

Nina sighs and tells him what they all think. “We could do the same. Fuck you, for lying to us. For hiding her. For breaking her heart. And fuck you, for telling her to fuck off. Fuck you, for letting her go with him.” She tells him and he´s silent, just glares at her. “But you know that´s *exactly* your problem.” She says.

“You can never do *anything* without leaving things in shreds.” She tells him.

“Don´t look at me like that.” He tells her. “Like what?” She asks. “Like you think I´m broken.” He says. “We *don´t* think you´re broken.” She tells him.

“You´re in love.” She says. “That´s what we think.” She nods and he shakes his head. “You´ll lose her.” She says concerned. “Because you did her wrong too. You both did.” She tells him gently. “Don´t let yourself lose her.” She tells him and their friends think the same. But he shakes his head with a grin, and they look at him like he lost his mind.

And he probably had already. Over the girl he just made leave.

“I lost her.” He tells them, facing the void that calls him. “When I made a secret out of her. When I didn´t told you, she´s the one that messed me up on Halloween. Shen I kissed her and acted like I didn´t. When we texted all night and I ignored her on the parties. When I didn´t kiss her on fucking New Year´s eve. Because I´m fucked up and a coward.” He rages. “I lost her when I didn´t kiss her, the months afterward. Cause I was too scared. I lost her every time she ran after me, and I pushed her away. I fucking lost her when I left. And after that I lost her over and over.” He lists.

“When I didn´t reach out, I lost her. I lost her when she fucked my best mate. And I lost her when I told everyone but her that I love her. I lost her when I promised I´ll try and failed. I lost her when I left again. Cause I´m bad in keeping good things." He growls.

"And when I got back, she had her guards up. She didn´t let me in. I lost her there. I just ignored it and pretended I didn´t. But she was gone long before I ever had a chance of having her. I was the one on the outside now. She didn´t trust me. And I lost her when she left me, and didn´t come back since." He shakes his head at the tears that spill. "I lost her when I pushed her away again after my mom died." He wipes his face. "I fucking lost her when she showed up with fucking Wren.." His voice breaks.

"I lost myself as I lost her." He says. "I lost her when she told me she had let go. That she moved on. That I can´t come back in. That she´ll fall for him." He nods, his lips trembling.

"And I lost her today when she told me to be *friends*." He yells. "I lost her for good when I told her to fuck off. And I pretty fucking much lost her when she walked out of that door with him." He clenches his jaw hard enough to hurt, but not enough to numb the pain he´s in. "So, don´t you *dare*, telling me that I´ll lose her." He faces her. "Cause I already lost her." He nods. "I lost her more than I had her. Before I even had her *once*." He spits.

"So, shut the fuck up about me losing her, cause I fucking lost her." He shakes his head again and wipes his mouth. "Already lost her." He says again and walks outside.

198

Kai

I walk outside. They´re on the street. *In the rain.*

He´s looking down at her and she looks up at him. And that sight hurts me more than anything. The ones I once thought of friends.

The ones I once thought I loved.. *but couldn´t.*

They talk and it feels like I watch a movie and I´m on the outside watching my girl falling for another guy. *For him. It pains me.*

As she senses me, because I know she does, she looks at me. But Wrens head snaps in my direction following her gaze. He throws his head back. "Oh, fuck no." He growls and steps in front of her, but I get in his face. "Let me talk to her." I say through clenched teeth, and he shakes his head. "*No.*" He declines like it´s his decision. He pushes me back, but I slap his hand off me. *It hurts.*

"She doesn´t want to talk to you." He tells me shielding her.

Fucking shields, her from me.

"Why can´t she, tell me that?" I snap but he ignores me and turns to her. He grabs his keys and hands it to her. Without any word she *takes* them and gets into his Ford GT. She didn´t even look at me. I fight the tears that burn their way from my skull to the back of my eyeballs. *I fucked up.*

"Are you searching revenge?" I ask him on edge, but he stiffs a laugh. "No, Dark. You´re the one playing games." He snorts. "I´m just the one killing, remember? You´re Peter. I´m James." He tells me like I could ever forget. I shake my head at the memories of our childhood and teen years.

The tale I thought I lived in. The tale I made darker. Into a horror.

"I don´t play games." I retort and he grunts. "Well then what was that the last three years then?" He asks grinning. "You *know* what it was." I tell him meaning *trying* but he frowns. "Do I?" He asks. "Or should I ask *do you*?" He laughs and I glare at him.

And say nothing.

Even if he´s taller I could beat him. *He knows.* I did once. *I´ll do it again.*

But I won´t.

"You mean *love*?" He asks and fuck him for that. "I *just* want to talk to her for a sec." I tell him, ignoring his question but he shakes his head. "Just let me talk to her." I insist. "She doesn´t want to, don´t you get it?" He asks.

"I fucked up, I know okay. But she´s my best friend. I shouldn´t have said those things and I need to apologize." I say.

"It won´t change things Kai don´t you get it?" He growls and I shake my head. "You mean it won´t change *me*, right?" I ask. "That´s what you meant." I nod.

"We both know you can´t love her the way she wants." He states. "In fact, you never did." He adds. *He means love.*

I should fucking kill him for saying that. Maybe I didn´t love before but I definitely love her. *He has no fucking idea. I´ve changed.*

"Look I don´t care about.. *you*." I tell him meaning *them* together even if it´s a lie. "Really?" He snorts. "Because it doesn´t look like it." He laughs and I shrug. "Yeah." I say. "So, you´re okay with us dating now?" He asks with raised eyebrows, and I nod.

Fucking liar.

He grins. He knows I´m full of shit. *Because he knows me.*

"How come?" He asks nodding his chin at me. "Because she´ll end up with me." I say cause I know. But he just grins like he *knows* something I don´t which pisses me off.

He nods a few times. "If you feel better that way." He shrugs with that shitty smirk on his face. I should punch him, but I don´t want her to nurse him.

"She loves me." I say using it as a threat even if I shouldn´t. *I feel sick.*

"So?" he smirks. "I know that." He adds and shrugs like it´s no big deal, but it is. "But we both know what *your* love means." He laughs. "*Nothing*." He spits. "*Pain*." He growls. "Hurting people." He adds. "And you´ve hurt.. her enough." He scowls but I ignore his words. "She wears my ring." I say because today she actually wore it.

I´m so pathetic.

He just keeps grinning like this is a fucking game he knows the cards of. "So?" He challenges. *Fuck him.*

"It means *something*." I add a bit pissed. *I´m so weak.*

"And what is that? Can´t you be more *precise*?" He tilts his head. "Wait, no, *actually* you can´t. I forgot." He has that half grin half threat on his face.

Once I admired it but now, it cuts me.

"I mean sure it means *something*." He licks his lips, and I stare at it. Tasting my own blood. *My own sins.*

"Cause you gave it to her, and it means a lot to her. Yeah, know that. So?" he grins.

I fucking hate him.

And I have no reasoning left why she should talk to me besides me wanting to.

"It´s a promise ring." I say and feel like an idiot. Trying to tell him he can´t get between us. But I´m a fool thinking he didn´t already. Because *clearly,* he did.

With him, it´s different than with Aidan. I can´t even name it. Like he´s actually good for her. *How I never was.*

"Look I know you two. I know what I´m into." He says. "You don´t know *shit*." I spit fearing I´m wrong. "Yeah, maybe whatever." He shrugs and gets closer speaking low. "But you just kicked her out and told her to fuck off." He says, smiling at me. "Told the girl you *love*.. your *best friend* that she´s not and never were." He adds with venom on his tongue I used to suck. *Because once we were a team.*

He nods acting impressed. "Seems like you´re going to keep her." He says, patting my shoulder and his touch is slicing me, so I step back.

"You both are not good for each other." He says what I already know. "You might have her heart or piece of her soul or some shit. But I´m in her head." He tells me and it wasn´t exactly a threat, but it sounded like one to me.

"You have her wrapped around your *dick* don´t you?" I ask hatefully and he scoffs shaking his head. "It´s not about the games anymore, Kai." He tells me and him calling my name instead of *Dark* makes my blood boil.

"I care about her." He says. "More than you ever did." He lies. "That´s why she doesn´t want to talk to you anymore. Because she knows that you´re a letdown. Always were." He lifts his chin and turns around to walk away but stops midway.

With that grin on his face, I know all too well. *It´s the devil speaking to you. I used to be that for him. And he was mine. Now he has his own.*

"But as you know best, *nobody smart plays fair*." He quotes me and I freeze.

No, he didn´t. Fuck him. For saying that to me.

I taste blood but it´s not just mine. *It´s ours.*

"I´m not done with her." I tell him swallowing the taste. With the hand on his car door, he looks at me. "What if she´s done with you?" He tilts his head. "Doesn´t matter." I say. "She won´t." I add and he shakes his head, licking his lips. His mouth twitches. "She already is Dark." He simply says and *fuck him* for that.

He gets in the car, and she looks at him like I was never part of her life.

Like I´m not even here. And maybe I´m not.

They drive off and I stand there. *Unable to move or breathe.*

The devil let the universe explode trying to save her. *But he killed her.*

199

Lia

We went to Wren. We sat on the couch, and he let me cry.

"Sometimes what you want stays in your head." He says. "I know." I say. "And you'll keep suffering if you won´t let it go." He adds. And with *it,* he means Kai. "I know." I repeat, swallowing *it* down.

"I watched you change, Lia." He tells me.

But all I can think of is that he doesn´t call me *Scar*. He never once called me that. And I never knew how much I´d like that. *Until he didn´t. Call me scar.*

Because for him, I am nothing like that. *I´m more to him.*

He breathes and wipes his mouth realizing I´m not listening.

"Look I´ve seen you fall in and out of love with him." He says and I freeze.

In *and* out. *Out? Did I fall out of love with him?* His words throw me off completely. And it hits me like Novocain. *I did.* I did fall out of love with Kai. *That´s why I left him. Why I moved on.* Why I want *this* to work.

Because I´m not in love anymore. *Because I fell out of it.* And I didn´t just fell out of it I realized once again that love *is* not enough. That´s what the past years have taught me. *That´s what Kai taught me.* That love is *never* enough. That love means *nothing.* It´s just a feeling not a constant. *It passes. It´s ephemeral.* It´s our *now* that passed.

I do love him.

But I´m not *in love* with him anymore. It happened and I didn´t even noticed. *Until I did.* Until seeing him with someone else didn´t feel as bad as I thought it would be. Until it didn´t made me jealous. *Just sad.* Until it didn´t hurt that much. Until he wanted in but I didn´t want him to be anymore. Until it was easy to let myself fall for Wren because I wanted him in. Until it almost felt like a relief when he cut the cords for good. Until letting go was no struggle anymore. Until I didn´t even want to talk to him anymore neither look at him. Until leaving with Wren was all I wanted. Until never coming back was all I wanted.

Until I realized I wasn´t in love anymore.

I blink out of it and look at Wren. He looks at me. "Maybe you should fall in love with yourself first." He whispers. "Or maybe with me." He says with such honesty and emotions I might. *If I didn´t already.*

"Because go ask him *now* if he wants you. If he´ll ask you to be his girlfriend. If he´ll tell you he loves, you. But I can tell you how you end." He says. "Because with him there´s nothing but pain. Because when it comes down to it, he runs. He did that the past *years* Lia." He says. *Because he knows him.*

I nod. "But I won´t run unless you´ll do." He tells me. I nod through tears.

"So, are you in?" He asks. "Or will you keep chasing after him?" He asks the question I should have asked myself years ago.

He told me to fuck off. That we aren´t friends.

I know he didn´t mean that. *But he said it.*

Because he wanted to hurt me. And Wren is right, there is just pain with Kai.

But I´m sick of hurting. I made myself believe I want pain. *But I don´t.*

I want love and I want in. *With Wren.*

He takes my silence as uncertainty.

"Look I know, you can´t just shake him off your mind and stuff. I don´t pressure you." He assures me. "I just need to know if you´ll try to let me in." He says softly. I look at him.

At the guy who *wants me*. Like genuine *wanting* me. *Communicating.*

Giving me space. *Safety. Love.*

"I´m in." I whisper. He blinks. A grin fights to surface. He takes my face. "You´re in?" He asks to make sure he heard right. I kiss him. *Because I´m in.*

- 27 -

Next day

I´m in his bedroom and look around, taking in his stuff.

Lots of basketball. I used to watch him when I was at the games. But I never thought I might be in his bed someday.

I look at the pictures on his walls. *His friends. His grandma. His sister. His dog.*

There is a picture of Kai and him too. They look a bit younger maybe seventeen or something. There are even pictures of them as a kid. I´ve seen some familiar pictures on Kai´s walls. But Kai´s look like he already had thrown them away and put them back on at some point. But Wren´s look untouched. A bit dusty, maybe but he didn´t threw them away.

Not like Kai did. With everything.

Because even if Wren hates him, he´s still grateful.

As far as I know about a year or two before I met them, they´ve parted. It´s sad how it all went down. But looking at that picture of them smiling and laughing together, it´s weird. Because they´ve been friends too at some point. I think even closer than Aidan and Kai ever were. *But now they aren´t anymore.*

I don´t know why but something tells me their fallout is Kai´s fault. He makes everything fall at some point.

And he made him the villain. *But in reality, Kai is.*

But there´s always another side of the story. I´ve come to learn that the hard way. But that way you learn fast. Maybe Wren tells me if I ask. I would like to know what went down.

I jump shrieking as Wren comes up to me and I smack him. "You scared me." I whine but he looks at the photo in my hands. *Frozen.*

His gaze hardens. "Sorry." I hush but he shakes his head, his features softening. "It´s okay." He says. "They wouldn´t hang there if I wouldn´t want anyone to see." He tells me and I nod. *Silence.*

"Why aren´t you friends anymore?" I ask him. He sighs and takes it from me. He looks at it with a slight smile. "We were a bad duo. Always nonsense on our minds. We made a whole lot of a mess as kids. And as teens.. well, it got even worse." He chuckles at the memories. *I love how it looks on him.*

But I´m sad for him that things have changed. But things between Kai and me changed too, so whatever. *Life changes.*

"We brought the worst out of each other." He shrugs. "But in a good way. We were invincible." He´s lost in memories. "Those games they play. He might tell everyone *he* invented them. But we did." He tells me, and I can imagine that.

Now he´s silent.

"What happened?" I ask and he inhales. "He betrayed me." He says with a frown. "How?" I ask. "I don´t really want to talk about it, Lia." He says, shaking his head. "But he did me wrong." He nods.

"And I couldn´t forgive him." He states. "And since *then,* we´re rivals." He shrugs. "That´s all you´ll give me?" I ask and he sighs but nods. "For now, it´s all you need to know." He tells me and I chew my lip, but he frees it with his thumb.

"Maybe someday I´ll tell you all of it." He whispers and places a kiss on my lips.

Maybe someday.

He tugs the picture back to the others and sits on his desk watching me. "Thanks for telling me." I say. "And I´m sorry. He let you down." I add and he nods. "Me too." He says voice thin.

I look around and spot a purge mask. I take it and smile. "That day was.. *something.*" I say as I klick it on and freeze. It´s pink. *Deja Vu.*

I frown and face him. "*You* were that?" I ask and he smirks. "You *were.*" I cry. "I said I watched you." He says, holding my eyes. "Wait." I say and gape at him. He walks silently over to his cupboard and takes another mask. It´s that crystallized scream mask with blood. The same mask the guy had on Halloween that´s been blocking my way and pressing me to the door. Staring down at me and choking me.

"That was you too?" I ask breathlessly and he nods with a grin. "You scared me." I yell and he chuckles. "What did you expect?" He asks with a laugh. "It was Halloween." He tells me smiling and I shake my head but can´t fight my own grin.

It was him. Those green eyes.

Always watching me.

"Should I be concerned?" I ask playfully and he smirks. "Just *scared.*" He hums.

"So, you´re my stalker, then?" I ask. "I´m your savior." He says and I swallow.

He is.

He puts it on and grabs me by the throat to drag me to him. A cry gets stuck in my throat. "I´ve seen you like being scared don´t you, Sky?" He murmurs and I smile at him.

He just called me Sky.

Five weeks later, September

I´m at Wren´s and the guy´s apartment.

They have a huge living room with windows high as the walls. And in front of that a piano. *A black piano.*

It´s polished and beautiful. But untouched since years.

He didn´t play for me. I asked him to. He said *he doesn´t play anymore*.

But *maybe someday*. So, I didn´t ask again.

But he sits there often. Just looking at the keys for hours as if he can´t touch them. Like he´s scared to touch them. *I don´t know why.*

One of the guys told me he didn´t play in years. They said he never dares to play. And they advised me not to ask him why because he wouldn´t tell anyway. *So, I didn´t.*

But I kept wondering anyway because I´ve seen his awards. He must have been a goddess. But for some reason he doesn´t play. *Not anymore.*

And today is one of those days he just sits there. We´re alone and I sit on the couch with a book and listen to the rain prattle against the windows.

But I don´t read but I watch him. He´s wearing all black today. Like most of the time besides grey and white. A T-shirt and black Jeans. His hair a mess.

Silent fighting some demons that keep him from playing.

I look down and continue to read.

But I freeze as I see his fingers run over the keys. *Softly not making a sound.*

I hold my breath and plead my heart to stop for a sec. His hands hover over them and then they settle in place, and he begins to play. My heart bursts and my eyes well up as I hear the song, he´s playing. I recognize it on the first cords.

It´s *Another love by Tom Odell.*

The sound echoes in the whole place. *Filling the apartment.*

Surrounding us like a blanket. Giving me chills and making my body shiver.

He doesn´t sing. *He never does.*

I never heard him sing once, not even in the car. *He just plays.*

And I listen as he lets the notes speak what he won´t sing. *Neither will I.*

The lyrics float around us silently. There´s a theater playing our drama. *A Tragedy.*

My vision blurs, but I blink it away not wanting to miss any second. Tears spill down my cheeks and I don´t breathe afraid I´d make a sound he´ll stop.

My body aches. *How can you hurt when you don´t mouth those things?*

Because you can feel em.

When he´s done he plays again. He plays it over and over. *Like a mantra.*

Like he can´t stop. Like he has to play it out. Like he has to process. Like he played it before. *And some say he did.*

He´s completely in the flow. *In his passion.*

Lost in the sound and the silence as his fingers wander over the keys as if they never stopped. *Not for years.*

The veins on his hands play along. And his head tilts as he gets lost.

It´s full of emotion without him saying any. He plays it slow and fast. Aggressive and gentle. Passionate and soft. Angry and sad. Happy and violent. *Over and over.*

And with each time he begins anew, he plays it differently.

Telling another story. About another love.

It´s a way of grieving and saying I know. Of letting me know it´s okay.

A way to assure me he´ll wait. A way to heal us. A way to say we´re enough. A way to tell me I care. A way to let me know he feels. A way for him to plead me to let him be my *another love.* And I listen as a way to tell him he is my *another love.*

He played the whole evening until the boys came.

They stopped in the hallway and froze as I did. They stood there watching. Hearing him play. *Like they didn´t in years.*

As he stopped we all went still. He got up and just looked at us, but no one dared to say a thing. "Stop fucking staring." He snapped at them. "It´s no big deal." He told us and went to the bathroom. The door slammed shut. *It was a big deal.*

Some moments we just stayed in silence. *The shower turned on.*

Then they walked over to me and asked *how I made him play?*

I told them I did nothing. They were shocked as I was. *Maybe even more.*

I mean they have seen him over years doing nothing. *And now he played.*

They looked like they´ve seen a ghost. *We all did.* The ghost of another love.

They made dinner and sat on the couch drinking beer. *I drank with em.*

We ate in silence and didn´t watch Tv. We listened to the shower running. Wren stayed in there for a long time. The shower ran but he never got under.

When he got out there was that weird silence. He grabbed a beer and sat down next to me. *They stared at him.*

He looked not good. His eyes red. Maybe he cried. *He did.*

But no one talked about it. *We knew he didn´t want to.*

So, one of his friends cleared his throat and told us about a girl he met.

We listened and the chatter started. *They laughed.*

Later Wren took my hand leading me to his room.

He cried and said sorry. I said he doesn´t need to apologize. Then he kissed me. And that night we had sex. It was our first time. *The first time with another love.*

She realized she liked the pirates more than the lost boys. So, she stayed with them. Because she found the love Peter refused to give her.

The past years felt like we were drowning. But something wouldn´t let us die. We clung onto each other, dragging one another down. I needed to swim without choking. To live without drowning. *So, I let him go and swam.*

I thought I couldn´t bear being apart from him. *But I can.*

I just live with the pain. Maybe it´s what keeps me going. I did it despite the pain.

Maybe cause of the pain.

Luca kept me in touch, but I asked her to stop because I had to go on. The threesome has changed things. I can´t stop but blame myself for it. I distanced myself, expecting them to want the same. They´re his friends not mine. Back then the parties felt like pure magic. Now all they felt was heavy.

I always thought it would be him in the end. But the story got out of hand. Someone else has written a book I didn´t want to read. *It was a sad story.*

But Wren is good for me. He´s the better version of Kai. Without hurt. He´s almost perfect. *Almost.*

But Kai was right, we weren´t friends. We confused hate with love.

I know Kai regretted what he did. When Pan regrets stabbing you. But this time I didn´t listen. To the lies Peter tells you to keep you in Neverland. *To trap you.*

I was mad Finn wasn´t there because he would have stopped him.

We started as a secret and ended as a play. *But a sad one.*

But Wren was the only one was able to stick up to him. Grab his bare bones and break them. He gets under his skin. Maybe that´s another reason why we get along. We´ve been hurt by the same man. *The same lost boy.*

But I´m not with the lost boys anymore. I´m with the pirates. It´s like I´m with the enemy now. But it´s their side of the story. *Mine is a different one.*

In this one Hook loved Wendy. And Wendy loved him.

[NOTEBOOK ENTRIES]

I always wanted to get away, but she was the reason to come back. But I never stayed. The good side to money. You can buy everything, even a personal therapist. I´ve had him all my life. He´s in a way family. He helped. But being away helped even more. I know I have to come back eventually. I´m just scared to see her.

I realized the way I coped after my mom´s death was wrong. I focused on her and became dependent.

I promised I´d be there for the birthdays. She´ll be there. And I don´t know if I can face her. She was okay with me leaving, despite she asked me to stay. Like she made peace with it. That I'll never stay. Or maybe when she left, she never really came back.

I started seeing that girl. I need distraction. I have a feeling she moved on because she would have called. Maybe trying to grieve without her was a mistake. I hope I'm wrong.

I've looked for her all night. And when I saw her, I wanted to die. Because she hugged Wren, and they smiled at each other. It was like another life with another love. If I have nine life's I lost one that moment. Why him? Does she want to piss me off? With him, I'm sure. I thought she had moved on, but this was worse. They flirted and I wanted to rip my eyes out. He touched her. Never in my life I've felt more pain. She looked happy. It's a wonder I still have my tongue, cause I'm pretty sure I've almost snapped that thing. That piece of shit wanted to kiss her. But as always, he had the upper hand. And with her, he had all. Then she kissed him. Knifes slit me. I had to look away. But I didn't forget. That played over and over in my head. She fucking dates Wren. The one I've always tried to keep away from her. But Hook would always steal lost girls. But not Scar.

She fucked the ones I hate. The ones I love and I didn't feel sorry. Not even when she cried. She wanted us to end and decided to give up. But of course, she didn't see. She didn't change. She did the same things as always. Fleeing to some guy.

They deserve each other. I had nothing left for her to stay.

He fucking killed me. They killed me.

It rained that day. The day I lost her. When I pushed her but should have hold on. Maybe it wouldn't have made a difference. And maybe in another lifetime I'm not a coward and can love her right. But not in this lifetime. Maybe another.

201

Three months later, December

With Wren, I'm happy. *And in love.*

But it'll never feel the same it felt with Kai.

That's what I know when I look at him. Because after three months of radio silence. We bump into each other on a party. At Wrens and the guy's apartment. *Our party.*

I heard someone call his name and my face fell. His eyes were already on me when mine met his. *It was really him. Why was he here?*

He did that nod thing he used to do, sending my heart on a blade. And that's when I knew. *With him, it's different.*

I'll never be free of him because the way I felt. *Happy. Sad. Angry. Confused.*

I went to the kitchen and took a beer out of the fridge. *I knew he followed.*

Also, a thing he used to do. Sometimes like a lost puppy, sometimes like a watch dog.

Never leaves me alone.

Always finds his way back to me. Like he´s *Hachiko.* With the difference I´m not dead.

But even if I were, he would follow.

He looks at me as we stand opposite. He nods his chin questioning what´s up but I say nothing and just shrug, because if I´ll speak I would burst out in tears.

He reads my expression. I hate how of an open book I am to him.

I see the exact pain in his eyes I saw the day I left. It isn´t *that* obvious anymore or written all over his face. *But I see it.*

And I feel embarrassed cause I still get emotional. But before he can say a thing, Wren comes in and I smile. He kisses my forehead. *He didn´t see him yet.*

"I`ll go now." He tells me and I hold onto his upper body. *We kiss.*

He turns and stops. He looks at Kai and nods at him. "Dark." He greets him and Kai nods. *They exchange a look.*

Then he turns to me again. *Silently asking if I´m fine.*

I give him a slight nod. "I´ll call you." He says and grabs his bag. Once more he looks at me before he disappears between the people, and I look after him. Of course, out of all days, he has to work tonight.

I wish he could stay. I can´t do this without him. But I have to.

I don´t even know who invited Kai. *Probably no one.*

Kai´s voice snaps me out of it. "So, you *and* beer now?" he chuckles, and I face him. "Huh?" I ask lost in thought, so he points to my hand. "That beer." He say and I look down. "Ah yeah.." I nod. "It´s not *that* bad. And the guys mostly buy that gin or whiskey, so I got used to it." I shrug. He nods and chews his lips. I´m not sure what to say, so I just look at him. He frowns. *He´s gonna ask me something.*

"So, you and Wren are a thing now?" he asks. *Knew it.*

"Yap." I manage to say. "Pretty serious." He states. *What does he want?*

At this point I think we will never reach the state where we don´t look at each other.

Where we don´t have *that* connection to read the other. That we have that longing, knowing damn well we won´t ever work. That there will never be a point where we don´t hurt.

This will never stop.

"So, do you love him?" He asks and I blink at him. "What?" I ask. "Are you in love with him?" He asks but I blink again. "Lia." He says. *Don´t call me that.*

"Why do you ask me that?" I snap but he says nothing. "Yes, Kai I do love Wren." I tell him and he nods, looking at my feet. *Why is he here?*

It hurts so much to see him and to be near him.

If it´s heavy, you have to let it go. *And I let go.*

But he´s here again making it worse.

"I´ll go." I say before I break, and he looks at me and nods. "Was nice to see you Scar." He says and I flinch at the nickname I haven´t heard in a while. But I give him a weak smile and walk out.

I lock myself in the bathroom and dial Wrens number. He picks up after one ring. "I thought you´d call." He says. "You, okay?" He asks. "No." I say with a shaking voice, and he sighs. "I´m confused." I say.

"Why´s he even here?" I groan. I hear him breathing. "I have no idea." He sighs.

"Did you talk?" He asks curiously. "No not really no." I say. *Silence.*

"You should go talk to him." He says. "*No.*" I say. "Talk to him Sky. It´s been months." He presses. "He won´t be here for no reason." He adds and I rub my face. "Come on." He assures me and I inhale deeply. "Okay." I say exhaling. "I´ll call you later." He says. "Love you." He adds. "Okay, love you." I say.

Iris – The Goo Goo Dolls

I go back but he´s gone.

I look out of the foggy windows. *It´s snowing outside.*

I take my jacket, throw on some boots and pace down the stairs. I see his footprints in the snow. It looks like he has turned around a few times but decided against it. My chest hurts as I walk around the building and down the street. I see him and he turns. Then he stops taking a double check.

"Wait Kai." I call.

He walks in my direction. "You wanna talk?" I ask and he looks at me, startled. But he nods and we walk a bit down the streets.

Before he speaks up and we stop. "Look.." he begins. "I´m sorry for what I said to you." He says. "For all." He adds and looks to the ground. "I shouldn´t have said those things." He says. The snow falls in slow motion as if someone stopped time.

"I mean it Lia. I am so sorry for everything. I didn´t mean to hurt you. *Never*." His eyes well up and mine too. "I hope you know that. And I really tried. But I get why you couldn´t take it anymore. Why you´re with him." He nods and I bite my lips. "I was wrong. We *are* friends. At least I hope somehow, we *can* be." He says and I wipe my tears.

He fights his own.

"Because I missed you." He says. "And I *want* to be friends." He tells me. "I want you in my life. *Need* you more over." He looks past me.

"It was just too much. You and him. That was.." he trails off. "It felt worse than with Aidan." He says. "I couldn´t.." He doesn´t finish.

"I just *know* you´re my best friend." He tells me lost in memories. *And so am I.*

"It´s still hard for me to see you. But I´ll get used to it." He tells me. "It´s a problem I have to deal with. I´m sorry Scar." He says. "I know it can´t be how things were. It´ll never be that way. I just want to start over." He says.

And when I think he´s done, I speak up. "I am sorry. I did you wrong too." I say and he shrugs. "I did. Really, I´m sorry. But I can´t change the way I feel about Wren." I tell him and he nods. "I know." He says, looking at the void between us.

"Missed it too." I say and he doesn´t look at me. But he´s relieved I can feel it. The energy shifts. *Cause it´s in me too.*

And for the first time in over three years, we´re clear. There is certainty and clarity in what we are. There is communication. *There is hope.*

There is friendship. *At least, it could be.*

He walked me back and I asked him to come up, but he said that´s all he wanted to do tonight. So, I watched him walk away. His black coat now white. His hair damp almost black, covered in snowflakes. And it was the first time it didn´t hurt to watch him leave. Because I knew he would come back. *And this time, for sure.*

I got back, and the boys plastered me with questions. They knew our story too. It wasn´t just Wren. *Somehow, they all knew.*

It seems like just Kai, and I were never able to see what *they* all saw.

As I got a free minute, I called him back.

"You talked?" he asks. "Yeah." I breathe. "You sound okay." He states but it´s more of a question. "Yeah." I repeat and he snorts. "*Words*, Lia use words." He laughs. "How did it go? What did he say?" He rakes further.

"He apologized." I say. "Okay. That´s good." He comments. "He said he missed me." I begin and hear him breathing. "He wants to be friends." I add. *Silence.*

"*Friends.*" He repeats. "Yeah. Uhm, I guess we´re friends now." I say.

"Okay.. That´s good I guess?" He asks unsure. "It is." I agree. "I´m really glad we talked." I say relieved. "Thought so." I hear his smile. *Silence.*

"Miss you." I whisper. "Miss you too, Sky." He says.

202

Eight months later, August 2024, Cocaine Jesus – Rainbow Kitten Surprise

Kai and I we are friends. *Like really.*

We saw each other almost weekly. The pirates started partying with the Lost boys again. And things were *somehow* normal.

Not how it used to be, but different. It was a new beginning. *It was something.*

I´m at Kai´s and we wanted to watch the sunset on his roof like we used to do. Maybe smoke some pod and listen to music. But as I stepped on his balcony I stopped. There were rows of jars. *Jars full of stones.*

Lined and stacked on the concrete next to some plants.

"What are..?" I ask frowning and he clears his throat. "Uhm.. those are 156 stones I collected since.. you left." He speaks up from behind me and I blink.

Since you left.

I look at him. "Every time I went somewhere without you.." He shrugs. "But wanted you with me. Or just thought of you." He rubs his neck. "Missing you." He adds quietly and I look away. *He never had something worth of collecting.*

My vision blurs painfully as I kneel and open one of the glass jars. I take some flat ones out. He has *written* something on each of them. I get some more out and read it. The date and sometimes the time. How he felt and where he was. Why he picked it up. Why *I* would have liked it there.

"I haven´t left you." I whisper as hot tears run down my face, wetting the stones in my hands. "You did." His voice husky and my throat blocks. *I did.*

We had some of those situations before. When we get reminded of the good times. *Sometimes the bad too.*

Where it is sometimes hard to pretend, we can be friends without that being weird or hurtful. *Because it is to this day. It still hurts.*

But we reached a point where we can communicate better. Where it doesn´t break or part us anymore. We learned to be there for each other as friends.

We just learned to live with it.

I get up and face him. His expression is pained. "I´m sorry." He says.

"I should have moved them." He tells me. "It´s okay." I say even if it´s not. It already feels too much to be with him alone. *That happens sometimes.*

Sometimes everything is fine. *Sometimes not.*

And today is one of those days. *Where it feels too heavy.*

It´s easier when the others are around.

"I shouldn´t have come." I say choking on my words and his face mirrors mine. The shimmer of shed tears. The red in the eyes. The chest heaving. The pain in the heart. The lump in the throat. *The ache in the soul.*

We don´t speak but we do. Through eyes or something higher we don´t get. *You´ll leave,* he says but I keep silent.

Don´t leave, he begs. *I know,* I tell him.

I don´t want to, I say him. *But you will,* he says but I say nothing.

I'll wait for you, his eyes say.

I'll come back for you, my eyes say. *But they hid lies.*

And after that I left.

It´s still hard but we´ll get there. We just know we don´t want to lose each other. It´s just hard to be friends. *That´s all.*

Some higher might has decided that our paths would cross thousands of times, but never align. And I´ll always be there for crossing that line. But we must accept that we´ll never align.

Maybe that´s what was our problem back then. We were too much at once.

We see each other regularly. But it´s not the same. We all knew it would never be. And the worst part was knowing all the changes started with me.

And sometimes it´s hard to be friends. Sometimes the easiest. Sometimes it makes me happy. Sometimes angry or sad.

For Scorpios, it´s hard to let go. They are loyal to death for the people they love. Maybe that´s a weakness. The strings we get attached to. Because when we bond, it´s for life and beyond. Everyone is frightened of us because of our sting. But we don´t use it out of spite, we use it out of fear. We feel backed into a corner, so we defend ourselves. We hurt from mortal fear, not the sake of hurting.

But two of them are fighting a battle they can´t win. And we stung each other enough. But we learned not to anymore.

We keep coming back for each other and I won´t fight it anymore. I have accepted it. I have to live with him. He´ll always be a part of me.

Always.

203

Kai

Like that she left sometimes.

Sometimes I had to leave. *But we´re not leaving each other.*

We just leave the situation. *The emotions. The memories.*

At least when we can´t let them pass or talk about them. But we love each other too much to not want this to work. We try harder than we ever did before. And I´m glad we´re friends. Although she´s not here that much. But at this point, I take all I can get.

Even if I don´t have her. Even if she´s with Wren.

I just have to be with her. That´s what I know. It´s a feeling I can´t explain like something higher than us to understand. Like it´s written in all the books. Like it´s a law of nature. A formula that is immutable. Like my soul´s mission.

My curse and blessing. My purpose as a human being. To have her in my life and to make this work. To be better for her. *To heal for her.*

That was the reason I always came back. Like a voice or an angel whispering, I have to keep reading because the story isn´t over yet.

I can´t let go but neither does she. We want to stay in the other´s life. That´s why I had to get used to them having a relationship. Even if it was hurting me constantly. I would take *everything* to keep her.

And I had to wrap my head around the possibility that maybe she´s right, and we are just friends. That we won´t *ever* be more. And honestly, I rather be her friend than no one in her life. I rather see her in love with someone else than never seeing her again. I rather sit in the front row of her wedding than losing her ever again.

Cause she´s, my Nirvana, and my ultimate destination. In whatever lifetime. She´s mine. And I´m hers. *Always.*

"Loving her is my death sentence. Isn´t it?" I ask the grey sky that now cries onto me.

Because she left. But I know she´ll come back. *Just as I will.* Always.

[NOTEBOOK ENTRIES]

Love is only true in fairy tales. In reality it´s just pain. That´s what I´ve always known. But now I´ve come to learn I was right.

For many, it´s music that heals them. For me, it´s her. Even if in the same breath, she hurts me. She saved me but I couldn´t save her once. Because a villain can try hard to be a hero but fails anyway. So, I watched her get saved from another man. But I couldn´t hurt her anymore. I´d rather hurt myself.

I still remember the day when she looked at the rain like others at the stars. That day I fell for her. I wanted her looking at me like that. I just couldn´t see she did. But it was too late. And I can´t even argue cause he´s good for her. And she needs good. But I was never good.

When it hurts, it´s worth it. And with her it burns.

Colson Herzog

She has that split in her bottom lip. It´s pretty small. You wouldn´t notice normally. But I did, and I´m anything but normal. I noticed it at the pool. Before I smashed the water bombs in her face. I wanted to touch it. Kiss it. Lick it. Bite it. Ask her about it. Was it a wound? A scar? It looked like she sliced her lip. A white scar. Almost invisible. And since that day. She was Scar. My scar. I called her that way. She never knew. But everyone started to call her that way. I didn´t want her to know. That I named her Scar. Cause that day I noticed her and things like her scar. And in ways she stayed a scar. Even after years. And I had that conviction scars could fade. They did and I saw it on my body before. But hers never did. Neither the scar that she left on me.

204

Four months later, December, Lia

Thick snowflakes fall around me.

Wren let me out because I wanted to have a walk in the snow. With *Berlin by RYX* on my ears, I stride down the lone streets home.

It´s always pure magic when the flakes fall like time stopped. Like little fairies, they dance and fall in slow motion.

My gaze on my feet as I walk up to my house. But when I look up, I stop. Seeing Kai sitting on my doorsteps. He´s leaned forward. His hands scratching each other. A black coat. His hair damp. Messy as always. But no sign of snow. So, he sat there a while.

Waiting. For me.

When his eyes meet mine, I feel my heart stab me, for ever leaving him behind. We haven´t had much contact since the stones. Once a month, maybe. On the birthdays or the parties. But we didn´t do much anymore. We decided we need a bit less contact. But we´re still friends. Just not the daily ones we used to be. *Or tried to be.*

That look on his face makes me want to cry. My heart on my sleeves as I speak with a shaky voice. *But I´m not freezing.*

"What are you doing here?" I ask. "Wanted to talk to you." He says and I just look at him for a moment. *Did we ever just talk?*

As I say nothing, he speaks up. "Have a walk?" he suggests, and I nod and turn; he gets up following me. I walk ahead trying to get some time to prepare for *him*, I guess. But the snow crunches under his steps telling me he´s right behind me.

After a few steps, he falls in beside me. His hands in his pockets and keeping his distance. He´s an arm length away from me. The left side of my body heats being aware of him anyways.

We don´t speak the first minutes and walk in silence.

"Haven´t seen you in a while." He says at some point. *It was on purpose.*

But I say nothing. I did it because despite all, I still feel for him. And I really have to force myself not to give in. Because I know that won´t work.

"I have something for you." He says and we stop.

I look at him and he hands me a package I haven´t even noticed he had because I haven´t really looked at him. It´s a packet but more of an envelope. In black sharpie "*Scar*" written.

"What´s that?" I frown. "I wrote a book." He says. *I knew he would.*

"You did?" I ask, surprised but smiling and he nods. The vein on his neck pulses.

I always told him the world has to hear his voice.

"It´s everything you wanted me to say. Everything you wanted to hear. Everything I couldn´t say." He says and I freeze. *What?*

My smile fell. *My heart with it.*

"Couldn´t show." He adds and shrugs. *He wrote a book.. for me?*

"It´s a bit different than any books I´ve seen or read. It´s a mixture of poems, quotes, lyrics, notebook entries, monolog, and flow text. It´s really messy. But it´s how it was for me. For us." He shrugs and rubs his neck. "These are all letters, mostly poems I wrote since I practically I met you." He says and my eyes widen. *He did what?*

"Cause at some point I knew I couldn´t say em, *like ever*." He tells me. "I was never the person to say *such* things and I could never be. But I could write them. Express them." He explains. "So, knowing you would never hear them I wrote them down." He says looking on the ground. "That someday you might read them." His voice raspy and my eyes well up.

"And after two years I had enough to fill a book." He says. "So, I kept writing." He nods. "I wrote when I met you. When I kissed you. When I messed up. When I dreamed about you. When I left you. When you left me. I wrote it all." He lists. "It´s all in it. *All*." He says and I look at him silently.

"For you to read about the voice I could never share." He tells me and I try not to fall.

"And I don´t give it to you to change anything." He shakes his head. "Really, I know we´re just friends." He nods. "And we´re good with that because it´s where we hurt the least." He says to himself.

"I just give it to you because I made it for you. I did this all for you. You´re the reason I made this." He looks at my hands. "The reason I found my voice. The reason

I´ve healed wounds I swore I would never touch." His voice breaks but he clears his throat.

"You helped me.. *process* a lot of things. And work on myself. Understand myself." He swallows and shrugs. "My therapist told me when I was nine that I should write it all down. My thoughts, secrets, emotions, and goals. And I did." He nods.

"I did that all my life." He throws his hands up. "But when you came around.." He shakes his head. "It just made sense *why*. It´s almost like.. just then I started to find my voice. To get it. To get me. To get life." He shrugs with a laugh.

"So, thank you." He nods. "You changed me. You were right. There would be a girl that changed everything." He half shrugs. "You were." He tells me and his eyes fill with tears.

He wipes over his mouth and clears his throat again. *Swallows. Blinks.*

"I never knew, but I *needed* that change." He speaks. "So, thank you, Scar for changing me." He nods and his tears break free. *I say nothing.*

I should say something. *But I can´t speak.*

I can´t even cry, even if my whole body wants to. *It´s all blocked.*

I thought many times before that it was too much. That I couldn´t bear the emotions, the hurt, the longing, the love. But this time it´s not like *anything* before.

It is too much.

As I still keep shut, he gives me a weak smile and turns but I´m rooted. And all I can do is watch him walk away from me. *Down the street.*

And with him, the thick snowflakes disappear.

I stand there. *Why do I stand? Why does he leave?*

I´m with the package trying to process what just happened. *But I can´t.*

Long after he left, I stood there blinking at the empty street he went along. Unable to do anything, but then I sit down in the snow because I can´t think straight anymore. My jacket is long enough anyway so I won´t freeze *that* fast.

Not that I care.

I open it and there it is. *A book.*

I cough because I feel like the air is gone. *But it isn´t. My body just can´t work.*

I take short breaths through my nose and close my eyes. *It´s just a book.*

I can do this.

I take it out. It´s a paperback. It´s somewhere between thick and thin. Maybe 300 to 400 pages. He wrote a hole book. *About me. For me.*

The cover is grey, blue, and greenish. *It´s rain.*

It´s rain on a window. *That´s my window.*

There are clouds, raindrops, and the sky. *It´s beautiful.*

I read the title.

"Petrichor and Pluviophile"

Us.

The subtitles.

"How are you supposed to fall in love when you have trust issues, fear of commitment, and fear of losing control?"

Same.

The back.

"He didn´t plan to fall in love or become dependent on her.
But he did anyway.
She tried not to love him too much, and he tried to love her right."

I open it and read the declaration.

"Everything you wanted to hear from me but I couldn´t tell you.
This is for you, Scar."

I cry.

I read the first line. *My hands shake.*

"My sickness is called not being able to love. Or at least not without hurt."

I gasp for air.

"I´ve hurt before, ones I love. But her I´ve hurt the most.
I´ve hurt her as much as I loved her."

My body aches with waves of sobs.

- 27 -

It is exactly how he said. It´s different than anything I´ve seen and read.

I read it in one sit. For hours, I sat there and I couldn´t put it down. For obvious reasons but it´s a total page turner. *It is great. I knew he would be great.*

I cried and laughed. I got angry and sad. I got hope but lost it. I got hurt but loved. But mostly I got peace. *Because I understood.*

I´ve reached the last page.

"She wanted to hear my voice, but I could only ever offer her my poems."

I cry some more.

I only ever got his poems. His stolen words. *A book.*

Everything I wanted to hear for years. *A piece of him.*

And I found a piece of me in there too. It got lost on the way. *I found it.*

I sit there like a mood ring and change the colors. *But rather emotions.*

I don´t know what to do. *Or to feel.*

I really wish I had a pen with me, so I could annotate, underline, and write in it. The fact that he didn´t think of that makes me angry until I realize he probably assumed I would go home and read it. And not sit there until my ass and my bones froze. But I reread it anyway. Probably more than I should.

I take out my phone and dial his number.

He answers on the second ring. "Hey." He speaks. "He wrote me a book." I blurt.

Silence.

"What?" He asks. "He wrote me a book." I repeat. "Kai wrote me a book." I speak. One, two, three, four, five seconds of silence. "He wrote you a book?" He asks. "Yeah." I say. "He wanted to talk. He didn´t *really* talk, though." I told him. "We just walked a bit and then he said he gave it to me." My voice sounds weird.

He probably can tell I cried.

"He told me he had no intention. He just wanted me to have it." I say. *Silence.*

"Have you read it?" He asks. *One, two three.*

"Yes." I answer. "After he left." I add.

"What is it about?" he asks, probably *knowing* the answer. "Poems, letters, some diary like entries, quotes, lyrics but also some stories." I list. "All about you." He concludes. "Yeah. For me, about me, I don´t know." I say and he thinks.

One, two, three, four.

"He *really* loves you." He says like he just now realized. "You figured?" I joke. "No. He loves you like.. *love.*" He whispers, but I don´t get it. And I don´t know what to say to that either. *So, silence.*

"You´ve cried." He states and I close my eyes. "Yeah. It´s.. *a lot.* It´s confusing." I tell him. One, two, three, four, five, six seconds of silence. "Does it change anything?" he asks.

And there it is. The great question. *Does it change anything?*

"I don´t know." I say truthfully. One, two second´s silence. "Then I think you should talk to him." He says. *He´s always like that.*

He trusts me. He loves me that much that if I´ll go back to him, he´d be happy for me.

Like genuine.

He wants me to be happy. If it´s with or without him. And that´s how I felt about my ex.

That´s true love. That´s not anxiety. No jealousy. Just real and pure love.

He always supports me when it comes to Kai.

He did when I tried to make him jealous. When Kai pushed me away. When he came back and wanted to stay friends. He *always* supported us. Because even if they hate each other, he still wants him to be happy.

"Yeah, I think so too. I'll talk to him." I say. *Silence.*

"Okay call me later." He says. "I will." I tell him and hang up.

I knew it was a hard pill to swallow for him. *That he wrote a book for me.*

He knew it wasn't *just* a book. But still, he listened to me. *To my feelings.*

That's what he's been doing since I met him. *He truly cares about me.*

And of course, he would say when he was concerned because of Kai and me being friends again. But he *never* tried to stop me. He never clung to me the way Kai did. With Wren, I was free. With Kai, I just held on as much as he held onto me. But Wren and I we let us be individuals. We don't hold unless the other wants us to. And Wren may be not what my heart wants but what my soul needs.

He's peace.

205

I said Hi – Amy Shark

My heart in my throat as I walk up the stairs to the house I felt home for years and still do to this day. I ring the door instead of texting or using the spare key I know about. Aidan is the one who opens the door. Looking over his shoulder shouting at someone. My heart sinks when he looks at me and his does too. *I see it on his face.*

We haven't seen each other in four months too. *It wasn't just Kai I ghosted.*

He stops and we silently stare at each other.

"Hi." He says. "Hi." I mimic him.

"You're partying?" I ask when he says nothing. "No, just hanging out." He says.

"Wanna come in?" he asks, and I nod. He walks back into the living room as I undress.

I hear them talk.

My heart is too loud to think. I round the corner and Aidan says to them. "Look who's back." And one after the other, all eyes move to me. Finn isn't there. But there is Luca on Andi's lap. *They started dating this summer.*

Leon with Nina stroking his head. And there is Ryan. *But no Kai.*

I give them a weak smile. They smile back but it's weird. "Wanna sit down?" asks Nina. "Uhm.. I was actually going to talk to.." I start, but Leon cuts in. "He's upstairs." He tells me and I nod. *My throat hurts.*

"I'll go talk to him." I say. "Was nice to see ya all." I add and get to the stairs.

I shut my eyes at the pain. I want to cry as I take the first steps. They weren´t really *happy* to see me. And that I just came for Kai annoyed them even more.

But was I ever here for them?

I walk slowly because I hear them talk. *About me.*

"She´s been crying." Nina states. "Yeah, she looked off." Aidan agrees.

"Haven´t seen her since Kai kicked her out." Andi snorts.

"Have they stayed in contact after that?" Ryan asks. "Don´t think so." Leon says. "They did." Aidan tells them. *Tears spill.*

But I wipe them with my hoodie and walk on, not wanting to hear anything else.

206

Every You, Every Me - Placebo

Kai´s door is ajar, but I knock. *No answer.*

I get in. *It smells like him.* I look around. *He´s not here.*

I spot some new photographs and books as I walk to the bed and take his shirt smelling it. My stomach sinks painfully at the sensation. *I lower my arms.*

I still hold it as he speaks up behind me. "Hey." He says soft, but I hear the surprise in his voice. *I turn and let it fall.*

"Hi." I say. "You´re here?" he asks standing by the door and I nod. "I read it." I tell him.

He closes the door. "Okay." He says. *I have no idea what to say.*

He´s silent too, but because he looks at my hoodie. *Which is not his.*

Of course, it´s not. *It´s Wrens.*

He stares at it as if he only *now* realized what the past years happened.

"You wrote a book for me." I say the obvious but for me less obvious because I still can´t believe it. "I did." He nods. "Why?" I ask and he frowns. "What why? I´ve told you why." He says confused. *He did. But also, didn´t.*

"Why did you give it to me?" I ask. "Told you." he replies. *No, you didn´t.*

"Why now?" I ask instead. "Cause, it came today." He says and I nod but shake my head. "You can´t just.." I start. "You can´t just run away. And then let me leave. Tell me you don´t wanna see me. But tell me you want to be friends. And then disappear on me. Cause I haven´t seen *you* in months too. And it wasn´t just *my* fault." I tell him upset.

"You can´t show up or write a *book* and give it to me just to leave." I say and he nods. "You can´t." I say upset. "I did." He says and I nod. *He did.*

"But you didn´t tell me why. You told me why you wrote it and why you gave it to me. *But why?*" I ask again. *He says nothing.*

"You cried." He says as if he didn´t notice. *Maybe he didn´t.*

He steps closer. "No." I say stopping him. "Don´t." I demand. "Tell me *why* you did it." I insist and he looks at me helplessly. "Tell me." I beg and he inhales. "Did you want me back?" I ask and he looks at me like he´s losing me all over. *Maybe he is.*

"I can´t tell you that." He admits quiet. "Why?" I cry. "I have no answer myself." He tells me. "I just *know* I had to." He says and I nod but shake my head.

"It´s just I don´t know how to feel about this." I hold my stomach. "It hurts." I tell him. "Your name hurts. Seeing you hurts. Being here hurts. This *book*.." I yell. "*Hurts*." I add. "Seeing *them* hurts." I choke gesturing downstairs.

"Cause we´re *not* friends." I let the tears fall like my confession. "We´re not." I shake my head. "Maybe we have never been." I shrug.

"Being here is weird and I don´t even know what to talk to you anymore." I say in tears, and he looks at me like he has no idea what to say. *Neither do I.*

I´m helpless and he´s pained. *Just as I am. For the past four years, to be exact.*

"I just can´t let go of all this." I look around. "You." I tell him but he´s silent as tears trace his jaw.

"But that book. It´s great." I tell him changing the subject like I didn´t just hurt him all over again. "It is a total page turner. And you were right, it is different." I nod. "I knew they would remember you." I say but he shakes his head. "I haven´t published it." He tells me. "I wrote it for *me*." He adds. "For us." He says but at the word *us* I flinch.

"Well, you should do it it´s awesome." I say and go on without thinking. "And keep writing. Because I want to know how the story ends. I want a second one." I tell him not knowing what that means for us. *Or for me.*

He doesn´t know how to act around me any more too. *He blinks.*

"You wanna sit down?" he asks looking lost. "No." I say. "I have street clothes on." I say and he smiles. *I do too.*

But it fades as we see it on one another. Like, we realized we make each other happy. It´s been long since we did that. *Were we ever just happy?*

"You can change." He suggests but I shake my head. "No, I think I should go now." I say and he looks at me like it´s his last chance. *And I think we both knew it was.*

"*Stay.*" He begs. "I´m still with Wren." I tell him although he knows. Since he saw me in his hoodie. "Yeah." He says hiding the pain. "Thought so." He nods.

As I want to say something, my phone rings. *It´s Wren.*

We both stare at the name. *Another name between us. Another love of one another.*

I answered the call. “Hey.” I say and Kai watches me silently; I hold his gaze. “At Kai´s.” I answer. “Can you get me?” I ask. *Kai looks away.*

“Okay see you in a minute.” I say and hang up. *He won´t look at me.*

Please look at me the sky pleaded. *He wouldn´t.*

“I´ll go.” I tell him. *Nothing.*

“We´ll text?” I ask and he nods. *Still not looking.*

“Bye Kai.” I say and go downstairs. *He says nothing.*

And without saying goodbye I leave. Sometimes I wish I stayed. Or didn´t accept Wren´s call. Maybe things would be different.

But what if they had been worse in the end? So, I left.

And that day none of them thought she would ever come back. Including herself.

They were wrong.

207

Devil and the deep blue sea – Mighty Oaks

I wait on the street for Wren as I hear the door open and freeze. I close my eyes.

Please don´t follow me.

But it´s Aidan that walks up to me. He sees me crying before I can turn. “What´s up with you?” He asks, and I look at him. “Hasn´t he told you?” I ask raising the package. He gives me a questioning look. *He didn´t. Of course, he didn´t.*

I hand it to him. “He wrote me a book.” I tell him. He frowns inspecting it. I can´t wrap my head around it.

He takes it out and looks at it. *Flips through. Reads some. Frowning.*

I wait silently. *Take in every reaction of him.*

“He wrote you a book.” He says and I nod. “He did.” I say. “Shit.” He says wiping his face. *The frown stays.*

“Right?” I agree and he blinks at me.

“Sorry I just left without saying bye but..” I don´t finish. “It´s strange.” He nods knowing what I´m feeling. *We stare at each other silently.*

Aidan and I had *always* something to say even during or after the triangle shit. What made us have *nothing* to say was Kai kicking me out. But he didn´t just kick me out of *his* life. *But out of theirs too.*

And I can´t seem to find my way back since. *It all changed.*

But change is the only constant in life, so I had to let it happen.

And let it finally go because it did happen months ago. *Some of it, years.*

The break happened when he kicked me out. Just like he did as we watched the basketball game in the beginning. But that time a year ago he didn´t took it back.

He didn´t ask me back in.

He let me leave because he never wanted me there in the first place. Even if he took it back. Part of him meant that. Like his words on the first party. That I don´t belong, don´t fit and he doesn´t want me. That I am not her friend.

Words can never hide the truth. You can only decide not to listen.

But their life´s have changed because I met them. Four years ago, I went to that party that changed my life. Now four years later I finally leave it behind for good. The lost boys and Wendy´s. *Neverland.*

And as Leon told me before, I fucked up their friend group. *I shouldn´t have.*

And right now, I feel the distance. Maybe we could pick up where we left off. Maybe I don´t want to, anymore. To be one of them. *Loved by him. Chosen by him.*

Maybe I made the decision long ago. When he left me. Because when he came back.

I was away.

It was just a matter of time till I left. And all the times I got back I was lost. A lost child searching the graveyard for his rotten body. Trying to find it living and loving, but it was dead. *Because those who Pan took were dead. Because we all know the tale, but it was a dark one and told by a child. The reality was bloody and deadly.*

Pan only loved dead ones.

But I was alive.

"So, what does that mean?" He asks and snaps me out of it. "Mean what?" I ask. "The book." He says and I shrug. "I don´t know." I say. *Silence.*

"So, you´re gonna leave or what are you doin out here?" He asks and I don´t have to say anything for him to know the answer.

"So, you leave again?" He asks pissed. "Will you ever stay?" He accuses me. "He´s the one leaving." I say but he shakes his head. "He stopped leaving you a long time ago. You always complained about him but you didn´t realize that you turned into the one who was constantly running away." He tells me and I frown at him. "As he started staying you wanted to flee." He tells me.

"Do we all forget he left me first?" I ask upset. "That´s not the issue." He stiffs a laugh. "You know that." He adds. "No, I don´t know." I retort and he laughs licking his lips.

He´s mad.

"Kai had changed." He tells me. "You didn´t. It´s *you,* not being able to let people in." He says. "You just push em away when you can´t handle things." He shrugs. "It´s you, not *wanting* friends." He nods. "It´s you, wanting to be the victim" He adds but I´m unable to speak.

"And you know when you left him two years ago. You left us too." He tells me. "You know that right?" He asks me and I look down. "What do you think it was for us?" He spits. "For Kai? Huh?" He snaps. "Did you ever think of what he felt? After he *tried* for you? He never tried for *anyone*." He almost yells.

"You can blame him as long as you want. Yes, it was bad. But you did shitty things too." He says. "He´s been with you after Andi, that with your ex and after me." He lists and shakes his head. "And even I stayed friends with you after you chose him." He nods.

"I was in love with you Lia and I´m still here to this day, *trying*. For you. For that friendship." He says upset. "But you don´t." He nods. "And even now after you´re with Wren, he´s trying to be friends with you." He says.

"If he´s trying to be my friend what is that book then?" I yell in tears. "Is *that* for you what wanting to be friends looks like?" I ask and he laughs. "What did you expect Scar?" he yells. "That he´ll move on as *you* did?" He raises his brows. "Of course, he wants you back. He´ll never stop wanting to be better or good enough for you. He loves you. He´s trying to show you." He shrugs.

"That man wrote a damn book for you and still you don´t want to see.." He stops and shakes his head. "You always disappear on us." He snaps. "That´s not true." I say. "It is Lia." He nods. "We were trying. But you didn´t let us in." He tells me and I shake my head. "No, you didn´t." I argue. "Yes, we did. You didn´t want *us* in." He nods.

"Kai isn´t the only one who made this a secret. You betrayed us too." He snaps. "That´s not what a friend does. We knew Kai´s reasons, but you did it on purpose." He shakes his head. "Well, maybe we aren´t friends. Maybe we never were." I say and he stiffs a laugh. "Maybe you´re just not a good one." He tells me and my chest hurts.

Maybe.

I nod. "You´ve changed Lia." He looks like he doesn´t recognize me. "No, I didn´t." I tell him. "You just never knew me." I nod and he cocks an eyebrow. "Yeah, and *who´s* fault is that?" He grins and I bite back the sobs. *He´s right.*

"I wanted things to be like they used to be, but they can´t be. It´s just too hurtful at this point." I say. "You mean, for *you*?" He cuts in and I shrug. "It just doesn´t feel right anymore. I feel like I don´t belong anymore. It´s like I have nothing to say to you any-more." I say and his face gets blank and that´s when I know I lost him and with that them. *For good.*

"That´s sad." He says with a nod but a hurt one. "It is." I say as Wren´s GT turns in. I do a low wave, and he gives me a weak smile. The weakest he has ever shown. Because even the weakest of Aidan´s smiles shine bright. *But not this one.*

It´s a smile of goodbye. Because he knows I won´t be back.

I even forgot the book. But with all the reasons in a book. *I still didn´t stay.*

I fell in love with words he never said. But now I realize he didn´t have to. He didn´t need to write me a book, for me to know how he feels about me. He didn´t have to because I knew. *All along.*

And I don´t know why, but it felt right. Maybe I am not a good friend. Maybe I´m not even good in love. *Or anything at all.*

Maybe it was how he said that he was never good enough. Because nothing he said or did was good enough for me. For my expectations.

I was never satisfied, so maybe I was the cruel one. *By wanting too much love.*

By wanting him to be different. Whereas in reality, he was enough.

And I was never. *Enough.*

PART TWO

[Pluviophile]

1

Kai Dark

✧ November 03.1998 – † September 22.2025

Pluviophile (n) *a lover of rain.*

someone who finds joy and peace of mind during rainy days.

One year later, 2025, The Funeral – Band of Horses

I´m choking and sobbing as I read the engraving of the black headstone. Underneath a sea of white roses covering the grave of the man I loved. *And lost.*

The six who carried him were his brother, Aidan, Leon, Ryan, Andi, and Wren. Wren played piano, Leon Bass-guitar, and Ryan Guitar. They sang the song.

~~But no one was ready for the funeral.~~

A picture of him in a black frame.

~~The sun shined.~~ It was drizzling. He didn´t belong to the rain. *Rain belonged to him.*

He wasn´t home in the rain. *Rain was home in him.*

The sound of rain always soothed me. *~~Now it just reminds me of his death.~~*

I was nineteen when I met him. I was twenty-one when he left me. I was twenty-two when I left him. I was twenty-three when I tried to get over him. I was twenty-four when I let him go. And I was twenty-five when he died. He died at 27.

I wish I never left him or let him go. I wish I could have let him love me and he would have let me in.

Maybe he would still be alive if we happened. But we only ever were an almost. A crossing line. A rain shower. Not for every day. *Just for almost every.*

Every time I pushed him and told him it´s not enough. I wish I could go back. As he always said you´re never anywhere else but the now. But there won´t ever be a now with him. It´s no now I want to be in. There´s no now without him. But the only now I have left.

And that now breaks me.

As I stood there to say *something* I forgot all the words.

I mean what could I say? What can you say?

So, I decided to say something he would. "He loved to quote." I said, trying to see through my tears. My hand shook, so I spun my ring but it didn´t help.

Maybe it would never again help. And never is quite infinite.

"That´s the way he communicated." I smiled as tears streamed down my face, mirroring the people I looked at. My voice shook as I spoke. "And to honor him, here a quote from Albert Einstein." I paused trying to find the strength to speak.

"Energy cannot be created or destroyed; it can only be changed from one to another." I said as strongly as I could manage.

"So, he isn´t gone, he just changed." I said, trying to swallow the thing I could never get down. *Kai´s Death.*

2

Dead – 228k

The first year after Kai´s death I wanted to commit suicide at the age of 25.

I found a script. *Of his second book.*

The declaration read.

"My voice ever since you walked away and never came back since."

He wrote two books to prove his love for me. *And what did I?*

I let someone else love me. *I didn´t read it.*

That day I tried to commit suicide. *But couldn´t. It didn´t work.*

It was the first time I entered his room after his death, and I had a panic attack after finding it. *Everything was too much. Even breathing. Even my heart beating.*

I had his flip knife. *I freaked out. Like hysterical. I blacked out.*

Finn had to carry me out of the room. He called an ambulance.

They had to seduce me.

After that we left his room untouched for almost a year.

My anxiety was bad before he died. After it got out of hand.

Before I wasn´t scared of death. Now I might have even looked forward to it. Because when the world changes you have to change with it.

But how was I supposed to change in a world where he wasn´t no longer in?

"Someday something will break you so badly that you´ll become unbreakable." At least that´s a saying. But I think that´s right. Your psyche will do *anything* to never feel that way again. Even if it means never feeling *anything* again.

Sometimes you focus on one emotion. Because that´s better than to feel nothing at all.

But I´ve chosen numbness.

3

Colson Herzog

I broke up with Wren.

Moreover, I ghosted him after he died. *Cruel. Awful. Heartless.*

But I couldn´t face him. Not after he died. *After he carried his coffin.*

He had so much respect for him. *Our past. Our friendship. Their story.*

But somehow everyone knew I was Kai´s. *Wren knew. Our friends knew.*

Maybe Kai and I were the only ones who didn´t. And I´ll have to live with that. That he died without knowing I was all along his.

...

Somewhen in the past

"I´m sorry." I said as I sat down next to Wren. "Don´t apologize." He said.

"It´s just.." I tried to explain, but he cut me off. "The man you *love* died." He said as if it would have erased the fact that I left him without telling him. And the way he said love instead of *loved* made me shatter into a million pieces Those I would never find again.

And never did since.

"I love you and I´ve never doubted my feelings for you." I told him. "I know." He responded. "Neither did I." He added. "But you also didn´t second guess your love for *him*." He said, and I had to nod because it was true.

"I´ve told you once. And I´ll tell you over and over if I have to." He locked eyes with me. "I´ve known you two. I knew what I´ve let myself in. I´ve known your love towards one another and I´ve known you missed him. That you loved me *and* him." He said. "*Love.*" I corrected him and he nodded. "Love." He agreed.

"I know, and I knew all along he´s your man." He said what I already knew.

We talked a lot about it all. He knew every feeling I had towards Kai. Because we had no secrets. But there was never a time when I wanted to leave him for Kai. Even if I did miss him and loved him. I stayed with Wren because I wanted him. And even after Kai gave me his book, I still chose Wren. And one year later Kai died and changed everything.

But Wren knew all along that he was *my another love*, but he loved me anyway.

"It´s okay. Lia." He assured me before he hugged me tight, and I cried as he held me. He knew I chose Kai even if he was dead now.

Because a year ago Wren had the Ace of hearts. But death changed the cards.

Kai´s death changed us all.

Wren realized I was never his. *Not fully. Not like was already Kai´s.*

I broke the man who healed me. But maybe you can love just one person for real in a lifetime. And all the others are just a bit of a love. But not *that* love.

I felt like in one of those movies, where the main character realized she loved the other guy. *But she realized too late.* Because her another love was already dead.

4

I couldn´t be alone anymore.

Finn saved me a lot. We saved each other. *A lot.*

One time he had to get me in the grocery store because I broke down thinking I saw him in someone else´s face. And I had to accompany him during his meetings when he started working again. Because he needed me to be there to function.

Finn has always been busy. Always more working than partying. And he was always so passionate about it. But now he´s just working. *A robot. A shell.*

We calmed each other or lost our minds together. Maybe he wanted to make sure I won´t try again. Or he really cared and needed me.

We broke down. We got back up. *All together.*

He was the last thing I had left of the boy I loved too much and not enough.

When we saw each other it´s been a bit triggering because when I looked at him, I saw Kai. And when he looked at me, he saw him.

- 27 -

The day the call came, and I knew what happened. I was instantly back years ago at that party when I first saw him. *Thinking I would never see him again.*

And I couldn´t remember what he said to me the last time I spoke to him. We haven´t spoken much since he gave me his book. Maybe twice a month but it wasn´t enough.

Never enough.

One fucking year we lost and then he died.

And I tried to remember everything. About what we spoke the last time we talked.

I didn´t know. I didn´t.

But I remembered what he first said to me at that party. *"Spirit."* He said as he saw me with his dog, he told me his name. He didn´t say that the other was named *Chakra.*

No, he told me *Spirit.*

And now he´s a spirit. *A ghost. Gone.*

And I´m wondering what the spirit of life is.

What´s the meaning? Suffering? Attachment?

~~Accepting. Letting go.~~ *I´ll never let him go.*

5

27 – Machine Gun Kelly

The second year after Kai died, I searched help at the age of 26 and went to therapy.

I sent him messages. I talked to his mailbox and sent him audios.

I got to his grave. *Daily.*

Every time it rained. *And every time it didn´t.*

I got 27 tattooed. On the inside of my right ring finger. Where his ring should have been. Next to the ring of his, that I wear on my pinky. And whenever I´m anxious or sad, I rub the skin with my thumb. *Reminding me how short the now is.*

I wanted to grow old with him, now he never would.

- 27 -

I went to his room, and it smelled like him.

How long his scent will last? How can he be dead if it still smells like him?

He can´t be gone. *I smelled him.*

But someday his scent was gone and only his clothes smelled like him. But it was the scent of the washing powder. *But his scent.*

The scent of his body I would never smell again. *Never him.*

I could smell on his perfume, deodorant, or shampoo. *But it wasn´t him.*

There was something missing. *Him.*

I´ve been before in his room without him. *Missing him. Crying.*

But now he´s gone for good. He´ll never come through his door. *Never.*

He will never sit on the concrete wall or lay on the rooftop with me again. He´ll never read his books. Never put on his hoodies or the shirts with those quotes. Never lay in the white sheets. *He´ll never be here again.*

He´ll never talk to me. *I´ll never feel him.*

I´ll never look into his black eyes again. *Kiss him. Hug him. Fight him. Never.*

He´ll never write in those books. He´ll never finish his script. Our story will never have an end. Our story won´t continue to write itself. *Which is an end.*

But I haven´t read it nor touched it yet not even his first book. I let it how it was. On his bookshelf. *Two copies. One for him, one for me.*

And in most cases people leave their room as they left it. And I too never touched his books once. I never opened his closet. I never laid between the sheets. I just sat or stood there. *Dying from the inside out.*

His room became a museum. No one dared to touch. *Too precious. Too Kai to touch.*

We wanted to preserve a piece of him. A piece of his soul. *Him.*

I didn´t even had a last voice mail. I didn´t have an audio to listen to cause he preferred to text or call. But I watched the videos we made. *The pictures we took.*

I held onto those things because they were all I had left.

And the way he was haunted by quotes I was haunted by his words. My mind kept throwing them at me. *Throwing me back.*

Breaking me again. Choking on tears that I couldn´t spill anymore.

Feeling grief is a way of loving without being able to head home.

Because the receiver is gone.

But I´ve came in touch with the others again. And this time I stayed. *We all did.*

Even Wren and his folks. The pirates and the lost boys made peace. They walked side by side because they all lost the one thing, they all had in common. *Him.*

Because the truth was without Peter, there was no war to fight. But you shouldn´t confuse defeat with peace.

6

The car crash. They said he was dead instantly.

But don´t they say that to all of the relatives to soothe them?

Did he hurt? Is he suffering?

Was he scared? Did he see it coming? Was it fast? Was it slow?

Is it lonely? Is he alone now? Is he really gone?

Does it rain there? Are there others? Is it quiet? Is it loud?

Is his mom there? Is he happy? Is he sad? Angry? Lonely?

Can he see us? Hear us? Feel us? Remember us?

Is it bright? Is it dark? Does he know he´s gone?

And how do you survive loss? Is loss worse than dying?

I´ve never had a loss in my closer family. And now the only family I ever wanted, died. But I was too afraid to live. Kai always tried to show me how to be in the now. He never told me his secret. *How he did it. How he stayed.*

After he died, I kept struggling with not getting lost in the past.

He didn´t gave me a future. He even refused to give me a tomorrow. But he gave me his now´s. *But I refused to live them.*

I wasted my now´s for a future without him. *I wasted my life. I wasted love.*

He took my fear of losing control because I lost it, and I survived. But then he gave me a new one. The fear of not being able to let go of him. And I knew for sure I would never. Because when he left me years ago, I always thought at least we´re under the same stars. But now that he´s dead I don´t even have that.

Because who knows where he is now? Now that he died.

And when horrible things like that happen, you start to look at things differently. And I realized that we were toxic and maybe weren´t good for each other. That´s why I left him in the first place.

But him being gone for good made everything seem different. Because you start wondering if things could have been different. *And they could have.*

But that´s been taken away from you. And that´s why you start to hold onto the good things. Because memories are all you have left. So, you hold on in order not to fall.

In order not to forget.

So, we all stuck together, and his death brought us back together. Which is beautiful and sad. But we appreciated life and our friendship even more.

Death makes you realize things the hard way. And his taught us many things.

Now I just sat on my couch with a good book and lost in worlds I never wanted to leave.

Was it weird that the love I got in books was enough?

They wouldn´t hurt me. *Not the way his death did.*

But I couldn’t hide from my friends. And our paths parted here and there over the years, but we *always* found our way back. *Or I did.*

Because Aidan was right, I left them. *They tried, I didn´t.*

But that had changed and in an awful way, it felt like his death had a higher meaning. Like we all learned a lesson from it. To live and to appreciate each other.

There was that one time when it came close to *something* happening between me and Aidan. We had a very weak moment. *But we couldn´t.*

Because the last time we had sex was with Kai. We even kissed the last time as he was with us, and we wanted to keep it that way. Because that summer was just the three of us and no one could take that away.

Sometimes I look at that Polaroid, which is now in my phone case.

Always with me. Flipped over like he did.

Because after his death I got his phone since he left it at home that day.

But that wasn´t unusual.

So, I took the Polaroid and now I have two of them. *Always with me.*

7

One time we had a talk about what happened over the past years or rather I apologized to all of them.

"I´m sorry I fucked with our friend group." I said. "*Literally.*" Leon joked. "Rude." I laughed. *But he had a point.*

"I´m sorry." I said. "For what?" She asked. "For not telling you." I said. "What was between me and Kai." I added. "Already forgotten." She assured me.

"I´m sorry too, Luca." I looked at her. "I haven´t told you either." I added. "I knew." She said and I frowned. "Don´t look at me like that." She smacked me. "I know you. *Of course*, I knew." She laughed.

"I think somehow, we all knew." She looked in the void. "You two were just.. *different.*" She said absently and the others nodded.

"Don´t get I an apology?" Ryan asked. "For what?" I wanted to know. "For.. that *I´m* the only one you never tried to hit on." He stated but I knew he was joking. "I haven´t hit on *everyone*." I said upset. "You *did*." Leon commented and I give him a look, but he smiled at me.

"Yeah, okay, maybe I did." I said giving in. "Sorry for not *trying* to get laid by you." I said to Ryan, and he grinned. And without thinking I continued. "As if I were ever your type anyways." *They all looked at me.*

Luca and Finn confused. But Ryan *knew* what I meant. And I caught him off guard there for a sec. He´s been madly in love with Nina since forever. He never hit on her besides the fucking. But he always waited for them to break up.

That day just never came.

Leon shot me a look. I promised to never tell which I didn´t. But one day Ryan told me on his own, so I knew. But the only one clueless was Nina. *To this day.*

I think even Andi and Aidan had to know.

"Don´t know what you´re talking about." Ryan laughed.

I gave him a *sorry, but you deserved it* look.

"You didn´t just *out* him, did you?" Luca hissed. "No." Ryan and I said at the same time. "Would have told you that." He assured her. "Then what´s your type?" Nina asked casually, but Leon looked mad and Ryan uncomfortable. I didn´t know how much time they have spent together the past years. So, I had no idea *how* recent those wounds were.

But I guessed they still bleed.

“Have none.” He brushed her off and she looked at him for a millisecond too long for me to know she felt the same way about him.

Then why did she stick to Leon all those years?

Because she loved Ryan too.

And he watched her going back to Leon every single time. He always watched her from distance. He never acted on his feelings.

Right? Or did anything beyond that happen? Something no one knew. Just the two of them. Did she consider leaving Leon?

“Okay. We all forgive you for being a shit friend.” Leon stated ending that conversation. And maybe after all I wasn´t the only one who *almost* fucked up our friend group. Because love does that shit. *Fuck´s everything up.*

But our friend group was kinda fucked. *Even before me.*

Ryan loved Nina. He´s been single since I met him. Nina secretly loved Ryan but stayed with Leon. And Leon loved Nina but couldn´t stop flirting and hooking up with others since he couldn´t commit.

Aidan was the one who had the most sex. Never in relationships and always flirty and in someone´s pants.

Finn had no one he wanted. Because mostly he had no time working towards his goals which were basketball and the company. Luca adored Finn but gave up on him and got into several relationships until she ended up with Andi. And Andi was the one always in relationships, but secretly liking Luca. They got together and broke up again. After Kai´s death, they tried it again and stayed.

Kai was the loner, breaking hearts. *Including myself.*

He barely fucked. Always closed up. *But he let me in.*

And he fucked me with his best friend. Until we didn´t work anymore. And he had to let me go. And I had made out with Andi, tried to get back with my ex and then fucked my best friend, loved Kai all along and moved on to Wren.

So, I´m the one who´s fucked up. *But in ways we all were.*

8

One day I asked Aidan something I wanted to ask a long time ago.

“What´s about that nickname anyways?” I asked. “What? *Scar*?” He asked. I nodded. “Thought you never asked.” He smirked.

“We all have em.” He said. “Come on *you* don´t have such a nickname.” I said annoyed. “None you know of.” He teased with a big ass smile.

"Tell me." I demanded. He nodded. "We all had some. *Scars.*" He said. "But you were one, no one of us could forget." He told me. "It´s what we all knew. You were *our* scar." He said and I frowned at him. "One that you have left on us. One that made ours complete." He told me, but I didn´t understood. "That´s why we called you that." He said. *I didn´t get it.* "Why Kai called you that." He added, and my head snapped at him.

What? He nods.

"*He* came up with that name." He shrugged. *He did?* I blinked trying to remember, but I´m sure Kai wasn´t the first one to call me that. They just started at some point, and then they all called me that way. It made sense that name was something Kai would have come up with. But they stopped calling me Scar after his death.

Not immediately but eventually they all stopped.

"That´s why you´ve stopped calling me that." I whispered in pain. He nodded. "We didn´t know why at first and he wouldn´t tell us, so we just adopted it." He said. "But later on, we understood." He smiled. "He told me." He looked at me. "He said that you were his deepest scar. He knew that the moment he saw you." He chuckled because it was pretty cheesy for Kai to say something like that.

"That you´ve cut him before ever touching him. You´ve cut in deep, and it was all he needed. A scar deep enough to care to heal instead of ripping." He said, and my smile fell. My eyes filled with tears.

"He tried to heal for the only scar on his body he cared about." He said, and I sobbed.

"That nickname was about you." He looked at me with a similar shine in his eyes.

But he died before he could heal the only scar, he wanted. *Mine.*

He left his mark on me too. The one I couldn´t cover nor forget.

I was his greatest scar, and his death made him mine.

9

It´s been the firsts that scared me. *Because they were without him.*

On his and my birthday, I went to Paris. Finn came with me, and we stayed at their apartment. The other year I just sat on his grave. *Reading to him.*

It was more crying because, I´ll never hear him reading to me again. Then I was in Bali. The next I was in Italy drowning in thunderstorms and rain. I wanted to feel close to him. But it was never close enough. People would say he would have wanted me to move on.

To stop being a zombie and live. *But I couldn´t.*

And no one knew what he wanted. *No one. Not even me.*

The first year I did something very stupid. I headed off in his car. I went to the tunnel we raced through so many times before. We did it every time one of us had to run from something. When we needed to feel alive. When we needed that thrill.

The death around the corner.

I turned on our two songs and raced off. I started crying at some point, so I had to slow down. I couldn´t feel the same without him. I couldn´t escape life without him.

With him gone.

I couldn´t escape, I was trapped. Trapped in this life I didn´t want to live without him. I couldn´t bear to drive back so I made a detour. I haven´t gone back there since years after that. I did it with Finn and I didn´t cry, but with a pain in my body that wished to release some of it. I wished for every fairy, every shooting star, every angel to bring him back. To let me do this just one more time with him.

Sometimes I wish I had never met him. *He wouldn´t be dead now.*

He got pieces of me. *In me.* Pieces I never planned on sharing or losing.

But then I met him. And we got lost in one another. *Tied to each other.*

Lost some of ourselves in the other. *Lost pieces. And he took them.*

I had no chance. And I took some of his too. But we haven´t got the chance to take them back. So, I carry around pieces of a dead one. Pieces that hold me together. That safe me from falling apart. Pieces that hurt me on a daily basis. Pieces that heal me in the same way they cut me.

10

Lonely – Machine Gun Kelly

The third year after his death, I was stoned constantly at the age of 27.

Kai was an addict. He would numb himself into oblivion. And I was an addict of him and love. *But I lost my drug the day he died.*

He couldn´t live without pain and I couldn´t live without anxiety.

He always said he loved pain. *Now I get it.*

The pain made him feel alive. *Anxiety makes you feel dead.*

Not the pain is your death to your life. *Fear is.*

But fear is the side effect of life. And I stopped living. Stopped risking and growing. He lived with pain, but he lived. *He risked. He grew.* I didn´t.

- 27 -

I can´t remember *anything* from the day the call came. *I suppressed it.*

But *some* things came back to me. I remembered the last thing he said to me. What one of our last conversations was. It wasn´t *the* last one of course but it was the last one where it was just about us. It was right after he gave me the book. When I went to him, and he asked me to stay. He asked me to stay and I didn´t. But if I hadn´t been such a coward, I would have stayed. *Because the truth was, I was never not his.*

He wasn´t the only one to leave all the time. *I was even worse.*

Because I never came back. He left me twice. He came back twice. I left him once.

And I never came back.

He let me be happy and love another. He let me go when I couldn´t hold on.

Everyone has their one-time love. And either they live it or miss it. My once in a lifetime wasn´t my ex. *It was Kai.*

The one I couldn´t let myself love. The great love that I crossed paths with often but still missed. *Once in a lifetime.*

Looking back, I realized I had butterflies. But they died every time we kissed. And I thought it was a bad thing. *But now I know it wasn´t.*

They died because with him my anxiety died, and I felt safe.

Butterflies are another form of anxiety. If you feel them, it´s the wrong person.

If you feel them die, it´s the right.

At least that´s what I´ve been telling myself to stay sane.

Dying butterflies were a sign of love.

But I couldn´t listen to the cries of the dying ones. *But I saw when he died.*

When I was left behind with dead butterflies and body that was a graveyard of our love.

Dead butterflies.

11

His father moved back in the day he died.

That´s when his death was real to me. *When I saw his father.*

Saw him break. Saw his regret. Saw the guilt. And saw him lose his son. Saw the love he had for him but refused to show him all his life. It was there now. *And I saw.*

I wished he showed him.

And after Kai died, their relationship broke too. Finn was mad at him for I don´t know what exactly. *Probably everything.*

Because now he seemed to regret all the things. But I did that too, so I guess I wasn´t better than his father. I refused to give my love at some point. But his father *never* showed him.

\- 27 -

First, we wanted to scatter his ashes on a rainy day on Bali. *But we didn´t.*

Somehow, we were selfish and wanted him in a place. A place we could come to. To hold onto the energy that´s left of him. Because if we had dispersed him, he would be gone.

Everywhere and nowhere.

But we needed him *somewhere.*

We did keep a little for Bali though. *He would have wanted that.*

That the Darks are pretty rich, I knew. But how much showed me when he had a special place for his grave. *Alone.*

Where no one else laid. He had a whole garden just for his grave. Because if you have enough money, *anything* is possible. *Even a private cemetery.*

A garden with trees, plants, and flowers. A place to grieve, cut off from the rest of the cemetery. *Separate entrance. Separate everything.*

The cemetery was in the next town. Near the place where I read with him. It lies high above the roofs of the city. On a hill below the castle. *Between woods.*

It was a cemetery for rich people. Every tombstone looked expensive and important. Between the trees, you could look down on the city. His grave was close to the railing on the slope. *But more to the forest.*

In the clearing, a stone floor graced the path to his grave and all the way over to the viewing area. There was that cement bench in front of the view. His grave had the highest point of the cemetery. There were stairs to that part and a gate. *It was quiet.*

You heard the birds. There was a small fountain. And an old gazebo. White roses adorned the structure. Across from that, the stature of an angel.

I liked it there and it felt like him. I think he would have liked it.

Every season was different. I liked it the most when it rained. *It was beautiful.*

It didn´t smell like death or graveyard. It smelled like the woods and fresh roses.

White ones. It was peaceful.

When it rained, I found shelter in that open gazebo. Staring at his headstone, I sat there often. Gazing at the city in the distance between the trees. It looked too precious than ashes to lay in this place. *It felt like life. But there wasn´t. Was there?*

His father bought him that place. *A piece of peace.*

He regretted a lot, and I still despised him. But I get along with him better than Finn now. He gave us a place we could feel close to him.

Where his black headstone was. Surrounded by white roses.

12

I stopped and got clean. I still smoked, but not on a daily.

But I started to write. The book from my perspective. I wrote everything I wanted to tell him but now could never. But I went to his grave and read to him. *Our story.*

And the day he died. *It rained. Like fate.* Like rain was his friend. *Or enemy.*

He came off track. His car was crashed. But he didn´t drove with his that day. He took his brothers car. No one really knows why. His BMW is still in the garage.

Where he left it.

Finn´s now gone with him. I drive Kai´s now. Finn said he would love me to have it.

Another piece of him.

I always thought that unrequited love was the worst, but I was wrong.

Death is worse.

Because I always had hope somewhere deep down that, when the time was right, we would find each other again. *Death took that away.*

But death doesn´t take away the love. It grows even after death. What it takes is the chance. It takes the chance to express it.

The definition of pain is someone you love dying.

And there were times I wondered if he committed suicide. Because he was a good driver. A safe driver. He wouldn´t have gotten off the road. He wouldn´t speed when it was pouring. The streets were floated. *But accidents happen.*

Maybe he was distracted. Maybe it was just a second. Maybe a deer ran over the streets. Maybe he had been scared and took off.

But he wouldn´t dodge. *You´ll have to go straight at it.*

A split second and you die. *Maybe he wanted to go straight.*

When he showed me his journal entries years ago I´ve read about him thinking of suicide.

But would he, do it? Did he, do it?

Is that why he took his brothers car and not his? Because he wanted us to have his?

Why did he leave his phone or his ring?

What do you think when you realize you die? Did he live it? His death?

Or did he blink and miss it?

The possibility of suicide was even worse than just his death.

I couldn´t let me think that.

And since he was a writer. I would assume he would have left us a message.

A letter. A something. A poetry. A sentence.

But there was nothing. *And if he decided at the moment? In the now?*

- 27 -

I saw it. *The book.*

The book he wrote me. Between his books as if it belonged there. *The two copies.*

His and the one I left when I left him. *Left them all.*

I wondered if Aidan had ever read it or Finn. *But I didn´t ask. It didn´t matter.*

I took his copy. *He annotated it. Wrote in it.*

I cried a lot reading it. It was even better with his scribble in it. It was something completely new. I haven´t read it since that day he gave it to me.

So, it hit me more over.

Then I took my copy. *I annotated it. Wrote in it. Drew in it.*

One day I looked up the script of his second book. And it broke me in ways I thought I was already broken.

Then I looked up his computer for a copy.

Maybe he wrote more and didn´t print it. *But nothing.*

Then I looked at his phone. *And found it.* He still had the same pin code.

03. of August.

The last time he opened the document was two days before he died. *I cried.*

He saved it at three in the morning. He still struggled with insomnia.

I cried some more.

I couldn´t open it though. Because then there wouldn´t stand the date and the time he laid hands on it for the last time. So, instead I sent it to me.

So, I could open it on my phone.

And leave his untouched. Leave that day untouched.

I scrolled down to the last thing he might have written before he died. Scared to find signs that he *did*, commit suicide.

…

She had the stars in her eyes. And her eyes in the stars. And I had my eyes on the deepest scar my body has ever seen.

All art is good cause you bleed. I bled on paper she bled on colors. But sometimes we still bleed on each other.

The reason I write poetry is because I'm looking for a way to tell her I love her. The reason she reads novels is to find love. Are we just two idiots? Or too blind to see?

She loved me when I tasted like pain. I almost killed her, and she almost killed me.

When I looked at her, I felt like I could start crying. Like I could smile forever. It felt like coming home and going on an adventure. It was love and hate. Calm and the storm. It started to spin and stand still. My heartbeat faster and slower. I couldn't breathe and I breathed. It felt like finally but like it's over. All and nothing. Hide and seek. Familiar and foreign. Ripping apart and piecing back together. Fearing and feeling safe. It was what I felt when I looked at her. But I was a fool and didn't say it. Not once. Not ever. Never.

After all this time it's still her. But we were only a moment. At least for her. For me, she was my lifetime. My now's. For her we were only ever almost.

She wasn't what I needed she was what I dreamed of. She was what I tried to deserve.

I tried to be her friend. To be the man she needs. I have thought about telling her I have changed. That I'm ready. But I promised to leave her alone. Although, I never stopped thinking about the what if's.

I never stopped writing hoping she would hear. I never stopped using my poems hoping she would hear.

I tried to be good. It just wasn't her good. The good for her was in someone else. They were destined to meet. We were too. We just weren't destined to be.

Like all the devils he did fall. He loved to fall, but he never knew it would be without her. But there was no fall that wasn't about her.

She didn't say goodbye. A part of me believed that was a sign she would come back. And she did. But the day I gave her my book she said goodbye, so I knew it was over.

There was never a time where I didn't want her. And there will never be a time I won't need her. But I'll try to become what she wants. Maybe someday.

I wrote her a book and it wasn't enough. Maybe she wasn't enough for me.

…

It was a bit rough and jumble. It was confusing and a mess. It wasn't in order and I think there were some old ones in it too. But that's how he writes cause it's the way he thinks.

The way he feels.

But there were no signs of suicide. Just proof that he was broken. *That I broke him.*

Nothing new. But something hurtful.

I read the whole script in one sitting. It was as good as the first one maybe even better. Even if it wasn´t finished or sorted. He wrote about the way back to me. It was his journey until we got back together. *But we didn´t. He died.*

When he gave me the book, it should have saved us. He probably intended that in the first place. *But it didn´t. Because of me.* Because I wouldn´t let it. *Let him.*

I´m the one to blame. He wrote me an entire fucking book and I gave him nothing. I left like it didn´t mean anything, but it meant everything. *That´s why I left.*

But he didn´t know that did he?

Maybe he wrote it because our story was worth writing. *He sensed a great story.*

No one want´s to read a boring book.

Why does the story end when the angry guy gets the sad girl?

Why doesn´t it start there?

It was the journey after I left him. It wasn´t the journey of him getting back to me. Maybe he didn´t want me back. Maybe he wanted feed for his book. Maybe he knew all along we wouldn´t end up. Maybe it was a way to set him free. Maybe he wanted to hurt me by writing it. And maybe I´m wrong all along. Because he didn´t want to publish it.

That´s what he said.

Maybe I´ll never know.

But thanks to his books I could reread our story.

But I wouldn´t ever be able to live it.

I decided to print the book. It already had two hundred and fifty-eight pages. And I decided to write my own. I didn´t publish his but mine. He never wanted the world to hear his words. He only ever wanted me to hear em. And I heart but too late. But he was right, maybe I was not enough for him. But sometimes I think I wasn´t even for myself.

13

I went unconscious after he died. Cause reality was too real.

I went down a spiral. *Until I woke up again.*

He didn´t kiss me awake. But his voice did. *Woke me.*

After years, I had another awakening. All because of this book. After I read his script, I noticed he often quoted *The Picture of Dorian Gray* from Oscar Wilde.

So, I got curious.

I wanted to read it. He carried that book with him like his phone. His own holy grail, his diary and like his mind. *His soul.*

He carried it around and I never looked. *I never read it.*

He never read that to me either. *I wish he did.*

The pages were underlined with bullpen. *Pages written. Dog-eared.*

Every single one.

I could count the pages he left untouched on two hands. He had tons of editions. And every single one annotated differently. *I read them all.*

Over the years I read *all* his books. *His whole shelf.*

I read the things he wrote in it. But I knew this was his favorite. But I didn´t read it once. He didn´t ask me to, but he on the other hand had read every single book I´ve read.

Did he love me more than I loved him? Or did he just care more about me than I for him? Did he pay more attention to the details about me than I did? Did he just love reading books more than I did? Would it have made any difference if I read it sooner? Would I have seen us between the annotated pages? Would I have loved the book as I did now?

And now that I have read it. I questioned the way he acted. Because if he read it. If it was *indeed* his favorite. If he internalized all of it.

Why did he act the way he did? Why did he let his fears control him? Why didn´t he had the courage to love me? For the same reasons you didn´t.

I clung to the lines of the book as if his soul were in it. *And I think it really was.*

I read his edition meticulously.

Trying to analyze by the way he underlined what he was thinking or feeling. All the things he wrote in there became my daily prayer. I studied them as if they were my dissertation. *All the crosses.*

Question marks and comments. Any ink on the pages. Every ripple in the paper. Every trace he left behind. Every bold underlined line. Every wiggle or piece of him I could find.

Every trace of his soul.

I had the feeling to find him between the lines. To smell him on the pages.

The weed. The sunscreen. The rain.

After reading the book I saw everything different. *I just saw it too late.*

Maybe I went a bit crazy.

And in ways I definitely did. But when crazy meant having him. *I wanted it.*

I realized he quoted more than I have thought. I recognized all the lines he once said to me. He spoke to me through books. *Through that book.*

Through all his books. And I made the mistake and didn´t read them. And didn´t hear the different ways he tried to make me listen. To read between the lines.

It was a new way to cope. I felt close to him again. Like as if I had strengthened the energetic connection by reading his words. It was stupid to think, but it made me feel less pained. *Less lost. Less empty.*

He loved me in ways I didn´t listen to. That´s what I regret the most. Not listening when he was screaming.

- 27 -

I went to all the places he´s been without me. *All the stones he collected.*

I went through all of them. I even went back to Bali to see the places he wanted to show me, because we didn´t. *He couldn´t.*

The bungalow we were back then I found out he bought it. And there were *rows* of stones. And he wrote on them too. So, I went to all the places I could make out. And I kept collecting stones too. All the stones I bring to his headstone. The earth on his grave isn´t covered in flowers. *It´s covered in stones.*

Sometimes I even left books. *As I said I went a bit crazy.*

But it helped so I did what I had to.

And the only flowers I brought him were white roses.

Because they smell like spring.

14

The fourth year after Kai´s death I fell in love with his brother at the age of 28.

But that´s not true. *I fell years before.*

Wren was right at the time, but then the story got passed on to someone else. Someone followed the wrong string. Or I made the wrong decisions. But however, the time ran out the day Kai died. *They all knew.*

I loved many boys. All for different reasons. *But it all felt different.*

You can love your ex. You can love someone you knew in kindergarten and never saw again. Your best friend. A one-night stand. Someone fictional. *An artist.* You can love an almost. *Toxic.* You can even love something that never happened. And you can love someone who is dead. You can love a memory. *A dream. A wish. A someday.*

Even a never.

You can love all of them and still don´t be with them. Because love sometimes is just there. There is no reason. *No start. No end.* It´s just there. *The love.*

Just as it was with the love for his brother. *Just there. Just love.* I loved Finn before I loved him. *Before I fell for him.* I loved him as a friend. *As Kai´s brother.*

As someone who was there when the boy, I loved left me. I loved him as a person. As someone who helped me get over losing the boy I love. We loved each other for more than just the loss. It was beyond friendship.

Beyond love. Beyond romantic. Beyond Sex.

Beyond everything. *Just beyond.*

We felt there was *something* creeping in on us. *The tension.*

It felt wrong in many ways. *But not in all.*

At the time years ago, when Kai thought his brother screwed me and not Aidan it didn´t end well. *What would he think now?*

So, we kept fighting what had happened. Denying and blaming it on the mourning process. But it was like everything exploded. As our lips collided. A brief and bright illumination. A massive star that is at the end of its lifetime. *Dying by explosion.*

In which the star itself is destroyed. The luminosity of the star increases billions of times, it becomes as bright as a whole fucking galaxy for a short amount of time. And that´s what it felt like. Nothing like a mistake or something wrong.

It felt like a supernova.

I cried as we kissed. *He did too.* He carried me to his bed. *He fucked me.*

And I wanted it so bad. *And so did he.* We grieved but betrayed. *But we loved.*

Like a supernova.

…

I found – Amber Run

Finn sat in front of his grave after the funeral. Arms on his knees. *Shaking.*

I got on my knees in seconds holding him and Aidan sat beside me clinging to me. Leon squatted down to the other side of Finn and grabbed his neck steadying him.

Nina, Andi, Ryan, Luca, and Wren came behind us onto the ground. We cried and held each other. *On the outside.* But on the inside, we fell apart. *We all did.*

I leaned against Finn and Aidan against me. My head laid on Finn´s shoulder and Aidan held my head.

Wren was the first to go.

Followed by Andi and Ryan who took Nina and Luca with him.

A while it was just the four of us. Until Leon took Aidan, and they left too.

Finn´s face was pale. His dark eyes are surrounded by red. Which reminded me of Kai, and it killed me. Tears spilled and dried just to run again. His lip trembled and I grabbed his head holding him to me. *He held onto me.*

I kissed his temple but then stood up. His gaze followed in panic.

He looked so pained.

So not himself.

He always had his shit together. I have never seen him like that before.

Of course, he died a few days ago.

And now he was a broken man. He lost his little brother.

And I lost the love of my life.

My best friend. My something. My everything.

But he reached for my hand. "Don´t go." He choked. I wanted to give him space and time alone, but he *wanted* me to stay, so I let myself down hugging him.

We sat there for hours. *All day long.* Trying to survive time. *The now.*

Kai being gone.

- 27 -

After we got up, he took my hand holding his last string to this world.

He drove home after I offered him to drive four times.

But he wanted to drive his BMW.

It was already dark outside. The others sat in the living room. Nina slept in the arms of Leon. *Next to them Ryan.*

Aidan and the others were tangled in each other. *Wren wasn´t there.*

Finn got upstairs first but I watched them sleep for a moment and stroked Aidan´s hair. I looked at their faces. *It did hurt.* All hurt. *Will it ever be different?*

But what did hurt the most was what came next. It hurt, as I went upstairs and looked at the door I went through many times before. *But wouldn´t anymore.*

Kai´s door. The door that´s always been ajar. *Now closed.* As he left it.

The day he died.

My heart always knocked at his door. *Until he wasn´t behind anymore.*

And I looked at it in a pain I couldn´t even name. But I didn´t go through. Instead, I walked down the hall and knocked at his brother´s door. *He didn´t say anything.*

But this door was ajar, so I went inside and closed it behind me. He stood with his back to me, and I walked up to him. I put my hands on his back. Then on his shoulders and laid my head against his body. He tensed for a second before he relaxed into it. After a moment I walked around him. Seeing his face mirroring mine. *Utterly pained.*

Branded with tears. *But also need.*

His chest rose and fell as if he wasn´t dead inside. He looked down on me and I reached for his face. *Tears spilled.*

He rested his forehead onto mine. His hands at my sides. Mine on his chest. I felt him harden on my stomach. And his hot breath on my face.

What came next should have hurt more than anything. But the truth is it didn´t. Not the way it should have. Not the way it could have stopped us.

Instead, it hurt the way it kept us going. Guilt ate us alive and had driven us. But we craved it more than anything. It felt too good to be wrong. *Too great to stop.*

That was how we coped. Falling for each other instead of out of world.

His lips crashed on mine, and we cried into each other´s mouths. A low grunt escaped him. *Moaning in relief. Choking and sobbing.*

We kissed because it was what we wanted at that moment. Because life fucks you anyways. Because life is nothing like in the books. Because life is cruel, and life is too fucking short to resist.

Because we craved each other like our own penalty. *Own death. Own rebirth.*

It didn´t feel as cruel as it should have. It wasn´t as evil as *fucking* his little brother´s girl should have felt like. Or how fucking the love of your life´s brother should have *fucking* felt like. Because it didn´t feel like we would regret it in the morning. Because we didn´t want it before, but now we *fucking* did. *So, we did it.*

He lowered himself onto one knee and I held onto his shoulders. He took of my heels and slipped out of his shoes. I tugged at his tie, and he turned me around opening my sip. He lifted the black dress over my head and unbuttoned his shirt. *I ripped it.*

He opened his belt and stepped out of his suit pants. He grabbed me and carried me to his bed. He lowered himself onto me. *Kissing me greedy.*

It felt like we took MDMA, LSD, crack, cocaine, heroin, weed, meth, ecstasy, mushrooms and ayahuasca at once. High and not at all low.

"Hold onto me." He pressed as he slipped on a condom. "Do the same." I breathed as he looked down at me and fell into me with one stroke. He buried himself inside of me and I clenched onto him wrapping my legs around him to press him closer. He held with one hand the back of my head and with the other my back.

He filled me up in ways I didn´t know I was empty. He was thick, hard and his length on the edge of what I could take. I was throbbing and damp. *Vibrating even.*

We filled each other with emotions. *Those I´ve never felt.*

And I thought I´ve had them all.

We cried and moaned. I scratched his back, and he kissed my neck. I told him to bite me, and he told me to do the same.

We learned some things that night about each other. *We loved pain.*

We loved scraping each other´s skins until we bleed on each other.

We loved it until we bled.

We were self-destructive. We were the villains. *Broken, horny, lost, and selfish.*

I came under his touch, and he came inside me claiming me with every inch. He marked me in places I would never forget. *Places I would never regret.*

We got under the shower and did there the same. *Harder this time.* We got back in his bed and did it again. *Slower this time.* Next morning, we did it again.

Twice this time.

We couldn´t stop. *We wouldn´t stop.* The only hurtful thing was we didn´t *want* to stop. Maybe it was a trauma bond. *Maybe not.*

But we wanted each other and we didn´t argue. *Didn´t run. We stayed.*

Not once before we wanted each other. Now we couldn´t not, want each other.

Maybe it was a way for us to have a piece of Kai back. It was an awful way.

We knew that.

But he was the last string I had of him, and I was his last too.

So, we knotted them. *Saved them. Saved us.*

We haven´t told the others. *We couldn´t. Not right away.*

Days have passed. Weeks have passed. Months have passed. *Years have passed.*

We still buried inside of each other. We didn´t talk about feelings. We didn´t need to. And with time there were some. *We knew.*

I remember how much we fucked. I remember how he told me to ride his dick on his suit making myself come after his meeting. How he fucked me before his meetings on his desk.

I remember the first time he said he loves me while he took me from behind. How he said how good I felt. How he told me I was his. How he claimed me. How I wanted to be his. How I wanted to be wanted and wanted to be claimed. *Loved.*

How he´s been the one that wanted me. *Fully. No games. No confusion. No hurt.*

Just want. Just love.

Someday the others knew. They probably have thought it was foreseeable at some point.

And it probably was.

That eventually we would fall for each other. *Just not the day after the funeral.*

We´ve spent every day with each other. But they didn´t know we fell for each other years ago. It took us time to admit it. To acknowledge it. *To adapt with it.*

First there was just fucking. *A lot.* But then there was more. We loved each other. In ways, we shouldn´t have. *But we did.*

We found something we never even searched. In a place we would have never even looked. *If he hadn´t die.*

But I think we knew why it happened. Why we didn´t feel guilty.

At least not enough.

Because what Kai´s death taught us was how fragile life is. That the now is important. So, we did what we wanted and not what we should.

We lived. Stayed in the now. We stayed.

And truth is I would have died for my ex. I would have killed for Kai. But I would have lived for Finn. And that´s what I did. *What we did. Live.*

And the only thing I regret was that I didn´t live when Kai was still alive. When I could have lived with him. But back then anxiety was too great to awake. I feared everything. Anxiety paralyzed me and I couldn´t love correctly. I couldn´t let me be loved. I couldn´t let people in. *I couldn´t live. I feared life.*

But the only thing we feared *now* was death. *So, we lived.*

And Finn knew my soul belonged to another. But it was okay and that´s why we did it.

Because we knew.

15

Finn and I had that habit. Every evening - if we managed, but we tried - we danced in the living room. We cut the lights and put on a record.

We dressed up. Sometimes we even had dinner before and pretend to date. On rare nights we danced in complete silence. *No music.*

Mostly when it rained. *We listened.*

Listened the house. *The world. Our breaths. Our hearts.*

He taught me to dance properly, and I really got better. He was as perfect as on my sister´s wedding. If I only knew back then, he´d be the one I´d dance on my own wedding. That it would be him and not his brother.

If I only knew he would die. *If I only knew.*

The night we danced the first time was something over a year after Kai died. He asked me to dance, and I was shy for some reason. *But he made it go away.*

He put on a song. It´s always been that one song. *And we danced.*

Sometimes I felt like I shouldn´t love him like I did.

"I know." He said as I looked at him afraid to love and scared not to.

That´s all he said.

He wasn´t him. *And it was okay.*

"I don´t think he´s mad." He whispered in my hair and a tear rolled. We still hid around the others with whatever was between us. "I miss him." I hushed. "I miss him too." He said in a whisper and kissed my head.

We lost someone we love and that brought us together. We weren´t destined for each other, soulmates, or twin flames. *We were just happening.*

There was no falling in love. *There was just love.* It was there. *Before and after.*

We never fought it. We never had fights. We communicated. We were good for each other. We were functioning because we didn´t need each other. We were whole without each other. We´re growing as individuals. *Walking next to each other.*

"I wish I could make you happy the way he did. I know I can´t." He told me. "But I want you to know that I want to. But it would be cruel to even try. I don´t replace.." He said, but I cut in. "It was my fault because I loved him too much." I said. "You *can´t* love too much. Either you do or you don´t." He said. "Then I love him." I said. "I know you do." He replied.

"You make me happy." I assured him. "And I love you." I said and he kissed me.

Then we cried. Sometimes that happened.

Maybe the tears were our way of guilt. *Our way to bleed.*

And maybe that´s what saved us. *We did let it go. Let it pass. And felt it.*

- 27 -

Finn reminded me a lot of him. I mean they´re brothers. *Obviously, they´re alike.*

But now I saw things I´ve never seen. I always thought they were so different and in ways they were but also not.

Eventually I moved in. But basically, I was already. *Always been.*

Because even years ago I´ve been more at their house than mine.

Finn asked me to marry him. *I wanted his name,* but I said yes. Kai haunted my dreams since. I always dreamed vividly. But the dreams about him were too real.

The first year I thought every morning that it all was just a dream. Because he was still there. *But he wasn´t.*

And he died every day anew with the realization that this is my life.

…

He took his thin silver ring off his pinky and got on his knees.

"Be mine." He said. "What?" I asked. "Marry me." He begged and I got on my knees to level him. "You wanted my name remember?" He asked and I nodded.

"That´s *your* ring." I stated. "I want *you* to have it." He told me. *It fit perfectly.*

"But I´ll buy you a Diamond if you want one." He added and I shook my head. "I want *that* one." I told him. "But we´ll have to get *you* a new one." I said with a smile, and he smiled back and kissed me.

I woke up in tears. *Hysterical screaming.*

Most of the dreams I had about him made me that.

16

The fifth year after Kai died, I got pregnant at the age of 29. A girl and a Boy. *Twins.*

My grandmother had twins and somehow, I always knew I´d have them too. I became a mother on the thirteenth of November. *Scorpios.*

They looked like him. They didn´t look much like me besides, he got my eyes. They both have dark hair. She has his dark eyes. We named him Kaidan which means the fighter just like his uncle. *A fighter.* We named her Rain which means the rainy night which was just how his uncle was. *A rainy night.*

His father, who is called Blake, retired the same year. *Blake Dark.* Blake means black, dark, and pale. *Which is kind of fitting.* And his wife´s name was Ava. *Ava Dark.* Ava means strong and water. I don´t know if that was fitting but I guess it was.

Blake became a great grandfather. I talked a lot with him. And he *really* gave in effort. He was very emotional after he knew we were pregnant. He tried to be there for us. For Finn and me. Finn and Blake did fight though. I got along with him better.

He really tried to deal with what he did to his lost son. He grieved the time he couldn´t have back. He didn´t break because of the death of his wife because he could prepare for that. But what broke him was death the of his son he rejected.

A death no one was prepared for.

I worked on my relationship with my parents too after he died.

He taught me many things. *Death did.* What matters in life.

...

The first trip we took with the twins was to the cemetery.

Finn helped me with the cribs. He placed them beside me and left me. He sat on the stairs to the gazebo and watched me.

I took Kaidan out. “This is Kaiden.” My vison blurred. “Say hi to your uncle Kai.” I sobbed and held him close to my chest adjusting his hat. “He looks so much like you.” I said into the cold air. “But he has my grey-greenish eyes.” I smiled and gently tugged him back in his crib.

Tears spilled as I got her out. “And this is Rain.” I said with a chuckle. “You can´t see now because her eyes are closed but she has the eyes of yours.” I laughed and choked on it while crying. “Isn´t she gorgeous?” I asked.

He didn´t answer. Of course, he couldn´t.

“I miss you so much.” I sobbed. “I wish you could see them.” I tried to breathe.

“Finn is great as a father.” I told him. “You should see him.” I smiled and laid her back down and watched them. “I hope I don´t traumatize them.” I laughed insecurely. “With my constant crying.” I clarified. “Or I don´t know me in general.” I said upset. “I´m just scared.” I admitted. “They´re so fragile. So pure. So beautiful. So tiny.” I whispered. *Silence.*

“I always thought it would be you. You know?” I asked. “I imagined us with two boys.” I gazed into the void and blinked. “I love them so much. I´m scared to become a bad mother. To lose them.” I cried.

“You *have* to watch over them.” I demanded. “You have to guide them. Collect your angel guides up there and send them on their way.” I laughed in tears.

“It´s their first trip.” I told him proud. “Yep, their first trip is to a cemetery.” I nodded feeling stupid. “You´re the first place they went.” I shrugged. “And I´ll bring them as much as I can.” I promised. “They won´t forget you.” I assured him. “They will know who their uncle was.” I swallowed the lump in my throat. “They gonna remember you.” I told him. “We all do.” I added.

“And their next trip will be to another graveyard. To your moms.” I said. “So, in a few weeks we´ll fly to London.” I nodded and waved Finn over and let him be alone with his brother and the babies.

I walked over to the viewpoint and looked down on the snowed in landscape.

“I wish you knew them.” I hushed. “I wish they could know you.” I cried.

17

Five years later, Play this when I´m gone – Machine Gun Kelly

I slept at the graveyard countless times. I needed to be somewhere he was.

Since he died, I was the one who couldn´t sleep anymore. *It did haunt me.*

My only escape was sleep. *To dream.* His only escape was life. *To live.*

Until he couldn´t. *Live.*

Sour brain sometimes can´t tell the difference between reality and imagination.

But why should we stay in reality? And how do you even define what is real?

Truth is up to a point I wasn´t bold enough to live. *So, I hid in dreams.*

Because I couldn´t find the entrance to mine anymore. And in ways he was still with me. In my dreams we were together. *I felt him. Smelled him. Heard him.*

Maybe it was just a way of my brain to deal with the loss or maybe it´s true and he was there. I never really believed in astral travel, but I think I did.

My dreams felt different. *Out of body. Out of world.*

Maybe we meet in another dimension. Where we could be together. Or maybe I was just slowly losing my mind. But I hoped it to be true. *Needed it even.*

I got into practicing lucid dreaming. I wanted to see him and talk to him. But every time I tried to imagine him it didn´t work. And every time I didn´t try, he came.

He reached for me.

He haunted my dreams. That´s why I kept dreaming. The dreams kept me alive. Kept me living by dreaming. I saw him every night.

Like I walked with him once upon a life.

Sometimes I saw him elder. How he would look like at my age. Sometimes he was a child. A teen and sometimes old. Sometimes he was still 27.

I started a dream journal. I couldn´t risk forgetting. I drew and painted pictures of those dreams. *Capturing him.*

I daydreamed about him a lot too. Sometimes I even saw him.

Maybe I´m just insane.

Because with his death, I lost a huge part of me. He would have been mad at me if he knew how less I was living. *But I tried for him.*

I just needed more time. The one thing he feared of running out. *Until it did.*

I did all the things he had on his bucket list and all I had on mine. I traveled the world. Every year I went back to Bali. I worked my ass off.

For my kids. For me. For Finn.

But I didn´t stop dreaming. *Hoping. Waiting. Suffering. Drowning.*

…

"You don´t understand me. And I can´t explain." He said. "You´ll get *insane* trying to understand." He added. "Let me try." I begged. "Don´t you get that you already failed?" He asked. "What?" I cried. *But he disappeared.*

And reappeared behind me. "I´m dead Lia." He said and I turned around. His eyes started bleeding. "I died." He said, as the red turned into black.

His face got pale, and I reached for him, but he dissolved like ash in the wind.

...

In all my dreams I couldn´t reach him. *At least in the bad ones.*

But I had good ones too. Both on a different level hurtful.

Sometimes we danced on clouds. Sometimes we fell.

Sometimes we ran. Sometimes we flew. But sometimes I found him dead. Sometimes I was with him in the car. Sometimes he survived. Sometimes, he forgot who I was.

But the thing that always stayed the same was me waking up. And those dreams did hurt even more than the fact that he was dead. Because they felt too real. They tricked me in believing it´s real.

I had this dream that Kai took me with him. *To Neverland.*

Kai was Peter who refused to grow up. But now he´s in Neverland. *At least, I hope.*

Maybe if I´ll dream enough, I´ll reach Neverland and my lost boy.

And just like Pan, he ran away from the things his parents had planned for his life. Just as Peter he was scared of love. He was mad because I wanted to change him. He didn´t like changes nor feelings. Feelings other than pain.

And maybe after all I wasn´t Tinker but Wendy because I left him. Wendy should have never stayed with the pirates. *But she did.*

I kept dreaming of the lost boy who quoted Oscar Wilde and his favorite authors and lyrics. And he told me I´ve changed. *But I told him I didn´t.* I told him he died and that he left me. *He told me I´m lying.*

I spent my entire life on dreaming of Neverland. But when I reached it. I kept dreaming and didn´t wake up. Nina was right there was never a way back.

...

"We never made it. Did we?" He asked me and I cried. "No." I shook my head. He cried too then, and I held him. "Why?" He asked. "You died." I told him in tears. "No." He said over and over. "No." He screamed and chanted. Then he stopped. *The crying.*

He was still and he looked at me blankly. "You left me." He told me. "You *never* came back." He accused me. "You left me for him." He said. "No." I cried. "Yes, you did." He replied. Now he was the younger version of himself. *Maybe nine.*

"You left me." He cried. "You all did." He shouted and ran away from me. I ran after him, but he disappeared in a thousand pieces. *And I with him.*

Then I woke up and fiercely searched for him running over to his room.

He wasn´t there.

Finn carried me back. *I couldn´t sleep for a week.*

...

Dear lost boy,

I left my rained in window open for you to come and get me.

Please take me back. I never wanted to grow up too. Not without you.

With love, your lost girl.

...

I never gave up on the hope that he might come back.

As a ghost or something. Even if it was silly.

Because out of all the lost souls why should he find his way back to me?

Lost boys never die they just grow up. But Pan never grew up he died. And I knew the ending of the story that Peter will lose Wendy. But what no one saw coming was him to die. And that *never* was an infinite *now.*

18

Seven years later, Snowfall (slowed + reverb) - reidenshi

I remembered the day the call came. *I remembered it all.*

I just suppressed it. But it all came back. *It always does.*

...

I drove down a hill on an empty street of a forest. The middle was wet because the last days it rained a whole lot. *It hadn´t rained in quite a while.*

Between the treetops, pink and orange clouds flashed through the sky, heralding the sunset. The puddle reflected the colors of the sky. *It was beautiful.* It felt real.

Almost too real.

I loved this road. Especially when it rained. The woods were magical. *Out of world.*

My music cut off and my heart sank as I saw Finn´s name on my display. I waited a second before I answered the call. *We haven´t talked in a while either.*

"Hello?" I asked checking if my speaker was working. "Lia." He said, and his voice sounded weird I remember that. "Yeah, Hi. Do you hear me?" I asked way too loud. After a silence he spoke again. "Yes, I hear you. You´re driving?" He asked. "Yup, I´m heading home." I responded. "Where are you?" He asked which was a weird question, but I told him. "Why?" I asked. *Silence.*

"Finn?" I called out frowning. *Silence.*

"Yeah, I´m here." He said but his voice was so weird and far away. Almost like it didn´t belong to his body. *I remember the way he sounded made me nervous.*

"You okay?" I asked. *No answer. Something was off.*

"Are you alone?" He asked ignoring what I just asked. "What´s wrong Finn?" I raked further and my hands began to sweat. I felt dizzy and nauseous. I felt my heartbeat everywhere. "Call me back when you´re home." He diverted. "No, Finn what´s wrong?" I insisted.

Silence. Too much silence. Finn wasn´t *that* quiet.

"Can you pull over?" Was all he asked, and my heart stopped. I swallowed something I couldn´t get down.

"Uhm yeah, wait a sec." I said, my voice shaky and I drove about two minutes in silence looking for some path to pull out. *But it felt so much longer. He didn´t speak.*

My feet tingled, and my hand felt weird. I started to slip out of my body.

I parked my car.

"Okay." I stammered, voice raspy. *Silence. Silence. Silence.*

"You´re there?" I asked. "Is your engine off?" He asked. "Yeah, it is Finn what´s up?" I urged. *Silence. God-damn.*

I heard him take a few unsteady breaths. "Kai had an accident." He said in a muffled sound, cause my ears shut down after he said his name. My mind felt like I was in space.

Floating. No grip to real life.

"He passed away." He said. My heart was in my throat choking me. Killing me with every beat. *It was so heavy. It vibrated in every cell.*

"When?" I asked breathlessly. "Yesterday." He said over the speaker, and I had that low buzzing inside my ear. *Or my head.*

I couldn´t understand what he said to me. *Yesterday.* My ears rang painfully.

Yesterday.

"He had a car accident." His voice broke in a way that shook me. I blinked the void away and opened my mouth, but nothing came out. "He died immediately." He said, his voice shaking.

Even if it was quiet out there it all screamed. There were noises I never knew existed.

I heard them all.

"The streets were wet." He said it in pieces like he wanted me to adjust to what he said but my head fell loose.

How could anyone ever adjust to those words of someone telling you someone died?

Kai had an accident.

"He came off the road." He said and I listened to my phone as if it were alienated.

Not from this world.

Waiting for the weird voice to tell me things I can´t believe. *He passed away.*

"He took my car." He said and I couldn´t feel my heartbeat anymore. I couldn´t breathe anymore. *Was I dead? I was sure I was dying. It felt like it.*

I pushed the car door open. *He had a car accident.* I unbuckled the seatbelt that choked me and ripped it off. *The streets were wet.*

I forgot how to breathe. *It all spun.* I was so sure I would die. *He came off the road.*

I held the door. *Bile rose up.* It went all black. *He died immediately.*

I vomited as the tears spilled and Finn said something I couldn´t hear.

I cried. I spat. I screamed. I sobbed. I choked. I shivered.

It was all muffled. Like some angel held his hands over my ears shielding me from everything on the outside. Or like the devil pressed my head underwater to penalize me.

To kill me slowly.

And at that moment, I hoped for it. *To end it all.* For me to *already* die.

Because Kai had an accident. He passed away. *Yesterday.*

He had a car accident. He died immediately. The streets were wet. He came off the road. He took my car. The things he said to me haunted me. Going on loop in my mind. Like a merry-go-round I couldn´t jump off. *Life.*

I always thought I would sense something like that. That I would feel that something is wrong. But I felt nothing. *Yesterday I felt nothing.*

It was just a normal rainy day. The day he died. *Was normal.*

And I didn´t feel anything. *He didn´t say goodbye.*

No windows blew open. No knocking on wood. No strange light. *Nothing.*

"Lia." He said my name. "You have to calm down." He said and I almost laughed but I just vomited again.

Let go – slowed - Dybbukk

"Listen to me." He said. "Focus on my voice." He said and I wiped my mouth straightening and closed the door. *The car locked.*

"I can´t breathe." I choked. "I know." He said his voice was weak. "Breathe with me." He told me. "In." He directed. "And out." He demanded. *I did as he said.*

He counted for me. *Breathed for me.* My brain followed, after many attempts. I learned how to breathe again without choking on it. Without feeling like I would die any moment. Maybe it was Kai choking me for not feeling *anything* as it happened. *Yesterday.*

"I should have waited for you to be home." He said with regret, but I shook my head. "He died." I said, voice breaking causing my tears to flow again. "He died." He repeated. "I´m sorry." I said hysterically. *His brother died.*

And I´m having a panic attack. I think I´ll die, but his little brother died.

I´m selfish. Always been.

“I´m so sorry.” I said over an over crying harder. “Lia, stop.” he said firmly, and I held my breath. “I´ll text Wren for you. He´ll come and get you.” He informed me. And I stopped. Wren. *My boyfriend.* Two years, we´ve been together. *I forgot.*

“Can you send me your location?” He asked and I nodded. My hands were shaking as I tried to navigate anything on my phone. “I´ll stay with you on the phone until he´s there, okay?” He offered. “Yeah.” I said zoned out.

“Okay.” I added because I managed to send it to him.

“He´ll be there in a few.” He told me. “Okay.” I said, even though I knew he wouldn´t be here before at least three quarters of an hour.

My hands were cold. My right knee did hurt and I couldn´t feel my feet.

What do you say when someone´s brother dies?

And what do you say when someone´s love of their life dies?

“This isn´t real.” I said. *Silence.*

I recognized the signs. My brain tried to shift my attention. *Denial. I shut down.*

My mind tried to protect myself. *But how´s that even possible?*

The tears dried. “Finn.” I whispered as my face burned. “He died.” He cried into the phone. Now my eyes filled again with tears. “I´m sorry.” I said again.

“He´s gone.” He choked on his words, and I held the phone to my ear. “I´m here.” I stupidly said. “Here for you.” I added. “What can I do?” I asked but it was a dumb question. There was nothing I could do. *Nothing.*

I was on autopilot, trying to be there for him without breaking down myself.

“Bring him back.” His voice broke heavily. He put his hands on his mouth to muffle his sobs and screams and my heart broke in a million pieces. I never knew pain until I heard him scream, because of his little brother´s death.

My whole body shivered, and I got so cold. Chills pained my skin.

We cried with each other.

I waited to wake up. Waited on the sky pealing down revealing this wasn´t life. Discovering we´re in *the Truman Show*. Or in a simulation. *The Matrix.* I waited for the book to be slammed shut. For the credits to roll. For the silence between the next song.

But nothing came.

My penalty on earth was to wait on that. Wait for life to become good again.

To make sense again. To wait for Kai Dark not to be dead. *To wait.*

- 27 -

I don´t wanna do this anymore (No beat no lyrics) 8D version – Ntz Prod., Marc Strain, baddie b

Long after the sun set, headlights appeared on the abandoned landscape.

"Wren´s here." I told him. "Okay." Finn said. "Call me when you got home." He begged. "Call me when you need." I told him and we hung up.

It wasn´t long, the silence between us hanging up and my car door opening.

But it felt like forever.

It felt like he was dead. *Kai was dead.* It felt like a void.

Nothing. Space. No time. Infinity.

But then the door opened. Wren held the door frame squatting down. He looked at me like it was true. *Like he was dead.*

The car drove away. *Someone has driven him.*

He picked me up. *No talking.* Just dying. *Just Kai being dead.*

He sat down with me and shut the door. I felt limb in his arms.

He felt from another world. A world I no longer inhabited. A world that was no longer accessible. A world with him dead. *A world I couldn´t accept.*

Wren cried with me. *I don´t know how long.*

He lost his lost best friend and his enemy. *And he lost me.*

After a while he opened the door and a friend of him took the seat behind the wheel. He walked with me to the passenger seat. The buddy pulled out onto the street. He must have waited outside. *In the rain. How long did we sit there?*

Wren held me. *The shell of me.*

The physical part of me. *Is that how Kai felt when his mother died?*

Something ripped me apart from the inside out.

Finn lost his mother and now his brother.

I think, somewhere I blacked out.

- 27 -

The beach (Instrumental + slowed + muffled) - mxpheebz

When I got back, we were still in the car. *Wren under me.*

He was so warm. It stung to me because I felt so cold.

How could he be warm? How could the world go on when he died?

The music was off the whole ride. Just pattering against the windows. And it felt like shots into my heart. He put a blanket over me. But it didn´t shield me.

Nothing could.

Nothing could shield me from him dying. *My shield was gone.*

My shield died. *Yesterday.*

The world became muted. *Shut down. Quiet.* But it wasn´t at all bearable.

It was wrong.

The world felt foreign. *Unreal. Meaningless.*

And I can´t remember anything after that. How I got through the next eleven days till the funeral. *Kai´s funeral.*

I was at the Dark´s a lot. The Avery´s were there too. Their father was. *We all were.*

But who ever lived those days wasn´t me. I had no Materia. *I wasn´t there.*

I lost my grip to the world. And never got it back fully.

Because it died with him. *Yesterday.*

19

Wren

When Finn texted me to get to her, it was like the world has changed. It felt like we shifted reality. It was life changing day obvious reasons. *Cruel ones.*

But also, for one outstanding. *The love of my life lost the love of her life.*

And with that I lost mine.

I never had her fully, but I had her. Now I wouldn´t ever have her. I knew that when the text came and the moment I opened the car door to see her already *dead.* I knew when I felt her limpness against my body and when I saw the void in her eyes.

The loss in her eyes.

But I had to be strong for her.

We did cry together but I couldn´t let it get to me fully. *I needed to guard her.*

And I knew when she didn´t hold onto me or the physical world because she had nothing to hold onto. *Not anymore.*

Her center shifted. It died to be exact. He took it with him.

Pan never dies how could he? Hook was supposed to be able to kill him.

Not death itself.

I felt so much pain for her. I wished I could bring him back for her. He needed to come back. He needed to come back to bring her back to life.

I questioned the years we´ve been together when *they* were apart. I felt guilty and wished I could have told her she should get back with him. Because that´s what we all should have told her. *That they belong.*

I wished they got their shit together and I told him that he´s good enough for her.

That he can love. That he did love. That he was loved.

But I was selfish and wanted to hurt him for what he did to me. I wanted something he loved and feared. I got between them and now he´s dead. I won´t ever forgive myself for being the reason they kept apart. Deep down we all knew she´ll always choose him. I wish I would have told her to go back to him. Because he loved her.

He loved right. He was able. He was enough. Always were.

But I knew there was not one time she didn´t want to be with me. But that changed when he was no longer with us. *I knew. And it was okay.*

But it wasn´t because it broke her. I knew I couldn´t have done *anything* to change that. The fact that her heart belonged to someone dead. *To her another love.*

She loved a ghost.

I lost her in ways I never had her. Death sucked all life out of her. I saw it happen and felt it. I never felt that helpless in my life. *I couldn´t help.*

But I knew *who* could. Because I knew soon I´ll be like that too. When it hit me and my mind processed. And before that happened, I had to get her safe.

Because I had no idea what would happen if I realized that Kai Dark was dead.

- 27 -

When we reached the Dark´s house, I carried her inside. I knew I had to bring her to her home. That was now haunted. *By the ghost of him.*

The Avery´s parents opened the door for us.

Leon and Aidan holding each other´s heads. And Finn holding his own. He sat on the couch, but his head lifted as he heard us. I saw the same void on his face as I saw in hers.

It was on all their faces. Even the air carried the void.

"Scar." He called her but she didn´t respond. *She was gone.*

But after a moment her head that was buried in my neck jerked like she was forced out of some other place or a dream. Her body felt like a body again. Still limb but there and she looked at him. I let her down as she made attempts to move. She crashed into his arms. They held each other falling apart. *I watched her leave. Gone.*

I wiped my face on the verge of crying. *For his death. For them.*

For the loss of a life and a love. *For all of them.*

I was unable to speak. *What could I have said? Nothing.* There is no right thing to say when someone dies. *When someone you love dies.*

There are things to say when you lose your girl, but not when she loves the one who´s dead. Not when she´s grieving, breaking, falling, and screaming. No feeling would ever replace what I felt in those hours. And I would pay on the last day of my life for it.

For them being apart.

I begged and prayed for a time machine for a gene and a miracle. But I wasn´t God.

I was just another love.

Hook was supposed to kill Pan or the other way round. But not him just dying.

He can´t die on me. *On us.*

"I´ll go." My voice was cracking, and I cleared my throat. *It burned so much.*

I didn´t want to leave her. *But I knew I had to.*

I already felt it creeping up on me. *Realization.*

Because being here and seeing all of them. *It was too much.*

"Uhm.. call me if.. I´m sorry.. If.. I can do anything.." I stammered and Leon reached for my shoulder. "Thanks man." He said in a tone I wish I could forget.

But I still hear it.

To this day, I still hear their cries, sobs, and screams. *And mine too.*

They were all falling apart and I couldn´t do anything.

I nodded, wiped my face, and looked at the girl that was once mine. *But never really.*

At my another love. *Because Wendy was always Peter´s, never Hook´s.*

They clamped each other not looking up. *I wasn´t expecting her to.* I just wanted to look at her. I wanted to hug her. Kiss her hair. *Say anything.*

But I knew I shouldn´t. *So, I turned and walked away.*

The chill air hit me like concrete. I wanted to scream. *But I couldn´t.* My chest hurt. It was open. *Bleeding. Pan had stabbed his dagger into Hook and left it there.*

Now he´s dead and can´t take it back. *It´ll stay there.*

The marks Hook had left on him, Pan left on me.

I left and it was the hardest and easiest thing I ever did. I wished I had left her with him. That was the one thing no one could do. *Be with him.*

I broke down. *He was dead.*

20

Lia, I found - acoustic – Amber Run

It came back to me. To be honest I remembered *everything*. I just didn´t *want* to remember.

I suppressed it.

And I felt guilty of the wrong reasons.

I remembered that it happened twelve days after he died. That there were things that led up to *that* happening. That we *knew* that would happen. That we wanted it to happen. Needed it to happen. *I remembered all of it.*

We had an attraction towards each other that wasn´t there before. *Not at all.*

He´s always been as pretty as his brother. But he was never Kai, and I never thought of him that way. Not until I lost his brother. Not until he was all I had left. Not until something has been switched. *A kill switch of life.*

...

Wren brought me to the Dark´s.

My memories are blurry, but I still remember how we held each other. How I fell into his arms but how unable we were on holding each other.

Because there was nothing left to save.

How I let Wren leave after what he did for me. *My savior.*

How we cried into each other´s necks and how after Wren left, Leon and Aidan laid down with us. We were tangled into and over each other.

How Addie and Logan watched us and waited for Blake to arrive. How they left us alone when he did. How we all fell asleep and how Leon laid on the one and Aidan on the other end of the couch. And how Finn and I were in between.

How the two of us constantly checked on each other for a functioning pulse and a normal breathing. How we collected the tears of the others like they needed to be saved.

Like they could have been saved.

How we held our faces, trying to find something else but void in our eyes. How there was a moment we *almost* kissed. But how instead buried our faces in our necks. How I caressed his head, and he stroked my hair. How it didn´t help anything but *everything*. How we made a bond on our trauma that night.

And how we two couldn´t sleep. How we tried not to lose our shit. How we clung to each other´s skins. How he had a hard on, holding me. How I didn´t move when I felt it. How I wanted to feel him. How I began throbbing *i*n places I shouldn´t and how he felt I did. How we saved each other by ruining each other and how we crossed a line we could never turn back to.

How in the early morning hours it began to rain and how I stood up and went outside. How he followed me. How we sat on the path like I once did with his little brother.

What horribly felt like lifetimes ago.

How we started crying the tears we dried for each. How after a while the others joined us and how Finn broke down, burying his head on his knees. How Leon held his neck, and I held his arms. How Aidan held his back and how we held each other as the sky cried onto us. *How he bled on us.*

How we saved each other that day by losing him. How his death brought us back together. How, after the others got back to their home we showered. How I did as Finn sat down in front of the door. How Finn did while I dried my hair, not wanting to be alone. How we laid in bed for the next days. How there were more groans pressing into my body and soul. How there were more body parts throbbing.

How we forced each other to stay hydrated and eat once a day. How we forced each other to go for a walk and to take a shower. How we clung to each other like we weren´t lost at all. How we saw our eyes dying. How we felt nothing. How we felt each other. How holding became cuddling. How looking became gazing.

How we started watching each other while showering. How we sat there by the door just watching. How we held our gaze. How his groan twitched, and he watched my nipples stiffen. How we realized we want each other without even planning to.

How he never spoke once to his father the days before the funeral. How we all helped to organize the funeral. Which song. Which coffin. Which picture. Which flowers.

Which everything.

How his father organized it without speaking to his only left son.

The only one he ever cared about. How that man broke because the son he never seemed to care about, died.

How we tried to endure how heavy time felt. How the day came closer. How we came closer. How friends became more. How we reached that line, we started to cross. How in the morning of the funeral my hand laid on his hard on, when I woke up and how he twitched under my touch. How I wondered if he was already awake. How I kept my hand there. How I let my hand wander up slowly and he took a sharp breath as I did. How I kept going and slipped my hand underneath his shorts. How he panted as I started stroking his warm flesh. How he moaned and I lifted my head to watch. How his eyes met mine and how they lost the void in their color. How I liked the want in his eyes. How he liked the same in mine.

How his chest heaved. How he asked what I´m doing. How I started pumping. How his body jerked as he murmured my name. How he hardened further and how big he felt. How he demanded to keep going and how I did. How he searched my gaze. How he bit his lips wanting to feel mine. How I wanted the same.

How he came in his pants. How he groaned my name. How he tried to catch his breath for minutes. How he let his head fall back and how he reached for my thigh. How I moved closer as his hand wandered up. How I clung to his arm. How he slipped his fingers under my lace. How a shiver run through my body as he touched me. How he began circling my clit. How my feet went numb.

How I dragged my nails in his muscles. How he held my face with his free hand. How I moved. How he inserted fingers while rubbing me. How I moaned while watching. How he pushed his thumb inside my mouth. How I sucked on it wishing it were something else.

How he forced me to look at him as I came. How he picked up pace when my back arched and how he held me after.

How we took a shower separately like nothing happened. How we got ready alone like we were afraid it might happen again. How I put on some make up and straightened my hair. How I slipped into my black dress and my high heels. How he was already in his suit when I came back.

How his tie hung loose on his neck. How I reached for it, trying to bind it. How he chuckled at my attempts. How I almost saw his dimples for the first time his brother died. How he grabbed my wrist, asking *you have no idea how to tie a cravat don´t you?* How I shook my head almost smiling. How I watched him tie it.

How he looked down on me. How I stepped closer, and his hands found my sides. How he told me *you can fasten it*. How I did and how he watched me.

How there was *that* silence after. How we both *knew* what would happen after the funeral. How we dragged it out until the last second to break away and drove to the funeral. And how I remembered everything.

How we happened. And how we both knew we would.

Did Kai see that we knew? Did he see it all?

21

Finn

I would be lying if I said I didn´t picture her in my bed before, because I did.

Occasionally.

I did in situations I shouldn´t have. *I know that.*

Like when he left her. When I undressed her and held her in my arms. When she fell asleep in mine, *not his*.

But I would have *never* acted on it. But that didn´t stop me from thinking of it. Because I knew I could treat her better. But I also knew she wanted him. And in a twisted way she was his, and he was hers. *It´s always been like that.*

Even though they weren´t even together once. *At least not really.*

I would have never tried to get between them. I wanted him to be happy and to find love. And he found it with her. *They found it.*

But somehow that prevented them from being together.

I knew he wrote a book for her. Well, I didn´t just know I pushed him to *actually* get through with it. He told me his idea but he wasn´t sure if it would make any difference. And I told him it would. *I was so sure.* But I was wrong. *So, fucking wrong.*

I never planned on hitting on her. Besides, she never looked at me that way.

Because why would she?

I wasn´t in love with her or something. It was an affection I couldn´t place. Maybe I liked her cause she liked my brother. Which sounds so stupid and wrong, but I mean it in a way of she saw in him what he didn´t see himself. She made him question himself and his beliefs. I know because I saw the influence she had.

I always felt for her in a way. In a weird and confusing way. But I saw her as a friend. I never saw her in that way until she saw me that way. *Until we did.*

All I can do is treat her better. All I could do was love her. And let her love me even if I was still struggling with that one.

...

Right after my meeting I drove to the cemetery. *Like every day.*

It was a warm day in April, as I stood in front of his grave, and I saw the white roses on the stones that she collected. The picture of him in that black frame and the book she left.

The Picture of Dorian Gray.

It was the book our father gave him when he was a teen. Since then, he read it over and over. Like he could find his father in there. Like it´s been the only connection he had to him. He got lost in the books since then. He read them all. But that one he read the most.

But a book can´t save you. No matter how much you reread it. *It couldn´t save him.*

Now she reads his books like they could save her. *I hope they can.*

I look at the stones. It´s the evidence of how much he loved and missed her. How much he couldn´t let go and hoped she would come back. I look at all the proof that she can´t let go either. That she hasn´t forgiven herself for leaving him. The proof of her loss. The proof that she couldn´t save him. *No one of us could.*

The only one that could have saved him was himself. But in the end, it didn´t matter because he died. And no one, not even God could have saved him that.

I look at the grave and think. *Could I have saved him?*

He wanted to take my car. I don´t even know why. I didn´t question it either. He never took my car. *Not willingly.*

But I was stressed and lost in work and didn´t think about it. *Maybe..*

My chest hurts. Maybe he knew. Maybe it *was* suicide. There were no skid marks. He was going too fast and came off. It was just seconds.

But why not doing it with his car, then? Did he love his car more than himself?

I smile weakly. *He did.* But no, I didn´t think he did. He loved the now´s too much to lose them. He loved her too much to leave her alone for good.

"I can´t save you. But I can save her." I told his headstone. "All of us." I said. "Your death was not in vain. I promise we´ll do better." I told him, my voice shaky. "I´ll treat her good." My throat did hurt. "I´ll look out for her." I choked and took a deep breath for the next one.

"I wanted to ask you about something." I wiped my mouth, and my eyeballs burned. "I wanted to ask you." I breathed to not fall. "To ask you for permission." I clarified, clearing my throat. "I want to marry her." I held my breath and tears I fought escaped painfully.

They sliced my skin. Writing *you fucked your brother´s girl.*

I shut my eyes to ease the pain. "I wanted to ask you *if* I can marry her." I stated and wiped my bloody face. *No answer.*

"I want to marry her." I said. *Silence.*

"Fuck." I smiled weakly. "I want to marry her, Kai." I said, blood dripping from my eyes. "I don´t have a ring yet." I said. "But I´ll get her one." I nodded. "Even if I know the one she wanted.." My voice cracked. "I think I´ll take one of yours." I said. "She wears them all the time." I smiled, but it fell when I reminded myself, he´s not here to see.

"I´ll take one of those and someday.." I held my face. "Fuck this is corrupt." I took a breath. "Someday she can have a piece of you." I said frowning. "You can be a fucking diamond in a few years from now." I joked as tears streamed down my face, but I shook my head. *Silence.*

"This is not enough." I held back a sob. "Fuck it hurts so much, Kai." I suffocated on my tears. "Come back." I said. "This isn´t.. I should have died before my little brother." I yelled. *Silence.*

"If you chose to die.." I warned. "I´ll fucking track you in hell and beat the shit out of you *little shit*." I snapped. "You can´t just die. You can´t." I told him. *Silence.*

"You left us." I accused him. "That´s all you ever did." I scowled. "You run and escape." I said upset.

"Why did you have to die?" I screamed. "I need you." I shouted. "She needs you." I cried. "We all do." I wiped my face aggressively because I couldn´t see his stone anymore.

"You needed us." I pointed out. "But you´re so stubborn." I said. *Silence.*

"I miss you." I whispered. "I´m sorry." I said. "I shouldn´t marry her. You should." I said. "She´s your girl." I said.

"I can´t." I choked. "I can´t. I need you. Get your ass down here." I yelled, facing the sky. "Come back. Marry her." I demanded and cried so hard, I thought I´d die right there on the grave of my brother. But I survived and breathed. And hated myself for it.

Cause he can´t. He stopped. He died.

And I´ll marry his girl.

22

Years before

After I slept with her the day after the funeral I went to his grave to tell her.

"I fucked her." I said. *Silence.*

"I want her." Not even the wind made a sound. "Your girl." I began. "I fucked her." I said once again. *Nothing.*

"I love her." I said even though I wasn´t sure. *No answer.*

He wasn´t here to beat me up. To kill me, yell at me or to do anything.

I wished he were. "I´ll take care of her." I promised. "I promise." I cried. "I promise I´ll do." I screamed. "Kai, I promise I´ll do."

…

The day after I slept with her. I sat in his car and drove somewhere. *Anywhere.*

I wanted to go straight to the cemetery, but I needed to get my head straight first.

What would I say to him?

So, I drove, listening to my thoughts until I couldn´t stand the silence anymore. I put the radio on to some oldies channel and *that* song came on.

Take good care of my Baby - Dion.

I almost lost it. I thought I got insane. *Like really.*

That my mind played tricks with me. But that song was on, and it felt like a bad joke. The universe making fun of me. Penalizing me. Torturing me.

It´s a coincidence, I told myself. *It´s just a random song.*

But I had to pull over next to some field and stared at the display. My hands shook as shivers ran down my spine. I froze and listened. The lump in my throat choked me. I think I didn´t breathe the whole song.

It scared the shit out of me. *Was that little shit talking to me? It couldn´t be.*

There are no such things as spirits. *Right?*

My body went cold at the last seconds of the song and then I cried. It felt like a horror movie. But I would be glad. Because it would mean he was there. Still here to punish me. He´ll haunt me and might kill me even. And I fucking hoped he would.

I deserved it.

I didn´t believe in signs, fate or anything and I wasn´t religious either. But at that moment, I knew *something* messed with me. If it was fortune, God, karma, or hell even my brother. Whatever the heck it was. *I fucking believed it.*

I freaked anyway because of what I did and his death. *It ate me alive.*

And if that song and those lines would take some of that guilt away. I wanted it and to stay sane, I needed that. And maybe I read too much into it. But I didn´t care.

This was my little brother talking to me. That song was made for us.

I sat the whole day in that car and after the song was over, I shut it out and sat in dead silence choking on my sobs. I texted her *I can´t do this*.

Then I went to his grave and later that night I went home and just hugged her.

Telling her I can. I´ll take care of her.

And since that it´s been the one song I dance with her.

…

I blinked at flashbacks.

The memory of the day he came back after he left for London and punched me in the face.

"You *fucked*, Scar?" He yelled at me. "No." I yelled back. "Sure, it *clearly* looked like it with your *hands* on her." He snapped. "I don´t fuck her." I told him. "But you´re attracted to her." He retorted and looked like I punched him in the face.

I looked down. "You are." He said realizing. "You fucking bastard." He came at me, but I stopped him, pushing him off me. "Listen. I love her, *yes*." He glared at me. "But as a friend. As the girl of *my* brother." I assured him. "You´re right she´s *my* girl and don´t fucking tell me you *love* her." He shouted.

"I do, but I would *never* do anything. She´s yours." I told him and he shook his head and laughed. "Well thank you brother for not doing anything." He quoted.

"But you already *fucking* did." He raged. "It was nothing." I told him. "What was it then?" he insisted, and I let out a groan. "She´s been crying on your shoulder the past months or what?" He scowled and I inhaled beat. "No. Just.. just talk to her." I said and went downstairs to tell her.

…

"I would have never done anything. I swear. I knew the love you had was no good, but it was love." I told his grave.

"She loved you. Still does." I said. "And if you wouldn´t have died.. I would have never.." I tried to explain. "I mean it. She´s been off limit. Kai, I knew." I choked. "I didn´t saw her that way. I mean I felt *something* for her. Adoration but she´s been family. Cause she had you." I said.

“I didn´t see *that* coming. It was just there. She wanted it too.” I said quietly. “She wouldn´t have wanted it before. It´s the truth. There were chances for *something* to happen between us before. When you left her over and over. But she *never* wanted it. Never wanted me. And I knew.” I yelled upset.

“And I knew you two would end up together.” I said. “But how should I have known that you die?” I asked him. *Silence.*

“When it happened. We both made the choice.” I said but couldn´t breathe normally. “It´s wrong. But it didn´t feel like that.” I admitted.

His death didn´t justify *any* of it. It just made it real. Because if he wasn´t it would have *never* happened. *But it did. And it was real. He was gone.*

That didn´t make it less corrupt. But she made the first step. She acted on it first. She did the morning of the funeral. *So, I acted on it too.*

23

Eight years later, Lia

It was hot outside. And the sun shined as we walked towards the grave. On the right Kaidan who walked with my pinky finger and to the left Rain on my arms.

“Say hi to Uncle Kai.” I said as I squatted down. “Hi uncle Kai.” Kaidan said but Rain said nothing, just patted the earth and picked up a stone. She´s a bit shy just like her mother was. *But she smiled.*

She handed me the stone. “You´re uncle loved to collect stones from all the places he went.” I told them. “Adventures?” Kaidan asked excitedly and I nodded with a big smile. “Lots of adventures. He traveled around the world collecting them.” I said and picked up the heart shaped one. *There was even the one he got me for my birthday.*

“Those are from Bali. An island in the Indian Ocean. There it rains a lot and it´s very warm.” I explained. “Uncle Kai liked rain.” Kaidan stammered. “Yeah, indeed he did.” I said with a smile. “You want to go on an adventure for Kai?” I asked whispering as if I was talking about some secret mission and Kaidan nodded exhilarated. So, I took his hands. “You can look around and search for a *special* stone for his collection.” I said and he nodded grinning.

“Take your sister with you..” I said but he already grabbed her hand, and they started investigating the area. *Kai would have loved them.*

…

The day of the Wedding

I walked with the train in my hands towards the cemetery.

I let it down before I reached the grave, as if he couldn´t have seen me before I got in sight of the headstone. *If he could see me at all.*

I walked towards the stone with a bouquet of white roses. It was a mermaid dress hugging my curves. With a heart neckline and I wore my hair in a low ponytail. Thin stains of hair hung into my face, and I was nervous. As if he would really be there.

In a suit marrying me.

As if I wouldn´t marry his brother today.

I spun the engagement ring and immediately cried as I spoke. "I wanted you to be the first to see me." I said through tears. "I´m not wearing any makeup though, because I knew I´d cry." I managed a laugh. "But everything else is how it will be." I explained and pressed my lips together. *Hands shaking. Feeling dumb.*

Standing alone in my wedding dress. *On my wedding day.*

In front of the grave of another man. *I felt pathetic. I felt weak.*

I risked ruining my dress with earth or grass stains just to come here. I really had outdone myself. I slept here, read here aloud, and talked to him. I did many crazy things here.

Out of grief.

And now I´m here in my wedding dress.

"I love your brother with all my heart. And I love our kids." I said and the lump in my throat grew at every word. "But I hate that it isn´t you." I admitted and felt a weight off my chest. It felt horrible but relieving. "As my boyfriend or husband. As the father of my child." I cried.

"I´m sorry it´s not you." I whispered. "I love you." I added. "I wish you could be here." I choked. "You´d be a great husband and a great father." I chewed my lip.

"But I know your brother will be great too." I said. "But he´s just not you." I whispered and wiped my tears. Grabbing my train, I walked away.

Over the years, I realized I can´t live like that. Like I could wait long enough for him to reappear. *If it was that easy.*

24

Nine years later

Years have passed but it didn´t really feel like it.

I still felt like nineteen, even if I wasn´t anymore. *My mind stayed in the past.*

I lost my heart there too. And my soul was stuck between worlds. I relived it constantly.

So, the hurting never stops.

Your brain thinks it´s happening now. You chose to suffer because to go on would be worse. *At least you think it would.*

I still remembered *every* conversation. Like movies, they played in my head. All the moments I had with Kai. My memories drowned me. Even after all this time things came up and dragged me down. *Down the rabbit hole.*

Making me fall. Swallowing me. Tapping me. Hurting me. *Changing me.*

How detached can you get to the physical world? And what says that about you? And how can you get out?

Trauma throws memories at you. Like how I was at the hospital cause of dehydration and how Finn stopped eating. How good the first drag of the joint felt and how all of a sudden, I could smoke on lungs. How we went to the accident scene. Placed a cross, a picture of him and roses. *White ones.*

How we sat there. Waiting for him to reappear. Waiting for a sign and a change in the air. Waiting for a dear to pass. Waiting for rain that never came.

But everything comes back. *Eventually. It always does.*

I went to Kai´s grave for every important moment. I told him about everything. I talked about him like he wasn´t already gone. But I was homesick for a person that couldn´t hold me anymore. I felt like I couldn´t heal without him. He left a wound that needed his touch. He was the person I always searched for in crowds but never found. But there is no such thing as *forever* when we die. Just forever missing and forever remembering.

25

Ten years later

After 10 years, mostly only bones are left.

10 years after Kai´s death, his father let him cremate. Now there´s a black urn. There´s still a coffin and a black casket. But there isn´t Kai in it. There are pieces of him. His boxing gloves, favorite books, cameras. One of his Notebooks. His soccer ball. A copy of his book. Pictures and a joint. We wrote letters. And other things we connected with him.

...

Finn got on one knee and gave me a small black velvet box.

"A piece of him." He said with red shot eyes. I opened it. *It was a ring.*

A thin one. 0.5 carat, and it was silver with a blueish pear diamond. It looked like a tear or a raindrop. *It was a piece of him.*

"They used part of his ash." He said and I got on my knees. *Crying.*

...

"What´s your Hook?" I asked Finn. "Huh?" He looked at me confused. "You know what I mean." I gave him a look. He realized what I meant and considered, as if he never thought about his greatest fear before. *And I think he didn´t.*

"Silence." He said. "Before you, I was scared of silence." He told me and I frowned. "I have always worked and when I didn´t I listened to music, work out or played basketball." He explained.

"Truth is, I kept myself busy. Always hustling. Every minute of my day planned, so I wouldn´t have time to feel." He told me and looked drained. "But I could never sit in silence." He said upset. "Sit with myself and the thoughts.." He shook his head. "It was what scared me the most." He said in a hush. "What my brain would tell me if I wasn´t busy all the time." He admitted.

"And when my brother died I was scared of the silence that´ll come." He told me. "Of the empty house." He whispered. "His room." He stared off. "His car." He nodded. "The silence at his grave." He blinked.

"When I was in the house the night it happened." He swallowed. "When there was that *dead* silence." He blinked once more. "When for a minute I closed my eyes pretending he´s upstairs.." He swallowed. "Writing in his books. Smoking pod and jamming music. Being mad at me for no reason." He had to stop.

"When there was for a minute no pain." He whispered, but his voice shook anyway. "When I could pretend, he was still alive. That there was no silence." His voice broke.

"The silence after his death.. was more than I could bear." He said and his hands covered his face muffling his sobs.

Then he looked at me. "But you were here. And you were silent. You always were. The two of you." He smiled weakly. "I envied you." He said. "You knew silence is power, not weakness." He locked eyes with me. "You forced me to be silent." He nodded. "You showed me silence." He told me.

"What made me mad with Kai, you showed me to love." He explained.

"You showed me love." I told him. Because what I realized is that I never experienced real love. *Selfless love.*

It´s always been obsession, codependency, and addiction. But when Finn and I came together we were broken but weren´t trying to make the other whole. Mostly because we knew we couldn´t. *But also because we knew we shouldn´t.*

...

"Come here, I have to show you something." Finn told me and I followed him into Kai´s room. There was a black box on the floor.

"*Scar"* was written on top in sharpie. I knelt and stared at it. "What´s that?" I asked. "It´s for you." He said. "I found it in his bed box." He shrugged.

"Tell me if you need something." He said and closed the door behind him.

I opened the lit and froze. The box was filled with things I recognized and things I didn´t. Things I remembered as I saw them. But most importantly, there were things I had. That belonged to me or I´ve touched. *Things that reminded him of me.*

Like hairbands, sketches, bills, scribbled notes, a pen, and stones. The one he kicked as he walked me home. There were the wrinkled white roses. And the rose he wore on the wedding. There were Polaroid´s and some letters. Concert and festival tickets. Parking and bus tickets. The picture of us on Halloween. The picture he took of me with that butterfly. Books and plane tickets. A joint and the lit of a beer. A paper of some energy bar and there was a ring I´ve lost years ago. He kept them all. And I never knew he did that.

There was even a napkin with my lipstick on it.

I can´t even remember when I wore lipstick.

But I tugged the things back and I cried, but mostly I was grateful.

26

Twenty-one years later

"What was he like?" Kaidan asked and I smiled to myself. "Like a storm." I told him. "Mom, you´re being cryptic." He rolled his eyes at me. "He was." I laughed.

"You´re a lot like him. Stubborn and fearless. Intelligent and bold. Sarcastic pared with confidence and humor." I said, looking at him and every time I did, I saw Kai.

It was like he had more from him than from me.

"Rain is much like me and your dad. But *you* are through and through Kai." I told him with a broad grin, and he looked at the headstone. "I would have liked to have known him." He said his voice small. "He would have adored you." I assured him. "He would have been the coolest uncle." I said knowing. "No one says *cool* anymore." He frowned at me, and I smiled. *Just like his uncle would.*

"You think he´s watching?" He asked after a while, and I sighed. "I hope so." I said. "It would be a shame. All those stones and books you´ve left." He said.

I left even more. My heart. Happiness. My love.

I rubbed the spot where the 27 starts to fade on my ring finger. Kaidan stared at the engagement ring. “You loved Uncle Kai didn´t you?” He asked the question he wanted to ask for a long time. And now that he was seventeen, he understood more why I grieved the way I did.

“I did.” I admitted and laid down a white rose and a new stone. “Why did you and dad come together of you loved his brother?” He asked. “Because if we wouldn´t I wouldn´t be here anymore. Your dad saved me.” I told him.

“Have you been with him before dad?” He raked further and I always feared the day they would ask me *that,* but I sighed. “We haven´t been together. Not really, we did no labels.” I said and Kaidan snorted. “Kind of unhealthy.” He commented. I nodded. “Yeah, our generation was pretty toxic. Lost to be exact.” I agreed.

“Social media, Smartphones, KI, and the internet in general made everything so fast moving. People were afraid of missing out.” I explained.

“Was that the issue between you and Uncle Kai?” He asked.

Uncle Kai. It still stung with me.

I shook my head. “No. We knew we wanted and loved each other. We were just too scared to admit it or let it happen.” I said with a shrug. “But your generation is different. You date more and do stuff outside the internet. You get what´s wrong with the digitalization. You see the world as what it is. Worth living.” I said.

“*Mom.*” He whined annoyed by my lecture. But I loved giving them my advice. I wanted them to learn about psychology, Buddhism, philosophy, and mindfulness. Because I knew it would be something Kai would have taught them. As many things, he would have. He would have played soccer with Kaiden while it rained. He would have watched the stars and fireflies with Rain and told her about the meaning of life.

He would teach them so much.

So, I had to do my best.

“I know. I know.” I said. “Just let me tell you this.” I pleaded and he nodded giving in. “If you love someone, go tell them. And if the love isn´t returned. It sucks, but it´s okay.” I said and he listened. *He knew why it was important to me.*

“The hurt is worth it. But what is not worth is not trying enough. Regretting is not worth it. Life is too fragile and too short. Always remember that when you think of your uncle. Be in the now. Do what you want and live.” I said.

“Promise.” He said and hugged me. Then I took my wristwatch off. *It was Kai´s.*

And gave it to him. “It was his.” I told him. “It´s broken.” He said and I nodded. “It stands for everything. But no time. Because you have all the now´s.” I said and he took it and put it on. “Thanks mom.” He said.

"And please watch your sister. Be there for her." I demanded. "I am mom. Always. You *know* that." He assured me, a bit annoyed. *They were inseparable.*

"And just because I loved your uncle doesn´t mean that I don´t love your dad. Our you two." I told him. "I know." He said. "I haven´t thought that." He added.

He looked at me. "Loved?" He asked. "You said *loved*." He clarified and I blinked. "I love him." I corrected and he watched me for a beat.

"I´m sorry mom." He said. "That you lost him." He added and I gave him a weak smile. "Me too." I said.

27

Twenty-two years later

The kids had their own room. Blake had his too.

I haven´t once made the bed. I covered it with a thin dust blanket. The bed was all those years untouched. The way he laid in the sheets was conserved. The wrinkles were still there.

I sat on the office chair as Kaidan walked in. "Mom?" He asked me as I stared. "Yeah." I said still unable to blink, and he waited a moment before he spoke. "You want something to eat?" He asked. "No honey." I said. *Now I was blinking.*

"You miss him." He said. "Every day." I responded and looked at him. "But you can´t live like that." He added. "Like what?" I asked and he hesitated but spoke. "*Waiting*." He said and I knew he was right. Waiting on death to come around to lead me the way back to my lost boy. But it stung with me that they noticed too.

Of course, they would.

Suffering on my own was okay but concerning them wasn´t.

I inhaled long, and it was refreshing because I held my breath as I sat there. "He´s dead mom." He said as if I didn´t know. *Sometimes I wondered if I did.*

"*The dead linger sometimes.*" I quoted. "Oscar Wilde." He recognized right away and my eyes watered. He was as into in books as his uncle was.

"Was his favorite author." I told him, but he knew that.

I got up and walked to the bookshelf and took out the two paperbacks he wrote and the one that I wrote. "What are you doing?" He asked, knowing no one is allowed to touch *anything* here.

"Have I ever told you your uncle wrote me a book?" I asked, ignoring his question. His eyes widened, but his frown deepened. He shook his head. "He did." I told him. "The second he couldn´t finish though." I said and he eyed them.

"Those are three." He remarked and I nodded. "I wrote one." I said. "After he passed away." I told him. "And if you want, you can read them." I offered holding them out to him. "Yeah." His voice cracked. "I´d loved to." He said. He always loved reading the books of his uncle. He thought I didn´t notice, but I did. He sneaked in and read. I wouldn´t have forbidden it but maybe because it was off limits, he enjoyed it even more. I knew that feeling.

So, I let him.

"Does dad know about them?" He asked before he left. "He does." I nodded slightly. "But he hasn´t read them." I added. "Why?" He asked and I shrugged. "Ask your dad." I told him.

- 27 -

I made dinner as Kaidan called out.

"Mom." I turned, and he already stood next to the kitchen island and clearly out of breath. He´s was almost as tall as Finn. *I don't know how he grew up that fast.*

He had the same messy hair as Kai. *He looked so much like them.*

Sometimes it hurt just to look at him. Rain looks more like me. *But Kaidan..*

It´s like part of him is still here. *In him.*

He walked up to me and hugged me to his chest resting his chin on my head. "I´m so sorry Mom." He said. "What´s wrong?" I asked. "I´m sorry you lost him." He said. "That Dad lost him. Grandpa, Aidan, Leon.. they all.." He continued. "I´m sorry." He repeated and his grip tightened once more before he let go of me.

"Now I have to go." He said in a rush. "Where you´re heading?" I asked. "Telling a girl, I love her." He said and I smiled. "Wait." I shouted as he was already halfway out the living room. "Here take these." I said and took the bouquet of white roses from the vase. I always kept them around. So, it would always smell like spring.

That maybe Kai came back now and then if he smelled them.

"Girls love roses." I said and dabbed them on a towel and wrapped them in parcel paper and handed them to him. "Thanks mom." He said, kissing my head. "They´re pretty." He said and I smiled at him before he left. My eyes watered. *They were.*

28

Fifty-eight years later, Kaidan, Lost Boy Instrumental - Climb the Vine

She cried as she died. On the grave of the love of her life. She didn´t die on the grave of her husband. *She died on the grave of Uncle Kai.*

She died at the age of eighty-three. When she knew it was time, she called me. It was late night as I sneaked her out of the nursing home and drove her to the cemetery. I carried her the way because her legs were weak, and she laid down on the ground and I sat on the stairs to the gazebo watching her. She held two stones in her hands. And her necklace with three rings she wore all her life. The engagement ring made from his ashes. The promise ring he gave her on Bali. And his silver ring she always wore.

She cried and talked to him as if she saw him.

As if he was here with her. I hope he was.

I cried as I watched my mom die. *She died in peace.*

She died next to him. Thinking he was there to get her. *And she let go.*

It started to rain. *She smiled.*

Until her own death she couldn´t let him go. She went every week to his grave, and I had to drive her when she couldn´t anymore. I even sneaked her out when she wasn´t allowed anymore. *I helped her die there.*

I watched her die there. And death broke her heart. *I hope it healed now.*

I hope he waited on her and they´re all on their own adventures in Neverland.

And what I learned from my mom was that you should never be not brave enough to love. What I learned from my uncle Kai is that you should never be not brave enough to live. What I learned from my dad is you should never feel guilty of what you want in life.

And what I learned is that you should never expect life to be fair. Looking back, I´ve told a lot of women that I loved them. And I got heartbroken a lot too. But I have never regretted any of it. That´s what they taught me. *Life.*

29

Somewhen in the past of between life, Lia

At the age of 25 I got homesick of a place and a person I could never return to. Kai Dark died at the age of 27. And at the age of 25 I died with him. In a way I stopped living when he died. *Haven´t lived since.*

I hope he finds me in the next life. I hope the sky isn´t the limit and that energy never runs out.

Where do you hide, when the one you love is gone?

When I reached 27, I wanted to stay like that. Getting older than he was scared me. I would even die without him. But the purpose of life is fearing not to live.

I thought losing control was my biggest fear. But losing him was. Regret it became. Death, it became. My sickness after all isn´t called love it´s called regret.

Maybe the trick to be in the now was to make believe. That´s what I learned from the boy I lost. To take a break to look around. To see the Merry go round. *Life.*

- 27 -

I found a Notebook in his car. It slipped under his seat.

There was a quote. *Just one.* I didn´t know when he wrote that in there.

"But inside my heart there´s a picture of a girl"

I looked it up on the internet. *It was a song.*

The devil´s tears - Angus & Julia Stone

...

It rained when you died my firefly.

And I cried when I died. I smiled because I felt him.

What a scent that lingered in the air. The smell after rain. The smell after him.

Petrichor. *And I´ll always be a* ***Pluviophile.***

30

Lia, Another Love – slowed down - Tom Odell

It was about one and a half years after Kai´s death when Wren and I met and talked.

He sat at his piano and I sat next to him.

Minutes passed before he spoke up. "I never told you that before. And I don´t really know why I didn´t." He began. "But Kai and I were best Friends." He told me. "I know that." I said with a laugh, but he shook his head. "Well not *just* that." He said intently and I frowned. "We were *more* than that." He said slowly. *Huh?*

"He was in love with me." He said to me. *What?*

"What do you mean?" I asked. "We sort of.." He cleared his throat. "We were best friends." He said again. "You already said that." I retorted and he nodded. "Just let me talk okay." He asked and I nodded.

He took some breaths.

"We were the ones starting those games." He said. "Those with girls." He clarified.

Yeah, I heard of those.

"We made bets who could get them first. And we snatched girls from each other." He paused. "We fucked the same girls. Not at the same time but next to each other. Or in the same room." He told me. *That´s new.*

"We got off on that." He shrugged and licked his lips. *I can imagine.*

"Later on, Andi joined us and other guys too. It was *known* that we do that. Play with them and have some kinks." He explained. "But they always wanted more." He said.

Just how I wanted more.

"But he could never give them that. *So, they went to me.* And I fucked them. Some I even dated. Some became my girlfriends. But I got bored easily and broke up with them." He said.

"Then one night." He took a breath. "Kai and I boozed and got stoned. He read and I played games." He chuckled. "I knew about the nightmares, so I was mostly with him." He trailed off, lost in thought. *Like he did with me.*

It´s sad that they weren´t friends anymore because when I met them, they hated each other. *No love.*

"We even shared a bed." He smiled, thinking back. "We grew up together. His and my father were best friends." He told me and cleared his throat once again.

"Well and that one night we talked about girls. What we did with them and got off on that." He said, voice thick. "We got hard." He said breathless. "And started jacking off together." He revealed and I held my breath. "We watched porn. Then we did it without porn and it became a habit." He said voice husky. "We did jerk off in the showers and did it for the other." He chewed his lips.

"When we talked to some girls, we looked at each other. Knowing we´re hard and what we´ll do later. Knowing we´ll get off harder than with those girls´ lips." He said, and my mouth went dry.

"Sometimes we watched the other making out with. We even watched when we fucked." He smiled. "Some time we fucked those girls in his car. Me in the backseat, he in the front and we held eyes in the rearview." He said and I was throbbing. "We did it in the jacuzzi. Once we fucked the same girl at a party. First, he than me. It was a game. A foreplay for what would happen after." He said.

"But we only ever jerked off." He said. "Sometimes we would kiss or bite each other´s necks if we needed to." He told me and my throat ached.

He wanted him to bite him. *Like I did.*

"And that´s how it went for a long time. We didn´t really address it though. It was just the way we wanted and liked it." He paused as if the story were about to change, and my gut told me it would.

"He was never the type for relationships. Like never." He said. "Everybody knew." He added. *Me included.*

He chewed on his lips shaking his head. "But I dated girls. And had relationships." He told me. "And one time I met a girl I fell in love with. Like hard." He smiled and I wondered if I knew her. "We got together. And Kai was.. *pissed*." He said, and I closed my eyes.

He had feelings for him.

"I stopped coming over. We stopped those jerk-off sessions. I had a girlfriend now and things changed." He sighed. "And I was serious about her. He knew and was mad at me because he thought he lost his friend." He shrugged. *But that wasn´t it.*

"I didn´t party that much and didn´t sleep next to him. I spent my time with her. And Kai´s now´s were his most precious thing but the thing I refused to share with him." He said losing focus. "And I know it was a shitty thing to do. To neglect him and my friends that way. But what should I say, I was in love. And the first time you´ll *always* tend to do stupid things." He shrugged. *I knew that one.*

He took a deep breath. "So, Kai started to mess with me. Really fucked up shit." He said struggling. "He started talking to her. Pretending to have nothing in mind. But I knew he wanted to play. Like we used to." He stiffed a laugh, but it was a spiteful one.

He wanted to hurt him. For hurting him.

"But *this* was different." He said angry remembering. "But it didn´t stop him." He smiled venomous. "We had fights, and he blamed me to leave him alone. I told him I´m in love but he laughed at me and told me there is no love." He told me. "I knew what he thought of love. I knew him." He said upset. "But he wanted to hurt me." His chin tilted back. "Like I hurt him." He nodded.

"But I didn´t know that back then. I thought he was mad because of our friendship." His voice was filled with old emotions. "He was in love with you." I whispered and he nodded. "I think he was. I *know* he was. I mean I loved him too. Maybe at some point the same way he loved me, but I met her then, and she changed it all. She threw me off." He said shaking his head.

"I knew he was sort of fucked. And I didn´t think he´ll *ever* love someone in *that* way. Like ever. So, I never considered.. Never until.." He trailed off again. "Until he fucked your girlfriend." I said having heard *that* story somewhere before, but I never knew it was about them. *That´s why they stopped playing those games.*

Did they all know?

"Until he fucked my girlfriend." He repeated. "He got her around somehow. She fell for him. Like they all did eventually." He said lost in the void. "She cheated on me with my best friend." He said with a lump in his throat. "But he.." He shook his head.

"I knew he didn´t do it for the cheating part. He did it to hurt me. Because he was in love with me." He nodded absently.

"She came to me after crying, and I knew the minute I saw her." He wiped his face. "She tried to explain and all, but I left her. I didn´t care about her anymore. But I went to him." He said. "Ready to fucking rip his heart out. But what I saw when I came to his room.. *was his heart already out*." He said and, he had to pause to catch his breath.

"That broke me in ways that would *never* heal. Because when I saw him still lying on those sheets, he just *fucked* my girl in. Half-naked, stoned, and red eyes.." He shook his head. "Knowing he did cut himself after because his boxer was hanging low." He shut his eyes.

His cuts. I´ve seen those.

I never knew but now I did.

"I saw it in his eyes, that he loved me." He said with tears. "That Kai Dark loved me." He chuckled and wiped his tears. "I didn´t saw before because he *never* let it show until then." He told me. "And my anger was all gone. I was just hurt. Hurt because instead of telling me, he did that." He looked at me unable to breathe. "Because that´s how he loves, through pain." He said with a nod and my eyes teared because he loved me that way too.

But he hurt him more.

"And we just stood there. *Not talking.* Not even breathing." He told me. "Tears rolled that we both let fall. *Silently.* Looking at each other´s hearts on the floor. His bleeding, mine crushed. His footprint on mine and my knife in his. He ruined my first love I ruined his." He said and his body shook.

"And what happened after that?" I asked. "I laid down next to him but didn´t let him touch me. Till we fell asleep." He licked the salt of his lips. "The next morning, I got up and left." He said. "That´s it?" I asked and he nodded. "We never talked about it. Never got back to where we were. Stopped being friends. Became enemies. Fucked with each other´s friend groups and parties." He shrugged.

"He knew it wasn´t because he loved me. Because I would have loved him back if he had told me. He knew that but could only ruin things." His shoulders twitched. And somehow, I´m sad they didn´t cleared things or ended up together. I mean I got it Kai did a horrible thing. Cheating is the lowest but it´s just so sad. He lost him because of his own fault.

I hope he didn´t think he lost me because of himself.

"I know what you´re thinking." Wren said to me. "But it wasn´t *that* easy. He knew he couldn´t love. He knew this was how he was." He shrugged. "We missed each other. Sometimes we spoke. But things weren´t the same after." He lowered his head.

"He was fucked up but I wasn´t innocent either. I tasted blood and I wanted him to taste it. So, when I got the chance to mess with them I would. I called the cops on them many times. I laid many bombs in his way. And he knew." He smiled weakly. "It was a game. But I could never hurt him the way he did. But I tried anyways." He shrugged. "It was a way of still having each other. But it was better than nothing." He told me and I knew that feeling.

"Our groups divided to his side and mine." He said and smiled halfway. "We were creative in making each other´s life´s hard and it was fun." He said and cleared his throat straightening up.

"And then you came along." He looked at me. "I still remember the day you showed up." He grinned lost in memories. "The way he looked at you." He laughed. "I fucking knew, he hated you the moment he saw you." He chuckled shaking his head. "And then you kissed Aidan his new buddy after me and that pissed him off even more." He smirked. "He wanted you gone." His eyes pierced mine.

"I saw it in your eyes that you fell for him the minute you saw him." He said. "You know it was really funny watching you guys." He told me. "But it was weird too because I´ve seen him change. He did even things with you, he never did with me." He said. "But you dated Andi, and it made him boil." He laughed aloud. "But he wouldn´t let it on because of the games we played. He wanted to protect you from all that. But of course, Andi knew what was going on." He smiled. "Andi was a good friend of mine, so he got back at him." He told me.

"Kai hid you but that wasn´t because he didn´t care. People hide things *because* they care. And he did that with me too. We hid what we did, too." He told me.

"But he fell hard for you. And he never wanted to fall anymore." He told me. "Not after you." I said and he nodded. "He got scared. *Like with me.* But he didn´t hurt you as much as he hurt me. But he has hurt you in other ways. Like leaving." He said, and my eyes teared up.

"He was made for breaking hearts. Because once I had broken his. So, he broke you because he didn´t think he could do it differently." He told me. "But you made him change and he tried. You were the one he loved *after me*." He said.

"And then you and Aidan happened, and I wanted to stop you but somehow I wanted to see.. *what he´ll do*." He smiled. "It forced him to deal with his emotions and to tell you he loves you. What he could *never* tell me." He said in a way that still pained him.

"I knew that you wanted to make him jealous. *So, I played along.*" He smirked. "I loved it. It was fun." He licked his lips.

"He had changed but not enough to replace the pain with love." He said the things I felt back then. "Then you wanted to use me again." He grinned. "And I loved to help *again*." He told me. "But things went *differently* than we expected." He smiled and I did too. "I didn´t plan on using you to hurt him." He told me.

"*But how could I not fall for you?*" He asked with a faint smile on his lips. "I just did." His mouth twitched. "I saw you search love in persons you´ll never get it." He shrugged. "So, I thought, why couldn´t I be that person for you? To give the love that means love and not pain." he trailed off.

"And Kai knew that *that* was my intent." He said. "And I knew he tried to get you back. He even talked to me, but you were over him and he knew." He shrugged. "He let me love you the way he could never. How he couldn´t love me neither." He said and tears rolled down my cheeks.

"You were the first girl I had fallen for *after* him." He told me and my heart broke "He tried to be friends with you. And even *that* was okay." He said in tears, and he bit his lips hard before he kept going. "And even when he wrote you that *damn* book it was okay because how could it not be okay when he tried to learn how to love without pain?" He yelled upset and my eyes watered. "Even then it was okay." He told me his lips trembling. "But when he died.." He stopped himself.

Oh my god.

"It wasn´t okay anymore." I finished for him my voice shaking with realization. He nodded and tears streamed down his face. He covered his mouth trying to stop it and I reached for him. His body shook with the loss, and we cried for the same boy that couldn´t love us.

We cried about him trying. We cried about him dying.

- 27 -

"The girl I fell for." He began. "Was one of Nina´s friends. Elena." He said and in the back of my mind a bell rung. "That´s why he started hating her bringing them. Because one of them was the reason he lost me. That´s why he hated you." He told me and I blinked at him. My throat clogged and I stared off, remembering. *Elena.*

Elena who asked if it was Kai´s cap I wore. Who told me Kai watched me dancing on Wren´s party. Elena who told me with her friend about Neverland.

What they do and that Hook and Pan were the worst. Elena, who *knew* they were. Because she was the one Wren fell in love with, and the one Kai fucked.

She never told me. *The truth.* She just warned me. *But I fell anyways.*

Maybe she knew I wouldn´t listen. She was Wendy. Kai was Pan. And Hook was all along Wren. *I just didn´t look.*

Wren snapped me out of my thoughts. "I hope you´re not mad at me for not telling you all this way sooner. I knew he never would. But it was on me to tell you, and I didn´t. I´m so sorry. It was just.. I never really got over it.." He sobbed.

"*Don´t.*" I told him. "It´s okay." I assured him. *Because it really was.*

"He loved you in his own way." I whispered. "He loved you the same way." He whispered back and I nodded. "I know." I said in tears. *I knew.*

I told Kai he I´m his first love. But in reality, he was. *Wren was his first love.*

"I just feel bad I left him when he tried." I cried. "I left him too, Lia. But he also hurt us. And I don´t think he´s mad you know. He wants us to be happy." He said sure and I laughed choking on it. "That´s what Finn said to me." I said. "That he thinks Kai´s not mad." I told him. "But how? That´s all he ever was." I asked upset. "He´s been hurt. But he loved us." He shrugged.

I never really understood Aidan when he told me he would have never started something with me if he had known about Kai and me. But now *knowing* Kai and Wren were a thing.

I understood.

And If I would have known I would have never, but I didn´t know. Because they didn´t tell me. And knowing our fucked-up friends, one, or the other knew of that too, I´m sure.

I can´t help but think about the time in the shower with Aidan and Kai. I told him he likes to be touched by him. And he did but he knew he liked it. He hesitated and fought it because he knew he would like it.

Because he knew what that could destroy. Because it *already* destroyed something once. Their friendship. *And maybe something more.*

I couldn´t imagine how it must have been for him. *Seeing him with me.*

Out of all the people who went to our parties I´ve chosen the one he fell in love with.

The one he hurt.

But he never said a thing. *How could we have not known?*

I blinked. *Once twice. Kai died.*

"I´m sorry." I said as I realized. "I.." I stammered. "I´m so sorry." I freaked. "When he died.. you.. you held me.." I sobbed hysterically. "You held *me*." I cried.

"You didn´t know." He reminded me but I shook my head. "Why didn´t you say anything?" I asked upset. "I was in shock too." He told me. "And I knew it was over. I needed to deal on my own. Just as you." He assured me and I bit my lip.

"I mean it." He told me lifting my chin to look in my eyes. "It´s okay. You hear me?" He hushed. "We loved him both. And he loved both of us. *And that is okay.*" He said what I need to hear, and we hugged because for the first time after his death it felt okay. And even if it just for that moment. *It was okay.*

"Will you play it once more?" I asked in tears. Because I needed to hear it again.

Now with the real meaning behind those notes.

He nodded and faced the piano. And played the song of his *another love*. The song he played before, but it was never about me. *It was all along about Kai.*

After he was done, we sat in silence for a time.

"You stopped playing.." I began and he nodded. "I stopped because of him." He told me. "He always loved hearing me play." He sniffed his nose. "Especially *that* one." He said with a weak smile.

I couldn´t help but think of the day he played and how he locked himself in the bathroom crying. It was all because of Kai. *I wish I knew.*

I also realized Wren made that cake on my birthday. The one with *another love* written on it. And I realized, Wren was his greatest fear. Because he was love. Because when I asked Kai what his Hook were. *He hesitated.* He looked at *someone. It was him.*

I wish I would have known. I wish I would have looked. But I didn´t because he told me it was time. *His Hook.*

When in reality it was a person, he had lost. A person he had loved.

And the person he had hurt. *His Hook. Wren.*

Peter loved Hook once. Once they were friends. *Until Pan betrayed Jamie.* Until they became enemies. *Until Wren became Hook.*

His greatest desire and greatest fear. *Love.*

And I asked what his Hook was. But I should have asked *who.*

And I knew the story that Pan had his enemy. *But I never questioned it.* I knew Wren was the leader of the pirates but, I never connected the dots.

Kai and Andi hated each other. *Like really.* But Kai and Wren, they didn´t hate each other. *They avoided each other.*

They didn´t speak if it wasn´t necessary. *They never looked at each other.*

They didn´t act like enemies. They acted like they lost each other. Like it hurt too much, to look to be around.

Kai was hurt and what hurt people do is hurt. But he tried not to.

But no one dared to look.

31

The day Wren told me about them, he gave me something. *Pages.*

And when I saw them, *I knew*. Those were from Kai´s journal and he gave them to him. But they didn´t change anything. Just like Kai´s book didn´t change anything for me.

…

Maybe I just couldn´t love girls. Maybe I could love him.

We were a team. Maybe even closer than Aidan and I ever were. Until he had a girlfriend. And cause I´m Peter, I wanted Jamie to play with only me. But all we had was over when I fucked her. I threw up afterwards and cut myself. Maybe I had a thing for him. I´ve always had those tendencies I never acted on. But he didn´t beat me how I imagined. Because he was hurt and felt the same as I did. Love and betrayal. That´s why I did it. That wasn´t fair play, he said. I said nobody smart plays fair. And then he left me. I wasn´t made for that kind of love. The good one. I only ever knew the bad. And since then, he might have waited for me to like a girl more than myself. He was the only one I loved. The only he could hurt me with. So, he left me. Because he knew that would hurt me. But not the way I deserved to be hurt.

…

After that, I searched his journals for something. *And I found some.*

…

I met her and she changed everything. I was scared. Because I knew I would hurt her too. But I wanted to make it right. But Andi and Wren too couldn´t let that opportunity go. Cause I had something I loved. They tried to take her from me. But only he did. He won. And I was stupid to think he did it just to hurt me. Maybe in the beginning. But I know he loves her. And she loves him. And that hurts even more. Cause I might have loved him once too. I could never love them. They could only love each other. I missed them every day. I missed my best friends. My pirate and my Scar. My lost girl and Hook. But I never told her that my deepest scar wasn´t her. It was him. And I was his.

…

Wren wasn´t off limit because he was a bad person. He was off limit because Kai loved him. Because they loved each other. *And lost.*

I wasn´t mad at Wren. I wanted to hurt Kai as bad as he wanted to.

I got myself distracted and fell for Wren. Kai really changed. I didn´t want to see because that made me realize I didn´t. That´s why I pushed him away. Because he was better, and ready for this. For the almost, we were never ready to have.

He was better. *Okay even. I wasn´t.*

So, no I wasn´t mad. I was glad he told me. Because I understood Kai better. But I felt worse because he´s been through so much shit. *I wasn´t.*

Hook wanted to bring Wendy home. *But Wendy wanted Pan.*

32

The past, Neverland – Christian Ford

I never knew why his father insisted on *that* specific cemetery. I never really questioned it, either. Until one day I saw. *The stone.* A white one. *His was black.*

There was a fairy graved and a boy that looked like Peter Pan.

Next to them two stars. One small. *One big.*

✧✦

"1998 *† Gone to watch her brother. Gone to be an angel. Gone to Neverland."*

...

I cried as I saw it but I couldn´t believe it and didn´t understand either.

The stone was hidden between the trees among roses.

If you went across his grave over to the gazebo into the forest. Where that stature of an angel covered in white roses was. And there was that stone. *It wasn´t big.*

You couldn´t see until you *really* looked. But there it was. *Her stone.*

A stone I´ve seen before but never paid attention to.

But it was never just a stone. *It was a headstone.*

It was a stone for a lost girl. A stone I could now never not see. *A stone.*

A white one. *His was black.*

- 27 -

I went straight to his father´s office. When he saw my face. *He knew.*

He started crying covering his mouth. *I cried too.*

When he caught himself, we went onto the balcony. The skyline ahead but for a long time, we stood there. We looked down on the world keep spinning and the sun still shining. It was a spring day. *They lost her in summer.*

"We always wanted kids." He began. "We had Finn at a very young age." As he spoke, he had that plain smile, and his gaze fixed on the horizon. *I looked away.*

"And then we awaited twins. A boy and a girl." He trailed off and my heart sunk. "Finn never knew." He said. "He was too young to understand." He told me and I shut my eyes as warm tears ran down my face. *Finn was three years old then.*

"We couldn´t tell them." He said then. "We went back to London after the first years. and Addison and Logan watched our kids. And we had Dr. Kunz." He told me and my eyes closed in realization. *His therapist. He had him all his life.*

"Then he kept monitoring Kai and Ava got in a clinic for a while." He made a pause. "I kept the company on going. But I had to cut short too and went shortly after her." He continued. "We got better." He said with a nod. "And got back. Commuting between London and home. But it was hard. Seeing him without her. For my wife it was the hardest." He said and breathed unsteadily but tried to cover it with a throat clear. "It got harder as he grew up." His voice broke, and he cleared his throat once again. "And we loved him with all we had, but we could never.." He trailed off.

They blamed him in a way.

I felt dizzy and my knees shook. *Seeing him meant never seeing her.*

He was silent for minutes.

"My wife made him watch those *Disney* movies." He kind of chuckled. "*Alice in Wonderland. Peter Pan*." He listed and the next I said soundlessly because I knew what would come next. "*Sleeping Beauty.*" My lips trembled, and I bit them until blood filled my mouth. "Ava always said that he was Peter." He smiled. "But she never said she was Tinker." He said like it was a silly thing.

It was painful. But not at all silly.

"She told him he will find his *Sleeping Beauty* that he will kiss awake." He said, and his voice was far away. *He wanted to kiss me awake, but I wanted to sleep.*

"She wanted him to run down the rabbit hole to hide from the world." He said, and I sobbed covering my mouth.

He always wanted to show me how deep it could get, but I refused to fall.

And the next he didn´t say, but I knew.

She wanted him to play games, follow the second star to the right and never grow up.

Silence passed like the wind the clouds.

"We never wanted to reject him in the way we did. In the way I did." He covered his face with his hands. It´s been a burden they carried to save them. *To save him.*

But with that they hurt him more.

"You *have* to tell him." I choked and he nodded. "I will." He promised.

He had to tell Finn. And this would break him. *Again.*

Because he didn´t just lose his brother but his little sister too.

"I´m sorry for.." I cried and he nodded once, knowing. And then he left to tell his only left child he had lost more.

I grabbed the edge and screamed. I choked, cried, and almost threw up.

Still holding on, I sank down and I closed my eyes. My forehead rested on the cold glass.

He had a sister. He was a twin. He never knew.

He didn´t feel loved of his own parents. *And he never knew why.*

He blamed himself for something, he never knew they blamed him for. He must have felt a loneliness he could never place. One he could never fill. And his therapist knew.

Doesn´t he had to tell? Or maybe he didn´t think he was ready for it.

But are you ever ready to hear?

He´s been to therapy all his life. *He never knew why.* Or the original reason behind all the other reasons. *I wish he knew.*

In the end I was never Tinker. Even if I told myself. *I never was.* I´ve been Wendy all along. Because his sister was. *Tinker.*

His light and fairy in the night. *The one that made him fly.*

Maybe that was why he never had the urge to grow up. To be anywhere else as in the now. *Because she never did.*

Maybe he felt that a part of him was somewhere else.

Maybe that´s why he created Neverland to be close to the call of the void.

The call of the now he never understood. But there was always something missing. And it wasn´t the love of his parents, mine, or Wren´s. *It was hers.*

Tink hated Wendy because she wanted Peter to grow up. *But he could never.*

And like Peter, Kai ran away the day he was born. But he never came back. Because what he was searching for, he could never find. *Peace.*

His biggest scar wasn´t Wren nor me. *It was his sister.*

I believed he´ll be with her. It made it easier. *In ways.* But in ways it made it worse. Because he never knew that all along he had a sister and was loved unconditionally.

I hope he knows now. Now that he´s to Neverland. *To that they never land.*

Epilogue

H*ow easily do you get addicted? How good can you resist?*

And, what says that about you?

I am an addict of drugs, of numbness. And addict of self-destruction.

Of hurting. Of pain.

At least I was. *Until I met her.*

Now I am an addict to her. The one drug that kept me high and low.

It was my downfall. My downfall into her arms. *But she couldn't hold me.*

The only thing that could hold me from falling apart was pain. *It saved me.*

Kept me alive and in the rain. With her, it felt like rain.

I wish we never left the street in the rain. *Some say we never did.*

And nor Neverland.

...

You were my favorite dream, but I had to wake myself up. *So, I did.*

But I know tonight, when I close my eyes, I'll see you again.

Lost in worlds that aren't mine.

...

✧✦

And then the smallest of the two stars screamed *Now*.

[**THE END**]

Author Commentary

W*hy would I write this?*

I asked myself that question but never found a real answer.

But I mostly wrote it for myself.

I struggled the most with the ending. *How will it end? How should it end?*

I could have written a happy ending and let them have their love story. I could have easily written something different. I could have *changed* their story. It was in my might, but at the same time it wasn´t. Like someone else wrote those lines.

I couldn´t take them back once I laid them. I felt them and they were real then. I cried while they burned themselves to life.

And maybe it was a form of self-destruction. Maybe I didn´t *want* a happy ending. Maybe I did it because there is no happy end in life either. Because you can´t rewrite your life once it happened and it wouldn´t have felt right to switch it up after it came to me. And some books just aren´t made for a happy ending.

They say *write what you fear.* And I feared not letting go. I feared losing and having love. I feared silence. I feared time and losing control. *So, I wrote it.*

But why would I write this?

Because I couldn´t stop once I started. Because every passion that drives you is worth pursuing. It wasn´t planned to be a book until it became one.

- 27 -

I want to thank my sister for listening to my jabber about the process of writing.

I need to thank myself for not giving up on the idea of picking up a book at all.

And most of all I wanna thank all of those who care and listen.

For believing and hearing. Thank you, all.

"Your first book holds your soul. Your second, your Art."

So, this is my soul. Now watch me make art.

Colson Herzog

Reading Group Guide

What´s your Hook? Why?

Who was worse Lia or Kai? Why?

Did Andi date Lia to piss off Kai? And did Wren the same?

Do you think the others really didn´t know about Kai and Lia?

Did Kai love? Did Lia love?

Would you have left Kai too? Why? Why would you have stayed?

Why did Kai write that book? Why didn´t it change anything?

Why did she choose Wren over him?

Was Lia a bad friend? Why?

Is it understandable that Lia broke up with Wren after Kai´s death?

Do you think Kai did commit suicide? Why?

Why did he take his brother´s car? Why did he leave his phone?

Do you think the others knew about Kai and Wren?

Did Finn love Lia all along?

Do you think Kai knew he had a sister?

If Kai wouldn´t have died, would they have ended up together?

Why couldn´t she let go?

With whom should Lia have ended up with?

⟡✧

Sometimes memories are just a star or two away.
They hide where the fairies play.

What happened between Hook and Pan?

How could friends become enemies? Did Wren lie? Or Kai? They all?

When did the pirates and the lost boys form?

How was it growing up as a lost one? And had he really no parents?

How did the parties and games form? And what went down to change it all?

How was Neverland before her?

Who was Kai Dark and Wren Fates? Was their story already written?

How can lifetime become afterlife?

And who was lost boy before he met lost girl?

Quotes, Lyrics, Paraphrasing and References

Chapter 10: Quote from Heath Ledger.
Chapter 13:
Quote from Albert Einstein.
Quote from the 1954 Broadway musical adaptation of *Peter Pan*, music by Mark *"Moose"* Charlap and Jule Styne, lyrics by Carolyn Leigh, Betty Comden, and Adolph Green. The line is part of the lyrics to the song *"Never Never Land"* sung by Peter Pan.
Quote from the movie *Peter Pan*, directed by P.J. Hogan., (2003).
Chapter 19: Quote from Albert Einstein.
Chapter 23:
Quote from *Pride and Prejudice*, the 2005 film adaptation of Jane Austen´s novel directed by Joe Wright.
Poetry Quote by JmStorm from Pinterest.
Lyric from *"Swing Life away"* by Machine Gun Kelly (MGK) (feat. Kellin Quinn), on Black Flag (Deluxe Edition).
Chapter 29: Lyric from *"Bad things"* by Machine Gun Kelly (MGK) (feat. Camila Cabello), on bloom.
Chapter 33: Lyric from *"Bad things"* by Machine Gun Kelly (MGK) (feat. Camila Cabello), on bloom.
Chapter 36: Quote from *Peter Pan*, by J.M. Barrie., (2013), PUFFIN BOOKS, Penguin Group (USA) Inc., 22nd Printing.
Chapter 48:
Lyric from *"Rehab"* by Machine Gun Kelly (MGK), on bloom (Deluxe Edition), [Pre-Chorus].
Quote from *Pride and Prejudice*, the 2005 film adaptation of Jane Austen´s novel directed by Joe Wrigh.
Notebook Entries 4: Quote from Heath Ledger.
Chapter 50:
Quote from *Pride and Prejudice*, the 2005 film adaptation of Jane Austen´s novel directed by Joe Wright.
Quote from *ACT LIKE A LADY, THINK LIKE A MAN – What Men Really Think About Love, Relationships, Intimacy and Commitment*, by Steve Harvey with Denene Millner, (2014), Amistad, HarperCollins *Publishers*.
Chapter 55: Lyric from *"Lonley"* by Machine Gun Kelly (MGK) and Travis Barker, on Tickets To My Downfall (Original).
Chapter 56:
Quote from Albert Einstein.
Quote from Friedrich Nietzsche.
Chapter 62: Lyric from *"Bad things"* by Machine Gun Kelly (MGK) (feat. Camila Cabello), on bloom.
Chapter 70: Lyric from *"I Think I´m OKAY"* by Machine Gun Kelly (MGK), YUNGBLUD & Travis Barker, on Tickets To My Downfall.
Chapter 71: Lyric from *"in these walls"* by Machine Gun Kelly (MGK), (feat. PVRIS).
Chapter 83: Quote from *The Picture of Dorian Gray*, by Oscar Wilde, (2003), PENGUIN BOOKS, Penguin Group.
Chapter 89:
Quote from Albert Einstein.
Referencing and paraphrasing a Quote from Erin Anastasia
Chapter 96: Quote from *ACT LIKE A LADY, THINK LIKE A MAN – What Men Really Think About Love, Relationships, Intimacy and Commitment*, by Steve Harvey with Denene Millner, (2014), Amistad, HarperCollins *Publishers*.
Notebook Entries 8:
Quote from *The Picture of Dorian Gray*, by Oscar Wilde, (2003), PENGUIN BOOKS, Penguin Group.
Quote from *DIARY OF AN OXYGEN THIEF*, by ANONYMOUS, (2016), CORSAIR.
Chapter 106: Quote from Carl Jung.
Chapter 113: Quote from *The Picture of Dorian Gray*, by Oscar Wilde, (2003), PENGUIN BOOKS, Penguin Group.
Chapter 123: Quotes from *The Butterfly Effect*, 2004 directed by Michael Suby.
Chapter 124:
Quote from *The Picture of Dorian Gray*, by Oscar Wilde, (2003), PENGUIN BOOKS, Penguin Group.
Quote from *ON WRITING, A MEMOIR OF THE CRAFT*, by Stephen King, (2020), Hodder & Stoughton.
Chapter 126: Lyric from *"Mary on a Cross"* by Ghost, on 13 Commandments.
Chapter 129: Lyric from *"Remind Me to Forget"* by Kygo & Miguel, on Kids in Love.
Chapter 146:
Lyric from *"Once Upon a Dream"* by Lana Del Ray, on Maleficent (Original Motion Picture Soundtrack) (2014).
Quote from *Sleeping Beauty*, 1959 directed by Wolfgang Reitherman, Clyde Geronimi, Eric Larson, and Les Clark.
Chapter 153:
Referencing and paraphrasing from *The Matrix*, 1999 directed by Lana Wachowski and Lilly Wachowski.
Quote from *The Matrix*, 1999 directed by Lana Wachowski and Lilly Wachowski.
Chapter 154: Quote from *The Picture of Dorian Gray*, by Oscar Wilde, (2003), PENGUIN BOOKS, Penguin Group.
Chapter 171: Quote from Oscar Wilde.
Chapter 174: Quote from Albert Einstein.
Chapter 175: Quotes from The Picture of Dorian Gray, by Oscar Wilde, (2003), PENGUIN BOOKS, Penguin Group.
Chapter 193: Quote from Vincent Van Gogh.
Chapter 1: Quote from Albert Einstein.
Chapter 29: Lyric from *"The devil´s tears"* by Angus & Julia Stone, on Down The Way (Deluxe Edition) (2010).
Epilogue: Referencing and paraphrasing from *Peter Pan*, by J.M. Barrie., (2013), PUFFIN BOOKS, Penguin Group (USA) Inc., 22nd Printing.

[If I missed anything feel free to contact me]

Colson Herzog

 Colson Herzog, 25 years old.

A European writer who loves to read and write. But also, gaming, art, and swim.

Primarily, I want to inspire people. I want to make them feel when they read. If I achieve that, I did everything right.

But moreover, I want to create and evolve. And I would love for you to take part on my journey as a writer.

Writing for me is a way to escape life. But it is also a way into life. Into a thousand life´s. It makes me want to run and hide from life, but also face and chase it even. If I can evoke that in the reader, I am happy. And if they highlight or annotate anything I reached everything.

I used to hate books all my life and now I write and read with all my heart. Because sometimes you can find love in hate. Sometimes people change.

FOLLOW ME ON

INSTAGRAM

colsonherzogwriter

TIKTOK

colsonherzogwriter

EMAIL

colson.herzog@gmx.de

Printed in Poland
by Amazon Fulfillment
Poland Sp. z o.o., Wrocław

47392215R00346